MISSING
JOSEPH

MISSING JOSEPH

ELIZABETH GEORGE

BANTAM BOOKS
New York   Toronto   London   Sydney   Auckland

FOR
DEBORAH

BOOK DESIGN BY SIGNET M DESIGN, INC.

ISBN 0-553-09253-7

Bantam Books are published by Bantam Books, a division of Bantam Doubleday
Dell Publishing Group, Inc. Its trademark, consisting of the words "Bantam
Books" and the portrayal of a rooster, is Registered in U.S. Patent and Trademark
Office and in other countries. Marca Registrada. Bantam Books, 1540 Broadway,
New York, New York. 10036.

PRINTED IN THE UNITED STATES OF AMERICA

ACKNOWLEDGMENTS

I OWE MANY THANKS TO THE PEOPLE IN ENGland who assisted with background material for this book. Most particularly, I thank Patricia Crowther, author of *Lid off the Cauldron*, who allowed me to visit with her in her home in Sheffield and who kindly provided me with a foundation in the Craft of the Wise; the Reverend Brian Darbyshire of St. Andrew's Church in Slaidburn, who counselled me on the ways of the Church of England and let me rub elbows with his congregation; John King-Wilkinson, whose family's abandoned Dunnow Hall became the model for my Cotes Hall; and Tony Mott, my remarkable English editor who never loses patience and who, for this book, provided me with everything from a copy of *Mists over Pendle* to the location of train stations.

In the United States, I thank Patty Gram for helping out with all things English; Julie Mayer for reading yet another rough draft; Ira Toibin for recognizing the process, respecting the effort, and always acting the part of both husband and friend; Kate Miciak for offering editorial encouragement, wisdom, and enthusiasm; and Deborah Schneider, for always being there. This is for you, Deborah, in friendship and with love.

I have done nothing but in care of thee,
Of thee my dear one, thee my daughter, who
Art ignorant of what thou art, naught knowing
Of whence I am. . . .

<small>THE TEMPEST</small>

NOVEMBER:
THE
RAIN

CAPPUCCINO. THAT NEW AGE ANSWER TO DRIVing one's blues momentarily away. A few tablespoons of espresso, a froth of steamed milk, an accompanying and generally tasteless dash of powdered chocolate and suddenly life was supposed to be all in order again. What drivel.

Deborah St. James sighed. She picked up the bill that a passing waitress had slid surreptitiously onto the table.

"Good Lord," she said and she stared, both dismayed and disgusted, at the amount she was going to have to pay. A block away, she could have ducked into a pub and acknowledged that importunate inner voice saying, "What's this chi-chi rot, Deb, let's just have a Guinness somewhere." But instead, she'd made her way to Upstairs, the stylish marble-glass-and-chrome coffee shop of the Savoy Hotel where those who imbibed in anything beyond water paid heavily for the privilege. As she was discovering.

She'd come to the Savoy to show her portfolio to Richie Rica, an up-and-coming producer employed by a newly formed entertainment conglomerate called L.A.SoundMachine. He had travelled to London for a brief seven days to select the photographer who would capture for posterity the likenesses of Dead Meat, a five-member band from Leeds whose most recent album Rica was shepherding all the way from creation to completion. She was, he told her, the "ninth frigging photog" whose work he'd seen. His patience, apparently, was wearing thin.

Unfortunately, it gained no girth from their interview. Straddling a delicate gilded chair, Rica went through her portfolio with all the interest and the approximate speed of a man dealing cards in a gambling casino. One after another, Deborah's pictures sailed to the floor. She watched them fall: her husband, her father, her sister-in-law, her friends, the myriad relations she'd gained through her marriage. There was no Sting or Bowie or George Michael among them. She'd only got the interview in the first place through the recommendation of a fellow photographer whose work had also failed to please the American. And from the expression on Rica's face, she could tell she was getting no further than anyone else.

This didn't actually disturb her as much as seeing the black-and-white tarpaulin of her pictures grow on the floor beneath Rica's chair. Among them was her husband's sombre face, and his eyes—so grey-blue light, so much at odds with his jet-coloured hair—seemed to be gazing directly into hers. This isn't the way to escape, he was saying.

She never wanted to believe Simon's words at any moment when he was most in the right. That was the primary difficulty in their marriage: her refusal to see reason in the face of emotion, warring with his cool evaluation of the facts at hand. She would say, God damn it, Simon, don't tell me how to feel, you don't *know* how I feel... And she would weep the hardest with the greatest bitterness when she knew he was right.

As he was now, when he was fifty-four miles away in Cambridge, studying a corpse and a set of X-rays, trying to decide with his usual dispassionate, clinical acuity what had been used to beat in a girl's face.

So when, in evaluation of her work, Richie Rica said with a martyred sigh at the monumental waste of his time, "Okay, you got some talent. But you want the truth? These pictures wouldn't sell shit if it was dipped in gold," she wasn't as offended as she might have been. It was only when he jockeyed his chair around prior to rising that her mild ember of irritation feathered into flame. For he slid his chair into the blanket of pictures he'd just created, and one of its legs perforated the lined face of Deborah's father, sinking through his cheek and creating a fissure from jaw to nose.

It wasn't even the damage to the photograph that brought the heat to her face. If the truth be told, it was Rica's saying, "Oh hell, I'm sorry. You can print another of the old guy, can't you?" before he heaved himself to his feet.

Which is largely why she knelt, keeping her hands steady by pressing them to the floor as she gathered her pictures together, placing them back into the portfolio, tying its strings neatly, and then looking up to say, "You don't look like a worm. Why is it you act like one?"

Which—the relative merit of her pictures aside—is even more largely why she hadn't got the job.

"Wasn't meant to be, Deb," her father would have said. Of course, that was true. Lots of things in life are never meant to be.

She gathered up her shoulder bag, her portfolio, her umbrella, and made her way out to the hotel's grand entry. A short walk past a line of waiting taxis and she was out on the pavement. The morning's rain had abated for the moment, but the wind was fierce, one of those angry London winds that blow from the southeast, pick up speed on the slick surface of open water, and shoot down streets, tearing at both umbrellas and clothes. In combination with the traffic rumbling by, it created a whip-howl of noise in the Strand. Deborah squinted at the sky. Grey clouds roiled. It was a matter of minutes before the rain began again.

She'd thought about taking a walk before heading home. She wasn't far from the river, and a stroll down the embankment sounded lovelier than did the prospect of entering a house made tenebrous by the weather and rebarbative by the memory of her last discussion with Simon. But with the wind dashing her hair into her eyes and the air smelling each moment heavier with rain, she thought better of the idea. The fortuitous approach of a number eleven bus seemed indication enough of what she ought to do.

She hurried to join the queue. A moment later, she was jostling among the crowd in the bus itself. However, within two blocks, an embankment stroll in a raging hurricane looked decidedly more appealing than what the bus ride had to offer. Claustrophobia, an umbrella being driven into her little toe by an Aquascutum-outfitted Sloane Ranger several miles out of territory, and the pervasive odour of garlic which seemed to be emanating from the very pores of a diminutive, grandmotherly woman at Deborah's elbow all joined forces to convince her that the day promised nothing more than an endless journey from bad to worse.

Traffic ground to a halt at Craven Street, and eight more people took the opportunity of jumping into the bus. It began to rain. As if in response to all three of these events, the grandmotherly woman gave a tremendous sigh and Aquascutum leaned heavily onto the umbrella's handle. Deborah tried not to breathe and began to feel faint.

Anything—wind, rain, thunder, or an encounter with all Four Horsemen of the Apocalypse—would be better than this. Another interview with Richie Rica would be better than this. As the bus inched forward towards Trafalgar Square, Deborah fought her way past five skinheads, two punk rockers, half a dozen housewives, and a happy group of chattering American tourists. She gained the door just as Nelson's Column came into view, and with a determined leap, she was back in the wind with the rain beating soundly against her face.

She knew better than to open her umbrella. The wind would take it like tissue and hurl it down the street. Instead, she looked for shelter. The square itself was empty, a broad expanse of concrete, fountains, and crouching lions. Devoid of its resident flock of pigeons and of the homeless and often friendless who lounged by the fountains and climbed on the lions and encouraged the tourists to feed the birds, the square looked, for once, like the monument to a hero that it was supposed to be. It did not, however, hold out much promise as a sanctuary in the middle of a storm. Beyond it stood the National Gallery where a number of people huddled into their coats, fought with umbrellas, and scurried like voles up the wide front steps. Here was shelter and more. Food, if she wanted it. Art, if she needed it. And the promise of distraction which she had been welcoming for the last eight months.

With the rainwater beginning to drizzle through her hair to her scalp, Deborah hurried down the steps of the subway and through the pedestrian tunnel, emerging moments later in the square itself. This she crossed quickly, her black portfolio clasped hard to her chest, while the wind tore at her coat and drove the rain in steady waves against her. By the time she reached the door of the gallery, she was sloshing in her shoes, her stockings were spattered, and her hair felt like a cap of wet wool on her head.

Where to go. She hadn't been inside the gallery in ages. How embarrassing, she thought, I'm supposed to be an artist myself.

But the reality was that she had always felt overwhelmed in museums, within a quarter of an hour a hopeless victim to aesthetic-overload. Other people could walk, gaze, and comment upon brushstrokes with their noses fixed a mere six inches from a canvas. But for Deborah, ten paintings into any visit and she'd forgotten the first.

She checked her belongings in the cloakroom, picked up a museum plan, and began to wander, happy enough to be out of the cold, content with the thought that the gallery contained ample scope for at least a temporary respite. A diverting photographic assignment may have been out of her reach at the moment, but the exhibitions here at least held out the promise of continued avoidance for another few hours. If she was truly lucky, Simon's work would keep him the night in Cambridge. Discussion between them couldn't resume. She would have purchased more time in that way.

She quickly scanned the museum plan, looking for something that might engage her. *Early Italian, Italian 15th Century, Dutch 17th Century, English 18th Century.* Only one artist was mentioned by name. *Leonardo,* it said, *Cartoon. Room 7.*

She found the room easily, tucked away by itself, no larger than Simon's study in Chelsea. Unlike the exhibition rooms she had passed through to reach it, Room 7 contained only one piece, Leonardo da Vinci's full-scale composition of the Virgin and Child with St. Anne and the infant St. John the Baptist. Additionally unlike the other exhibition rooms, Room 7 was chapel-like, dimly illuminated by weak protective lights directed upon only the artwork itself, furnished with a set of benches from which admirers could contemplate what the museum plan called one of da Vinci's most beautiful works. There were, however, no other admirers contemplating it now.

Deborah sat before it. A tightness began to curl in her back and to form a coiled spring of tension at the base of her neck. She was not immune to the excellent irony of her choice.

It grew from the Virgin's expression, that mask of devotion and selfless love. It grew from St. Anne's eyes—deeply understanding in a face of contentment—cast in the Virgin's direction. For who would understand better than St. Anne, watching her own beloved daughter loving the wondrous Infant she'd borne. And the Infant Himself, leaning out of His mother's arms, reaching for His cousin the Baptist, leaving His mother even now, even now . . .

That would be Simon's point, the leaving. That was the scientist speaking in him, calm, analytical, and given to looking at the world in terms of the objective practicalities implied by statistics. But his worldview—indeed, his world itself—was different from hers. He could say, Listen to me, Deborah, there are other bonds besides those of blood . . . because it was easy for him, of all people, to possess that particular philosophical bent. Life was defined in different terms for her.

Effortlessly, she could conjure up the image of the photograph that Rica's chair leg had punctured and destroyed: how the spring breeze blew at her father's sparse hair, how a tree branch cast a shadow like a bird's wing across the stone of her mother's grave, how the daffodils he was placing in the vase caught the sun like small trumpets and furled against the back of his hand, how his hand itself held the flowers with his fingers curled tightly round their stems just as they'd been curling every fifth of April for the last eighteen years. He was fifty-eight years old, her father. He was her only connection of blood and bone.

Deborah gazed at the da Vinci cartoon. Its two female figures would have understood what her husband did not. It was the power the blessing the ineffable awe of a life created and brought forth from one's own.

I want you to give your body a rest for at least a year, the doctor had told her. This is six miscarriages. Four spontaneous abortions in the last nine months alone. We're encountering physical stress, a dangerous blood loss, hormonal imbalance, and—

Let me try fertility drugs, she'd said.

You're not listening to me. That's beyond consideration at the moment.

In vitro, then.

You know impregnation isn't the problem, Deborah. Gestation is.

I'll stay in bed for nine months. I won't move. I'll do anything.

Then get on an adoption list, start using contraceptives, and try again this time next year. Because if you continue to carry on in this fashion, you'll be looking at a hysterectomy before you're thirty years old.

He wrote out the prescription.

But there has to be a chance, she said, trying to pretend the remark was casual. She couldn't allow herself to become upset. There must, after all, be no demonstration of mental or emotional stress on the part of the patient. He would note it on the chart, and it would count against her.

The doctor was not unsympathetic. There *is*, he said, next year. When your body's had an opportunity to heal. We'll look at all the options then. In vitro. Fertility drugs. Everything else. We'll do all the tests we can. In a year.

So dutifully she began with the pills. But when Simon brought home the adoption forms, she drew the line on cooperation.

There was absolutely no point in thinking of it now. She forced herself to study the cartoon. The faces were serene, she decided. They seemed well-defined. The rest of the piece was largely impression, drawn like a series of questions that would remain forever unanswered. Would the Virgin's foot be raised or lowered? Would St. Anne continue to point towards the sky? Would the Infant's plump hand cradle the Baptist's chin? And was the background Golgotha, or was that a future too unsavoury for this moment of tranquillity, something better left unsaid and unseen?

"No Joseph. Yes. Of course. No Joseph."

Deborah turned at the whisper and saw that a man—still fully dressed for the out-of-doors in a great wet overcoat with a scarf round his neck and a trilby on his head—had joined her. He didn't seem to notice her presence and had he not spoken she probably wouldn't have noticed his. Dressed completely in black, he faded into the farthest corner of the room.

"No Joseph," he whispered again, resigned.

Rugby player, Deborah thought, for he was tall and looked hefty beneath his coat. And his hands, clasping a rolled-up museum plan in front of him like an unlit candle, were square and blunt fingered and fully capable, she imagined, of shoving other players to one side in a dash down the field.

He wasn't dashing anywhere now, although he did move forward, into one of the muted cones of light. His steps seemed reverential. With his eyes on the da Vinci, he reached for his hat and removed it as a man might do in church. He dropped it onto one of the benches. He sat.

He wore thick-soled shoes—serviceable shoes, country shoes— and he balanced them on their outer edges as he dangled his hands between his knees. After a moment, he ran one hand through thinning hair that was the slow-greying colour of soot. It didn't seem so much a gesture of seeing to his appearance as it did one of rumination. His face, raised to study the da Vinci, looked both worried and pained, with crescent bags beneath his eyes and heavy lines on his brow.

He pressed his lips together. The lower one was full, the upper one thin. They formed a seam of sorrow on his face, and they seemed to be acting as inadequate containment for an inner turmoil. Fellow struggler, Deborah thought. She was touched by his suffering.

"It's a lovely drawing, isn't it?" She spoke in the sort of hushed whisper one automatically uses in places of prayer or meditation. "I'd never seen it before today."

He turned to her. He was swarthy, older than he had seemed at first. He looked surprised to have been spoken to out of the blue by a stranger. "Nor I," he said.

"It's awful of me when you think that I've lived in London for the last eighteen years. It makes me wonder what else I've been missing."

"Joseph," he said.

"Sorry?"

He used the museum plan to gesture at the cartoon. "You're missing Joseph. But you'll always be missing him. Haven't you noticed? Isn't it always Madonna and Child?"

Deborah glanced again at the artwork. "I'd never thought of that, actually."

"Or Virgin and Child. Or Mother and Child. Or Adoration of the Magi with a cow and an ass and an angel or two. But you rarely see Joseph. Have you never wondered why?"

"Perhaps... well, of course, he wasn't really the father, was he?"

The man's eyes closed. "Jesus God," he replied.

He seemed so struck that Deborah hurried on. "I mean, we're taught to believe he wasn't the father. But we don't know for certain. How could we? We weren't there. She didn't exactly keep a journal of her life. We're just told that the Holy Ghost came down with an angel or something and... Naturally, I don't know how it was supposed to be managed but it was a miracle, wasn't it? There she was a virgin one minute and pregnant the next and then in nine months— there was this little baby and she was holding him probably not quite believing he was real and counting his fingers and toes. He was hers, really hers, the baby she'd longed for... I mean, if you believe in miracles. If you do."

She hadn't realised that she'd begun to cry until she saw the man's expression change. Then the sheer oddity of their situation made her want to laugh instead. It was wildly absurd, this psychic pain. They were passing it between them like a tennis ball.

He dug a handkerchief out of a pocket of his overcoat, and he pressed it, crumpled, into her hand. "Please." His voice was earnest. "It's quite clean. I've only used it once. To wipe the rain from my face."

Deborah laughed shakily. She pressed the linen beneath her eyes and returned it to him. "Thoughts link up like that, don't they? You don't expect them to. You think you've quite protected yourself. Then all of a sudden you're saying something that seems so reasonable and safe on the surface, but you're not safe at all, are you, from what you're trying not to feel."

He smiled. The rest of him was tired and ageing, lines at the eyes and flesh giving way beneath his chin, but his smile was lovely. "It's the same for me. I came here merely for a place to walk and think that would be out of the rain, and I stumbled on this drawing instead."

"And thought of St. Joseph when you didn't want to?"

"No. I'd been thinking of him anyway, after a fashion." He tucked his handkerchief back into his pocket and went on, his tone becoming more determinedly light. "I'd have preferred a walk in the park, actually. I was heading to St. James's Park when the rain began again. I generally like to do my thinking out of doors. I'm a countryman at heart and if ever there're thoughts to be had or decisions to be made, I always try to get myself outside to think them or to make them. A proper tramp in the air clears the head, I find. And the heart as well. It makes the rights and wrongs of life—the yes's and the no's—easier to see."

"Easier to see," she said. "But not to deal with. Not for me, at least. I can't say yes just because people want me to, no matter how right it may be to do so."

He directed his gaze back to the cartoon. He rolled the museum plan tighter in his hands. "Nor can I always," he said. "Which is why I head out for a tramp in the air. I was set on feeding the sparrows from the bridge in St. James's, watching them peck at my palm and letting every problem find its solution from there." He shrugged and smiled sadly. "But then there was the rain."

"So you came here. And saw there was no St. Joseph."

He reached for his trilby and set it on his head. The brim cast a triangular shadow on his face. "And you, I imagine, saw the Infant."

"Yes." Deborah forced her lips into a brief, tight smile. She looked about her, as if she too had belongings to gather in preparation for leaving.

"Tell me, is it an infant you want or one that died or one you'd like to be rid of?"

"Be *rid*—"

Swiftly, he lifted his hand. "One that you want," he said. "I'm sorry. I should have seen that. I should have recognised the longing. Dear God in heaven, why are men such fools?"

"He wants us to adopt. I want my child—his child—a family that's real, one that we create, not one that we apply for. He's brought the papers home. They're sitting on his desk. All I have to do is fill out my part and sign my name, but I find that I just can't do it. It wouldn't be mine, I tell him. It wouldn't come from me. It wouldn't come from us. I couldn't love it the same way if it wasn't mine."

"No," he said. "That's very true. You wouldn't love it the same way at all."

She grasped his arm. The wool of his coat was damp and scratchy beneath her fingers. "You understand. He doesn't. He says there're connections that go beyond blood. But they don't for me. And I can't understand why they do for him."

"Perhaps it's because he knows that we humans ultimately love something that we have to struggle for—something that we give up everything to have—far more than the things that fall our way through chance."

She released his arm. Her hand fell with a thud to the bench between them. Unwittingly, the man had spoken Simon's own words. Her husband may as well have been in the room with her.

She wondered how she had come to unburden herself in the presence of a stranger. I'm desperate for someone to take my part, she thought, looking for a champion to bear my standard. I don't even care who that champion is, just so long as he sees my point, agrees, and lets me go my own way.

"I can't help how I feel," she said hollowly.

"My dear, I'm not sure anyone can." The man loosened his scarf and unbuttoned his coat, reaching inside to his jacket pocket. "I should guess you need a tramp in the air to think your thoughts and clear your head," he said. "But you need fresh air. Wide skies and broad vistas. You can't find that in London. If you've a mind to do your tramping in the North, you've a welcome in Lancashire." He handed her his card.

Robin Sage, it read, *The Vicarage, Winslough.*

"The Vic—" Deborah looked up and saw what his coat and scarf had hidden before, the white solid collar encircling his neck. She should have realised at once from the colour of his clothes, from his talk of St. Joseph, from the very reverence with which he'd regarded the da Vinci cartoon.

No wonder she'd found it so easy to reveal her troubles and her sorrows. She'd been confessing to an Anglican priest.

DECEMBER: THE SNOW

BRENDAN POWER SPUN ROUND AS THE DOOR creaked open and his younger brother Hogarth entered the glacial cold of the vestry of St. John the Baptist Church in the village of Winslough. Beyond him the organist, accompanied by a single, tremulous, and no doubt utterly uninvited voice, was playing "All Ye Who Seek for Sure Relief," as a follow-up to "God Moves in a Mysterious Way." Brendan had little doubt that both pieces constituted the organist's sympathetic but unsolicited comment upon the morning's proceedings.

"Nothing," Hogarth said. "Not a ginger. Not a git. And no vicar to be found. Everyone on *her* side's in a real twist, Bren. Her mum was moaning about the wedding breakfast being ruined, *she* was hissing about getting revenge on some 'rotten sow,' and her dad's just left to 'hunt that little rat down.' Quite the folks they are, these Townley-Youngs."

"Maybe you're off the hook, Bren." Tyrone—his older brother and best man and, by rights, the only other person who should have been in the vestry aside from the vicar—spoke with guarded hope as Hogarth closed the door behind him.

"No way," Hogarth said. He reached in the jacket pocket of his hired morning coat that, despite all efforts by the tailor, failed to make his shoulders look like anything other than the sides of Pendle Hill incarnate. He took out packet of Silk Cuts and lit up, flicking the match onto the cold stone floor. "She has him by the curlies, she does,

Ty. Make no mistake about it. And let it be a lesson to you. Keep it in your trousers till it's got a proper home."

Brendan turned away. They both loved him, they both had their own way of offering consolation. But neither Hogarth's joking nor Tyrone's optimism was going to change the reality of the day. Come hell or high water—and between the two it was more likely to be hell—he would be married to Rebecca Townley-Young. He tried not to think about it, which is what he'd been doing since she'd first dropped by his office in Clitheroe with the results of her pregnancy test.

"I don't know how it happened," she said. "I've never had a regular period in my life. My doctor even *told* me that I'd have to go on some sort of medication just to get myself regular if I ever wanted a family. And now...Look where we are, Brendan."

Look what you did to me was the underlying message, as was *And you, Brendan Power, a junior partner in Daddy's own solicitor's firm! Tsk, tsk. What a shame it might be to be given the sack.*

But she didn't need to say any of that. All she needed to say, head lowered penitently, was, "Brendan, I simply don't know what I'm going to tell Daddy. What shall I do?"

A man in any other position would have said, "Just get rid of it, Rebecca," and gone on with his work. A different sort of man in Brendan's own position might have said the same thing. But Brendan was eighteen months away from St. John Andrew Townley-Young's decision as to which of the solicitors would handle his affairs and his fortune when the current senior partner retired from the firm, and the perquisites that went with that decision were of the sort that Brendan could not turn from lightly: an introduction to society, the promise of other clients from Townley-Young's class, and stellar advancement in his career.

The opportunities promised by Townley-Young's patronage had prompted Brendan to involve himself with the man's twenty-eight-year-old daughter in the first place. He'd been with the firm just short of a year. He was eager to make his place in the world. Thus, when through the senior partner, St. John Andrew Townley-Young had extended an invitation to Brendan to escort Miss Townley-Young to the horse and pony sales of the Cowper Day Fair, it had seemed too much a stroke of good fortune for Brendan to demur.

At the time, the idea hadn't been repellent. While it was true that even under the best of conditions—after a good night's sleep and an hour and a half with her make-up and her hair curlers and her very best clothes—Rebecca still tended to resemble Queen Victoria in her declining years, Brendan had felt he could tolerate one or two mutual encounters with good grace and the guise of camaraderie. He counted heavily on his ability to dissemble, knowing that every decent lawyer had at least several drops of dissimulation in his blood. What he did not count on was Rebecca's ability to decide, dominate, and direct the course of their relationship from its very inception. The second time he was with her, she took him to bed and rode him like the master of the hunt with a fox in sight. The third time he was with her, she rubbed him, fondled him, skewered herself on him and came up pregnant.

He wanted to blame her. But he couldn't avoid the fact that as she panted and bobbed and bounced against him with her odd skinny breasts hanging down in his face, he had closed his eyes and smiled and called her God-what-a-woman-you-are-Becky and all the time thought of his future career.

So they would indeed be married today. Not even the failure of the Reverend Mr. Sage to appear at the church was going to stop the tide of Brendan Power's future from flooding right in.

"How late is he?" he asked Hogarth.

His brother glanced at his watch. "It's gone half an hour now."

"No one's left the church?"

Hogarth shook his head. "But there's a whisper and a titter that *you're* the one who's failed to show. I've been doing my part to save your reputation, lad, but you might want to pop your head into the chancel and give a bit of a wave to reassure the masses. I can't say what that'll do to reassure your bride, though. Who's this sow she's after? Are you already having a bit of stuff on the side? Not that I'd blame you. Getting it up for Becky must be a real treat. But you were always one for a challenge, weren't you?"

"Stow it, Hogie," Tyrone said. "And put out the fag. This is a church, for God's sake."

Brendan walked to the vestry's single window, a lancet set deeply into the wall. Its panes were as dusty as was the room itself, and he cleared a small patch to look out at the day. What he saw was the graveyard, its cluster of stones like malformed slate thumbprints against the snow, and in the distance, the looming slopes of Cotes Fell that rose cone-shaped against a grey sky.

"It's snowing again." Absently, he counted how many graves were topped by seasonal sprays of holly, their red berries glistening against the spiked, green leaves. Seven of them that he could see. The greenery would have been brought this morning by wedding guests, for even now the wreaths and sprays were only lightly sprinkled with snow. He said, "The vicar must have gone out earlier this morning. That's what's happened. And he's caught somewhere."

Tyrone joined him at the window. Behind them, Hogarth ground his cigarette into the floor. Brendan shivered. Despite the fact that the church's heating system was busily grinding away, the vestry was still unbearably cold. He put his hand to the wall. It felt icy and damp.

"How are Mum and Dad doing?" he asked.

"Oh, Mum's a bit nervous but as far as I can tell, she still thinks it's a match made in heaven. Her first child to get married and glory-to-God he's hopping into the arms of the landed gentry, if only the vicar'll show his face. But Dad's watching the door like he's had enough."

"He hasn't been this far from Liverpool in years," Tyrone noted. "He's just feeling nervous."

"No. He's feeling who he is." Brendan turned from the window and looked at his brothers. They were mirrors of him and he knew it. Sloped shoulders, beaked noses, and everything else about them undecided. Hair that was neither brown nor blond. Eyes that were neither blue nor green. Jaws that were neither strong nor weak. They were all of them perfectly cast for potential serial killers, with faces that faded into a crowd. And that's how the Townley-Youngs reacted when they'd met the whole family, as if they'd come face to face with their worst expectations and their most dreaded dreams. It was no wonder to Brendan that his father was watching the door and counting the moments till he could escape. His sisters were probably feeling the same. He even felt some envy for them. An hour or two and it would be over. For him, it was a lifetime proposition.

■   ■   ■

Cecily Townley-Young had accepted the role of her cousin's chief bridesmaid because her father had instructed her to do so. She hadn't wanted to be part of the wedding. She hadn't even wanted to come to the wedding. She and Rebecca had never shared anything other than their relative positions as the daughters of sons on a scrawny family tree, and as far as Cecily was concerned, things could have pretty much stayed that way.

She didn't like Rebecca. First, she had nothing in common with her. Rebecca's idea of an afternoon of bliss was to crawl round four or five pony sales, talking about withers and lifting rubbery equine lips to have a sharp look at those ghastly yellow teeth. She carried apples and carrots like loose change in her pockets, and she examined hooves, scrotums, and eyeballs with the sort of interest most women give to clothes. Second, Cecily was tired of Rebecca. Twenty-two years of enduring birthdays, Easter, Christmas, and New Year's on her uncle's estate—all in the name of a spurious family unity that absolutely no one felt—had ground to gravel whatever affection she might have harboured for an older cousin. A few exposures to Rebecca's incomprehensible extremes of behaviour had kept Cecily at a safe distance from her whenever they occupied the same house for more than a quarter of an hour. And third, she found her intolerably stupid. Rebecca had never boiled an egg, written a cheque, or made a bed. Her answer for every little problem in life was, "Daddy'll see to it," just the sort of lazy, parental dependence that Cecily loathed.

Even today Daddy was seeing to it in finest form. They'd done their part, obediently waiting for the vicar in the ice-floored, snow-speckled north porch of the church, stomping their feet, with their lips turning blue, while the guests rustled and murmured inside among the holly and the ivy, wondering why the candles weren't being lit and why the wedding march hadn't begun. They'd waited for an entire quarter of an hour, the snow making its own lazy bridal veils in the air, before Daddy had stormed across the street and pounded furiously on the vicarage door. He'd returned, his usual ruddy skin gone white with rage, in less than two minutes.

"He's not even home," St. John Andrew Townley-Young had snapped. "That mindless cow"—this was his manner of identifying the vicar's housekeeper, Cecily decided—"said he'd already gone out when she arrived this morning, if you can believe it. That incompetent, foul little..." His hands formed fists in their dove-coloured gloves. His top hat trembled. "Get inside the church. All of you. Get out of this weather. I'll handle the situation."

"But Brendan's here, isn't he?" Rebecca had asked anxiously. "Daddy, Brendan's not missing as well!"

"We should be so lucky," her father replied. "The whole family's here. Like rats who won't leave a sinking ship."

"St. John," his wife murmured.

"Get inside!"

"But people will see me," Rebecca wailed. "They'll see the bride."

"Oh, for Christ's sake, Rebecca." Townley-Young disappeared into the church for another, utterly freezing two minutes, and came back with the announcement, "You can wait in the bell tower," before he set off again to locate the vicar.

So at the base of the bell tower they were waiting still, hidden from the wedding guests by a gate of walnut balusters that was covered by a dusty, foul-smelling red velvet curtain whose nap was so worn that they could see the lights from the church chandeliers shining through. They could hear the rising ripple of concern as it flowed through the crowd. They could hear the restless shuffling of feet. Hymnals opened and shut. The organist played. Beneath their feet in the crypt of the church, the heating system groaned like a mother giving birth.

At the thought, Cecily gazed speculatively at her cousin. She'd never believed Rebecca would find any man fool enough to marry her. While it was true that she stood to inherit a fortune and she'd already been given that ghoulish monstrosity Cotes Hall in which to retire in connubial ecstasy once the ring was on her finger and the register was signed, Cecily couldn't imagine how the fortune itself—no matter how great—or the crumbling old Victorian mansion—no matter how distinct its potential for revival—would have induced any man to take on a lifetime of dealing with Rebecca. But now . . . She recalled her cousin just this morning in the loo, the noise of her retching, the sound of her shrill "Is it going to be like this every goddamned morning?" followed by her mother's soothing "Rebecca. Please. We've guests in the house." And then Rebecca's "I don't care about them. I don't care about anything. Don't *touch* me. Let me out of here." A door slammed. Running footsteps pounded along the upstairs passage.

Preggers? Cecily wondered idly at the time as she carefully applied mascara and smoothed on some blusher. She marvelled at the idea that a man might actually have taken Rebecca to bed. Lord, if that was the case, anything was possible. She examined her cousin for telltale signs of the truth.

Rebecca didn't exactly look like a woman fulfilled. If she was supposed to blossom with pregnancy, she was adrift somewhere in the prebudding stage, somewhat given to jowls, with eyes the size and shape of marbles and hair permed into a helmet on her head. To her credit, her skin was perfect, and her mouth was rather nice. But somehow, nothing really *worked* together, and Rebecca always ended up looking as if her individual features were at war with each other.

It wasn't really her fault, Cecily thought. One ought to have at least a titbit of sympathy for someone so ill-favoured by looks. But every time Cecily tried to dig up one or two empathetic stirrings from her heart, Rebecca did something to quash them like bugs.

As she was doing now.

Rebecca paced the tiny enclosure below the church bells, furiously twisting her bouquet. The floor was filthy, but she did nothing to hold her dress or her train away from it. Her mother did this duty, following her from point A to point B and back again like a faithful dog, with satin and velvet clutched in her hands. Cecily stood to one side, surrounded by two tin pails, a coil of rope, a shovel, a broom, and a pile of rags. An old Hoover leaned against a stack of cartons near her, and she carefully hung her own bouquet from the metal hook that would otherwise have been used to accommodate its cord. She lifted her velvet dress from the floor. The air was fusty in the space beneath the bells, and one couldn't move in any direction without touching something absolutely black with grime. But at least it was warm.

"I *knew* something like this would happen." Rebecca's hands strangled her bridal flowers. "It's not going to come off. And they're laughing at me, aren't they? I can *hear* them laughing."

Mrs. Townley-Young made a quarter turn as Rebecca did the same, bunching more of the satin train and the bottom of the gown into her arms. "No one's laughing," she said. "Don't worry yourself, darling. There's simply been some sort of unfortunate mistake. A misunderstanding. Your father will put things right straightaway."

"How could there be a mistake? We *saw* Mr. Sage yesterday afternoon. The last thing he said was, 'See you in the morning.' And then he forgot? He went off somewhere?"

"Perhaps there's been an emergency. Someone could be dying. Someone wishing to see—"

"But Brendan held back." Rebecca stopped pacing. Eyes narrowing, she looked thoughtfully at the west wall of the bell tower, as if she could see through it to the vicarage across the street. "I'd gone to the car and he said he'd forgotten one last thing he'd wanted to ask Mr. Sage. He went back. He went inside. I waited for a minute. Two or three. And—" She whirled, began her pacing again. "He wasn't talking to Mr. Sage at all. It's that bitch. That witch! And she's behind this, Mother. You know she is. By God, I'll get her."

Cecily found this an interesting twist in the morning's events. It held out the tantalising promise of diversion. If she had to endure this day somehow in the name of the family and with one eye fixed on her uncle's will, she decided she might as well do something to enjoy her act of sufferance. So she said, "Who?"

Mrs. Townley-Young said, "Cecily," in a pleasant but determined-to-discipline voice.

But Cecily's question had been enough. "Polly Yarkin." Rebecca said the name through her teeth. "That miserable little sow at the vicarage."

"Vicar's housekeeper?" Cecily asked. This was a twist to be explored at length. Another woman already? All things considered, she couldn't blame poor old Brendan, but she did think he might have set his sights a bit low. She continued the game. "Gosh, what's she got to do with anything, Becky?"

"Cecily, dear." Mrs. Townley-Young's voice had a less pleasant ring.

"She pushes those dugs into every man's face and just waits for him to react to the sight," Rebecca said. "And he wants her. He does. He can't hide it from me."

"Brendan loves you, darling," Mrs. Townley-Young said. "He's marrying you."

"He had a drink with her at Crofters Inn last week. Just a quick stop before he headed back to Clitheroe, he said. He didn't even know she'd be there, he said. He couldn't exactly pretend he didn't recognise her, he said. It's a village, after all. He couldn't act like she was a stranger."

"Darling, you're working yourself up over nothing at all."

"You think he's in love with the vicar's housekeeper?" Cecily asked, widening her eyes to wear the guise of naiveté. "But, Becky, then why is he marrying you?"

"Cecily!" her aunt hissed.

"He isn't marrying me!" Rebecca cried out. "He isn't marrying anyone! We haven't got a vicar!"

Beyond them, a hush fell over the church. The organ had stopped playing for a moment, and Rebecca's words seemed to echo from wall to wall. The organist quickly resumed, choosing "Crown with Love, Lord, This Glad Day."

"Mercy," Mrs. Townley-Young breathed.

Sharp footsteps sounded against the stone floor beyond them and a gloved hand shoved the red curtain aside. Rebecca's father ducked through the gate.

"Nowhere." He slapped the snow from his coat and shook it from his hat. "Not in the village. Not at the river. Not on the common. Nowhere. I'll have his job for this."

His wife reached out to him but didn't make contact. "St. John, good Lord, what'll we do? All these people. All that food at the house. And Rebecca's condi—"

"I know the bloody details. I don't need reminding." Townley-Young flipped the curtain to one side and gazed into the church. "We're going to be the butt of every joke for the next decade." He looked back at the women, at his daughter particularly. "You got yourself into this, Rebecca, and I damn well ought to let you get yourself out."

"Daddy!" She said his name as a wail.

"Really, St. John . . ."

Cecily decided this was the moment to be helpful. Her father would no doubt be rumbling down the aisle to join them at any time—emotional disturbances were a special source of delectation to him—and if that was the case, her own purposes would best be served by demonstrating her ability to be at the forefront of solving a family crisis. He was, after all, still temporising on her request to spend the spring in Crete.

She said, "Perhaps we ought to phone someone, Uncle St. John. There must be another vicar not far."

"I've spoken to the constable," Townley-Young said.

"But he can't *marry* them, St. John," his wife protested. "We need to get a vicar. We need to have the wedding. The food's waiting to be eaten. The guests are getting hungry. The—"

"I want Sage," he said. "I want him here. I want him now. And if I have to drag that low church twit up to the altar myself, I'll do it."

"But if he's been called out somewhere..." Mrs. Townley-Young was clearly trying to sound like the voice of perfect reason.

"He hasn't. That Yarkin creature caught me up in the village. His bed hadn't been slept in last night, she said. But his car's in the garage. So he's somewhere nearby. And I've no doubt at all as to what he's been up to."

"The *vicar?*" Cecily asked, achieving horror while feeling all the delight of an unfolding drama. A shotgun wedding performed by a fornicating vicar, featuring a reluctant bridegroom in love with the vicar's housekeeper and a frothing bride hellbent on revenge. It was almost worth having to be chief bridesmaid just to be in the know. "No, Uncle St. John. Surely not the vicar. Heavens, what a scandal."

Her uncle glanced her way sharply. He pointed a finger at her and was beginning to speak when the curtain was drawn to one side once more. They turned as one to see the local constable, his heavy jacket flaked with snow, his tortoiseshell spectacles spotted with moisture. He wasn't wearing a hat, and his ginger hair wore a cap of white crystals. He shook them off, running a hand back over his head.

"Well?" Townley-Young demanded. "Have you found him, Shepherd?"

"I have," the other man replied. "But he's not going to be marrying anyone this morning."

JANUARY:
THE
FROST

CHAPTER ONE

WHAT DID THAT SIGN SAY? DID YOU SEE IT, SImon? It was some sort of placard at the edge of the road." Deborah St. James slowed the car and looked back. They'd already rounded a bend, and the thick lattice of bare branches from the oaks and horse chestnuts hid both the road itself and the lichenous limestone wall that had been edging it. Where they were now, the roadside's demarcation consisted of a skeletal hedge, denuded by winter and blackened by twilight. "It wasn't a sign for the hotel, was it? Did you see a drive?"

Her husband shook off the reverie in which he'd spent much of the long drive from Manchester airport, half-admiring the winter landscape of Lancashire with its subdued blend of moorland russets and farmland sage, half-brooding over the possible identification of the tool which had cut a thick electrical wire prior to its being used to bind together the hands and the feet of a female body found last week in Surrey.

"A drive?" he asked. "There might have been one. I didn't notice. But the sign was for palm reading and a psychic in residence."

"You're joking."

"I'm not. Is that a feature of the hotel you've not told me about?"

"Not that I know." She peered through the windscreen. The road began to slope upwards, and the lights from a village shimmered in the distance, perhaps a mile farther on. "I suppose we haven't gone far enough."

"What's the place called?"

"Crofters Inn."

"Decidedly, then, the sign didn't say that. It must be an advertisement for someone's line of employment. This is Lancashire, after all. I'm surprised the hotel isn't called The Cauldron."

"We wouldn't have come had it been, my love. I'm becoming superstitious in my advancing years."

"I see." He smiled in the growing darkness. *Her advancing years.* She was only twenty-five. She had all the energy and the promise of her youth.

Still, she looked tired—he knew she hadn't been sleeping well— and her face was wan. A few days in the country, long walks, and rest were what she needed. She'd been working too much in the past several months, working more than he, keeping late hours in the darkroom and going out far too early on assignments only marginally connected to her interests in the first place. I'm trying to broaden my horizons, she would say. Landscapes and portraits aren't enough, Simon. I need to do more. I'm thinking of a multimedia approach, perhaps a new show of my work in the summer. I can't get it ready if I don't get out there and see what's what and try new things and stretch myself and make some more contacts and . . . He didn't argue or try to hold her back. He just waited for the crisis to pass. They'd weathered several during the first two years of their marriage. He always tried to remember that fact when he began to despair of their weathering this.

She pushed a tangle of coppery hair behind her ear, put the car back into gear, and said, "Let's go on to the village, then, shall we?"

"Unless you'd like to have your palm read first."

"For my future, you mean? I think not, thank you."

He'd intended it as nothing. From the false brightness of her reply, he knew she hadn't taken it that way. He said, "Deborah . . . "

She reached for his hand. Driving, her eyes on the road, she pressed his palm to her cheek. Her skin was cool. It was soft, like the dawn. "I'm sorry," she said. "This is our time together. Don't let me mess it about."

But she didn't look at him. More and more, at tense moments she wasn't meeting his eyes. It was as if she believed that the act of doing so would give him an advantage she did not want him to have, while all the time he felt every single advantage between them was hers.

He let the moment pass. He touched her hair. He rested his hand on her thigh. She drove on.

From the palm reader's sign, it was little over a mile into the small village of Winslough, which was built along the acclivity of a hill. They passed the church first—a Norman structure with crenellation on its tower and along its roofline and a blue-faced clock permanently displaying the time as three twenty-two—then the primary school, then a row of terraced houses facing an open field. At the peak of the hill, in a Y where the Clitheroe Road met the west-east junctions leading to Lancaster or to Yorkshire, Crofters Inn sat.

Deborah idled the car at the junction. She wiped at some condensation on the windscreen, squinted at the building, and sighed. "Well. It's not much to speak of, is it? I thought . . . I was hoping . . . It sounded so romantic in the brochure."

"It's fine."

"It's from the fourteenth century. It's got a great hall where they used to hold a Magistrate's Court. The dining room's got a timbered ceiling, and the bar hasn't been changed in two hundred years. The brochure even said that—"

"It's fine."

"But I *wanted* it to be—"

"Deborah." She finally looked at him. "The hotel's not the point of our being here, is it?"

She looked back at the building. In spite of his words, she was seeing it through the lens of her camera, weighing each area of composition. How it was situated on its triangle of land, how it was placed in the village, how it was designed. She did it as a second-nature response, like breathing.

"No," she said at last, although she sounded reluctant. "No. It's not the point. I suppose."

She drove through a gate at the inn's west end and stopped in the car park behind it. Like all the other structures in the village, the building was a combination of the county's tan limestone and millstone grit. Even from behind, aside from white woodwork and green window boxes that were filled with a motley array of winter pansies, the inn bore no truly distinguishing features and no adornments. Its most significant distinction seemed to be an ominous portion of concaved slate roof that St. James earnestly hoped wasn't over their room.

"Well," Deborah said again with some resignation.

St. James leaned towards her, turned her to face him, and kissed her. "Did I mention I've been wanting to see Lancashire for years?"

She smiled at that. "In your dreams," she replied and got out of the car.

He opened the door, feeling the cold, damp air lap against him like water, smelling woodsmoke and the peaty odours of wet earth and decomposing leaves. He lifted out his braced bad leg and thumped it to the cobbles. There was no snow on the ground, but frost rimed the lawn of what would otherwise be a seasonal beer garden. It was abandoned now, but he could imagine it filled with summertime tourists who came to walk on the moors, to climb the hills, and to fish in the river that he could hear but not see, coursing noisily some thirty yards away. A path led towards it—he could see this as well since its frosty flagstones reflected the lights at the rear of the inn—and although the inn's property clearly did not include the river, a boundary wall had an access gate built into it. The gate was open and as he watched, a young girl hurried through it, stuffing a white plastic bag into the over-size anorak she was wearing. This was neon orange, and, despite the girl's considerable height, it hung down to her knees and drew attention to her legs which were encased in enormous, muddy green Wellingtons.

She started when she saw Deborah and St. James. But rather than hurry by them, she marched right up and, without ceremony or introduction, grabbed the suitcase that St. James had lifted from the boot of the car. She peered inside and snatched up his crutches as well.

"*Here* you are," she said, as if she'd been searching them out by the river. "Bit late, aren't you? Didn't the register say you'd be here by four?"

"I don't think I gave any time at all," Deborah replied, in some confusion. "Our plane didn't land until—"

"No matter," the girl said. "You're here now, aren't you? And there's plenty of time before dinner." She glanced at the misty lower windows of the inn, behind which an amorphous shape was moving under the distinctive bright lights of a kitchen. "A word to the wise is in order. Skip the beef bourguignon. It's the cook's name for stew. Come on. This way."

She began lugging the suitcase towards a rear door. With it in one hand and St. James' crutches under her arm, she walked with a peculiar, hobbling gait, her Wellingtons alternately squishing and slapping against the cobbles. There seemed to be nothing to do but follow, and St. James and Deborah did so, trailing the girl across the car park, up a set of back stairs, and through the rear door of the inn. This gave way to a corridor off of which opened a room whose door was marked with a hand-lettered sign saying *Residents' Lounge.*

The girl thumped the suitcase onto the carpet and leaned the crutches against it with their tips pressing onto a faded Axminster rose. "There," she announced and brushed her hands together in an I've-done-my-part gesture. "Will you tell Mum that Josie was waiting for you outside? Josie. That's me." This last she said stabbing a thumb to her chest. "It'd be a favour, actually. I'll pay you back."

St. James wondered how. The girl watched them earnestly.

"Okay," she said. "I can see what you're thinking. To be honest, she's 'had it with me,' if you know what I mean. It's nothing that I *did.* I mean, it's lots of stupid stuff. But mostly it's my hair. I mean, it doesn't generally *look* like this. Except it will for a while. I s'pose."

St. James couldn't decide if she was talking about the style or the colour, both of which were dreadful. The former was an ostensible attempt at a wedge which seemed to have been rendered by someone's nail scissors and someone else's electric razor. It made her look remarkably like Henry V as depicted in the National Portrait Gallery. The latter was an unfortunate shade of salmon that did battle with the neon jacket she wore. It suggested a dye job applied with more enthusiasm than expertise.

"Mousse," she said apropos of nothing.

"I beg your pardon?"

"Mousse. You know. The stuff for your hair. It was s'posed to just give me red highlights, but it didn't actually work." She drove her hands into the pockets of her jacket. "I got just about everything going against me, see. Try finding a fourth form bloke *my* height sometime. So I thought if I made my hair look better, I'd get some notice from a fifth or lower sixth bloke. Stupid. I know. You don't have to tell me. Mum's been doing that for the last three days. 'What am I go'n' to *do* with you, Josie?' Josie. That's me. Mum and Mr. Wragg own the inn. *Your* hair's awful pretty, by the way." This last was addressed to Deborah whom Josie was inspecting with no little interest. "And you're tall as well. But I expect you've stopped growing."

"I think I have. Yes."

"I haven't. The doctor says I'll be over six feet. A throwback to the Vikings, he says and he laughs and pats me on the shoulder like I ought to get the joke. Well, what the *H* were the Vikings doing in Lancashire, that's what I want to know."

"And your mother, no doubt, wants to know what you were doing by the river," St. James noted.

Josie looked flustered and waved her hands. "It's not the river, exactly. And it's nothing bad. Really. And it's only a favour. Just a mention of my name. 'Young girl met us in the car park, Mrs. Wragg. Tall. Bit gawky. Said her name was Josie. Quite pleasant she was.' If you'd drop it like that, Mum might unknot her knickers for a bit."

"Jo-se-*phine!*" A woman's voice shouted somewhere in the inn. "Jo-se-phine Eugenia Wragg!"

Josie winced. "I hate it when she does that. It reminds me of school. 'Josephine Eugene. She looks like a bean.' "

She didn't, actually. But she was tall, and she moved with the clumsiness of a young teenager who has suddenly become aware of her body before she's got used to it. St. James thought of his own sister at this very same age, cursed by height, by the aquiline features into which she hadn't yet grown, and by a wretchedly androgynous name. Sidney, she would introduce herself sardonically, the last of the St. James boys. She'd borne the brunt of her schoolmates' teasing for years.

Gravely, he said, "Thank you for waiting in the car park, Josie. It's always nice to be met when one gets where one's going."

The girl's face lit. "Ta. Oh, *ta*," she said and headed for the door through which they'd come. "I'll pay you back. You'll see."

"I've no doubt of that."

"Just go on through the pub. Someone'll meet you there." She waved them in the general direction of another door across the room. "I've got to get out of these Wellies quick." And with another querying look at them, "You won't mention the Wellies, will you? They're Mr. Wragg's."

Which went a long way to explain why she'd been flopping about like a swimmer wearing flippers. "My lips are sealed," St. James said. "Deborah?"

"The very same."

Josie grinned in response and slipped through the door.

Deborah picked up St. James' crutches and looked about at the L-shaped room that served as the lounge. Its collection of overstuffed furniture was tatty, and several lampshades were askew. But a break-front sideboard held an array of magazines for guests to peruse, and a bookcase was crammed with a good fifty volumes. Above pine wain-scotting the wallpaper appeared recently hung—poppies and roses twining together—and the air bore the decided fragrance of potpourri. She turned to St. James. He was smiling at her.

"What?" she said.

"Just like home," he replied.

"Someone's, at least." She led the way into the pub.

They had arrived, apparently, during off-hours, for no one was present behind the mahogany bar or at any of the matching pub-issue tables which beer mats dotted in small round splodges of orange and beige. They dodged their way past these and their accompanying stools and chairs, under a ceiling that was low, its heavy timbers blackened by generations of smoke and decorated with a display of intricate horse brasses. In the fireplace, the re-mains of an afternoon's blaze was still glowing, giving an occasional snap as final pockets of resin burst.

"Where'd she get off to, that blasted girl?" a woman was de-manding. She spoke from what was apparently an office. Its door stood open to the left of the bar. Immediately next to it, a stairway rose, with steps oddly slanted as if strained from bearing weight. The woman came out, yelled "Jo-se-*phine!*" up the stairs, and then caught sight of St. James and his wife. Like Josie, she started. Like Josie, she was tall and thin, and her elbows were pointed like arrow heads. She raised one self-conscious hand to her hair and removed a plastic barrette of pink rosebuds which held it haphazardly off her cheeks. She lowered the other to the front of her skirt and brushed aimlessly at a snowfall of lint. "Towels," she said in apparent explanation of the latter activity. "She was supposed to fold them. She didn't. I had to. That sums up life with a fourteen-year-old girl."

"I think we just met her," St. James said. "In the car park."

"She was waiting for us," Deborah added cooperatively. "She helped us in with our things."

"Did she?" The woman's eyes went from them to their suitcase. "You must be Mr. and Mrs. St. James. Welcome. We've given you Skylight."

"Skylight?"

"The room. It's our best. A bit cold, I'm afraid, at this time of year, but we've put in an extra heater for you."

Cold didn't really do justice to the condition of the room to which she led them, two flights up, at the very top of the hotel. Although the free-standing electric heater was ticking away, sending out palpable streams of warmth, the room's three windows and two additional skylights acted like transmitters for the cold outside. Two feet in any direction from them, one walked into a shield of ice.

Mrs. Wragg drew the curtains. "Dinner's from half past seven till nine. Will you be wanting anything prior to that? Have you had your tea? Josie can pop up with a pot, if you like."

"Nothing for me," St. James said. "Deborah?"

"No."

Mrs. Wragg nodded. She rubbed her hands up the sides of her arms. "Well," she said. She bent to pick a length of white thread from the carpet. She wound it round her finger. "Bath's through that door. Mind your head, though. The lintel's a bit low. But then all of them are. It's the building. It's old. You know the sort of thing."

"Yes, of course."

She went to the chest of drawers between the two front windows and made minute adjustments to a cheval mirror and more adjustments to the lace doily beneath it. She opened the clothes cupboard, saying, "Extra blankets here," and she patted the chintz upholstery of the room's only chair. When it became apparent that there was nothing more to be done, she said, "London, aren't you?"

"Yes," St. James said.

"We don't get lots here from London."

"It's quite a distance, after all."

"No. It's not that. Londoners head south. Dorset or Cornwall. Everyone does." She went to the wall behind the chair and fussed with one of two prints hanging there, a copy of Renoir's *Two Girls at the Piano*, mounted on a white mat going yellow at the edges. "There's not a lot likes the cold," she added.

"There's some truth in that."

"Northerners move to London as well. Chasing dreams, I think. Like Josie does. Did she . . . I wonder did she ask about London?"

St. James glanced at his wife. Deborah had unlocked the suitcase and opened it on the bed. But at the question, she slowed what she was doing and stood, a single feathery grey scarf in her hands.

"No," Deborah said. "She didn't mention London."

Mrs. Wragg nodded, then flashed a quick smile. "Well, that's good, isn't it? Because that girl's got a mind for mischief when it comes to anything that'll take her from Winslough." She brushed her hands together and balled them at her waist and said, "So then. You've come for country air and good walks. And we've plenty of both. On the moors. Through the fields. Up into the hills. We had snow last month—first time it's snowed in these parts in ages—but we've only frost now. 'Fool's snow,' my mum called it. Makes things muddy, but I expect you've brought your Wellies."

"We have."

"Good. You ask my Ben—that's Mr. Wragg—where's the best place to walk. No one knows the lay of the land like my Ben."

"Thank you," Deborah said. "We'll do that. We're looking forward to some walks. And to seeing the vicar as well."

"The vicar?"

"Yes."

"Mr. Sage?"

"Yes."

Mrs. Wragg's right hand slithered from her waist to the collar of her blouse.

"What is it?" Deborah asked. She and St. James exchanged a glance. "Mr. Sage's still in the parish, isn't he?"

"No. He's . . ." Mrs. Wragg pressed her fingers into her neck and completed her thought in a rush. "I suppose he's gone to Cornwall himself. Like everyone else. In a manner of speaking."

"What's that?" St. James asked.

"It's . . ." She gulped. "It's where he was buried."

CHAPTER TWO

POLLY YARKIN RAN A DAMP CLOTH ACROSS THE work top and folded it neatly at the edge of the sink. It was a needless endeavour. No one had used the vicar's kitchen in the last four weeks, and from the looks of things no one was likely to use it for several weeks more. But she still came daily to the vicarage as she had been doing for the last six years, seeing to things now just as she had seen to things for Mr. Sage and his two youthful predecessors who had both given precisely three years to the village before moving on to grander vistas. If there *was* such a creature as a grander vista in the C of E.

Polly dried her hands on a chequered tea towel and hung this on its rack above the sink. She'd waxed the linoleum floor that morning, and she was pleased to note that when she looked down, she could see her reflection on its pristine surface. Not a perfect reflection, naturally. A floor isn't a mirror. But she could see well enough the shadowy crinkles of carrot hair that escaped the tight binding of scarf at the back of her neck. And she could see—far too well—her body's silhouette, slope-shouldered with the weight of her watermelon breasts.

Her lower back ached as it always ached, and her shoulders stung where the overfull bra pulled its dead weight against the straps. She prised her index finger under one of these and winced as the resulting release of pressure from one shoulder only made the other feel that much worse. You're so lucky, Poll, her mates had cooed enviously as undeveloped girls, lads go all woozy at the thought of you. And her mother had said, Conceived in the circle, blessed by the Goddess, in her typical crypto-maternal fashion, and she swatted Polly's bum the first and final time the girl had spoken about having surgery to reduce the burden dangling like lead from her chest.

She dug her fists into the small of her back and looked at the wall clock above the kitchen table. It was half past six. No one was going to come to the vicarage this late in the day. There was no reason to linger.

There was no real reason at all, in fact, for Polly's continued presence in Mr. Sage's home. Still, she came each morning and stayed beyond dark. She dusted, cleaned, and told the church wardens that it was important—indeed, it was crucial at this time of year—to keep up the house for Mr. Sage's replacement. And all the time that she worked, she kept an eye watching for a movement from the vicar's nearest neighbour.

She'd been doing that daily since Mr. Sage's death when Colin Shepherd had first come round with his constable's pad and his constable's questions, sifting through Mr. Sage's belongings in his quiet, knowing constable's way. He'd only glance at her when she answered the door to him each morning. He'd say Hullo Polly and slide his eyes away. He'd go to the study or to the vicar's bedroom. Or sometimes he'd sit and sort through the post. He'd jot down notes and stare for long minutes at the vicar's diary, as if an examination of Mr. Sage's appointments somehow contained the key to his death.

Talk to me, Colin, she wanted to say when he was there. Make it like it was. Come back. Be my friend.

But she didn't say anything. Instead, she offered tea. And when he refused—No thanks, Polly. I'll be off in a moment.—she returned to her work, polishing mirrors, washing the insides of windows, scrubbing toilets, floors, basins, and tubs till her hands were raw and the whole house glowed. Whenever she could, she watched him, cataloguing the details designed to make her lot lighter to bear. Got too square of a chin, does Colin. His eyes are nice green but far too small. Wears his hair silly, tries to comb it straight back and it always parts in the middle and then flops forward so it covers his brow. He's always messing it about, he is, raking his fingers through it in place of a comb.

But the fingers generally stopped her dead, and there the useless catalogue ended. He had the most beautiful hands in the world.

Because of those hands and the thought of them gliding their fingers across her skin, she'd always end up where she started from at first. Talk to me, Colin. Make it like it was.

He never did, which was just as well. For she didn't really want him to make it like it had been between them at all.

Too soon for her liking, the investigation ended. Colin Shepherd, village constable, read out his findings in an untroubled voice at the coroner's inquest. She'd gone because everyone in the village had done so, filling up the space in the great hall at the inn. But unlike everyone else, she'd gone only to see Colin and to hear him speak.

"Death by misadventure," the coroner announced. "Accidental poisoning." The case was closed.

But closing the case didn't put an end to the titillated whispers, the innuendoes, or the reality that in a village like Winslough *poisoning* and *accidental* constituted a sure invitation to gossip and an indisputable contradiction in terms. So Polly had stayed in her place at the vicarage, arriving at half past seven each morning, expecting, hoping day after day, that the case would reopen and that Colin would return.

Wearily, she dropped onto one of the kitchen chairs and eased her feet into the work boots she'd left early that morning on the growing pile of newspapers. No one had thought to cancel Mr. Sage's subscriptions yet. She'd been too caught up with thinking of Colin to do so herself. She'd do it tomorrow, she decided. It would be a reason to return once more.

When she closed the front door, she spent a few moments on the vicarage steps to loosen her hair from the scarf that bound it. Freed, it crinkled like rusty steel wool round her face, and the night breeze shifted it the length of her back. She folded the scarf into a triangle, making sure the words *Rita Read Me Like A Book In Blackpool!* were hidden from view. She put it over her head and knotted its ends beneath her chin. Thus restrained, her hair scratched her cheeks and her neck. She knew it couldn't possibly look attractive, but at least it wouldn't fly about her head and catch in her mouth as she made the walk home. Besides, stopping on the steps beneath the porch light, which she always left burning once the sun went down, gave her the opportunity for an unimpeded look at the house next door. If the lights were on, if his car was in the drive . . .

Neither was the case. As she trudged across the gravel and plunged into the road, Polly wondered what she would have done had Colin Shepherd actually been at home this evening.

Knock on the door?

Yes? Oh, hullo. What is it, Polly?

Press her thumb against the bell?

Is there something wrong?

Cup her eyes to the windows?

Are you needing the police?

Walk direct in and start up talking and pray that Colin would talk as well?

I don't understand what you want with me, Polly.

She buttoned her coat beneath her chin and blew grey steamy breath on her hands. The temperature was falling. It had to be less than five degrees. There'd be ice on the roads and sleet if it rained. If he didn't drive careful coming round a curve, he'd lose control of the car. Perhaps she'd come upon him. She'd be the only one near enough to help. She'd cradle his head in her lap and press her hand to his brow and brush his hair back and keep him warm. Colin.

"He'll be back to you, Polly," Mr. Sage had said just three nights before his death. "You stand firm and be here for him. Be ready to listen. He's going to need you in his life. Perhaps sooner than you think."

But all of that was nothing more than Christian mumbo-jumbo, reflecting the most futile of Church beliefs. If one prayed long enough, there was a God who listened, who evaluated requests, who stroked a long white beard, looked thoughtful, and said, "Yesssss. I see," and fulfilled one's dreams.

It was a load of rubbish.

Polly headed south, out of the village, walking on the verge of the Clitheroe Road. The going was rough. The path was muddy and clogged with dead leaves. She could hear the squish of her footsteps over the wind that creaked above her in the trees.

Across the street, the church was dark. There would be no even-song till they got a new vicar. The Church Council had been inter-viewing for the past two weeks, but there seemed to be a scarcity of priests who wanted to take up life in a country village. No bright lights and no big city seemed to equate with no souls needing to be saved, which was hardly the case. There was plenty of scope for salvation in Winslough. Mr. Sage had been quick to see that, especially—and perhaps most of all—in Polly herself.

For she was a long time, long ago sinner. Skyclad in the cold of winter, in the balmy nights of summer, in the spring and fall, she had cast the circle. She had faced the altar north. Placing the candles at the circle's four gates and using the water, the salt, and the herbs, she created a holy, magical cosmos from which she could pray. All the elements were there: the water, the air, the fire, the earth. The cord snaked round her thigh. The wand felt strong and sure in her hand. She used cloves for the incense and laurel for the wood and she gave herself—heart and soul, she declared—to the Rite of the Sun. For health and vitality. Praying for hope where the doctors had said there was none. Asking for healing when all they promised was morphine for the pain until death finally closed all.

Lit by the candles and the burning laurel's flame, she had chanted the petition to Those whose presence she had earnestly invoked:

> *Annie's health restor-ed be.*
> *God and Goddess grant my plea.*

And she had told herself—convinced herself utterly—that her every intention was wholesome and pure. She prayed for Annie, her friend from childhood, sweet Annie Shepherd, darling Colin's own wife. But only the spotless could call upon the Goddess and expect response. The magic of those who made the petition had to be pure.

Impulsively, Polly traced her steps back to the church and entered the graveyard. It was as black as the inside of the Horned God's mouth, but she needed no light to show her the way. Nor did she need it to read the stone. ANNE ALICE SHEPHERD. And beneath it the dates and the words *Dearest Wife*. There was nothing more and nothing fancy, for more and fancy were not Colin's way.

"Oh Annie," Polly said to the stone that stood in the even deeper shadows where the wall of the yard skirted round a thick-branched chestnut tree. "It's come upon me three-fold like the Rede says it would. But I swear to you, Annie, I never meant you harm."

Yet even as she swore, the doubts were upon her. Like a plague of locusts, they laid her conscience bare. They exposed the worst of what she had been, a woman who wanted someone's husband for her own.

"You did what you could, Polly," Mr. Sage had told her, covering her hand with his own large mitt. "No one can truly pray away cancer. One can pray that the doctors have the wisdom to help. Or that the patient develops the strength to endure. Or that the family learns to cope with the sorrow. But the disease itself... No, dear Polly, one can't pray away that."

The vicar had meant well, but he didn't really know her. He wasn't the sort who could comprehend her sins. There was no absolution saying *go in peace* for what she had longed for in the foulest part of her heart.

Now she paid the three-fold price of having invited upon herself the wrath of the Gods. But it wasn't cancer that they sent to afflict her. It was a finer vengeance than Hammurabi could ever have wrought.

"I'd trade places with you, Annie," Polly whispered. "I would. I *would*."

"Polly?" A low, disembodied whisper in return.

She jumped back from the grave, her hand at her mouth. A rush of blood beat against her eyes.

"Polly? Is that you?"

Footsteps crunched just beyond the wall, gumboots snapping on the icy dead leaves that lay on the ground. She saw him then, a shadow among shadows. She smelled the pipe smoke that clung to his clothes.

"Brendan?" She didn't need to wait for confirmation. What little light there was shone itself on Brendan Power's beak of a nose. No one else in Winslough had a profile to match it. "What're you doing out here?"

He seemed to read in the question an implicit and unintended invitation. He vaulted the wall. She stepped away. He approached her eagerly. She could see he held his pipe in his hand.

"I've been out to the Hall." He tapped the pipebowl against Annie's gravestone, dislodging burnt tobacco like ebony freckles on the frozen skin of the grave. He appeared to realise the impropriety of what he had done in the very next instant, because he said, "Oh. Damn. Sorry," and he squatted and brushed the tobacco away. He stood, buried the pipe in his pocket, and shuffled his feet. "I was walking back to the village on the footpath. I saw someone in the graveyard, and I—" He lowered his head and seemed to be studying the barely discernible tops of his black gumboots. "I hoped it was you, Polly."

"How's your wife?" she asked.

He raised his head. "The renovation at the Hall's been tampered with again. A bathroom tap left on. Some carpet's got ruined. Rebecca's worked herself into a state."

"Understandable, isn't it?" Polly said. "She wants a home of her own. It can't be easy, living at her mum and dad's, with a baby on the way."

"No," he said. "It's not easy. For anyone. Polly."

At the warmth of his tone, she looked away, in the distant direction of Cotes Hall where for the last four months a team of decorators and craftsmen had been pounding away at the long-abandoned Victorian structure, attempting to ready it for Brendan and his wife. "I can't think why he doesn't arrange for a night watchman."

"He won't be bullied into a watchman, he says. He's got Mrs. Spence right on the grounds. He's paying her to be there. And by God she ought to be bloody enough. Or so he says."

"And does—" She worked at saying the name and betraying nothing as she said it. "Does Missus Spence never hear any mischief being made?"

"Not from her cottage. It's too far behind the Hall, she says. And when she makes rounds, no one's ever there."

"Ah."

They were silent. Brendan shifted his weight. Icy soil crackled beneath him. A gust of night wind soughed through the chestnut's branches and blew at the back of Polly's hair where the scarf couldn't manage to hold it in place.

"Polly."

She heard both the urgency and the plea in his voice. She'd seen them before on his face when he asked to join her at her table in the pub, appearing as if with preternatural knowledge of her movements each time she went to Crofters Inn for a drink. Now, as on those other occasions, she felt her stomach knot and her limbs grow cold.

She knew what he wanted. It was no different from what everyone wanted: rescue, escape, a secret to cling to, a half-formed dream. What did it matter to him if she was hurt in the process? On what account book was ever written the payment exacted for damage to a soul?

You're married, Brendan, she wanted to say in a tone that combined both patience and compassion. Even if I loved you—which I don't, you know—you've got a wife. Go on home to her now. Climb into bed and make love to Rebecca. You were willing enough to do that at one time.

But she was cursed with being a woman not naturally given to either rejection or cruelty. So instead, she said only, "I'll be off now, Brendan. My mum's waiting supper," and she headed out the way she had come.

She heard him following. He said, "I'll walk with you. You shouldn't be out here alone."

"It's too far," she said. "And you've just come that way, haven't you?"

"But on the footpath," he said with an assurance suggesting he believed his answer was the height of logic. "Across the meadow. Over the walls. I didn't walk along the road." He matched his steps to hers. "I've got a torch," he added, pulling it out of his pocket. "You shouldn't be walking at night without a torch."

"It's only a mile, Brendan. I can cope with that."

"So can I."

She sighed. She wanted to explain that he couldn't simply take a walk with her in the dark. People would see them. They'd misunderstand.

But she knew in advance how he would respond to her explanation. They'll just think I'm walking to the Hall, he'd answer, I go out there every day.

What an innocent he was. How imperfect was his understanding of village life. It would matter little to anyone who saw them that Polly and her mother had lived twenty years in the gabled lodge at the mouth of the drive that led to Cotes Hall. No one would stop to think of that, or to think that Brendan was checking on the Hall's renovation in anticipation of moving there with his bride. *Assignation by night*, the villagers would label it. Rebecca would hear of it. There'd be hell to pay.

Not that Brendan wasn't paying already. Polly had little doubt of that. She'd seen enough of Rebecca Townley-Young throughout their lives to know that marriage to her under the best of conditions would not be a particularly nurturing affair.

So among other things, she felt sorry for Brendan which is why she allowed him to join her at Crofters Inn in the evening, which is why she now just kept walking along the verge, with her eyes fastened on the steady, bright beam from Brendan's torch. She didn't attempt to make conversation. She had a fairly good idea where any conversation with Brendan Power would ultimately lead.

A quarter of a mile along, she slipped on a stone, and Brendan took her arm.

"Careful," he said.

She could feel the back of his fingers pressing against her breast. With each of her footsteps, the fingers rose and fell, acting the part of distant cousin to caress.

She shrugged, hoping to disengage his hand. His grip grew firmer.

"It was Craigie Stockwell," Brendan said diffidently into the growing silence between them.

She drew her eyebrows together. "Craigie what?"

"The carpet at the Hall. Craigie Stockwell. From London. It's a ruin now. The drain in the basin was plugged with a rag. Friday night, I should guess. It looked as if the water had run all weekend."

"And no one *knew*?"

"We'd gone down to Manchester."

"Doesn't anyone go inside when the workmen aren't there? Check things're in order?"

"Mrs. Spence, you mean?" He shook his head. "She generally just checks the windows and doors."

"But isn't she supposed to be—"

"She's a caretaker. Not a security guard. And I imagine she's nervous out there alone. Without a man, I mean. It's a lonely spot."

But she'd frightened off intruders at least once, Polly knew. She'd heard the shotgun herself. And then a few minutes later came the thudding of two or three frantic, shouting runners, and the gunning of a motorbike afterwards. The word went out to the village after that. People didn't mess Juliet Spence about.

Polly shivered. The wind was rising. It blew in brief, frigid gusts through the bare hawthorn hedge that bordered the road. It promised a heavier frost in the morning.

"You're cold," Brendan said.

"No."

"You're shivering, Polly. Here." He put his arm round her and drew her snugly next to him. "Better, isn't it?" She didn't reply. "We walk together at the same pace, don't we? Have you noticed that? But if you put your arm round my waist, it's even easier going."

"Brendan."

"You haven't been to the pub this week. Why?"

She didn't respond. She moved her shoulders. His grip remained firm.

"Polly, have you been up Cotes Fell?"

She felt the cold on her cheeks. It insinuated itself like tentacles down her neck. Ah, she thought, here it comes at last. Because he'd seen her there one evening last autumn. He'd heard her petition. He knew the worst.

But he went on easily. "I find I like hiking more and more every week. I've been out to the reservoir three times, you know. I've done a long tramp through the Trough of Bowland and another near Claughton, up Beacon Fell. The air smells so fresh. Have you noticed that? When you reach the top? But then, I suppose you're too busy to do much walking."

Now he'll say it, she thought. Now comes the price I'll have to pay him to hold his tongue.

"With all the men in your life."

The allusion was a puzzle.

He shot her a glance. "There must be men. Lots, I'd guess. That's probably why you've not been in the pub. Busy, aren't you? Dating, I mean. Someone special, no doubt."

Someone special. Without consideration, Polly gave a weary chuckle.

"There *is* someone, isn't there? A woman like you. I mean. I can't imagine a bloke who wouldn't. Given half a chance. *I* would. You're terrific. Anyone can see that."

He switched off the torch and put it in his pocket. Freed, his other hand grasped her arm.

"You look so good, Polly," he said and bent closer. "You smell good. You feel good. Chap doesn't see that needs his head examined."

His steps slowed then stopped. There was reason for this, she told herself. They had reached the drive at one side of which sat the lodge where she lived. But then he turned her to him.

"Polly," he said urgently. He caressed her cheek. "I feel so much for you. I know you've seen it. Won't you please let me—"

A car's headlamps caught them like rabbits in its beam, not coming along the Clitheroe Road but bumping and jolting along the lane that led beyond the lodge up to Cotes Hall. And just like rabbits, they froze in position, Brendan's one hand on Polly's cheek, his other on her arm. There could be no real mistaking his intentions.

"Brendan!" Polly said.

He dropped his hands and put a careful two feet between them. But it was too late. The car came upon them slowly, then slowed even more. It was an old green Land Rover, mud-spattered and grimy, but its windscreen and windows were perfectly clean.

Polly turned her head away from the sight of it, not so much because she didn't want to be seen and gossiped over—she knew that nothing would spare her that—but so she wouldn't have to see the driver or the woman next to him with her blunt greying hair and her angular face and, Polly could see it all so vividly without even trying, with her arm stretched out so that the tips of her fingers rested on the back of the driver's neck. Touching and twining through that slicked-back, undisciplined, ginger hair.

Colin Shepherd and Missus Spence were having another lovely evening together. The Gods were reminding Polly Yarkin of her sins.

■　　■　　■

Damn the air and the wind, Polly thought. There was no justice. No matter what she did, it came out wrong. She slammed the door behind her and drove her fist into it once.

"Polly? That you, luv-doll?"

She heard the roll of her mother's heavy footsteps trundling across the sitting room floor. The sound of wheezing accompanied this, as did the clink and clatter of jewellery—chains, necklaces, gold doubloons, and anything else her mother saw fit to deck herself out with when she made her wintertime morning toilette.

"Me, Rita," Polly answered. "Who else?"

"I dunno, luv. Some good-looking chappie with a sausage to share? Got to keep yourself open to the unexpected. 'At's my motto, that is." Rita laughed and wheezed. Her scent preceded her like an olfactory harbinger. Giorgio. She sprayed it on by the tablespoon. She came to the door of the sitting room and filled it, so large a woman that she ballooned out in a shapeless mass from her neck to her knees. She leaned against the jamb, working hard to catch her breath. The entry light glistened against the necklaces on her massive chest. It cast a grotesque Rita-shadow on the wall and made a fleshy beard of one of her chins.

Polly squatted to unlace her boots. They were thick-soled with mud, a fact that did not escape her mother.

"Where you been, luv-doll?" Rita jingle-jangled one of her necklaces, an affair of large cat heads fashioned in brass. "You go for a hike?"

"Road's muddy," Polly said with a grunt as she forced off one boot and worked on the other. Their laces were sodden, and her fingers were stiff. "Wintertime. You forget what it's like?"

"Wish I could, I do," her mother said. "So how's things in the metropolis today?"

She pronounced it metro-POH-lis. Deliberately. It was part of her persona. She wore a guise of spurious ignorance while in the village, an extension of the general style she adopted when she came home for her winters in Winslough. Spring, autumn, and summer, she was Rita Rularski, reader of tarot, thrown stones, and palms. From her shopfront in Blackpool, she foresaw the future, expounded on the past, and made sense of the troubled, fractious present for anyone willing to part with the cash. Residents, tourists, holiday-makers, curious housewives, fine ladies looking for a giggle and a thrill, Rita saw them all with equal aplomb, dressed in a kaftan big enough to fit an elephant, with a bright scarf covering her grizzled brambles of hair.

But in winter she became Rita Yarkin again, back in Winslough for a three-month stay with her only child. She put her hand-painted sign on the verge of the road and waited for custom which seldom developed. She read magazines and watched the telly. She ate like a docker and painted her nails.

Polly glanced at these curiously. Purple today, with a tiny strip of gold crossing each one diagonally. They clashed with her kaftan—it was pumpkin orange—but they were a decided improvement over yesterday's yellow.

"You tiff with someone this evenin', luv-doll?" Rita asked. "You got an aura shrivelled to nothing, you do. That a'nt good, is it? Here. Lemme take a look at your face."

"It's nothing." Polly made herself busier than she needed to be. She banged her boots against the inside of the woodbox next to the door. She took off her scarf and folded it neatly into a square. She put this square in the pocket of her coat and then brushed the coat itself with the flat of her hand, removing both speckles of lint and nonexistent splatters of mud.

Her mother wasn't to be easily side-tracked. She pushed her huge mass from the door-jamb. She waddled to Polly and turned her round. She peered at her face. With her hand palm-open and an inch away, she traced the shape of Polly's head and her shoulders.

"I see." She pursed her lips and dropped her arm with a sigh. "Stars and earth, girl, stop being such a fool."

Polly stepped to one side and headed for the stairs. "I need my slippers," she said. "I'll be down in a minute. I can smell supper. Have you done goulash like you said?"

"Listen here, Pol. Mr. C. Shepherd a'nt so special," Rita said. "He got nothing to offer a woman like you. Do you not see that yet?"

"Rita . . ."

"It's living that counts. *Living,* you hear? You got life and knowledge like blood in your veins. You got gifts beyond anything I ever had or seen. Use them. Damn it all, don't throw them away. Gods above, if I had half what you have, I'd own the world. Stop climbing those stairs and listen to me, girl." She slammed her hand down on the banister.

Polly felt the stairs tremble. She turned, blowing out a gust of resigned breath. It was only the three months of winter that she and her mother were together, but in the last six years, day tended to drag upon day as Rita used every excuse she could find to examine the manner in which Polly was living her life.

"That was him went by in the car just now, wasn't it?" Rita asked. "Mr. C. Shepherd his precious self. With *her,* wasn't he? From up at the Hall. That's what you're feeling the pain of now, isn't it?"

"It's nothing," Polly said.

"And there you've got it right. It's nothing. He's nothing. Where's the sorrow in that?"

But he wasn't nothing to Polly. He never had been. How could she explain this to her mother, whose only experience of love had ended abruptly when her husband left Winslough on the rainy morning of Polly's seventh birthday, headed to Manchester "to get something special for my extra-special little girl," and never came home.

Deserted was not a word Rita Yarkin ever used to describe what had happened to her and her only child. *Blessed* she called it. If he didn't have the sense to know what kind of women he was walking out on, they were both better off without the ugly toad.

Rita had always seen her life in those terms. Every difficulty, trial, or misfortune could be easily redefined as a blessing in disguise. Disappointments were wordless messages from the Goddess. Rejections were merely indications that the most desired pathway was not the best. For long ago, Rita Yarkin had given herself—heart, mind, and body—into the safekeeping of the Craft of the Wise. Polly admired her for such trust and devotion. She only wished she could feel the same.

"I'm not like you, Rita."

"You are," Rita said. "You're more like me than me in the first place. When did you last cast the circle? Not since I've been home, surely."

"I have done. Yes. Since then. Two or three times."

Her mother raised one sceptical, line-drawn eyebrow. "You're the discreet one, aren't you? Where you been casting?"

"Up Cotes Fell. You know that, Rita."

"And the Rite?"

Polly felt prickly heat on the back of her neck. She'd have chosen not to answer, but her mother's power was becoming stronger every time she made a reply. She could feel it quite distinctly now, as if it were oozing from Rita's fingers, slithering up the banister and through Polly's palm.

"Venus," she said miserably and tore her eyes from Rita's face. She waited for the mockery.

It did not come. Instead Rita took her hand from the banister and studied her daughter thoughtfully. "Venus," she said. "This i'n't about making love potions, Polly."

"I know that."

"Then—"

"But it's still about love. You don't want me to feel it. I know that, Mum. But it's there all the same and I can't make it go away just because you'd have me. I love him. Don't you think I'd stop it if only I could? Don't you think I pray to feel nothing for him . . . or at least to feel for him nothing more'n what he feels for me? D'you think I *choose* to be tortured like this?"

"I think we all choose our tortures." Rita lumbered to an ancient rosewood Canterbury made lopsided by the absence of two of its wheels. It leaned against one of the walls in the entry beneath the stairs, and with a grunt to rock her weight to one side, Rita bent as much as her legs would allow and wrestled open its single drawer. She brought out two rectangles of wood. "Here," she said. "Take 'em."

Without question or protest, Polly took the wood. She could smell its unmistakable odour, sharp but pleasant, a permeative scent.

"Cedar," she said.

"Correct," said Rita. "Burn it to Mars. Pray for strength, girl. Leave love to those who don't have your gifts."

CHAPTER THREE

RS. WRAGG LEFT THEM IMMEDIATELY AFTER making her announcement about the vicar. To Deborah's dismayed "But what happened? How on earth did he die?" she said guardedly, "I couldn't quite say. A friend of his, are you?"

No. Of course. They hadn't been friends. They'd only shared a few minutes' conversation in the National Gallery on a rainy, blowing November day. Still, the memory of Robin Sage's kindness and his anxious concern made Deborah feel leaden—struck by a mixture of surprise and dismay—when she was told he was dead.

"I'm sorry, my love," St. James said when Mrs. Wragg closed the door upon her own departure. Deborah could see the worry darkening his eyes, and she knew he was reading her thoughts as only a man who had known her all her life could have possibly read them. He didn't go on to say what she knew he wanted to say: It isn't you, Deborah. You haven't death's touch, no matter what you think... Instead, he held her.

They finally descended the stairs between the bar and the office at half past seven. The pub was apparently in the process of serving its regular evening crowd. Farmers leaned against the bar engaged in conversation. Housewives gathered at tables enjoying an evening out. Two ageing couples compared walking sticks while six noisy teenagers joked loudly in a corner and smoked cigarettes.

From the midst of this latter group—among which, accompanied by the ribald comments of their mates, one couple necked heavily, with an occasional pause from the girl to nip at a flask and from the boy to drag deeply on a cigarette—Josie Wragg emerged. She'd changed for the evening into what appeared to be a work uniform. But part of her black skirt's hem was falling out and her red bow tie was hopelessly askew, dribbling a long, unravelling string down the prairie expanse of her chest.

She ducked behind the bar where she scooped up two menus, and she said formally, with a wary eye in the direction of the balding man who pulled the pub's taps with the sort of authority that suggested he had to be Mr. Wragg the proprietor, "Good evening, sir. Madam. You've settled in good?"

"Perfectly," St. James replied.

"Then I expect you'll want to have a look at these." She handed the menus over with a low-voiced "But mind you. Don't forget what I said about the beef."

They skirted past the farmers, one of whom was shaking a monitory fist, red-faced and talking about "telling him tha's a public footpath . . . *public*, you hear me" and wound their way through the tables to the fireplace where flames were rapidly working on a cone-shaped pile of silver birch. They met curious glances as they crossed the room—tourists were unusual in Lancashire at this time of year—but to their pleasant *good evening,* the men nodded brusquely in wordless greeting and the women bobbed their heads. And while the teenagers remained in their far corner of the pub, happily oblivious of everyone but themselves, it seemed less group-egocentricity than it was interest in the continuing entertainment provided by the blonde flask-nipper and her companion, who was at this moment busy snaking his hand under the bright yellow sweat shirt she wore. The material undulated as his fist rose like a mobile third breast.

Deborah sat on a bench beneath a faded and decidedly unpointillistic needlepoint rendering of *A Sunday Afternoon on the Grand Jatte.* St. James took the stool opposite her. They ordered sherry and whisky, and when Josie brought the drinks to their table, she positioned her body to block the young entwined lovers from their view.

"Sorry about that," she said with a wrinkle of her nose as she placed the sherry in front of Deborah and adjusted it just so. She did the same with the whisky. "Pam Rice, that is. Playing tart for the night. Don't ask me why. She's not a bad sort. Just when she gets with Todd. *He's* seventeen."

This last was offered as if the boy's age explained all. But perhaps thinking it might not have done, Josie continued. "Thirteen. Pam, that is. Fourteen next month."

"And thirty-five sometime next year, no doubt," St. James noted drily.

Josie squinted over her shoulder at the young couple. Despite her previous look of disdain, her bony chest rose tremulously. "Yes. Well . . . " And then she turned back to them with what seemed like effort. "What'll you have, then? Besides the beef. The salmon's quite good. So's the duck. And the veal's"—The pub's outer door opened, letting in a gust of cold air that puffed round their ankles like moving silk—"cooked with tomatoes and mushrooms, and we've got a sole tonight done with capers and . . . " Josie's recitation faltered as, behind her, the hubbub from the Crofters Inn patrons dissolved with remarkable speed into silence.

A man and woman stood just inside the door, where an overhead light shone down upon the contrast they made. First hair: his roughly the colour of ginger; hers salt and pepper, thick, straight, and bluntly cut to touch her shoulders. Then face: his youthful and handsome but with a pugnacious prominence to the jaw and chin; hers strong and forceful, untouched by make-up to hide middle age. And clothes: his a barbour jacket and trousers; hers a worn navy pea jacket and faded blue jeans with a patch on one knee.

For a moment, they remained side by side in the entry, the man's hand resting on the woman's arm. He wore tortoiseshell spectacles whose lenses caught the light and effectively hid his eyes and his reaction to the hush that greeted his entrance. She, however, looked round slowly, making deliberate contact with every face that had the courage to hold her gaze.

" . . . capers and . . . and . . . " Josie appeared to have forgotten the rest of her prepared recitation. She poked the pencil into her hair and scratched it against her scalp.

From behind the bar, Mr. Wragg spoke as he scooped the froth off a glass of Guinness. "Evening to you, Constable. Evening, Missus Spence. Cold night, in't it? We're in for a bad snap, you ask me. You, Frank Fowler. Another stout?"

At last one of the farmers turned from the door. Others began to do the same. "Wouldn't say no, Ben," Frank Fowler replied, and knuckled his glass across the bar.

Ben pulled on the tap. Someone said, "Billy, you got some fags on you?" A chair scraped against the floor like an animal's howl. The double ring of the telephone sounded from the office. Slowly the pub returned to normal.

The constable went to the bar where he said, "Black Bush and a lemonade, Ben," while Mrs. Spence found a table set apart from the others. She walked to it without hurry, quite a tall woman with her head held up and her shoulders straight, but instead of sitting on the bench against the wall, she chose a stool that presented her back to the room. She removed her jacket. She was wearing an ivory wool turtleneck beneath it.

"How's things, Constable?" Ben Wragg asked. "Your dad get settled into the pensioners' home yet?"

The constable counted out some coins and laid them on the bar. "Last week," he said.

"Quite a man, your dad was in his day, Colin. Quite a copper."

The constable pushed the money towards Wragg. He said, "Yes. Quite. We all had years to get to know that, didn't we," and he picked up the glasses and went to join his companion.

He sat on the bench, so his face was to the room. He looked from the bar to the tables, one at a time. And one at a time, people looked away. But the conversation in the pub was hushed, so much so that the sound of banging pots in the kitchen was quite distinct.

After a moment, one of the farmers said, "Guess that'll be it for the evening, Ben," and another said, "Got to pop round to see my old gran." A third merely tossed a five-pound note on the bar and waited for his change. Within minutes of the arrival of the constable and Mrs. Spence, most of the other patrons of Crofters Inn had vanished, leaving behind one lone man in tweeds who swirled his gin glass and slumped against the wall, and the group of teenagers who moved to a fruit machine at the far end of the pub and began to try their luck with its spinning dials.

Josie had stood by the table during all of this, her lips parted and her eyes wide. It was only Ben Wragg's barking, "Josephine, be about it," that brought her back to her explanation of dinner. Even then, all she managed was, "What'll . . . for dinner?" But before they had a chance to make their selections, she went on with "The dining room's just this way, if you'll follow me."

She led them through a low door next to the fireplace where the temperature dropped a good ten degrees and the predominant scent was of baking bread rather than the pub's cigarette smoke and ale. She put them next to a simmering wall heater and said, "You'll have the place all to yourselves this evening. No one else is staying here tonight. I'll just pop into the kitchen and tell them what you've—" whereupon she finally seemed to realise that she had nothing at all to tell anyone. She chewed her lip. "Sorry," she said. "I'm not thinking right. You've not even ordered."

"Is something wrong?" Deborah asked.

"Wrong?" The pencil went back into her hair, lead first this time and twirling, as if she were drawing a design on her scalp.

"Is there some sort of problem?"

"Problem?"

"Is someone in trouble?"

"Trouble?"

St. James put an end to the game of echo. "I don't think I've ever seen a local constable clear out a public house so quickly. Without time being called, of course."

"Oh, no," Josie said. "It's not Mr. Shepherd. I mean . . . It's not actually . . . It's just that . . . Things've happened round here and you know how it is in a village and . . . Gosh, p'raps I ought to take your order. Mr. Wragg gets himself in a real fret if I chunter too much with the residents. 'They haven't come to Winslough to have their ears gnawed off by the likes of you, Miss Josephine.' That's what he says. Mr. Wragg. You know."

"Is it the woman with the constable?" Deborah asked.

Josie flicked a look towards a swinging door that appeared to give access to the kitchen. "I really oughtn't talk."

"Perfectly understandable," St. James said and consulted his menu. "Stuffed mushrooms to start and the sole for me. And for you, Deborah?"

But Deborah felt reluctant to be put off. She decided that if Josie was hesitant to talk about one subject, a switch to another might loosen her tongue. "Josie," she said, "can you tell us anything about the vicar, Mr. Sage?"

Josie's head flew up from her writing pad. "How'd you know?"

"What?"

She flung her arm in the direction of the pub. "Out there. How'd you know?"

"We don't know anything. Except that he's dead. We'd come to Winslough in part to see him. Can you tell us what happened? Was his death unexpected? Had he been ill?"

"No." Josie dropped her eyes to her writing pad and gave all her concentration to the writing of *stuffed mushrooms and sole.* "Not exactly ill. Not for long, that is."

"A sudden illness, then?"

"Sudden. Yes. Right."

"A heart condition? A stroke? Something like that."

"Something . . . quick it was. He went off quick."

"An infection? A virus?"

Josie looked pained, clearly torn between holding her tongue and spilling her guts. She fiddled her pencil across her pad.

"He wasn't murdered, was he?" St. James asked.

"No!" the girl gasped. "It wasn't like that at all. It was an accident. Really. Honest and true. She didn't mean . . . She couldn't have . . . I mean I know her. We all do. She didn't mean him any harm."

"Who?" St. James asked.

Josie's eyes went towards the door.

"It's that woman," Deborah said. "It's Mrs. Spence, isn't it?"

"It wasn't murder!" Josie cried.

                    ■   ■   ■

She offered them the story in bits and pieces between serving the dinner, pouring the wine, bringing the cheese board, and presenting the coffee.

Food poisoning, she told them, December last. The story came in gulps, fits, and starts, with frequent glances in the direction of the kitchen, apparently to make sure no one would catch her in the midst of telling the tale. Mr. Sage had been making his rounds of the parish, visiting each family for afternoon tea or an evening meal—

"Eating his way towards righteousness and glory, according to Mr. Wragg, but you got to ignore him if you know what I mean because he never goes to church 'less it's Christmas or a funeral."

—and he went to Mrs. Spence on a Friday night. It was just the two of them because Mrs. Spence's daughter—

"She's my best mate Maggie."

—was spending the evening with Josie right here. Mrs. Spence had always made it clear to anyone who asked that she didn't think much of going to church as a general rule despite its being the sole, dependable social event in the village, but she wasn't one to be rude to a vicar, so when Mr. Sage wanted to try to talk her into giving the C of E another chance in her life, she was willing to listen. She was always polite. That was her way. So the vicar went out to her cottage for the evening, prayer book in hand, all ready to bring her back to religion. He was supposed to be at a wedding the next morning—

"Tying up that skinny cat Becca Townley-Young and Brendan Power... him that's out there in the bar drinking gin, did you see him?"

—but he never showed up and that's how everyone found out he was dead.

"Dead and stiff with his lips all bloody and his jaws locked up like they was wired shut."

"That certainly sounds like an odd bit of food poisoning," St. James remarked doubtfully. "Because if food's gone bad—"

It wasn't *that* kind of food poisoning, Josie informed them with a pause to scratch her bottom through her threadbare skirt. It was real food poisoning.

"You mean poison in the food?" Deborah asked.

The poison *was* the food. Wild parsnip picked down by the pond near Cotes Hall. "Only it wasn't wild parsnip like Missus Spence thought. Not at all. Not—at—all."

"Oh no," Deborah said as the circumstances of the vicar's death began to take on more clarity. "How dreadful. What a terrible thing."

"It was water hemlock," Josie said in breathless summation. "Like what Socrates drunk with his tea in Greece. She thought it was parsnip, did Missus Spence, and so did the vicar and he ate it and..." She grabbed her throat and made appropriate death noises after which she glanced round furtively. "Only don't tell Mum I did like that, will you? She'll tan me if she knows I made light of his dying. It's sort of a black joke 'mongst the blokes in the village: See-cute-a-now and see-you-dead-in-a-minute."

"See-what?" Deborah asked.

"*Cicuta*," St. James said. "The Latin name for its genus. *Cicuta maculata. Cicuta virosa.* The species depends on the habitat." He frowned and absently toyed with the knife that he had used to cut a wedge of double Gloucester, pressing its point into a fragment of the cheese that was left on his plate. But instead of seeing it, for some reason he found himself teasing a memory from the edge of his sub-conscious. Professor Ian Rutherford at the University of Glasgow, who insisted upon wearing surgical garb even to lectures, whose by-words had been *y'can't take a scunner to a corpse, lads and lassies*. Where the hell had he come from, St. James wondered, swirling like a Scots banshee out of the past.

"He never showed up for the wedding next morning," Josie was continuing affably. "Mr. Townley-Young's still got himself in a twist over that. It took till half past two to get another vicar, and the wedding breakfast was a total ruin. More'n half the guests had already left the church. Some people think it was Brendan's doing—'cause it was a forced marriage, and no one can imagine any bloke facing a lifetime of marriage to Becca Townley-Young without trying to do something desperate to stop it—but then that's making light of things again and if Mum knows I'm doing it, I'll be in real trouble. She liked Mr. Sage, did Mum."

"And you?"

"I liked him as well. Everyone did 'cept for Mr. Townley-Young. *He* said the vicar was 'too low church by half' because Mr. Sage wouldn't use incense and he wouldn't tart himself up in satin 'n' lace. But there's more important stuff'n that in being a proper vicar, if you ask me. And Mr. Sage saw to the important stuff."

St. James half-listened to the girl prattle on. She was pouring coffee and presenting them with a decorative, porcelain plate upon which lay six petit fours with remarkable and gastronomically ques-tionable rainbow icings.

The vicar was a great one for visiting in the village, Josie ex-plained. He started a youth group—*she* was social chair and vice-president, by the way—and he looked in on the housebound and he tried to get people to come back to church. He knew everyone in the village by name. On Tuesday afternoons, he read to the children in the primary school. He answered his own front door when he was home. He didn't put on airs.

"I met him briefly in London," Deborah said. "He did seem quite nice."

"He was. Truly. And that's why when Missus Spence comes round, things get a bit difficult." Josie leaned over their table and made an adjustment to the paper doily under the petit fours, centring it carefully on the plate. The plate itself she pushed closer to the table's small tassel-shaded lamp, the better to highlight the confections' icing. "I mean, it's not like just *anyone* made the mistake, is it? Crimminy-crimeny, it's not like Mum did it."

"But surely no matter who made the mistake, that person would have spent some time being looked on with a leery eye," Deborah noted. "Especially as Mr. Sage was well-liked."

"Isn't like that," Josie said in quick reply. "She's a herbalist, is Missus Spence after all, so she should have bloody well known what she was digging out of the ground before she put it on the flaming table. That's what people say, at least. In the pub. You know. They chew on the story and they won't let it go. Doesn't matter to them what the inquest said."

"A herbalist who didn't recognise hemlock?" Deborah asked.

"That's what's got them in a dither all right."

St. James listened silently, tilting the fragment of double Gloucester with his knife, gazing at the crater-like surface of the cheese. Unbidden, Ian Rutherford returned, lining up on the worktable specimen jars which he removed from a trolley with a connoisseur's care while all the time the smell of formaldehyde that emanated from him like a ghoulish perfume put a premature end to anyone's thoughts of lunch. *On to primary symptoms, my luvlies,* he was announcing gaily as he produced each jar with a flourish. *Burning pain in th' gullet, excessive salivation, nausea. Next, giddiness before the convulsions begin. These are spasmodic, rendering the musculature rigid. Vomition's precluded by convulsive closure of the mouth.* He gave a satisfied rap on the metallic lid of one of the jars in which appeared to be floating a human lung. *Death in fifteen minutes, or up to eight hours. Asphyxia. Heart failure. Complete respiratory shutdown.* Another rap on the lid. *Questions? No? Good. Enough of cicutoxin. On to curare. Primary symptoms . . .*

But St. James was having symptoms of his own and he felt them even as Josie chattered on: disquiet at first, a distinct unease. *Now here's a case in point,* Rutherford was saying. But the point he was making and the nature of the case were elusive as eels. St. James set down his knife and reached for one of the petit fours. Josie beamed her apparent approval of his choice.

"Iced them myself," she said. "I think the pink-and-green ones look best."

"What sort of herbalist?" he asked her.

"Missus Spence?"

"Yes."

"The doctoring sort. She picks stuff in the forest and up on the hills and she mixes it good and mashes it up. For fevers and cramps, head colds and stuff. Maggie—Missus Spence's her mum and she's *my* best mate and she's ever so nice—she's never even been to a doctor, far's I know. She gets a sore, her mum whips up a plaster. She gets a fever, her mum makes some tea. She made me a throat wash from creeping jenny when I was out to the Hall on a visit— that's where they live, up by Cotes Hall—and I gargled for a day and the soreness was gone."

"So she knows her plants."

Josie's head bobbed. "That's why when Mr. Sage died, it looked real bad. How could she not know, people've wondered. I mean, *I* wouldn't know wild parsnip from hay but Missus Spence..." Her voice drifted off and she held out her hands in a what's-a-body-to-think sort of gesture.

"But surely the inquest dealt with all that," Deborah said.

"Oh yes. Right above stairs in the Magistrate's Court—have you seen it yet? Pop in for a look before you go to bed."

"Who gave evidence?" St. James asked. The answer promised a renewal of disquiet, and he was fairly certain what that answer would be. "Other than Mrs. Spence herself."

"Constable."

"The man who was with her tonight?"

"Him. Mr. Shepherd. That's right. He found Mr. Sage—the body, I guess—on the footpath that goes to Cotes Hall and the Fell on Saturday morning."

"Did he conduct the investigation alone?"

"Far's I know. He's our constable, isn't he?"

St. James saw his wife turning to him curiously, one of her hands raising to finger a twisted curl of her hair. She said nothing, but she understood him well enough to realise where his thoughts were heading.

It was, he thought, none of their business. They'd come to this village for a holiday. Away from London and away from their home, there would be no professional or domestic distractions to prevent the dialogue in which they needed to engage.

Yet it wasn't that easy to walk away from the two dozen scientific and procedural questions that were second nature to him and shouting to be answered. It was even less easy to walk away from the persistent monologue of Ian Rutherford. Even now, it was playing like a nagging, nameless melody inside his skull. *I've got to hae the thickened portion of the plant, m' luvlies. Very characteristic, this little beauty, stem and root. Stem is thickened as y' will note and not one but several roots are attached. When we cut into the surface of the stem like so, we have oursel's the very scent of raw parsnip. Now, to review . . . who sh'll do the honours?* And under eyebrows that looked like wild plants themselves, Rutherford's blue eyes would dart round the laboratory, always on the look-out for the hapless student who appeared to have assimilated the least information. He had a special gift for recognising both confusion and ennui, and whoever was experiencing either reaction to Rutherford's presentation was most likely to be called upon to review the material at the lecture's end. *Mr. Allcourt-St. James. Enlighten us. Please. Or do we ask too much of you this fair morning?*

St. James heard the words as if he still stood in that room in Glasgow, all of twenty-one years old and thinking not of organic toxins but of the young woman he'd finally taken to bed on his last visit home. His reverie disturbed, he made a valiant attempt at bluffing his way through a response to the professor's request. *Cicuta virosa,* he said and he cleared his throat in an effort to buy time, *toxic principle cicutoxin, acting directly on the central nervous system, a violent convulsant, and . . .* The rest was a mystery.

And, Mr. St. James? And? And?

Alas. His thoughts were too firmly attached to the bedroom. He remembered nothing more.

But here in Lancashire, more than fifteen years later, Josephine Eugenia Wragg gave the answer. "She always kept roots in the cellar. Potatoes and carrots and parsnips and everything, each in their separate bin. So a whisper went round that if she didn't feed it to the vicar on purpose, someone might've snuck in and mixed the hemlock with the other parsnips and just waited till it was cooked and eaten. But *she* said at the inquest that couldn't have happened 'cause the cellar was always locked up tight. So then everyone said all right we'll accept that that's the case but then she should have *known* it wasn't wild parsnip in the first place 'cause . . . "

Of course she should have known. Because of the root. And

that had been Ian Rutherford's main point. That was what he'd been waiting impatiently for his daydreaming, negligent student to say.

Ye don't have a prayer in science, my lad.

Yes. Well. They would see about that.

CHAPTER FOUR

THERE IT WAS, THAT NOISE AGAIN. IT SOUNDED like hesitant footsteps treading on gravel. At first she had thought it was coming from the courtyard, and although she knew it wasn't proper to be relieved at the idea, her fears were at least moderately soothed by the fact that whoever it was creeping round in the dark, he seemed to be heading in the direction not of the caretaker's cottage but of Cotes Hall. And it had to be a *he*, Maggie Spence decided. Prowling about old buildings at night wasn't the sort of behaviour a *she* would engage in.

Maggie knew she ought to be on the alert, considering everything that had gone on at the Hall over the past few months, considering especially the ruination of that fancy-pants carpet only last weekend. Being on the alert was, after all, the only thing aside from her school prep that Mummy had asked her to do prior to leaving with Mr. Shepherd this evening.

"I'll only be gone a few hours, darling," Mummy had said. "If you hear anything, don't go outside. Just phone. All right?"

Which is, by rights, what Maggie knew she ought to do now. After all, she had the numbers. They were downstairs next to the telephone in the kitchen. Mr. Shepherd's home, Crofters Inn, and the Townley-Youngs just in case. She had looked them over as Mummy left, wanting to say in mock innocence, "But you're just going to the inn, aren't you, Mummy? So why've you given me Mr. Shepherd's number as well?" But she knew the answer to that question already, and if she asked, it would only have been to embarrass the both of them.

Sometimes, though, she wanted to embarrass them. She wanted to shout, March twenty-third! I know what happened, I know that's when you did it, I even know where, I even know how. But she never did. Even if she hadn't seen them in the sitting room together—having arrived home too early after a tiff in the village with Josie and Pam—and even if she hadn't slipped away from the window with her legs gone all peculiar at the sight of Mummy and what she'd been doing, and even if she hadn't gone to sit and think about it all on the weed-choked terrace of Cotes Hall with Punkin curled in a mangy ball of tabby-orange at her feet, she still would have known. It was pretty obvious, with Mr. Shepherd looking at Mummy ever since with his eyes all bleary and his mouth gone soft and Mummy being careful as careful not to look at him.

"They're *doing* it?" Josie Wragg had whispered breathlessly. "And you actually in reality without a doubt in the world *saw* them doing it? Naked and stuff? In the *sitting* room? Maggie!" She lit a Gauloise and lay back on her bed. All the windows were open to remove the smoke so that her mummy wouldn't know what she was getting up to. But Maggie couldn't see how all the breeze in the world could come close to eliminating the foul odour produced by the French cigarettes that Josie favoured. She placed her own between her lips and filled her mouth with smoke. She blew it out. She hadn't mastered the inhaling part yet and wasn't sure she wanted to.

"They didn't have all their clothes off," she said. "Mummy didn't, at least. I mean, she wasn't actually undressed at all. She didn't really need to be."

"Didn't *need* . . . ? Then what were they doing?" Josie demanded.

"Oh God, Josephine." Pam Rice yawned. She tossed her head of perfectly bobbed blond hair and it fell, as it always did, perfectly in place. "Develop a clue in life, won't you? What d'you think they were doing? I thought you were supposed to be the expert round here."

Josie frowned. "But I don't see how . . . I mean if she had all her clothes on."

Pam raised her eyes to the ceiling in a display of martyred patience. She drew in deeply on her cigarette and exhaled and inhaled in something she called Frenching. "It was in her mouth," she said. "M-o-u-t-h. Do I have to draw you a picture, or do you get it now?"

"In her . . . " Josie looked flustered. She touched her fingertips to her tongue as if doing so would allow her to understand more completely. "You mean his thing was actually—"

"His *thing*? God. It's called a penis, Josie. P-e-n-i-s. All right?" Pam rolled onto her stomach and gazed with narrowed eyes at the glowing tip of her cigarette. "All I can say is I hope *she* got something, which she probably didn't if she was wearing all her clothes." Again, a toss of that perfect head of hair. "Todd knows better than to finish it off before I've come and that's a fact."

Josie's forehead creased. She was obviously still trying to come to terms with the information. Always presenting herself as the living authority on female sexuality—courtesy of a dog-eared copy of *The Female Sexual Animal Unleashed At Home* (Vol. I), which she'd pinched from the rubbish bin where her mother had deposited it after, at the insistence of her husband, she had spent two months attempting to "become lidibinous or something like that"—she was out of her depth with this one.

"Were they—" She seemed to struggle for a word. "Were they moving or anything, Maggie?"

"Christ in dirty knickers," Pam said. "Don't you know anything? No one needs to move. *She* just needs to suck."

"To . . . " Josie mashed out her cigarette on the windowsill. "Maggie's mum? With a bloke? That's disgusting!"

Pam chuckled languidly. "No. It's *Unleashed*. Right and proper, if you ask me. Didn't your book get round to mentioning that, Jo? Or was it all about dipping your tits in clotted cream and serving them up with the strawberries at tea? You know the sort of thing. 'Make life for your man a constant surprise.' "

"There's nothing wrong with a woman becoming attuned to her sensual nature," Josie replied with some dignity. She lowered her head and picked at a scab on her knee. "Or to a man's, for that matter."

"Yes. Too right. A real woman ought to know what gives who a tickle and where. Don't you think so, Maggie?" Pam used her unnerving ability to make her eyes look at once both purely innocent and bluer than blue. "Don't you think it's important?"

Maggie crossed her legs Indian fashion and gave a pinch to the heel of her hand. It was the way she reminded herself to admit to nothing. She knew what information Pam wanted from her—she could see that Josie knew it as well—but she'd never sneaked on a soul in her life, and she wasn't about to sneak on herself.

Josie came to the rescue. "Did you say anything? After you saw them, I mean."

She hadn't, not then at least. And when she finally brought it up, as a shrill accusation hurled half in anger and half in self-defence, Mummy had reacted by slapping her face. Not once but twice and as hard as she could. One second afterwards—and maybe it was seeing the expression of surprise and shock on Maggie's face because Mummy had never hit her in her life—she'd cried out like she'd been struck herself, grabbed Maggie to her, and hugged her so fiercely Maggie felt her breath leave. But still, they hadn't talked about any of it. "It's my business, Maggie," Mummy had said firmly.

Fine, Maggie thought. And my business is mine.

But it wasn't, really. Mummy wouldn't let it be. She had brought the sludgy tea to Maggie's bedroom every morning for a fortnight after their row. She had stood and made sure Maggie drank every drop. To her protestations, she said, "I know what's best." To her whimpers when the pain cramped through her stomach, she said, "It will pass, Maggie." And she wiped her brow with a cool, soft cloth.

Maggie studied the inky shadows in her bedroom and listened again, concentrating in order to discern the sound of footsteps from the wind jostling an old plastic bottle against the gravel outside. She hadn't turned on any of the lights upstairs, and she crept to the window and peered out into the night, feeling secure in the knowledge that she could see without being seen. Below her in the courtyard, shadows from the east wing of Cotes Hall made great caves of dark. Cast from the mansion's gables, they loomed like open pits and offered more than ample protection for anyone wishing to hide himself. She squinted at them one by one, trying to distinguish whether a hulking form against a far wall was only a yew bush in need of clipping or a prowler trying the window. She couldn't tell. She wished Mummy and Mr. Shepherd would return.

She'd never minded being left alone in the past, but early on after their arrival in Lancashire, she'd developed a dislike of staying in the cottage by herself, either day or night. Perhaps it was baby-stuff to feel that way, but the minute Mummy drove off with Mr. Shepherd, the minute she slipped into the Opel to go off on her own, or headed in the direction of the footpath, or went into the oak wood on a search for plants, Maggie felt the walls start inching close about her. She was uniquely aware of being by herself on the grounds of Cotes Hall, and while Polly Yarkin lived just at the far end of the drive, it was nearly a mile away and no matter how she screamed and shouted, if she ever needed Polly's help for any reason, she wouldn't hear.

It didn't matter to Maggie that she knew where Mummy kept her pistol. Even if she had used it before for target practice—which she never had—she couldn't imagine actually pointing it at anyone, let alone pulling the trigger. So instead, when she was by herself, she burrowed into her bedroom like a mole. If it was night, she kept the lights off and waited for the sound of a returning car or of Mummy's key scraping in the locked front door. And while she waited, she listened to Punkin's soft feline snores rising like steady puffs of auditory smoke from the centre of her bed. With her vision fixed on the small birch bookcase atop of which lumpy old Bozo the elephant presided among the other stuffed animals with comforting grace, she clutched her scrapbook to her chest. She thought about her father.

He existed in fantasy, Eddie Spence, dead before he was thirty, his body twisted along with the wreckage of his racing car in Monte Carlo. He was the hero of an untold story Mummy had hinted at a single time, saying, "Daddy died in a car crash, darling" and "Please, Maggie. I can't speak of it to anyone," with her eyes filled with tears when Maggie tried to ask more. Maggie often tried to conjure up his face from her memory, but she failed in the effort. So what there was of Daddy she held in her arms: the pictures of formula-one race cars she clipped and collected, placing them into her Important Events Book along with careful notations about every Grand Prix.

She plopped onto the bed, and Punkin stirred. He raised his head, yawned, and then pricked his ears. They turned like radar in the direction of the window, and he rose in a single, lissome movement and leapt silently from the bed to the sill. There, he hunkered, his tail making restless, tapping movements as it circled round his front paws.

From the bed, Maggie watched him surveying the courtyard much as she had done, his eyes blinking slowly as his tail continued to tap in silence. She knew from studying up on the subject in his kitten-days that cats are hypersensitive to changes in the environment, so she rested more easily in the knowledge that Punkin would tell her the very moment there was anything outside that she ought to fear.

An old lime tree stood just beyond the window, and its branches creaked. Maggie listened hard. Twigs scratched in vibrato against the glass. Something rasped on the old tree's furrowed bark. It was only the wind, Maggie told herself, but even as she thought this, Punkin gave the signal that something wasn't right. He rose with an arching back.

Maggie's heart thumped jerkily. Punkin launched himself from the window-sill and landed on the rag rug. He was through the door in a streak of orange locomotion before Maggie had time to realise that someone must have climbed the tree.

And then it was too late. She heard the soft thud of a body landing on the slate roof of the cottage. The quiet tread of footsteps followed. Then came the sound of gentle rapping on the glass.

This last made no sense. As far as she knew, housebreakers didn't announce themselves. Unless, of course, they were trying to see if anyone was at home. But even then, it seemed more sensible to think that they'd just knock on the door or ring the front bell and wait for an answer.

She wanted to shout, You've got the wrong place, whoever you are, you want the Hall, don't you? But instead she lowered her scrapbook to the floor next to the bed and slid along the wall into the deeper shadows. Her palms felt itchy. Her stomach rolled. She wanted more than anything to call out for her mummy, but that would be of less than no use. A moment later she was glad of the fact.

"Maggie? Are you there?" she heard him call softly. "Open up, will you? I'm freezing my bum off."

Nick! Maggie dashed across the room. She could see him, crouched on the slope of roof just outside the dormer window, grinning at her, his silky black hair brushing against his cheeks like soft bird's wings. She fumbled with the lock. Nick, Nick, she thought. But just as she was about to fling up the sash, she heard Mummy saying, "I don't want you alone with Nick Ware again. Is that clear, Margaret Jane? No more of that. It's over." Her fingers failed her.

"Maggie!" Nick whispered. "Let me in! It's cold."

She'd given her word. Mummy had been driven close to tears during their row, and the sight of her eyes red-rimmed and full over

Maggie's behaviour and Maggie's stinging words had wrung the promise from her without a thought of what it would really mean to give it.

"I can't," she said.

"What?"

"Nick, Mummy isn't home. She's gone into the village with Mr. Shepherd. I promised her—"

He was grinning more widely. "Great. Excellent. Come on, Mag. Let me in."

She swallowed past a raw spot in her throat. "I can't. I can't see you alone. I promised."

"Why?"

"Because . . . Nick, you know."

His hand was against the window glass, and he dropped it to his side. "But I just wanted to show you . . . Oh what the hell."

"What?"

"Nothing. Forget it. Never mind."

"Nick, tell me."

He turned his head away. He wore his hair bobbed, overlong on the top the way the rest of the boys did, but it never looked trendy on him. It looked right, as if he'd been the style's inventor.

"Nick."

"Just a letter," he said. "It doesn't matter. Forget it."

"A letter? From who?"

"It isn't important."

"But if you've come all this way—" Then she remembered. "Nick, you've not heard from Lester Piggott? Is that it? Has he answered your letter?" It was hard to believe. But Nick wrote to jockeys as a matter of course, always adding to his collection of letters. He'd heard from Pat Eddery, Graham Starkey, Eddie Hide. But Lester Piggott was a plum, to be sure.

She flung up the sash. The cold wind gusted like a cloud into the room.

"Is that it?" she asked.

From his ancient leather jacket—long claimed to be a gift to his great-uncle from an American bombardier during World War II—Nick took an envelope. "It isn't much," he said. "Just 'nice to hear from you, lad.' But he signed it real clear. No one thought he'd answer, remember, Mag? I wanted you to know."

It seemed mean-spirited to leave him outside when he'd come on such an innocent errand. Even Mummy couldn't object to this. Maggie said, "Come in."

"Not if it'll make trouble with your mum."

"It's all right."

He squeezed his lanky frame through the window and made a deliberate point of not closing it behind him. "I thought you'd gone to bed. I was looking in the windows."

"I thought you were a prowler."

"Why'n't you turn on the lights?"

She dropped her eyes. "I get scared. Alone." She took the envelope from him and admired the address. *Mr. Nick Ware, Esq.*, *Skelshaw Farm* was written clearly in a firm, bold hand. She returned it to Nick. "I'm glad he wrote back. I thought he would."

"I remembered. That's why I wanted you to see." He flipped his hair off his face and looked round the room. Maggie watched, in dread. He'd be noticing all the stuffed animals and her dolls sitting upright in the wicker chair. He'd go to the bookshelves and see *The Railway Children* along with the other favourite titles from her childhood. He'd realise what a baby she was. He wouldn't want to take her about then, would he. He probably wouldn't want to know her at all. Why hadn't she thought before letting him in?

He said, "I've never been in your bedroom before. It's real nice, Mag."

She felt dread dissolve. She smiled. "Ta."

"Dimple," he said and touched his index finger to the small depression in her cheek. "I like it when you smile." Tentatively, he dropped his hand to her arm. She could feel his cold fingers, even through her pullover.

"You're ice," she said.

"Cold outside."

She was acutely aware of being in the dark in forbidden territory. The room seemed smaller with him standing in it, and she knew the proper thing to do was to take him downstairs and let him out by the door. Except that now he was here, she didn't want him to go, not without giving her some kind of sign that he was still hers in spite of everything that had happened in their lives since last October. It wasn't enough to know that he liked it when she smiled and he could touch the dimple in her cheek. People liked babies' smiles, they said so all the time. She wasn't a baby.

"When's your mum coming home?" he asked.

Any minute was the truth. It was after nine. But if she told the truth, he'd be gone in an instant. Perhaps he'd do it for her sake, to keep her from trouble, but he'd do it all the same. So she said, "I don't know. She went off with Mr. Shepherd."

Nick knew about Mummy and Mr. Shepherd, so he knew what that meant. The rest was up to him.

She made a move to close the window, but his hand was still on her arm, so it was easy enough for him to stop her. He wasn't rough. He didn't need to be. He merely kissed her, flicking his tongue like a promise against her lips, and she welcomed him.

"She'll be a while then." His mouth moved to her neck. He gave her the shivers. "She's been getting hers regular enough."

Her conscience told her to defend her mummy from Nick's interpretation of the village gossip, but the shivers were running along her arms and her legs each time he kissed her and they kept her from thinking as straight as she'd like. Still, she was in the process of gathering her wits to make a firm reply when his hand moved to her breast and his fingers began to play with her nipple. He rolled it gently back and forth until she gasped with the hurt and the tingling heat and he relinquished the pressure and started the process all over again. It felt so good. It felt beyond good.

She knew she ought to talk about Mummy, she ought to explain. But she couldn't seem to hold on to that thought for longer than the instant in which Nick's fingers released her. Once they began to tease her again, she could think only of the fact that she didn't want to risk any discussion standing in the way of the sign that things were right between them. So she finally said from somewhere outside of herself, "We've got an understanding now, my mum and I," and she felt him smiling against her mouth. He was a clever boy, Nick. He probably didn't believe her for a moment.

"Missed you," he whispered and pulled her tight to him. "God, Mag. Give me some hard."

She knew what he wanted. She wanted to do it. She wanted to feel It through his blue jeans again, going rigid and big because of her. She pressed her hand against It. He moved her fingers up and down and around.

"Jesus," he whispered. "Jesus. Mag."

He slid her fingers along Its length to the tip. He circled them round It. He felt heavy against her. She squeezed It gently, then harder when he groaned.

"Maggie," he said. *Mag.*"

His breathing was loud. He tugged her pullover off. She felt the night wind against her skin. And then she felt only his hands on her breasts. And then only his mouth as he kissed them.

She was liquid. She was floating. The fingers on his blue jeans weren't even hers. She wasn't the one easing down the zip. She wasn't the one making him naked.

He said, "Wait. Mag. If your mum comes home—"

She stopped him with her kiss. She groped blindly for the sweet full weight of him, and he helped her fingers stroke down and round his globes of flesh. He groaned, his hands went under her skirt, his fingers rubbed hot circles between her legs.

And then they were on the bed together, Nick's body a pale sapling above her, her own body ready, hips lifted, legs spread. Nothing else mattered.

"Tell me when to stop," he said. "Maggie, all right? We won't do it this time. Just tell me when to stop." He put It against her. He rubbed It against her. The tip of It, the length of It. "Tell me when to stop."

Just once more. Just this once. It couldn't be such a horrible sin. She pulled him closer, wanting him near.

"Maggie. Mag, don't you think we ought to stop?"

She pressed It closer and closer with her hand.

"Mag, really. I can't hold off."

She lifted her mouth to kiss him.

"If your mum comes home—"

Slowly, deeply, she rotated her hips.

"Maggie. We can't." He plunged It inside.

■   ■   ■

Scrubber, she thought. Scrubber, slut, tart. She lay on the bed and stared at the ceiling. Her vision blurred as tears slid from her eyes, forking across her temples and down into her ears.

I'm nothing, she thought. I'm a slut. I'm a tart. I'll do it with anyone. Right now it's only Nick. But if some other bloke wants to stick It in me tomorrow, I'll probably let him. I'm a scrubber. A tart.

She sat up and swung her legs over the edge of the bed. She looked across the room. Bozo the elephant wore his usual expression of pachydermatous bemusement, but there seemed to be something else in his face tonight. Disappointment, no doubt. She'd let Bozo down. But that was nothing compared to what she'd done to herself.

She eased off the bed and onto the floor where she knelt, feeling the ridges of the worn rag rug pressing into her knees. She clasped her hands together in the attitude of prayer and tried to think of the words that would lead to forgiveness.

"I'm sorry," she whispered. "I didn't mean it to happen, God. I just thought to myself: If only he'll kiss me then I'll *know* things're still right between us, no matter what I promised Mummy. Except when he kisses me that way I don't want him to stop and then he does other things and I want him to do them and then I want more. I don't want it to end. And I know it's wrong. I know it. I do. But I can't help how I feel. I'm sorry. God, I'm sorry. Don't let bad come out of this please. It won't happen again. I won't let him. I'm sorry."

But how many times could God forgive when she knew it was wrong and He knew she knew it and she did it anyway because she wanted Nick close? One couldn't make endless bargains with God without Him wondering about the nature of the deal He was striking. She was going to pay for her sins in a very big way, and it was only a matter of time before God decided that an accounting was due.

"God doesn't work that way, my dear. He doesn't keep score. He's capable of endless acts of forgiveness. This is why He's our Supreme Being, the standard after which we model ourselves. We can't hope to reach His level of perfection, of course, and He doesn't expect us to. He merely asks that we keep trying to better ourselves, to learn from our mistakes, and to understand others."

How simple Mr. Sage had made it all sound when he'd come upon her in the church that evening last October. She'd been kneeling in the second pew, in front of the rood screen, with her forehead resting on her two clenched fists. Her prayer had been much the same as tonight's, only it had been the first time then, on a mound of paint-stiffened wrinkled tarpaulins in a corner of the Cotes Hall scullery. With Nick easing her clothes off, easing her to the floor, easing easing

easing her ready. "We won't actually do it," he'd said, just like tonight. "Tell me when to stop, Mag." And he kept repeating *tell me when to stop Maggie tell me tell me* while his mouth covered hers and his fingers worked magic between her legs and she pressed and pressed herself against his hand. She wanted heat and closeness. She needed to be held. She longed to be part of something more than herself. He was the living promise of all she desired, there in the scullery. She merely had to accept.

It was the aftermath that she hadn't expected, that moment when all the *nice girls don't*'s came rushing through her conscience like Noah's flood: boys don't respect girls who . . . they tell all their mates . . . just say no, you can do that . . . who steals my purse . . . they only want one thing, they only think of one thing . . . do you want a disease . . . what if he gets you pregnant, do you think he'll be so hot for you then . . . you've given in once, you've crossed a line with him, he'll be after you now again and again . . . he doesn't love you, if he did, he wouldn't . . .

And so she had come to St. John the Baptist's for evensong. She'd half-listened to the reading. She'd half-heard the hymns. Mostly, she'd looked at the intricate rood screen and the altar beyond it. There, the Ten Commandments—etched into looming, individual bronze tablets—comprised the reredos, and she found her attention helplessly riveted on commandment number seven. It was harvest festival. The altar steps were spread with an array of offerings. Sheaves of corn, marrows of yellow and green, new potatoes in baskets, and several bushels of beans filled the church air with the fertile scent of autumn. But Maggie was only imperfectly aware of this, as she was only imperfectly aware of the prayers being said and the organ being played. The light from the main chandelier in the chancel seemed to glitter directly onto the bronze reredos, and the word *adultery* quivered in her vision. It seemed to grow larger, seemed to point and accuse.

She tried to tell herself that committing adultery meant that at least one of the parties had to be in possession of wedding vows to break. But she knew that an entire school of loathsome behaviours rested beneath the awning of that single word, and she was guilty of most of them: impure thoughts about Nick, infernal desire, sexual fantasies, and now fornication, the worst sin of all. She was black and corrupt, headed straight for damnation.

If only she could recoil from her behaviour, writhing in disgust over the act itself or how it made her feel, God might forgive her. If only the act had made her feel unclean, He might overlook this one small lapse. If only she didn't want it—and Nick and the indescribable warmth of their bodies' connection—all over again, now, right here in the church.

Sin, sin, sin. She lowered her head to her fists and kept it there, oblivious of the rest of the service. She began to pray, making fervent supplications for God's forgiveness, with her eyes squeezed shut so tight she saw stars.

"I'm sorry, I'm sorry, I'm sorry," she whispered. "Don't let bad happen to me. I won't do it again. I promise. I promise. I'm sorry."

It was the only prayer that she could devise, and she repeated it mindlessly, caught up in her need for direct communication with the supernatural. She heard nothing of the vicar's approach, and she didn't even know the service was over and the church empty until she felt a hand curving firmly round her shoulder. She looked up with a cry. All of the chandeliers had been extinguished. The only light remaining came in a greenish glow from an altar lamp. It touched one side of the vicar's face and cast long, crescent shadows from the bags beneath his eyes.

"He is forgiveness itself," the vicar said quietly. His voice was soothing, just like a warm bath. "Never doubt that. He exists to forgive."

The serenity of his tone and the kindness of his words brought tears to her eyes. "Not this," she said. "I don't see how He can."

His hand squeezed her shoulder, then dropped. He joined her in the pew, sitting not kneeling, and she slid back onto the bench herself. He indicated the rood atop its screen. "If the Lord's last words were, 'Forgive them, Father,' and if His Father did indeed forgive—which we may be assured that He did—then why wouldn't He forgive you as well? Whatever your sin may be, my dear, it cannot equal the evil of putting to death the Son of God, can it?"

"No," she whispered, although she had begun to cry. "But I knew it was wrong and I did it anyway because I wanted to do it."

He fished a handkerchief from his pocket and handed it to her. "That's the nature of sin. We face a temptation, we have a choice to make, we choose unwisely. You aren't alone in this. But if you're resolved in your heart not to sin again, then God forgives. Seventy times seven. You may rely upon that."

Possessing resolution in her heart was the problem. She wanted to promise. She wanted as much to believe in her promise. Unfortunately she wanted Nick more. "That's just it," she said. And she told the vicar everything.

"Mummy knows," she finished, plaiting his handkerchief back and forth through her fingers. "Mummy's so angry."

The vicar dropped his head and seemed to be examining the faded needlework fleur-de-lis on the kneeler. "How old are you, my dear?"

"Thirteen," she said.

He sighed. "Dear God."

More tears rose in her eyes. She blotted them away and hiccupped as she spoke. "I'm bad. I know it. I *know* it. So does God."

"No. It isn't that." He covered her hand briefly. "It's the rush to adulthood that disturbs me. It's taking on such troubles when you're still so young."

"It's not a trouble to me."

He smiled gently. "No?"

"I love him. He loves me."

"And that's generally where the trouble starts, isn't it?"

"You're making fun," she said stiffly.

"I'm speaking the truth." He moved his gaze from her to the altar. His hands were on his knees, and Maggie saw his fingers tense as he gripped them more firmly. "Your name is?"

"Maggie Spence."

"I've not seen you in church before tonight, have I?"

"No. We ... Mummy isn't taken much with going to church."

"I see." Still he held the grip on his knees. "Well, you've come upon one of mankind's biggest challenges at a fairly young age, Maggie Spence. How to cope with the sins of the flesh. Even before the time of our Lord, the ancient Greeks recommended moderation in everything. They knew, you see, the sort of consequences one faces through giving in to one's appetites."

She frowned, confused.

He caught the look and went on with, "Sex is an appetite as well, Maggie. Something like hunger. It begins with mild curiosity rather than a rumble in the stomach, to be sure. But it quickly becomes a

demanding taste. And unfortunately, it isn't like overeating or intox-
ication from drink, both of which provide a rather immediate physical
discomfort that can later act as a reminder of the fruits of impetuous
indulgence. Instead, it provides a sense of well-being and release,
one that we come to wish to experience again and again."

"Like a drug?" she asked.

"Very much like a drug. And just like many drugs, its harmful
properties aren't immediately apparent. Even if we know what they
are—intellectually—the promise of pleasure is often too seductive
for us to abstain when we should. That's when we must turn to the
Lord. We must ask Him to infuse us with the strength to resist. He
faced His own temptations, you know. He understands what it is to
be human."

"Mummy doesn't talk about God," Maggie said. "She talks about
AIDS and herpes and warts and getting pregnant. She thinks I won't
do it if I'm scared enough."

"You're being harsh on her, my dear. These are far from unrealistic
concerns on her part. Cruel facts are associated with sexuality these
days. Your mother is wise—and kind—to share them with you."

"Oh, too right. But what about her? Because when she and Mr.
Shepherd—" Her automatic protest died unfinished. No matter her
feelings, she couldn't betray Mummy to the vicar. That wouldn't be
right.

The vicar cocked his head but made no other indication that he
understood in what direction Maggie's words had been heading.
"Pregnancy and disease are the long-term potential consequences we
face when we submit ourselves to the pleasures of sex," he said. "But
unfortunately, when we're in the midst of an encounter leading up
to intercourse, we rarely think of anything save the moment's
exigency."

"Sorry?"

"The need to do it. At once." He lifted the fleur-de-lis kneeler
from its hook on the back of the pew in front of him and placed it
on the uneven stone floor. "Instead, we think in terms of *it couldn't,
I won't,* and *it can't.* Out of our desire for physical gratification comes
the denial of possibility. I won't become pregnant; he couldn't give
me a disease because I believe he doesn't have one. And it is from
these little acts of denial that our deepest sorrow ultimately springs."

He knelt and gestured that she was to join him. "Lord," he said quietly, eyes on the altar, "help us to see Your will in all things. When we are sorely tried and tempted, allow us to realise it is through Your love that we are so tested. When we stumble and sin, forgive us our wrongs. And give us the strength to avoid all occasion of sin in the future."

"Amen," Maggie whispered. Through the thick fall of her hair, she felt the vicar's hand rest lightly on the back of her neck, a comradely expression that imparted the first real peace she'd had in days.

"Can you resolve to sin no more, Maggie Spence?"

"I want to."

"Then I absolve you in the name of the Father, and the Son, and the Holy Spirit."

He walked out with her into the night. The lights were on in the vicarage across the street, and Maggie could see Polly Yarkin in the kitchen, setting the vicar's table for dinner.

"Of course," the vicar was saying, as if in continuation of a previous thought, "absolution and resolve are one thing. The other's more difficult."

"Not doing it again?"

"And keeping yourself active in other areas of your life so the temptation's not there." He locked the church door and pocketed the key in his trousers. Although the night was quite cool, he wasn't wearing an overcoat and his clerical collar gleamed in the moonlight like a Cheshire smile. He observed her thoughtfully, pulling on his chin. "I'm starting a youth group here in the parish. Perhaps you'd like to join us. There'll be meetings and activities, things to keep you busy. It might be a good idea, all things considered."

"I'd like to, except... We're not members of the Church, actually, Mummy and I. And I can't think that she'd let me join. Religion... She says religion leaves a bad taste in the mouth." Maggie dropped her head when she revealed this last. It seemed particularly unfair, considering the vicar's kindness to her. She went on to add in a rush, "I don't feel that way myself. At least I don't think I do. It's just that I don't know much about it in the first place. I mean ... I've hardly ever been. To Church, that is."

"I see." His mouth turned down, and he fished in his jacket pocket to bring out a small white card which he handed to her. "Tell your mummy I'd like to visit with her," he said. "My name's on the

card. My number as well. Perhaps I can make her feel more comfortable with the Church. Or at least pave the way for you to join
us." He walked out of the churchyard at her side and touched her
shoulder in farewell.

The youth group seemed like something Mummy would agree
to, once she got over her disapproval of its being tied to the Church.
But when Maggie pressed the vicar's card upon her, Mummy had
stared down at it for the longest time, and when she looked up, her
face was pasty and her mouth looked queer.

You went to someone else, her expression said, as clearly as if she'd
spoken. *You didn't trust your mummy.*

Maggie tried to soothe her feelings as well as avoid the unspoken
accusation by hurriedly saying, "Josie knows Mr. Sage, Mummy. Pam
Rice does as well. Josie says he's only been in the parish for three
weeks now, and he's trying to get people back to the Church. Josie
says the youth group—"

"Is Nick Ware a member?"

"I don't know. I didn't ask."

"Don't lie to me, Margaret."

"I'm not. I just thought . . . The vicar wants to talk to you about
it. He wants you to phone."

Mummy walked to the rubbish basket, ripped the card in half,
and buried it—with a savage little twist of her wrist—among the
coffee grounds and grapefruit rinds. "I have no intention of speaking
to a priest about anything, Maggie."

"Mummy, he only—"

"This discussion is over."

But despite Mummy's refusal to phone him, Mr. Sage had come
three times to the cottage. Winslough was a small village, after all,
and discovering where the Spence family lived was as easy as asking
in Crofters Inn. When he'd shown up unexpectedly one afternoon,
doffing his trilby to Maggie as she opened the door, Mummy had
been alone in the greenhouse repotting some herbs. She'd greeted
Maggie's nervous announcement of the vicar's visit by saying tersely,
"Go to the inn. I'll phone when you can come home." And the anger
in her voice and the hardness of her face told Maggie it was wiser
not to ask any questions. She had long known Mummy didn't like
religion. But it was just like trying to gather the facts about her father:
She didn't know why.

Then Mr. Sage died. Just like Daddy, Maggie thought. And he liked me just like Daddy. I know he did. I do.

Now in her bedroom, Maggie found she had run out of words to send to heaven. She was a sinner, a slut, a tart, a scrubber. She was the vilest creature God ever put on earth.

She got to her feet and rubbed her knees where they were red and sore from the rug's digging into them. Wearily, she wandered to the bathroom and rustled through the cupboard to find what Mummy kept hidden there.

"What happens is this," Josie had explained confidentially when they'd come upon the odd plastic container with its even odder spout, deeply buried among the towels. "After they have sex, the woman fills this bottle thing with oil and vinegar. Then she sort of sticks this nozzle part up inside and pumps it real hard and then she won't have a baby."

"But she'll smell like a tossed salad," Pam Rice put in. "I don't think you've got your facts straight, Jo."

"I most certainly do, Miss Pamela Know-it-all."

"Right."

Maggie examined the bottle. She shuddered at the thought. Her knees weakened a bit, but she would have to do it. She carried it downstairs and into the kitchen where she set it on the work top and took down the oil and vinegar. Josie hadn't said how much to use. Half and half, most likely. She uncapped the vinegar and began to pour.

The kitchen door opened. Mummy walked in.

CHAPTER FIVE

HERE WAS NOTHING TO SAY, SO MAGGIE KEPT pouring, keeping her eyes on the vinegar as its level rose. When it reached halfway, she recapped the bottle and unstoppered the oil. Her mother spoke.

"What in God's name are you doing, Margaret?"

"Nothing," she said. It seemed obvious enough. The vinegar. The oil. The plastic bottle with its detachable, elongated spout lying next to it. What else could she be doing but preparing to rid her body of all the internal traces of a man? And who else would that man be but Nick Ware?

Juliet Spence shut the door behind her with a *snick* of the lock. At the sound, Punkin appeared from the darkness of the sitting room and glided across the kitchen to rub against her legs. He mewled softly.

"The cat wants feeding."

"I forgot," Maggie said.

"How did you forget? What were you doing?"

Maggie didn't reply. She poured the oil into the bottle, watching it bob and swirl in graceful amber orbs as it met the vinegar.

"Answer me, Margaret."

Maggie heard her mother's handbag drop onto one of the kitchen chairs. Her heavy pea jacket followed. Then came the sharp *plit plot* of her boots as she crossed the room.

Never had Maggie been more aware of the advantage her mother had in height than when Juliet Spence joined her at the work top.

She seemed to tower above her like an angel of vengeance. One false move and the sword would fall.

"What exactly are you planning to do with that concoction?" Juliet asked. Her voice sounded careful, the way someone spoke just before he was sick.

"Use it."

"For?"

"Nothing."

"I'm glad of it."

"Why?"

"Because if you're developing a bent towards feminine hygiene, you're going to have quite a mess on your hands if you douche with oil. And I take it that we *are* talking about hygiene, Margaret. There's nothing else behind this, I'm sure. Aside, of course, from a curious and rather sudden compulsion to be certain your private parts are fresh and clean."

Maggie studiously set the oil on the work top next to the vinegar. She stared at the undulating mixture she'd made.

"I saw Nick Ware pedalling his bicycle along the Clitheroe Road on my way home," her mother went on. Her words were coming faster now, each one sounding as if her teeth clipped it off. "I don't particularly want to think what that—combined with this fascinating experiment you're apparently conducting in emulsification—might actually mean."

Maggie touched her index finger to the plastic bottle. She observed her hand. Like the rest of her, it was small, dimpled, and plump. It couldn't possibly be less like her mother's. It was unsuited for housework and heavy toil, unused to digging and working with the earth.

"This oil-and-vinegar business isn't connected with Nick Ware, is it? Tell me it was purely coincidence that I should have seen him heading back towards the village not ten minutes ago."

Maggie jiggled the bottle and watched the oil slip and slide across the surface of the vinegar. Her mother's hand clamped over her wrist. Maggie felt the immediate answering numbness in her fingers.

"That hurts."

"Then talk to me, Margaret. Tell me Nick Ware hasn't been here tonight. Tell me you haven't had sex with him again. Because you reek of it. Are you aware of that? Do you realise you smell like a whore?"

"So what? You smell of it, too."

Her mother's fingers contracted convulsively, her short nails creating sharp pressure points of pain on the soft underside of Maggie's wrist. Maggie cried out and tried to pull away but only succeeded in flinging their locked hands against the plastic bottle so that it slipped into the sink. The pungent mixture arced out to form an oleaginous pool. As it drained away, it left red and gold beads against the white porcelain.

"I suppose you think I deserve that remark," Juliet said. "You've decided sex with Nick is the perfect way to get an eye for an eye. Which is what you want, isn't it? Isn't it what you've been wanting for months? Mummy's taken a lover and you'll fix her good if it's the last thing you do."

"It's nothing to do with you. I don't care what you do. I don't care how you do it. I don't even care when. I love Nick. He loves me."

"I see. And when he makes you pregnant and you're faced with having his baby, will he love you then? Will he leave school in order to support the two of you? And how will it feel, Margaret Jane Spence—motherhood before your fourteenth birthday?"

Juliet released her and went into the old-fashioned larder. Maggie rubbed her wrist and listened to the angry pop and snap of airtight containers being opened and closed on the chipped marble work top. Her mother returned, brought the kettle to the sink, set it to boil on the cooker. "Sit down," she said.

Maggie hesitated, running her fingers through the oil and vinegar that remained in the sink. She knew what was to follow—it was exactly what had followed her first encounter with Nick in the Hall in October—but unlike October, this time she understood what those two words presaged, and the understanding was a sickness to her that quickly ran ice down her back. How stupid she'd been just three months ago. What had she been thinking? Each morning Mummy had presented her with the cup of thick liquid she passed off as her special female tea, and Maggie had screwed up her face and drunk it obediently, believing it was the vitamin supplement Mummy claimed it to be, something every girl needed when she became a woman. But now, in conjunction with her mother's words this evening, she remembered a hushed conversation that Mummy had had with Mrs. Rice in this very kitchen nearly two years ago, with Mrs. Rice begging for something to "kill it, stop it, I beg you, Juliet" and with Mummy saying, "I can't do that, Marion. It's a private oath, to be sure, but it's an oath nonetheless, and I mean to keep it. You must go to a clinic if you want to be rid of it." At which Mrs. Rice began to weep, saying, "Ted won't hear of it. He'd kill me if he thought I did anything at all . . . " And then six months later her twins were born.

"I said sit down," Juliet Spence repeated. She was pouring the water over the dried, crushed bark root. Its acrid odour wafted up with the steam. She added two tablespoons of honey to the drink, stirred it vigorously, and took it to the table. "Come here."

Maggie felt the angry cramps without use of the stimulant, a phantom pain that grew from her memory. "I won't drink that."

"You will."

"I won't. You want to kill the baby, don't you? *My* baby, Mummy. Mine and Nick's. That's what you were doing before, in October. You said it was vitamins, to make my bones strong and to give me more energy. You said women need more calcium than little girls and I wasn't a little girl any longer so I needed to drink it. But you were lying, weren't you? *Weren't* you, Mummy? You wanted to make sure I didn't have a baby."

"You're being hysterical."

"You think it's happened, don't you? You think there's a baby inside me, don't you? Isn't that why you want me to drink?"

"We'll make it un-happen if it's happened. That's all."

"To a baby? My baby? No!" The edge of the work top dug into her spine as Maggie backed away from her mother.

Juliet set the mug on the table, resting a hand on her hip. With the other hand, she rubbed her forehead. In the kitchen light, her face looked gaunt. The streaks of grey in her hair seemed at once duller and more pronounced. "Then what exactly is it that you were planning to do with the oil and vinegar if not try—no matter how ineffectively—to stop a baby's conception?"

"That's . . . " Maggie turned miserably back to the sink.

"Different? Why? Because it's easy? Because it washes things away without any pain, stopping things before they start? How convenient for you, Maggie. Unfortunately, that's not the way it's going to be. Come here. Sit down."

Maggie pulled the oil and vinegar towards her in a protective and largely meaningless gesture. Her mother continued.

"Even if oil and vinegar were efficacious contraceptives—which they are not, by the way—a douche is completely useless much more than five minutes after intercourse."

"I don't care. I wasn't using it for that. I just wanted to be clean. Like you said."

"I see. Fine. Whatever you wish. Now, are you going to drink this, or are we going to argue, deny, and play with reality for the rest of the night? Because neither of us is leaving this room until you've drunk it, Maggie. Depend upon that."

"I won't drink it. You can't make me. I'll have the baby. It's mine. I'll have it. I'll love it. I will."

"You don't know the first thing about loving anyone."

"I do!"

"Really? Then what does it mean to make a promise to someone you love? Is it just words? Is it something you say to get you through the moment? Something without meaning mouthed to soothe feelings? Something to get what you want?"

Maggie felt tears building behind her eyes, in her nose. Everything on the work top—a dented toaster, four metal canisters, a mortar and pestle, seven glass jars—shimmered as she began to cry.

"You made a promise to me, Maggie. We had an agreement. Shall I recall it for you?"

Maggie grabbed on to the kitchen sink's tap and shoved it back and forth, having no purpose for doing so other than experiencing the certainty of contact with something that she could control. Punkin leapt to the work top and approached her. He wove in and out of the bottles and jars, pausing to sniff at some crumbs on the toaster. He gave a plaintive mew and rubbed against her arm. She reached for him blindly and lowered her face to the back of his neck. He smelled of wet hay. His fur adhered to the trail her tears were making on her cheeks.

"If we didn't leave the village, if I agreed that we wouldn't move on this time, you'd see I never regretted it. You'd make me proud. Do you remember that? Do you remember giving me your solemn word? You were sitting at this very table last August, crying and pleading to stay in Winslough. 'Just this once, Mummy. Please don't let's move again. I've got such good mates here, special mates, Mummy. I want to finish school. I'll do anything. Please. Let's just stay.' "

"It was the truth. My mates. Josie and Pam."

"It was a variation on truth, less than a half-truth if you will. Which is no doubt why within the next two months you were having it off on the floor in Cotes Hall with a fifteen-year-old farmboy and God knows who else."

"That isn't true!"

"Which part, Maggie? Having it off with Nick? Or pulling down your knickers for any one of his randy little mates who wanted to give you a poke?"

"I hate you!"

"Yes. Ever since this started, you've been making that clear. And I'm sorry about that. Because I don't hate you."

"You're doing the same." Maggie swung back to her mother. "You preach about being good and not having babies and all the time you're doing no better than me. You do it with Mr. Shepherd. Everyone knows."

"Which is what this is all about, isn't it? You're thirteen years old. During your entire life I've never taken a lover. And you're bound and determined that I won't take one now. I'm to go on living solely for you, just as you're used to. Right?"

"No."

"And if you have to get pregnant to keep me in line, then that's just fine."

"No!"

"Because what is a baby after all, Maggie? Just something you can use to get what you want. You want Nick tied to you? Fine, give him sex. You want Mummy preoccupied with your concerns? Good. Get yourself pregnant. You want everyone to notice how special you are? Open your legs for any bloke who sniffs you up. You want—"

Maggie grabbed up the vinegar and hurled the bottle to the floor where it exploded against the tile. Glass shards shot the length of the room. At once the air was eye-stingingly sour. Punkin hissed, backing into the canisters, his fur on end and his tail a plume.

"I'll love my baby," she cried. "I'll love it and take care of it and it'll love me. That's what babies do. That's all babies do. They love their mummies and their mummies love them."

Juliet Spence ran her eyes over the mess on the floor. Against the tiles—which were cream coloured—the vinegar looked like diluted blood.

"It's genetic." She sounded worn out. "My God in heaven, it's inbred at your core." She pulled out one of the kitchen chairs and sank onto it. She cupped her hands round the mug of tea. "Babies aren't love machines," she said to the mug. "They don't know how to love. They don't know what love is. They only have needs. Hunger, thirst, sleep, and wet nappies. And that's the end of it."

"It's not," Maggie said. "They love you. They make you feel good inside. They belong to you. One hundred percent. You can hold them and sleep with them and cuddle them close. And when they get big—"

"They break you in pieces. One way or another. It comes down to that."

Maggie rubbed the back of her wrist across her wet cheeks. "You just don't want me to have something to love. That's what it is. You can have Mr. Shepherd. That's fine and good for you. But I'm not supposed to have anything at all."

"Do you really believe that? You don't think you have me?"

"You're not enough, Mummy."

"I see."

Maggie picked up the cat and cradled it against her. She saw defeat and sorrow in her mother's posture: slumped into the seat with her long legs outstretched. She didn't care. She pressed the advantage. What did it matter? Mummy could get comfort from Mr. Shepherd if she felt hurt. "I want to know about Daddy."

Her mother said nothing. She merely turned the mug in her hands. On the table lay a packet of snapshots that they'd taken over Christmas, and she reached for this. The holiday had fallen before the inquest, and they'd worked hard at good spirits and happiness, trying to forget what frightening possibilities the future held for them both if Juliet stood trial. She flipped through the pictures, all of the two of them. It had always been that way, years and years of the two of them, a relationship that had brooked no interference from any third party.

Maggie watched her mother. She waited for an answer. She'd been waiting like this for all of her life, afraid to demand, afraid to push, overcome with guilt and apologies if her mother's reaction verged upon tears. But not tonight.

"I want to know about Daddy," she repeated.

Her mother said nothing.

"He isn't dead, is he? He's never been dead. He's been looking for me. That's why we've kept on the move."

"No."

"Because he wants me. He loves me. He wonders where I am. He thinks about me all the time. Doesn't he?"

"This is fantasy, Maggie."

"Doesn't he, Mummy? I want to know."

"What?"

"Who he is. What he does. What he looks like. Why we're not with him. Why we've never been with him."

"There's nothing to tell."

"I look like him, don't I? Because I don't look like you."

"This sort of discussion won't do anything to make you miss having a father."

"Yes it will. It *will*. Because I'll know. And if I want to find him—"

"You can't. He's gone."

"He isn't."

"Maggie, he is. And I won't talk about it. I won't make up a story. I won't tell you lies. He's gone from both our lives. He's always been gone. Right from the first."

Maggie's lips trembled. She tried to control them and failed. "He loves me. Daddy loves me. And if you'd let me find him, I could prove it to you."

"You want to prove it to yourself. That's all. And if you can't prove it with your father, you're set to prove it with Nick."

"No."

"Maggie, it's obvious."

"That isn't true! I love him. He loves me." She waited for her mother to respond. When Juliet did nothing more than give the mug of tea a half turn on the table, Maggie felt herself harden. A small black place seemed to grow on her heart. "If there's a baby, I'll have it. Do you hear me? Only I won't be like you. I won't have secrets. My baby'll know who her daddy is."

She swept past the table and out of the room. Her mother made no attempt to detain her. Her anger and righteousness carried her to the top of the stairs where she finally paused.

Below in the kitchen, she heard a chair scrape back. The water went on in the sink. The cup clinked against the porcelain. A cupboard opened. The patter of dry cat nibbles poured into a bowl. The bowl clicked on the floor.

After that, silence. And then a harsh gasp and the words "Oh God."

■   ■   ■

Juliet hadn't said a prayer for nearly fourteen years, not because she had been without the need for theurgy—there had, in fact, been times when she was desperate for it—but because she no longer believed in God. She had at one time. Daily prayer, attendance at church, heartfelt communication with a loving deity, were as much a part of her as were her organs, her blood, and her flesh. But she'd lost the blind faith so necessary to belief in the unknowable and the unknown when she began to realise that there was no justice, divine or otherwise, in a world in which the good were made to suffer torments while the bad went untouched. In her youth, she'd held on to the belief that there was a day of accounting for everyone. She had realised that perhaps she would not be made privy to the manner in which a sinner was brought before the bar of eternal justice, but brought before that bar he would be, in one form or another, in life or after death. Now she knew differently. There was no God who listened to prayers, righted wrongs, or attenuated suffering in any way. There was just the messy business of living, and of waiting for those ephemeral moments of happiness that made the living worthwhile. Beyond that, there was nothing, save the struggle to ensure that no one and nothing endangered the possibility of those moments' periodic advents in life.

She dropped two white towels onto the kitchen floor and watched the vinegar soak through them in growing blossoms of pink. While Punkin observed the entire operation from his perch on the work top, his expression solemn and his eyes unblinking, she dumped the towels in the sink and went for a broom and a mop. This latter was unnecessary—the towels had managed to absorb the mess and the broom would take care of the glass—but she had learned long ago that physical toil alleviated any bent towards rumination, which is why she worked in her greenhouse every day, clambered through the oak wood at dawn with her collection baskets, tended her vegetable garden with a zealot's devotion, and watched over her flowers more with need than with pride.

She swept up the glass and dumped it in the rubbish. She decided to forgo the mop. Better to scrub the tile floor on her hands and knees, feeling the dull circles of ache centring on her kneecaps and beginning to throb the length of her legs. Below physical labour on the list of activities designed to serve as substitutes for thought, resided physical pain. When labour and pain were conjoined by either chance or design, one's mental processes slowed to nothing. So she scrubbed the floor, pushing the blue plastic pail before her, forcing her arm out in wide sweeping motions that strained her muscles, kneading wet rags against tile and grout with such energy that her breath became short. When the job was completed, perspiration made a damp semicircle round her hairline and she wiped it away with the arm of her turtleneck. Colin's scent was still on it: cigarettes and sex, the private dark musk of his body when they loved.

She pulled the turtleneck over her head and dropped it on top of her pea jacket on the chair. For a moment, she told herself Colin was the problem. Nothing would have happened to alter the substance of their lives had not she, in an instant of egocentric need, given in to the hunger. Dormant for years, she had long ago stopped believing she had the capacity to feel desire for a man. When it came upon her without expectation or warning, she found herself without adequate defence.

She railed against herself for not having been stronger, for forgetting the lessons that parental discourses from her childhood—not to mention a lifetime of reading Great Books—had laid before her: Passion leads inescapably to destruction, the only safety lies in indifference.

But none of this was Colin's fault. If he had sinned, it was only in loving and in the sweet blindness of that loving's devotion. She understood this. For she loved as well. Not Colin—because she would never be able to allow herself the degree of vulnerability necessary to allow a man to enter her life as an equal—but Maggie, for whom she felt all her lifeblood flowing, in a kind of anguished abandon that bordered on despair.

My child. My lovely child. My daughter. What wouldn't I do to keep you from harm.

But there was a limit to parental protection. It made itself known the moment the child struck out on a path of her own devising: touching the top of the cooker despite having heard the word *no!* a hundred thousand times, playing too near the river in winter when the water was high, pinching a nip of brandy or a cigarette. That Maggie was choosing—wilfully, deliberately, with an inchoate understanding of the consequences—to forge her way into adult sexuality while she was still a child with a child's perceptions of the world, was the single act of adolescent rebellion that Juliet had not prepared herself to face. She'd thought about drugs, about raucous music, about drinking and smoking, about styles of dress and ways of cutting hair. She'd thought about make-up, arguments, curfews, and growing responsibility and *you don't understand you're too old to understand*, but she had never once thought about sex. Not yet. There would be time to think of sex later. Foolishly, she didn't connect it with the little girl who still had her mummy brush her hair in the morning, fixing back its long russet mass with an amber barrette.

She knew all the governing principles behind a child's progression from infant to autonomous adult. She'd read the books, determined to be the best possible mother. But how to deal with this? How to develop a delicate balancing act between fact and fiction to give Maggie the father she wanted and at the same time set her own mind at rest? And even if she was able to do that much for her daughter and herself—which she could not do and would not even consider doing, no matter the cost—what would Maggie have learned from her mother's capitulation: that sex is not an expression of love between two people but a powerful ploy.

Maggie and sex. Juliet didn't want to think about it. Over the years she'd grown more and more adept at the art of repression, refusing to dwell upon anything that evoked unhappiness or turmoil. She moved forward, she moved on, she kept her attention on the distant horizon where existed the promise of exploration in the form of new places and new experiences, where existed the promise of peace and sanctuary in the form of people who, through centuries of habit and custom, kept their distance from taciturn strangers. And until last August, Maggie had always been perfectly happy to keep her eyes on this horizon as well.

Juliet let the cat out and watched him disappear into the shadows cast by Cotes Hall. She went upstairs. Maggie's door was closed, but she didn't tap on it as she otherwise might on another sort of night, going in to sit on her daughter's bed, smoothing back her hair, allowing her fingertips to graze against that peach-soft skin. Instead, she went to her own room across the landing and took off the rest of her clothes in the darkness. In doing so on another sort of night, she might have thought about the pressure and warmth of Colin's hands on her body, allowing herself just five minutes to relive their lovemaking and recall the sight of him etched above her in the semidarkness of his room. But tonight, she moved like an automaton, grabbing up her woollen dressing gown and making her way to the bathroom to draw a bath.

You smell of it, too.

How could she in conscience counsel her daughter against a behaviour she engaged in—looked forward to, longed for—herself? The only way to do it was to give him up and then to move on as they had done in the past, no looking back, cutting every tie. It was the only answer. If the vicar's death had not been enough to bring her to her senses about what was and was not possible in her life—had she actually believed even for an instant that she might make a go of it as the loving wife of the local constable?—Maggie's relationship with Nick Ware would.

Mrs. Spence, my name is Robin Sage. I've come to talk to you about Maggie.

And she'd poisoned him. This compassionate man who had meant only good to her and her daughter. What kind of life could she hope to have in Winslough now when every heart doubted her, every whisper condemned her, and no one save the coroner himself had had the courage openly to ask how she had come to make such a fatal mistake.

She bathed slowly, permitting herself only the immediate physical sensations attendant to the act: the flannel on her skin, the steam rising round her, the water in rivulets between her breasts. The soap smelled of roses, and she breathed its fragrance to obliterate all others. She wanted the bathing to wash away memory and to free her of passion. She looked to it for answers. She asked it for equanimity.

I want to know about Daddy.

What can I tell you, my dearest love? That running his fingers through your downy hair meant nothing. That the sight of your eye-lashes lying like feathery shadows against your cheeks when you slept did not make him want to hold you close. That your grubby hand clutching a dripping ice lolly would never have made him laugh with delight and dismay. That your place in his life was quiet and sleeping in the rear seat of a car with no muss and no fuss and no demands, please. That you were never as real to him as he was to himself. You were not the centre of his world. How can I tell you that, Maggie? How can I be the one to destroy your dream?

Her limbs felt heavy as she towelled herself off. Her arm seemed weighted as she brushed her hair. The bathroom mirror wore a thin skin of steam, and she watched the movements of her silhouette in it, a faceless image whose only definition was dusky hair fast going to grey. The rest of her body she could not see in reflection, but she knew it well enough. It was strong and durable, firm of flesh and unafraid of hard work. It was a peasant's body, made for the easy delivery of children. And there should have been many. They should have tumbled round her feet and cluttered the house with their mates and belongings. They should have played, learned to read, skinned their knees, broken windows, and wept their confusion at life's in-consistencies in her arms. But there had been only one life given into her care and one chance to mould that life into maturity.

Had it been her failure, she wondered not for the first time. Had she let parental vigilance lapse in the cause of her own desires?

She set her hairbrush on the edge of the basin and went across the landing to the closed door of her daughter's room. She listened. No light shone from beneath the door, so she turned the knob quietly and entered.

Maggie was asleep, and she did not awaken when the dim oblong of light from the landing fell across her bed. As she so often did, she'd kicked off the blankets, and she was curled on her side, her knees drawn up, a child-woman wearing pink pyjamas with the top two buttons of the jacket missing so that the crescent of a full breast showed, the nipple an aureole flushed against her white skin. She'd taken her stuffed elephant from the bookcase on which he'd resided since their coming to Winslough. He lay in a lump bunched into her stomach, his legs sticking straight out like a soldier's at attention and his old mangled trunk prehensile no longer, but loved down to a stub from years of wear and tear.

Juliet eased the blankets back over her daughter and stood gazing down at her. The first steps, she thought, that odd, teetering baby walk of hers as she discovered what it was to be upright, clutching onto a handful of Mummy's trousers and grinning at the miracle of her own awkward gait. And then the run, hair flapping and flying and chubby arms extended, full of confidence that Mummy would be there with her own arms outstretched to catch and to hold. That way of sitting, legs splayed out stiffly with the feet pointing northeast and northwest. That utterly unconscious posture of squatting, scooting her compact little body closer to the ground to pick a wildflower or examine a bug.

My child. My daughter. I don't have all the answers for you, Margaret. Most of the time I feel that I'm merely an older version of a child myself. I'm afraid, but I cannot show you my fear. I despair, but I cannot share my sorrow. You see me as strong—the master of my life and my fate—while all the time I feel as though at any moment the unmasking will occur and the world will see me—and you will see me—as I really am, weak and riven by doubt. You want me to be understanding. You want me to tell you how things are going to be. You want me to make things right—life right—by waving the wand of my indignation over injustice and over your hurts, and I can't do that. I don't even know how.

Mothering isn't something one learns, Maggie. It's something one does. It doesn't come naturally to any woman because there is nothing natural about having a life completely dependent upon one's own. It's the only kind of employment that exists in which one can feel so utterly necessary and at the same moment so entirely alone. And in moments of crisis—like this one, Maggie—there is no sagacious volume in which one looks up answers and thus discovers how to prevent a child from harming herself.

Children do more than steal one's heart, my dear. They steal one's life. They elicit the worst and the best that we have to offer, and in return they offer their trust. But the cost of all this is insurmountably high and the rewards are small and long in coming.

And at the end, when one prepares to release the infant, the child, the adolescent into adulthood, it is with the hope that what remains behind is something bigger—and more—than Mummy's empty arms.

WHAT FOLLOWS SUSPICION

CHAPTER SIX

THE SINGLE MOST PROMISING SIGN WAS THAT when he reached out to touch her—smoothing his hand along the bare pathway of her spine—she neither flinched nor shrugged off the caress in irritation. This gave him hope. True, she neither spoke to him nor discontinued her dressing, but at the moment Detective Inspector Thomas Lynley was willing to accept anything that wasn't an outright rejection leading to her departure. It was, he thought, decidedly the down side of intimacy with a woman. If there was supposed to be a happily-ever-after associated with falling in love and having that love returned, he and Helen Clyde had not yet managed to find it.

Early days, he tried to tell himself. They were still unused to the role of lover in each other's life after having, for more than fifteen years, been resolutely living the role of friend. Still, he wished she would stop dressing and come back to bed where the sheets were still warm from her body and the scent of her hair still clung to his pillow.

She hadn't switched on a lamp. Nor had she opened the curtains to the watery morning light of a London winter. But despite these facts, he could see her plainly in what little sun managed to seep first through the clouds and then through the curtains. Even if this had not been the case, he had long ago committed to memory her face, each one of her gestures, and every part of her body. Had the room been dark, he could have described with his hands the curve of her waist, the precise angle at which she dipped her head a moment before she shook back her hair, the shape of her calves, her heels, and her ankles, the swell of her breasts.

He had loved before, more often in his thirty-six years than he would have liked to admit to anyone. But never before had he felt such a curious, utterly Neanderthal need to master and possess a woman. For the last two months since Helen had become his lover, he'd been telling himself that this need would dissolve if she agreed to marry him. The desire to dominate—and to have her submit—could hardly flourish in an atmosphere of power sharing, equality, and dialogue. And if these were the hallmarks of the sort of relationship he wanted with her, then the part of him that needed to control how things would be in the here and now was the part of him that was going to have to be immolated soon.

The problem was that even now when he knew that she was upset, when he knew the reason why and could not begin with any degree of honesty to fault her for it, he still found himself irrationally wanting to browbeat her into a submissive and apologetic admission of error, one for which the most logical expiation would be her willing return to bed. Which was, in and of itself, the second and more imperative problem. He'd awakened at dawn, aroused by the warmth of her sleeping body pressed against his. He'd run his hand along the curve of her hip, and even in sleep she'd turned into his arms to make slow, early-in-the-morning love. Afterwards, they'd lain among the pillows and the tousled blankets, and with her head on his chest and her hand on his breast and her chestnut hair spilling like silk between his fingers, she'd said:

"I can hear your heart."

To which he'd answered: "I'm glad. That means you've not broken it yet."

To which she'd chuckled, gently bitten his nipple, then yawned and asked her question.

To which, like the utterly besotted fool he was, he'd given an answer. No prevarication. No equivocation. Just a hem and a haw, a clearing of the throat, and then the truth. From which rose their argument—if the accusation of "objectifying women, objectifying me, *me*, Tommy, whom you claim to love" could be called an argument. From which rose Helen's present determination to be dressed and be gone without further discussion. Not in anger, to be sure, but in yet another instance of her need to "think things out for myself."

God, how sex makes fools of us, he thought. One moment of release, and a lifetime to regret it. And the hell of it was that, as he watched her dressing—hooking together the bits of silk and lace that posed as women's underwear—he felt the heat and tightening of his own desire. His body was itself the most damning evidence of the basic truth behind her indictment of him. For him, the curse of being male seemed to be entrenched inextricably in dealing with the aggressive, mindless, animal hunger that made a man want a woman no matter the circumstances and sometimes—to his shame—because of the circumstances, as if a half hour's successful seduction were actually proof of something beyond the body's ability to betray the mind.

"Helen," he said.

She walked to the serpentine chest of drawers and used his heavy silver-backed brush to see to her hair. A small cheval mirror stood in the midst of his family photographs, and she adjusted it from his height to hers.

He didn't want to argue with her, but he felt compelled to defend himself. Unfortunately, because of the subject she'd chosen for their disagreement—or if the truth be admitted, the subject which his behaviour and then his words had ultimately propelled her into choosing—his only defence appeared to have its roots in a thorough examination of her. Her past, after all, was no more unsullied than was his own.

"Helen," he said, "we're two adults. We have history together. But we each have separate histories as well, and I don't think we gain anything by making the mistake of forgetting that. Or by making judgements based upon situations that might have existed prior to our involvement with each other. I mean, this current involvement. The physical aspect." Inwardly, he grimaced at his bumbling attempt at putting an end to their contretemps. Goddamn it, we're lovers, he wanted to say. I want you, I love you, and you bloody well feel the same about me. So stop being so blasted sensitive about something which has nothing whatsoever to do with you, or how I feel about you, or what I want from you and with you for the rest of our lives. Is that clear, Helen? Is it? Is it clear? Good. I'm glad of it. Now get back into bed.

She replaced the hairbrush, rested her hand upon it, and didn't turn from the chest of drawers. She hadn't yet put on her shoes, and

Lynley took additional, if tenuous, hope from that. As he did from the certainty of his belief that she no more wanted any form of estrangement between them than did he. To be sure, Helen was exasperated with him—perhaps only marginally more than he was exasperated with himself—but she hadn't written him off entirely. Surely she could be made to see reason, if only through being urged to consider how in the past two months he himself could have easily misconstrued her own erstwhile romantic attachments should he ever have been so idiotic as to evoke the spectral presence of her former lovers as she had done with his. She would argue, of course, that she wasn't concerned with his former lovers at all, that she hadn't, as a matter of fact, even brought them up. It was women in general and his attitude towards them and the great ho-ho-ho-I'm-having-another-hot-one-tonight that she believed was implied by the act of draping a tie on the outer knob of his bedroom door.

He said, "I haven't lived as a celibate any more than have you. We've always known that about each other, haven't we?"

"What's that supposed to mean?"

"It's just a fact. And if we start trying to walk a tightrope between the past and the future in our life together, we're going to fall off. It can't be done. What we have is now. Beyond that, the future. To my way of thinking, that ought to be our primary concern."

"This has nothing to do with the past, Tommy."

"It does. You said not ten minutes ago that you felt just like 'his lordship's squalid little Sunday-night score.' "

"You've misunderstood my concern."

"Have I?" He leaned over the edge of the bed and scooped up his dressing gown which had fallen to the floor in a heap of blue paisley sometime during the night. "Are you angrier about a tie on the door knob—"

"About what the tie implies."

"—or more specifically about the fact that, by my own extremely cretinous admission, it's a device I've used before?"

"I think you know me well enough not to have to ask a question like that."

He stood, shrugged his way into the dressing gown, and spent a moment picking up the clothing he'd been in such a tearing hurry to divest himself of at half past eleven on the previous night. "And I think you're at heart more honest with yourself than you're being at the moment with me."

"You're making an accusation. I don't much like that. Nor do I like its connotation of egocentricity."

"Yours or mine?"

"You know what I mean, Tommy."

He crossed the room and pulled open the curtains. It was a bleak day outside. A gusty wind was scudding heavy clouds from east to west in the sky above, while on the ground a thin crust of frost lay like fresh gauze on the lawn and the rose bushes that comprised his rear garden. One of the neighbourhood cats perched atop the brick wall against which heavy solanum climbed. He was hunched into dual humps of head and body with his calico fur rippling and his face looking shuttered, demonstrating that singularly feline quality of being at once imperious and untouchable. Lynley wished he could say the same about himself.

He turned from the window to see that Helen was watching his movements in the mirror. He went to stand behind her.

"If I choose," he said, "I could drive myself mad with thinking of the men you've had as your lovers. Then in direct avoidance of the madness, I could accuse you of using them to meet your own ends, to gratify your ego, to build your self-esteem. But *my* madness would still be there all the time, just beneath the surface, no matter the strength of my accusations. I'd merely be diverting and denying it by focussing all my attention—not to mention the force of my righteous indignation—on you."

"Clever," she said. Her eyes were on his.

"What?"

"This way of avoiding the central issue."

"Which is?"

"What I don't want to be."

"My wife."

"No. Lord Asherton's little dolly bird. Detective Inspector Lynley's hot new piece. The cause of a little wink and a smirk between you and Denton when he sets out your breakfast or brings you your tea."

"Fine. Understandable. Then marry me. I've wanted that for the last twelve months and I want it now. If you'll agree to legitimatising this affair in the conventional manner—which is what I've proposed from the first and you know it—then you'll hardly have to concern yourself with idle gossip and potential derogation."

"It's not as easy as that. Idle gossip's not even the point."

"You don't love me?"

"Of course I love you. You know that I love you."

"Then?"

"I won't be made an object. I *won't*."

He nodded slowly. "And you've felt like an object these past two months? When we've been together? Last night perhaps?"

Her glance faltered. He saw her fingers close round the handle of the brush. "No. Of course not."

"But this morning?"

She blinked. "God, how I hate to argue with you."

"We're not arguing, Helen."

"You're trying to trap me."

"I'm trying to look at the truth." He wanted to run his fingers the length of her hair, turn her to him, cup her face in his hands. He settled for resting his hands on her shoulders. "If we can't live with each other's past, then we have no future. That's the real bottom line no matter what else you claim it to be. I can live with your past: St. James, Cusick, Rhys Davies-Jones, and whomever else you've slept with for a night or a year. The question is: Can you live with mine? Because that's really what this is all about. It has nothing to do with how I feel about women."

"It has everything to do with it."

He heard the intensity in her tone and saw the resignation on her face. He turned her to him then, understanding and mourning the fact at once. "Oh God, Helen," he sighed. "I haven't had another woman. I haven't even wanted one."

"I know," she said, resting her head against him. "Why doesn't that help?"

■   ■   ■

After reading it, Detective Sergeant Barbara Havers crumpled up the second page of Chief Superintendent Sir David Hillier's lengthy memorandum, rolled it into a ball, and lobbed it neatly across the width of Inspector Lynley's office, where it joined the previous page in the rubbish bin which she'd placed, for a bit of an athletic challenge, next to the door. She yawned, rubbed her fingers vigorously against her scalp, rested her head on her fist, and continued reading. "Pope Davy's Encyclical on Keeping Yer Nose Clean," MacPherson had called the memorandum *sotto voce* in the officers' mess.

Everyone agreed that they had better things to do than to read Hillier's epistle on the Serious Obligations Of The National Police Force When Investigating A Case With Possible Connection To The Irish Republican Army. While they all recognised that Hillier was taking his inspiration from the release of the Birmingham Six—and while few of them had any sympathy for those members of the West Midlands police force who had been the focus of Her Majesty's Investigation as a result—the fact remained that they were far too burdened by their individual workloads to spend time committing to memory their Chief Superintendent's prescriptive treatise.

Barbara, however, wasn't currently floundering in the middle of half a dozen cases, as were some of her colleagues. Rather, she was engaged in experiencing a long-anticipated two-week holiday. During this time, she had planned to work on her childhood home in Acton, preparing to hand it over to an estate agent and move herself to a tiny studio-cum-cottage she'd managed to find in Chalk Farm, tucked behind a large Edwardian house in Eton Villas. The house itself had been subdivided into four flats and a spacious ground floor bed-sit, none of which were within Barbara's limited budget. But the cottage, sitting in the rear of the garden beneath a false acacia tree, was practically too small for anyone but a dwarf to live in comfortably. And while Barbara was not a dwarf, her living aspirations were definitely dwarf-ish: She did not look to entertain visitors, she did not anticipate marriage and family, she worked long hours and simply needed a place to lay her head at night. The cottage would do.

She had signed the lease with no little excitement. This would be the first home she had had away from Acton in the last twenty of her thirty-three years. She thought of how she would decorate it, where she would buy her furniture, what photographs and prints she would hang on the walls. She went to a garden centre and looked at plants, making note of what grew well in window boxes and what needed sun. She paced the length of the cottage and then the width, she measured the windows and examined the door. And she returned to Acton with her mind awash with plans and ideas, all of which seemed unrealistic and impossible to attain when she was confronted with the amount of work that needed to be done to her family's home.

Interior painting, exterior repairs, replacing wallpaper, refinishing woodwork, extirpating an entire rear garden of weeds, cleaning old carpets . . . the list seemed endless. And beyond the fact that she was only one person attempting to see to the renovation of a house that had gone uncared for since she'd left secondary school—which was depressing enough in and of itself—there was the vague sense of unease that she felt each time a project was actually completed.

At issue was her mother. For the past two months, she had been living in Greenford, some distance out of London on the Central line. She'd made the adjustment to Hawthorn Lodge fairly well, but Barbara still wondered how much she would be tempting fate if she sold the old house in Acton and set herself up in a more desirable neighbourhood, in an intriguingly bohemian little cottage that wore the label *new life—enter hopes and dreams,* in which her mother would have no real place. For wasn't she doing more than merely selling an overlarge house in order to finance what might be her mother's lengthy stay in Greenford? Indeed, wasn't the very idea of selling the house in order to do that merely a blind for her own selfishness? Or were these occasional twinges of conscience that accompanied her pursuit of freedom really nothing more than a convenient focal point for her attention so that she didn't have to face what lay beneath them?

You have your own life, she'd been telling herself stoutly more than a dozen times each day. There's no crime in getting on with it, Barbara. But it felt like a crime, when the project itself didn't feel more overwhelming than she could bear. She fluctuated among making lists of everything that needed to be done, despairing that she would be able to do it, and fearing the day when the work was completed and the house was sold and she was finally on her own.

In her rare introspective moments, Barbara admitted that the house gave her something to cling to, a last vestige of security in a world in which she no longer had relations into whom she could sink even the slightest hook of emotional dependence. No matter that she had not been able to sink a hook into any relation's empathy or reliability for years—her father's lingering illness and her mother's mental deterioration had long precluded that—living in the same old house in the same old neighbourhood at least bore the appearance of security. To give it up and forge ahead into the unknown . . . Sometimes Acton seemed infinitely preferable.

There are no easy answers, Inspector Lynley would have said, there's only living through the questions. But the thought of Lynley made Barbara shift restlessly in his desk chair and force herself to read the first paragraph on the third page of Hillier's memorandum.

The words meant nothing. She couldn't concentrate. Having inadvertently conjured up the presence of her superior officer, she was going to have to deal with him.

How to do so? She squirmed, lay the memorandum down among the various reports and folders that were stacking up during his absence, and sank her hand into her shoulder bag in search of her cigarettes. She lit one and blew smoke at the ceiling, eyes narrowed against the smoke's acrid sting.

She was in Lynley's debt. He would deny it, naturally, no doubt with an expression of such bemusement that she would momentarily distrust her own deductions. But scanty as they were, she had the facts, and she didn't much like the position in which they placed her. How to repay him when he would never allow it as long as their circumstances were so imbalanced? He would never begin to entertain the word *debt* as a given between them.

Damn him, she thought, he sees too much, he knows too much, he's too flaming clever to get caught in the act. She swivelled the chair to face a cabinet on top of which sat a picture of Lynley and Lady Helen Clyde. She scowled at him.

"Get knotted," she said, flicking ash to the floor. "Stay out of my life, Inspector."

"Now, Sergeant? Or will later do as well?"

Barbara spun round quickly. Lynley stood in the doorway, his cashmere overcoat slung over one shoulder and Dorothea Harriman—their divisional superintendent's secretary—bobbing up and down behind him. *Sorry*, Harriman mouthed at Barbara with wildly exaggerated and decidedly apologetic movements of her arms, *I didn't see him coming. I couldn't warn you.* When Lynley glanced over his shoulder, Harriman waggled her fingers, smiled brilliantly at him, and disappeared in a blaze of heavily lacquered blonde hair.

Barbara got to her feet at once. "You're on holiday," she said.

"As are you."

"So what're you . . . ?"

"What are *you?*"

She dragged long on her cigarette. "Thought I'd stop by. I was in the area."

"Ah."

"You?"

"The same." He entered and hung his coat on the rack. Unlike herself, who had at least kept up the I'm-on-holiday pretence by coming to the Yard wearing blue jeans and a tatty sweat shirt across which had been stencilled *Buy British, By George* beneath a faded depiction of that saint making hash of an extremely dispirited-looking dragon, Barbara saw that Lynley was dressed for work in his customary fashion: three-piece suit, crisp shirt, silk maroon tie, with the ubiquitous watch chain looped across his waistcoat. He went to his desk—the immediate vicinity of which she quickly vacated—favoured the smouldering tip of her cigarette with a look of displeasure as he passed her, and began sorting through the folders, reports, envelopes, and numerous departmental directives. "What's this?" he asked, holding up the remaining eight pages of the memorandum which Barbara had been reading.

"Hillier's thoughts on working with the IRA."

He patted his jacket pocket, brought out his spectacles, and ran his eyes down the page. "Odd. Is Hillier losing his touch? It appears to start in the middle," he noted.

Sheepishly, she reached into the rubbish and rescued the two top pages which she smoothed out against her chunky thigh and handed to him, dropping cigarette ash on the cuff of his suit jacket in the process.

"Havers . . ." His voice was patience itself.

"Sorry." She flicked the ash off. A spot of it remained. She rubbed it into the material. "Good for it," she said. "Old wives' tale."

"Put out that blasted thing, will you?"

She sighed and squashed the remaining stub of tobacco against the heel of her left plimsoll. She flicked the butt in the direction of the rubbish bin, but it missed its mark and landed on the floor. Lynley lifted his head from Hillier's memorandum, observed the butt over the tops of his spectacles, and raised a single, querying eyebrow.

"Sorry," Havers said and went to place the offending article in the rubbish. She returned the bin to its original position at the side of his desk. He murmured his thanks. She plopped onto one of the visitor chairs and began to worry an incipient hole in the right knee of her jeans. She stole a look or two at him while he continued to read.

He appeared perfectly refreshed and entirely untroubled. His blond hair lay neatly against his head in its usual well-scissored fashion—she'd always wanted to know who saw to the miraculous cutting that produced the effect of its never growing so much as a millimetre beyond an established length—his brown eyes were clear, no circles darkened the skin beneath them, no new lines of fatigue or worry had joined the age lines on his brow. But the fact remained that he was supposed to be on a holiday that had long been arranged with Lady Helen Clyde. They were off to Corfu. They were supposed to be leaving, in fact, at eleven. But it was now a quarter past ten, and unless the Inspector was planning on a trip to Heathrow via helicopter within the next ten minutes, he wasn't going anywhere. At least not to Greece. At least not today.

"So," she said breezily, "is Helen with you, sir? Did she stop to chat up MacPherson in the mess?"

"No to both." He continued reading. He'd just concluded the third page of the tract, and he was balling it up as she had done with the first two, although in his case, the action appeared to be unconscious, merely something to do with his hands. He'd made it a full year off the evil weed, but there were times when his fingers seemed to need something to do in place of holding the cigarette he'd been used to.

"She's not ill? I mean, weren't you two heading off to—"

"We were supposed to, yes. Plans change sometimes." He looked at her over the rims of his spectacles. It was one of his now-that-we're-getting-down-to-it looks. "And what about your plans, Sergeant? Have they changed as well?"

"Just taking a break. You know how it is. Work, work, work and a girl's hands just start to look like dead lobsters. I'm giving them a rest."

"I see."

"Not that I need to give them a rest from painting."

"What?"

"Painting. You know. The interior of the house. Three blokes showed up at my place two days ago. Contractors, they were. Had a deal all drawn up and signed to paint the inside of my house. Odd, that was, you know, because I hadn't called a contractor. Odder still when you think the job had been paid for in advance."

Lynley frowned and placed the memorandum on top of a bound PSI report on the relationship between civilians and police in London. "Decidedly odd," he said. "You're certain they were at the right house."

"Dead certain," she said. "One hundred percent certain. They even knew my name. They even called me *sergeant*. They even asked what it was like for a woman to work in CID. Chatty blokes, they were. But I did wonder how they could ever have known I work here at the Met."

As expected, Lynley's face was a study in wonderment. She half-expected him to go all Miranda on her, exclaiming on the braveness and newness of a world they both knew to be generally corrupt and largely hopeless. "And you read the contract? You made certain they were in the right place?"

"Oh yes. And they were bloody good, sir, the lot of them. Two days and the house was painted like new."

"How intriguing." He went back to the report.

She let him read for the amount of time it took her to count from one to one hundred. Then, "Sir."

"Hmm."

"What'd you pay them?"

"Whom?"

"The painters."

"What painters?"

"Give over, Inspector. You know what I'm talking about."

"The chaps who painted your house?"

"What'd you pay them? Because I know you did, don't bother to lie about it. Besides you, only MacPherson, Stewart, and Hale know that I'm working on the place during my holiday, and they can't exactly put their hands on the kind of lolly we're talking about to do this job. So what'd you pay them and how much time do I have to pay you back?"

Lynley set the report aside and allowed his fingers to play with his watch chain. They removed the watch from his pocket, flipped it open, and he made a show of examining the time.

"I don't want your bleeding charity," she said. "I don't want to feel like anyone's pet project. I don't want to *owe*."

"It does make demands on one, owing," he said. "One always ends up putting the debt onto a scale in which future behaviours are weighed. How can I lash out in anger when I owe him something? How can I go my own way without discussion when I'm in his debt? How can I maintain a safe businesslike distance from the rest of the world if I have a connection somewhere?"

"Owing money isn't a connection, sir."

"No. But gratitude generally is."

"So you were buying me? Is that it?"

"Assuming I had anything to do with it in the first place—which, I feel compelled to warn you, is not an inference that will be supported by any evidence you may attempt to glean—I generally don't purchase my friendships, Sergeant."

"Which is your way of saying that you paid them cash, and you probably paid them a bonus as well to keep their mouths shut." She leaned forward, slapping her hand lightly against his desk. "I don't want your help, sir, not in this way. I don't want anything from you that I can't return. And besides . . . Even if that wasn't the case, I'm not exactly ready—" She blew out her breath in a gust of sudden nerve loss.

Sometimes she forgot he was her superior officer. Worse, sometimes she forgot the one thing she'd once sworn to keep in the forefront of her mind every instant she was with him: The man was an earl, he had a title, there were people in his life who actually called him *my lord*. Given, none of his colleagues at the Yard had considered him anything other than Lynley for more than ten years, but she didn't possess the sort of sang-froid that allowed her to feel on equal footing with someone whose family had been rubbing elbows with the sort of blokes who were used to being referred to as *your highness* and *your grace*. It gave her the crawlies when she thought about it, it raised her hackles when she dwelt upon it. And when it caught her unawares—such as now—it made her feel like a perfect fool. One didn't unburden one's soul to a blue blood. One wasn't really sure that blue bloods were possessed of souls themselves.

"And even if that weren't the case," Lynley picked up her thought with an unconscious—if typical—correction of her grammar, "I expect as the day when you leave Acton looms closer, the prospect looms larger. It's one thing to have a dream, isn't it? It's quite another when it becomes reality."

She sank back in her chair, staring at him. "Christ," she said. "How the hell does Helen put up with you?"

He smiled briefly and removed his spectacles which he returned to his pocket. "She doesn't, at the moment, actually."

"No trip to Corfu?"

"I'm afraid not. Unless she goes alone. Which, as we both know, she's been perfectly willing to do before."

"Why?"

"I upset her equilibrium."

"I don't mean why then. I mean why now."

"I see." He swivelled the chair, not towards the cabinet and the picture of Helen, but towards the window where the upper floors of the dreary post-war construction that was the Home Office nearly matched the colour of the leaden sky. He steepled his fingers beneath his chin. "We fell out over a tie, I'm afraid."

"A tie?"

As a means of clarification, he gestured to the one he was wearing. "I'd hung a tie on the door knob last night."

Barbara frowned. "Force of habit, you mean? Like squeezing toothpaste from the middle of the tube? Something that gets on one's nerves once the stars of romance start twinkling less brightly?"

"I only wish."

"Then what?"

He sighed. She could tell he didn't want to go into it. She said, "Never mind. It's none of my business. I'm sorry it didn't work out. I mean the holiday. I know you were looking forward to it."

He played with the knot at his throat. "I'd left my tie on the door knob—outside the door—before we went to bed."

"So?"

"I didn't pause to think she might notice, and beyond that it's something I'm used to doing on occasion."

"So?"

"And she didn't notice, actually. But she did ask how it was that Denton has never once disturbed us in the morning since we've been . . . together."

Barbara saw the dawn. "Oh. I get it. He sees the tie. It's a signal. He knows that someone's with you."

"Well . . . yes."

"And you told her that? Jesus, what an idiot, Inspector."

"I wasn't thinking. I was wandering like a schoolboy in that blithering state of sexual euphoria when *no one* thinks. She said, 'Tommy, how is it that Denton has never once stumbled in with your morning tea on the nights I've stayed?' And I actually told her the truth."

"That you'd been using the tie to tell Denton that Helen was in the bedroom?"

"Yes."

"And that you'd done it with other women in the past?"

"God no. I'm not that much of an idiot. Although it wouldn't have made any difference had I said it. She assumed I'd been using it that way for years."

"And had you?"

"Yes. No. Well, not recently, for God's sake. I mean, only with her. Which isn't meant to imply that I didn't put a tie on the knob for someone else. But there hasn't been anyone else since she and I . . . Oh blast it." He waved off the rest.

Barbara nodded solemnly. "I'm certainly getting the idea of how the old grave was dug."

"She claims it's an example of my inherent misogyny: my valet and I exchanging a lubricious chuckle over breakfast about who's been moaning the loudest in my bed."

"Which you've never done, of course."

He swung his chair back to her. "What exactly do you take me for, Sergeant?"

"Nothing. Just yourself." She poked at the hole on her knee with more interest. "Of course, you always could have given up early morning tea all together. I mean, once you started having women spend the night. That way you'd never have needed a signal. Or you could have started brewing morning tea yourself and nipping back up to your bedroom with the tray." She pressed her lips together at the thought of Lynley stumbling round his kitchen—assuming he even knew where it was in the first place—trying to find the kettle and to work the cooker. "I mean, it would have been sort of liberating for you, sir. You might even have ultimately ventured into toast."

And then she giggled, although it sounded more like a snort, slipping out from between her pressed lips. She covered her mouth and watched him over the top of her hand, half in shame at her making a joke of his situation and half in amusement at the thought of him—in the midst of frenzied, determined seduction—surreptitiously hanging a tie on his door knob in such a way that his lady love wouldn't notice and question why he was doing it.

His face was wooden. He shook his head. He fingered the rest of Hillier's report. "I don't know," he said gravely. "I don't see how I could ever manage toast."

She guffawed. He chuckled.

"At least we don't have that sort of trouble in Acton." Barbara laughed.

"Which is, no doubt, partially why you're reluctant to leave."

What a marksman, she thought. He wouldn't miss an opening if he was wearing a blindfold. She got up from her chair and walked to the window, slipping her fingers into the rear pockets of her jeans.

"Isn't that why you're here?" he asked her.

"I told you why. I was in the area."

"You were looking for distraction, Havers. As was I."

She gazed out the window. She could see the tops of the trees in St. James's Park. Completely bare, rustling in the wind, they looked like sketchings against the sky.

"I don't know, Inspector," she said. "It seems like a case of be-careful-what-you-wish-for. I know what I want to do. I'm scared to do it."

The telephone rang on Lynley's desk. She started to answer it.

"Leave it," he said. "We're not here, remember?" They both watched it as it continued to ring, the way people do when they expect their collective will to have some small influence over another's actions. It finally stopped.

"But I suppose you can relate to that," Barbara went on as if the telephone had not interrupted them.

"It's something about the gods," Lynley said. "When they want to make you mad, they give you what you most desire."

"Helen," she said.

"Freedom," he said.

"We're one hell of a pair."

"Detective Inspector Lynley?" Dorothea Harriman stood in the doorway, wearing a trim black suit relieved by grey piping on collar and lapels. A pillbox hat was perched on her head. She looked ready for an appearance on the balcony of Buck House on Remembrance Sunday should she be summoned to dwell among the royals. Only the poppy was missing.

"Yes, Dee?" Lynley asked.

"Telephone."

"I'm not here."

"But—"

"The sergeant and I are unavailable, Dee."

"But it's Mr. St. James. He's phoning from Lancashire."

"St. James?" Lynley looked at Barbara. "Haven't he and Deborah gone on holiday?"

Barbara raised her shoulders. "Haven't we all?"

CHAPTER SEVEN

LYNLEY WAS DRIVING UP THE ACCLIVITY OF the Clitheroe Road towards the village of Winslough by late afternoon. Mellow sunlight, fading as day drew towards night, pierced the winter mist that lay over the land. In narrow bands, it glanced against the old stone structures—church, school, houses, and shops that rose in a serried display of Lancashire's stalwart architecture—and it changed the colour of the buildings to ochre, from their normally sombre tan-soaked-with-soot. Beneath the tyres of the Bentley, the road was wet, as it always seemed to be in the North at this time of year, and pools of water from both ice and frost, which gathered and melted and gathered again on a nightly basis, glimmered in the light. Upon their surfaces the sky was reflected, as were the vertebral forms of hedges and trees.

He slowed the car some fifty yards from the church. He parked on the verge and got out into the knife-sharp air. He could smell the smoke from a fresh, dry-wood fire nearby. This argued for dominance with the prevalent odours of manure, turned earth, wet and rotting vegetation which emanated from the expanse of open land lying just beyond the brambly hedge that bordered the road. He looked past this. To his left, the hedge curved northeast with the road, giving way to the church and then, perhaps a quarter of a mile farther on, to the village itself. To his far right, a stand of trees thickened into an old oak wood above which rose a hill that was sided by frost and topped by a wavering wreath of mist. And directly in front of him, the open field dipped languidly down to a crooked stream from which the land lifted again on the other side in a patchwork of drystone walls. Among these stood farms, and from them even at this distance Lynley could hear the bleating of sheep.

He leaned against the side of the car and gazed at St. John the Baptist's. Like the village itself, the church was a plain structure, roofed in slate and ornamented only by its clock-faced bell tower and Norman crenellation. Surrounded by a graveyard and chestnut trees, backdropped by a misty egg-shell sky, it didn't much look like a player in a set piece with murder at its core.

Priests, after all, were supposed to be minor characters in the drama of life and death. Theirs was the role of conciliator, counsellor, and general intermediary between the penitent, the petitioner, and the Lord. They offered a service elevated both in efficacy and importance as a result of its connection to the divine, but because of this fact there was a measured distance between them and the members of their congregation, one which seemed to preclude the sort of intimacy that led to murder.

Yet this chain of thought was sophistry, Lynley knew. Everything from the monitory aphorism about the wolf in sheep's clothing to that time-worn hypocrite the Reverend Arthur Dimmesdale bore evidence of that. Even if this were not the case, Lynley had been a policeman long enough to know that the most guileless exterior—not to mention the most exalted position—had the fullest potential to hide culpability, sin, and shame. Thus, if murder had shattered the peace of this somnolent countryside, the fault did not lie in the stars or in the ceaseless movement of the planets, but rather at the centre of a guarded heart.

"There's something peculiar going on," St. James had said on the phone that morning. "From what I've been able to gather, the local constable apparently managed to avoid calling in his divisional CID for anything more than a cursory investigation. And he seems to be involved with the woman who fed this priest—Robin Sage— the hemlock in the first place."

"Surely there was an inquest, St. James."

"There was. The woman—she's called Juliet Spence—admitted doing it and claimed it was an accident."

"Well, if the case went no further and the coroner's jury brought in a verdict of accidental poisoning, we have to assume that the autopsy and whatever other evidence there was—no matter who gathered it—verified her account."

"But when you consider the fact that she's a herbalist—"

"People make mistakes. Consider how many deaths have risen from a putative fungi expert's picking the wrong sort of wild mushroom in the woods and cooking it up for dinner and death."

"This isn't quite the same."

"You said she mistook it for wild parsnip, didn't you?"

"I did. And that's where the story goes bad."

St. James set forth the facts. While it was true, he said, that the plant was not immediately distinguishable from a number of other members of its family—the *Umbelliferae*—the similarities among the genera and the species were confined largely to the parts of the plant that one wouldn't be drawn to eating in the first place: the leaves, the stems, the flowers, and the fruit.

Why not the fruit, Lynley wanted to know. Didn't this entire situation arise from the act of picking, cooking, and eating the fruit?

Not at all, St. James told him. Although the fruit was as poisonous as the rest of the plant, it consisted of dry, two-part capsules that, unlike a peach or an apple, weren't fleshy and hence gastronomically attractive. Someone harvesting water hemlock, thinking it was wild parsnip, would not be eating the fruit at all. Rather, he'd be digging up the plant and using the root.

"And that's the rub," St. James said.

"The root bears the distinguishing characteristics, I take it."

"It does."

Lynley had to admit that, while the characteristics weren't legion, they were enough to rouse his own sleeping disquiet. This was, in part, why he unpacked the clothing he'd put in his suitcase for a week in the mild winter of Corfu, repacked it for the insidious bone-chill of the North, and made his way up the M1 to the M6 and thence deep into Lancashire with its desolate moors, its cloud-covered fells, and its antique villages from which more than three hundred years ago had sprung his country's ugliest fascination with witchcraft.

Roughlee, Blacko, and Pendle Hill were none of them too distant in either miles or memory from the village of Winslough. Nor was the Trough of Bowland through which twenty women were marched to their trials and their deaths at Lancaster Castle. It was historical fact that persecution raised its nasty head most often when tensions rose and a scapegoat was needed to diffuse and displace them. Lynley wondered idly if the death of the local vicar at the hands of a woman was tension enough.

He turned from his contemplation of the church and went back to the Bentley. He switched on the ignition, and the tape he'd been listening to since Clitheroe resumed. Mozart's *Requiem*. Its sombre combination of strings and woodwinds, accompanying the solemn, low intonation of the choir, seemed appropriate to the circumstances. He guided the car back into the road.

If it wasn't a mistake that killed Robin Sage, it was something else, and the facts suggested that *something else* was murder. As did the plant, that conclusion grew from the root.

"One distinguishes water hemlock from other members of the *Umbelliferae* by the root," St. James had explained. "Wild parsnip has a single root stock. Water hemlock has a tuberous bundle of roots."

"But isn't it within the realm of possibility that this particular plant had only one root stock?"

"It's possible, yes. Just as another sort of plant might have its opposite: two or three adventitious roots. But statistically speaking, it's unlikely, Tommy."

"Still, one can't discount it."

"Agreed. But even if this particular plant had been an anomaly of that sort, there are other characteristics to the underground portion of the stem that one would think a herbalist would notice. When cut open lengthwise, the stem of water hemlock displays nodes and internodes."

"Help me out here, Simon. Science isn't my field."

"Sorry. I suppose you'd call them chambers. They're hollow, with a diaphragm of pith tissue running horizontally across the cavity."

"And wild parsnip doesn't have these chambers?"

"Nor does it exude a yellow oily liquid when its stem is cut."

"But would she have cut the stem? Would she have opened it lengthwise?"

"The latter, no. I admit it's doubtful. But as to the former: How could she have removed the root—even if it was the anomaly, a single one—without cutting the stem in some way? Even breaking the root off from the stem would have produced that singular oil."

"And you believe that's enough of a warning to a herbalist? Isn't it possible that she might have been distracted from noticing? What if someone was with her when she was digging it up? What if she were talking to a friend or arguing with her lover or distracted in some way? Perhaps even deliberately distracted."

"Those are possibilities. And they bear looking into, don't they?"

"Let me make a few phone calls."

He had done so. The nature of the answers he'd managed to dig up had piqued his interest. Since the holiday in Corfu had turned into another one of life's promises unkept, he threw tweeds, blue jeans, and sweaters in his suitcase and stowed that along with gumboots, hiking shoes, and anorak into the boot of his car. He'd been wanting to get out of London for weeks. While he'd have preferred his escape to be effected by a flight to Corfu with Helen Clyde, Crofters Inn and Lancashire would have to do.

He rolled past the terraced houses that signalled entry into the village proper and found the inn at the junction of the three roads, just where St. James had told him it would be. St. James himself, along with Deborah, Lynley found in the pub.

The pub itself was not yet open for its evening business. The iron wall sconces with their small tasselled shades hadn't been lit. Near the bar, someone had set out a blackboard upon which the night's specialities had been printed in a hand that employed oddly pointed letters, sloping lines, and a devotion to fuchsia-coloured chalk. *Lasagnia* was offered, as were *Minuet Steak* and *Steamed Toffy Pudding*. If the spelling was any indication of the cooking, things didn't look promising. Lynley made a mental note to try the restaurant in lieu of the pub.

St. James and Deborah were seated beneath one of the two windows that looked out onto the street. On the table between them, the remains of an afternoon tea mixed with beer mats and a stapled sheaf of papers that St. James was in the act of folding and stuffing into his inside jacket pocket. He was saying:

"Listen to me, Deborah," to which she was replying, "I won't. You're breaking our agreement." She crossed her arms. Lynley knew that gesture. He slowed his steps.

Three logs burned in the fireplace next to their table. Deborah turned in her chair and looked into the flames.

St. James said, "Be reasonable."

She said, "Be fair."

Then one of the logs shifted and a shower of sparks rained onto the hearth. St. James worked the fire brush. Deborah moved away. She caught sight of Lynley. She said, "Tommy" with a smile and looked a mixture of saved and relieved as he stepped into the greater light that the fire provided. He set his suitcase by the stairway and went to join them.

"You've made excellent time," St. James said as Lynley offered his hand in greeting and then brushed a kiss against Deborah's cheek.

"The wind at my back."

"And no trouble getting away from the Yard?"

"You've forgotten. I'm on holiday. I'd just gone into the office to clear off my desk."

"And we've taken you from your holiday?" Deborah asked. "Simon! That's dreadful."

Lynley smiled. "A mercy, Deb."

"But surely you and Helen had plans."

"We did. She changed her mind. I was at a loose end. It was either a drive to Lancashire or a prolonged rattle round my house in London. Lancashire seemed to hold infinitely more promise. It's a diversion, at least."

Deborah shrewdly assessed the final statement. "Does Helen know you've come?"

"I'll phone her tonight."

"Tommy . . ."

"I know. I've not behaved well. I've picked up my marbles and run away."

He dropped into the seat next to Deborah and picked up a shortbread still left on the plate. He poured some tea for himself into her empty cup and stirred in sugar as he munched. He looked about. The door to the restaurant was shut. The lights behind the bar were switched off. The office door was open a crack, but no movement came from within, and while a third door—set at an angle behind the bar—was open far enough to emit a lance of light that pierced the labels of the spirit bottles that hung upside down awaiting use, no sound came from beyond it.

"No one's here?" Lynley asked.

"They're about somewhere. There's a bell on the bar."

He nodded but made no move to go to it.

"They know you're the Yard, Tommy."

Lynley raised an eyebrow. "How?"

"You had a phone message during lunch. It was the talk of the pub."

"So much for incognito."

"It probably wouldn't have served us well, anyway."

"Who knows?"

"That you're CID?" St. James leaned back and let his glance wander, as if trying to remember who had been in the pub when the call came through. "The owners, certainly. Six or seven locals. A group of hikers who're no doubt long gone."

"You're certain about the locals?"

"Ben Wragg—he's the owner—was chatting some of them up at the bar when his wife brought the news from the office. The rest got the information with their lunches. At least Deborah and I did."

"I hope the Wraggs charged extra."

St. James smiled. "They didn't, that. But they did give us the message. They gave everyone the message. Sergeant Dick Hawkins, Clitheroe Police, phoning for Detective Inspector Thomas Lynley."

" 'I asked him where this Detective Inspector Thomas Lynley was from, I did,' " Deborah added in her best Lancashire accent. " 'And wouldn't you know'—with a wonderfully dramatic pause, Tommy—'he's from New Scotland Yard! Staying right here at the inn, he'll be. He booked a room hisself not three hours past. *I* took the call. Now what you s'pose he's come to look into?' " Deborah's nose wrinkled with her smile. "You're the week's excitement. You've turned Winslough into St. Mary Mead."

Lynley chuckled. St. James said pensively, "Clitheroe's not the regional constabulary for Winslough, is it? And this Hawkins said nothing about being attached to anyone's CID, because if he had, we surely would have heard that bit of news along with everything else."

"Clitheroe's just the divisional police centre," Lynley said. "Hawkins is the local constable's superior officer. I spoke to him this morning."

"But he's not CID?"

"No. And you were right in your conclusions about that, St. James. When I spoke to Hawkins earlier, he affirmed the fact that Clitheroe's CID did nothing more than photograph the body, examine the crime scene, collect physical evidence, and arrange for autopsy. Shepherd himself did the rest: investigation and interviews. But he didn't do them alone."

"Who assisted?"

"His father."

"That's deucedly odd."

"Odd and irregular but not illegal. From what Sergeant Hawkins told me earlier, Shepherd's father was Detective Chief Inspector at the regional constabulary in Hutton-Preston at the time. Evidently he pulled rank on Sergeant Hawkins and gave the order how things would be."

"*Was* Detective Chief Inspector?"

"This Sage affair was his last police case. He retired shortly after the inquest."

"So Colin Shepherd must have arranged with his father to keep Clitheroe's CID out of it," Deborah said.

"Or his father wanted it that way."

"But why?" St. James mused.

"I dare say that's what we're here to find out."

·   ·   ·

They walked down the Clitheroe Road together, in the direction of the church, past the front of terraced houses whose white, transomed windows were edged by a hundred years of grime that no mere washing could ever remove.

They found Colin Shepherd's house next to the vicarage, just across the street from St. John the Baptist Church. Here, they separated, Deborah crossing to the church itself with a quiet "I haven't seen it yet anyway," leaving St. James and Lynley to conduct their interview with the constable on their own.

Two cars stood on the drive in front of the sorrel brick building, a muddy Land Rover at least ten years old and a splattered Golf that looked relatively new. No car stood on the neighbouring drive, but as they skirted past the Rover and the Golf on their way to Colin Shepherd's door, a woman came to one of the front windows in the vicarage, and she watched their progress with no attempt to hide herself from view. One hand was freeing kinky, carrot-coloured hair from a scarf that bound it at the base of her neck. The other was buttoning a navy coat. She didn't move from the window even when it was obvious that Lynley and St. James had seen her.

A narrow, rectangular sign jutted from the side of Colin Shepherd's house. Blue and white, it was printed with the single word *POLICE*. As was the case in most villages, the local constable's home was also the business centre of his policing area. Lynley wondered idly if Shepherd had brought the Spence woman here to do his questioning of her.

A dog began to bark in answer to their ringing of the bell. It was a sound that started at one end of the house, rapidly approached the front door, and took up a raucous position behind it. A large dog by the sound of it, and none too friendly.

A man's voice said, "Quiet, Leo. Sit," and the barking ceased at once. The porch light flicked on—although it wasn't yet completely dark—and the door swung open.

With a large black retriever sitting at attention at his side, Colin Shepherd looked them over. His face reflected neither the anticipation attendant to greeting a request for his professional services nor the general curiosity attached to finding strangers at one's door. His words explained why. He said them with a quick, formal nod. "Scotland Yard CID. Sergeant Hawkins said you might pay me a call today."

Lynley produced his warrant card and introduced St. James, to whom Shepherd said after an evaluative glance, "You're staying at the inn, aren't you? I saw you last night."

"My wife and I came to see Mr. Sage."

"The red-headed woman. She was out by the reservoir this morning."

"She'd gone there to walk on the moor."

"The mist comes down fast in these parts. It's no place for a walk if you don't know the land."

"I'll tell her."

Shepherd stepped back from the door. The dog rose in response, a rumbling in his throat. Shepherd said, "Be quiet. Go back to the fire," and the dog trotted obediently into another room.

"Use him for your work?" Lynley asked.

"No. Just for hunting."

Shepherd nodded to a coat rack that stood at one end of the elongated entry. Beneath it, three pairs of gumboots lined up, two of them smeared with fresh mud on the sides. Next to these, a metal milk basket stood, with an empty cocoon of some long-departed insect dangling by a thread from one of its bars. Shepherd waited while

Lynley and St. James hung up their coats. Then he led the way down the corridor in the direction the retriever had taken.

They went into a sitting room where a fire burned and an older man was laying a small log on top of the flames. Despite the years that separated them in age, it was obvious that this was Colin Shepherd's father. They shared many similarities: the height, the muscular chest, the narrow hips. Their hair was different, thinning in the father and fading to the colour of sand in the way that blonds do as they move towards grey. And the long fingers, sensitivity, and sureness of the hands in the son had in the father become large knuckles and split nails with age.

The latter man slapped his palms together briskly as if to rid them of wood dust. He offered his hand in greeting. "Kenneth Shepherd," he said. "Detective Chief Inspector, retired. Hutton-Preston CID. But I expect you know that already, don't you?"

"Sergeant Hawkins passed the information on to me."

"As well he ought. It's good to meet you both." He shot a glance at his son. "Have you something to offer these good gentlemen, Col?"

The constable's face did not change its expression despite the affability of his father's tone. Behind his tortoiseshell spectacles, his eyes remained guarded. "Beer," he said. "Whisky. Brandy. I've a sherry here that's been collecting dust for the last six years."

"Your Annie *was* a one for her sherry, wasn't she?" the Chief Inspector said. "God rest her sweet soul. I'll have a go with that. And you?" to the others.

"Nothing," said Lynley.

"Nor for me," St. James said.

From a small fruitwood side table, Shepherd poured the drink for his father and something from a spirit decanter for himself. As he did so, Lynley glanced round the room.

It was sparsely furnished, in the manner of a man who shops at jumble sales when a pressing need arises and doesn't give much thought to the look of his possessions. The back of a beleaguered sofa was covered by a handknit blanket of multicoloured squares that managed to hide most of the large but mercifully faded pink anemones that decorated its fabric. Nothing beyond their own worn upholstery covered either of the two mismatched wing chairs, the arms of which were threadbare and the backs of which were permanently dented from serving as the resting place for generations of heads. Aside from a bentwood coffee table, a brass floor lamp, and the side table on which the liquor bottles stood, the only other item of interest hung on the wall. This was a cabinet that housed a collection of rifles and shotguns. They were the only things in the room that looked cared for, no doubt companion pieces to the retriever who had sunk onto an ancient, stained duvet in front of the fire. His paws, like the gumboots in the hall, were clotted with mud.

"Game birds?" Lynley asked with a look at the guns.

"Deer at one time as well. But I've given that up. The killing never lived up to the stalking."

"It seems that it should. But it never does, does it?"

His sherry glass in hand, the Chief Inspector gestured towards the sofa and chairs. "Sit," he said, sinking into the sofa. "We've just come in from a tramp ourselves and can do with taking a load off our feet. I'm off in about a quarter of an hour. I've got a sweet young thing of fifty-eight years waiting dinner for me at the pensioner's flat. But there's time enough for a natter first."

"You don't live here in Winslough?" St. James asked.

"Haven't in years. I like a bit of action and a bit of willing, soft girl-flesh to go with it. There's none of the first to be found in Winslough and what there is of the second's long been tied up."

The constable took his drink to the fire, squatted down on his haunches, and ran his hand over the retriever's head. In response, Leo opened his eyes and moved to rest his chin against Shepherd's shoe. His tail skittered in contentment against the floor.

"Got yourself in the mud," Shepherd said, giving a gentle tug to the retriever's ears. "A fine mess you are."

His father snorted. "Dogs. Christ. They get under your skin about as bad as do women."

It was an opening from which Lynley's question rose naturally, although he was as certain the Chief Inspector hadn't intended it to be used that way as he was certain the man's visit to his son had little to do with an afternoon's hike on the moors. "What can you tell us about Mrs. Spence and the death of Robin Sage?"

"Not exactly a Yard concern, is it?" Although he said it in a friendly enough fashion, the Chief Inspector's response came too quickly upon the heels of the question. It spoke of having been prepared in advance.

"Formally? No."

"But informally?"

"Surely you're not blind to the irregularity of the investigation, Chief Inspector. No CID. Your son's attachment to the perpetrator of the crime."

"Accident, not crime." Colin Shepherd looked up from the dog, his glass clasped in an easy grip in his hand. He remained squatting next to the fire. A countryman born and bred, he could no doubt maintain the position for hours without the slightest discomfort.

"An irregular decision, but not illegal," the Chief Inspector said. "Colin felt he could handle it. I agreed. Handle it he did. I was with him through most of it, so if it's the lack of CID input that's got the Yard in a dither, CID was here all the time."

"You sat in on all the interviews?"

"The ones that mattered."

"Chief Inspector, you know that's more than irregular. I don't need to tell you that when a crime's been committed—"

"But no crime was," the constable said. He kept one hand on the dog, but his eyes were on Lynley. He didn't move them. "The crime-scene team came out to crawl round the moors and overturn stones, and they saw the situation well enough in an hour. This wasn't a crime. It was a clear-cut accident. I saw it that way. The coroner saw it that way. The jury saw it that way. End of story."

"You were certain of that from the first?"

The dog stirred restlessly as the hand on him tightened. "Of course not."

"Yet aside from the initial presence of the crime-scene team, you made the decision not to involve your divisional CID, the very people who are trained to determine if a death is an accident, a suicide, or murder."

"I made the decision," the Chief Inspector said.

"Based upon?"

"A phone call from me," his son said.

"You reported the death to your father? Not to the divisional headquarters in Clitheroe?"

"I reported to both. I told Hawkins I would handle it. Pa confirmed. Everything seemed straightforward enough once I'd talked to Juliet . . . to Mrs. Spence."

"And Mr. Spence?" Lynley asked.

"There is none."

"I see."

The constable dropped his eyes, swirled the liquor in his glass. "This has nothing to do with our relationship."

"But it adds a complication. I'm sure you see that."

"It wasn't a murder."

St. James leaned forward in the wing chair he'd chosen. "What makes you so certain? What made you so certain a month ago, Constable?"

"She had no motive. She didn't know the man. It was only the third time they'd even met. He was after her to start going to church. And he wanted to talk about Maggie."

"Maggie?" Lynley asked.

"Her daughter. Juliet had been having some trouble with her and the vicar got involved. He wanted to help. Mediate between them. Offer advice. That's it. That's their relationship in a nutshell. Should I have called in CID and had them read her the caution over that? Or would you have preferred a motive first?"

"Means and opportunity are powerful indicators in themselves," Lynley said.

"That's a lot of balls and you know it," the Chief Inspector put in.

"Pa . . ."

Shepherd's father waved him off with his sherry glass. "I have the means for murder every time I get behind the wheel of my car. I have opportunity when I step on the pedal. Is it murder, Inspector, if I hit someone who dodges into the path of my car? Do we need to call in CID for that, or can we deem it an accident?"

"Pa . . ."

"If that's your argument—and I can't deny its tenability at the moment—why involve CID in the person of yourself?"

"Because he *is* involved with the woman, for God's sake. He wanted me here to make sure he kept his mind clear. And he did. Every moment."

"Every moment you were here. And by your own admission, you weren't here for each interview."

"I damn well didn't need—"

"Pa." Shepherd's voice was sharp. It altered to quiet reason when he went on. "Obviously it looked bad when Sage died. Juliet knows her plants, and it was hard to believe she could have mistaken water hemlock for wild parsnip. But that's what happened."

"You're certain of that?" St. James asked.

"Of course I am. She got ill herself the night Mr. Sage died. She was burning with fever. She was sick four or five times, until two the next morning. Now you can't tell me that without having a blessed motive in the world she'd *knowingly* eat a few bites of the deadliest natural poison there is in order to paint a murder an accident. Hemlock's not like arsenic, Inspector Lynley. One doesn't build up an immunity to it. If Juliet wanted to kill Mr. Sage, she bloody well wouldn't have been such a fool as to deliberately eat part of the hemlock herself. She could have died. She was lucky she didn't."

"You know for a fact she was ill?" Lynley asked.

"I was there."

"At the dinner?"

"Later. I stopped by."

"What time?"

"Towards eleven. After I made my last patrol."

"Why?"

Shepherd tossed back the rest of his drink and placed the glass on the floor. He took off his spectacles and spent a moment polishing the outer right lens against the sleeve of his flannel shirt.

"Constable?"

"Tell him, lad," the Chief Inspector said. "It's the only way he's going to be satisfied."

Shepherd gave a shrug, replacing the spectacles. "I wanted to see if she was alone. Maggie'd gone to spend the night with one of her mates..." He sighed, shifted his weight.

"And you thought Sage might be doing the same with Mrs. Spence?"

"He'd been there three times. Juliet gave me no reason to think she'd taken him as a lover. I wondered. That's all. I wondered. It's nothing I'm proud of."

"Would it be likely that she'd take on a lover after so brief an acquaintance, Constable?"

Shepherd picked up his glass, saw it was empty, put it back down. A spring creaked on the sofa as the Chief Inspector stirred.

"Would she, Mr. Shepherd?"

The constable's spectacles flashed briefly in the light as he lifted his head to meet Lynley's gaze. "That's hard to know about any woman, isn't it? Especially a woman you love."

There was truth to that, Lynley admitted. More than he liked to think about. People expatiated on the virtues of trust all the time. He wondered how many of them actually lived by it, with no doubts ever camping like restless gypsies just at the edge of their consciousness.

He said: "I take it Sage was gone when you arrived?"

"Yes. She said he'd left at nine."

"Where was she?"

"In bed."

"Ill?"

"Yes."

"But she let you in?"

"I knocked. She didn't answer. I let myself in."

"The door was unlocked?"

"I have a set of keys." He saw St. James glance quickly in Lynley's direction. He added, "She didn't give them to me. Townley-Young did. Keys to the cottage, Cotes Hall, the whole estate. He owns it. She's the caretaker."

"She knows you have the keys?"

"Yes."

"As a security precaution?"

"I suppose."

"Do you use 'em often? As part of your evening patrol?"

"Not generally, no."

Lynley saw that St. James was looking thoughtfully at the constable, his brows drawn together as he pulled at his chin. He said: "It was a bit risky, that, wouldn't you say, letting yourself into her cottage at night? What if she had been in bed with Mr. Sage?"

Shepherd's jaw tightened but he answered easily. "I suppose I would have killed him myself."

CHAPTER EIGHT

DEBORAH SPENT THE FIRST QUARTER OF AN hour inside St. John the Baptist Church. Beneath the hammer-beam ceiling, she wandered down the central aisle towards the chancel, tracing a mittened finger along the scroll-work that edged each pew. On the far side of the pulpit, one of them was boxed, separated from the rest by a gate of barley-sugar columns on the top of which a small bronze plaque bore blackened letters reading *Townley-Young.* Deborah lifted its latch and stepped inside, wondering what sort of people would want to maintain the unpleasant, centuries-old custom of segregating themselves from those they considered their social inferiors.

She sat on the narrow bench and looked about. The air in the church was musty and frigid, and when she exhaled, her breath hung whitely before her face for a moment, then dissipated like a cirrus in the wind. On a pillar nearby, the hymnboard hung, listing a selection for some previous service. Number 388 was at the top, and idly she opened one of the hymnals to it, reading

> *Lord Christ, who on thy heart didst bear*
> *the burden of our shame and sin,*
> *and now on high dost stoop to share*
> *the fight without, the fear within,*

after which she dropped her eyes to

that we may care, as thou hast cared,
for sick and lame, for deaf and blind,
and freely share, as thou hast shared,
in all the sorrows of mankind

and then stared at the words with her throat aching-tight, as if they had been written precisely for her. Which they had not. Which they had *not.*

She slapped the book closed. To the left of the pulpit a banner hung limply from a metal rod, and she scrutinised this. *Winslough* was stitched across a faded blue background in letters of yellow. Below them *St. John the Baptist Church* was rendered in quilted patchwork from which several tufts of stuffing leaked like snow against the bell tower and on the face of the clock. She wondered what the banner was used for, when it had been hung, if it had ever seen the light of day, how old it was, who had made it and why. She pictured an elderly woman of the parish at work on the design, stitching her way into the good graces of the Lord by making an offering for His place of worship. How long had it taken her? What sort of thread had she used for the quilting? Did anyone help? Did anyone know? Was there anyone who kept that sort of history of a church?

Such games, Deborah thought. What an effort she made to keep her mind in check. How important it was to feel the tranquillity suggested by a visit to a church and communion with the Lord.

She hadn't come here for that. She had come because a walk down the Clitheroe Road in the late afternoon with her husband and the man who was his closest friend, who was her own former lover, who was the father of the child she might have had—would never have—seemed the best way to escape the feeling of having been betrayed.

Dragged up to Lancashire on false pretences, she thought and gave a weak chuckle at the idea, she who had been the ultimate betrayer.

She had found the sheaf of adoption papers tucked between his pyjamas and his socks, and she'd felt indignation pinch at her spine at the thought of his deception and at this intrusion into their time away from their real life in London. He wanted to talk about it, he explained when she flung the papers on the chest of drawers. He felt it was time that they sorted things out.

There was nothing to sort. To talk about it was to engage in the kind of conversation that spun like a cyclone, gathering speed and energy from misunderstanding, wreaking destruction from words hurled in anger and self-defence. A family isn't blood, he would say so reasonably because God knew that Simon Allcourt-St. James was scientist, scholar, and reason incarnate. A family is people. People bond to one another out of time, exposure, and experience, Deborah. We form our connections from the give and take of emotion, from the growing sensitivity to another's needs, from mutual support. A child's attachment to his parents has nothing to do with who gave him birth. It comes from living day to day, from being nurtured, from being guided, from having someone there—someone consistent— that he can trust. You know this. You do.

It isn't that, it isn't that, she would want to say, even as she felt the tears which she so much despised cutting off her ability to speak.

Then what is it? Tell me. Help me understand.

Mine . . . it wouldn't be . . . yours. It wouldn't be us. Can't you see that? Why won't you see?

He would look at her without speaking for a moment, not to punish her with withdrawal as she'd once thought his silences meant, but to think and to problem-solve. He would be considering a recommendation on a course of action for them to take when all she wanted was that he too would weep and display through his tears that he understood her grief.

Because he'd never do that, she couldn't say the final unsayable to him. She hadn't even yet said it to herself. She didn't want to feel the sorrow that would accompany the words. So she fought against their encroachment on her consciousness and she fended them off by railing against what she knew very well was his greatest strength: that he never allowed a single circumstance to defeat him, that he took life as he found it and bent it to his will.

You don't even care, would be the words she chose. This means nothing to you. You don't want to understand me.

What a convenience a cyclone-argument was.

She'd gone walking that morning to avoid confrontation. Out on the moors with the wind in her face, hiking across the uneven ground, dodging the occasional spines of furze and tramping through heather gone brown with winter, she'd kept everything at bay but the exercise itself.

Now, however, the quiet church admitted no such means of avoidance. She could examine the memorials, watch the dying light darken the colours in the windows, read the bronze Ten Commandments that formed the reredos and decide how many she'd broken so far. She could scrape her feet across the age-warped floor of the Townley-Young pew and count the moth holes dotting the red mantle on the pulpit. She could admire the woodwork of the rood screen and the tester. She could wonder about the tonal quality of the bells. But she could not avoid the voice of her conscience that spoke the truth and forced her to hear it:

Filling out those papers means I'm giving up. It's admitting defeat. It tells me I'm a failure, not a woman at all. It says the ache will fade but it'll never end. And it isn't fair. This is the one thing that I want . . . this single, simple, unattainable thing.

Deborah stood and pushed open the box-pew's gate. With the sound of its creaking came Simon's words:

Are you punishing yourself, Deborah? Does your conscience say you've sinned and the only expiation is to replace one life with another which you yourself create? Is that what you're doing? And are you doing it for me? Do you think you owe me that?

Perhaps, in part. For he was, if anything, forgiveness itself. If he had been some other kind of man—railing occasionally or throwing into her face the fact that she was at fault in this failure—she might have been able to bear it more easily. It was because he did nothing save look for solutions and express his growing alarm about her health that she found it so difficult to forgive herself.

On the worn red carpet, she retraced her steps down the aisle to the north door of the church. She stepped outside. She shivered in the growing cold and tucked her scarf inside the collar of her coat. Across the street, two cars were still parked in the constable's drive. A light was on in the porch. But no one was stirring behind the front window.

Deborah turned away and entered the graveyard. It was lumpy like the moorland, tangled at the edges with blackberry and bramble, the stark red of dogwood growing in a thicket round one tomb. On top of this an angel stood with head bowed and arms extended, as if in final readiness to throw himself into the fire-coloured stems.

Nothing much had been done to see to the upkeep of the graves. Mr. Sage had been dead for a month, but the lack of concern for the church's immediate surroundings seemed to have its genesis further back in time than that. The path was overgrown with weeds. The graves were mottled with black, dead leaves. The stones were splattered with mud and green with lichen.

Among them, one grave lay like a soundless reproach to the state to which time and lack of interest had reduced the others. It was swept clean. Its blanket of tough, moorland grass was clipped. Its stone was unblemished. Deborah went to inspect it.

Anne Alice Shepherd, the carving read. She'd been twenty-seven years old at her death. She'd also been someone's *dearest wife* in life, and if the condition of her grave was any indication, she was someone's dearest wife in death as well.

A glint of colour caught Deborah's eye. It seemed as misplaced as did the red dogwood in the otherwise chromatic congruence of the graveyard, and she bent to examine the base of the gravestone where two bright pink interlocking ovals shone against a nest of something grey. Upon her first inspection, the grey seemed to flow out of the marble marker as if the stone were disintegrating to dust. But on a closer look, she saw that it was a small mound of ashes into whose centre an even smaller, smooth stone had been carefully laid. On this were painted the interlocking ovals which had first caught her eye, two rings of neon pink, perfectly executed, each the same size.

It seemed an odd offering to make to the dead. Winter called for holly wreaths and made do with juniper. At the worst, it accepted those ghastly plastic flowers encased in plastic cases that grew mildew inside. But ashes and stone and, she now saw, four slivers of wood holding the stone in place?

She touched her finger to it. It was smooth as glass. It was almost perfectly flat as well. It had been placed on the ground directly at the centre of the gravestone, but it lay among the ashes like a message for the living and not a fond remembrance of the dead.

Two rings, interlocked. Gently, without disturbing the ashes in which the stone lay, Deborah picked it up, its size and weight no more than that of a pound coin in her hand. She removed one mitten and she felt the stone lie cold, like a pool of standing water in her palm.

Despite their odd colour, the rings reminded her of wedding

bands, the sort one saw engraved in gold or embossed on invitations. Like their counterparts on paper, they were the same sort of perfect circles that priests always seemed to speak of, perfect circles of both the union and the unity that a strong marriage was supposed to embody. "A union of bodies, of souls, and of minds," the minister had said at her own wedding more than two years ago. "These two before us shall now become one."

Except that it never quite happened that way in anyone's life, as far as Deborah could tell. There was love, and with it came growing trust. There was intimacy, and with it came the warmth of assurance. There was passion, and with it came moments of joy. But if two hearts were to beat as one and if two minds were to think in like manner, such integration had not occurred between herself and Simon. Or if it had, the triumph of its accomplishment had been evanescent.

Yet there was love between them. It was vast, subsuming most of her life. She could not imagine a world without it. What she wondered was if the love between them was enough to forge through fear in order to reach understanding.

Her fingers closed round the stone with its two pink rings painted brightly upon it. She would keep it as a talisman. It would serve as a fetish for what the unity of marriage was supposed to produce.

■   ■   ■

"You've made a real cock-up of things this time. You know that, don't you? They've settled themselves in to reinvestigate the death and you've not got yourself a sinner's chance in hell of stopping them. You understand that, don't you?"

Colin carried his whisky glass into the kitchen. He placed it directly beneath the tap. Although there were no other dishes in the sink and none at the moment that wanted washing on either the work top or the table, he squirted a lemon-scented detergent into the glass and ran water into it until soap bubbles frothed. They slid over the rim and down one side while the water churned up more like foam in a Guinness.

"Your career's on the line now. Everyone from Constable Nit chasing boys from Borstal to Hutton-Preston's CC is going to hear about this. You realise that, don't you? You've a blot on you, Col, and when next there's an opening in CID, no one's likely to forget it. You see that, don't you?"

Colin unwound the striped dish cloth from the base of the tap and lowered it into the glass with the sort of precision he might have used when cleaning one of his shotguns. He knuckled it into a wad, shimmied it round and round, and ran it carefully along the rim. Funny, how he could still miss Annie at an unexpected moment like this. It always came without warning—a quick surge of grief and longing that rose from his loins and ended near his heart—and it always came from something so ordinary that he never considered how insidious was the action that precipitated it. He was always unarmed and never unaffected.

He blinked. A tremor shook him. He rubbed the glass harder.

"You think I can help you at this point, don't you, boy?" his father was continuing. "I stepped in once—"

"Because you wanted to step in. I didn't need you here, Pa."

"Are you out of your mind? Have you bloody gone daft? Has she got you in blinkers or just smiling like a prat with your trousers unzipped?"

Colin rinsed the glass, dried it with the same care he'd used in washing it, and placed it next to the toaster which, he noted, was dusty and littered on its top with crumbs. Only then did he look at his father.

The Chief Inspector was standing in the doorway as was his habit, blocking escape. The only way to avoid conversation was to push past him, to find employment in the pantry off the kitchen, or to mess about in the garage. In any case, his father would follow. Colin recognised when the Chief Inspector was building up a good head of steam.

"What in hell were you thinking of?" his father asked. "What in God's-name-bloody-stinking hell were you thinking of?"

"We've been through this before. It was an accident. I told Hawkins. I followed procedure."

"Bleeding hell you did! You had a corpse on your hands with the stench of murder oozing from every pore. Tongue chewed to shreds. Body bloated like a pig. The whole area beat down like he'd been wrestling with the devil. And you call it an accident? You report that to your superior officer? Christ, I can't think why they haven't sacked you by now."

Colin folded his arms across his chest, leaned against the work top, and made his breathing slow. They both knew why. He put the answer into words. "You didn't give them the chance, Pa. But for that matter, you didn't give me a chance, either."

His father's face flamed. "Jesus God! A chance? This isn't a game. This is life and death. It's *still* life and death. Only this time, boy-o, you're on your own." He'd rolled up the sleeves of his shirt upon entering the house when they'd returned from their hike. Now he began unrolling them, shoving the material down his arms and battering it into place. On the wall to his right, Annie's cat clock wagged its black pendulum tail as its eyes shifted with every tick and tock. It was just about time for him to leave. He had his sweet piece of girl-flesh to see to. All Colin had to do was wait him out.

"Suspicious circumstances call for CID. You know that, boy, don't you?"

"I had CID."

"You had their bleeding photographer!"

"The crime team came. They saw what I saw. There was no indication that anyone other than Mr. Sage had been there. No footprints in the snow but his. No witness who saw anyone else on the footpath that night. The ground was thrashed up because he'd had convulsions. It was obvious from the look of him that he'd had some sort of seizure. I didn't need any DI to tell me that."

His father's fists clenched. He raised his arms then dropped them. "You're as stubborn an ass as you were twenty years ago. As stupid as well."

Colin shrugged.

"You have no choice now. You know that, don't you? You've the whole sodding village in a quagmire over this wet fanny you've got such a fancy for."

Colin's own fist clenched. He forced himself to release it. "That's it, Pa. Be on your way. As I recall, you've a fanny of your own waiting somewhere this evening."

"You're not too old to be beaten, boy."

"True. But this time, you'd probably lose."

"After what I did—"

"You didn't need to do anything. I didn't ask you to be here. I didn't ask you to follow me round like a hound with a good scent of fox up his nose. I had it under control."

His father gave a sharp, derisive nod. "Stubborn, stupid, and blind as well." He left the kitchen and went to the front door where he battled his way into his jacket and shoved his left foot into one of his boots. "You're lucky they've come."

"I don't need them. She did nothing."

"Save poison the vicar."

"By accident, Pa."

His father jerked on the second boot and straightened up. "You'd better pray on that, son. Because there's one hell of a cloud hanging over you now. In the village. In Clitheroe. All the way to Hutton-Preston. And the only way it's about to clear off is if the Yard's CID don't smell something nasty in your lady friend's bed."

He fished his leather gloves from his pocket and began to pull them on. He didn't speak again until he'd squashed his peaked cap on his head. Then he peered at his son sharply.

"You've been straight with me, haven't you? You've done no holding back?"

"Pa—"

"Because if you've covered up for her, you're through. You're sacked. You're indicted. That's the number. You understand that, don't you?"

Colin saw the anxiety in his father's eyes and heard it beneath the anger in his voice. He knew there was a measure of paternal solicitude in it, but he also knew that beyond the reality that a cover-up would lead to an investigation and a trial, it was the complete incomprehensibility of the fact that he wasn't hungry that picked at his father's peace. He had never been restless. He didn't yearn for a higher rank and the right to sit comfortably behind a desk. He was thirty-four years old and still a village constable and as far as his father was concerned, there had to be a good reason why. *I like it* wasn't good enough. *I love the countryside* would never do. The Chief Inspector might have bought *I can't leave my Annie* a year ago, but he'd fly into a rage if Colin spoke of Annie while Juliet Spence was part of his life.

And now, there was the potential humiliation of his son's involvement in the cover-up of a crime. He'd rested easy when the coroner's jury had reached their verdict. He'd be in a hornets' nest of dread until Scotland Yard completed their investigation and verified that there had been no crime.

"Colin," his father said again. "You've been straight with me, haven't you? Nothing held back?"

Colin met his gaze directly. He was proud he could do so. "Nothing held back," he said.

It was only when he'd closed the door upon his father that Colin felt his legs weaken. He grasped onto the knob and leaned his forehead against the wood.

It was nothing to concern himself with. No one would ever need to know. He'd not even thought of it himself until the Scotland Yard DI had asked his question and triggered the memory of Juliet and the gun.

He'd gone to speak to her after receiving three angry phone calls from three frightened sets of parents whose sons had been out for a frolic on the grounds of Cotes Hall. She'd been living at the Hall in the caretaker's cottage just a year then, a tall, angular woman who kept to herself, made her money from growing herbs and brewing up potions, hiked vigorously across the moors with her daughter, and seldom came into the village for anything. She bought groceries in Clitheroe. She bought gardening supplies in Burnley. She examined crafts and sold plants and dried herbs in Laneshawbridge. She took her daughter on the occasional excursion, but her choices were always a margin off-beat, like the Lewis Textile Museum rather than Lancaster Castle, like Hoghton Tower's collection of dolls' houses rather than Blackpool's diversions by the sea. But these were things he discovered later. At first, bucking down the rutted lane in his old Land Rover, he thought only of the idiocy of a woman who'd shoot into the darkness at three young boys making animal noises at the edge of the woods. And a shotgun at that. Anything could have happened.

The sun was filtering through the oak wood on that afternoon. Beads of green lined the branches of trees as a late winter day gave way to spring. He was rounding a bend in the blasted road that the Townley-Youngs had been refusing to repair for the better part of a decade when through the open window came the sharp scent of cut lavender and with it one of those stabbing memories of Annie. So blinding it was, so momentarily real that he trod on the brake, half expecting her to come at a run from the woods, there where the lavender had been planted thickly at the edge of the road more than one hundred years ago when Cotes Hall lay in readiness for its bridegroom who had never arrived.

They'd been out here a thousand times, he and Annie, and she usually plucked at the lavender bushes as she made her way along the lane, filling the air with the scent of both the flowers and the foliage, collecting the buds to use in sachets among the wools and the linens at home. He remembered those sachets as well, clumsy little gauze pouches tied with frayed purple ribbon. They always came apart within a week. He was always picking bits of lavender out of his socks and brushing them off the sheets. And despite his protest of "Come on, girl. What good do they do?" she kept industriously tucking the pouches into every corner of the house, even once into his shoes, saying, "Moths, Col. We can't have moths, can we?"

After she died, he rid the house of them in an ineffective attempt to rid the house of her. Directly he swept her medicines from the bedside table, directly he pulled her clothes from their hangers and pushed her shoes into rubbish bags, directly he took her scent bottles into the rear garden and smashed them one by one with a hammer as if by that action he could smash away the rage, he went on a search for Annie's sachets.

But the smell of lavender always thrust her before him. It was worse than at night when his dreams allowed him to see her, remember, and long for what she once had been. In the day, with only the scent to haunt him, she was just out of reach, like a whisper carried past him on the wind.

He thought *Annie, Annie* and stared at the lane with his hands gripping the steering wheel.

So he didn't see Juliet Spence at once, and thus she had the initial advantage over him, which he sometimes thought she maintained to this day. She said, "Are you quite all right, Constable?" and he snapped his head to the open window to see that she had come out of the woods with a basket on her arm and the knees of her blue jeans crusted with mud.

It didn't seem the least odd that Mrs. Spence should know who he was. The village was small. She would have seen him before now even though they had never been introduced. Beyond that, Townley-Young would have told her that he made periodic visits to the Hall as part of his evening rounds. She might even have noticed him on occasion from her cottage window when he rumbled through the courtyard and shone his torch here and there against the boarded windows of the mansion, checking to make sure that its crumble to ruin stayed in the hands of nature and was not usurped by man.

He ignored her question and got out of the Rover. He said, although he knew the answer already, "It's Mrs. Spence, isn't it?"

"It is."

"Are you aware of the fact that last night you discharged your shotgun in the direction of three twelve-year-old boys? In the direction of children, Mrs. Spence?"

She had odd bits of greenery, roots, and twigs in her basket, along with a trowel and a pair of secateurs. She picked up the trowel, dislodged a heavy clod of mud from its tip, and rubbed her fingers along the side of her jeans. Her hands were large and dirty. Her fingernails were clipped. They looked like a man's. She said, "Come to the cottage, Mr. Shepherd."

She turned on her heel and walked back into the woods, leaving him to jostle and jolt the last half mile along the road. By the time he'd crunched into the courtyard across the gravel and pulled to a halt in the shadow of the Hall, she'd got rid of her basket, brushed the mud from her jeans, washed her hands so thoroughly that her skin looked abraded, and set a kettle to boil on the cooker.

The front door stood open and when he mounted the single step that did for a porch, she said, "I'm in the kitchen, Constable. Come in."

Tea, he thought. Questions and answers all controlled through the ritual of pouring, passing sugar and milk, shaking Hob Nobs onto a chipped floral plate. Clever, he thought.

But instead of making tea, she poured the boiling water slowly into a large metal pan in which glass jars stood in water of their own. She set the pan onto the cooker as well.

"Things need to be sterile," she said. "People die so easily when someone is foolish and thinks of making preserves without sterilising first."

He looked round the kitchen and tried to get a glimpse of the larder beyond it. The time of year seemed decidedly odd for what she was proposing. "What are you preserving?"

"I might ask the same of you."

She went to a cupboard and took down two glasses and a decanter from which she poured a liquid that was in colour somewhere just between dirt-toned and amber. It was cloudy, and when she placed a glass in front of him on the table where he'd gone to sit unbidden in an attempt to establish some sort of authority over her, he picked it up suspiciously and sniffed. What did it smell like? Bark? Old cheese?

She chuckled and swallowed a healthy portion of her own. She put the decanter on the table, sat down across from him, and circled her hands round her glass. "Go ahead," she said. "It's made from dandelion and elder. I drink it every day."

"What's it for?"

"I use it for purging." She smiled and drank again.

He lifted the glass. She watched. Not his hands as he lifted, not his mouth as he drank, but his eyes. That was what struck him later when he thought about their first encounter: how she never took her eyes from his. He himself was curious and gathered quick impressions about her: she wore no make-up; her hair was greying but her skin was lined only faintly so she couldn't be that much older than he; she smelled vaguely of sweat and earth, and a smudge of dirt made a patch above her eye like an oval birth mark; her shirt was a man's, over-large, frayed at the collar and ripped at the cuffs; at the *V* made where it buttoned, he could see the initial arc of one breast; her wrists were large; her shoulders were broad; he imagined the two of them could wear each other's clothes.

"This is what it's like," she said quietly. Dark eyes she had, with pupils so large that the eyes themselves looked black. "At first it's the fear of something larger than yourself—something over which you have no control and only limited understanding—that's inside her body with a power of its own. Then it's the anger that some rotten disease cut into her life and yours and made a mess out of both. And then it's the panic because no one has any answers that you can believe in and everyone's answer is different from everyone else's anyway. Then it's the misery of being saddled with her and her illness when what you wanted—signed up for, made your vows to cherish—was a wife and a family and normality. Then it's the horror of being trapped in your house with the sights and the smells and the sounds of her dying. But oddly enough, in the end it all becomes the fabric of your life, simply the way you live as man and wife. You become accustomed to the crises and to the moments of relief. You become accustomed to the grim realities of bed pans, commodes, vomit, and urine. You realise how important you are to her. You're her anchor and her saviour, her sanity. And whatever needs you have of your own, they become secondary—unimportant, selfish, nasty even—in light of the role you play for her. So when it's over and she's gone, you don't feel released the way everyone thinks you probably feel. Instead, you feel like a form of madness. They tell you it's a blessing that God finally took her. But you know there isn't a God at all. There's just this gaping wound in your life, the hole that was the space she took up, the way she needed you, and how she filled your days."

She poured more of the liquid into his glass. He wanted to make some sort of response, but he wanted even more to run so that he wouldn't have to. He removed his spectacles—turning his head away from them rather than simply drawing them off the bridge of his nose—and in doing so he managed to remove his eyes from hers.

She said, "Death isn't a release for anyone but the dying. For the living it's a hell whose face just keeps on changing all the time. You think you'll feel better. You think you'll let the grief go someday. But you never do. Not completely. And the only people who can understand are the ones who've gone through it as well."

Of course, he thought. Her husband. He said, "I loved her. Then I hated her. Then I loved her again. She needed more than I had to give."

"You gave what you could."

"Not in the end. I wasn't strong when I should have been. I put myself first. While she was dying."

"Perhaps you'd borne enough."

"She knew what I'd done. She never said a word, but she knew." He felt confined, the walls too close. He put on his spectacles. He pushed away from the table and walked to the sink where he rinsed out his glass. He looked out the window. It faced not the Hall but the woods. She'd planted an extensive garden, he saw. She'd repaired the old greenhouse. A wheelbarrow stood to one side of it, filled with what looked like manure. He imagined her shoveling it into the earth, with the strong, bold movements that her shoulders promised. She'd sweat as she did it. She'd pause to wipe her forehead on her sleeve. She wouldn't wear gloves—she'd want to feel the wooden handle of the shovel and the sunlit heat of the earth—and when she was thirsty the water she drank would pour down the sides of her mouth to dampen her neck. A slow trickle of it would run between her breasts.

He made himself turn from the window to face her. "You own a shotgun, Mrs. Spence."

"Yes." She stayed where she was, although she changed her position, one elbow on the table, one hand curved round her knee.

"And you discharged it last night?"

"Yes."

"Why?"

"The land's posted, Constable. Approximately every one hundred yards."

"There's a public footpath superseding any posting. You know that very well. As does Townley-Young."

"These boys weren't on the path to Cotes Fell. Nor were they headed back towards the village. They were in the woods behind the cottage, circling up towards the Hall."

"You're sure of that."

"From the sound of their voices, of course I'm sure."

"And you warned them off verbally?"

"Twice."

"You didn't think to phone for help?"

"I didn't need help. I just needed to be rid of them. Which, you must admit, I did fairly well."

"With a shotgun. Blasting into the trees with pellets that—"

"With salt." She ran her thumb and middle finger back through her hair. It was a gesture that spoke more of impatience than vanity. "The gun was loaded with salt, Mr. Shepherd."

"And do you ever load it with anything else?"

"On occasion, yes. But when I do, I don't shoot at children."

He noticed for the first time that she was wearing earrings, small gold studs that caught the light when she turned her head. They were her only jewellery, save for a wedding band that, like his own, was unadorned and nearly as thin as the lead of a pencil. It too caught the light when her fingers tapped restlessly against her knee. Her legs were long. He saw that she'd taken off her boots somewhere and wore nothing now but grey socks on her feet.

He said, because he needed to say something to keep his focus, "Mrs. Spence, guns are dangerous in the hands of the inexperienced."

She said, "If I had wanted to hurt someone, believe me, I would have done, Mr. Shepherd."

She stood. He expected her to cross the kitchen, bringing her glass to the sink, returning the decanter to the cupboard, invading his territory. Instead, she said, "Come with me."

He followed her into the sitting room, which he'd passed earlier on his way to the kitchen. The late afternoon's light fell in bands on the carpet, flashed light and dark against her as she walked to an old pine dresser against one wall. She pulled open the left top drawer. She took out a small package of towelling that was done up with twine. Uncoiled and unwrapped, the towelling fell away to expose a handgun. A revolver, looking particularly well-oiled.

She said again, "Come with me."

He followed her to the front door. It still stood open, and the March air was crisp with a breeze that lifted her hair. Across the courtyard, the Hall stood empty—broken windows boarded, old rain-pipes rusted, stone walls chipped. She said, "Second chimney pot from the right, I think. Its left corner." She lifted her arm, aimed the gun, and fired. A wedge of terra cotta shot off the second chimney like a missile launched.

She said once again, "If I had wanted to hurt someone, I would have done, Mr. Shepherd." She returned to the sitting room and placed the gun on its wrapping which lay on the dresser top, between a basket of sewing and a collection of photographs of her daughter.

"Do you have a licence for that?" he asked her.

"No."

"Why not?"

"It wasn't necessary."

"It's the law."

"Not for the way I bought it."

She was standing with her back against the dresser. He stayed in the doorway. He thought about saying what he ought to say. He considered doing what the law required of him. The weapon was illegal, she was in possession of it, and he was supposed to remove it from the premises and charge her with the crime. Instead, he said:

"What do you use it for?"

"Target practice mostly. But otherwise protection."

"From whom?"

"From anyone who isn't warned off by a shouting voice or a shotgun blast. It's a form of security."

"You don't seem insecure."

"Anyone with a child in the house is insecure. Especially a woman on her own."

"Do you always keep it loaded?"

"Yes."

"That's foolish. That's asking for trouble."

A smile flickered briefly round her mouth. "Perhaps. But I've never fired it in the company of anyone other than Maggie before today."

"It was foolish of you to show it to me."

"Yes. It was."

"Why did you?"

"For the same reason I own it. Protection, Constable."

He stared at her across the room, feeling his heart beating rapidly and wondering when it had begun to do so. From somewhere in the house he heard water dripping, from out-of-doors the sharp trill of a bird. He saw the rise and fall of her chest, the *V* of her shirt where her skin seemed to glisten, the stretch of blue jeans across her hips. She was gangly and sweaty. She was more than unkempt. He couldn't have left her.

Without a single coherent thought, he took two strides, and she met him in the centre of the room. He pulled her into his arms, his fingers diving through her hair, his mouth on hers. He hadn't known that such hunger for a woman could even exist. Had she resisted in the least, he knew he would have forced her, but she didn't resist and she clearly didn't want to. Her hands were in his hair, at his throat, against his chest and then her arms encircled him as he pulled her closer, cradling her buttocks and grinding grinding grinding against her. He heard the snap of buttons falling away as he pulled off her shirt, seeking her breasts. And then his own shirt was off and her mouth was on him, kissing and biting a trail to his waist where she knelt, fumbled with his belt, and pushed down his trousers.

Jesus God, he thought. Jesus Jesus Jesus. He knew only two terrors: that he might actually explode into her mouth, that she might release him before he could do so.

CHAPTER NINE

SHE COULDN'T POSSIBLY HAVE BEEN LESS LIKE Annie. Perhaps that had been the initial attraction. In place of Annie's soft, willing compliance, he had put Juliet's independence and strength. She was easily taken and eager to be taken, but not easily known. During the first hour of their love-making on that March afternoon, she'd said only two words: *God* and *harder*, the second of which she repeated three times. And when they'd had enough of each other—long after they'd moved from the sitting room up the stairs to her bedroom where they'd tried out both the floor and the bed—she turned on her side with one arm cradling her head, and she said, "What's your Christian name, Mr. Shepherd, or am I to go on calling you Mr. Shepherd?"

He traced the faint lightning bolt of skin that puckered her stomach and was the only indication—besides the child herself—that she'd given birth. He felt there wasn't sufficient time in his life to come to know every inch of her body well enough, and as he lay beside her, having had her four times already, he began to ache to have her again. He'd never made love to Annie more than once in any twenty-four-hour period. He'd never thought to try. And while the loving of his wife had been tender and sweet, leaving him feeling at once at peace and somehow in her debt, the loving of Juliet had ignited his senses, unearthing a desire that no amount of having her seemed to sate. After an evening, a night, an afternoon together, he could catch the scent of her—on his hands, on his clothes, when he combed his hair—and find himself wanting her, driven to telephone her, saying only her name to which her low voice would respond, "Yes. When."

But to her first question, he merely said, "Colin."

"What did your wife call you?"

"Col. And your husband?"

"I'm called Juliet."

"And your husband?"

"His name?"

"What did he call you?"

She ran her fingers along his eyebrows, the curve of his ear, his lips. "You're terribly young," was her reply.

"I'm thirty-three. And you?"

She smiled, a small, sad movement of her mouth. "I'm older than thirty-three. Old enough to be..."

"What?"

"Wiser than I am. Far wiser than I've been this afternoon."

His ego replied. "You wanted it, didn't you?"

"Oh yes. As soon as I saw you sitting in the Rover. Yes. I wanted. It. You. Whatever."

"Was that some sort of potion you had me drink?"

She raised his hand to her mouth, took his index finger between her lips, sucked on it gently. He caught his breath. She released him and chuckled. "You don't need a potion, Mr. Shepherd."

"How old are you?"

"Too old for this to be anything more than a single afternoon."

"You don't mean that."

"I have to."

Over time, he'd chipped away at her reluctance. She revealed her age, forty-three, and she surrendered time and again to desire. But when he talked of the future, she turned to stone. Her answer was always the same.

"You need a family. Children to raise. You were meant to be a father. I can't give that to you."

"Rot. Women older than you have babies."

"I've had my baby, Colin."

Indeed. Maggie was the equation to be solved if he was to win her mother, and he knew it. But she was elusive, a sprite-child who had watched him solemnly from across the courtyard when he left the cottage on that first afternoon. She was clutching a mangy cat in her arms, and her eyes were solemn. She knows, he thought. He said hello and her name, but she disappeared round the side of the Hall. And ever since then, she'd been polite—a very model of good breeding—but he could see the judgement on her face and he could have predicted the manner in which she would exact retribution from her mother long before Juliet realised where Maggie's infatuation with Nick Ware was heading.

He could have interceded in some way. He knew Nick Ware, after all. He was well-acquainted with the boy's parents. He could have been useful, had Juliet let him.

Instead, she'd allowed the vicar to enter their lives. And it hadn't taken Robin Sage long to forge what Colin himself had been unable to create: a fragile bond with Maggie. He saw them talking together outside the church, strolling into the village with the vicar's heavy hand at rest on the girl's shoulder. He watched them perched on the graveyard wall with their backs to the road, their faces towards Cotes Fell, and the vicar's arm arcing out to illustrate the curve of the land or some point he was making. He noted the visits Maggie had paid to the vicarage. And he used these last to broach the subject with Juliet.

"It's nothing," Juliet said. "She's looking for her father. She knows it can't be you—she thinks you're too young and besides you've never left Lancashire, have you—so she's trying out Mr. Sage for the role. She thinks her father's out searching for her somewhere. Why not as a vicar?"

Which gave him the opening: "Who is her father?"

Her face settled into the familiar, firm lines of withdrawal. He sometimes wondered if her silence was a way she maintained his level of passion for her, keeping herself more intriguing than other women and thus challenging him to prove an entirely nonexistent dominance over her by cooperatively continuing to perform in her bed. But she seemed unaffected by that as well, saying only, "Nothing lasts forever, does it, Colin," whenever his desperation to know the truth forced him to allude to leaving her. Which he never would, which he knew he never could.

"Who is he, Juliet? He isn't dead, is he?"

The most she had ever said, she said in bed one June night with a wash of moonlight against her skin, making a dappled pattern from the summer leaves outside the window. She said, "Maggie wants to think that."

"Is it the truth?"

She closed her eyes briefly. He lifted her hand, kissed its palm, rested it against his chest. "Juliet, is it the truth?"

"I think it is."

"Think . . . ? Are you married to him still?"

"Colin. Please."

"Were you ever married to him?"

Her eyes closed again. He could see the faint glimmer of tears beneath the lashes, and for a mindless moment he couldn't understand the source of either her pain or her sadness. Then he said, "Oh God. Juliet. Juliet, were you raped? Is Maggie . . . Did someone—"

She whispered. "Don't humiliate me."

"You were never married, were you?"

"Please, Colin."

But that fact made no difference. Still she wouldn't marry him. *Too old for you* was the excuse she gave.

Not, however, too old for the vicar.

Standing in his house, his head pressed against the cool front door, the sound of his father's departure long faded, Colin Shepherd felt Inspector Lynley's question bouncing round his skull like a persistent echo of all his doubts. *Was it likely she'd take on a lover after so brief an acquaintance?*

He squeezed his eyes shut.

What difference did it make that Mr. Sage had gone out to Cotes Hall just to talk about Maggie? The village constable had merely gone out there to caution a woman about discharging a shotgun, only to find himself tearing off her clothes in a fever to mate after less than an hour in her company. And she didn't protest. She didn't try to stop him. If anything, she was as aggressive as he. When one considered it, what kind of a woman was that?

A siren, he thought and he tried to turn away from his father's voice. *You got to take the upper hand with a woman, boy-o, and you got to keep it. Right from the first. They'll make you a ninny, give 'em the chance.*

Had she done that with him? With Sage as well? She'd said he was visiting her to talk about Maggie. He meant well, she said, and she ought to listen. She'd declared herself at the end of her rope when it came to reasonable discussion with the girl, so if the vicar had ideas, who was she to turn a deaf ear to them?

And then she'd searched his face. "You don't trust me, Colin, do you?"

No. Not an inch. Not a moment of being alone with another man in that isolated cottage where the solitude itself was a call for seduction. Nonetheless, he'd said, "Of course I do."

"You can come as well, if you'd like. Sit between us at the table. Make certain I don't take off my shoe and rub my foot against his leg."

"I don't want that."

"Then what?"

"I just want things settled between us. I want people to know."

"Things can't be settled in the way you'd like."

And now they never would be, unless and until Scotland Yard cleared her name. Because all her protests of their age difference aside, he knew he couldn't marry Juliet Spence and maintain his position in Winslough while so many doubts filled the atmosphere with whispered speculations whenever they appeared in public together. And he couldn't leave Winslough married to Juliet if he hoped to keep peace with her daughter. He was caught in a trap of his own devising. Only New Scotland Yard CID could spring him.

The doorbell rang above his head, so shrill and unexpected a sound that he started. The dog began barking. Colin waited for him to trot out of the sitting room.

"Quiet," he said. "Sit." Leo complied, head cocked to one side, waiting. Colin opened the door.

The sun was gone. Dusk was drawing quickly towards night. The light on the porch which he'd switched on to welcome New Scotland Yard now shone on the wiry hair of Polly Yarkin.

She was clutching a scarf twined between her fingers and pinching closed the collar of her old navy coat. Her felt skirt dangled overlong to her ankles which were themselves encased in battered boots. She moved uneasily from foot to foot. She offered a quick smile.

"I was finishing up in the vicarage, wasn't I, and I couldn't help but notice . . ." She cast a look back in the direction of the Clitheroe Road. "I saw th' two gentlemen leave. Ben at the pub said Scotland Yard. I wouldn't have known except Ben phoned—him being a church warden, you know—and told me they'd probably want to have themselves a poke through the vicarage. He said for me to wait. But they didn't come. Is everything all right?"

One hand squeezed her collar more tightly, and the other grappled with the loose ends of the scarf. He could see her mother's name upon it, and he recognised it as a souvenir advertising her business in Blackpool. She'd gone through scarves, beer mats, printed match-book covers—like she was running some posh hotel—and she'd even given out free chopsticks for a while when she was "purely truly positive" that tourism from the Orient was about to reach an all-time high. Rita Yarkin—aka Rita Rularski—was nothing if not a born entrepreneur.

"Colin?"

He realised he was staring at the scarf, wondering why Rita had chosen neon lime green and decorated that colour with crimson diamonds. He stirred, glanced down, saw that Leo was wagging his tail in welcome. The dog recognised Polly.

"Is everything all right?" she asked again. "I saw your dad leave as well and I spoke to him—I was sweeping the porch—but he didn't seem to hear because he didn't say anything. So I wondered is everything all right?"

He knew he couldn't leave her standing on the porch in the cold. He'd known her from childhood after all, and even if that had not been the case, she'd come on an errand that at least wore the guise of a friend's concern. "Come in."

He closed the door behind her. She stood in the entry, balling up her scarf, rolling it round and round in her hands before shoving it into her pocket. She said, "I've got these muddy old boots on, don't I?"

"It's all right."

"Sh'll I leave them here?"

"Not if you've just put them on at the vicarage."

He returned to the sitting room with the dog at his heels. The fire was still burning, and he added another log to it, watching fresh wood settle into flame. He felt the heat reaching out in waves towards his face. He remained where he was and let it bake his skin.

Behind him, he heard Polly's hesitant footsteps. Her boots squeaked. Her clothing rustled.

"Haven't been here in a while," she said diffidently.

She would find it considerably changed: Annie's chintz-covered furniture gone, Annie's prints off the wall, Annie's carpet torn out, and everything replaced helter-skelter without taste, merely to meet need. It was functional, which was all he'd required of the house and its furnishings once Annie had died.

He expected her to remark upon it, but she said nothing. He finally turned from the fire. She hadn't removed her coat. She had only come three paces into the room. She smiled at him tremulously.

"Bit cold in here," she said.

"Stand by the fire."

"Ta. Think I will." She held her hands out towards the flames, then unbuttoned her coat but didn't remove it. She was wearing an overlarge lavender pullover that clashed with both the rust of her hair and the magenta of her skirt. A faint odour of mothballs seemed to rise from its wool. "You all right, Colin?"

He knew her well enough to realise she'd go on asking the question until he answered it. She'd never been one to make the connection between refusal to respond and reluctance to reveal. "Fine. Would you like a drink?"

Her face lit. "Oh, yes. Ta."

"Sherry?"

She nodded. He went to the table and poured her some, taking nothing for himself. She knelt by the fire and petted the dog. When she took the glass from him, she stayed where she was, on her knees, resting on the heels of her boots. There was a substantial crust of dried mud upon them. Speckles of it had settled on the floor.

He didn't want to join her, although it would have been the natural thing to do. They'd sat with Annie in a ring before this fireplace many times before she died, but their circumstances had been different then: No sin made a lie of their friendship. So he chose the armchair and sat on the edge of it, resting his arms against his knees, his hands clasped loosely like a barrier in front of him.

"Who phoned them?" she asked.

"Scotland Yard? The crippled man phoned for the other, I imagine. He'd come to see Mr. Sage."

"What do they want?"

"To re-open the case."

"They said?"

"They didn't have to say it."

"But do they know something . . . Has something new come up?"

"They don't need anything new. They just need to have doubts. They share them with Clitheroe CID or Hutton-Preston Constabulary. They start nosing about."

"Are you worried?"

"Should I be?"

She dropped her gaze from him to her glass. She had yet to take a drink of the sherry. He wondered when she would.

"Your dad's a bit hard on you is all," she said. "He's always been that, hasn't he? I thought he might use this to ride you rough. He looked real cheesed off when he left."

"I'm not worried about Pa's reaction, if that's what you mean."

"That's good then, isn't it?" She pivoted the small sherry glass on her palm. Next to her, Leo yawned and settled his head on her thighs. "He's always liked me," she said, "ever since he's a pup. He's a nice dog, is Leo."

Colin made no reply. He watched the flames dance the light against her hair and cast a golden hue on her skin. She was attractive in a quirky sort of way. The fact that she didn't seem to realise this had at one time been part of her charm. Now it served as the key to a memory he'd long tried to forget.

She looked up. He moved his eyes away. She said in a low, uncertain voice, "I cast the circle for you last night, Colin. To Mars. For strength. Rita wanted me to petition for myself, but I didn't. I did it for you. I want the best for you, Colin."

"Polly . . ."

"I remember things. We used to be such friends, didn't we? We'd hike out by the reservoir. We'd see films in Burnley. We went to Blackpool once."

"With Annie."

"But we were friends as well, me and you."

He gazed at his hands so that he wouldn't have to meet her eyes. "We were. But we made a mess of it all."

"We didn't. We only—"

"Annie knew. Directly I walked into the bedroom, she knew. She could read it all over me. And I could see that reading on her face. She said, How was your picnic, did you have a nice time, did you get some fresh air, Col? She knew."

"We didn't mean to hurt her."

"She never asked me to be faithful. Did you know that? She didn't expect it once she knew she was going to die. She reached for my hand one night in bed and she said, Take care of yourself, Col, I know how you're feeling, I wish we could be that way again with each other but we can't, dear lover, so you must take care of yourself, it's all right."

"Then why don't you see—"

"Because that night I swore to myself that whatever it took, I wouldn't betray her. And I did it anyway. With you. Her friend."

"We didn't intend it. It wasn't like it was planned."

He looked at her again, a sharp movement of lifting his head that she apparently didn't expect him to make because she flinched in response. A bit of the sherry she held slopped over the side of her glass and onto her skirt. Leo sniffed at it curiously.

"What does it matter?" he said. "Annie was dying. You and I were fucking in a barn on the moors. We can't change either one of those facts. We can't make them pretty and we can't tart them up."

"But if she told you—"

"No. Not . . . with . . . her . . . friend."

Polly's eyes grew bright, but she didn't shed the tears. "You closed your eyes that day, Colin, you turned your head away, you never touched me and barely spoke to me ever again. How much more do you want me to suffer for what happened? And now you . . ." She gulped for breath.

"Now I?"

She dropped her eyes.

"Now I? What now?"

Her answer sounded like a chant. "I burnt cedar for you, Colin. I put the ashes on her grave. I put the ring stone with them. I gave Annie the ring stone. It's sitting on her grave. You can see it if you want. I gave up the ring stone. I did it for Annie."

"What now?" he asked again.

She bent to the dog, rubbed her cheek against his head.

"Answer me, Polly."

She raised her head. "Now you're punishing me more."

"How?"

"And it isn't fair because I love you, Colin. I loved you first. I've loved you longer than her."

"Her? Who? How am I punishing you?"

"I know you better than anyone ever could. You need me. You'll see. Mr. Sage even told me."

Her final statement brought gooseflesh upon him. "Told you what?"

"That you need me, that you don't know it yet but you will soon enough if I just stay true. And I have been true. All these years. Always. I live for you, Colin."

Her avowal of devotion was less than important when the implication behind *Mr. Sage even told me* demanded exploration and action.

"Sage talked to you about Juliet, didn't he?" Colin asked. "What did he say? What did he tell you?"

"Nothing."

"He gave you some sort of assurance. What was it? That she would end things between us?"

"No."

"You know something."

"I don't."

"Tell me."

"There's nothing—"

He stood. He was three feet from her but still she shrank back. Leo raised his head, his ears perking up, a growl in his throat as he sensed the tension. Polly set her sherry glass on the hearth and kept her eyes and one hand on its base, as if it might take flight should she not keep watch.

"What do you know about Juliet?"

"Nothing. I told you. I said that already."

"About Maggie?"

"Nothing."

"About her father? What did Robin Sage tell you?"

"Nothing!"

"But you were sure enough about me and Juliet, weren't you? He made you sure. What did you do to get the information from him, Polly?"

Her hair sailed round her shoulders as her head flew up. "What's that supposed to mean?"

"Did you sleep with him? You were alone with the man for hours in the vicarage every day. Did you try some kind of spell?"

"I never!"

"Did you see a way to ruin things between us? Did he give you an idea?"

"No! Colin—"

"Did *you* kill him, Polly? Is Juliet taking the blame?"

She jumped to her feet, planted them apart, punched her fists to her hips. "Just listen to yourself. You talk about me. She's got you bewitched. She put you in place, got you eating from her hand, murdered the vicar, and got away with it clean. And you're so blinded by your own stupid lust that you can't even see how she's used you."

"It was an accident."

"It was murder, murder, murder and she did it and everyone knows she did it. No one can think you could be such a fool as to believe a single word that she says. Except we all know why you believe her, don't we, we all know what you're getting, we even know when, so don't you imagine she might have been giving our precious little vicar just a bit of the same?"

The vicar . . . the vicar . . . Colin felt it all at once: bones, blood, and heat. His muscles coiling and his mother's voice shouting *No, Ken, don't!* as his arm soared up right palm to left shoulder and he made the primary lunge to strike. Lungs full, heart raging, wanting contact and pain and retribution and—

Polly cried out, staggered back. Her boot hit the sherry glass. It flew towards the fire and broke on the fender. The sherry dripped and sizzled. The dog began to bark.

And Colin stood there at the ready, aching to strike. With Polly not Polly and himself not himself and the past and the present howling round him like the wind. Arm raised, features twisted into an expression he'd seen a thousand times but never felt on his face, never thought to feel, never dreamed to feel. Because he couldn't actually be the man he'd sworn to himself would never exist.

Leo's barking turned to yelps. They sounded wild and fearful.

"Quiet!" Colin snapped.

Polly cringed. She took another step backwards. Her skirt skimmed the flames. Colin grabbed her arm to draw her from the fire. She jerked away. Leo backed off. His nails scraped on the floor. Aside from the fire and Colin's torn breathing, they made the only sound in the room.

Colin held his hand up at the level of his chest. He stared at the shaking fingers and palm. He'd never struck a woman in his life. He wouldn't have thought he was even capable of doing so. His arm dropped like a weight.

"Polly."

"I cast the circle for you. For Annie as well."

"Polly, I'm sorry. I'm not thinking right. I'm not thinking at all."

She began to button her coat. He could see that her hands were trembling worse than his, and he made a move to help her but stopped when she cried *No!* as if with the expectation of being struck.

"Polly..." His voice sounded desperate, even to himself. But he didn't know what he wanted to say.

"She's got you not thinking," Polly said. "That's what it is. But you don't see that, do you? You don't even want to. 'Cause how can you face it if the very same thing that makes you hate me is what keeps you from seeing the truth about her." She took out her scarf, made a shaky attempt to fold it into a triangle, and flipped it over her head to hold down her hair. She knotted its ends beneath her chin. She moved past him without a glance, squeaking across the room in her ancient boots. She paused at the door and spoke without looking back.

"While you were fucking that day in the barn," she said quite clearly, "I was making love."

■ ■ ■

"On the sitting room sofa?" Josie Wragg asked incredulously. "You mean right here? With your mum and dad in the house? You never!" She got as close as she could to the mirror above the basin and applied the eyeliner with an inexpert hand. A blob of it went into her lashes. She blinked, then squinted when it made contact with her eyeball. "Ooooh. It stings. Oh crikey Moses. Now look what I've done." She'd given herself a make-up black eye. She rubbed it with a tissue and spread the mess across her cheek. "You didn't really," she said. "I don't believe it."

Pam Rice balanced on the edge of the bathtub and blew cigarette smoke towards the ceiling. To do it, she let her head hang back on her neck in a lazy movement that Maggie was sure she'd seen in an old American film. Bette Davis. Joan Crawford. Maybe Lauren Bacall.

"Want to see the stain for yourself?" Pam asked.

Josie frowned. "What stain?"

Pam flicked ash into the bathtub and shook her head. "Lord. You don't know anything, do you, Josephine Bean?"

"I most certainly do."

"Really? Great. You tell me what stain."

Josie worked this one over. Maggie could tell she was trying to think up a reasonable answer even though she pretended to be concentrating on the mess she'd made of her eyes. This was second to the mess she'd already made of her nails last night, having purchased a do-it-yourself acrylic nail kit through the post when her mother had refused to allow her to make a trip to Blackpool in order to have artificial nails put on by a stylist. The result of Josie's attempt to extend her own stubs to what she called drive-men-wild length looked like elephant-man-of-the-fingers.

They were in the upstairs and only bathroom of Pam Rice's terraced house, across the street from Crofters Inn. While directly below them in the kitchen Pam's mummy fed the twins an afternoon tea of scrambled eggs and beans on toast—to the accompaniment of Edward's happy shouting and Alan's laughter—they watched Josie experiment with her most recent cosmetic acquisition: a half-bottle of eyeliner purchased from a fifth former who'd pinched it from his sister's chest of drawers.

"Gin," Josie finally announced. "Everyone knows you drink it. We've seen the flask."

Pam laughed and did her smoke-at-the-ceiling routine again. She flipped her cigarette into the toilet. It made a sound like *psst* as it sank. She held on to the edge of the bathtub and leaned back again, farther this time so that her breasts jutted towards the ceiling. She still wore her school uniform—all three of them did—but she'd removed the jersey, unbuttoned the blouse to expose her cleavage, and rolled up the sleeves. Pam had the ability to make an inanimate white cotton blouse just scream to be stripped from her body.

"God, I'm horny as a she-goat," she said. "If Todd doesn't want to do it tonight, I'm getting it off with some other bloke." She swivelled her head in the direction of the door where Maggie sat on the floor, cross-legged. "How's our Nickie?" she asked, casual and cool.

Maggie rolled her cigarette in her fingers. She'd taken six obligatory puffs—in by the mouth, out through the nose, nothing in the lungs—and was waiting for the rest to burn itself down so that she could let it join Pam's in the toilet. "Fine," she said.

"And big?" Pam asked, swinging her head so that her hair moved like a single curtain of blonde. "Just like a salami, that's what I've heard. Is it true?"

Maggie looked at Josie's reflection in the mirror. She made a wordless plea for rescue.

"Well, is it?" Josie said in Pam's direction.

"What?"

"The stain. Gin. Like I said."

"Semen," Pam said, looking largely bored.

"See-what?"

"Come."

"Where?"

"Christ alive, you're a twit. That's what it is."

"What?"

"The stain! It's from him, okay? It drips out, all right? When you're done, understand?"

Josie studied her reflection, making another heroic attempt with the eyeliner. "Oh *that*," she said and dipped the brush into the bottle. "From the way you were talking, I thought it was s'posed to be something weird."

Pam snagged up her shoulder bag that lay on the floor. She pulled out her cigarettes and lit up again. "Mum was frothing like a dog when she saw it. She even smelled it. Do you believe that? She started in with 'You miserable little tart,' went on to 'You're a real cheap piece for any one of these blokes,' and finished with 'I can't hold my head up in the village any longer. Neither can your dad.' I told her if I had my own bedroom, I wouldn't have to use the sofa and she wouldn't have to see the stains." She smiled and stretched. "Todd goes on and on so long, he must come a bloody quart every time." And with a sly look at Maggie, "What about Nick?"

"All *I* can say's I hope you're taking precautions," Josie put in quickly, ever Maggie's friend. "Because if he does it as many times as you said and if he makes you—well, you know—get *fulfilled* each time, then you're heading for trouble, Pam Rice."

Pam's cigarette stopped midway to her lips. "What're you talking about?"

"You know. Don't act like you don't."

"I don't, Jose. Explain it to me." She took a deep drag, but Maggie could see that she did it mostly to hide her smile.

Josie took the bait. "If you have a—*you* know—"

"Orgasm?"

"Right."

"What about it?"

"It helps the swimmy things get up inside you more easy. Which is why lots of women don't—you know—"

"Have an orgasm?"

"Because they don't want the swimmy things. Oh, and they can't relax. That too. I read it in a book."

Pam hooted. She swung off the bathtub and opened the window through which she shouted, "Josephine Eugene, the brains of a bean," before dissolving into laughter and sliding down the wall to sit on the floor. She took another hit from her cigarette, pausing now and then to give in to the giggles.

Maggie was glad she'd opened the window. It was getting harder and harder to breathe. Part of her knew it was just because of the amount of cigarette smoke in the little room. The other part knew it was because of Nick. She wanted to say something to rescue Josie from Pam's fun-making. But she wasn't sure what would serve to deflect the ridicule at the same time as it revealed nothing about herself.

"When was the last time *you* read anything about it?" Josie asked, recapping her bottle of eyeliner and examining in the mirror the fruits of her labour.

"I don't need to read. I experience," Pam replied.

"Research is as important as experience, Pam."

"Really? And exactly what sort have you done?"

"I know things." Josie was combing her hair. It made no difference. No matter what she did to it, it flopped right back into the same frightful style: fringe high on the forehead, bristles on the neck. She should never have tried to cut it herself.

"You know things from books."

"And observation. Imperial evidence, that's called."

"Provided by?"

"Mum and Mr. Wragg."

This piece of information seemed to strike Pam's fancy. She kicked off her shoes and drew her legs beneath her. She flicked her cigarette into the toilet and made no comment when Maggie took the opportunity of doing the same. "What?" she asked, eyes dancing happily at the potential for gossip. "How?"

"I listen at the door when they're having relations. He keeps saying, 'Come on, Dora, come on, come on, come on, baby, come on, love' and she never makes a sound. Which is also, by the way, how I know for a fact that he isn't my dad." When Pam and Maggie greeted this news blankly, she went on with, "Well, he can't be, can he? Look at the evidence. She's never once been—you know, fulfilled by him. I'm her only kid. I was born six months after they got married. I found this old letter from a bloke called Paddy Lewis—"

"Where?"

"In the drawer where she keeps her knickers. And I could tell she'd done it with him. *And* been fulfilled. Lots. *Before* she married Mr. Wragg."

"How long before?"

"Two years."

"So what were you?" Pam asked. "The longest pregnancy on record?"

"I don't mean they only did it once, Pam Rice. I mean they were doing it regular two years before she married Mr. Wragg. And she kept the letter, didn't she? She must still love him."

"But you look exactly like your dad," Pam said.

"He isn't—"

"All right, all right. You look like Mr. Wragg."

"That's just coincidence," Josie said. "Paddy Lewis must look like Mr. Wragg as well. And that makes sense, doesn't it? She'd be looking for someone to remind her of Paddy."

"So then Maggie's dad must look like Mr. Shepherd," Pam announced. "All her mum's lovers must have looked like him."

Josie said, "Pam," in a pained fashion. Fair was only fair. One could speculate indefinitely about one's own parents, but it wasn't proper to do the same about anyone else's. Not that Pam ever worried much about what was proper before she opened her mouth.

Maggie said softly, "Mummy never had a lover before Mr. Shepherd."

"She had at least one," Pam corrected.

"She didn't."

"She did. Where else did you come from?"

"From my dad. And Mummy."

"Right. Her lover."

"Her husband."

"Really? What was his name?"

Maggie picked at a loose thread on her jersey. She tried to poke it through the knitting to the other side.

"What was his name?"

Maggie shrugged.

"You don't know because he didn't have a name. Or maybe she didn't know it. Because you're a bastard."

"Pam!" Josie took a quick step forward, with the eyeliner bottle closed in her fist.

"What?"

"Watch your mouth."

Pam flipped back her hair with a languid movement of her hand. "Oh, stop the drama, Josie. You can't tell me that *you* believe all this rot about race car drivers and mummies running off and daddies out looking for their darling little girls for the next thirteen years."

Maggie felt the room growing larger about her, felt herself shrinking with a hollowness inside. She looked at Josie but couldn't quite see her because she seemed to be standing in a mist.

"If they were married at all," Pam was continuing conversationally, "she probably gave him his cards along with some parsnip at dinner one night."

"Pam!"

Maggie pushed herself against the door and from there to her feet. She said, "I have to be going, I think. Mummy will be wondering—"

"God knows we wouldn't want that," Pam said.

Their coats were in a pile on the floor. Maggie pulled hers out but could not make her fingers and hands work well enough to get it on. It didn't matter. She was feeling rather hot.

She threw open the door and hurried down the stairs. She heard Pam saying with a laugh, "Nick Ware better watch he doesn't cross Maggie's mum."

And Josie responding, "Oh, shove it, won't you?" before she came clattering down the stairs herself. "Maggie!" she called.

Out on the street it was dark. A cold breeze from the west funnelled down the road from north Yorkshire and turned into a gust at the centre of the village where Crofters Inn and Pam's house stood.

Maggie blinked and wiped the wet from beneath her eyes as she thrust one arm into her coat and started walking.

"Maggie!" Josie caught her up less than ten steps from Pam's front door. "It's not what you think. I mean it is, but it isn't. I didn't know you good then. Pam and I talked. I told her about your dad, it's true, but that's all I ever told her. I swear it."

"It was wrong of you to tell."

Josie dragged her to a halt. "It was. Yes, yes. But I didn't tell her in fun. I wasn't making fun. I told her 'cause it made us alike, you and me."

"We aren't alike. Mr. Wragg's your father, and you know it, Josie."

"Oh, maybe he is. That would be my luck, wouldn't it? Mum running off with Paddy Lewis and me stuck in Winslough with Mr. Wragg. But that's not what I mean. I mean we dream. We're different. We think bigger thoughts. We got our sights set on stuff bigger than this village. I used you as a point of illustration, see? I said, I'm not the only one, Pamela Bammela. Maggie has thoughts about *her* dad too. And she wanted to know what your thoughts were and I told her and I shouldn't have. But I wasn't making fun."

"She knows about Nick."

"Never! Not from me. I never said a word and I never will."

"Then why does she ask?"

"Because she thinks she knows something. She keeps hoping she can make you say."

Maggie scrutinised her friend. There wasn't much light, but in what little shed itself upon Josie's face from a single street lamp that stood at the drive of the Crofters Inn car park across the road, she looked earnest enough. She looked a little odd as well. The eyeliner hadn't dried thoroughly when she opened her eyes after having applied it, so her eyelids were streaked in the way ink runs when water pours over it.

"I didn't tell her about Nick," Josie said again. "That's between me and you. Always. I promise."

Maggie looked down at her shoes. They were scuffed. Above them her navy tights were speckled with mud.

"Maggie. It's true. Really."

"He came over last night. We . . . It happened again. Mummy knows."

"No!" Josie grasped her arm and led her across the street and into the car park. They side-stepped a glossy silver Bentley and headed down the path that led to the river. "You never said."

"I wanted to tell you. I was waiting all day to tell you. But she kept hanging about."

"That Pam," Josie said as they went through the gate. "She's just like a bloodhound when it comes to gossip."

A narrow path angled away from the inn and descended towards the river. Josie led the way. Some thirty yards along, an old ice-house stood, built into the bank where the river plunged sharply through a fall of limestone, sending up a spray that kept the air cool on the hottest days of summer. It was fashioned from the same stone used in the rest of the village, and like the rest of the village its roof was slate. But it had no windows, just a door whose lock Josie had long ago broken, turning the ice-house into her lair.

She shouldered her way inside. "Just a sec," she said, ducking beneath the lintel. She fumbled about, bumped into something, said, "Holy hell on wheels," and struck a match. Light flared a moment later. Maggie entered.

A lantern stood atop an old nail barrel, sending out an arc of hissing yellow light. This fell upon a patchwork of carpet—worn through here and there to its straw-coloured backing—two three-legged milking stools, a cot covered by a purple eiderdown, and an up-ended crate overhung by a mirror. This last made do for a dressing table, and into it Josie placed the bottle of eyeliner, new companion to her contraband mascara, blusher, lipstick, nail polish, and assorted hair-goo.

She hustled up a bottle of toilet water and sprayed it liberally on walls and floor like a libation offered to the goddess of cosmetics. It served to mask the odours of must and mildew that hung in the air.

"Want a smoke?" she asked, once she made sure the door was closed snugly upon them.

Maggie shook her head. She shivered. It was clear why the ice-house had been built in this spot.

Josie lit a Gauloise from a packet she took from among her cosmetics. She flopped onto the cot and said, "What'd your mum say? How'd she find out?"

Maggie pulled one of the two stools closer to the lantern. It gave off a substantial amount of heat. "She just knew. Like before."

"And?"

"I don't care what she thinks. I won't stop. I love him."

"Well, she can't follow you everywhere, can she?" Josie lay on her back, one arm behind her head. She raised her bony knees, crossed one leg over the other, and bounced her foot. "God, you're so lucky." She sighed. The tip of her cigarette glowed fire-red. "Is he . . . well, you know . . . like they say? Does he . . . fulfill you?"

"I don't know. It goes sort of fast."

"Oh. But is he . . . *you* know what I mean. Like Pam wanted to know."

"Yes."

"*God*. No wonder you don't want to stop." She squirmed deeper into the eiderdown and held out her arms to an imaginary lover. "Come 'n' get me, baby," she said past the cigarette that bobbed in her lips. "It's waiting right here and it's all—for—you." And then squirming on her side, "You're taking precautions, aren't you?"

"Not really."

Her eyes became saucers. "Maggie! I never! You got to take precautions. Or he does at least. Does he wear a rubber?"

Maggie cocked her head at the oddity of the question. A rubber? What on earth. . . . "I don't think so. Where would he . . . ? I mean, he may have one in his pocket from school."

Josie bit her lip but didn't quite manage to catch the grin. "Not *that* kind of rubber. Don't you know what it is?"

Maggie stirred uneasily on the stool. "I know. Of course I do. I know."

"Right. Look, it's like this squishy plastic stuff he puts on his Thing. Before he puts it in you. So you don't get pregnant. Is he using that?"

"Oh." Maggie twisted a lock of her hair. "That. No. I don't want him to use it."

"Don't want . . . Are you crazy? He *has* to use one."

"Why?"

"Because if he doesn't, you'll have a baby."

"But you said before that a woman needs to be—"

"Forget what I said. There are always exceptions. I'm here, aren't I? I'm Mr. Wragg's, aren't I? Mum was panting and moaning with this bloke Paddy Lewis, but I came along when she was cold as ice.

That's pretty much proof that anything can happen no matter if you get fulfilled or not."

Maggie thought this over, running her finger round and round the last button on her coat. "Good then," she said.

"*Good?* Maggie, bleeding saints on the altar, you can't—"

"I want a baby," she said. "I want Nick's baby. If he tries to use a rubber, I won't even let him."

Josie goggled at her. "You're not yet fourteen."

"So?"

"So you can't be a mummy when you haven't finished school."

"Why not?"

"What would you do with a baby? Where would you go?"

"Nick and I would get married. Then we'd have the baby. Then we'd be a family."

"You can't want that."

Maggie smiled with real pleasure. "Oh yes I can."

CHAPTER TEN

L YNLEY MURMURED, "GOOD GOD," AT THE sudden drop in temperature when he crossed the threshold between the pub and the dining room of Crofters Inn. In the pub, the large fireplace had managed to disperse enough heat to create pools of at least moderate warmth in its farthest corners, but the weak central heating of the dining room did little more than provide the uncertain promise that the side of one's body closest to the wall heater would not go numb. He joined Deborah and St. James at their corner table, ducking his head each time he passed beneath one of the low ceiling's great oak beams. At the table, an additional electric fire had been thoughtfully provided by the Wraggs, and from it semisubstantial waves of heat lapped against their ankles and floated towards their knees.

Enough tables were laid with white linen, silverware, and inexpensive crystal to accommodate at least thirty diners. But it appeared that the three of them would be sharing the room only with its unusual display of artwork. This consisted of a series of gilt-framed prints which depicted Lancashire's most prominent claim to fame: the Good Friday gathering at Malkin Tower and the charges of witchcraft that both preceded and followed it. The artist had depicted the principals in an admirably subjective fashion. Roger Nowell, the magistrate, looked suitably grim and barrel-chested, with wrath, vengeance, and the power of Christian Justice incised upon his features. Chattox looked appropriately decrepit: wizened, bent, and dressed in rags. Elizabeth Davies, with her rolling eyes uncontrolled by ocular muscles, looked deformed enough to have sold herself for the devil's kiss. The rest of them comprised a leering group of demon-lovers, with the exception of Alice Nutter who stood apart, eyes lowered, ostensibly maintaining the silence she had taken with her to her grave, the only convicted witch among them who had sprung from the upper class.

"Ah," Lynley said in acknowledgement of the prints as he shook out his table napkin, "Lancashire's celebrities. Dinner and the prospect of disputation. Did they or didn't they? Were they or weren't they?"

"More likely the prospect of loss of appetite," St. James said. He poured a glass of fumé blanc for his friend.

"There's truth in that, I suppose. Hanging half-witted girls and helpless old women on the strength of a single man's apopleptic seizure does give one pause, doesn't it? How can we eat, drink, and be merry when dying's as close as the dining room wall?"

"Who are they exactly?" Deborah asked as Lynley took an appreciative sip of the wine and reached for one of the rolls which Josie Wragg had only moments before deposited on the table. "I know they're the witches, but do you recognise them, Tommy?"

"Only because they're in caricature. I doubt I'd know them if the artist had done a less Hogarthian job of it." Lynley gestured with his butter knife. "You have the God-fearing magistrate and those he brought to justice. Demdike and Chattox—they're the shrivelled ones, I should think. Then Alizon and Elizabeth Davies, the mother-daughter team. The others I've forgotten, save Alice Nutter. She's the one who looks so decidedly out of place."

"Frankly, I thought she looked like your aunt Augusta."

Lynley paused in buttering a portion of roll. He gave the print of Alice Nutter a fair examination. "There's something in that. They have the same nose." He grinned. "I'll have to think twice about dining at aunt's next Christmas Eve. God knows what she'll serve in disguise for wassail."

"Is that what they did? Mix some sort of potion? Cast a spell on someone? Make it rain toads?"

"That last sounds vaguely Australian," Lynley said. He looked the other prints over as he munched on his roll and sifted through his memory for the details. One of his papers at Oxford had touched upon the seventeenth-century hue and cry over witchcraft. He remembered the lecturer vividly—twenty-six years old and a strident feminist who was as beautiful a woman as he had ever seen and approximately as approachable as a feeding shark.

"We'd call it the domino effect today," he said. "One of them burgled Malkin Tower, the home of one of the others, and then had the audacity to wear in public something she'd stolen. When she was brought before the magistrate, she defended herself by accusing the Malkin Tower family of witchcraft. The magistrate might have concluded that this was a ridiculous stab at deflecting culpability, but a few days later, Alizon Davies of that same tower cursed a man who within minutes was stricken with an apoplectic seizure. From that point on, the hunt for witches was on."

"Successfully, it seems," Deborah said, gazing at the prints herself.

"Quite. Women began confessing to all sorts of ludicrous misbehaviours once they were brought before the magistrate: having familiars in the form of cats, dogs, and bears; making clay dolls in the persons of their enemies and stabbing thorns into them; killing off cows; making milk go bad; ruining good ale—"

"Now there's crime worthy of punishment," St. James noted.

"Was there proof?" Deborah asked.

"If an old woman mumbling to her cat is proof. If a curse overheard by a villager is proof."

"But then why did they confess? Why would anyone confess?"

"Social pressure. Fear. They were uneducated women brought before a magistrate from another class. They were taught to bow before their betters—if only metaphorically. What more effective way to do it than to agree with what their betters were suggesting?"

"Even though it meant their death?"

"Even though."

"But they could have denied it. They could have kept silent."

"Alice Nutter did. They hanged her anyway."

Deborah frowned. "What an odd thing to celebrate with prints on the walls."

"Tourism," Lynley said. "Don't people pay to see the Queen of Scots' death mask?"

"Not to mention some of the grimmer spots in the Tower of London," St. James said. "The Chapel Royal, Wakefield Tower."

"Why bother with the Crown Jewels when you can see the chopping block?'' Lynley added. "Crime doesn't pay, but death brings them running to part with a few quid.''

"Is this irony from the man who's made at least five pilgrimages to Bosworth Field on the twenty-second of August?" Deborah asked blithely. "An old cow pasture in the back of beyond where you drink from the well and swear to Richard's ghost you would have fought for the Yorks?"

"That's not death," Lynley said with some dignity, lifting his glass to salute her. "That's history, my girl. Someone's got to be willing to set the record straight.''

The door that led to the kitchen swung open, and Josie Wragg presented them with their starters, muttering, "Smoked salmon *here*, pâté *here*, prawn cocktail *here*,'' as she set each item on the table, after which she hid both the tray and her hands behind her back. "Enough rolls?" She asked the question of everyone in general, but she made a poor job of surreptitiously examining Lynley.

"Fine," St. James said.

"Get you more butter?"

"I don't think so. Thanks."

"Wine okay? Mr. Wragg's got a cellarful if that's gone off. Wine does that sometimes, you know. You got to be careful. If you don't store it right, the cork gets all dried up and shrivelled and the air gets in and the wine turns salty. Or something."

"The wine's fine, Josie. We're looking forward to the bordeaux as well."

"Mr. Wragg, he's a connoisseur of wine." She pronounced it con-NOY-ser and bent to scratch her ankle, from which activity she looked up at Lynley. "You're not here on holiday, are you?"

"Not exactly."

She straightened up, reclasping the tray behind her. "That's what I thought. Mum said you were a detective from London and I thought at first you'd come to tell her something about Paddy Lewis which she, of course, wouldn't be likely to share with me for fear I'd spread it to Mr. Wragg which, of course, I would definitely not do even if it meant she was to run off with him—Paddy, that is—and leave me here with Mr. Wragg. *I* know what true love's about, after all. But you're not that kind of detective, are you?"

"What kind is that?"

"You know. Like on the telly. Someone you hire."

"A private detective? No."

"I thought that's what you were at first. Then I heard you talking on the phone just now. I wasn't exactly eavesdropping. Only, your door was open a crack and I was taking fresh towels to the rooms and I happened to hear." Her fingers scratched against the tray as she grasped it more tightly behind her before going on. "She's my best friend's mum, you see. She didn't mean any harm. It's like if someone is making preserves and they put in the wrong stuff and a bunch of people get ill. Say they buy the preserves at a church fête even. Strawberry or blackberry. Well, they might do that, huh? And then they take them home and spread them on their toast the next morning. Or on their scones at tea. Then they get sick. And everyone knows it was an accident. See?"

"Naturally. That could happen."

"And that's what happened here. Only it wasn't a fête. And it wasn't preserves."

None of them replied. St. James was idly twirling his wineglass by the stem, Lynley had stopped tearing apart his roll, and Deborah was looking from the men to the girl, waiting for one of them to respond. When they didn't, Josie went on.

"It's just that Maggie's my best mate, see. And I've never had a best mate before. Her mum—Missus Spence—she keeps to herself lots. People call that queer, and they want to make something of it. But there's nothing to make. You got to remember that, don't you think?"

Lynley nodded. "That's wise. I'd agree with that."

"Well then . . . " She bobbed her ill-clipped head and looked for a moment as if she intended to dip into a curtsy. Instead, she backed away from the table in the direction of the kitchen door. "You'll want to start eating, won't you? The pâté's mum's own recipe, you know. The smoked salmon's real fresh. And if you want anything . . . " Her voice faded when the door closed behind her.

"That's Josie," St. James said, "in case you haven't been introduced. A strong advocate of the accident theory."

"So I noticed."

"What did Sergeant Hawkins have to say? I take it that's the conversation Josie overheard you having."

"It was." Lynley speared a piece of salmon and was pleasantly surprised to find it—as Josie had declared—quite fresh. "He wanted to restate that he was following Hutton-Preston's orders from the first. Hutton-Preston Constabulary got involved through Shepherd's father, and as far as Hawkins was concerned, everything from that moment was on the up and up. Still is, in fact. So he's backing his man in Shepherd, and he's none too pleased that we're poking about.''

"That's reasonable enough. He's responsible for Shepherd, after all. What falls on the village constable's head isn't going to look good on Hawkins' record either.''

"He also wanted me to know that Mr. Sage's bishop had been entirely satisfied with the investigation, the inquest, and the verdict.''

St. James looked up from his prawn cocktail. "He attended the inquest?''

"He sent someone, evidently. And Hawkins seems to feel that if the investigation and inquest had the blessing of the Church, they damn well ought to have the Yard's blessing as well.''

"He won't cooperate, then?''

Lynley speared more salmon onto his fork. "It isn't a question of cooperation, St. James. He knows the investigation was a bit irregular and the best way to defend it, himself, and his man is to allow us to prove their conclusions correct. But he doesn't have to like any of it. None of them do.''

"They're going to start liking it a great deal less when we take a closer look at Juliet Spence's condition that night.''

"What condition?'' Deborah asked.

Lynley explained what the constable had told them about the woman's own illness on the night the vicar died. He explained the ostensible relationship between the constable and Juliet Spence. He concluded with, "And I have to admit, St. James, that you might have got me here on a fool's errand after all. It looks bad that Colin Shepherd handled the case by himself with only his father's intermittent assistance and a cursory glance at the scene by Clitheroe CID. But if she was ill too, then the accident theory bears far more weight than we originally thought.''

"Unless,'' Deborah said, "the constable's lying to protect her and she wasn't ill at all.''

"There's that, of course. We can't discount it. Although it does suggest collusion between them. But if alone she had no motive to murder the man—a point, of course, which we know is moot—what on earth would theirs together have been?''

"There's more to it than uncovering motives if we're looking for culpability," St. James said. He pushed his plate to one side. "There's something peculiar about her illness that night. It doesn't hold together."

"What do you mean?"

"Shepherd told us that she was repeatedly sick. She was burning with fever as well."

"And?"

"And those aren't symptoms of hemlock poisoning."

Lynley toyed a moment with the last piece of salmon, squeezed some lemon on top of it, but then decided against eating. After their conversation with Constable Shepherd, he'd been on the path to dismissing most of St. James' earlier concerns regarding the vicar's death. Indeed, he'd been well on his way to chalking the entire adventure up to one hell of a long drive away from London to cool himself off from his morning's altercation with Helen. But now...
"Tell me," he said.

St. James listed the symptoms for him: excessive salivation, tremors, convulsions, abdominal pain, dilation of the pupils, delirium, respiratory failure, complete paralysis. "It acts on the central nervous system," he concluded. "A single mouthful can kill a man."

"So Shepherd's lying?"

"Not necessarily. She's a herbalist. Josie told us that last night."

"And you told me this morning. It was largely the reason why you had me tearing up the motorway like Nemesis on wheels. But I don't see what—"

"Herbs are just like drugs, Tommy, and they act like drugs. They're circulatory stimulants, cardioactives, relaxants, expectorants... Their functions run the virtual gamut of what a chemist supplies under a doctor's prescription."

"You're proposing she took something to make herself ill?"

"Something to induce fever. Something to induce vomiting."

"But isn't it possible that she ate some of the hemlock thinking it was wild parsnip, began to feel ill once the vicar left, and mixed herself a purgative to relieve her discomfort, without connecting her discomfort to what she thought was wild parsnip? That would account for the constant vomiting. And couldn't the constant vomiting have raised her temperature?"

"It's possible, yes. Marginally so. But if that's the case—and frankly, I wouldn't lay money on it, Tommy, considering how quickly water hemlock works on the system—wouldn't she have told the constable that she'd drunk a purgative after eating something that didn't agree with her? And wouldn't the constable have passed that message on to us today?"

Lynley raised his head once again to the prints on the wall. There was Alice Nutter as before, maintaining her obdurate silence, her complexion becoming more perfect gallows with every moment she refused to speak. A woman of secrets, she carried all of them to her grave. If it was an outlawed Roman Catholicism which held her tongue, if it was pride, if it was the angry knowledge that she had been framed by a magistrate with whom she had quarrelled, no one knew. But in an isolated village, there was always an aura of mystery about a woman with secrets who was unwilling to share them. There was always a pernicious little need to smoke the creature out in an unrelated fashion and make her pay for what she kept to herself.

"One way or another, something's not right here," St. James was saying. "I tend to think Juliet Spence dug up the water hemlock, knew exactly what it was, and cooked it up for the vicar. For whatever reason."

"And if she had no reason?" Lynley asked.

"Then someone else surely did."

. . .

After Polly had gone, Colin Shepherd drank the first of the whiskies. Got to get the hands to stop shaking, he thought. He gulped the initial shot down. It raced fire through his gullet. But when he set the glass upon the side table, it chattered like a woodpecker knocking bark for its food. Another, he decided. The decanter shivered against the glass.

The next he drank to make himself think of it. The Great Stone of Fourstones, then Back End Barn. The Great Stone was a hulking oblong of granite, an unexplained country oddity sitting on the rough grassland of Loftshaw Moss a number of miles to the north of Winslough. There they had gone for their picnic on that fine spring day when the harsh moor's wind blew only as a breeze and the sky was brilliant with its fleece of clouds and its blue forever. Back End Barn was the object of their walk when the meal was eaten and the wine was drunk. Hiking had been Polly's suggestion. But he'd chosen the direction, and he knew what was there. He, who had walked on these moors since his childhood. He, who recognised every spring and rivulet, knew the name of every hill, and could find the location of each pile of stones. He'd led them directly towards Back End Barn, and he'd been the one to suggest they have a look inside.

The third whisky he drank to bring all of it back. The feel of a splinter piercing his shoulder as he pushed open the weather-pitted door. The strong scent of sheep and the feathery tufts of wool clinging to the mortar between the stones that made up the walls. The two shafts of light that fell from gaps in the old slate roof, making a perfect *V* at whose point Polly had gone to stand with a laugh, saying, "Looks like a spotlight, doesn't it, Colin?"

When he shut the door, the rest of the barn seemed to recede with the dimming of the light. With the barn, receded the world so that all that was left were those two, simple, yellow-gold shafts provided by the sun, and at their juncture Polly.

She looked from him to the door he'd closed. Then she ran her hands down the sides of her skirt and said, "Like a secret place, isn't it? With the door shut and all. D'you and Annie come here? I mean, did you come here? Before. You know."

He shook his head. She must have taken his quiet for a reminder of the anguish that waited for him back in Winslough. She said impulsively, "I've brought the stones. Let me cast them for you."

Before he could reply, she dropped to her knees and from her skirt pocket she brought forth a little black velvet bag embroidered with red and silver stars. She unloosed its drawstrings and poured the eight rune stones into her hand.

"I don't believe in that," he said.

"That's because you don't understand it." She settled onto her heels and patted the floor at her side. It was stone, uneven, rutted, and pock-marked from the hooves of ten thousand sheep. It was utterly filthy. He knelt to join her. "What d'you want to know?"

He made no reply. Her hair was all ablaze in the light. Her cheeks were flushed.

"Come on with you, Colin," she said. "There must be something."

"There's nothing."

"There must be."

"Well, there isn't."

"Then I shall cast them for myself." She shook the stones like dice in her hand and closed her eyes, head cocked to one side. "Now. What shall I ask?" The stones clicked and rattled. Finally she said in a rush, "If I stay in Winslough, shall I meet my true love?" And then to Colin with an impish smile, " 'Cause if he's there, he's being a bit skittish about introducing himself." With a snap of her wrist, she threw the stones away from her. They clattered and skipped across the floor. Three stones showed their decorated sides. Polly leaned forward to see them and clasped her hands at her bosom in delight. "You see," she said, "the omens are good. Here's the ring stone farthest. That's for love and marriage. And the Lucky stone next. See how it looks like an ear of corn? That means wealth. And the three birds in flight nearest to me. That means sudden change."

"So you'll have a sudden marriage to someone with money? That sounds like you're heading for Townley-Young."

She laughed. "Wouldn't he be in a fright to know that, our Mr. St. John?" She scooped up the stones. "Your turn now."

It didn't mean anything. He didn't believe. But he asked it anyway, the only question he wanted to ask. It was the one he asked each morning when he rose, each night when he finally made his way to bed. "Will Annie's new chemotherapy help her?"

Polly's brow furrowed. "Are you sure?"

"Throw the stones."

"No. If it's your question, you throw them."

He did so, casting them away as she had done, but looking to see that only one stone showed its decorated side, painted with a black *H*. Like the ring stone that Polly had thrown, this one lay farthest from him.

She gazed upon them. He saw her left hand begin to gather the material of her skirt. She reached forward as if to sweep the stones into a single pile. "You can't read only one stone, I'm afraid. You'll have to try again."

He clasped her wrist to stop her. "That isn't the truth, is it? What's it mean?"

"Nothing. You can't read one stone."

"Don't lie."

"I'm not."

"It says *no*, doesn't it? Only we didn't have to ask the question to know the answer." He released her hand.

She picked up the stones one by one and replaced them in the bag until only the black one remained on the floor.

"What's it mean?" he asked once again.

"Grief." Her voice was hushed. "Parting. Bereavement."

"Yes. Well. Right." He raised his head to gaze at the roof, trying to relieve the odd pressure behind his eyes, concentrating on how many slates it would take to obliterate the sunlight that streamed to the floor. One? Twenty? Could it even be done? If one stepped on the roof to repair the damage, wouldn't the entire structure collapse?

"I'm sorry," Polly said. "It was stupid of me. I'm stupid like that. I don't think when I ought."

"It's not your fault. She's dying. We both know it."

"But I wanted today to be special for you. Just a few hours away from everything. So you wouldn't have to think about it for a while. And then I brought out the stones. I didn't think you'd ask . . . But what else *would* you ask. I'm so stupid. Stupid."

"Stop it."

"I made it worse."

"It can't be any worse."

"It can. I made it."

"You didn't."

"Oh, Col . . ."

He lowered his head. He was surprised to see his own pain reflected in her face. His eyes were hers, his tears were hers, the lines and shadows that betrayed his grief were etched on her skin and shaded onto her temples and along her jaw.

He thought, No I can't, even as he reached out to cup her face. He thought, No I won't, even as he began to kiss her. He thought, Annie Annie, as he pulled her to the floor, felt her hovering over him, felt his mouth seek the breasts that she freed for him—freed for him—even as his hands slid up her skirt, slipped off her panties, pulled down his own trousers, urged her down to him, down to him, needing her, wanting her, the heat, so soft, and that first night together what a wonder she was, not timid at all like he'd thought she'd be but open to him, loving him, gasping at first at the strangeness of it before she moved with his body and rose to meet him and caressed the length of his naked back and cradled his buttocks and forced him deeper inside her with each thrust deeper and all the time all the time her eyes on his liquid with happiness and love as all his energy gathered its force from the pleasure of her body from the heat from the wet from the silky prison that held him that wanted him even as he wanted and wanted and wanted, crying "Annie! Annie!" as he reached his orgasm inside the body of Annie's friend.

Colin drank a fourth whisky to try to forget. He wanted to blame her when he knew the responsibility was his. Slut, he'd thought, she didn't have the decency to be loyal to Annie. She was ready and willing, she didn't try to stop him, she even pulled off her blouse and took off her bra, and when she knew that he wanted inside, she let him without a murmur of protest or afterwards even a word of regret.

Except he'd seen her expression when he opened his eyes only moments after crying out Annie's name. He'd recognised the magnitude of the blow he had dealt her. And selfishly he'd considered it her just deserts for that afternoon's seduction of a married man. She brought the stones deliberately, he'd thought. She planned it all. No matter how they fell when he cast them to the floor, she would have interpreted them in such a way that fucking her would be the logical outcome. She was a witch, was Polly. Every moment, every day, she knew what she was doing. She had it all planned.

Colin knew that *I'm sorry* did nothing to mitigate his sins committed against Polly Yarkin on that spring afternoon in Back End Barn and every day since then. She had reached out to him with the hand of friendship—no matter how complicated it might have been by the fact of her love—and time and again, he had turned away, caught up in the need to punish her, because he lacked the courage to admit the worst that he was to himself.

And now she'd given up the ring stone, laying it and all her simple hopes for the future on Annie's grave. He knew she'd done it as yet another act of contrition, attempting to pay for a sin in which she'd played only a minor role. It wasn't right.

"Leo," Colin said. By the fire, the dog perked up his head, expectant. "Come."

He grabbed a torch and his heavy jacket from the entry. He went out into the night. Leo walked at his side, unleashed, his nose quivering with the scents of the icy winter air: woodsmoke, damp earth, the lingering exhaust fumes of a car that passed, a faint smell of frying fish. For him, a walk at night lacked the excitement of a walk in the day when there were birds to chase and the occasional ewe to startle with his bark. But still, it was a walk.

They crossed the road and entered the graveyard. They wound their way towards the chestnut tree, Colin directing them with the torch's cone of light, Leo snuffling along just ahead of him, to the right, out of its beam. The dog knew where they were going. They'd been there often enough before. So he reached Annie's grave before his master and he was sniffing round the marker—and sneezing—when Colin said, "Leo. No."

He shone the light on the grave. And then all round it. He squatted to get a better look.

What had she said? *I burnt cedar for you, Colin. I put the ashes on her grave. I put the ring stone with them. I gave Annie the ring stone.* But it wasn't here. And the only thing that could possibly be interpreted as ashes from cedar was a faint coating of grey flecks on the frost. While he admitted that these could have come from the ashes if they'd been blown by the wind and disturbed by the dog's snuffling through them, the rune stone itself couldn't have been blown away. And if that was the case . . .

He walked round the grave slowly, wanting to believe Polly, willing to give her every chance. He thought the dog might have knocked it to one side, so he searched with the light and turned over every stone that appeared the right size, looking upon each for the interlocking pink rings. He finally gave up.

He chuckled with derision at his own gullibility. How guilt makes us want to believe in redemption. Obviously, she had offered the first thought that had come into her head, putting herself forward, trying as always to make him take the blame. And—as everyone appeared to be doing—at the same time she was giving it her all to wrest him away from Juliet. It wasn't going to work.

He lowered the torch to shine in a white, bright circle on the ground. He gazed first to the north in the direction of the village where lights climbed the hillside in a pattern so familiar that he could have named each family behind every point of illumination. He gazed then to the south where the oak wood grew and where, beyond it, Cotes Fell rose like a black-cloaked figure against the night sky. And at the base of the fell, across the meadow, tucked into a clearing that had long ago been made among the trees, Cotes Hall stood, and with it the cottage and Juliet Spence.

What a damn fool's errand he had come on to the churchyard. He stepped over Annie's grave, reached the wall in two strides. With a third he was over it, calling for the dog and swiftly moving in the direction of the public footpath that led from the village to the top of Cotes Fell. He could have gone back for the Rover. It would have been faster. But he told himself that he wanted the walk, needing to feel completely grounded in the choice he was making. And what better way to do that than to have the solid earth beneath his feet, to have his muscles working and his blood at the flow?

He brushed aside the thought that fluttered against his mind like a wet-winged moth as he strode along the path: In his position, going the back way to the cottage implied not only a clandestine visit to Juliet but also collusion between them as well. Why was he using the back way to the cottage when he had nothing whatsoever to hide? When he had a car? When it was faster in a car? When the night was cold?

As it had been in December when Robin Sage made the identical walk, with the identical destination in mind. Robin Sage, who had a car, who could have driven, who chose to walk, despite the snow that already lay upon the ground and in ignorance of or indifference to the fact that more had been promised before morning. Why had Robin Sage walked that night?

He liked exercise, fresh air, a ramble on the moors, Colin told himself. In the two months Sage had lived in the village prior to his death, he'd seen the vicar often enough in his crusty Wellingtons with a walking stick stabbing into the ground. He called upon all the villagers by foot. He went to the common by foot when he fed the ducks. What reason was there to conclude he would have done anything but walk when it came to the cottage?

The distance, the weather, the time of year, the growing cold, the night. The answers presented themselves to Colin, as rose the one fact he kept trying to discount. He'd never seen Sage do his walking at night. If the vicar made a call outside the village after dark, he took his car. He'd done as much the single time he'd gone out to Skelshaw Farm to meet Nick Ware's family. He'd done the same when he'd made the rounds of the other farms.

He'd even driven to dine at the Townley-Young estate shortly after his arrival in Winslough, before St. John Andrew Townley-Young had fully comprehended the extent of the vicar's low church leanings and cut him off his list of acceptable acquaintances. So why had Sage walked to see Juliet?

The same moth fluttered its wet-winged answer. Sage hadn't wanted to be seen, just as Colin himself didn't want to be seen paying a call at the cottage on the very night of the day that New Scotland Yard had come to the village. *Admit it, admit it . . .*

No, Colin thought. That was the venomous, green-eyed monster making its attack on trust and belief. Surrendering to it in any way meant a sure death to love and a certain extinction of his hopes for the future.

He determined to think no more about it, and made good that promise by turning off the torch. Although he had walked the footpath for nearly thirty years, he had to concentrate on something beyond Robin Sage in order to anticipate a sudden dip in the land and to find his way over the occasional stile. The stars assisted. They were brilliant in the sky, a dome of crystals that flickered like beacons on a distant landmass, across an ocean of night.

Leo led the way. Colin couldn't see him, but he could hear the dog's feet breaking through the skin of frost on the ground, and the sound of him scrambling over a wall with a happy yelp made Colin smile. A moment later the dog began to bark in earnest. And then a man's voice called, "No! Hey, there! Steady on!"

Colin switched on the torch and picked up the pace. Against the next wall, Leo was bounding back and forth, leaping up towards a man who sat atop the stile. Colin shone the light on his face. The man squinted and shrank back in response. It was Brendan Power. The solicitor had a torch with him, but he wasn't using it. Instead, it lay next to him, its light extinguished.

Colin ordered the dog down. Leo obeyed, although he lifted one front leg and pawed rapidly at the wall's rough stones as if greeting the other man. "Sorry," Colin said. "He must have given you a start."

He saw that the dog had interrupted Power in the midst of a sit and a smoke, which explained why he hadn't been using his torch. His pipe still glowed weakly, and what was left of the burning tobacco gave off the odour of cherries.

Bum-boy's tobacco, Colin's father would have called it with a scoff. If you're going to smoke, boy-o, at least have the sense to choose something that makes you smell like a man.

"Quite all right," Power said, extending his hand to let the dog sniff his fingers. "I was out for a walk. I like to get out in the evening if I can. Get in a bit of exercise after sitting behind a desk all day. Keep myself in shape. That sort of thing." He sucked on the pipe and seemed to be waiting for Colin to make some sort of similar reply.

"Out to the Hall?"

"The Hall?" Power reached in his jacket and brought forth a pouch which he opened and sank the pipe into, packing it with fresh tobacco without having cleared the bowl of the old. Colin watched him curiously. "Yes. The Hall. Right. Checking things. The work and all. Becky's getting anxious. Things haven't gone well. But you know that already."

"There's been no more trouble since the weekend?"

"No. Nothing. But one can't be too careful. She likes me to check. And I don't mind the walk. Fresh air. Breeze. Good for the lungs." He took a deep breath as if to prove his point. Then he tried to light the pipe with only a moment's success. The tobacco caught, but the clogged bowl prevented the stem from drawing. He gave up the effort after two tries and replaced pipe, pouch, and matches in his jacket. He hopped off the wall. "Becky'll be wondering where I've got off to. I suppose. Good evening, Constable." He began to walk off.

"Mr. Power."

The man turned abruptly. He kept himself clear of the light which Colin was directing his way. "Yes?"

Colin picked up the torch which still lay on the wall. "You've forgotten this."

Power bared his teeth in what passed for a smile. He gave a short laugh. "Fresh air must have gone right to my head. Thanks."

When he reached for the torch, Colin held on a moment longer than was absolutely necessary. Testing the waters because they needed to be tested, because New Scotland Yard would be doing its own testing soon enough, he said, "Do you know this is the spot where Mr. Sage died? Just on the other side of the stile?"

Power's Adam's apple seemed to travel the length of his neck. He said, "I say . . . "

"He did his best to make it over but he was having convulsions. Did you know? He hit his head on the lower step."

Power's glance shifted quickly from Colin to the wall. "I didn't know. Only that he was found . . . that you found him somewhere on the footpath."

"You saw him the morning before he died, didn't you? You and Miss Townley-Young."

"Yes. But you know that already. So—"

"That was you with Polly in the lane last night, wasn't it? Outside the lodge?"

Power didn't answer at once. He looked at Colin with some curiosity and when he replied, the answer came slowly, as if with some thought as to why the question had been asked in the first place. He was, after all, a solicitor. "I was on my way out to the Hall. Polly was on her way home. We walked together. Is there a problem with that?"

"And the pub?"

"The pub?"

"Crofters. You've been there with her. Drinking in the evenings."

"Once or twice, while I was out for a walk. When I stopped by the pub on my way home, Polly was there. I joined her." He played the torch from one hand to the other. "What of it, anyway?"

"You met Polly before your marriage. You met her at the vicarage. Did she treat you well?"

"What's that supposed to mean?"

"Did she seek you out? Ask you any favours?"

"No. Of course not. What are you getting at?"

"You've access to keys to the Hall, haven't you? To the caretaker's cottage as well? She never asked to borrow them? She never made any offer in return for the loan of them?"

"That's some *bloody* cheek. What in hell are you trying to suggest? That Polly . . . ?" As his words died, Power looked towards Cotes Fell. "What's all this about? I thought it was over."

"No," Colin said. "Scotland Yard's come to call."

Power's head turned. His gaze was even. "And you're looking to misdirect them."

"I'm looking for the truth."

"I thought you did that already. I thought we heard it at the inquest." Power removed his pipe from his jacket. He tapped the bowl against the heel of his shoe, dislodged the tobacco, and all the time kept his eyes on Colin. "You're in hot water, aren't you,

Constable Shepherd? Well, let me make a suggestion. Don't look to pour any of it on Polly Yarkin." He strode off without another word, pausing some twenty yards away to repack and relight his pipe. The match flared, and from the glow that followed, it was clear that the tobacco had caught.

CHAPTER ELEVEN

COLIN KEPT THE TORCH LIT FOR THE REST OF the walk to the cottage. Using darkness as a means of distraction was futile at this point. Brendan Power's final words had made further avoidance impossible.

He was hedging his bets and he knew it, setting up a secondary set of possibilities, and arranging an unexamined point of departure. He was looking for a viable direction in which he could lead the London police.

Just in case, he told himself. Because the *what if*'s were increasing their restless murmur inside his skull, and he had to do something to quell them. He had to take an action that was well within his purview, called for under the circumstances, and guaranteed to set his mind at rest.

He hadn't considered what that direction would be until he saw Brendan Power and realised—with a rush of intuition so powerful that he could feel its certainty in the hollow of his gut—what could have happened, what *must* have happened, and how Juliet was blaming herself for a death she had only indirectly caused.

Right from the start, he'd believed that the death was accidental because he couldn't consider any other explanation and continue to look at himself in the mirror every morning. But now he saw how wrong he might have been and what an injustice he had done to Juliet in those dark and isolated moments when he—like everyone else in the village—wondered how she of all people could possibly have made such a fatal mistake. Now he saw how she might have been manipulated into believing that she had made a mistake in the first place. Now he saw how it all had been done.

That thought and the rising desire to avenge the wrong committed against her drove him forward at new speed along the footpath, with Leo happily loping ahead. They veered off into the oak wood a short distance beyond the lodge in which Polly Yarkin and her mother lived. How easy it was to slip from the lodge to Cotes Hall, Colin realised. One didn't even need to walk along the gouged disaster of a lane to get there.

The path led him beneath the trees, across two footbridges whose wood was mossy and slowly rotting with each winter's damp, and over a spongy drugget of leaves that lay in sodden decomposition under a delicate coating of frost. It ended where the trees made way for the rear garden of the cottage, and when Colin reached this point, he watched Leo bound through the piles of compost and the fallow earth to scratch at the base of the cottage door. He himself directed the torchlight here and there, assessing the details: the greenhouse to his immediate left, detached from the cottage, no lock on its door; the shed beyond it, four wooden walls and a tarpaper roof where she kept the tools which she used for her gardening and for the forays she made into the woods for her plants and roots; the cottage itself with the green cellar door—its thick paint flaking away in large chips—that led to the dark, loam-scented cavity beneath the cottage where she stored her roots. He fixed the torchlight on this and kept it fixed steadily as he crossed the garden. He gazed down at the padlock that held the door closed. Leo joined him, bumping his head against Colin's thigh. The dog walked across the sloping surface of the door. His nails scraped the wood, and a hinge creaked in answer.

Colin flashed the light to this. It was old and rusty, quite loose against the wooden jamb that was itself bolted to the angled stone plinth that served as its base. He played the hinge in his fingers, back and forth, up and down. He dropped his hand to the lower hinge. It held firmly to the wood. He shone the light against it, examined it closely, wondering if the marks he saw could be construed as scratches against the screws or merely an indication of some sort of abrasive used against the metal to remove the stains left by a slipshod worker when he painted the wood.

He should have seen all this before, he realised. He shouldn't have been so desperate to hear "death by accidental poisoning" that he overlooked the signs which might have told him that Robin Sage's death had been something else. Had he argued with Juliet's own frantic conclusions, had his mind been clear, had he trusted her loyalty, he could have spared her the stain of suspicion, the subsequent gossip, and her own distorted belief that she had killed a man.

He turned off the torch and walked to the back door. He knocked. No one answered. He knocked a second time, and then tried the knob. The door swung open.

He said, "Stay," to Leo who obediently sank onto his haunches. He entered the cottage.

The kitchen smelled of dinner—the fragrance of roasted chicken and newly baked bread, of garlic sautéed in olive oil. The odour of the food reminded him that he hadn't eaten since the previous night. He'd lost appetite along with self-assurance the moment Sergeant Hawkins phoned him this morning and told him to expect a visit from New Scotland Yard.

"Juliet?" He flipped on the kitchen light. A pot was on the cooker, a salad on the work top, two places laid on the old Formica table with its burn mark shaped like a crescent moon. Two glasses held liquid— one milk, one water—but no one had eaten, and when he touched his fingers to the glass filled with milk, he could feel from its temperature that it had stood there, undrunk, for quite some time. He called her name again and went through the passage to the sitting room.

She was by the window in the dark, just a shadow herself, standing with her arms crossed beneath her breasts, looking out at the night. He said her name. She replied without turning from the glass.

"She hasn't come home. I've phoned around. She was with Pam Rice earlier. Then with Josie. And now—" She let out her breath in a brief, bitter laugh. "I can guess where she's gone. And what she's up to. He was here last night, Colin. Nick Ware. Again."

"Shall I go out and have a look for her?"

"What would be the point? She's made up her mind. We can drag her back now and lock her in her room, but that would only be postponing the inevitable."

"What?"

"She means to get herself pregnant." Juliet pressed the tips of her fingers against her forehead, rubbed them up to her hairline, grasped the front of her hair and pulled hard as if to give herself pain.

"She doesn't know anything about anything. God in heaven, neither do I. Why did I ever think I'd be good for a child?"

He crossed the room, stood behind her, and reached round her to loose her fingers from her hair. "You are good for her. This is just a stage she's in."

"One I've set in motion."

"How?"

"With you."

He felt an odd settling within him, one churn of the stomach and nothing more, presage of a future he wouldn't consider. "Juliet," he said. But he had no idea of what would reassure her.

Along with her blue jeans, she was wearing an old work shirt. It smelled faintly like a herb. Rosemary, he thought. He didn't want to think of anything else. He pressed his cheek against her shoulder and felt the material, soft, against his skin.

"If her mummy can take a lover, why can't she?" Juliet said. "I let you into my life and now I'm to pay."

"She'll grow past this. Give it time."

"While she's having regular sex with a fifteen-year-old boy?" She pulled away from him. He felt the cold sweep in to take the place of the pressure of her body against his. "There isn't time. And even if there were, what she's doing—what she's after—is complicated by the fact that she wants her father, and if I can't produce him in double quick time, she'll make a father out of Nick."

"Let me be her father."

"That isn't the point. She wants *him*, the real thing. Not a stars-in-his-eyes substitute ten years too young who's blithering with some sort of idiotic love, who thinks marriage and babies are the answer to everything, who—" She stopped herself. "Oh, God. I'm sorry."

He tried to sound unaffected. "It's a fair enough description. We both know that."

"It wasn't. It was cruel. She hasn't been home. I've been phoning everywhere. I feel caught on the edge and . . . " She balled her hands together and pressed them to her chin. In the meagre light that came from the kitchen, she looked like a child herself. "Colin, you can't understand what she's like—or what I'm like. The fact that you love me won't change that."

"And you?"

"What?"

"Don't love me in return?"

She squeezed her eyes shut. "*Love* you? What a joke on the both of us. Of course, I love you. And look where it's brought me to with Maggie."

"Maggie can't run your life."

"Maggie *is* my life. Why can't you see that? This isn't about us—about you and me, Colin. This isn't about our future because we don't have a future. But Maggie does. I won't let her destroy it."

He heard only part of her words and said in careful repetition to make certain he'd understood, "We don't have a future."

"You've known that from the first. You just haven't wanted to admit it to yourself."

"Why?"

"Because love makes us blind to the real world. It makes us feel so complete—so much part of someone else—that we can't see its equal power to destroy."

"I didn't mean why haven't I wanted to admit it. I meant why don't we have a future," he said.

"Because even if I weren't too old, even if I wanted to give you babies, even if Maggie could live with the idea of our getting married—"

"You don't know she can't."

"Let me finish. Please. This once. And listen." She waited for a moment, perhaps to bring herself under control. She held her hands out towards him, cupped together, as if she would give him the information. "I killed a man, Colin. I can't stay here in Winslough any longer. And I won't let you leave this place you love."

"The police have come," he said in answer. "From London."

At once, she dropped her hands to her sides. Her face altered, as if she were drawing a mask into place. He could feel the distance it created between them. She was invulnerable and unreachable, her armour secure. When she spoke, her voice was utterly calm.

"From London. What do they want?"

"To find out who killed Robin Sage."

"But who . . . ? How . . . ?"

"It doesn't matter who phoned them. Or why. It only matters that they're here. They want the truth."

She lifted her chin fractionally. "Then I'll tell it. This time."

"Don't make yourself look guilty. There isn't any need."

"I said what you wanted me to say before. I won't do that again."

"You're not hearing me, Juliet. There isn't any need for self-sacrifice in this. You're no more guilty than I am."

"I . . . killed . . . this . . . man."

"You fed him wild parsnip."

"What I thought was wild parsnip. Which I myself dug up."

"You can't know that for sure."

"Of course I know it for sure. I dug it up that very day."

"All of it?"

"All . . . ? What are you asking?"

"Juliet, did you take some parsnip from the root cellar that evening? Was it part of what you cooked?"

She took a step backwards, as if to distance herself from what his words implied. The action cast her into deeper shadow. "Yes."

"Don't you see what that means?"

"It means nothing. There were only two roots left when I checked the cellar that morning. That's why I went out for more. I . . ."

He could hear her swallow as she began to understand. He went to her. "So you see, don't you?"

"Colin . . ."

"You've taken the blame without cause."

"No. I haven't. I didn't. You can't believe that. You mustn't."

He smoothed his thumb along her cheekbone, ran his fingers round the curve of her jaw. God, she was like an infusion of life. "You don't see it, do you? That's the goodness of you. You don't even want to see it."

"What?"

"It wasn't Robin Sage at all. It was never Robin Sage. Juliet, how can you be responsible for the vicar's death when you were the one who was meant to die?"

Her eyes grew wide. She began to speak. He stopped her words—and the fear which he knew lay behind them—with his kiss.

          ▪   ▪   ▪

They were scarcely out of the dining room, making their way through the pub to the residents' lounge, when the older man accosted them. He gave Deborah a cursory glance that took in everything from her hair—always somewhere in the evolutionary cycle between haphazardly disarrayed and absolutely dishevelled—to the splotchy stains of ageing on her grey suede shoes. Then he moved his attention to St. James and Lynley, both of whom he scrutinised with the sort of care one generally gives to assessing a stranger's potential for committing a felony.

"Scotland Yard?" he asked. His tone was peremptory. It managed to suggest that only a hand-wringing, obsequious response to the question would do. At the same time it implied, "I know your sort," "Walk two steps to the rear," and "Pull at your forelock." It was a lord-of-the-manor voice, the sort that Lynley himself had spent years trying to shed, and thus it was guaranteed to raise his hackles the moment he heard it. Which it did.

St. James said quietly, "I'm having a brandy. You, Deborah? Tommy?"

"Yes. Thank you." Lynley allowed his gaze to follow St. James and Deborah to the bar.

The pub appeared to be serving its regulars, none of whom seemed to be paying much attention to the older man who stood before Lynley waiting for a response. Yet everyone seemed at the same time to be aware of him. Their effort to ignore his presence was too studied, their eyes darting towards him then just as quickly flitting away.

Lynley looked him over. He was tall and spare, with thinning grey hair and a fair complexion made ruddy round the cheeks through an exposure to the out-of-doors. But this was a hunting-and-fishing exposure, for there was nothing about the man to suggest that the time he spent exposed to the elements was anything other than leisure's employment. He wore good tweeds; his hands looked manicured; his air was sure. And from the expression of distaste he cast in the direction of Ben Wragg who was slapping the bar and laughing heartily at a joke he himself had just told St. James, it was clear that coming to Crofters Inn constituted something of a descent from on high.

"Look here," the man said. "I asked a question. I want an answer. Now. Is that clear? Which of you is from the Yard?"

Lynley took the brandy that St. James brought him. "I am," he said. "Detective Inspector Thomas Lynley. And something tells me that you're Townley-Young."

He loathed himself even as he did it. The man would have had no way of determining a thing about him or about his background from a simple examination of his clothes because he hadn't bothered much about dressing for dinner. He wore a burgundy pullover over his pinstriped shirt, a pair of grey wool trousers, and shoes that still had a thin crease of mud along the seam. So until Lynley spoke—until he made the decision to employ the Voice whose every inflection shouted public school educated, blue blood born, and bred to possess a series of cumbersome, useless titles—Townley-Young would have had no way of knowing that he was addressing his questions to a belted earl. He still didn't, exactly. No one was whispering *Eighth Earl of Asherton* into his ear. No one was listing the accoutrements of fortune, class, and birth: the town house in London, the estate in Cornwall, a seat in the House of Lords if he wished to take it, which he decidedly did not.

Into Townley-Young's startled silence, Lynley introduced the St. Jameses. Then he sipped his brandy and observed Townley-Young over the rim of his glass.

The man was undergoing a major adjustment in attitude. The nostrils were unpinching, and the spine was loosening. It was clear that he wanted to ask half a dozen questions absolutely verboten in the situation and that he was attempting to look as if he'd known from the first that Lynley was less *them* and more *us* than Townley-Young himself would ever be.

"May I speak to you privately?" he said and then added hastily with a glance at the St. Jameses, "I mean out of the pub. I should hope your friends would join us." He managed the request with considerable dignity. He may have been surprised to discover that more than one class of individual could rest at ease beneath the title of Detective Inspector, but he wasn't about to go all Uriah Heepish in an effort to mitigate the scorn with which he'd first spoken.

Lynley nodded towards the door to the residents' lounge at the far side of the pub. Townley-Young led the way. The lounge was, if anything, colder than the dining room had been and without the extra electric fires placed strategically to cut the chill.

Deborah switched on a lamp, straightened its shade, and did the same to another. St. James removed an unfolded newspaper from one of the armchairs, tossed it to the sideboard on which Crofters Inn kept its supply of other reading material—mostly ancient copies of *Country Life* that looked as if they'd crumble if opened precipitately—

and sat in one of the armchairs. Deborah chose a nearby ottoman for her own seat.

Lynley noted that Townley-Young glanced once at St. James' disability, a swift look of curiosity that moved quickly on its way to find a place for himself in the room. He chose the sofa above which hung a dismal reproduction of *The Potato Eaters.*

"I've come to you for help," Townley-Young said. "I'd got the word at dinner that you'd appeared in the village—that sort of news passes like a blaze in Winslough—and I decided to come round and see you myself. You're not here on holiday, I take it?"

"Not exactly."

"This Sage business, then?"

Comrades in class did not constitute an invitation to professional disclosure as far as Lynley was concerned. He answered with a question of his own. "Do you have something to tell me about Mr. Sage's death?"

Townley-Young pinched the knot of his kelly-green tie. "Not directly."

"Then?"

"He was a good enough chap in his way, I suppose. We just didn't see eye-to-eye on matters of ritual."

"Low church versus high?"

"Indeed."

"Surely not a motive for his murder, however."

"A motive . . . ?" Townley-Young's hand dropped from his tie. His tone remained icily polite. "I've not come here to confess, Inspector, if that's what you mean. I didn't much like Sage, and I didn't much like the austerity of his services. No flowers, no candles, just the bare bones. Not what I was used to. But he wasn't a bad sort for a vicar, and his heart was in the right place as far as church-going was concerned."

Lynley took up his brandy and let the balloon glass warm in the palm of his hand. "You weren't part of the church council who interviewed him?"

"I was. I dissented." Townley-Young's ruddy cheeks grew momentarily ruddier. That the apparent Lord of the Manor had held no sway with the council on which he was undoubtedly the most important member went leagues to reveal his position in the hearts of the villagers.

"I dare say you don't especially mourn his passing, then."

"He wasn't a friend, if that's what you're getting at. Even if friendship had been possible between us, he'd only been in the village for two months when he died. I realise that two months count for two decades in some arenas of our society these days, but frankly, I'm not of the generation that takes to calling its fellows by their Christian names on a moment's notice, Inspector."

Lynley smiled. Since his father had been dead for some fourteen years and since his mother was nothing if not decidedly given to breaking her way past traditional barriers, he sometimes had occasion to forget the older generation's reliance upon the choice of name as an indicator of intimacy. It always caught him off-guard and amused him mildly to come up against it in his work. What's in a name indeed, he thought.

"You mentioned that you had something to tell me that was indirectly involved with Mr. Sage's death," Lynley reminded Townley-Young, who looked as if he was about to embellish upon his nominal theme.

"In that he was a visitor on the grounds of Cotes Hall several times prior to his death."

"I'm not sure I follow you."

"I've come about the Hall."

"The Hall?" Lynley glanced at St. James. The other man lifted one hand fractionally in a don't-ask-me gesture.

"I'd like you to look into what's been happening out there. Malicious mischief being made. Pranks being pulled. I've been trying to renovate it for the past four months, and some group of little hooligans keep getting in the way. A quart of paint spilled here. A roll of wallpaper ruined there. Water left running. Graffiti on the doors."

"Are you assuming that Mr. Sage was involved? That hardly seems likely for a clergyman."

"I'm assuming someone with a bone to pick with me is involved. I'm assuming you—a policeman—will get to the bottom of it and see that it's stopped."

"Ah." As he felt himself bristle beneath the final, imperious statement—their relative positions in an ostensibly classless society brushed aside in the man's exigent need to have his personal problems resolved post-haste—Lynley wondered how many people in the immediate vicinity felt they had serious bones to pick with Townley-Young. "You've a local constable to see to things of this sort."

Townley-Young snorted. "He's been dealing"—the word heavy with the weight of Townley-Young's sarcasm—"with this from the first. He's done his investigating after every incident. And after every incident, he's turned up nothing."

"Have you given no thought to hiring a guard until the work is finished?"

"I pay my bloody taxes, Inspector. What else are they to be used for if I can't call upon the assistance of the police when I have a need?"

"What about your caretaker?"

"The Spence woman? She frightened off a group of young thugs once—and quite competently, if you want my opinion, despite the ruckus it caused round here—but whoever's at the bottom of this current rash of mischief has managed to do it with a great deal more finesse. No sign of forced entry, no trace left behind save for the damage."

"Someone with a key, I dare say. Who has them?"

"Myself. Mrs. Spence. The constable. My daughter and her husband."

"Any of you wishing that the house go unfinished? Who's supposed to live there?"

"Becky . . . My daughter and her husband. Their baby in June."

"Does Mrs. Spence know them?" St. James asked. He'd been listening, his chin in his palm.

"Know Becky and Brendan? Why?"

"Might she prefer it if they didn't move in? Might the constable prefer it? Might they be using the house themselves? We've been given to understand they're involved with each other."

Lynley found that this line of questioning did indeed lead in an interesting direction, if not exactly the one intended by St. James. "Has someone dossed there in the past?" he asked.

"The place was locked and boarded."

"A board is fairly easy to loosen if one needs entry."

St. James added, obviously continuing with his own line of thought, "And if a couple were using the place for an assignation, they might not take lightly to having it denied them."

"I don't much care who's using it and for what. I just want it stopped. And if Scotland Yard can't do it—"

"What sort of ruckus?" Lynley asked.

Townley-Young gaped at him blankly. "What the devil . . . ?"

"You mentioned that Mrs. Spence caused a ruckus when she frightened someone off the property. What sort of ruckus?"

"Discharging a shotgun. Got the little beasts' parents in a snit over that." He gave another snort. "Let their lads run about like hooligans, they do, this lot of parents in the village. And when someone tries to show them a touch of discipline, you'd think Armageddon had begun."

"A shotgun's rather heavy discipline," St. James remarked.

"Aimed at children," Deborah added.

"These aren't exactly children and even if they were—"

"Is it with your permission—or perhaps your advice—that Mrs. Spence uses a shotgun to carry out her duties as caretaker of Cotes Hall?" Lynley asked.

Townley-Young's eyes narrowed. "I don't particularly appreciate your efforts to turn this round on me. I came here for your assistance, Inspector, and if you're unwilling to give it, then I'll be on my way." He made a movement as if to rise.

Lynley raised a hand briefly to stop him, saying, "How long has the Spence woman worked for you?"

"More than two years now. Nearly three."

"And her background?"

"What of it?"

"What do you know about her? Why did you hire her?"

"Because she wanted peace and quiet and I wanted someone out there who wanted peace and quiet. The location's isolated. I didn't want to employ as caretaker anyone who felt compelled to mingle with the rest of the village on a nightly basis. That would hardly have served my interests, would it?"

"Where did she come from?"

"Cumbria."

"Where?"

"Outside of Wigton."

"Where?"

Townley-Young sat forward with a snap. "Look here, Lynley, let's get one thing straight. I came here to employ you, not the opposite. I won't be spoken to as if I'm a suspect, no matter who you are or where you're from. Is that clear?"

Lynley placed his balloon glass on the birch side table next to his chair. He regarded Townley-Young evenly. The man's lips had flattened to broom-straw width and his chin jutted out pugnaciously. If Sergeant Havers had been in the residents' lounge with them, she would have yawned widely at this point, flipped her thumb towards Townley-Young, said, "Get this bloke, will you?" and followed that up with a less-than-friendly and more-than-bored "Answer the question before we have you in the nick for failure to cooperate in a police investigation." It was always Havers' way to stretch the truth to serve her purposes when hot on the scent of a piece of information. Lynley wondered whether that approach would have worked with someone like Townley-Young. If nothing else, it would have afforded him a moment of pleasure just to see Townley-Young's reaction to being spoken to in such a way and with such an accent as Havers'. She didn't have the Voice by any stretch of the imagination, and she generally made the most of that fact when confronted with someone who did.

Deborah moved restlessly on the ottoman. Out of the corner of his eye, Lynley saw St. James' hand move to her shoulder.

"I realise why you've come to see me," Lynley said at last.

"Good. Then—"

"And it's one of those unfortunate quirks of fate, that you've walked into the middle of an investigation. You can, of course, telephone your solicitor if you'd prefer to have him here while you answer the question. Where, exactly, did Mrs. Spence come from?" It bent the truth only partially. Lynley gave a mental salute to his sergeant. He could live with that.

The question was whether Townley-Young could do also. They engaged in a silent skirmish of wills, their eyes locked in combat. Townley-Young finally blinked.

"Aspatria," he said.

"In Cumbria?"

"Yes."

"How did she come to work for you?"

"I advertised. She applied. She came to interview. I liked her. She's got common sense, she's independent, she's fully capable of taking whatever action is necessary to protect my property."

"And Mr. Sage?"

"What about him?"

"Where was he from?"

"Cornwall." And before Lynley could press the point with a further question, "Via Bradford. That's all I recall."

"Thank you." Lynley got to his feet.

Townley-Young did likewise. "As to the Hall . . . "

"I'll be speaking to Mrs. Spence," Lynley said. "But my suggestion is to follow the keys and to think about who might not want your daughter and her husband to move into the Hall."

Townley-Young hesitated at the door to the residents' lounge, his hand on the knob. He seemed to be studying it because he kept his head bent for a moment and his forehead was creased as if with thought. He said, "The wedding."

"Sorry?"

"Sage died the night before my daughter's wedding. He was to perform the ceremony. We none of us knew where to find him, and we had the devil of a time finding someone else." He looked up. "Someone who doesn't want Becky at the Hall could be someone who didn't want her to marry in the first place."

"Why?"

"Jealousy. Revenge. Thwarted desire."

"For?"

Townley-Young gazed back at the door, an act of seeing through it to the pub beyond. "For what Becky already has," he said.

■   ■   ■

Brendan found Polly Yarkin in the pub. He went to the bar for his gin and bitters, bobbed his head in good evening to three farmers and two maintenance men from Fork Reservoir, and joined her at her table near the fireplace where she was toeing the bark from a piece of birch at her feet. He didn't wait for an invitation to sit with her. Tonight, at least, he had an excuse.

She looked up as he decisively placed his glass on the table and lowered himself onto the three-legged stool. Her eyes moved from him to the far door that gave way to the residents' lounge. She kept them fixed on it as she said, "Bren, you mustn't sit here. You best go on home."

She didn't look well. Although she was sitting right next to the fire, she hadn't removed either her coat or her scarf, and as he un-buttoned his jacket and slid his stool closer to hers, she seemed to draw her body inward protectively. She said, "Bren," in a low, in-sistent voice, "mind what I say."

Brendan cast a casual glance round the pub. His conversation with Colin Shepherd—and especially the parting remark he'd shot at the constable as he sauntered off—had given Brendan a surge of confi-dence he hadn't experienced in months. He felt invulnerable to stares or gossip or even direct confrontation itself. "What have we got here, Polly? Day labourers, farmers, a few housewives, the local teen gang. I don't care what they think. They'll think what they want no matter what, won't they?"

"It's not just them, all right? Di'n't you see his car?"

"Whose?"

"His. Mr. Townley-Young's. He's in there." She gave a nod in the direction of the residents' lounge, her eyes still averted. "With them."

"With whom?"

"The London police. So be off with you before he comes out and—"

"And what? What?"

She replied with a shrug. He could see what she thought of him in the movement of her shoulders and the settling of her mouth. It was the very same thing that Rebecca thought. It was what they all thought: every man jack of them in the whole bloody village. They saw him under Townley-Young's thumb, under everyone's thumb. Like a cart horse in bridle and blinkers for life.

He took an irritated gulp of his drink. The liquor washed back in his throat too quickly, misdirected itself, and made him cough. He fished in his pocket for a handkerchief. His pipe, tobacco, and matches spilled onto the floor.

"God *damn*." He snatched them back. He coughed and hacked. He could see Polly looking round the pub, smoothing her scarf, trying to achieve some distance by ignoring his plight. He found his hand-kerchief and pressed it to his mouth. He took a second, slower sip of the gin. It roared across his tongue and down his throat, leaving fire in its wake. But it warmed him this time, both to his topic and to the situation.

"I'm not afraid of my father-in-law," he said tersely. "Despite what everyone thinks, I'm fully capable of standing my ground with him. I'm fully capable of a hell of a lot more than this lot round here gives me credit for." He considered adding an if-they-only-knew innuendo to give his assertion an air of credibility. But Polly Yarkin was nobody's fool. She'd question and probe and he'd end up revealing what he most wanted to keep to himself. So instead he said, "I have a right to be here. I have a right to sit wherever I please. I have a right to speak to whomever I like."

"You're acting the fool."

"Besides, this is business." He threw back more gin. It went down smoothly. He considered a trip to the bar for a second glass. He'd toss that down and perhaps have a third and bugger anyone who tried to stop him.

Polly was toying with a stack of beer mats, concentrating on them as if by that action she could continue to avoid an open acknowledgement of his presence. He wanted her to look at him. He wanted her to reach over and touch his arm. He was important in her life now and she didn't even know it. But she would soon enough. He would make her see.

"I was out at Cotes Hall," he said.

She didn't reply.

"I came back on the footpath."

She stirred on the stool as if to leave. One hand went to the back of her neck. Her fingers dug into its nape.

"I saw Constable Shepherd."

Her movement ceased. Her eyelids seemed to tremble, as if she wanted to look at him but couldn't allow herself even that much contact. "So?" she said.

"So you'd better watch where you're stepping, all right?"

Contact at last. She met his gaze. But it wasn't curiosity he read in her face. It wasn't a need to possess information or obtain clarity. A slow, ugly flush was climbing her neck and spreading streaks of crimson up from her jaw.

He was disconcerted. She was supposed to ask what he meant by his statement, which was supposed to lead to a request for his advice, which he would be only too happy to give, which would lead to her gratitude. Gratitude would prompt her to establish a place for him in her life. Obtaining that would lead her to love. And if it wasn't love exactly that she ended up feeling, desire would do.

Except that his statement wasn't engendering anything close to that primary domino of curiosity that would topple the defences she'd kept raised against him from the instant he'd met her. She looked enraged.

"I've done *nothing* to her or to anyone," she hissed. "I don't know nothing about her, all right?"

He drew back. She leaned forward. "About her?" he said blankly.

"Nothing," she repeated. "And if a chat with Constable Shepherd on the footpath makes you think Mr. Sage told me something I could use to—"

"Kill him," Brendan said.

"What?"

"He thinks you're responsible. For the vicar's death. He's looking for evidence Shepherd is."

She sat back on her stool. Her mouth opened and closed, opened again. She said, "Evidence."

"Yes. So watch where you're stepping. And if he questions you, Polly, you phone me at once. You've got the number of my office, don't you? Don't talk to him alone. Don't be with him alone. Do you understand?"

"Evidence." She said it as if to convince herself, as if to try out the word for size. The menace behind it didn't seem to reach her.

"Polly, answer me. Do you understand? The constable's looking for evidence to establish the fact that you're responsible for the vicar's death. He was heading out towards Cotes Hall when I saw him."

She stared at him without appearing to see him. "But Col was only angry," she said. "He didn't mean it. I pushed him too far—I do that sometimes—and he said something he didn't really mean. I knew that. He knew it as well."

She was speaking Greek as far as Brendan was concerned. She was drifting in space. He needed to bring her back to earth, and more importantly, back to him. He took her hand. Eyes still unfocussed, she didn't withdraw it. He twined his fingers with hers.

"Polly, you've got to listen."

"No, it's nothing. He didn't mean a thing."

"He asked me about keys," Brendan said. "Whether I'd given a set of keys to you, whether you'd asked for them."

She frowned, said nothing.

"I didn't answer him, Polly. I told him that line of enquiry wasn't on. I told him to bugger off as well. So if he comes to see you—"

"He can't think that." She spoke so low that Brendan had to lean forward to hear her. "He knows me, does Colin. He *knows* me, Brendan."

Her hand tightened round his, pulled his towards her breast. He was startled, delighted, and more than ready to be of whatever assistance he could.

"How can he think I would ever, ever... No matter what... Brendan!" She flung his hand to one side. She backed her stool into the corner. She said, "Now it's worse," and just as Brendan was about to question her, seeking to understand how anything could possibly be worse if she'd finally started to accept him, a heavy hand descended on his shoulder.

Brendan looked up into the face of his father-in-law. "Flaming bloody hell," St. John Andrew Townley-Young said concisely. "Get outside before I thrash you to pieces, you miserable worm."

.   .   .

Lynley shut the door of his room and stood with his back to it, his eyes on the telephone next to the bed. On the wall above it, the Wraggs continued to display their love affair with the Impressionists and Post-Impressionists: Monet's tender *Madame Monet and Child* made an odd companion piece to Toulouse-Lautrec's *At the Moulin Rouge*, both of them mounted and framed with more enthusiasm than care, the latter hanging at an angle that suggested all of Montmartre had been hit by an earthquake just as the artist was rendering immortal its most famous nightclub. Lynley straightened the Toulouse-Lautrec. He pinched a cobweb that seemed to be dangling from Madame Monet's hair. But neither a contemplation of the prints nor a few minutes' consideration of their quixotic pairing was sufficient to prevent his reaching for the telephone and punching in her number.

He dug in his pocket for his watch. It was just after nine. She wouldn't be in bed. He couldn't even use the hour as a plausible reason for avoidance. He had no excuse for not placing the call.

Except cowardice, which he had in spades whenever it came to dealing with Helen. Did I really want love, he wondered wryly, and if so when did I want it? And wouldn't an affair—a dozen affairs— be less difficult and more convenient than this? He sighed. What a monstrosity love was; it was nothing so simple as the beast with two backs.

The sex part had been effortless between them from the first. He'd driven her home from Cambridge on a Friday in November. They'd not stirred from her flat until Sunday morning. They didn't even have a meal until Saturday night. He could close his eyes—even now as he thought of it—and still look up into her face, see the way her hair framed it in a colour not so different from the brandy he'd just drunk, feel her moving against him, sense the warmth beneath his palms as he ran them from her breasts to her waist to her thighs, and hear the way her breathing caught then changed altogether as it rose with her climax and she cried out his name. He'd touched his fingers beneath her breast and felt her heart pounding. She laughed, a little embarrassed at the ease of it all between them.

She was what he wanted. Together, they were what he wanted. But life never took a permanent definition from the hours they spent with each other in bed.

Because one could love a woman, make love to her, and have her make love completely in return and, with considerable care and a refusal to reveal, still never be touched at the core of one's being. For that was a final breaking of barriers from which one never walked away the same. And both of them knew it, because both of them had crossed all conceivable boundaries with other people before.

How do we learn to trust, he wondered. How do we ever develop the courage to make the heart vulnerable a second or third time, exposing it to yet another chance of breaking? Helen didn't want to do that, and he couldn't blame her. He wasn't always certain that he could risk it himself.

He thought with chagrin about his behaviour that day. He'd been eager enough to take the first opportunity to dash out of London this morning. He knew his motivations well enough to admit that, in part, he'd snatched at the promise of distance from Helen as well as the chance to punish her. Her doubts and fears exasperated him, perhaps because they so accurately mirrored his own.

Wearily, he sank onto the edge of the bed and listened to the steady *plink...plink* of water dripping from the tap in the bath. In the way of all night noises, it dominated as it could never do at any other time, and he knew that if he didn't do something to stop it, he would toss, turn, and fight with the pillow once he put out the light and attempted to sleep. He decided it probably wanted a washer, if bath taps had washers the way basin taps did. Ben Wragg could no doubt provide him with one. All he needed to do was pick up the phone and ask. What would it take to repair the thing, anyway? Five minutes? Four? And he could think while he did it, taking the time to engage his hands with an odd job so that his mind was free to make a decision regarding Helen. He couldn't, after all, telephone her without knowing what his objective was in doing so. Five minutes would prevent him from rushing in thoughtlessly and just as thoughtlessly taking the risk of exposing himself—not to mention Helen who was far more sensitive than he—to . . . He paused in the mental colloquy with himself. To what? *What?* Love? Commitment? Honesty? Trust? God alone knew how either one of them might survive the challenges of that.

He laughed sourly at his own capacity for self-deception and reached for the telephone just as it rang.

"Denton told me where to find you," was the first thing she said.

The first thing he said was, "Helen. Hullo, darling. I was just about to phone you," realising that she probably wouldn't believe him and that he couldn't blame her if that was the case.

But she said, "I'm glad of it."

And then they grappled with the silence. In it, he could imagine where she was—in her bedroom in the Onslow Square flat, on the bed, with her legs curled beneath her and the ivory-and-yellow counterpane acting as contrast to her hair and her eyes. He could see how she was holding the phone—two-handed and cradled as if she would protect it, herself, or the conversation she was having. He could guess at her jewellery—earrings that she'd already removed and placed on the walnut table by the bed, a thin gold bracelet still encircling her wrist, a matching chain round her neck that her fingers touched talisman-like when they moved the scant inches from the phone to her throat. And there at the hollow of her throat was the scent she wore, something between flowers and citrus.

They both spoke at once, saying,

"I shouldn't have—"

"I've been feeling—"

—and then breaking off with the quick laughter of nerves that serves as the underpinning of a conversation between lovers who are both afraid of losing what they've so recently found. Which is why in an instant Lynley mentally abjured every plan he'd just been pondering before she had phoned.

He said, "I love you, darling. I'm sorry about all this."

"Were you running away?"

"This time, I was. Yes. After a fashion."

"I can't be angry over that, can I? I've done it often enough myself."

Another silence. She would be wearing a silk blouse, wool trousers, or a skirt. Her jacket would be lying where she'd laid it, at the foot of the bed. Her shoes would be sitting nearby on the floor. The light would be on, casting its inverted triangular glow against the blossoms and stripes of the wallpaper at the same time as it diffused through the lampshade to touch her skin.

"But you've never run away to hurt me," he said.

"Is that why you've gone off? To hurt me?"

"Again, after a fashion. It's nothing I'm proud of." He reached for the cord of the telephone and twined it between his fingers, restless for something of substance to touch since he'd placed himself more than two hundred and fifty miles to the north, and he couldn't touch her. He said, "Helen, about that blasted tie this morning..."

"That wasn't the issue. You knew it at the time. I didn't want to admit it. It was just an excuse."

"For?"

"Fear."

"Of what?"

"Moving forward, I suppose. Loving you more than I do at the moment. Making you too much of my life."

"Helen—"

"I could easily lose myself in the love of you. The problem is I don't know if I want to."

"How can something like that be bad? How can it be wrong?"

"It's neither. But grief comes with love, eventually. It has to. It's only the timing that no one can be sure of. And that's what I've been trying to come to terms with: whether I want the grief and in what proportion. Sometimes..." She hesitated. He could see her fingers move to rest on her collar bone—her gesture of protection—before she went on. "It's closer to pain than anything I've ever experienced. Isn't that mad? I'm afraid of that. I suppose I'm actually afraid of you."

"You have to trust me, Helen, at some point in all this, if we're ever to go on."

"I know that."

"I won't cause you grief."

"Not deliberately. You won't. I know that as well."

"Then?"

"If I lose you, Tommy."

"You won't. How could you? Why?"

"In a thousand different ways."

"Because of my job."

"Because of who you are."

He felt the sensation of being swept away from everything, but most of all from her. "So it is the tie after all," he said.

"Other women?" she said. "Yes. Marginally. But it's more a worry over the day-to-day, the business of living, the way people grind at each other and wear the best parts down over time. I don't want that. I don't want to wake up some morning and discover I stopped loving you five years in the past. I don't want to look up from dinner one night and find you watching me and read on your face the very same thing."

"That's the risk, Helen. It all comes down to a leap of faith. Although God knows what's in store for us if we can't even manage to get to Corfu together for a week's holiday."

"I'm sorry about that. About me as well. I was feeling boxed in this morning."

"Well, you're free of that now."

"And I don't want to be. Free of that. Free of you. I don't want that, Tommy." She sighed. It caught on the edge of what he wanted to believe was a stifled sob. Except that Helen had only sobbed once in her life that he knew of—as a girl of twenty-one with her world smashed to bits by a car which he himself had driven—and he seriously doubted that she would begin sobbing again for his benefit now. "I wish you were here."

"My wish as well."

"Will you come back? Tomorrow?"

"I can't. Denton didn't tell you? There's a case, of sorts."

"Then you won't want me there to bother with, either."

"You wouldn't be a bother. But it wouldn't work."

"Will anything ever? Work, that is."

That was the question. Indeed it was. He looked down at the floor, at the mud on his shoes, at the floral carpet, at the patterns it made. "I don't know," he said. "And that's the full hell of it. I can ask you to risk it all with a jump into the void. I simply can't guarantee what you'll find there."

"But then no one can."

"No one who's truthful. That's the bottom line. We can't predict the future. We can only use the present to guide us hopefully in its direction."

"Do you believe that, Tommy?"

"With all my heart."

"I love you."

"I know. That's why I believe."

CHAPTER TWELVE

MAGGIE WAS LUCKY. HE CAME OUT OF THE PUB alone. She'd been hoping he would ever since she saw his bicycle propped against the white gates that led into the Crofters Inn car park. It was hard to miss it, an odd girl's bike with big balloon tyres, once the treasure of his older sister but since her marriage appropriated by Nick without a care in the world as to the queer sight he made on it, pedalling through the village towards Skelshaw Farm with his old leather bomber's jacket flapping round his waist and the radio–tape player hanging from one of the handlebars. Usually something by Depeche Mode was rock-and-rolling from the speakers. Nick was particularly fond of them.

He was fiddling with the radio as he left the pub, all his concentration apparently given to finding a station that he could tune in with minimum static and maximum volume. Simple Minds, UB40, an ancient piece by Fairground Attraction all bleeped by like people interrupted in the midst of a conversation before he found something that he settled with. It consisted mostly of high, screeching notes on an electric guitar. She heard Nick say, "Clapton. All *right*," as he slipped the radio's grip piece over the bicycle's handlebars. He stooped to tie his left shoelace, and as he did so, Maggie melted out of the doorway shadows of The Pentagram Tearoom across the street from the inn.

She'd stayed in Josie's lair by the river long after the other girl had left to set the tables in the restaurant and to act the part of waitress there. She'd intended to go home eventually, when dinner was long past ruined and her continuing absence couldn't be rationally assigned to anything other than murder, abduction, or in-your-face rebellion. Two hours past dinner would do nicely for that. Mummy deserved it.

Despite what had happened between them last night, she'd put another cup of that horrid tea on the table in front of Maggie this morning, saying, "Drink this, Margaret. Now. Before you leave." She sounded hard—not like Mummy at all—but at least there was no more of her saying it was good for her bones no matter the taste, filled to the brim with the vitamins and minerals that a woman's developing body had to have. That lie was gone. But Mummy's determination was not.

Neither was Maggie's, however. "I won't. You can't make me. You did it before. But you *can't* make me drink it again." Her words were high and shrill. Even to her own ears, she sounded like a mouse being swung by its tail. And when Mummy had held the cup to her lips, with her other hand locked on the back of Maggie's neck, saying, "You *will* drink this, Margaret. You'll sit here till you do," Maggie had flung up her arms, dashing the cup and its liquid, hot and steaming, against Mummy's chest.

Her wool jersey soaked it up like a desert in June and moulded itself into a scalding second skin. Mummy cried out and rushed to the sink. Maggie watched in horror.

She said, "Mummy, I didn't—"

"Get out of here. Get out," Mummy gasped. And when Maggie didn't move, she dashed back to the table and yanked her chair away from it. "You heard me. Get out."

It wasn't Mummy's voice. It wasn't anybody's voice that she'd ever known. It wasn't Mummy at the sink with the ice-cold water flooding out of the tap, taking handfuls, throwing them against the wool jersey, with her teeth clamped over her lower lip. She was making noises like she couldn't breathe. At last when she was through and the jersey was soaked with new water over old, she bent over and began to pull it off. Her body shuddered.

"Mummy," Maggie had said in that same mouse voice.

"Get out. I don't even know who you are," the reply.

She'd stumbled into the grey morning, had sat by herself in a corner of the bus all the way to school. She had slowly come to terms with the extent of her loss over the course of the day. She recovered.

She developed a brittle little shell to protect herself from the whole situation. If Mummy wanted her out, she would get out. She would. And it wouldn't be hard to do at all.

Nick loved her. Hadn't he said it over and over again? Didn't he say it every day, when he had the chance? She didn't need Mummy. How dim it was to think she ever had. And Mummy didn't need her. When she was gone, Mummy could have her nice private life with Mr. Shepherd, which is probably what she wanted in the first place. In fact, maybe *that's* why she kept trying to make Maggie drink that tea. Maybe . . .

Maggie shivered. No. Mummy was good. She was. She was.

It was half past seven when Maggie left the river lair. It would be after eight by the time she made the walk home to the cottage. She'd go inside, majestic and silent. She'd go up to her room and close the door. She'd never once speak to Mummy again. What was the point?

Then the sight of Nick's bicycle had changed her purpose, taking her across the street to the tearoom with its recessed doorway out of the wind. She would wait for him there.

She hadn't thought the wait would be so long. Somehow, she'd believed that Nick would sense she was lingering outside and would leave his mates to find her. She couldn't go in to him in case Mummy phoned the pub on a search for her, but she didn't mind waiting. He'd be out soon enough.

Nearly two hours later, he'd emerged. And when she sneaked up beside him and slipped her arm round his waist, he jumped with the shock of it and gave a cat's yowl. He whirled around. The movement and the wind caught his hair and flung it into his eyes. He flipped it back, saw her.

"Mag!" He grinned. The guitar on the radio climbed a few high, wild notes.

"I was waiting for you. Over there."

He turned his head. The wind dashed his hair about his head once again. "Where?"

"The tearoom."

"Outside? Mag, are you daft? In this weather? I bet you've gone all ice. Why di'n't you come in?" He glanced at the lighted windows of the inn, nodded once, and said, "Because of the police. That's it, isn't it?"

She frowned. "Police?"

"New Scotland Yard. Got here round five, from what Ben Wragg was saying. Di'n't you know? I thought for certain you would."

"Why?"

"Your mum."

"Mummy? What . . . ?"

"They're here to sniff round Mr. Sage's death. Look, we need to talk." His eyes darted down the road to North Yorkshire in the direction of the common where the car park across the street was supplied with an old stone shed of public toilets. There was shelter there from the wind, if not the cold, but Maggie had a better idea.

"Come with me," she said and with a pause for him to grab the radio—whose volume he lowered as if in understanding of the clandestine nature of their movements—she led him through the gates of the Crofters Inn car park. They wove between the cars. Nick low-whistled his admiration of the same silver Bentley that had been parked there several hours before when Josie and Maggie had walked to the river.

"Where are we—"

"Special place," Maggie said. "It's Josie's. She won't mind. Have you a match? We'll need one for the lantern."

They descended the path carefully. It was slick with the night's developing coat of ice, with rushes and weeds made constantly damp by the river that tumbled through the limestone boulders below. Nick said, "Let me," and went on ahead, his hand extended back to her, to keep her steady and on her feet. Each time he slid an inch or two, he said, "Steady on, Mag," and firmed up his grip. He was taking care of her, and the thought of that made her warm inside to out.

"Here," she said as they reached the old ice-house. She pushed against the door. It creaked on its hinges and scraped against the floor, rucking up part of the patchwork carpet. "This is Josie's secret place," Maggie said. "You won't tell anyone about it, Nick?"

He ducked inside the door as Maggie fumbled for the nail barrel and the lantern on top of it. She said, "I'll need the matches," and felt him press a book of them into her hand. She lit the lantern, lowered its glow to a candle's softness, and turned back to him.

He was gazing about. "Wizard," he said with a smile.

She moved past him to shut the door and, as she had seen Josie do earlier, she sprayed the floor and the walls with toilet water.

"It's colder in here than outside," Nick said. He zipped his bomber's jacket and beat his hands against his arms.

"Here," she said. She sat on the cot and patted the spot next to her. When he dropped down beside her, she took up the eiderdown that served as a coverlet, and they wore it like a cape.

He loosed himself from it long enough to produce the Marlboros he favoured. Maggie returned him his matches and he lit two cigarettes at once, one for each of them. He inhaled deeply and held his breath. Maggie pretended to do the same.

More than anything, she liked the nearness of him. The sound of his leather jacket rustling, the pressure of his leg against hers, the heat of his body, and—when she gave a quick look—the length of his eyelashes and the heavily lidded, sleepy shape of his eyes. "Bedroom eyes," she'd heard one of the teachers call them. "Bet that bloke'll be giving the ladies something nice to remember in a few more years." Another had added, "I wouldn't mind something nice from him now, actually," and they all had laughed, stopping abruptly when they realised Maggie was close enough to hear. Not that they knew anything about Maggie and Nick. No one knew about them except Josie and Mummy. And Mr. Sage.

"There was an inquest," Maggie said reasonably. "They said it was an accident, didn't they? And once the inquest says it's an accident, no one can say anything else. Isn't that it? They can't do another. Don't the police know that?"

Nick shook his head. The cigarette glowed. He tapped ash onto the carpet and ground it in with the toe of his shoe. "That's the trial part, Mag. You can't be tried twice for the same crime, unless there's new evidence. Sort of. I think. But that doesn't matter because there wasn't any trial in the first place. An inquest's not a trial."

"Will there be one? Now?"

"Depends on what they find."

"Find? Where? Are they looking for something? Will they come to the cottage?"

"They'll be talking to your mum, that's for sure. They've already been holed up tonight with Mr. Townley-Young. I got money says he must've phoned for them in the first place." Nick gave a little chuckle. "You should've been there, Mag, when he came out of the lounge. Poor ol' Brendan was having a gin with Polly Yarkin and T-Y went white to his lips and dead-cod stiff when he saw them.

They weren't *doing* nothing but drinking, but T-Y had Bren outa that pub faster 'n anything. His eyes just sort of shot laser blasts at him. Like in a film."

"But Mummy didn't do anything," Maggie said. She felt a small, burning point of fear in her chest. "It wasn't on purpose. That's what she said. The jury agreed."

"Sure. Based on what they were told. But someone might've lied."

"Mummy didn't lie!"

Nick seemed to recognise her fears immediately. He said, "It's okay, Mag. There's nothing to worry about. Except that they'll probably want to talk to you."

"The police?"

"Right. You knew Mr. Sage. You and him were mates in a way. When the police investigate, they always talk to all the dead bloke's mates."

"But Mr. Shepherd never talked to me. The inquest man didn't. I wasn't there that night. I don't know what happened. I can't tell them anything. I—"

"Hey." He took a final, deep drag of his cigarette before he squashed it against the stone wall behind them and did the same to hers. He put his arm round her waist. At the far side of the ice-house, Nick's radio was hissing spasmodically, its station lost. "It's okay, Mag. It's nothing to worry about. It's nothing to do with you at all. I mean, you didn't exactly kill the vicar, did you?" He chuckled at the very impossibility of the thought.

Maggie didn't join him. At heart, it was all about responsibility, wasn't it? Responsibility with a capital *R*.

She could remember Mummy's anger when she'd been told of Maggie's visits to Mr. Sage's house. To the shrill, outraged defence of "Who told you? Who's been spying on me?"—which Mummy wouldn't answer but it didn't really matter, did it, because Maggie knew precisely who had done the spying—Mummy had said, "Listen to me, Maggie. Have some common sense. You don't actually know this man. And he *is* a man, not a boy. He's at least forty-five years old. Are you aware of that? What are you doing paying visits alone to a forty-five-year-old man? Even if he's a vicar. Especially because he's a vicar. Can't you see the position you're putting him in?" And to the explanation "But he said I could come for tea when I wanted.

And he gave me a book. And—," her mother said, "I don't care what he gave you. I don't want you to see him. Not in his house. Not alone. Not at all." When Maggie had felt the tears rise in her eyes, when she let them trickle down her cheeks while she said, "He's my friend. He says so. You don't want me to have any friends, do you," Mummy had grabbed her arm in a grip that meant listen-and-don't-you-dare-argue-with-me-missy, saying, "You stay away from him." To the petulant question "Why," she released her and said only, "Anything could happen. Everything *does* happen. That's the way of the world, and if you don't know what I mean, start reading the newspaper." Those words closed the discussion between them that night. But there were others:

"You were with him today. Don't lie about it, Maggie, because I know it's the truth. As from now, you're gated."

"That's not fair!"

"What did he want with you?"

"Nothing."

"Don't be sullen with me or you'll regret it more than having disobeyed in the first place. Is that clear? What did he want with you?"

"Nothing."

"What did he say? What did he do?"

"We just talked. We ate some Jaffa Cakes. Polly made tea."

"She was there?"

"Yes. She's always—"

"In the room?"

"No. But—"

"What did you talk about?"

"Stuff."

"Such as?"

"School. God." Mummy made a noise through her nose. Maggie countered it with "He asked did I ever go to London? Do I think I'd like to see it? He said I'd like London. He said he's been there lots. He even went for a two days' holiday last week. He says people who get tired of London oughtn't be alive. Or something like that."

Mummy didn't reply. Instead, she watched her hands grating and grating and grating some cheese. So fast she held the block of cheddar that her knuckles were white. But not as white as her face.

Maggie felt comfortable with the advantage indicated by Mummy's silence, and she pressed it. "He said we might go to London sometime on an excursion with the youth group. He said there's families in London who'd let us stay so we wouldn't even have to find a hotel. He said London's grand and we could go to museums and see the Tower and go to Hyde Park and have lunch at Harrod's. He said—"

"Go to your room."

"Mummy!"

"You heard me."

"But I was only—"

Mummy's hand stopped her words. It moved in less than an eyeblink to slap her face. Shock and surprise, far more than pain, brought the tears to her eyes. Anger came with them, as did the desire to hurt back in kind.

"He's my friend," she cried. "He's my friend and we talk and you don't want him to like me. You never want me to have any friends at all. That's why we move, isn't it? Over and over. So no one will like me. So I'll always be alone. And if Daddy—"

"Stop it!"

"I won't, I won't! If Daddy finds me, I'll go with him. I will. Wait and see. You won't be able to stop me, no matter what."

"I wouldn't depend on that, Margaret."

Then Mr. Sage died, just four days later. Who was really responsible? And what was the crime?

"Mummy's good," she said in a low voice to Nick. "She didn't mean anything bad to happen to the vicar."

"I believe you, Mag," Nick replied. "But someone round here doesn't."

"What if they put her on trial? What if she goes to gaol?"

"I'll take care of you."

"Truly?"

"A fact."

He sounded strong and certain. He *was* strong and certain. He felt good to be near. She worked one arm round his waist and rested her head on his chest.

"I want us to be like this always," she said.

"Then that's the way it'll be."

"Really?"

"Really. You're my number one, Mag. You're the only one. Don't worry about your mum."

She slid her hand from his knee to his thigh. "Cold," she said and snuggled closer to him. "You cold, Nick?"

"Bit. Yeah."

"I can warm you nice."

She could feel his smile. "Bet you can at that."

"Want me to?"

"Wouldn't say no."

"I can. I like to." She did it just the way he had shown her, her hand making the slow, sinuous friction. She could feel It growing hard in response. "Feel good, Nick?"

"Hmm."

She rubbed the heel of her hand from base to tip. Then her fingers lightly retraced the pathway. Nick gave a shaky sigh. He stirred.

"What?"

He was reaching in his jacket. There was crackling in his hand. "Got this from one of the blokes," he said. "We can't do it any more without a Durex, Mag. It's crazy. Too risky."

She kissed his cheek and then his neck. Her fingers sank between his legs where she remembered he felt the most. He lost his breath in a groan.

He lay back on the cot. He said, "We got to use the Durex this time."

She worked the zip of his blue jeans, worked the jeans below his hips. She slipped off her tights, lay down next to him, and lifted her skirt.

"Mag, we got to use—"

"Not yet, though, Nick. In a minute. All right?"

She draped a leg over his. She began to kiss him. She began to caress and caress and caress It without using her hands.

"That good?" she whispered.

His head was thrown back. His eyes were closed. He moaned for reply.

A minute was more than enough time, she found.

•   •   •

St. James sat in the bedroom's only chair, an overstuffed wing-back. Aside from the bed, it was the most comfortable piece of furniture he'd yet to encounter at Crofters Inn. He drew his dressing gown round him against the pervasive chill descending from the glass of the bedroom's two skylights and settled himself.

Behind the closed door of the bathroom, he could hear Deborah splashing away in the tub. She usually hummed or sang as she bathed, for some reason invariably choosing either Cole Porter or one of the Gershwins and rendering them with the enthusiasm of an undiscovered Edith Piaf and all the talent of a street hawker. She couldn't carry a tune if King's College Choir were trying to assist her. Tonight, however, she bathed in silence.

Normally, he would have welcomed any extended interlude between "Anything Goes" and "Summertime," especially if he was trying to read in their bedroom while she was paying tribute to old American musicals in the adjoining bath. But tonight he would have preferred to hear her cheerful dissonance rather than listen to her quiet bathing and be forced to consider not only how best to interrupt it but also whether he wanted to do so.

Aside from a brief skirmish over tea, they'd declared and maintained an unspoken truce upon her return from her extended tramp on the moors that morning. It had been easy enough to effect, with Mr. Sage's death to consider and Lynley's arrival to anticipate. But now that Lynley was with them and the machinery of an investigation oiled and ready, St. James found that his thoughts kept returning to the unease in his marriage and what he himself was doing to contribute to it.

Where Deborah was all passion, he was all reason. He had liked to believe this basic difference in their natures constituted the bedrock of fire and ice upon which their marriage was soundly fixed. But they had entered an arena in which his ability to reason seemed not only a disadvantage but also the very spark that ignited her refusal to approach conflict in any way other than pig-headedly. The words *about this adoption business, Deborah* were enough to send up every one of her defences against him. She moved from anger to accusation to tears with such dizzying speed that he didn't know where to begin to contend with it or with her. And because of this, when discussions concluded with her banging out of the room, the house, or this morning the hotel, he more often breathed a sigh of relief than did he

wonder what he himself could do to approach the problem from another angle. I tried, he would think, when the reality was that he'd
gone through the motions without trying much at all.

He rubbed the stiff muscles at the base of his neck. They were
always the primary indicator of the amount of stress he was currently
refusing to acknowledge. He shifted in the chair. His dressing gown
slid partially open with his movement. The cold air climbed his good
right leg and forced his attention to his left, which as always felt
nothing. He made a disinterested observation of it, an activity in
which he'd engaged only rarely in the past several years, but one
which he'd obsessively pursued day after day in the years before his
marriage.

The object was always the same: to inspect the muscles for their
degree of atrophy, intent upon fending off the disintegration that was
the eventual by-product of paralysis. He'd regained the use of his left
arm over time and through months of teeth-grating physical therapy.
But the leg had been a different creature altogether, resistant to every
effort at rehabilitation, like a soldier unable to heal from psychic war
wounds as if they alone could prove he'd seen action.

"Many of the workings of the brain are still veiled in mystery,"
the doctors had said in contemplative explanation of why the use of
his arm would return but not that of his leg. "When the head under-
goes as serious an injury as yours did, the prognosis for a full recovery
has to be couched in the most guarded terms."

Which was their way of beginning the list of perhapses. Perhaps
he would regain complete use of it over time. Perhaps he would walk
unassisted one day. Perhaps he would awaken one morning and have
sensation restored, flexing muscles, moving toes, and bending the
knee. But after twelve years, it wasn't likely. So he held on to what
was left after the first four years of obstinate delusion had been
stripped away: the appearance of normality. As long as he could keep
atrophy from doing its worst to the muscles, he'd declare himself
satisfied and dismiss the dream.

He'd fended off the disintegration with electrical current. The
fact that this was an act of vanity was something which he never
denied, telling himself that it wasn't such a sin to want to look like
a perfect physical specimen, even if he could no longer be one.

Still, he hated the oddity of his gait, and despite the number of
years that he had lived with it, he sometimes still grew momentarily

sticky on the palms when exposed to the curiosity in a stranger's eyes. *Different*, they said, *not quite one of us*. And while he was different in the limited fashion described by his disability and he couldn't deny it, in a stranger's presence it was always underscored—even for an instant—a hundredfold.

We have certain expectations of people, he thought as he idly evaluated the leg. They'll be able to walk, to talk, to see, and to hear. If they can't—or if they do it in a way that defies our preconceived notions about them—we label them, we shy away from contact, we force them to want to be part of a whole that is in itself without distinction.

The water in the bathroom began to drain, and he glanced at the door, wondering if that's what was at the root of the difficulty he and his wife were having. She wanted what was her due, the norm. He had long believed normality had little intrinsic value.

He pushed himself to his feet and listened to her movements. The surge of water told him she had just stood. She would be stepping out of the tub, reaching for a towel, and wrapping it round her. He tapped against the door and opened it.

She was wiping the mirror free of steam, her hair spilling tendrils against her neck from the turban she'd fashioned from a second towel. Her back was to him, and from where he stood, he could see that her back was lightly beaded with moisture. As were her legs, which looked smooth and sleek, softened by the bath oil that filled the room with the scent of lilies.

She looked at his reflection and smiled. Her expression was fond. "I suppose it's well and truly over between us."

"Why?"

"You didn't join me in the bath."

"You didn't invite me."

"I was sending you mental invitations all through dinner. Didn't you get them?"

"Was that your foot under the table, then? It didn't feel much like Tommy's, come to think of it."

She chuckled and uncapped her lotion. He watched her smooth it against her face. Muscles moved with the circular motion of her fingers, and he made an exercise out of identification: *trapezius, levator scapulae, splenius cervicis*. It was a form of discipline to keep his mind heading in the direction in which he wished it to go. The prospect of deferring conversation with Deborah till another time was always heightened by the sight of her, freshly out of her bath.

"I'm sorry about bringing the adoption papers," he said. "We made a bargain and I didn't keep my part of it. I was hoping to romance you into talking about the problem while we were here. Ascribe it to male ego and forgive me, if you will."

"Forgiven," she said. "But there isn't a problem."

She capped the lotion and began to towel herself off with rather more energy than the task required. Seeing this, he felt the palm of caution flatten itself against his chest. He said nothing else until she had slid into her dressing gown and freed her hair from its towel. She was bent from the waist, combing her fingers through the tangles in lieu of using a brush, when he spoke again. He chose his words carefully.

"That's an issue of semantics. What else can we call what's been happening between us? Disagreement? Dispute? Those don't seem to hit the mark particularly well."

"And God knows we can't stumble in the process of applying scientific labels."

"That isn't fair."

"No?" She raised herself and rooted through her make-up case to produce the slender jacket of pills. She popped one from its plastic casing, held it up in presentation to him between her thumb and index finger, and put it into her mouth. She turned on the tap with such decided force that the water hit the bottom of the basin and rose up like spume.

"Deborah."

She ignored him. She drank the pill down. "There. Now you can set your mind at rest. I've just eliminated the problem."

"Taking the pills or not is going to be your decision, not mine. I can stand over you. I can attempt to force you. I choose not to do so. I choose only to make certain you understand my concern."

"Which is?"

"Your health."

"You've made that clear for two months now. So I've done what you wanted, and I've taken my pills. I won't be getting pregnant. Aren't you satisfied with that?"

Her skin was beginning to mottle, always a primary sign that she was feeling backed into a corner. Her movements were becoming clumsy as well. He didn't want to be the cause of her panic, but at the same time he wanted to clear the air between them. He knew he was being as obstinate as she was, but still he pressed on. "You make it sound as if we don't want the same thing."

"We don't. Are you asking me to pretend I don't realise that?" She moved past him into the bedroom where she went to the electric heater and made an adjustment that took too much time and concentration. He followed her, keeping his distance by resuming his place in the wingback chair, a careful three feet away.

"It's family," he said. "Children. Two of them. Perhaps three. Isn't that the goal? Wasn't that what we wanted?"

"*Our* children, Simon. Not two that Social Services condescends to give us, but two that we have. That's what I want."

"Why?"

She looked up. Her posture stiffened and he realised he had somehow cut to the quick with a question he'd simply not thought to ask before. In their every discussion, he'd been too intent upon pressing home his own points to wonder at her single-minded determination to *have* a baby no matter the cost.

"Why?" he asked again, leaning towards her, his elbows on his knees. "Can't you talk about it with me?"

She looked back at the heater, reached for one of its knobs, twisted it fiercely. "Don't patronise me. You know I can't stand that."

"I'm not patronising you."

"You are. You psychologise everything. You probe and twist. Why can't I just feel what I feel and want what I want without having to examine myself under one of your damned microscopes?"

"Deborah . . ."

"I want to have a baby. Is that some sort of crime?"

"I'm not suggesting that."

"Does it make me a madwoman?"

"No. Of course not."

"Am I pathetic because I want that baby to be ours? Because I want it to be the way we send down roots? Because I want to know we created it—you and I? Because I want to be connected to it? Why does this have to be such a crime?"

"It isn't."

"I want to be a real mother. I want to experience it. I want the child."

"It shouldn't be an act of ego," he said. "And if it is for you, then I think you've mistaken what being a parent is all about."

Her head turned back to him. Her face was aflame. "That's a nasty thing to say. I hope you enjoyed it."

"Oh God, Deborah." He reached out to her but couldn't manage to bridge the space between them. "I don't mean to hurt you."

"You've a fine way of hiding it."

"I'm sorry."

"Yes. Well. It's been said."

"No. Not everything." He sought the words with a fair degree of desperation, walking the line between trying not to hurt her further and trying himself to understand. "It seems to me that if being a parent is more than just producing a baby, then you can have that experience with any child—one you have, one you merely take under your wing, or one you adopt. If the act of parenting and not simply producing is indeed what you want in the first place. Is it?"

She didn't reply. But she also didn't look away. He felt it safe to go on.

"I think a great many people go into it without the slightest consideration given to what will be asked of them over the course of their children's lives. I think they go into it without consideration given to anything at all. But seeing an infant through to adulthood and beyond takes its own special kind of toll on a person. And you have to be prepared for that. You have to want the entire experience. Not simply the act of producing a baby because you feel otherwise incomplete without having done so."

He didn't need to add the rest: that he'd had the experience of parenting a child to back up his words, that he'd had it with her. She knew the facts of their shared history: Eleven years her senior, he'd made her one of his primary responsibilities from the time he was eighteen years old. Who she was today was in large part due to the influence he'd had in shaping her life. The fact that he'd been a second father of sorts was part blessing in their marriage, and larger part curse.

He drew upon the blessing of it now, hoping that she could fight her way through the fear or anger or whatever it was that kept getting in the way of their reaching each other, banking on their shared past to help them find a way into the future.

"Deborah," he said, "you don't have to prove anything to anyone.

Not to the world. And certainly not to me. Never to me. So if this is all about proving, for God's sake let it go before it destroys you."

"It's not about proving."

"What then, if not that?"

"It's just that...I always pictured what it would be like." Her lower lip trembled. She pressed her fingertips to it. "It would grow inside me all those months. I'd feel it kick and I'd put your hand on my stomach. You'd feel it as well. We'd talk about names and make a nursery ready. And when I delivered, you'd be there with me. It would be just like an act of forever between us, because we'd made this...this little person together. I wanted that."

"But that's fiction, Deborah. That's not the binding. The stuff of life is the binding. This—between us now—this is the binding. And we're the forever." He held out his hand once again. This time she took it, although she remained where she was, those careful three feet away. "Come back to me," he said. "Race up and down the stairs with your knapsack and your cameras. Clutter up the house with your photographs. Play music too loudly. Leave your clothes on the floor. Talk to me and argue and be curious about everything. Be alive to your fingertips. I want you back."

Her tears spilled over. "I've forgotten the way."

"I don't believe that. It's all there inside you. But somehow—for some reason—the idea of a baby has taken its place. Why, Deborah?"

She lowered her head and shook it. Her fingers loosened in his. Their hands dropped to their sides. And he realised that, despite his intentions and all of his words, there was more to be said that his wife wasn't saying.

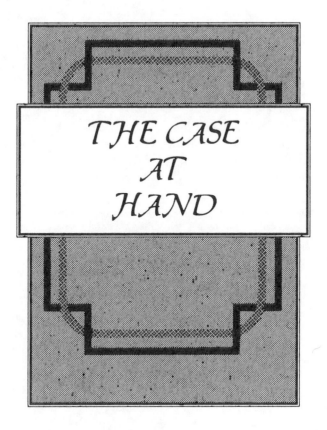

THE CASE
AT
HAND

CHAPTER THIRTEEN

I N BEST VICTORIAN FASHION, COTES HALL WAS a structure that seemed to consist solely of weather-vanes, chimneys, and gables from which bay and oriel windows reflected the ashen morning sky. It was built of limestone, and the combination of neglect and exposure to weather had caused the exterior to grow unappealingly lichenous, with streaks of grey-green descending from the roof in a pattern that resembled a vertical alluvial fan. The land that immediately surrounded the Hall had been taken over by weeds, and while it commanded an impressive view of the forest and the hills to its west and its east, the bleak winter landscape in conjunction with the property's general condition made the idea of living there more repellent than welcome.

Lynley eased the Bentley over the last of the ruts and into the courtyard round which the Hall loomed like the house of Usher. He gave a moment's thought to St. John Townley-Young's appearance at Crofters Inn on the previous night. On the way out he'd encountered his son-in-law plainly having a drink with a woman who was not his wife, and from Townley-Young's reaction it appeared that this was not the younger man's first such transgression. At the time, Lynley had thought that they'd unwittingly stumbled upon the motive behind the pranks at the Hall as well as the identity of the prankster. A woman who was the third point of a love-triangle might go to extreme lengths to disrupt the tranquillity and the marriage of a man she wanted for herself. However, as he ran his eyes from the Hall's rusting weathervanes to the great gaps in its rainpipes to the snarl of weeds and patches of damp where the base of the structure met the ground, Lynley was forced to admit that that had been a facile and largely chauvinistic conclusion. He, who didn't even have to face it, shuddered at the thought of having to live here. No matter the renovation inside, the exterior of the Hall, as well as its gardens and park, would take years of devoted labour to turn round. He couldn't blame anyone, wedded blissfully or otherwise, for trying to avoid it in whatever way he could.

He parked the car between an open-back lorry stacked high with lumber and a minivan with *Crackwell and Sons, Plumbing, Ltd.* emblazoned in orange letters on its side. From inside the house came the mixed sounds of hammer, saw, cursing, and "March of the Toreadors" at medium volume. In unconscious time to the music, an elderly man in rust-stained coveralls teetered out a rear door, balancing a roll of carpet on his shoulder. It appeared to be sodden. He dumped it along the side of the lorry, nodding at Lynley. He said, "Help you with something, mate?" and lit a cigarette while waiting for the answer.

"The caretaker's cottage," Lynley said. "I'm looking for Mrs. Spence."

The man lifted his bristly chin in the direction of a carriage house across the courtyard. Abutting it was a smaller building, an architectural miniature of the Hall itself. But unlike the Hall, its limestone exterior had been scrubbed clean and there were curtains in the windows. Round the front door someone had planted winter irises. Their blooms made a bright screen of yellow and purple against the grey walls.

The door was closed. When Lynley knocked and no one answered, the man called out, "Try the garden. The greenhouse," before he trudged back into the Hall.

The garden proved to be a plot of land behind the cottage, separated from the courtyard by a wall into which a green gate was recessed. This opened easily despite the rust on its hinges, and it gave way to what was clearly Juliet Spence's demesne. Here the earth was ploughed and free of weeds. The air smelled of compost. In a flower bed along the side of the cottage, twigs crisscrossed over a covering of straw that protected the crowns of perennials from the frost. It was clear that Mrs. Spence was preparing to do some sort of planting at the far side of the garden, for a large vegetable patch had been marked out with boards pounded into the earth, and pinewood stakes stood at the head and the foot of what would be rows of plants some six months from now.

The greenhouse was just beyond this. Its door was closed. Its glass panes were opaque. Behind these, Lynley could see the form of a woman moving, her arms extended to tend to some sort of plant that was hanging on a level with her head. He crossed the garden. His Wellingtons sank into damp soil that formed a path from the cottage to the greenhouse and ultimately into the wood beyond.

The door wasn't latched. The pressure of a single, light tap swung it soundlessly open. Mrs. Spence apparently neither heard the tap nor immediately noticed the influx of cooler air, because she went on with her work, giving him the welcome opportunity to observe.

The hanging plants were fuchsias. They grew from wire baskets lined with some sort of moss. They'd been trimmed for the winter but not stripped of all their leaves, and it was these that Mrs. Spence appeared to be attending to. She was pumping a malodorous spray upon them, pausing to turn each basket so that she doused the plant thoroughly before moving on to the next one. She was saying, "Take that, you little bastards," and working the pump swiftly.

She looked harmless enough, poking round the greenhouse among her plants. True, her choice of headgear was a little bit odd, but one couldn't judge and condemn a woman for wearing a faded red bandana round her forehead. If anything, it made her look like an American Navajo. And it served its purpose, anchoring her hair away from her face. This bore smudges of dirt, which she further smeared by rubbing the back of her hand—protected by a frayed and fingerless mitten—across one cheek. She was middle-aged, but her activity had the concentration of youth, and watching her, Lynley found it difficult to call her *murderess.*

This marked hesitation made him uneasy. It forced him to consider not only the facts he already had but also those in the process of unveiling themselves as he stood in the doorway. The greenhouse was a hotchpotch of plants. They stood in both clay and plastic pots along a central table. They lined the two work tops that ran the length of the greenhouse sides. They came in all shapes and sizes, in every imaginable type of container, and as he worked his eyes through them, he wondered how much of Colin Shepherd's investigating had gone on in here.

Juliet Spence turned from the last of the hanging baskets of fuchsias. She started when she saw him. Her right hand reached instinctively for the loose cowl-neck of her black pullover in an inherently
female defensive manoeuvre. Her left hand still held the pump, however. Obviously, she had the presence of mind not to set it down
when she could use it on him if necessary.

"What do you want?"

"Sorry," he said. "I knocked. You didn't hear me. Detective
Inspector Lynley. New Scotland Yard."

"I see."

He reached for his identification. She waved him off, revealing a
large hole in her pullover's armpit. It acted as companion, evidently,
to the threadbare condition of her muddy jeans.

"That's unnecessary," she said. "I believe you. Colin told me
you'd probably come round this morning." She placed the pump on
the work top amid the plants and fingered the remaining leaves of
the nearest fuchsia. He could see that they were abnormally ragged.
"Capsids," she said in explanation. "They're insidious. Like thrips.
You generally can't tell they're attacking the plant until the damage
is evident."

"Isn't that always the case?"

She shook her head, giving another blast of insecticide to one of
the plants. "Sometimes the pest leaves a calling card. Other times
you don't know he's come for a visit until it's too late to do anything
but kill him and hope you don't kill the plant in the process. Except
that I don't suppose I ought to be talking to you about killing as if I
enjoy it, even when I do."

"Perhaps when a creature is the instrument of another's destruction, it has to be killed."

"That's certainly my feeling. I've never been one to welcome
aphids into my garden, Inspector."

He started to enter the greenhouse. She said, "In there first,
please," and pointed to a shallow plastic tray of green powder just
inside the door. "Disinfectant," she explained. "It kills micro-
organisms. There's no sense in bringing other unwelcome visitors
inside on the soles of one's shoes."

He obliged her, closing the door and stepping into the tray in
which her own footprints had already left their mark. He could see

the residue of disinfectant speckling the sides and crusting the seams of her round-toed boots.

"You spend a great deal of time in here," he noted.

"I like to grow things."

"A hobby?"

"It's very peaceful—raising plants. A few minutes with one's hands in the soil and the rest of the world seems to fade away. It's a form of escape."

"And you need to escape?"

"Doesn't everyone at one time or another? Don't you?"

"I can't deny it."

The floor consisted of gravel and a slightly elevated path of brick. He walked along this between the central table and the peripheral work top and joined her. With the door closed, the air in the greenhouse was some degrees warmer than the air outside. It was heavily tinctured with the scent of potting soil, fish emulsion, and the odour of the insecticide she'd been pumping.

"What sorts of plants do you grow in here?" he asked. "Aside from the fuchsias."

She leaned against the work top as she spoke, pointing out the examples with a hand whose nails were clipped like a man's and crusted with dirt. She didn't appear to mind or even to notice. "I've been babying along some cyclamen for ages. They're the ones with the stems that look nearly transparent, lined up over there in the yellow pots. The others are philodendrons, grape ivy, amaryllis. I've got African violets, ferns, and palms, but something tells me you probably recognise them well enough. And these"—she moved to a shelf above which a grow-light glowed over four wide, black trays where tiny plants were sprouting—"are my seedlings."

"Seedlings?"

"I start my garden in here in the winter. Green beans, cucumbers, peas, lettuce, tomatoes. These are carrots and onions. I'm trying Vidalias although every gardening book I've read predicts utter failure there."

"What do you do with it all?"

"The plants I generally offer in Preston's car-boot sale. The vegetables we eat. My daughter and I."

"And parsnips? Do you grow those as well?"

"No," she said and folded her arms. "But we've come to it, haven't we?"

"We have. Yes. I'm sorry."

"There's no need to apologise, Inspector. You've a job to do. But I hope you won't mind if I work while we talk." She gave him little choice in the minding. She picked up a small cultivator from among the clutter of gardening utensils which filled a tin pail underneath the central table. She began to move along the potted houseplants, gently loosening their soil.

"Have you eaten wild parsnip from this area before?"

"Several times."

"So you know it when you see it."

"Yes. Of course."

"But you didn't last month."

"I thought I did."

"Tell me about it."

"The plant, the dinner? What?"

"Both. Where did the water hemlock come from?"

She pinched a straggly stem from one of the larger philodendrons and threw it into a plastic sack of rubbish beneath the table. "I thought it was wild parsnip," she clarified.

"Accepted for the moment. Where did it come from?"

"Not far from the Hall. There's a pond on the grounds. It's terribly overgrown—you probably noticed the state things are in—and I found a stand of wild parsnip there. What I thought was parsnip."

"Had you eaten parsnip from the pond before?"

"From the grounds. But not from that location by the pond. I'd only seen the plants."

"What was the root stock like?"

"Like parsnip, obviously."

"A single root? A bundle?"

She bent over a particularly verdant fern, parted its fronds, examined its base, and then lifted the plant to the work top opposite. She went on with her cultivating. "It must have been a single, but I don't actually recall the look of it."

"You know what it should have been."

"A single root. Yes. I know that, Inspector. And it would make it far easier on both of us if I just lied and declared it was definitely a single root I dug up. But the fact is I was in a rush that day. I'd gone to the cellar, discovered I had only two small parsnips, and hurried out to the pond where I thought I'd seen more. I dug one up and came back to the cottage. I assume the root I brought with me was a single, but I can't recall for a fact that it was. I can't picture it dangling from my hand."

"Odd, wouldn't you say? It is, after all, one of the most important details."

"I can't help that. But I would appreciate being given some credit for telling the truth. Believe me, a lie would be far more convenient."

"And your illness?"

She set down her cultivator and pressed the back of her wrist to the faded red headband. She dislodged upon it a speckling of soil. "What illness?"

"Constable Shepherd said you were ill yourself that night. He said you'd eaten some of the hemlock as well. He claimed to have dropped by that evening and found you—"

"Colin's trying to protect me. He's afraid. He's worried."

"Now?"

"Then as well." She replaced the cultivator among the other tools and went to adjust a dial on what appeared to be the irrigation system. The slow dripping of water began a moment later, somewhere to their right. She kept her eyes and her hand on the dial as she continued. "That was part of the convenience, Inspector, Colin's saying he'd just dropped by."

Lynley followed the previously established euphemism. "I take it he didn't drop by at all."

"Oh, he did. He was here. But it wasn't a coincidence. He didn't just happen to be on his rounds. That's what he told the inquest. That's what he told his father and Sergeant Hawkins. That's what he told everyone. But that's not what happened."

"You arranged for him to come?"

"I telephoned him."

"I see. The alibi."

She looked up at that. Her expression seemed resigned rather than culpable or afraid. She took a moment to strip off her tattered mittens and tuck them into the sleeves of her sweater before saying, "That's exactly what Colin said people would think: that I was phoning him to establish a form of innocence. 'She ate the stuff as well,' he'd have to say at the inquest. 'I was at the cottage. I saw for myself.' "

"Which is what he said, as I understand it."

"He'd have said the rest, if I'd had my way. But I couldn't convince him of the necessity of saying I'd phoned him because I'd been sick three times, I wasn't handling the pain of it very well, and I wanted him near. So he ended up putting himself at risk by colouring the truth. And I don't much like living with that knowledge."

"He's at risk in any number of ways at this point, Mrs. Spence. The investigation is filled with irregularities. He needed to hand the case over to a CID team from Clitheroe. Since he didn't do that, he'd have been wise to conduct any interrogations with an official witness present. And considering his involvement with you, he should have stepped out of the process altogether."

"He wants to protect me."

"That may be the case but it looks a far sight nastier than that."

"What do you mean?"

"It looks as if Shepherd's covering up his own crime. Whatever that may have been."

She pushed herself abruptly from the central table against which she had been leaning. She walked two paces away from him, then back again, pulling off her headband. "Look. Please. These are the facts." Her words were terse. "I went out to the pond. I dug up water hemlock. I thought it was parsnip. I cooked it. I served it. Mr. Sage died. Colin Shepherd had no part of this."

"Did he know Mr. Sage was coming to dinner?"

"I said he had no part of this."

"Did he ever ask you about your relationship with Sage?"

"Colin's done nothing!"

"Is there a Mr. Spence?"

She balled the bandana into her fist. "I . . . No."

"And your daughter's father?"

"That's none of your business. This has absolutely nothing to do with Maggie. Not at all. She wasn't even here."

"That day?"

"For the dinner. She was in the village, spending the night with the Wraggs."

"But she was here that day, earlier, when you went out to look for the wild parsnip in the first place? Perhaps while you were cooking?"

Her face seemed rigid. "Hear me, Inspector. Maggie isn't involved."

"You're avoiding the questions. That tends to suggest you've something to hide. Something about your daughter?"

She moved past him towards the door of the greenhouse. The space was confined. Her arm brushed against him as she passed, and it would have taken little enough effort to detain her, but he chose not to do so. He followed her out. Before he could ask another question, she spoke.

"I'd gone to the root cellar. There were only two left. I needed more. That's the extent of it."

"Show me, if you will."

She led him across the garden to the cottage where she opened the door to what appeared to be the kitchen and removed a key from a hook just inside. Not ten feet away, she unfastened the padlock on the sloping cellar door and lifted it.

"A moment," he said. He lowered and lifted it for himself. Like the gate in the wall, it moved easily enough. And like the gate, it moved without noise. He nodded and she descended the steps.

There was no electricity in the root cellar. Light was supplied from the doorway and from a single small window at the level of the ground. This was the size of a shoe carton and partially obstructed by the straw which covered the plants outside. The result was a chamber of moisture and shadow, comprising perhaps an eight-foot square. Its walls were an unfinished mixture of stone and earth. Its floor was the same, although some effort had been expended at one time to make it even.

Mrs. Spence gestured towards one of four roughly hewn shelves bolted to the wall that was farthest from the light. Aside from a neat stack of bushel baskets, the shelves were all the room contained save what they themselves held. On the top three sat rows of canning jars, their labels indecipherable in the gloom. On the bottom stood five small wire bins. Potatoes, carrots, and onions filled three. The other two held nothing.

Lynley said, "You've not replenished your supply."

"I don't think much of eating parsnips any longer. And certainly not wild ones."

He touched the rim of one of the empty bins. He moved his hand to the shelf that held it. There was no sign of either dust or disuse.

He said, "Why do you keep the cellar door locked? Have you always done?"

When she didn't reply at once, he turned from the shelves to look at her. Her back was to the muted light of morning that shone through the door, so he couldn't read her expression.

"Mrs. Spence?"

"I've kept it locked since October last."

"Why?"

"It has nothing to do with any of this."

"I'd appreciate an answer nonetheless."

"I've just given one."

"Mrs. Spence, shall we pause to look at the facts? A man is dead at your hands. You've a relationship with the police official who investigated the death. If either of you thinks—"

"All right. Because of Maggie, Inspector. I wanted to give her one less place to have sex with her boyfriend. She'd already used the Hall. I'd put a stop to that. I was trying to eliminate the rest of the possibilities. This seemed to be one of them, so I locked it up. Not that it mattered, as I've since discovered."

"But you kept the key on a hook in the kitchen?"

"Yes."

"In plain sight?"

"Yes."

"Where she could get to it?"

"Where I could get to it quickly as well." She ran an impatient hand back through her hair. "Inspector, please. You don't know my daughter. Maggie tries to be good. She thought she'd been wicked enough already. She gave me her word that she wouldn't have sex with Nick Ware again, and I told her I'd help her keep the promise. The lock itself was sufficient to keep her out."

"I wasn't thinking about Maggie and sex," Lynley said. He saw her glance move from his face to the shelves behind him. He knew what she was looking at largely because she didn't allow her eyes to rest upon it longer than an instant. "When you go out, do you lock your doors?"

"Yes."

"When you're in the greenhouse? When you make your rounds of the Hall? When you leave to look for wild parsnips?"

"No. But then I'm not out for long. And I'd know if someone were prowling round."

"Do you take your handbag? Your car keys? The keys to the cottage? The cellar key?"

"No."

"So you didn't lock up when you went out to look for parsnips on the day that Mr. Sage died?"

"No. But I know where you're heading and it isn't going to work. People can't come and go here without my knowing. That simply doesn't happen. It's like a sixth sense. Whenever Maggie met with Nick, I *knew*."

"Yes," Lynley said. "Quite. Please show me where you found the water hemlock, Mrs. Spence."

"I've told you I thought it was—"

"Indeed. Wild parsnip."

She hesitated, one hand lifted as if there was a point she wanted to make. She dropped both, saying, "This way," quietly.

They went out through the gate. Across the courtyard, three of the workers were having morning coffee in the bed of the open-back lorry. Their Thermos jugs were lined up on one stack of lumber. Another they used as their chairs. They watched Lynley and Mrs. Spence with undisguised curiosity. It was clear that this visit was going to be fuel for the fires of gossip by the end of the day.

In the better light, Lynley took a moment to evaluate Mrs. Spence as they crossed the courtyard and walked round the gabled east wing of the Hall. She was blinking rapidly as if in an effort to free her eyes of soot, but the cowl-neck of her pullover showed how the muscles of her neck were straining. He realised that she was trying not to cry.

The worst part of policework lay buried in the effort it took not to empathise. An investigation required a heart that attached itself to the victim alone or to a crime whose commission called out for justice. While Lynley's sergeant had mastered the ability to wear emotional blinkers when it came to a case, Lynley found himself, more often than not, torn in a dozen unlikely directions as he gathered information and came to know the facts and the principals involved. They were rarely black or white, he had come to find. It was, inconveniently, not a black-or-white world.

He paused on the terrace outside the east wing. The paving stones here were cracked and clotted with winter-dead weeds and the view was of a frost-coated hillside. This sloped down to a pond beyond which another hillside rose steeply, its summit hidden by the mist.

He said, "You've had trouble here, as I understand. Work disrupted. That sort of thing. It sounds as if someone doesn't want the newlyweds to take over the Hall."

She seemed to misunderstand his intentions in speaking, seeing it as another attempt at accusation rather than as an opportunity for a moment's reprieve. She cleared her throat and rebounded from whatever distress she was feeling. "Maggie used it less than half a dozen times. That's all."

He briefly toyed with the idea of reassuring her about the nature of his comments. He rejected it, and followed her lead. "How did she get in?"

"Nick—her boyfriend—loosened a board covering one of the windows in the west wing. I've nailed it shut since. Unfortunately, that hasn't put a stop to the mischief."

"You didn't know at once that Maggie and her friend were using the Hall? You couldn't tell someone had been prowling round?"

"I was referring to someone prowling round the cottage, Inspector Lynley. Surely you yourself would be aware if some sort of intruder had been in your own home."

"If he conducted a search or took something, yes. Otherwise, I'm not certain."

"Believe me, I am."

With the toe of her boot, she dislodged a tangle of flowerless dandelions from between two of the terrace stones. She picked up the weed, examined several rosettes of the scratchy, toothed leaves, and hurled it aside.

"But you've never managed to catch the prankster here? He—or she—has never made a sound to attract your attention, never stumbled into your garden by mistake?"

"No."

"You've never heard a car or a motorbike?"

"I haven't."

nd your rounds have been varied enough that someone bent

on mischief wouldn't be able to predict when you'd be likely to take another turn round the grounds?"

Impatiently, she shoved her hair behind her ears. "That's correct, Inspector. May I ask what this has to do with what happened to Mr. Sage?"

He smiled affably. "I'm not entirely sure." She looked in the direction of the pond at the base of the hill, her intention clear. But he found that he wasn't quite ready to move on. He gave his attention to the east wing of the house. Its lower bay windows were boarded over. Two of the upper ones bore seamlike cracks. "It looks as if it's stood vacant for years."

"It's never been lived in, aside from three months shortly after it was built."

"Why not?"

"It's haunted."

"By whom?"

"The sister-in-law of Mr. Townley-Young's great-grandfather. What does that make her? His great-grandaunt?" She didn't wait for reply. "She killed herself here. They thought she'd gone out for a walk. When she didn't return by evening, they began a search. It was five days before they thought of searching the house."

"And?"

"She'd hanged herself from a beam in the luggage room. Next to the garret. It was summer. The servants were tracking down the smell."

"Her husband couldn't face continuing life here?"

"A romantic thought, but he was dead already. He'd been killed on their wedding trip. They said it was a hunting accident, but no one was ever particularly forthcoming about how it happened. His wife returned alone, so everyone thought. They didn't know at first she brought syphilis with her, his gift to their marriage, evidently." She smiled without humour, not at him but at the house. "According to legend, she walks the upper corridor, weeping. The Townley-Youngs like to think it's with remorse for having killed her husband. I like to think it's with regret for having married the man in the first place. It was 1853 after all. There was no easy cure."

"For syphilis."

"Or for marriage."

She strode off the terrace in the direction of the pond. He watched her for a moment. She took long steps despite her heavy boots. Her hair lifted with her movement, in two greying arcs sweeping back from her face.

The slope he followed her down was icy, its grass long defeated by purslane and furze. At its base, the pond lay in the shape of a kidney bean. It was thickly overgrown, resembling a marsh, with water that was murky and, no doubt in the summer, a breeding ground for everything from insects to disease. Unkempt reeds and denuded weeds grew waist-tall round it. The latter sent out tendrils to grasp at clothes. But Mrs. Spence seemed oblivious of this. She waded into their midst and brushed the clinging bits of them aside.

She stopped less than a yard from the water's edge. "Here," she said.

As far as Lynley could tell, the vegetation she indicated was indistinguishable from the vegetation everywhere else. In the spring or summer, perhaps, flowers or fruit might give an indication of the genera—if not the species—that now appeared to be little more than skeletal shrubs and brambles. He recognised nettle easily enough because its toothed leaves still clung to the stem of the plant. And reeds were the same in shape and size from season to season. But as for the rest, he was mystified.

She apparently saw this, for she said, "Part of it is knowing where the plants grow when they're in season, Inspector. If you're looking for roots, they're still in the ground even when the stems, leaves, and flowers are gone." She pointed to her left where an oblong of ground resembled nothing more than a mat of dead leaves from which a spindly bush grew. "Meadowsweet and wolfbane grow there in the summer. Farther up there's a fine patch of chamomile." She bent and rooted through the weeds at her feet, saying, "And if you're in doubt, the leaves of the plant don't go much farther than the ground beneath it. They disintegrate ultimately, but the process takes ages and in the meantime, you've got your source of identification right here." She extended her hand. In it she held the remains of a feathery leaf not unlike parsley in appearance. "This tells you where to dig," she said.

"Show me."

She did so. No trowel or hoe was necessary. The earth was damp. It was simple enough for her to uproot a plant by pulling on the crown and the stems that remained of it above the ground. She knocked the root stock sharply against her knee to dislodge the clods of earth that were still clinging to it, and both of them stared, without speaking, at the result. She was holding a thickened stock of the plant from which a bundle of tubers grew. She dropped it immediately, as if, without even being ingested, it still had the power to kill.

"Tell me about Mr. Sage," Lynley said.

CHAPTER FOURTEEN

ER EYES COULDN'T SEEM TO MOVE FROM THE hemlock she had dropped. "Surely I would have seen the multiple tubers," she said. "I would have known. Even now, I'd *remember*."

"Were you distracted? Did someone see you? Did someone call out to you while you were digging?"

Still she didn't look at him. "I was in a rush. I came down the slope, made for this spot, cleared away the snow, and found the parsnip."

"The hemlock, Mrs. Spence. Just as you did now."

"It had to have been a single root. I would have seen otherwise. I would have known."

"Tell me about Mr. Sage," he repeated.

She raised her head. Her expression seemed bleak. "He came to the cottage several times. He wanted to talk about the Church. And Maggie."

"Why Maggie?"

"She'd grown fond of him. He'd taken an interest in her."

"What sort of interest?"

"He knew she and I were having our troubles. What mother and daughter don't? He wanted to intercede."

"Did you object to this?"

"I didn't particularly enjoy feeling inadequate as a mother, if that's what you mean. But I let him come. And I let him talk. Maggie wanted me to see him. I wanted to make Maggie happy."

"And the night he died? What happened then?"

"Nothing more than had happened before. He wanted to counsel me."

"About religion? About Maggie?"

"About both, actually. He wanted me to join the Church, and he wanted me to let Maggie do the same."

"That was the extent of it?"

"Not exactly." She wiped her hands on the faded bandana which she took from the pocket of her jeans. She balled it up, tucked it into the sleeve of her sweater to join her mittens, and shivered. Her pullover was heavy, but it would not be enough protection against the cold. Seeing this, Lynley decided to continue the interview right where they were. Her uprooting of the water hemlock had given him the whip hand, if only momentarily. He was determined to use it and to strengthen it by whatever means were available. Cold was one of them.

"Then what?" he asked.

"He wanted to talk to me about parenthood, Inspector. He felt I was keeping too tight a rein on my daughter. It was his belief that the more I insisted upon chastity from Maggie, the more I'd drive her away. He felt if she was having sex, she should be taking precautions against pregnancy. I felt she shouldn't be having sex at all, precautions or not. She's thirteen years old. She's little more than a child."

"Did you argue about her?"

"Did I poison him because he disagreed with how I was bringing her up?" She was trembling, but not from distress, he thought. Aside from the earlier tears which she had managed to control within moments of being tested by them, she didn't really appear to be the sort of woman who would allow herself an overt display of anxiety in the presence of the police. "He didn't have children. He wasn't even married. It's one thing to express an opinion growing out of a mutual experience. It's quite another to offer advice having no basis in anything but reading psychology texts and possessing a glorified ideal of family life. How could I possibly take his concerns to heart?"

"Despite this, you didn't argue with him."

"No. As I said, I was willing to hear him out. I did that much for Maggie because she was fond of him. And that's the extent of it. I had my beliefs. He had his. He wanted Maggie to use contraceptives.

I wanted her to stop complicating her life by having sex in the first place. I didn't think she was ready for it. He thought it was too late to turn her behaviour around. We chose to disagree."

"And Maggie?"

"What?"

"Where did she stand in this disagreement?"

"We didn't discuss it."

"Did she discuss it with Sage?"

"I wouldn't know."

"But they were close."

"She was fond of him."

"Did she see him often?"

"Now and again."

"With your knowledge and approval?"

She lowered her head. Her right foot dug at the weeds in a spasmodic, kicking motion. "We've always been close, Maggie and I, until this business with Nick. So I knew about it when she saw the vicar."

The nature of the answer said everything. Dread, love, and anxiety. He wondered if they went hand in hand with motherhood.

"What did you serve him for dinner that night?"

"Lamb. Mint jelly. Peas. Parsnips."

"What happened?"

"We talked. He left shortly after nine."

"Was he feeling ill?"

"He didn't say. Only that he had a walk ahead of him and since it had been snowing, he ought to be off."

"You didn't offer to drive him."

"I wasn't feeling well. I thought it was flu. I was just as happy to have him leave, frankly."

"Could he have stopped somewhere along the way home?"

Her eyes moved to the Hall on its crest of land, from there to the oak wood beyond it. She appeared to be evaluating this as a possibility, but then she said firmly, "No. There's the lodge—his housekeeper lives there, Polly Yarkin—but that would have taken him out of his way, and I can't see what reason he'd have to stop by and visit with Polly when he saw her every day at the vicarage. Beyond that, it's easier to get back to the village on the footpath. And Colin found him on the footpath the next morning."

"You didn't think to phone him that night when you yourself were being sick?"

"I didn't attach my condition to the food. I said already, I thought I'd got flu. If he'd mentioned feeling unwell before he left, I might have phoned him. But he hadn't mentioned it. So I didn't make the connection."

"Yet he died on the footpath. How far is that from here? A mile? Less? He'd have been stricken rather quickly, wouldn't you say?"

"He must have been. Yes."

"I wonder how it was that he died and you didn't."

She met his gaze squarely. "I couldn't say."

He gave her a long ten seconds of silence in which to move her eyes off him. When she didn't do so, he finally nodded and directed his own attention to the pond. The edges, he saw, wore a dingy skin of ice like a coating of wax that encircled the reeds. Each night and day of continued cold weather would extend the skin farther towards the centre of the water. When entirely covered, the pond would look like the frosty ground that surrounded it, appearing to be an uneven but nonetheless innocuous smear of land. The wary would avoid it, seeing it clearly for what it was. The innocent or oblivious would attempt to cross it, breaking through its false and fragile surface to encounter the foul stagnation beneath.

"How are things between you and your daughter now, Mrs. Spence?" he asked. "Does she listen to you now that the vicar's gone?"

Mrs. Spence took the mittens from the sleeves of her pullover. She thrust her hands into them, her fingers bare. It was clear she intended to go back to work. "Maggie isn't listening to anyone," she said.

■　　■　　■

Lynley slipped the cassette into the Bentley's tape player and turned up the volume. Helen would have been pleased with the choice, Haydn's Concerto in E-flat Major, with Wynton Marsalis on the trumpet. Uplifting and joyful, with violins supplying the counterpoint to the trumpet's pure notes, it was utterly unlike his usual selection of "some grim Russian. Good Lord, Tommy, didn't they compose anything just the merest bit listener-friendly? What made them so ghoulish? D'you think it was the weather?" He smiled at the thought of her. "Johann Strauss," she would request. "Oh, all right. I know. Simply too pedestrian for your lofty taste. Then compromise. Mozart." And in would pop *Eine Kleine Nachtmusik*, the only piece by Mozart which Helen could invariably identify, announcing that her ability to do so kept her free of the epithet *absolute philistine*.

He drove south, away from the village. He put the thought of Helen aside.

He passed beneath the bare tree branches and headed for the moors, thinking about one of the basic tenets of criminology: There is always a relationship between the killer and the victim in a pre-meditated murder. This is not the case in a serial killing where the killer is driven by rages and urges incomprehensible to the society in which he lives. Nor is it always the case in a crime of passion when a murder grows out of an unexpected, transitory, but nonetheless virulent blaze of anger, jealousy, revenge, or hate. Nor is it like an accidental death in which the forces of coincidence bring the killer and the victim together for one moment of inalterable time. Pre-meditated murder grows out of a relationship. Sort through the re-lationships that the victim has had, and inevitably the killer turns up.

This bit of knowlege was part of every policeman's bible. It went hand in glove with the fact that most victims know their killers. It was second cousin to the additional fact that most killings are com-mitted by one of the victim's immediate relatives. Juliet Spence may well have poisoned Robin Sage in a horrible accident the conse-quences of which she would have to wrestle with for the rest of her life. It would not be the first time someone with a bent towards the natural and organic life picked up a wild-grown bit of root or fungi, flowers or fruit and ended up killing himself or someone else as a result of an error in identification. But if St. James was correct—if Juliet Spence couldn't have realistically survived even the smallest ingestion of water hemlock, if the symptoms of fever and vomiting couldn't be attached to hemlock poisoning in the first place—then there had to be a connection between Juliet Spence and the man who had died at her hands. If this was the case, then the superficial connection appeared to be Juliet's daughter, Maggie.

The grammar school, an uninteresting brick building that sat at the triangle created by the juncture of two converging streets, was not far from the centre of Clitheroe. It was eleven-forty when he pulled into the car park and slid carefully into the space left between an antique Austin-Healey and a conventional Golf of recent vintage with an infant's safety seat riding as passenger. A small homemade sticker reading *Mind The Baby* was affixed to the Golf's rear window.

Lessons were in progress inside the school, judging from both the emptiness of the long linoleum-floored corridors and the closed doors that lined them. The administration offices were just inside, facing one another to the left and the right of the entrance. At one time suitable titles had been painted in black upon the opaque glass that comprised the upper half of their doors, but the passing years had reduced the letters to speckles the approximate colour of wet soot, from which one could barely make out the words *headmistress, bursar, masters' common room,* and *second master* in self-important Graeco-Roman printing.

He chose the headmistress. After a few minutes' loud and repetitive conversation with an octogenarian secretary whom he found nodding over a strip of knitting that appeared to be the sleeve of a sweater appropriate in size for a male gorilla, he was shown into the headmistress' study. *Mrs. Crone* was engraved across a placard that sat on her desk. An unfortunate name, Lynley thought. He spent the moments until her arrival considering all the possible sobriquets the pupils probably had invented for her. They seemed infinite in both variety and connotation.

She turned out to be the antithesis of all of them, in a pencil-tight skirt hemmed a good five inches above the knee and an overlong cardigan with padded shoulders and enormous buttons. She wore discoidal gold earrings, a necklace to match, and shoes whose skyscraper heels directed the eye inexorably to an outstanding pair of ankles. She was the sort of woman who asked for the once-over twice or more, and as he forced his eyes to remain on her face, Lynley wondered how the school's board of governors had ever settled upon such a creature for the job. She couldn't have been more than twenty-eight years old.

He managed to make his request with the minimum of time given to speculating what she looked like naked, forgiving himself for the instant of fantasy by telling himself it was the curse of being male. In the presence of a beautiful woman, he had always experienced that knee-jerk reaction of being reduced—if only momentarily—to skin, bone, and testosterone. He liked to believe that this response to an exposure to feminine stimuli had nothing to do with who he really was and where his loyalties lay. But he could imagine Helen's reaction to this minor and assuredly inconsequential battle with lust-in-the-heart, so he engaged in a mental explanation of his behaviour, using terms like *idle curiosity* and *scientific study* and *for God's sake stop overreacting to things, Helen*, as if she were present, standing in the corner, silently watching, and knowing his thoughts.

Maggie Spence was in a Latin lesson, Mrs. Crone told him. Couldn't this wait until lunch? A quarter of an hour?

It couldn't, actually. And even if it could, he'd prefer to make contact with the girl in complete privacy. At lunch, with other pupils milling about, there was the chance they'd be seen. He'd like to spare the girl whatever potential embarrassment he could. It couldn't be easy for her, after all, with her mother having been under police scrutiny once already and now under it again. Did Mrs. Crone know her mother, by the way?

She'd met her on Speech Day in Easter term last year. A very nice woman. A firm disciplinarian, but very loving towards Maggie, obviously devoted to the child's every interest. Society could use a few more parents like Mrs. Spence behind our nation's youth, couldn't it, Inspector.

Indeed. Mrs. Crone would get no disagreement from him. Now about seeing Maggie . . . ?

Did her mother know he'd come?

If Mrs. Crone would like to phone her . . .

The headmistress eyed him carefully and scrutinised his warrant card with such attention that he thought she was going to try it for gold between her teeth. At last she handed it back to him and said she would send for the girl if the Inspector would be so good as to wait here. They could use this study as well, she informed him, as she herself was on her way to the dining hall where she would remain on duty while the pupils had their lunch. But she expected the In-spector to allow Maggie time for hers, she warned in parting, and if the girl wasn't in the dining hall by a quarter past twelve, Mrs. Crone would send someone to fetch her. Was that clear? Did they understand each other?

They certainly did.

In less than five minutes, the study door opened and Lynley stood as Maggie Spence came into the room. She shut the door behind her with unnecessary care, turning the knob to make certain the activity was done in perfect silence. She faced him across the room, hands clasped behind her back, head lowered.

He knew that in comparison with today's youth, his own introduction to sexual activity—enthusiastically orchestrated by the mother of one of his friends during the half-term at Lent in his final year at Eton—had been relatively late. He'd just turned eighteen. But despite the change in mores and the bent towards youthful profligacy, he found it difficult to believe that this girl was engaged in sexual experimentation of any kind.

She looked too like a child. Part of this was her height. She couldn't have been much more than an inch over five feet tall. Part was her posture and demeanour. She stood slightly pigeon-toed with her navy stockings bunched a bit at her ankles, and she shuffled on her feet, bent her ankles outwards, and looked as if she expected to be caned. The rest was personal appearance. The rules of the school may have forbidden the wearing of make-up, but surely nothing prevented her from taking a more adult approach with her hair. This was thick, the only attribute she shared with her mother. It fell to her waist in a wavy mass and was drawn back from her face and held in place with a large amber barrette shaped like a bow. She wore no bob, no shelf-cut, no sophisticated French braid. She made no attempt to emulate an actress or a rock-and-roll star.

"Hello," he said to her, finding that he spoke as gently as he would have done to a frightened kitten. "Has Mrs. Crone told you who I am, Maggie?"

"Yes. But she needn't have done. I knew already." Her arms moved. She seemed to be twisting her hands behind her back. "Nick said last night you'd come to the village. He saw you in the pub. He said you'd be wanting to talk to all of Mr. Sage's good mates."

"And you're one of them, aren't you?"

She nodded.

"It's rough to lose a friend."

She made no reply, merely shuffled again on her feet. This appeared to be another similarity to her mother. He was reminded of Mrs. Spence's digging at the terrace weeds with the toe of her boot.

"Join me," he said. "I'd prefer to sit down, if you don't mind."

He drew a second chair to the window, and when she sat, she

finally looked up at him. Her sky-blue eyes regarded him frankly, with hesitant curiosity but no trace of guile. She was sucking on the inside of her lower lip. The action deepened a dimple in her cheek.

Now that she was closer to him, he could more easily recognise the budding woman that was altering forever the shell of the child. She had a generous mouth. Her breasts were full. Her hips were just wide enough to be welcoming. Hers was the sort of body that was probably going to fight off weight in middle age. But now, under the staid school uniform of skirt, blouse, and jumper, it was ripe and ready. If it was at the insistence of Juliet Spence that Maggie used no make-up and wore a hairstyle more suited to a ten-year-old than to a teenager, Lynley found he couldn't blame her.

"You weren't at the cottage the night that Mr. Sage died, were you?" he asked her.

She shook her head.

"But you were there during the day?"

"Off and on. It was Christmas hols, see."

"You didn't want to have dinner with Mr. Sage? He was your mate, after all. I wonder you didn't welcome the chance."

Her left hand covered her right. She held them balled in her lap. "It was the night of the monthly doss-round," she said. "Josie, Pam, and me. We spent the night with each other."

"Something you do every month?"

"In alphabetical order. Josie, Maggie, Pam. It was Josie's turn. That's always the funnest because if they aren't booked up, Josie's mum lets us choose whatever room in the inn we fancy. We took the skylight room. It's up under the eaves. It was snowing and we liked to watch it settle on the glass." She was sitting up straight, her ankles properly crossed. Wisps of russet hair uncontrolled by the barrette curled against her cheeks and her forehead. "Dossing at Pam's is the worse because we have to sleep in the sitting room. That's on account of her brothers. They have the upstairs bedroom. They're twins. Pam doesn't like them much. She thinks it's disgusting that her mummy and dad made more babies at their age. They're forty-two, Pam's mummy and dad. Pam says it gives her the creeps to think of her mum and dad like that. But I think they're sweet. The twins, I mean."

"How do you organise the doss-round?" Lynley asked.

"We don't, ac'shully. We just do it."

"With no plan?"

"Well, we know it's the third Friday of the month, don't we? And we just follow the alphabet like I said. Josie-Maggie-Pam. Pam's next. We did my house this month already. I thought maybe Josie and Pam's mummies wouldn't let them doss with me this time round. But they did."

"You were worried because of the inquest?"

"It was over, wasn't it, but people in the village . . . " She looked out the window. Two grey-hooded jackdaws had landed on the sill and were pecking furiously at three crusts of bread, each bird trying to jockey the other from the perch and hence claim the remaining crust. "Mrs. Crone likes to feed the birds. She's got a big cage-thing in her garden where she raises finches. And she always puts seed or something else to eat on the window-sill here. I think that's nice. Except birds quarrel over food. Have you ever noticed? They always act like there won't be enough. I can't think why."

"And the people in the village?"

She said, "I see them watching me sometimes. They stop talking when I pass. But Josie and Pam's mummies don't do that." She dismissed the birds and offered him a smile. The dimple made her face both lopsided and endearing. "Last spring we had a doss-round in the Hall. Mummy said we could, so long as we didn't mess anything about. We took sleeping bags. We dossed in the dining room. Pam wanted to go upstairs but Josie and I were afraid we'd see the ghost. So Pam went up the stairs with a torch 'n slept by herself in the west wing. Only we found out later she wasn't by herself at all. Josie didn't think much of that, did she? She said this was supposed to be just for *us*, Pamela. No men allowed. Pam said you're just jealous because you've never had a man, have you? Josie said I've had plenty of men, Miss-Any-Bloke's-Scrubber—which wasn't exactly the truth—and they had such a quarrel that for the next two months Pam wouldn't come to the doss-round at all. But then she did again."

"Do all of your mums know which night the doss-round is set for?"

"The third Friday of the month. Everyone knows."

"Did you know you'd be missing a dinner with the vicar if you went to Josie's for the December doss-round?"

She nodded. "But I sort of thought he wanted to see Mummy alone."

"Why?"

She played her thumb back and forth against the sleeve of her jumper, rolling and unrolling it against her white blouse. "Mr. Shepherd does, doesn't he. I thought p'rhaps it would be like that."

"Thought or hoped?"

She looked at him earnestly. "He'd come before, Mr. Sage. Mummy sent me to visit with Josie, so I thought she was interested. They talked, him and Mummy. Then he came again. I thought if he fancied her, I could help out by being off. But then I found out he didn't fancy her at all. Not Mummy. And she didn't fancy him."

Lynley frowned. A small alarm was buzzing in his head. He didn't like the sound of it.

"What do you mean?"

"Well, they didn't do anything, did they. Not like her and Mr. Shepherd."

"They'd only seen each other a few times, though. Isn't that the case?"

Her head bobbed in agreement. "But he never talked about Mummy when I saw him. And he never asked after her like I thought he would if he fancied her."

"What did he talk about?"

"He liked films and books. He talked about them. And the Bible. Sometimes he read me stories from the Bible. He liked the one about the old men who watched the lady taking a bath in the bushes. I mean the old men were in the bushes, not the lady. They wanted to have sex with her because she was so young and beautiful and even though they were old, it wasn't like they'd stopped feeling desires themselves. Mr. Sage explained it. He was good at that."

"What other things did he explain?"

"Mostly about me. Like why I was feeling how I felt about . . . " She gave the wrist of her jumper a little twist. "Oh, just stuff."

"Your boyfriend? Having intercourse with him?"

She dropped her head and concentrated on the jumper. Her stomach growled. "Hungry," she mumbled. Still, she didn't look up.

"You must have been close to the vicar," Lynley said.

"He said it wasn't bad, what I felt for Nick. He said desire was natural. He said everyone felt it. He even felt it, he said."

Again the buzzing, that insidious alarm. Lynley observed the girl carefully, trying to read behind every word she was uttering, wondering how much she was leaving unsaid. "Where did you have these conversations, Maggie?"

"In the vicarage. Polly'd make tea and bring it into the study. We'd eat Jaffa Cakes and talk."

"Alone?"

She nodded. "Polly didn't much like to talk about the Bible. She doesn't go to church. Course, we don't either."

"But he talked about the Bible with you."

"Mostly because we were friends. You can talk about stuff with your friends, he said. You can tell who your friends are because they listen."

"You listened to him. He listened to you. You were special to each other."

"We were mates." She smiled. "Josie said the vicar liked me better'n anyone in the parish and I didn't even go to church. She was miffed at that, was Josie. She said why does he want *you* for tea and for walks on the moors, Miss Maggie Spence? I said he was lonely and I was his friend."

"Did he tell you he was lonely?"

"He didn't have to. I knew. He was always glad to see me. He always gave me a hug when I left. He was good at hugs."

"You liked them."

"Yes."

He let a moment pass as he considered how best to approach the subject without frightening her off. Mr. Sage had been her friend, her trusted companion. Whatever they had shared had been sacred to the girl.

"It's nice to be hugged," he said musingly. "Few things are nicer, if you ask me." He could tell she was watching him, and he wondered if she sensed his hesitation. This type of interview wasn't his forte. It required the surgical skill of a psychologist, touching as it did upon fear and taboo. He was feeling his way forward on precarious ground and not particularly happy about being there. "Friends have secrets sometimes, Maggie, things they know about each other, things they say, things they do together. Sometimes it's the secrets and the promise of keeping them that make them friends in the first place. Was that how it was between you and Mr. Sage?"

She was silent. He saw that she had gone back to sucking on the inside of her lower lip. A wedge of mud had fallen to the floor from between the heel and the sole of one of her shoes. In her restless movement on the chair, she had crushed the mud to brown shards on the Axminster carpet. Mrs. Crone wouldn't be pleased with that.

"Were they a worry to your mum, Maggie? The promises perhaps? The secrets?"

"He liked me better'n anyone," she said.

"Did your mum know that?"

"He wanted me to be in the social club. He said he'd speak with her so she would let me join. They were going to take an excursion to London. He asked me special did I want to go. They were going to have a Christmas party as well. He said surely Mummy would let me come to that. They talked on the phone."

"The day he died?"

It was too quick a question. She blinked rapidly and said, "Mummy didn't do anything. Mummy wouldn't hurt anyone."

"Did she ask him for dinner that night, Maggie?"

The girl shook her head. "Mummy didn't say."

"She didn't invite him?"

"She didn't say she asked him."

"But she told you he was coming."

Maggie weighed an answer. He could see her doing so, the action evident from the manner in which her eyes lowered to the level of his chest. He needed no additional reply.

"How did you know he was coming if she didn't tell you?"

"He phoned. I heard."

"What?"

"It was about the social club, the party, like I said. Mummy sounded cross. 'I have no intention of letting her go. There's no point in discussing this any further.' That's what she said. Then he said something. He went on and on. And she said he could come for dinner and they'd talk about it then. But I didn't think she was going to change her mind."

"That very night?"

"Mr. Sage always said one had to strike while the poker could get to the wood." She frowned thoughtfully. "Or something like that. He never took a first no to mean an always no. He knew I wanted to be in the club. He thought it was important."

"Who directs the club?"

"No one. Not now that Mr. Sage's dead."

"Who was in it?"

"Pam and Josie. Girls from the village. Some from the farms."

"No boys?"

"Just two." She wrinkled her nose. "The boys were being stubborn about joining. 'But we shall win them over in the end,' Mr. Sage said. 'We shall put our heads together and develop a plan.' That's part of the reason why he wanted me in the club, you see."

"So that you could put your heads together?" Lynley asked blandly.

She didn't react. "So that Nick would join. 'Cause if Nick joined, the rest would follow. Mr. Sage knew that. Mr. Sage knew everything."

.   .   .

Rule One: Trust your intuition.
Rule Two: Back it up with the facts.
Rule Three: Make an arrest.

Rule Four had something to do with where an officer of the law should relieve himself after consuming four pints of Guinness at the conclusion of a case, and Rule Five referred to the single activity most highly recommended as a form of celebration once the guilty party was brought to justice. Detective Inspector Angus MacPherson had handed out the rules, printed on garish hot-pink cards with suitable illustrations, during a divisional meeting at New Scotland Yard one day, and while the fourth and fifth rules had been the cause of general guffawing and lewd remarks, the first three Lynley had clipped from the rest during an idle moment while waiting on hold on the telephone. He used them for a bookmark. He considered them an addendum to the Judges' Rules.

The intuitive deduction that Maggie was central to Mr. Sage's death had brought him to the Clitheroe grammar school in the first place. Nothing she had said during their conversation disabused him of that belief.

A lonely, middle-aged man and a young girl poised on the brink of womanhood made for an uneasy combination, no matter the man's ostensible rectitude and the girl's overt naiveté. If sifting through the ashes of Robin Sage's death disclosed a meticulous approach to the seduction of a child, Lynley would not be at all surprised. It wouldn't be the first time molestation had worn the guise of friendship and sanctity. It wouldn't be the last. The fact that the violation was perpetrated upon a child was part of its insidious allure. And in this case, because the child was already sexual, whatever guilt might otherwise stay the hand of captivation could be easily ignored.

She was eager for friendship and approval. She yearned for the warmth of contact. What better fodder could possibly exist to satiate a man's mere physical desire? It wouldn't necessarily have been an issue of power with Robin Sage. Nor would it have naturally been a demonstration of his inability to forge or maintain an adult relationship. It could have been human temptation, pure and simple. He was good at hugs, as Maggie had said. She was a child who welcomed them. That she was actually far more than a child might have been something the vicar discovered to his own surprise.

And what then, Lynley wondered. Arousal and Sage's failure to master it? The itch in the palms to peel back clothing and expose bare flesh? Those two traitors to detachment—heat and blood—pulsing in the groin and demanding action? And that clever whisper in the back of the brain: What difference does it make, she's already doing it, she's nobody's innocent, it's not as if you're seducing a virgin, if she doesn't like it she can tell you to stop, just hug her close so she can feel you and know, graze her breasts quickly, glide a hand between her thighs, talk about how nice it is to be cuddled, just the two of us, Maggie, our special secret, my finest little mate...

It all could have happened over a few short weeks. She was at odds with her mother. She needed a friend.

Lynley pulled the Bentley into the street, drove to the corner, and made the turn to head back into the centre of the town. It was possible, he thought. But at this point so was anything else. He was running before his horse to market. Rule One was crucial. There was no doubting that. But it could not overshadow Rule Two.

He began to look for a phone.

CHAPTER FIFTEEN

NEAR THE SUMMIT OF COTES FELL, FROM above the standing stone they called Great North, Colin Shepherd gathered what he hadn't previously added to his storehouse of facts surrounding the death of Robin Sage: When the mist dissipated or when the wind made it drift, one could see the grounds of Cotes Hall quite clearly, especially in winter when the trees bore no leaves. A few yards below, leaning against the stone for a smoke or a rest, one was limited to viewing the old mansion's roof with its mishmash of chimney-pots, dormer windows, and weathervanes. But climb a bit higher to the summit and sit in the shelter of that limestone outcropping that curved like the punctuation of a question which no one would ask, and one could see everything, from the Hall itself in all its ghoulish decrepitude, to the courtyard it surrounded on three sides, from the grounds that crept out from it, reclaimed by nature, to the outbuildings intended to serve its needs. Among these last was the cottage, and it was to the cottage and into its garden that Colin had watched Inspector Lynley go.

While Leo dashed from one point of canine interest to another at the summit of the fell, led by his nose into a happy exploration of scent, Colin followed Lynley's movements across the garden and into the greenhouse, marvelling at the clear vista he had. From below, the mist had looked much like a solid wall, impedimentary to movement and impenetrable to vision. But here, what had seemed both impassable and opaque proved to have the substance of cobwebs. It was damp and cold but otherwise of little account.

He watched everything, counting the minutes they spent inside the greenhouse, taking note of their exploration of the cellar. He filed away the fact that the kitchen door of the cottage had been left unlocked behind them when they made their way into the courtyard and across the grounds, just as it had been unlocked while Juliet worked in solitude in her greenhouse and when she opened it to fetch the cellar key. He saw them pause for conversation upon the terrace, and when Juliet gestured towards the pond, he could have predicted what would follow.

Throughout it all, he could hear as well. Not their conversation, but the distinct sound of music. Even when a sudden gust of wind altered the density of the mist, he could still hear that spritely march playing.

Anyone who took the trouble to climb Cotes Fell would know of the comings and goings at the Hall and at the cottage. It wasn't even necessary to take the risk of trespassing on the Townley-Young land. The hike to the summit was a public footpath, after all. While the going was occasionally steep—especially the last stretch above Great North—it wasn't enough to tax the endurance of anyone Lancashire born and bred. It was especially not enough to tax the endurance of a woman who made it a regular climb.

When Lynley had reversed his monster of a car out of the courtyard in preparation for the return drive through the potholes and mud that kept most visitors away, Colin turned from the view and walked over to the question-mark limestone outcropping. He squatted in its shelter, thoughtfully scooped up a handful of shards and pebbles, and let them spill back onto the ground from his loosened fist. Leo joined him, giving the exterior of the outcropping a thorough olfactory examination and dislodging a miniature landslide of shale. From his jacket pocket, Colin removed a chewed-up tennis ball. He played it back and forth beneath Leo's nose, hurled it into the mist, and watched the dog trot happily in pursuit. He moved with perfect sure-footed grace, did Leo. He knew his job and had no trouble doing it.

A short distance from the outcropping, Colin could see a thin, earthen scar marking the hardy grass that was indigenous to the moors and the hillsides. It formed a circle approximately nine feet in diameter, its circumference delineated by stones that were spaced out evenly, perhaps twelve inches apart. At the circle's centre lay an oblong of granite, and he didn't need to approach and examine it to know it would bear the leavings of melted wax, the scratches made by a gypsy-pot, and the distinct etching of a five-pointed star.

It was no secret to anyone in the village that the top of Cotes Fell was a sacred place. It was heralded by Great North, long reputed to be capable of giving psychic answers to questions if the questioner both asked and listened with a pure heart and a receptive mind. Its oddly shaped outcropping of limestone was seen by some as a fertility symbol, the stomach of a mother, swollen with life. And its finial of granite—so like an altar that the similarities could not be easily ignored—had been well-established as a geological oddity in the early decades of the last century. This, then, was a place of ancients where the old ways endured.

The Yarkins had been chief practitioners of the Craft and worshippers of the Goddess for as long as Colin could remember. They had never made a secret of it. They went about the business of chants, rituals, candle or cord spells, and incantations with a devotion that had garnered them, if not respect, at least a higher degree of toleration than one would normally expect from villagers whose circumscribed lives and limited experience often promoted a conservative bias towards God, monarch, country, and nothing else. But in times of desperation, anyone's influence with any Almighty was generally welcome. So if illness struck a beloved child, if a farmer's sheep were dropping with disease, if a soldier was due to be posted in Northern Ireland, no one ever declined Rita or Polly Yarkin's offer to cast the circle and petition the Goddess. Who really knew, after all, which Deity listened? Why not hedge one's religious bets, cover every one of the supernatural bases, and hope for the best?

He'd even done it himself, allowing Polly to climb this hill time and again for Annie's sake. She wore a gold robe. She carried laurel branches in a basket. She burned them along with cloves for incense. With an alphabet he couldn't read and didn't truly believe was real, she carved her request into a thick orange candle and burned it down, asking for a miracle, telling him that anything was possible if the heart of the witch was pure. After all, hadn't Nick Ware's mum got her boy-child at last, and her all of forty-nine years old when she had him? Hadn't Mr. Townley-Young seen fit to grant an unheard of pension to the men who worked his farms? Hadn't Fork Reservoir been developed to provide new jobs for the county? These, Polly said, were the boons of the Goddess.

She never permitted him to watch a ritual. He wasn't a practitioner, after all. Nor was he an initiate. Some things, she said, couldn't be allowed. So if the truth be faced, he never knew what she actually did when she reached the top of the fell. He had never once heard her make a request.

But from the top of the fell, where from the wax drippings on the granite altar Colin knew she still was practising the Craft, Polly could see Cotes Hall. She would have been able to monitor movements in the courtyard, on the grounds, and in the cottage garden. No arrival or departure would have gone unnoticed, and even if someone headed from the cottage into the wood, she could see that from here.

Colin stood and whistled for Leo. The dog came bounding out of the mist. He carried the tennis ball in his mouth and dropped it playfully at Colin's feet, his snout a mere inch or two away, ready to snatch it back should his master reach for it. Colin entertained the retriever with the bit of tug-and-pull that he wanted, smiling at the artificiality of the dog's protective growls. Finally, Leo released the ball, backed off a few steps, and waited for the throw. Colin hurled it down the hillside in the direction of the Hall and watched as the dog gambolled after it.

Colin followed slowly, keeping to the footpath. He paused by Great North and put his hand against it, feeling the quick shock of cold that the ancients would have called the rock's magical power.

"Did she?" he asked and closed his eyes for the answer. He could feel it in his fingers. *Yes . . . yes . . .*

The descent wasn't consistently sharp. The walk was a cold one, but it wasn't impossible. So many feet had carved out the track over time that the grass, which was slippery with frost in other areas, was worn through to the earth and stones on the path. The resulting friction against the soles of one's shoes eliminated much risk. Anyone could make the walk up Cotes Fell. One could walk it in the mist. One could walk it at night.

It switched back on itself three times so that the vista it provided was continually changing. A view of the Hall became one of the dale with Skelshaw Farm in the distance. A moment later, the sight of Skelshaw Farm gave way to the church and cottages of Winslough.

And finally, as the slope became pasture at the bottom of the fell, the footpath edged the grounds of Cotes Hall.

Colin paused here. There was no stile in the drystone wall to allow a hiker easy access to the Hall. But like many areas of the countryside that have gone untended, the wall was in marginal disrepair. Brambles overgrew it in some sections. Others gaped open with small pyramids of rubble lying beneath them. It would take little effort to climb through the gap. He did it himself, whistling for the dog who followed.

The land here dipped a second time, in a gradual slope that ended at the pond, some twenty yards away. Reaching this, Colin looked back the way he had come. He could make out Great North, but beyond it nothing. The mist and the sky were monochromatic, and the frost on the land provided no contrast. They hid without even appearing to hide. An observer couldn't have asked for more.

He skirted the pond with the dog at his heels, stopping to crouch and examine the root that Juliet had unearthed for Lynley. He rubbed its surface, disclosing the dirty-ivory flesh, and he pressed his thumbnail against the stem. A thin bleeding of oil the width of a needle oozed out. *Yes . . . yes.*

He flung it into the middle of the pond and watched it sink. The water undulated in growing circles that lapped at the edges of the grimy ice. He said, "Leo. No," when the dog's instincts to fetch took him too close to the water's edge. He took the tennis ball from him, threw it the distance to the terrace, and followed him after it.

She would be back in the greenhouse. He'd seen her return there when Lynley left, and he knew she'd be seeking the release that came from potting, trimming, and otherwise working with her plants. He thought about stopping. He felt the urge to share with her what he knew so far. But she wouldn't want to hear it. She would protest and find the idea repellent. So instead of crossing the courtyard and entering the garden, he headed down the lane. When he came to the first gap in the bordering lavender, he slipped through it with the dog and went into the wood.

A quarter of an hour's walk brought him to the rear of the lodge. There was no garden, just an open plot of land comprising leaves, mud, and one anemic Italian cypress that appeared to be longing for transplantation. This leaned at a windblown angle against the lodge's only outbuilding, a ramshackle shed with gaps in the roof.

The door bore no lock. It also possessed neither knob nor handle, just a rusty ring, survivor of neglect and the vicissitudes of weather. When he pushed upon it, one hinge came apart from the frame, screws tumbled out of the rotten wood, and the door sagged into a narrow depression in the soggy ground where it fit quite naturally as if used to the place. The resulting aperture was large enough for him to slip through.

He waited for his eyes to adjust to the change in light. There was no window, just the gray illumination of the day, filtering through the poorly sealed walls and streaking in a thin seam from the door. Outside, he heard the dog sniffing round the base of the cypress. Inside, he heard nothing save the sound of his own breathing, amplified as it struck the wall in front of him and returned.

Forms began to emerge. What was first a slab of wood at waist height, jammed with an odd assortment of shapes, became a workbench holding sealed gallon tins of paint. Among these lay stiffened brushes, petrified rollers, and a stack of aluminum trays. Two cartons of nails lay behind the paint, along with a quart jar on its side, spilling out an assortment of screws, nuts, and bolts. Everything was covered with what appeared to be at least a decade of grime.

Between two of the paint tins, a spider's web hung. It trembled with his movement but held no spider lying in wait at its centre. Colin passed his hand through it, feeling the ghost-touch of the strands against his skin. They bore no trace of the mucilage produced to trap flying insects. The web's solitary architect was long since gone.

None of that mattered. One could enter the shed without disturbing its appearance of disuse and its air of decay. He had done so himself.

He ran his eyes over the walls where nails held tools and gardening implements: a rusty saw, a hoe, a rake, two shovels, and one balding broom. Beneath them a green hose pipe coiled. At its centre stood a dented pail. He looked inside. The pail held only a pair of gardening gloves with thumb and index finger worn through on the right hand. He examined these. They were large, a man's. They fitted his own hands. And in the spot where they had laid at the bottom of the pail, the metal shone bright and winked clean in the light. He returned them and went back to the search.

A sack of lawnseed, another of fertiliser, and a third of peat leaned against a black wheelbarrow which was upended into the farthest corner. He moved these to one side and pulled the barrow away from the wall to look behind it. A small wooden crate filled with rags gave off a faint odour of rodents. He upended the crate, saw two small creatures scurry for cover under the workbench, and rustled through the rags with the toe of his boot. He found nothing. But the barrow and the bags had looked as undisturbed as the rest of the objects in the shed, so he wasn't surprised, just thoughtful.

There were two possibilities, and he mulled them over as he returned everything to its appropriate place. One was implied by the unmistakable absence of small handtools. He had seen no hammer for the nails, no driver for the screws, no spanner for the nuts and the bolts. More importantly, he had seen neither trowel nor cultivator despite the presence of rake, hoe, and shovels. Disposing of either the trowel or the cultivator would have been too obvious, of course. Disposing of them all was decidedly clever.

The second possibility was that there had been no handtools in the first place, that the long-departed Mr. Yarkin had removed them along with himself upon his hasty flight from Winslough more than twenty-five years ago. They would have made an odd addition to his baggage, to be sure, but perhaps he'd wanted them for his work. What had it been? Colin tried to recall. Was it carpentry? Then why leave the saw, if that was the case?

He carried his developing scenario further. If there were no handtools here at the lodge, she would have known where to borrow what she needed. She would have known when to do the borrowing since she could have waited for the moment from her perch on Cotes Fell. For that matter, she could even have watched for her moment from the lodge. It sat on the edge of the estate grounds, after all. She would have heard any car pass, and a quick trip to the window would have told her who was driving.

That made the most sense. Even if she had her own tools, why would she run the risk of using them when she could use Juliet's and replace them in the greenhouse with no one's being the wiser? She'd have to go into the garden anyway, in order to get to the cellar. Yes. That was it. She had motive, means, and opportunity, and although Colin felt certainty quicken his pulse, he knew he couldn't afford to proceed along this line of suspicion without making solid a few more facts.

He eased the door closed and tramped through the mud to the

lodge. Leo trotted out of the wood, a picture of complete dog bliss with his coat hung with small clods of humus and his ears decorated with blackened, dead leaves. This was a day to be celebrated for the dog: a hike up the fell, a bit of run-and-chase, a chance to get thoroughly filthy in the wood. Forget retrieving when he could root round the oaks like a pig after truffles.

"Stay," Colin said to him, pointing to a beaten-down patch of weeds by the door. He knocked and hoped the day would be one of celebration for himself as well.

He heard her before she opened the door. The sound of her footsteps rumbled on the floor. The sound of her wheezing accompanied her action of unfastening bolts. Then she stood before him like a walrus on ice, one hand spread out on her massive chest as if its pressure could relieve her breathing. He could see that he had interrupted her in the process of painting her nails. Two were aquamarine, three were uncoloured. All were inhumanly long.

She said, "By the stars and sun, if it a'nt Mr. C. Shepherd hisself," and she looked him over from head to foot, her eyes lingering longest upon his groin. Under her gaze, he felt the oddest sensation of heat throbbing in his testicles. As if she knew this, Rita Yarkin smiled and emitted a sigh of what appeared to be pleasure. "So. What're you about, Mr. C. Shepherd? You here as the hopeful answer to a maiden's prayers? Myself being the maiden, of course. Wouldn't want you to misapprehend my meaning."

"I'd like to come in, if that's all right," he said.

"Would you now?" She shifted her bulk against the door-jamb. The wood groaned. She reached out—at least a dozen bangles rattling like manacles round her wrist—and ran her fingers over his hair. He did his best not to cringe. "Cobwebs," she said. "Mmmmm. Here's another. Where you been putting this pretty head, luv?"

"May I come inside, Mrs. Yarkin?"

"Rita." She looked him over. "I s'pose it depends on what you mean by 'come inside.' Now there's lots of women would welcome you coming wherever you want and just about whenever the fancy takes you. But me? Well, I'm just a bit p'rticular about my toy boys. Always have been."

"Is Polly here?"

"It's Polly you're after, is it, Mr. C. Shepherd? Now I wonder why? Is she good enough for you, all of a sudden? Did you get thrown over by her up the lane?"

"Look, Rita, I don't want a row with you. Are you going to let me in or shall I come back later?"

She played with one of the three necklaces she wore. It was beads and feathers with the wooden head of a goat as its pendant. "I can't think we got anything here as will interest you."

"Perhaps. When did you come this year?" He saw his error in vocabulary from the way her mouth twitched in response. He headed her off by saying, "When did you arrive in Winslough?"

"Twenty-fourth of December. Same as always."

"After the vicar's death."

"Yeah. Never got to meet the bloke. From the way Polly talked about him and everything that happened, I would've liked to read his palm." She reached for Colin's hand. "Have yours done, luv?" And when he freed himself from her grip, "Scared to know the future, are you? So's most people. Let's have a look. The news is good, you pay. The news is bad, I keep my mug tight shut. Sound like a deal?"

"If you'll let me in."

She smiled and waddled back from the door. "Have at me, luv. Have you ever poked a woman weighing twenty stone? I got more places you can stick it than you got time to explore."

"Right," Colin said. He squeezed past her. She was wearing enough perfume to permeate the entire lodge. It came off her in waves, like heat from a coal fire. He tried not to breathe.

They stood in a narrow entrance that did duty as a service porch. He untied his muddy boots and left them among the Wellingtons, umbrellas, and mackintoshes. He took his time about this process of untying and removing, using the activity as a means of observing what the porch held. He made particular note of what stood next to a rubbish bin of mouldy brussels sprouts, mutton bones, four empty packets for Custard Cremes, the remains of a breakfast of fried bread and bacon, and a broken lamp without its shade. This was a basket, and it contained potatoes, carrots, marrows, and a head of lettuce.

"Polly's done the shopping?" he asked.

"That's day before yesterday's. Brought it by at noon, she did."

"Does she bring you parsnips for dinner occasionally?"

"Sure. 'Long with everything else. Why?"

"Because one doesn't need to buy them. They grow wild here-abouts. Did you know that?"

Rita's talon nail was tracing the pendant-head of the goat. She played with one horn, then the other. She gave a sensual stroke to the beard. She regarded Colin thoughtfully. "And what if I do?"

"Did you tell Polly, I wonder. It would be a waste of money to have her buy from the greengrocer what she could dig up herself."

"True. But my Polly's not much for rooting, Mr. Constable. We like the natural life, make no mistake there, but Polly's a girl who draws the line at grubbing round the wood on her hands and knees. Unlike some as I could name, she's got better things to do, does Polly."

"But she knows her plants. It's part of the Craft. You have to know all the different woods for burning. You'd have to recognise your herbs as well. Doesn't the ritual call for their use?"

Rita's face became blank. "Ritual calls for the use of more'n you know or understand, Mr. C. Shepherd. And none of it I'll be likely to share with you."

"But there's magic in herbs?"

"There's magic in lots of things. But all of it springs from the will of the Goddess, praised be Her name, whether you're using the moon, the stars, the earth, or the sun."

"Or the plants."

"Or water or fire or anything. It's the mind of the petitioner and the will of the Goddess that make the magic. It's not to be found in mixing potions and drinking'm down." She lumbered through the far doorway and into the kitchen where she went to the tap and held a kettle beneath a dismal trickle of water.

Colin took the opportunity to complete his examination of the service porch. It held a bizarre variety of Yarkin possessions, everything from two bicycle wheels minus their tyres to a rusty anchor with one prong missing. A basket for a long-departed cat occupied one corner, and it was heaped with a mound of tattered paperback books whose covers appeared to feature women of impressive bosom caught up in the arms of men on the verge of ravishing them. *Love's Savage Desperation* blazed across one cover. *Passion's Lost Child* adorned another. If a set of handtools were secreted in the porch among the cardboard cartons of old clothes, the antique Hoover, and the ironing board, it would take a thirteenth labour of Heracles in order to find them.

Colin joined Rita in the kitchen. She'd gone to the table where, among the remains of her mid-morning coffee and crumpets, she had returned to painting her nails. The scent of the polish was making a valiant effort to dominate both her perfume and the smell of bacon grease that seemed to be crackling in a frying pan on the cooker. Colin switched the pan's place with the kettle of water. Rita gestured her thanks with the nail-polish brush, and he wondered what had inspired her choice of colour and where she had managed to purchase it in the first place.

He said by way of edging cagily towards the purpose of his visit, "I came in the back way."

"So I noticed, sweet face."

"I mean through the garden. I had a look at your shed. It's in bad shape, Rita. The door's come off its hinges. Shall I fix it for you?"

"Why, that's a first-rate, bang-on idea, Mr. Constable."

"Have you any tools?"

"Must have. Somewhere." She examined her right hand, languidly holding it out at arm's length.

"Where?"

"Don't know, sweet."

"Would Polly?"

She waggled her hand.

"Does she use them, Rita?"

"Could be. Could not. But it's not like we're dead interested in home improvement, is it?"

"That's typical, I'd think. When women don't have a man in the house for a long period of time, they—"

"I didn't mean me and Polly," she said. "I mean me and you. Or is that part of your job these days, popping through back gardens and checking on sheds and offering to fix them for helpless ladies?"

"We're old friends. I'm happy to be of help."

She sputtered with a laugh. "I bet you are. Happy as a ram at the rut, Mr. Constable, just being helpful. Bet if I ask Polly, she'll tell me you been stopping by once or twice a week for years, ready to help her out with her chores." She laid her left hand on the table and reached for her polish.

The kettle began to boil. He fetched it from the cooker. She had already prepared two thick mugs for the water. A glittering heap of what appeared to be instant coffee crystals lay at the bottom of each. One mug had already been used, if the ring of red lipstick was any indication. The other—printed with the word *Pisces* above which a silvery green fish swam in a current of cracked azure glaze—apparently was intended for him. He hesitated fractionally before pouring the water, tilting the mug towards him as surreptitiously as possible for examination.

Rita eyed him and gave him a wink. "G'on, luv-bunny. Take a little chance. We all got to go sometime, don't we?" She chuckled and bent her head to the work of painting her nails.

He poured the water. There was only one teaspoon on the table, already used by the look of it. His stomach felt queasy at the thought of putting it into his mug, but considering the boiling water as a steriliser, he dipped it in quickly and made a few rapid, conciliatory revolutions. He drank. It was definitely coffee.

He said, "I'll have a look for those tools now," and took the mug with him to the dining room, where he placed it on the table and intended to forget it.

"You have a look for whatever you like," Rita called after him. "We got nothing much to hide but what's under our skirts. Let me know if you want a look there."

Her shriek of laughter followed him from the dining room, where a hasty exploration through a dresser disclosed a set of dishes and several tablecloths redolent of moth balls. At the foot of the stairs, a battle-weary Canterbury held yellowing copies of a London tabloid. A quick glance proved that one of the Yarkins had saved only the more delectable issues, featuring two-headed babies, corpses giving birth inside coffins, wolf-children of the circus, and the authorised account of extra-terrestrial visitations to a convent in Southend-on-Sea. He pulled out the single drawer and found himself fingering through small chunks of wood. He recognised the scent of cedar and pine. A leaf was still attached to the laurel. The others he would have been hard pressed to name. But Polly and her mother would have no trouble with the identification. They would know by the colour, the density, the scent.

He climbed the stairs, moving quickly, knowing that Rita was bound to put an end to his search as soon as she'd discovered its limit in amusement value. He looked right and left, assessing the possibilities presented by a bath and two bedrooms. Immediately in front of him stood a leatherbound chest upon which sat an unappealing squat bronze of someone male, priapic, and horned. Across the passage from this a cupboard gaped open, spilling forth linens and assorted jumble. Fourteenth labour of Heracles, he thought. He went for the first bedroom as Rita called his name.

He ignored her, stood in the doorway, and cursed. The woman was a sloth. She'd been in the lodge for more than a month, and she was still living from her mammoth suitcase. What wasn't oozing from this was lying on the floor, on the backs of two chairs, and at the foot of the unmade bed. A dressing table next to the window looked as if it had once been a set-piece in a criminal investigation. Cosmetics and a colour wheel of nail-polish bottles crowded its surface, with an impressive patina of face powder dashed across everything, much like fingerprint dust. Necklaces hung from the door knob and from one of the posters of the bed. Scarves snaked on the floor through discarded shoes. And every inch of the room seemed to emanate Rita's characteristic scent: part ripe fruit on the verge of going bad, part ageing woman in need of a bath.

He made a cursory check of the chest of drawers. He moved on to the wardrobe and then knelt to examine the space beneath the bed. His sole discovery was that the latter served as repository for an extensive array of slut's wool as well as one stuffed black cat with its back arched, its fur at the bristle, and *Rita Knows And Sees* printed on a banner that extended from its tail.

He went to the bath. Rita called his name a second time. He made no reply. He shoved his hands through to the rear of a stack of towels that sat on one of the recessed shelves along with cleanser, scrubbing rags, two kinds of disinfectant, a half-torn print of some Lady Godiva type standing in a clam shell—covering her privates and looking coy—and a pottery toad.

Somewhere in the lodge there had to be something. He felt the fact's certainty just as solidly as he felt the lumpy green linoleum beneath his feet. And if it wasn't the tools, whatever else it might be, he would be able to recognise its significance.

He slid open the mirror of the medicine chest and rooted through aspirin, mouth wash, toothpaste, and laxatives. He went through the pockets of a terry bathrobe that hung limply on the back of the door.

He picked up a stack of paperback books on the top of the toilet's cistern, flipped through them, and set them on the edge of the tub. And then he found it.

The colour caught his eye first: a streak of lavender against the yellow bathroom wall, wedged behind the cistern to keep it out of sight. A book, not large, perhaps five by nine inches, and thin, with its title worn from the spine. He used a toothbrush from the medicine chest to force the book upwards. It flopped onto the floor face up, next to a balled-up washing flannel, and for a moment he merely read its title, savouring the sensation of having his suspicions vindicated.

Alchemical Magic: Herbs, Spices, and Plants.

Why had he thought the proof might be a trowel, a three-pronged cultivator, or a box of tools? Had she used any of those, had she even owned them in the first place, what a simple thing it would have been to dispose of them somewhere. Dig a hole on the estate grounds, bury them in the wood. But this slim volume of incrimination spoke to the truth of what had happened.

He flipped the book open haphazardly, reading chapter titles and feeling each moment ever more sure. "The Harvest's Magic Potential," "Planets and Plants," "Magical Attribution and Application." His eye fell upon descriptions of use. He read the warnings appended as well.

"Hemlock, hemlock," he murmured and riffled through the pages. His hunger for information grew, and facts about hemlock leapt out as if they'd only been waiting for the opportunity to sate him. He read, turned more pages, read again. The words flew up at him, glowed as if rendered in neon against a night sky. And finally the phrase *when the moon is full* stopped him.

He stared at this, unprepared for memory, thinking no, no, no. He felt rage and grief make a knot in his chest.

She'd been lying in bed, she'd asked him to open the curtains wide, she'd watched the moon. It was the bloody orange of autumn, a lunar disc so huge it looked within grasp. Harvest moon best, Col, Annie had whispered. And when he turned from the window, she had sunk into the coma that led to her death.

"No," he whispered. "Not Annie. No."

"Mr. C. Shepherd?" Rita's voice, calling imperiously from below, closer than before. She was near the stairs. "You having a bit of fun with me undies?"

He fumbled with the buttons of his woollen shirt, slipped the book inside, flat against his stomach, and tucked it into the waistband of his trousers. He felt dizzy. A glance in the mirror and he saw the high colour smearing palm prints across his cheeks. He removed his spectacles and bathed his face, holding the icy water against his skin until, from out of the pain of the chill, anaesthesia spread.

He dried his face and studied his reflection. He ran both hands through his hair. He looked at his skin and examined his eyes, and when he was ready to face her with equanimity, he went to the stairs.

She was standing at the bottom, and she slapped the banister. Her bangles rattled. Her triple chin bounced.

"What're you up to, Mr. Constable Shepherd? This a'nt about shed doors and it a'nt a social call."

"Do you know the signs of the zodiac?" he asked her as he descended. He marvelled at the calm of his words.

"Why? Want to see if me and you's compatible? Sure, I know'm. Aries, Cancer, Virgo, Sagi—"

"Capricorn," he said.

"That's you?"

"No. I'm Libra."

"The scales. Nice one, that. Just the thing for your line of work."

"Libra's October. When does Capricorn fall in the calendar year? Do you know, Rita?"

"Course I know. Who d'you think you're jawing, some yobbo on the street? It's December."

"When?"

"Starts the twenty-second, runs for a month. Why? Is her up the lane more goat than you thought?"

"It's just a fancy I had."

"I've one or two of my own." She trundled her enormous weight around and headed back in the direction of the kitchen where she positioned herself at the door to the service porch and wiggled her fingers at him in a come-to-mama gesture made awkward by her care to make certain that the still-tacky nail polish didn't smudge. "Your half of the bargain," she said.

The thought of what she might mean made his legs quiver unexpectedly. "Bargain?" he asked.

"C'mere, luv-bunny. Nothing to fear. I only bite fellahs whose sign is the bull. Give us your palm."

He remembered. "Rita, I don't believe in—"

"The palm." Again, she gestured, more come-hither than come-to-mama this time.

He cooperated. She was, after all, blocking the only reasonable access to his boots.

"Oh, nice hand, this." She ran her fingers the length of his and crossed his palm with a feathery touch. She whispered a circular caress on his wrist. "Very nice," she said, her eyes fluttering closed. "Very nice indeed. A man's hands, these. Hands that belong on a woman's body. Pleasure hands, these. They light fires in the flesh."

"This doesn't sound much like a fortune to me." He tried to pull away. She tightened her grip, one hand on his wrist and the other holding his fingers flat.

She turned his hand and placed it on one of her mounds of flesh that he took to be her breast. She forced his fingers to squeeze. "Like some of that, wouldn't you, Mr. Constable-person. Never had anything quite like it, have you?"

There was truth in that. She didn't feel like a woman. She felt like a quadruple batch of lumpy bread dough. The caress had the approximate appeal of gripping onto a fistful of drying clay.

"Make you want more, luv-bunny? Mmm?" Her eyelashes were painted thick with mascara. They made a crescent of spider legs against her cheek. Her chest rose and fell with a tremulous sigh, and the odour of onions whiffed into his face. "Horned God make him ready," Rita murmured. "Man to a woman, plough to a field, giver of pleasure and the force of life. Aaahhi-oooo-uuuu."

He could feel her nipple, huge and erect, and his body was responding despite the revolting prospect of the two of them . . . himself and Rita Yarkin . . . this whale in a turban of scarlet and pink . . . this mass of fat with fingers that slid up his arm, cast a blessing on his face, and began a suggestive descent down his chest . . .

He pulled his hand away. Her eyes popped open. They seemed dazed and unfocussed, but a shake of her head cleared them. She studied his face and seemed to read what he couldn't hide. She chuckled, then guffawed, then leaned against the kitchen work top and howled.

"You thought . . . You thought . . . Me and you . . ." Between the words, more laughter spewed forth. Tears formed in the creases near her eyes. When she finally controlled herself, she said, "I told you,

Mr. C. Shepherd. When I want it from a man, I get it from a bull."
She blew her nose on a grimy-looking tea towel and held out her
hand. "C'mere. Give it. No more prayers to get your poor little bowels
in an uproar."

"I've got to go."

"Don't you, though." She snapped her fingers for his hand. She
was still blocking egress, so he offered it to her. He made certain his
expression telegraphed how little to his liking this game-playing was.

She pulled him to the sink where the light was better. "Good
lines," she said. "Nice indication of birth and marriage. Love is—"
She hesitated, frowning, absently pulling at one of her eyebrows.
"Get behind me," she said.

"What?"

"Do it. Slip your hand beneath my arm so I can get a better look
at this right side up." When he hesitated, she snapped, "I don't mean
no funny business. Just do it. Now."

He did so. Because of her girth, he couldn't see what she was
doing, but he could feel her fingernails tracing his palm. Finally, she
balled up his hand and released it.

"So," she said briskly. "Not much to see, after all your grumbling.
Just the regular bit. Nothing of importance. Nothing to worry you."
She turned on the tap in the sink and made a project out of rinsing
out three glasses on which a residue of milk had formed a skin.

"You're keeping your part of the bargain, aren't you?" Colin
asked.

"Wha's that, pretty face?"

"Your mug's shut tight."

"'S nothing, is it? You don't believe in it anyways."

"But you do, Rita."

"I believe in lots of things. Don't mean they're real."

"Given. So tell me. I'll be the judge."

"I thought you had important stuff to do, Mr. Constable. Wasn't
that you in a rush to be gone?"

"You're avoiding the answer."

She shrugged.

"I want it."

"You can't have everything you want, sugar pie, much as you've
been currently getting it." She held the glass up to the light of the
window. It was nearly as dirty as when she began. She reached for

some liquid detergent and poured a few drops in. She returned to the water and used a sponge, exerting some rather serious pressure.

"What's that supposed to mean?"

"Don't ask ninny questions. You're a clever enough bloke. You figure it out."

"That's the reading? Convenient for you, the phrasing of it, Rita. Is that the sort of thing you tell the twits who pay you for their fortunes in Blackpool?"

"Steady on," she said.

"It all follows the same pattern, this mumbo-jumbo that you and Polly play at. Stones, palms, and tarot cards. None of it's anything more than a game. You look for a weakness and use it to benefit yourselves with money."

"Your ignorance a'nt worth the effort of response."

"And that's a manoeuvre as well, isn't it? Turn the other cheek but still score a hit. Is that what the Craft's all about? Dried-up women with nothing to live for but the thought of damaging others' lives? A spell here, a curse there, and what does it matter because if someone gets hurt only another member of the Craft will know. And you all hold your tongues, don't you, Rita? Isn't that the blessing of a coven?"

She continued washing one glass after another. She'd chipped one nail. The polish was scarred on another. "Love and death," she said. "Love and death. Three times."

"What?"

"Your palm. A single marriage. But love and death three times. Death. Everywhere. You belong to the priesthood of death, Mr. Constable."

"Oh, quite."

She turned her head from the sink, but her hands went on washing. "It's on your palm, my boy. And the lines don't lie."

CHAPTER SIXTEEN

S T. JAMES HAD BEEN AT A LOSS THE PREVIOUS night. Lying in bed and gazing through the skylight at the stars, he thought about the maddening futility of marriage. He knew that the slow-motion, running-towards-each-other-along-the-beach-for-the-passionate-embrace-before-fade- out celluloid depiction of relationships led the romantic in everyone to anticipate a lifetime of happily-ever-after. He also knew that the reality taught, inch by merciless inch, that if there was a happily of any kind, it never came for an extended stay, and when one opened the door to its ostensible knock, one faced the possibility of admitting instead grumpily, angrily, or a host of others all clamouring for attention. It was sometimes extremely disheartening to have to contend with the messiness of life. He'd been at the point of deciding that the only reasonable way to deal with a woman was not at all when Deborah moved towards him from across the bed.

"I'm sorry," she had whispered and slipped her arm across his chest. "You're my number-one bloke."

He turned to her. She buried her forehead against his shoulder. He put his hand on the back of her neck, feeling the heavy weight of her hair as well as the childlike softness of her skin.

"I'm glad of it," he whispered in return. "Because you're my number-one bit of fluff. Always have been, you know. Always will be."

He could feel her yawn. "It's hard for me," she murmured. "The path's there, isn't it, but it's the first step that's difficult. It keeps messing me up."

"That's the way of things. I suppose it's how we learn." He cradled her. He felt the sleep start to take her. He wanted to call her back from it, but he kissed her head and let her go.

Over breakfast, he'd still maintained caution, however, telling himself that while she was his Deborah, she was also a woman, more mercurial than most. Part of what he savoured about life with her was the unexpected. A newspaper editorial alluding to the possibility of the police manufacturing a case against an IRA suspect was enough to send her into a fury out of which she might decide to organise a photographic odyssey to Belfast or Derry to "find out what's what for myself, by God." A report about cruelty to animals took her to the streets to join in a protest. Discrimination against sufferers from AIDS dispatched her to the first hospice she could find which accepted volunteers to read to patients, to talk, and to be a friend. Because of this, from one day to the next, he was never quite certain what sort of mood he might find her in when he descended the stairs from his lab to join her for lunch or for dinner. The only certainty about life with Deborah was that nothing was particularly certain at all.

He generally revelled in her passionate nature. She was more alive than anyone he knew. But living completely demanded that she feel completely as well, so while her highs were delirious, infused with excitement, her lows were correspondingly empty of hope. And it was the lows that worried him, making him want to advise her to rein herself in. *Try not to feel so deeply* was the counsel he always found himself ready to voice. He'd learned long ago to keep that prescription to himself, however. Telling her not to feel was as good as telling her not to breathe. Besides, he liked the whirl of emotion in which she lived. If nothing else, it kept him from ever being bored.

So when she said, finishing up her grapefruit wedges, "Here's what it is. I need a direction. I don't like the way I've been floundering about. It's time I narrowed my field of vision. I need to make a commitment and go with it," he made a vaguely supportive reply as he wondered what on earth she was talking about.

He said, "Good. That's important." He buttered a triangle of toast. She nodded vigorously at his approval and, with gastronomical enthusiasm, tapped her spoon against the top of her boiled egg. When she didn't appear to be forthcoming with any additional information, he said, in a tentative reconnaissance of her meaning, "Floundering makes one feel as if there's no foundation, don't you think?"

"Simon, that's just exactly it. You always understand."

He mentally patted himself on the back, saying, "A decision about direction gives the foundation, doesn't it?"

"Absolutely." She munched happily on her toast. She was looking out the window at the grey day, damp street, and bleak, sooty buildings. Her eyes were alight with whatever obscure possibilities the icy weather and dismal surroundings promised.

"So," he said, walking a fine line between expansive conclusion and information gathering, "what have you narrowed your vision to?"

"I haven't entirely decided," she said.

"Oh."

She reached for the strawberry jam and plopped a teaspoonful onto her plate. "Except just look at what I've been doing so far. Landscapes, still lifes, portraits. Buildings, bridges, the interior of hotels. I've been eclecticism personified. No wonder I'm not developing a reputation." She smeared jam on the toast and waved it at him. "It's this. I need to make a decision about what sort of photography gives me the most pleasure. I need to follow my heart. I've got to stop striking out in every direction whenever someone offers me work. I can't excel at everything. No one does, really. But I can excel at something. I thought it would be portraits at first, when I was in school, d'you know. Then I got sidetracked onto landscapes and still lifes. Now I'm just dabbling in whatever commercial assignment comes to hand. But that's no good. It's time to commit."

So during their morning walk to the common where Deborah took the ducks the rest of her toast, and while they examined the World War I memorial with its solitary soldier, head bowed, rifle extended, she chatted about her art. Still lifes presented a wealth of opportunity—did he know what the Americans were currently doing with flowers and paint? had he seen the studies of metal scored, heated, and treated with acid? was he aware of Yoshida's depictions of fruit?—but on the other hand, they did seem rather distant, didn't they? Not much emotional risk involved in shooting a tulip or a pear. Landscapes were lovely—what a treat to be a travel photographer and go on assignment to Africa or the Orient, wouldn't that be smashing?—but they demanded only an eye for composition, the skill for lighting, the knowledge of filters and film, all of it technique. Whereas portraits—well, there was an element of trust that had to be established between artist and subject. And trust required risk. Portraits forced both parties to come out of themselves. You took a picture of a body, but if you were good, you captured the personality beneath. Now there was real living, didn't he think so, engaging the heart and mind of the sitter, earning his trust, capturing his realness.

Something of a cynic, St. James wouldn't have put money on most people having much "realness" under their surface personae. But he was happy enough to be involved in Deborah's conversation. When she first began chatting, he tried to evaluate her words, tone, and expression for the likelihood of their being avoidance. She'd been upset last night with his intrusion into her territory. She wouldn't want a repeat of that. But the more she talked—weighing this possibility, rejecting that, exploring her motivations for each—the more he felt reassured. There was an energy to her that he hadn't seen in the last ten months. Whatever her reasons for entering into a discussion of her professional future, the mood it seemed to engender in her was a far sight better than her previous depression. So when she set up her tripod and Hasselblad, saying, "The light's good right now," and wanted him to pose in the deserted beer garden of Crofters Inn so that she might test her regard for portraits, he let her snap away at every possible angle, for more than an hour despite the cold, until they received Lynley's call.

She was saying, "You see, I don't think I want to do conventional studio portraits. I mean, I don't want people coming in and posing for their anniversary snaps. I wouldn't mind being called out to do something special, but largely I think I want to work on the street and in public places. I want to find interesting faces, and let the art grow from there," when Ben Wragg announced from the rear door of the inn that Inspector Lynley was wanting to speak to Mr. St. James.

The result of that conversation—Lynley shouting over the noise of some sort of roadwork that appeared to call for minor explosives—was a drive to the cathedral at Bradford.

"We're looking for a connection between them," Lynley had said. "Perhaps the bishop can provide it."

"And you?"

"I've an appointment with Clitheroe CID. After that, the forensic pathologist. It's formality mostly, but it's got to be done."

"You saw Mrs. Spence?"

"The daughter as well."

"And?"

"I don't know. I'm uneasy. I've not much doubt that the Spence woman did it and knew what she was doing. I've plenty of doubt it was conventional murder. We need to know more about Sage. We need to unearth the reason he left Cornwall."

"Are you on to something?"

He heard Lynley sigh. "In this case, I hope not, St. James."

Thus, with Deborah at the wheel of their hired car and a phone call made to ensure their reception, they drove the considerable distance to Bradford, skirting Pendle Hill and swinging to the north of Keighley Moor.

The secretary to the Lord Bishop of Bradford admitted them into the official residence not far from the fifteenth-century cathedral that was the seat of his ministry. He was a toothy young man who carried a maroon leather diary under one arm and continually riffled through its gold-edged pages as if to remind them how limited was the bishop's time and how fortunate were they that a half-hour had been carved out for them. He led the way not into a study, library, or conference room, but through the wood-panelled residence to a rear stairway that descended to a small, personal gym. In addition to a wall-size mirror, the room contained an exercise bike, a rowing machine, and a complicated contraption for lifting weights. It also contained Robert Glennaven, Bishop of Bradford, who was occupied with pushing, shoving, climbing, and otherwise tormenting his body on a fourth machine that consisted of moving stairs and rods.

"My Lord Bishop," the secretary said. He made the introductions, snapped a turn on his heel, and went to sit in a straight-backed chair by the foot of the stairs. He folded his hands over the diary—now opened meaningfully to the appropriate page—took his watch off his wrist and balanced it on his knee, and placed his narrow feet flat on the floor.

Glennaven nodded at them brusquely and wiped a rag across the top of his sweat-sheened bald head. He was wearing the trousers to a grey sweat suit along with a faded black T-shirt on which *TENTH UNICEF JOG-A-THON* was printed above the date 4 May. Both trousers and shirt were mottled by rings and streaks of perspiration.

"This is His Grace's exercise time," the secretary announced unnecessarily. "He has another appointment in an hour, and he'll need an opportunity to shower prior to that. If you'll be so good as to keep it in mind."

There were no other seats in the room aside from those provided by the equipment. St. James wondered how many other unexpected or unwanted guests were encouraged to limit their visits to the bishop by having to conduct them standing up.

"Heart," Glennaven said, jabbing his thumb to his chest before he adjusted a dial on the stair machine. He puffed and grimaced as he spoke, no exercise enthusiast but a man without options. "I've another quarter of an hour. Sorry. Can't let up or the benefits diminish. So the cardiologist tells me. Sometimes I think he has profit sharing going with the sadists who create these infernal machines." He pumped, lunged, and continued to sweat. "According to the deacon"—with a tilt of his head to indicate his secretary—"Scotland Yard wants information in the usual fashion of people wanting something in this new age. By yesterday, if possible."

"True enough," St. James said.

"Don't know that I can tell you anything useful. Dominic here"— another head tilt towards the stairs—"could probably tell you more. He attended the inquest."

"At your request, I take it."

The bishop nodded. He grunted with the effort of addressing the additional tension he'd added to the machine. The veins became swollen on his forehead and arms.

"Is that your usual procedure, sending someone to an inquest?"

He shook his head. "Never had one of my priests poisoned before. I had no procedure."

"Would you do it again if another priest died under questionable circumstances?"

"Depends on the priest. If he was like Sage, yes."

Glennaven's introduction of the topic made St. James' job easier. He celebrated this fact by taking a seat on the bench of the weight machine. Deborah went to the exercise bike and made it her perch. At their movement, Dominic looked disapprovingly at the bishop. The best-laid plans gone awry, his expression said. He tapped the face of his watch as if to make sure it was still in working order.

"You mean a man likely to be deliberately poisoned," St. James said.

"We want priests who are dedicated to their ministry," the bishop said between grunts, "especially in parishes where the temporal rewards are minimal at best. But zeal has its negatives. People find it offensive. Zealots hold up mirrors and ask people to look at their own reflections."

"Sage was a zealot?"

"In some eyes."

"In yours?"

"Yes. But not offensively so. I've a high tolerance for religious activism. Even when it's not politically sound. He was a decent sort. He had a good mind. He wanted to use it. Still, zeal causes problems. So I sent Dominic to the inquest."

"I've been given to understand that you were satisfied by what you heard," St. James said to the deacon.

"Nothing that was recorded by the adjudicating party indicated Mr. Sage's ministry to be wanting in any way." The deacon's monotone, a demonstration of hear-no-evil, speak-no-evil, and step-on-no-toes, no doubt served him well in the political-religious arena in which he worked. It did little to add to their knowledge, however.

"As to Mr. Sage himself?" St. James asked.

The deacon ran his tongue over his protruding teeth and picked a piece of lint from the lapel of his black suit jacket. "Yes?"

"Was he himself wanting?"

"As far as the parish was concerned, and from the information I was able to gather from my attendance at the inquest—"

"I mean in your eyes. Was he wanting? You must have known him as well as heard about him at the inquest."

"We none of us are capable of achieving perfection," was the deacon's prim response.

"Actually, non sequiturs aren't of much help in examining an untimely death," St. James said.

The deacon's neck seemed to lengthen as he lifted his chin. "If you're hoping for more—perhaps something detrimental—then I must tell you I am not in the habit of sitting in judgement upon fellow clerics."

The bishop chuckled. "What balderdash, Dominic. Most days you sit in judgement like St. Peter himself. Tell the man what you know."

"Your Grace—"

"Dominic, you gossip like a ten-year-old schoolgirl. Always have done. Now, stop equivocating before I climb off this damnable machine and box your bloody ears. Pardon me, dear madam," to Deborah who smiled.

The deacon looked as if he smelled something unpleasant but had just been told to pretend it was roses. "All right," he said. "It seemed to me that Mr. Sage had a rather narrow field of vision. His every reference point was specifically biblical."

"I shouldn't think that a limitation in a priest," St. James noted.

"It is perhaps the most serious limitation a priest can take with him into his ministry. A strict interpretation of and consequent adherence to the Bible can be perfectly blinding, not to mention severely alienating to the very flock whose membership one might be trying to increase. We are not Puritans, Mr. St. James. We do not harangue from the pulpit any longer. Nor do we encourage religious devotion based upon fear."

"Nothing we've heard about Sage indicates that he was doing that either."

"Not yet in Winslough, perhaps. But *our* last meeting with him here in Bradford certainly stands as monumental evidence of the direction in which he was determined to head. There was trouble brewing all round that man. One sensed it was just a matter of time before it came to a boil."

"Trouble? Between Sage and the parish? Or a member of the parish? Do you know something specific?"

"For someone who'd spent years in the ministry, he had no essential grasp of the concrete problems faced by his parishioners or anyone else. Example: He took part in a conference on marriage and the family not a month before he died and while a professional—a psychologist, mind you, here in Bradford—attempted to give our brothers some guidance on how to deal with parishioners having marital problems, Mr. Sage wanted to engage in a discussion of the woman taken in adultery."

"The woman . . . ?"

"John, chapter eight," the bishop said. " 'And the scribes and Pharisees brought unto him a woman taken in adultery . . . ' etcetera, etcetera. You know the story: Feel free to throw stones, if you've not sinned yourself."

The deacon continued as if the bishop hadn't spoken. "There we were in the middle of discussing the best approach to take with a couple whose ability to communicate is clouded by the need to control each other, and Sage wanted to talk about what was moral versus what was right. Because the laws of the Hebrews declared it to be so, it was moral to stone this woman, he said. But was it necessarily right? And oughtn't that be what we explore in our conferences together, brothers: the dilemma we face between that which is moral in the eyes of our society and that which is right in the eyes of God? It was all perfect rubbish. He didn't want to talk about anything concrete because he lacked the ability to do so. If he could keep our heads up in the air and fill up our time with nebulous discussions, his own weaknesses as a priest—not to mention his deficiencies as a man—might never be revealed." In conclusion, the deacon waved his hand in front of his face as if whisking away a pesky fly. He gave a derisive tut. "The woman taken in adultery. Should we or shouldn't we stone sinners in the market-place. My God. What drivel. This is the twentieth century. Nearly the twenty-first."

"Dominic always has his fingers on the pulse of the obvious," the bishop noted. The deacon looked miffed.

"You disagree with his assessment of Mr. Sage?"

"No. It's accurate. Unfortunate, but true. His zealotry had a distinctly biblical flavour. And frankly, that's off-putting, even for clerics."

The deacon bowed his head briefly in humble acceptance of the bishop's laconic approbation.

Glennaven continued to pump away on the stair machine, adding ever more to the increasing stains of sweat on his clothes. It clicked and whirred. The bishop panted. St. James thought about the oddity of religion.

All forms of Christianity sprang from the same source, the life and words of the Nazarene. Yet the ways of celebrating that life and those words seemed as infinite in variety as the individuals who were the celebrants. While St. James recognised the fact that tempers could flare and dislikes could brew over interpretations and styles of worship, it seemed more likely that a priest whose mode of devotion irritated parishioners would be replaced rather than eliminated. St. John Townley-Young may have found Mr. Sage too low church for his taste. The deacon may have found him too fundamental. The parish may have been irked by his passion. But none of these seemed significant enough reasons to murder him. The truth had to lie in another direction. Biblical zealotry did not appear to be the connection that Lynley was hoping to unearth between killer and victim.

"He came to you from Cornwall, as I understand it," St. James said.

"He did." The bishop used the rag to scour his face and to sponge the sweat from his neck. "Nearly twenty years there. Round three months here. Part of it with me whilst he went on his interviews. The rest in Winslough."

"Is that the ordinary procedure, to have a priest stay here with you during the interview process?"

"Special case," Glennaven said.

"Why?"

"A favour to Ludlow."

St. James frowned. "The town?"

"Michael Ludlow," Dominic clarified. "Bishop of Truro. He asked His Grace to see to it that Mr. Sage was . . . " The deacon made much of sifting through the chaff of his thoughts for a wheat-like euphemism. "He felt Mr. Sage needed a change of environment. He thought a new location might increase his chance of success."

"I had no idea a bishop might be so involved in the work of an individual cleric. Is that typical?"

"In the work of this cleric, yes." A buzzer sounded from the stair machine. Glennaven said, "Saints be praised," and reached for a knob that he turned anticlockwise. He slowed his pace for a cool-down period. His breathing began to return to normal. "Robin Sage was Michael Ludlow's archdeacon originally," he said. "He'd spent the first seven years of his ministry climbing to that position. He was only thirty-two when he received the appointment. He was an unqualified success. He made *carpe diem* his personal watchword."

"That doesn't sound at all like the man from Winslough," Deborah murmured.

Glennaven acknowledged her point with a nod. "He made himself indispensable to Michael. He served on committees, involved himself in political action—"

"Church-approved political action," Dominic added.

"He lectured at theological colleges. He raised thousands of pounds for the maintenance of the cathedral and for the local churches. And he was fully capable of mingling without either effort or discomfort in any level of society."

"A jewel. A real catch, in other words," Dominic said. He didn't seem overly pleased with the thought.

"It's odd to think a man like that would suddenly be satisfied, living the life of a village cleric," St. James said.

"That was Michael's thought exactly. He hated to lose him, but he let him go. It was Sage's request. He went to Boscastle for his first posting."

"Why?"

The bishop wiped his hands on the rag and folded it. "Perhaps he'd been to the village on holiday."

"But why the sudden change? Why the desire to go from a position of power and influence to one of relative obscurity? That's hardly the norm. Even for a priest, I dare say."

"He'd travelled on a personal road to Damascus a short time before, evidently. He'd lost his wife."

"His wife?"

"Killed in a boating accident. According to Michael, he was never the same afterwards. He saw her death as a punishment from God for his temporal interests, and he decided to eschew them."

St. James looked at Deborah across the room. He could tell she was thinking his very same thought. They'd all of them made an uninformed assumption based upon limited information. They had assumed the vicar hadn't been married because no one in Winslough had mentioned a wife. He could see from Deborah's thoughtful expression that she was reflecting upon the day in November when she'd had her only conversation with the man.

"So I assume that his passion for success was replaced with a passion to make up for his past in some way," St. James said to the bishop.

"But the problem was that the latter passion didn't translate as well as the former had. He went through nine placements."

"In what period of time?"

The bishop looked at his secretary. "Some ten to fifteen years, wasn't it?" Dominic nodded.

"With no success anywhere? A man with his talents?"

"As I said, the passion didn't translate well. He became the zealot we spoke of earlier, vehement about everything from the decline in church attendance to what he called the secularisation of the clergy. He lived the Sermon on the Mount, and he wasn't accepting of a fellow clergyman or even a parishioner who failed to do the same. If that wasn't enough to cause him problems, he firmly believed that God shows His will through what happens to people in their lives. Frankly, that's a difficult draught of medicine to swallow if you're the victim of a senseless tragedy."

"Which he himself was."

"And which he believed to be his just deserts."

" 'I was self-centred,' he'd say," the deacon intoned. " 'I cared only for my own need for glory. God's hand moved to change me. You can change as well.' "

"Unfortunately, true though his words may have been, they didn't constitute a recipe for success," the bishop said.

"And when you heard that he was dead, did you think there was a connection?"

"I couldn't avoid considering it," the bishop replied. "That's why Dominic went to the inquest."

"The man had inner demons," Dominic said. "He chose to wrestle them in a public forum. The only way he could make expiation for his own worldliness was to castigate everyone he met for theirs. Is that a motive for murder?" He snapped closed the bishop's appointment diary. It was clear that their interview was at an end. "I suppose it depends upon how one reacts when confronted with a man who seemed to feel that his was the only correct way to live."

∎   ∎   ∎

"I've never been good at this, Simon. You know that." They'd finally stopped for a rest in Downham, on the other side of the Forest of Pendle. They parked by the post office and walked down the sloping lane. They circled round a storm-stricken oak that had been reduced to trunk and truncated branches and headed back towards the narrow stone bridge they'd just crossed in the car. Pendle Hill's grey-green slopes hulked in the distance with fingers of frost curling down from the summit, but they were not intent upon a hike towards this. Rather they had spied a small green on the near side of the bridge, where a stream cut a scythe's curve along the lane and flowed behind a neat line of cottages. Here a worn bench backed up to a drystone wall, and perhaps two dozen mallards quacked happily on the grass, explored the roadside, and paddled in the water.

"Don't worry about it. This isn't a contest. Remember what you can. The rest will come when it comes."

"Why are you so obnoxiously undemanding?"

He smiled. "I've always thought it was part of my charm."

The ducks came to greet them with the expectation of food on their minds. They quacked and set about examining footwear, investigating and rejecting Deborah's boots, moving onto St. James' shoelaces. These caused a flurry of interest, as did the metal crosspiece of his brace. However, when none of this produced the tiniest, edible morsel, the ducks fluffed and resettled their feathers reproachfully and from that moment displayed a disappointed aloofness to the human presence altogether.

Deborah sat on the bench. She nodded a hello to a parka-clad woman who trudged by them in red Wellingtons with an energetic black terrier on a lead. Then she rested her chin on her fist. St. James joined her. He touched his fingers to the ridge that she was creating between her eyebrows.

"I'm thinking," she said. "I'm trying to remember."

"So I noticed." He put up the collar of his coat. "I'm merely wondering if it's a requirement of the process that it be conducted in temperatures falling below ten degrees."

"What a baby you are. It's not even that cold."

"Tell that to your lips. They're turning blue."

"Pooh. I'm not shivering."

"I'm not surprised. You've gone far beyond that. You're in the final stages of hypothermia and you don't even know it. Let's go back to that pub. There's smoke coming from the chimney."

"Too many distractions."

"Deborah, it's cold. Doesn't brandy sound comforting?"

"I'm thinking."

St. James shoved his hands into his overcoat pockets and gloomily gave his refrigerated attention to the ducks. They seemed oblivious of the cold. But then, they'd had a whole summer and autumn to fatten themselves up in preparation for it. Besides, they were naturally insulated with down, weren't they? Lucky little devils.

"St. Joseph," Deborah finally announced. "That's what I remember. Simon, he was devoted to St. Joseph."

St. James raised a doubtful eyebrow and hunched further into his coat. "It's a start, I suppose." He tried to sound encouraging.

"No, really. It's important. It must be." Deborah went on to explain her meeting with the vicar in Room 7 of the National Gallery. "I was admiring the da Vinci—Simon, why is it that you've never taken me to see it before?"

"Because you hate museums. I tried when you were nine. Don't you recall? You preferred to go rowing on the Serpentine and became quite unruly when I took you to the British Museum instead."

"But those were mummies. Simon, you wanted me to look at the mummies. I had nightmares for weeks."

"So did I."

"Well, you shouldn't have let a little bit of temper defeat you so easily."

"I'll keep that in mind for the future. Back to Sage."

She used the sleeves of her coat as a muff, tucking her hands inside. "He pointed out that the da Vinci cartoon didn't have St. Joseph in it. He said that St. Joseph hardly ever was in a painting with the Virgin and wasn't that sad? Or something like that."

"Well, Joseph was just the breadwinner, after all. The good old bloke, the right-hand man."

"But he seemed so . . . so *sad* about it. He seemed to take it personally."

St. James nodded. "It's the meal-ticket syndrome. Men like to think they're more important than that in the general scheme of their women's lives. What else do you recall?"

She sank her chin to her chest. "He didn't want to be there."

"In London?"

"In the gallery. He'd been heading somewhere else—was it Hyde Park?—when it started to rain. He liked nature. He liked the country. He said it helped him think."

"About what?"

"St. Joseph?"

"Now there's a subject for ample consideration."

"I *told* you I wasn't any good at this. I don't have a memory for conversation. Ask me what he wore, what he looked like, the colour of his hair, the shape of his mouth. But don't ask me to tell you what he said. Even if I could remember every word, I'd never be able to delve for hidden meanings. I'm no good at verbal delving. I'm no good at any delving. I meet someone. We talk. I like him or I don't. I think: This is someone who might be a friend. And that's the end of it. I don't expect him to turn up dead when I come to call, so I don't remember every detail of our first encounter. Do you? *Would* you?"

"Only if I'm conversing with a beautiful woman. And even then I find I'm distracted by details having nothing to do with what she has to say."

She eyed him. "What sort of details?"

He cocked his head thoughtfully and examined her face. "The mouth."

"The mouth?"

"I find women's mouths a study. I've been readying myself for the last several years to posit a scientific theory on them." He settled back against the bench and regarded the ducks. He could feel her bristling. He contained a smile.

"Well, I won't even ask what the theory is. You want me to. I can tell by your expression. So I won't."

"Just as well."

"Good." She wriggled next to him, duplicating his position on the bench. She held out her feet and scrutinised the tops of her boots. She clicked her heels together. She did the same with her toes. She said, "Oh all right. Damn it. Tell me. *Tell* me."

"Is there a correlation between size and significance of utterance?" he asked solemnly.

"You're joking."

"Not at all. Have you never noticed that women with small mouths invariably have little of importance to say?"

"What sexist rubbish."

"Take Virginia Woolf as an example. Now there was a woman with a generous mouth."

"Simon!"

"Look at Antonia Fraser, Margaret Drabble, Jane Goodall—"

"Margaret Thatcher?"

"Well, there are always exceptions. But the general rule, and I argue that the facts will uphold it absolutely, is that the correlation exists. I intend to research it."

"How?"

"Personally. In fact, I thought I'd begin with you. Size, shape, dimension, pliability, sensuality . . . " He kissed her. "Why is it I've a feeling you're the best of the lot?"

She smiled. "I don't think your mother beat you enough when you were a child."

"We're even then. I know for a fact that your father never laid a hand upon you." He got to his feet and extended his hand to her. She slipped hers into the crook of his arm. "How does a brandy sound?"

She declared it sounded fine, and they began to retrace their steps up the lane. Much like Winslough, just beyond the village the open land rose and fell in gentle hills parcelled out in farms. Where the farms ended, the moors began. Sheep grazed here. Among them, the occasional border collie moved. The occasional farmer worked.

Deborah paused on the threshold of the pub. St. James, holding the door for her, turned back to find her staring at the moors and tapping the knuckle of her index finger contemplatively against her chin.

"What is it?"

"Walking. Simon, he said he liked to walk on the moors. He liked to be outside when he had to make a decision. That's why he wanted to go to the park. St. James's Park. He'd planned to feed the sparrows from the bridge. And he knew about the bridge. Simon, he must have been there before."

St. James smiled and drew her into the doorway of the pub.

"D'you think it's important?" she asked.

"I don't know."

"D'you think perhaps he had a reason for talking about the Hebrews wanting to stone that woman? Because we know he was married. We know his wife met with an accident...Simon!"

"Now you're delving," he said.

CHAPTER SEVENTEEN

F OR SPENCE. DIDN'T YOU HEAR?"

"The headmistress sent for her and . . . "

". . . see his *car?*"

"It was about her mum."

Maggie hesitated on the school steps when she realised that more than one speculative glance was being directed her way. She'd always liked the time between the last lesson and the departure of the school bus. It presented the best opportunity to gossip with the pupils who lived in other villages and in the town. But she'd never considered that the giggles and whispers that accompanied the afternoon chit-chat might one day be about her.

Everything had seemed outwardly normal at first. Pupils were gathered on the tarmac in front of the school in their usual fashion. Some were lingering by the school bus. Others were lounging against cars. Girls were combing their hair and comparing shades of contra-band lipstick. Boys were sparring with each other or trying to look cool. When Maggie came through the doors, threaded her way down the steps, and searched the assembly for Josie or Nick, her mind was engaged with the questions the London detective had asked her. She didn't even stop to wonder about it when a ripple of whispers slid through the crowd. She'd been feeling rather dirty ever since the conversation in Mrs. Crone's study, and she couldn't exactly under-stand why. So her mind was taken up with turning over every possible reason as if each were a stone, and she was mostly conscious of waiting to see if a slug of previously unconscious guilt would slither away from exposure to the light.

She was used to feeling guilty. She kept on sinning, she tried to convince herself she wasn't sinning, she even excused the worst of her behaviour by telling herself it was Mummy's fault. Nick loves me, Mummy, even if you don't. See how he loves me? See? See?

In reply, her mother had never used look-at-everything-I've-done-for-you-Margaret in the sort of play upon conscience that Pam Rice's mother tried with no effect. She never talked in terms of deep disappointment as Josie reported her mother had done on more than one occasion. Nonetheless, prior to this very day, her mother had been the consistent, major source of Maggie's guilt: She was disappointing Mummy; she was causing Mummy's anger; she was adding torture to Mummy's pain. Maggie knew all this without having to hear it. She had always been extremely adept at reading reactions on her mother's face.

Which was why Maggie had come to realise last night precisely how much power she had in this war with her mother. She had power to punish, to hurt, to warn, to avenge . . . the list stretched on to forever. She wanted to feel triumphant in the knowledge that she'd wrested the ship's wheel of her life away from her mother's controlling hands. But the truth was, she felt troubled about it. So when she arrived home late the previous night—outwardly proud of the purple love bruises which Nick had sucked to the surface of her neck—the flames of pleasure Maggie had expected to warm her at Mummy's frantic worry were instantly extinguished at the sight of her face. She made no reproach. She just came to the door of the darkened sitting room, and she gazed upon her as if from a place where she couldn't be reached. She looked a hundred years old.

Maggie had said, "Mummy?"

Mummy had placed her fingers on Maggie's chin, had turned it gently to expose the bruises, had then released her and climbed the stairs. Maggie heard her door click shut softly behind her. It was a sound that hurt more than the slap she deserved.

She was bad. She knew it. Even when she felt warmest and closest to Nick, even when he loved her with his hands and his mouth, when he was pressing It to her, holding her, opening her, saying Maggie, Mag, Mag, she was black and she was bad. She was filled with blame. She was becoming every day more used to the shame of her behaviour, except that she had never expected to be made to feel it over her friendship with Mr. Sage.

What she felt was like the prickles from nettle leaves. But they scratched at her spirit instead of her skin. She kept hearing the detective ask about secrets, and that made her feel dry and itchy inside. Mr. Sage had said, You're a good girl, Maggie, don't ever forget that, believe it completely. He said, We get confused, we lose our way, but we can always find our way back to God through our prayers. God listens, he said, God forgives everything. Whatever we do, Maggie, God will forgive.

He was comfort itself, was Mr. Sage. He was understanding. He was goodness and love.

Maggie had never betrayed the confidence of their times together. She had held them precious. And now she was faced with the London detective's suspicions that what was most special about her friendship with the vicar was also what had led to his death.

This was the slug that writhed beneath the last stone of implication she turned over in her mind. The fault was hers. And if that was the case, then Mummy had known all along what she was doing when she fed the vicar dinner that night.

No. Maggie argued the point with herself. Mummy couldn't have known she was feeding him hemlock. She took care of people. She didn't hurt them. She made unguents and poultices. She mixed special teas. She brewed decoctions, infusions, and tinctures. Everything she did was to help, not to harm.

Then the whispers of her schoolmates rising round her made delicate fissures in the shell of her thoughts.

"She poisoned the bloke."

". . . didn't get away with it after all."

"The police came from London."

". . . devil-worshippers, I heard and . . ."

Maggie was startled into sudden comprehension. Dozens of eyes were on her. Faces were bright with speculation. She clutched her rucksack of schoolbooks to her chest and looked about for a friend. Her head felt weightless, oddly and suddenly divorced from her body. All at once it was the most important thing in the world to pretend she didn't realise what they were talking about.

"Seen Nick?" she asked. Her lips felt chapped. "Seen Josie?"

A fox-faced girl with a large pimple on the side of her nose became the group spokesman. "They don't want to hang about with you, Maggie. They're not so dim they can't see the risk."

A murmur of approval lapped round the girl like a small wave, then receded in kind. The faces seemed to move closer to Maggie.

She held her rucksack tighter. A book's sharp corner dug into her hand. She knew they were teasing—didn't one's mates always like to tease whenever they could?—and she drew herself taller to meet the challenge. "Right," she said with a smile as if she herself approved of whatever joke they were trying to make. "Quite. Come on. Where's Josie? Where's Nick?"

"They've gone off already," Fox-face said.

"But the bus . . ." It was sitting where it always sat, waiting for departure, just a few yards away, inside the gate. There were faces at the windows, but from the steps of the school, Maggie couldn't tell if her friends were among them.

"They made their own arrangements. During lunch. When they knew."

"Knew what?"

"Who you were with."

"I wasn't with anyone."

"Oh right. Whatever you say. You lie about as good as your mum."

Maggie tried to swallow, but her tongue got stuck on the roof of her mouth. She took a step towards the bus. The group let her go but closed ranks right behind her. She could hear them talking as if to each other, but all of it intended for her.

"They went off in a car, did you know?"

"Nick and Josie?"

"And that girl who's been after him. *You* know who I mean."

Teasing. They were teasing. Maggie walked faster. But the schoolbus seemed farther and farther away. There was a shimmer of light dancing in front of it. It started as a beam and turned into bright speckles.

"He'll stay clear of her now."

"If he's got any brains. Who wouldn't?"

"It's true. If her mum doesn't take a fancy to her mates, she just invites them for dinner."

"Like that fairy story. Have an apple, dearie? It'll help you sleep."

Laughter.

"Only you won't wake up real soon."

Laughter. Laughter. The bus was too far.

"Here, eat this. I cooked it up special. Just for you."

"Now, don't be shy about second helpings. I can see you're just *dying* for more."

Maggie felt a hot ember at the back of her throat. The bus glimmered, got small, became the size of her shoe. The air closed round it and swallowed it up. Only the wrought iron gates of the school were left.

"It's my own recipe. Parsnip pie, I call it. People say it's *dead* good."

Beyond the gates lay the street—

"They call me Crippen, but don't let that put you off your dinner."

—and escape. Maggie began to run.

■　■　■

She was pounding towards the centre of town when she heard him calling her. She kept going, dashing up to the high street and then across it, tearing towards the car park at the base of the hill. What she was planning to do there, she couldn't have said. It was only important to get away.

Her heart was slamming into her chest. She had a folding and pulling pain in her side. She skidded on a patch of slick pavement and wobbled, but she caught herself against a lamppost and ran on.

"Watch yourself, luv," warned a farmer who was getting out of his Escort next to the kerb.

"Maggie!" shouted someone else.

She heard herself sob. She saw the street blur. She kept rushing forwards.

She passed the bank, the post office, some shops, a tea room. She dodged a young woman pushing a pram. She heard the thud of footsteps behind her, and then another shout of her name. She gulped away tears and plunged on.

Fear pumped energy and speed through her body. They were following her, she thought. They were laughing and pointing. They were only waiting for the opportunity to encircle her and begin the whispers all over again: What her mum did . . . do you know, do you know . . . Maggie and the vicar . . . a vicar? . . . that bloke? . . . Cor, he was old enough to be . . .

No! Drop the thought, trample it, bury it, shove it away. Maggie hurtled down the pavement. She didn't stop until a blue sign hanging from a squat brick building brought her up short. She wouldn't have seen it at all had she not lifted her head to make her eyes stop watering. And even then the word swam, but she could still make it out. *Police.* She stumbled to a halt against a rubbish bin. The sign seemed to grow larger. The word glittered and throbbed.

She shrank away from it, half crouched on the pavement, trying to breathe and trying not to cry. Her hands were numb. Her fingers were tangled in the straps of her rucksack. Her ears felt so cold that steel spikes of pain were shooting down her neck. It was the end of the day, the temperature was dropping, and never in her life had she felt so alone.

She didn't, she didn't, she didn't, Maggie thought.

But somewhere shouted a chorus: She did.

"Maggie!"

She cried out. She tried to make herself small, like a mouse. She hid her face in her arms and slid down the side of the rubbish bin until she was sitting on the pavement, balling herself up as if reducing her size somehow served as a form of protection.

"Maggie, what's going on? Why'd you run off? Didn't you hear me calling?" A body joined her on the pavement. An arm went round her.

She smelled the old leather of his jacket before she processed the fact that the voice was Nick's. She thought in nonsensical but none-theless rapid succession how he always kept the jacket crumpled up in his rucksack during school hours when he had to be in uniform, how he always took it out during lunch to "give it a breather," how he always wore it the minute he was able, before and after school. It was odd to think she would know the smell of him before she'd recognise the sound of his voice. She gripped his knee.

"You went off. You and Josie."

"Went off? Where?"

"They said you'd gone. You were with . . . You and Josie. They said."

"We were on the bus like always. We saw you run off. You looked dead cut up about something, so I came after you."

She lifted her head. She'd lost her barrette somewhere in the flight from the school, so her hair hung round her face and partially screened him from her.

He smiled. "You look done in, Mag." He thrust his hand inside his jacket and brought out his cigarettes. "You look like a ghost was chasing you."

"I won't go back," she said.

He bent his head to shelter cigarette and flame, and he flipped the used match into the street. "No point to that." He inhaled with the deep satisfaction of someone for whom a change in circumstances has allowed a smoke sooner rather than later. "Bus is gone anyway."

"I mean back to school. Tomorrow. To lessons. I won't go. Ever."

He eyed her, brushing his hair back from his cheeks. "This about that bloke from London, Mag? The one with the big motor that got all the chappies in a fuss today?"

"You'll say forget it. You'll say ignore them. But they won't let up. I'm never going back."

"Why? What's it to you what those twits think?"

She twisted the strap of her rucksack round her fingers until she saw that her nails were turning blue.

"Who cares what they say?" he asked. "You know what's what. That's all that matters."

She squeezed her eyes shut against the truth and pressed her lips together to keep from saying it. She felt more tears leak out from beneath her eyelids, and she hated herself for the sob which she tried to disguise with a cough.

"Mag?" he said. "You know the truth, right? So what those loobies say in the schoolyard don't amount to nothing but twaddle, right? What they say's not important. What you know is."

"I *don't* know." The admission burst from her like a sickness she could no longer contain. "The truth. What she . . . I don't know. I don't *know*." Even more tears spilled out. She hid her face on her knees.

Nick whistled low, between his teeth. "You never said before now."

"We always move. Every two years. Only this time I wanted to stay. I said I'd be good, I'd make her proud, I'd do good in school. If we could just stay. This once. Just stay. And she said yes. And then I met the vicar after you and I . . . after what we did and how hateful Mummy was and how bad I felt. And he made me feel better and . . . She was in a rage about that." She sobbed.

Nick flung his cigarette into the street and held her with the other arm as well.

"He found me. That's what it is, Nick. He finally found me. She didn't want that. It's why we always ran. But this time we didn't and he had enough time. He came. He came like I always knew he would."

Nick was silent for a moment. She could hear him draw a breath. "Maggie, you're thinking the vicar was your dad?"

"She didn't want me to see him and I saw him anyway." She raised her head and grabbed onto his jacket. "And now she doesn't want me to see you. So I won't go back there. I won't. You can't make me. No one can. If you try—"

"Is there a problem here, kids?"

They both drew back from the sound of a voice. They turned to see the speaker. A rail-thin policewoman stood above them, heavily cloaked for the weather and wearing her hat at a rakish angle. She carried a notebook in one hand and a plastic cup of something steaming in the other. She sipped from this as she waited for response.

"A blow-up at school," Nick said. "It's nothing much."

"Needing some help?"

"Nah. It's girl stuff. She'll be okay."

The policewoman studied Maggie with what looked more like curiosity than empathy. She shifted her attention to Nick. She made a show out of watching them over the rim of her cup—its lazy cat's-tail of steam fogging up her spectacles—as she took another sip of whatever was in it. Then she nodded and said, "You'd best be off home then," and held her ground.

"Yeah, right," Nick said. He urged Maggie to her feet. "C'mon then. We're off."

"Live round here?" the policewoman asked.

"Just a ways from the high."

"I've not seen you before."

"No? I've seen you lots. You have a dog, right?"

"A Corgi, yes."

"See. I knew. Seen you out for your walk." Nick tapped his index finger out from his temple in a form of salute. "Afternoon," he said.

Arm round Maggie, he shepherded her back in the direction of the high street. Neither of them looked to see if the policewoman was watching.

At the first corner, they ducked right. A short distance down the street and another right led through a walkway that lay between the back of the public buildings and the overgrown rear gardens of a line of council cottages. Then they were heading down the slope once more. They emerged in less than five minutes into Clitheroe's car park. It was largely empty of vehicles at this time of day.

"How'd you know about her dog?" Maggie asked.

"I just went with the odds. A lucky break for us."

"You're clever. And good. I love you, Nick. You take care of me."

They stopped in the shelter of the public lavatory. Nick blew on his hands and tucked them underneath his arms. "Going to be cold tonight," he said. He looked in the direction of the town where smoke feathered up from chimneys, becoming lost against the sky. "You hungry, Mag?"

Maggie read the desire beneath the words. "You c'n go on home."

"I won't. Not 'less you—"

"I'm not going."

"Then neither am I."

They were at an impasse. The evening wind was starting to blow, and it had an easy time of finding them. It gusted across the car park, unimpeded, and scattered bits of trash about their feet. A Moment's bag glittered greenly against Maggie's leg. She used her foot to brush it away, leaving a streak of brown against the navy of her tights.

Nick brought out a handful of coins from his pocket. He counted.

"Two pounds sixty-seven," he said. "What about you?"

She dropped her eyes, said, "Nothing," then raised them in a hurry. She tried to make her voice sound proud. "So you don't have to stay. Go on. I can manage."

"I already said—"

"If she finds me with you, it'll go that much worse on us both. Go home."

"Won't happen. I'm staying. I said."

"No. I don't want to be at fault. I'm already . . . because of Mr. Sage . . . " She wiped her face on her coat sleeve. She was tired to the bone and longing for sleep. She wondered about trying the lavatory door. She did so. It was locked. She sighed. "Go on," she said again. "You know what c'n happen if you don't."

Nick joined her in the doorway of the ladies'. It was recessed about six inches so they gained some ground against the cold. "You believe that, Mag?"

She hung her head. She felt the misery of the knowledge lie across her shoulders, heavy and cumbersome, like sacks of sand.

"You think she killed him because he came for you? Because he was your dad?"

"She never talked about my dad. She wouldn't ever say."

Nick's hand touched her head. His fingers made an attempt at caressing, but they were thwarted by the snarls in her hair. "I don't think he was, Mag. Your dad, that is."

"Sure, because—"

"No. Listen." He took a step closer. He put his arms round her. He spoke into her hair. "His eyes were brown, Mag. So's your mum's."

"So?"

"So he can't be your dad, can he? Because of the odds." She stirred to speak but he continued. "Look, it's like sheep. My dad explained it. They're all white, right? Well, sort of white. But every once in a while out pops a black one. Didn't you ever wonder how? It's a recessive gene, see? It's something inherited. The lamb's mum and dad both had a black gene somewhere inside them, and when they mated out came a black lamb instead of a white one, even though they were white themselves. But the odds are against it happening. Which is why most sheep are white."

"I don't—"

"You're like the black sheep because your eyes are blue. Mag, what d'you think the odds are of two brown-eyed people having a kid with blue eyes?"

"What?"

"Must be a million to one. Maybe more. Maybe a billion to one."

"You think?"

"I know. The vicar wasn't your dad. And if he wasn't your dad, then your mum didn't kill him. And if she didn't kill him, she won't be trying to kill anyone else."

There was a *that's that* quality to his voice that urged her to accept his words. Maggie wanted to believe him. It would make everything so much easier to live with if she knew that his theory comprised the truth. She would be able to go home. She would be able to face Mummy. She wouldn't think about the shape of her nose and her hands—were they like the vicar's, *were* they?—nor would she wonder about why he had held her out at arm's length and studied her so. It would be a relief to know something for certain, even if it didn't answer her prayers. So she wanted to believe. And she would have believed if Nick's stomach hadn't rumbled noisily, if he hadn't shivered, if she hadn't seen in her mind's eye his father's enormous flock of sheep, drifting like slightly soiled clouds against a green Lancashire hillside sky. She pushed him away.

"What?" he said.

"There's more'n one black sheep born in a flock, Nick Ware."

"So?"

"So those aren't any billion to one odds."

"It isn't like sheep. Not exactly. We're people."

"You want to go home. Go on. Go home. You're lying to me, and I don't want to see you."

"Mag, I'm not. I'm trying to explain."

"You don't love me."

"I do."

"You just want your tea."

"I was only saying—"

"And your scones and your jam. Well, go ahead. Get them. I can take care of myself."

"With no money?"

"I don't need money. I'll get a job."

"Tonight?"

"I'll do something. See if I won't. But I'm not going home and I'm not going back to school and you can't talk about sheep like I was so dim I couldn't figure it out. Because if two white sheep could have a black one then two brown-eyed people could have me and you know it. Isn't that right? Well, isn't that right?"

He drove his fingers through his hair. "I didn't say it wasn't possible. I just said the odds—"

"I don't care about the odds. This isn't like some horse race. This is *me*. We're talking about my mum and dad. And she killed him. You know it. You're just lording it over me and trying to make me go back."

"I'm not."

"You are."

"I said I wouldn't leave you and I won't. Okay?" He looked about. He squinted against the cold. He stamped his feet to warm them. "Look, we need something to eat. You wait here."

"Where're you going? We don't have even three pounds. What kind of—"

"We can get some crisps. Some biscuits and stuff. You're not hungry now but you will be later and we won't be near any shop by then."

"We?" She made him look at her. "You don't have to go," she said a last time.

"Do you want me?"

"To go?"

"And other stuff."

"Yes."

"Do you love me? Trust me?"

She tried to read his face. He was anxious to be off. But perhaps he was only hungry after all. And once they started walking, he would be warm enough. They could even run.

"Mag?" he said.

"Yes."

He smiled, brushed his mouth against hers. His lips were dry. It didn't feel like a kiss. "Then wait here," he said. "I'll be right back. If we're gonna bunk off, it's best that no one see us together in town and remember for when your mum phones the police."

"Mummy won't. She won't dare."

"I wouldn't take odds on that." He turned up the collar of his jacket. He looked at her earnestly. "You okay here, then?"

She felt her heart warm. "Okay."

"Don't mind sleeping rough tonight?"

"Not so long as I'm sleeping with you."

CHAPTER EIGHTEEN

COLIN ATE HIS TEA AT THE KITCHEN SINK. SARdines on toast, with the oil slipping through his fingers and splatting onto the pot-scarred porcelain. He didn't feel hungry in the least, but he'd been light-headed and weak in the limbs for the past thirty minutes. Food seemed the obvious solution.

He'd made his walk back to the village along the Clitheroe Road, which was closer to the lodge than was the Cotes Fell footpath. His pace was brisk. He told himself that a need to avenge was what drove him so rapidly onwards. He kept repeating her name in his head as he walked: Annie, Annie, Annie my girl. It was a way to avoid hearing the words *love and death three times* pulse with the blood in his skull. By the time he reached his house, he was hot in the chest but ice to the bone in his hands and feet. He could hear his heart's erratic thumping inside his eardrums, and his lungs couldn't seem to get enough air. He ignored the symptoms for a good three hours but when there was no improvement, he decided to eat. Teatime, he thought in irrational response to his body's behaviour, that'll take care of it, must have a bite to eat.

He washed down the fish with three bottles of Watney's, drinking the first one while the bread was toasting. He pitched the bottle into the rubbish and opened another as he rooted in the cupboard for the sardines. The tin gave him trouble. Curling the metal lid round the key required a steadiness that he wasn't able to muster. He got it halfway unrolled when his fingers slipped and the sharp edge of the top sliced into his hand. Blood spurted out. It mixed with the fish oil, started to sink, then formed perfect small beads that floated like scarlet lures for the fish. He felt no pain. He wrapped his hand in a tea towel, used the end of it to sop the blood off the surface of the oil, and tilted the beer bottle up to his mouth with the hand that was free.

When the toast was ready, he dug the fish from the tin with his fingers. He lined them up on the bread. He added salt and pepper and a thick slice of onion. He began to eat.

There was no particular taste or smell to it, which he found rather odd because he could distinctly remember how his wife once complained about the scent of sardines. Makes my eyes water, she would say, that fish smell in the air, Col, it makes my stomach go peculiar.

Her cat clock ticked on the wall above the AGA, wagging its tail and moving its eyes. It seemed to be repeating her name with the sound of its clicking wheels and gears: No longer tick-tock but An-nie, An-nie, An-nie, it said. Colin concentrated intently on this. Just like the rhythm of his earlier footsteps, the repetition of her name drove other thoughts away.

He used the third beer to clear his mouth of the fish that he couldn't taste. Then he poured a small whisky and drank that down in two swallows to try to bring back feeling to his limbs. But still he couldn't quite vanquish the cold. This caused him confusion because the furnace was on, he still wore his heavy jacket, and by all rights he should have been soaking in sweat.

Which he was, in a manner of speaking. His face was so fiery that his skin was throbbing. But the rest of him trembled like a birch in the wind. He drank another whisky. He moved from the sink to the kitchen window. He looked across to the vicar's house.

And then he heard it again, as distinctly as if Rita were standing directly behind him. *Love and death three times.* The words were so clear that he swung round with a cry which he strangled the instant he saw that he was alone. He cursed aloud. The sodding words meant nothing. They were merely a stimulus of the sort used by every palm-reader in the world, giving you a small piece of a nonexistent life jigsaw and whetting your incipient desire to have more.

Love and death three times needed no elucidation from anyone as far as Colin was concerned. It translated to *pounds and pence each week*, hard-earned coins pressed into the palm of the palmist by dried-up spinsters, naive housewives, and lonely widows, all seeking meaningless reassurance that their lives weren't as futile as they appeared to be.

He turned back to the window. Across his drive, across the vicar's, the other house watched him in return. Polly was within, as she had continued to be in the weeks since Robin Sage's death. She was no doubt doing what she always did—scrubbing, polishing, dusting, and waxing in a fervent display of her utility. But that wasn't all, as he finally understood. For Polly was also biding her time, patiently waiting for the moment when Juliet Spence's blind need to take blame resulted in her incarceration. While Juliet in gaol wasn't quite the same as Juliet dead, it was better than nothing. And Polly was too clever in her ways to make another attempt on Juliet's life.

Colin wasn't a religious man. He'd given up on God during the second year of Annie's dying. Still, he had to acknowledge that the hand of a greater power than his own had been active in the Cotes Hall cottage on that night in December when the vicar had died. By all rights, it should have been Juliet eating alone in the vicar's place. And if it had been, the coroner would have affixed the label *accidental poisoning/self-administered* to her dying, with no one wise to the manner in which that convenient accident had been brought about.

She would have rushed in to minister to his grief, would have Polly. More than anyone he knew, she excelled at sympathy and fellow-feeling.

Roughly, he rubbed his hands clean of sardine oil and used two plasters to cover the cut. He paused to pour himself one more swallow of whisky which he gulped down before heading out the door.

Bitch, he thought. Love and death three times.

She didn't come to the door when he knocked, so he pressed his finger to the bell and held it. He took some satisfaction from the shrill jangle it made. The sound grated on the nerves.

The inner door opened. He could see her form, behind the opaque glass. Top-heavy and inflated by too many garments, she looked like a miniature of her mother. He heard her say, "Glory. Get off the bell, will you," and she yanked the door open, ready to speak.

She didn't, when she saw him. Instead, she looked beyond him to his house, and he wondered if she'd been watching as usual, if she'd stepped away from the window for a moment and thus missed his approach. She'd missed little else in the past few years.

He didn't wait for her to ask him in. He squeezed past her. She shut both the outer and the inner doors behind him.

He followed the narrow corridor to the right and walked straight along to the sitting room. She'd been working in here. The furniture gleamed. A tin of beeswax, a bottle of lemon oil, and a box of rags sat in front of an empty bookshelf. There wasn't a trace of dust anywhere. The carpet was vacuumed. The lace window curtains hung crisp and clean.

He turned to face her, unzipping his jacket. She stood awkwardly in the doorway—the sole of one sock-clad foot pressed to the other's ankle, the toes moving in an unconscious scratch—and she followed his movements with her eyes. He threw his jacket on the sofa. It fell just short and slid to the floor. She moved towards it, eager to put everything in its rightful place. Just doing her job, was Polly.

"Leave it be."

She stopped. Her fingers gripped the ribbing on the bottom edge of her bulky, brown pullover. It hung, loose and misshapen, to her hips.

Her lips parted when he began to unbutton his shirt. He saw her catch her tongue between her teeth. He knew well enough what she was thinking and wanting, and he took a distinctly gut-warming pleasure from the knowledge that he was about to disappoint her. He drew out the book from against his stomach and flipped it to the floor between them. She didn't look at it immediately. Instead, her fingers moved from her pullover to grasp the folds of the insubstantial gypsy skirt hanging unevenly beneath it. Its colours—bright red, gold, and green—caught the light of a floor lamp standing next to the sofa.

"Yours?" he said.

Alchemical Magic: Herbs, Spices, and Plants. He saw her lips form the first two words.

She said, "Glory. Where'd you get that ol' thing?" sounding all the world full of curious confusion and nothing more.

"Where you left it."

"Where I—?" Her gaze moved from the book to him. "Col, what're you about?"

Col. He felt his hand tremble with the need to strike. Her show of guilelessness seemed less of an outrage than did the familiarity implied by her saying that name.

"Is it yours?"

"Was. I mean I s'pose it still is. Except I haven't seen it for ages."

"I'd expect that," he said. "It was well enough out of sight."

"What's that supposed to mean?"

"Behind the cistern."

The light flickered in the lamp, a bulb going bad. It made a tiny hissing sound and went out, inviting the day's exterior gloom to seep past the lace curtains. Polly didn't react, didn't seem to notice. She appeared to be mulling over his words.

He said, "You would have been wiser to throw it away. Like the tools."

"Tools?"

"Or did you use hers?"

"Whose tools? What're you about here, Colin?" Her voice was wary. She inched away from him so subtly that he might not have noticed had he not been anticipating every sign of her guilt. Her fingers even stopped themselves in the midst of flexing. He found that of interest. She knew better than to allow them to fist.

"Or perhaps you didn't use any tools at all. Perhaps you loosened the plant—gently, you know how I mean, you know how to do it—and then lifted it from the soil, root and all. Is that what you did? Because you'd know the plant, wouldn't you, you'd recognise it just as well as she'd do."

"This is about Missus Spence." She spoke slowly, as if to herself, and she didn't appear to be seeing him although she was looking in his direction.

"How often do you use the footpath?"

"Which one?"

"Don't play games with me. You know why I'm here. You didn't expect it. And Juliet's taking the blame made it unlikely that anyone would ever come looking for you. But I've smoked you out, and I want the truth. How often do you use the footpath?"

"You're mad." She managed to put another inch between them. Her back was to the door, and she was clever enough to know that a glance over her shoulder would announce her intentions and give him the advantage which she currently seemed to believe was hers.

"Once a month at least, I should guess," he said. "Is that right? Doesn't the ritual have more power if it's performed when the moon is full? And isn't the power more potent if the ritual takes place in the direct light of that moon? And isn't it true that communication with the Goddess is more profound if you perform the ritual on a holy site? Like the top of Cotes Fell?"

"You know I worship on the top of Cotes Fell. I make no secret of that."

"But you've other secrets, haven't you? Here. In this book."

"I haven't." Her voice was weak. She seemed to realise what weakness implied, because she roused herself to say, "And you're frightening me, you are, Colin Shepherd," with an edge of defiance.

"I was up there today."

"Where?"

"Cotes Fell. The summit. I hadn't been in years, not since before Annie. I'd forgotten how well you can see from there, Polly, and what you can see."

"I go there to worship. That's all and you know it." She put another inch between them, saying more quickly, "I burned the laurel for Annie. I let the candle melt down. I used cloves. I prayed—"

"And she died. That very night. How convenient."

"No!"

"During the harvest moon, while you prayed on Cotes Fell. And before you prayed, you brought her soup to drink. Do you remember that? You called it your special soup. You said to make sure she ate every bit."

"It was only vegetables, for both of you. What're you thinking? I had some myself. It wasn't—"

"Did you know that plants are most potent when the moon is full? The book says that. You must harvest them then, no matter what part you want, even the root."

"I don't use plants that way. No one does in the Craft. It's not about evil. You know that. P'rhaps we find herbs for incense, yes, but that's all. Incense. For part of the ritual."

"It's all in the book. What to use for revenge, what will alter the mind, what to use for poison. I've read it."

"No!"

"And the book was behind the cistern where you've kept it hidden . . . how long has it been?"

"It wasn't hidden. If it was there, it just fell. There was lots of things on the cistern, wasn't there? A whole stack of books and magazines. I didn't hide this—" She touched it with her toe and withdrew, gaining yet another inch of distance from him. "I didn't hide a thing."

"What about Capricorn, Polly?"

That stopped her cold. She repeated the word without making a sound. He could see the panic beginning to take hold of her as he forced her closer and closer to the truth. She was like a rogue dog when at last it's cornered. He could feel her spine stiffening and her legs wanting to splay.

"Hemlock's strength is in Capricorn," he said.

Her tongue whisked across her lower lip. Fear was a scent on her, sour and strong.

"The twenty-second of December," he said.

"What about it?"

"You know."

"I don't. Colin, I don't."

"The first day of Capricorn. The night the vicar died."

"This is—"

"And one thing more. The moon was full that night. And the night before. So it all fits together. You had the instructions, your how-to for murder, printed in the book: dig the root out when the plant is dormant; know its strength is in Capricorn; know it's deadly poison; know it's most potent when the moon is full. Shall I read it all for you? Or would you prefer to read it yourself? Look under *H* in the index. For hemlock."

"No! She put you up to this, didn't she? Missus Spence. I c'n see it on your face as big as c'n be. She said go see that Polly, go ask her what she knows, go ask her where she's been. And she left it to you to think up the rest. That's how it is, isn't it? Isn't it, Colin?"

"Don't even say her name."

"Oh, I'll say it all right. I'll say it and more." She stooped and snatched the book from the floor. "Yes, it's mine. Yes, I bought it. I used it as well. And she knows that—damn her—because I was fool enough once—more'n two years back when she first came to Winslough—to ask her about making a tincture from bryony. And more the fool I was, I even told her why." She shook the book at him. "Love, Colin Shepherd. Bryony's for love. So's apple in a charm. Here, want to see?" She flipped a silver chain from beneath her pullover. A small globe hung from it, its surface filigree. She yanked it from her neck and threw it to the floor where it bounced against his foot. He could see the dried bits of the fruit inside. "And aloe for sachets and benzoins for perfume. And cinquefoil for a potion that you wouldn't ever drink. It's all in the book, with everything else. But you only see what you want to see, don't you? That's the way it is now. That's the way it's always been. Even with Annie."

"I won't talk about Annie with you."

"Oh, won't you? AnnieAnnieAnnie with a halo on her head. I'll talk about her just as much as I want because I know what it was like. I was there just like you. And she wasn't a saint. She wasn't a noble patient suffering in silence with you sitting at the bedside, putting flannels on her brow. That wasn't how it was."

He took a step towards her. She held her ground.

"Annie said, Go ahead, Col, you take care of yourself, my precious love. And she never let you forget it when you did."

"She never said—"

"She didn't *need* to say. Why won't you see it? She lay in her bed with all the lights off. She said, I was too ill to reach for the lamp. She said, I thought I would die today, Col, but it's all right now because you're home and you're not to worry a jot about me. She said, I understand why you need a woman, my love, you do what you must do and don't think about me in this house, in this room, in this bed. Without you."

"That's not how it was."

"And when the pain was bad, she didn't lie there like a martyr. Don't you remember? She screamed. She cursed you. She cursed the doctors. She threw things at the wall. And when it was worst, she said, You did this to me, you made me rot, and I'm dying and I hate you, I *hate* you, I wish you were dying instead."

He made no response. It felt as if a siren were sounding in his head. Polly was there, mere inches away, but she seemed to be speaking from behind a red veil.

"So I prayed on the top of Cotes Fell, I did. At first for her health. And then for... And then for you alone after she died, hoping that you would see... would know... Yes, I got this book"—She shook it again—"but it was because I loved you and I wanted you to love me back and I was willing to try anything to make you whole. Because you weren't whole with Annie. You hadn't been for years. She bled you in her dying, but you don't want to face it because then you might have to face what living with Annie was like as well. And it wasn't perfect. Because nothing is."

"You don't know the first thing about Annie's dying."

"That you emptied her bedpans and hated the thought of it. Don't I know that? That you wiped her bum with your stomach at the boil. Don't I know that? That just when you needed most to get out of the house for a breath of air, she knew and would cry and take a bad turn and you always felt guilty because *you* weren't ill, were you? You didn't have the cancer. You weren't going to die."

"She was my life. I loved her."

"At the end? Don't make me laugh in your face. At the end was bitterness and a rage of anger. Because no one lives without joy for that long and feels anything else at the end of it."

"You bloody bitch."

"Yes, all right. That and more, if you like. But I face the truth, Colin. I don't tart it up with hearts and flowers like you."

"Then let's take the truth another step, all right?" He reduced the distance between them another few inches when he kicked the amulet to one side. It clattered against the wall and broke open, spilling its contents onto the carpet. The bits of apple looked like shrivelled skin. Human skin, even. And he wouldn't put its collection past her. He'd put nothing past Polly Yarkin. "You prayed for her to die, not to live. When it didn't come quick, you helped it along. And when her dying didn't get you what you wanted the moment you wanted it—and when was that, Polly? Was I supposed to fuck you the day of the funeral?—you decided to try potions and charms instead. Then Juliet came. She threw your plans awry. You tried to use her. And it was bloody clever to let her know I wasn't truly available just in case she was interested and got in your way. But we found each other anyway—Juliet and I—and you couldn't bear that. Annie was gone. The final barrier to your happiness was buried in the churchyard. And here was another. You saw what was happening between us, didn't you? The only solution was to bury her as well."

"No."

"You knew where to find the hemlock. You walk by the pond each time you hike Cotes Fell. You dug it up, you put it in the root cellar, and you waited for Juliet to eat it and die. And if Maggie died as well, that would have been a shame, but she's expendable, isn't she? Everyone is. You just didn't count on the vicar's presence. That was the misfortune. I imagine you had a few uneasy days once he was poisoned, while you waited for Juliet to take the blame."

"So what did I gain, if that's how it happened? Coroner said it was an accident, Colin. She's free. So are you. And you've been stuffing her like some randy farmboy eyeing his daddy's ewes ever since. So what did I gain?"

"What you've waited and hoped for, ever since the vicar died by mistake. The London police. The case re-opened. With every bit of circumstantial evidence pointing to Juliet." He snatched the book from her fingers. "Except this, Polly. You forgot about this." She made a lunge for it. He threw the book to the corner of the room and caught her arm. "And when Juliet's safely put away for good, you'll have what you want, what you tried to get while Annie was alive, what you prayed for when you prayed for her death, what you mixed your potions and wore your amulets for, what you've been after for years." He took a step closer. He felt her trying to pull away. He experienced a distinct tingling of pleasure at the thought of her fear. It shot down his legs. It began to work unexpected magic in his groin.

"You're hurting m' arm."

"This isn't about love. This was never about love."

"Colin!"

"Love has no part in what you've been after since that day—"

"No!"

"You remember it, then, don't you? Don't you, Polly?"

"Let me go." She twisted beneath him. She was breathing in tiny baby gasps. No more than a child, so easy to subdue. Squirming and writhing. Tears in her eyes. She knew what was coming. He liked her knowing.

"On the floor of the barn. Where the animals do it. You remember that."

She wrenched her arm away and spun around to run. He caught her skirt as it flared with her movement. He jerked her towards him. The material ripped. He twirled it round his hand and pulled harder. She stumbled but didn't fall.

"With my cock inside and you grunting like a sow. You remember that."

"Please. No." She was starting to cry and he found that the sight of her tears inflamed him more than had the thought of her fear. She was penitent sinner. He was avenging god. And her punishment would be a godly justice.

He grabbed more of the skirt, pulled on it savagely, and heard the satisfactory sound of it giving way. Another pull. Then another.

And every time Polly struggled to escape him, the skirt ripped more. "Just like that day in the barn," he said. "Just what you want."

"No. I don't. Not like this. Col. Please."

The name. The name. His hands shot out and tore the rest of the skirt from her body. But she seized the moment of release and ran. She made it to the corridor. She was close to the door. Another three feet and she would escape.

He leapt and tackled her as her hand grasped the knob of the inner door. They crashed to the floor. She began to flail at him wildly. She didn't speak. Her arms and legs thrashed. Her body convulsed.

He struggled to pin down her arms, grunting, "Fuck...you... so...hard."

She screamed, "No! Colin!" but he cut her off with his mouth. He drove his tongue inside her, with one hand on her neck pressing and pressing while the other ripped at her underwear. He used his knee to force her legs apart. Her hands tore at his face. She found his spectacles, flung them off. She sought his eyes. But he was close on her, powering his face into hers, filling her mouth with his tongue and then spitting, spitting and every moment fired more and more with the need to show, to master, to punish. She would crawl and beg. She would pray for mercy. She would call upon her Goddess. But *he* was her god.

"Cunt," he grunted into her mouth. "Bitch...cow." He fumbled with his trousers while she rolled and struggled, kicking against him, her every breath a shriek. She drove her knee upwards, missing his testicles by less than an inch. He slapped her. He liked the feel of the slap—how it brought life and power back to his hand. He hit her again, harder this time. He used his knuckles and admired the red bruising they brought to her skin.

She was weeping and ugly. Her mouth hung open. Her eyes squeezed shut. Mucous dripped from her nose. He liked her that way. He wanted her weeping. Her terror was a drug. He shoved her legs apart and he fell upon her. He celebrated her punishment like the god he was.

■   ■   ■

She thought, This is what it's like to die. She lay as he had left her, one leg crooked and the other extended, her pullover shoved up beneath her armpits, her bra jerked down to bare one breast where his bite still throbbed like a brand. A sheer piece of nylon edged with lace—"Got yerself some fancies I see," Rita had chuckled. "Looking for a bloke who likes it wrapped up pretty?"—looped round her left ankle. A shredded ribbon of skirt draped across her neck.

She stared upwards and followed the threading of a crack that began above the door and spread out like veins against the skin of the ceiling. Somewhere in the house a metallic crank-rattle sounded, followed by a whirring that was steady and low. The boiler, she thought. She wondered why it was heating water since she couldn't recall having used any that day. She pondered everything she had done in the vicarage, taking each project one step at a time because it seemed so important to know why the boiler was heating water right now. It couldn't realise, after all, how filthy she was. It was just a machine. Machines didn't anticipate a body's needs.

She made a list. Newspapers first. She'd bound them up like she'd promised herself and discarded them all in the rubbish bin. She'd phoned and cancelled the subscription as well. Potted plants next. There were only four of them, but they were looking poorly and one had lost nearly all of its leaves. She'd been giving them water religiously every day, so she couldn't understand why they were turning all yellow. She'd taken them to the rear garden and set them on the porch, thinking the poor little things might like some sun, if it ever came out which it hadn't. Bedding after that. She'd changed the sheets on all three beds—two singles, one double—just like she'd been doing every week since she'd first come to work. Didn't make any difference that no one used the beds. One had to change the linen to keep it fresh. But she hadn't done any laundry, so the boiler shouldn't be at work over that. What was it, then?

She tried to picture each of her movements that day. She tried to make them appear among the cracks in the ceiling. Newspapers. Telephone. Plants on the porch. And after that . . . It was too much effort to think beyond the plants. Why? Was it water? Was she frightened of water? Had something happened with water? No, how silly. Think of rooms with water.

She remembered. She smiled but it hurt because her skin felt stiff like glue had dried upon it so she hurried in her mind from the bedrooms to the kitchen. Because that was it. She'd washed all the dishes, the glassware, the pots, and the pans. She'd scrubbed the cupboards as well. Which is why the boiler was working now. And anyway, didn't a boiler always work? Didn't it fire itself up when it felt the water inside start to cool? No one switched it on. It just worked. Like magic.

Magic. The book. No. She must have no thoughts like that. They painted nightmare pictures in the back of her head. She didn't want to see.

The kitchen, the kitchen, she thought. Washing dishes and cupboards and then on to the sitting room which was already clean and tidy as could be but she polished the furniture because she couldn't seem to make herself leave this place, let go, find another way to live, and then he was with her. And his face wasn't right. His back seemed too stiff. His arms didn't hang, they just waited.

Polly rolled to her side, drew her legs up, and tried to cradle herself. Hurts, she thought. Her legs felt torn away from her body. A hammer pounded down low where he'd slammed and slammed her. And inside, acid burned at her flesh. She felt throbbing and scraped. She was nothing.

Slowly, she became aware of the cold, a thin current of air that flowed insistently against her bare skin. She shivered. She realised he'd left the inner door open upon his leaving, and the outer door was not completely latched. Her fingers plucked aimlessly at the pullover, and she tried to work it down as a cover, but she got it no farther than beneath her breasts before giving up. It didn't feel right. The wool abraded her skin.

From where she lay she could see the stairway, and she began to inch towards it with no thought in mind but to get out of the draught, to find somewhere safe that was dark. But once she rested her head on the bottom stair, she looked up and the light seemed brighter at the top. She thought, Bright means warm, better than dark. It was getting late, but the sun must have come out one final time. It would be a winter sun—milky and distant—but if it fell on the carpet in one of the bedrooms, she could curl within its golden boundaries and let her dying continue there.

She began to climb. She found she couldn't manage her legs, so she pulled herself up, hand over hand on the banister. Her knees bumped on the stairs. When she lolled to one side, her hip thudded against the wall which is how she saw the blood. She interrupted her progress to look at it curiously, to touch a finger to its crimson smear, marvelling at how quickly it was able to dry, and how it turned to mahogany when mixed with air. She saw that it was oozing from between her legs, and that it had been oozing quite long enough to create palmate patterns on her inner thighs and crooked rivulets down one leg.

Dirty, she thought. She would have to bathe.

The idea of washing inflated in her mind, driving the nightmare pictures away. Holding on to the thought of water and its warmth, she made it to the top of the stairs and crawled to the bath. She shut the door and sat on the cold white tile with her head against the wall, her knees drawn up, and the blood seeping out against the fist she pressed between her legs.

After a moment, she rolled her shoulders against the wall, flipped herself two feet, and thus gained the tub. She lowered her head to its side and reached one hand to the tap. Her fingers grappled with it, failed to make it turn, and slipped off altogether.

She knew somehow she'd be whole again if she could only wash. If she could wash off the scent of him and scrub away the touch of his hands, if the soap could cleanse the inside of her mouth. And as long as she could think about washing—what it would feel like, how the water would rise to her breasts, how long she would lie in the tub and just dream—she wouldn't have to think about anything else. If she could only make the water run.

She reached again for the tap. Again she failed. She was doing it by feel because she didn't want to open her eyes and have to see herself in the mirror that she knew was hanging on the back of the bathroom door. If she saw the mirror, she would have to think, and she was determined not to think again. Except about washing.

She'd get into the tub and never come out, just letting the water rise and fall. She'd watch its bubbles, she'd listen to its flow. She'd feel it glide between her fingers and toes. She'd love it, hold it, be good to it. That's what she'd do.

Only, nothing was forever, not even the washing, and when it was over she would have to feel, which is the one thing she didn't want to do, didn't want to face, didn't want to live through. Because this was dying no matter what she pretended, this was the real ending of things. How funny to think she'd always expected it to come in old age with her lying in a bed all snowy with linens and her grand-children there and someone who loved her holding her hand so she wouldn't do her leaving all alone. She saw now that it was all about being alone in the first place, living was. And if living was all about being alone, dying wouldn't be anything different.

She could deal with that. Dying alone. But only if it was here and now. Because then it would be over. She wouldn't have to get up, get into the water, wash him away, and walk out the door. She'd never have to make her way home—oh Goddess, the long walk—and face her mother. More, she would never have to see him, never have to look in his eyes, and never remember over and over, like a film running back and forth in her brain, the moment when she knew he was going to hurt her.

I don't know what it means to love anyone, she realised. I thought it was goodness, a wanting to share. I thought it meant like you hold out your hand and someone takes it, holds it hard, and pulls you safe from the river. You talk. You tell him bits of yourself. You say here's where I hurt and you give it to him and he holds it and gives you where he hurts in return and you hold it and that's how you learn to love. You lean where he's strong. He leans where you're strong. And there's a joining somewhere. But it's not like this, not like it was today, here, in this house, it's not like this.

That was the worst of it, the filth of loving him that no amount of washing could cleanse. Even through the terror, even in the instant when she knew exactly what he meant to do, even when she begged him not to and he did it anyway—ramming her, tearing her flesh from her flesh, and leaving her lying like used rags on the floor—the worst was that he was the man she loved. And if the man she loved could know that she loved him and still do this to her and grunt with the pleasure of showing her who would dominate and who would submit, then what she had thought was love was nothing. Because it seemed to her that if you loved someone and if he knew you loved him, he'd take care not to hurt you. Even if he didn't love you full in return, he'd cherish your feelings, hold them to his heart, and feel a fondness of some kind. Because that was what one did for people.

Only if that wasn't the truth of living, then she didn't want to live any more. She'd get into the bath and let the water take her. Let it cleanse her and kill her and carry her off.

CHAPTER NINETEEN

"TAKE A LOOK AT THESE."

Lynley passed the folder of photographs across the coffee table to St. James. He picked up his pint of Guinness and thought about straightening *The Potato Eaters* or cleaning the dust from both the frame and the glass of *Rouen Cathedral* in order to see if it was actually *in Full Sunlight* as it appeared to be. Deborah seemed to read his mind at least partially. She muttered, "Oh bother, this is driving me crazy," and dealt with the Van Gogh print before plopping back down on the sofa next to her husband. Lynley said, "Bless you, my child," and waited for St. James' reaction to the crime-scene material which Lynley had brought back with him from Clitheroe.

Dora Wragg had been good enough to see to their needs in the residents' lounge. While the pub was already closed for the latter part of the afternoon, two elderly women in heavy tweeds and hiking boots had still been sitting by what remained of the fire when Lynley returned from his visits with Maggie, the police, and the medical examiner. Although the two women had been engaged in a sombre but enthusiastic discussion about "Hilda's sciatica . . . and isn't the poor dear a martyr to it, luvvie?" and seemed unlikely to eavesdrop on any conversation unconnected to Hilda's hips, Lynley had taken one look at their eager, sharp faces and decided that discretion was the better part of conversing openly about anyone's death.

So he waited until Dora placed a Guinness, a Harp, and an orange juice on the coffee table in the residents' lounge and took herself off to the nether regions of the inn before he handed over the folder to his friend. St. James studied the photographs first. Deborah gave them a glance, suffered a frisson of aversion, and quickly looked away. Lynley couldn't blame her.

The photographs of this particular death seemed more disquieting than many others he had seen, and at first he couldn't understand why. He was, after all, no stranger to the myriad ways in which an unexpected death occurs. He was used to the result of strangulations—the cyanosed face, the bulging eyes, the blood-froth at the mouth. He had seen his share of blows to the head. He'd examined a variety of knife wounds—from cut throats to one virtual disembowelment not unlike the Whitechapel murder of Mary Kelly. He'd seen victims of bombings and victims of shootings, their limbs torn off and their bodies mutilated. But there was something personally horrifying about this death, and he couldn't put his finger on what it was. Deborah did it for him.

"It went on and on," she murmured. "It took some time, didn't it? Poor man."

And that was it. Death hadn't come in an instant for Robin Sage, a moment's violent visitation via gun, knife, or garrotte with oblivion following hard on its heels. It had taken him slowly enough for him to realise what was happening and for his physical suffering to be acute. The crime-scene pictures illustrated that.

They'd been taken in colour by the Clitheroe police, but what they captured was predominantly black and white. The latter constituted a good six inches of newly fallen snow covering the ground and powdering the wall next to which the body lay. The former constituted the body itself, dressed in black clerical garb beneath a black overcoat that was bunched round the waist and hips as if the vicar had tried to slither out of it. But even here the black did not achieve complete ascendancy over the white, for the body itself—like the wall its hand reached towards—wore a thin but thorough membrane of snow. This had been documented in seven photographs before the crime-scene team had brushed the snow from the body into the collection jars that would later be deemed non-evidential, considering the circumstances of the death. And once the body was brushed free of snow, the photographer had gone to work once again.

The rest of the pictures spelled out the nature of Robin Sage's death agony. Dozens of deep arcing gouges in the ground, thick mud on his heels, earth and flakes of grass beneath his nails testified to the manner in which he had tried to escape the convulsions. Blood on his left temple, three slits on his cheek, one shattered eyeball, and a heavily ensanguined stone beneath his head suggested the strength of those same convulsions and how little he was able to do to master them once he understood there was no escape. The position of his head and neck—thrown back so far that it seemed inconceivable no vertebrae were broken—indicated a frantic battle for air. And the tongue, a swollen mass chewed nearly in half, protruded from the mouth in an eloquent statement about the man's final moments.

St. James went through the pictures twice. He set two aside, a close-up of the face and a second of one of the hands. He said, "It's heart failure if you're lucky. Asphyxia if you're not. Poor bastard. He was unlucky as the devil."

Lynley didn't need to examine the photographs St. James had chosen to support his point. He'd seen the bluish colour of the lips and ears. He'd noted the same of the fingernails. The undamaged eye was prominent. Lividity was well-developed. All were indications of respiratory failure.

"How long do you suppose it took him to die?" Deborah asked.

"Too long by half." St. James glanced at Lynley over the autopsy report. "You spoke with the pathologist?"

"Everything was consistent with hemlock poisoning. No specific lesions of the stomach's mucous membrane. Gastric irritation and oedema of the lungs. Time of death between ten that night and two the next morning."

"What did Sergeant Hawkins have to say? Why did Clitheroe CID buy the accidental-poisoning conclusion so quickly and back off from an investigation? Why did they let Shepherd handle it on his own?"

"CID had been at the site while Sage's body was still there. It was clear that, the external injuries he'd done to his face aside, his death was caused by some sort of seizure. They didn't know what sort. The detective constable on the scene actually thought it was epilepsy when he saw the tongue—"

"Good God," St. James muttered.

Lynley nodded agreement. "So after they took the photographs, they left it up to Shepherd to gather the details leading up to Sage's death. Essentially, it was his call. At the time, they didn't even know Sage had been out in the snow all night as no one had even reported him missing until he failed to show up to perform the Townley-Young wedding."

"But once they knew he'd been to dinner at the cottage? Why didn't they step in?"

"According to Hawkins—who frankly was a bit more forthcoming when I was standing before him, warrant card in hand, than when I had him on the phone—three factors influenced the decision: the involvement of Shepherd's father in the constable's investigation, what Hawkins honestly assumed to be the pure coincidence of Shepherd's visit to the cottage on the night Sage died, and some additional input from forensic."

"The visit wasn't a coincidence?" St. James asked. "Shepherd wasn't making rounds?"

"Mrs. Spence phoned him to come to her," Lynley replied. "She told me she wanted to testify as much for the coroner's jury at the inquest, but Shepherd insisted on claiming he'd just dropped by on his rounds. She said he lied because he wanted to protect her from local gossip and unfriendly speculation after the verdict was in."

"That doesn't seem to have worked, if the other night in the pub is any indication."

"Quite. But here's what I find intriguing, St. James: She was perfectly willing to admit to the truth of phoning Shepherd when I spoke to her this morning. Why bother to do that? Why didn't she stick with the story they'd agreed on, one that was generally accepted and believed, even if the villagers aren't particularly in love with it?"

"Perhaps she never agreed to Shepherd's story in the first place," St. James offered. "If he testified before she did at the inquest, I doubt she would have wanted to perjure him by telling the truth."

"But why not agree to the story? Her daughter wasn't home. If only the two of them—she and Shepherd—knew that she'd phoned him, what possible reason could she have now for telling me a different story, even if it's the truth? She's damning herself by the admission."

"You won't think I'm guilty if I admit I'm guilty," Deborah murmured.

"Christ, but that's a dangerous game to play."

"It worked on Shepherd," St. James said. "Why not on you? She fixed in his mind the image of her vomiting. He believed her and he took her part."

"That was the third factor that influenced Hawkins' decision to call off the CID. The sickness. According to forensic . . . " Lynley set down his glass, put on his spectacles, and picked up the report. He scanned the first page, the second, and found what he was looking for on the third, saying, "Ah, here it is. 'Prognosis for recovering from hemlock poisoning is good if vomition can be obtained.' So the fact that she was sick supports Shepherd's contention that she ate some of the hemlock accidentally."

"Purposely. Or, what's more likely, not at all." St. James took up his pint of Harp. "*Obtained* is the operative word, Tommy. It indicates that vomition isn't a natural by-product of ingestion. It must be induced. So she'd have had to take a purgative of some sort. Which means she would have had to know that she'd ingested poison in the first place. And if that's the case, why didn't she phone Sage to warn him or send someone out looking for him?"

"Could she have known something was wrong with her but not that it was hemlock? Could she have assumed it was something else? Some milk gone bad? A bad piece of meat?"

"She could have assumed anything, if she's innocent. We can't get away from that."

Lynley sailed the report back to the coffee table, removed his spectacles, ran his hand through his hair. "Then we're nowhere, essentially. It's a case of yes-you-did, no-I-didn't unless there's a motive somewhere. Can I hope the bishop gave you one in Bradford?"

"Robin Sage was married," St. James said.

"He wanted to talk to his fellow priests about the woman taken in adultery," Deborah added.

Lynley leaned forward in his chair. "No one's said . . . "

"Which seems to mean no one knew."

"What happened to the wife? Was Sage divorced? That would be an odd thing for a priest, surely."

"She died some ten or fifteen years ago. A boating accident in Cornwall."

"What sort?"

"Glennaven—he's Bradford's bishop—didn't know. I phoned Truro but couldn't get through to the bishop there. And his secretary wasn't forthcoming with anything other than the basic fact: a boating accident. He wasn't free to give out information on the telephone, he said. What sort of boat it was, what the circumstances were, where the accident occurred, what the weather was like, if Sage was with her when it happened . . . nothing."

"Protecting one of their own?"

"He didn't know who I was, after all. And even if he did, I hardly have the right to the information. I'm not CID. And what we're engaged in here is hardly an official endeavour, even if I were."

"But what do you think?"

"About the idea that they're protecting Sage?"

"And through him the reputation of the Church."

"It's a possibility. The connection to the woman taken in adultery is hard to ignore, isn't it?"

"If he killed her . . ." Lynley mused.

"Someone else might have waited for an opportunity for revenge."

"Two people alone on a sailboat. A rough day. A sudden squall. The boom shifts in the wind, cracks the woman on the head, and she's overboard in an instant."

"Could that sort of death be faked?" St. James asked.

"A murder posing as an accident, you mean? No boom at all but a blow to the head? Of course."

"What poetic justice," Deborah said. "A second murder posing as an accident. It's symmetrical, isn't it?"

"It's a perfect sort of vengeance," Lynley said. "There's truth to that."

"But then who is Mrs. Spence?" Deborah asked.

St. James listed possibilities. "A former housekeeper who knew the truth, a neighbour, an old friend of the wife."

"The wife's sister," Deborah said. "His own sister even."

"Being urged back to the Church here in Winslough and finding him a hypocrite she couldn't endure?"

"Perhaps a cousin, Simon. Or someone who worked for the Bishop of Truro as well."

"Why not someone who was involved with Sage? Adultery cuts both ways, doesn't it?"

"He killed his wife to be with Mrs. Spence but once she discovered the truth, she wouldn't have him? She ran off?"

"The possibilities are endless. Her background's the key."

Lynley turned his pint glass thoughtfully on the table. Concentric rings of moisture marked its every position. He'd been listening but felt disinclined to dismiss all his previous conjectures. He said, "Nothing else peculiar in his background, St. James? Alcohol, drugs, an unseemly interest in something disreputable, immoral, or illegal?"

"He had a passion for Scripture, but that doesn't seem out of character in a priest. What are you looking for?"

"Something about children?"

"Paedophilia?" When Lynley nodded, St. James went on. "Not a hint of that."

"But would there be a hint, if the Church was protecting him and saving its own reputation to boot? Can you see the bishop admitting to the fact that Robin Sage had a penchant for choirboys, that he had to be moved—"

"And he moved continually, according to the Bishop of Bradford," Deborah noted.

"—because he couldn't keep his hands to himself? They'd get him help, they'd insist upon that. But would they ever admit to the truth in public?"

"I suppose it's as likely as anything else. But it seems the least plausible of the explanations. Who are the choirboys here?"

"Perhaps it wasn't boys."

"You're thinking of Maggie. And Mrs. Spence killing him to put an end to . . . what? Molestation? Seduction? If that's the case, why wouldn't she say?"

"It's still murder, St. James. She's the girl's only parent. Could she depend upon a jury seeing it her way, acquitting, and leaving her free to care for the child who depends upon her? Would she take that risk? Would anyone? Would you?"

"Why not report him to the police? To the Church?"

"It's her word against his."

"But the daughter's word . . ."

"What if Maggie chose to protect the man? What if she wanted the involvement in the first place? What if she fancied herself in love with him? Or fancied he loved her?"

St. James rubbed the back of his neck. Deborah sank her chin into the palm of her hand. Both of them sighed. Deborah said, "I feel like the Red Queen in *Alice*. We need to run twice as fast, and I'm already out of breath."

"It's not looking good," St. James agreed. "We need to know

more, and all they need to do is hold their tongues to keep us permanently in the dark."

"Not necessarily," Lynley said. "There's still Truro to consider. We've plenty of room to manoeuvre there. We've got the wife's death to dig into, as well as Robin Sage's background."

"God, that's a hike. Will you go there, Tommy?"

"I won't."

"Then who?"

Lynley smiled. "Someone on holiday. Just like the rest of us."

*   *   *

In Acton, Detective Sergeant Barbara Havers turned on the radio that sat on the top of the refrigerator, and interrupted Sting in the midst of warbling about his father's hands. She said, "Yeah, baby. Sing it, you hunk," and chuckled at herself. She liked listening to Sting. Lynley claimed her interest was rooted solely in the fact that Sting appeared to shave only once a fortnight, in a display of putative virility that was geared to attract a largely feminine following. Barbara pooh-poohed this. She argued that, for his part, Lynley was a musical snob, saying that if a piece had been composed within the last eighty years, he wouldn't offend his aristocratic ears by exposing them to it. She herself had no real predilection for rock and roll, but given her preference, she always chose it over classical, jazz, blues, or what Constable Nkata referred to as "honky Grandma tunes" which usually featured something from the forties inoffensively rendered by a full orchestra with a heavy emphasis on the strings. Nkata himself was devoted to blues, although Havers knew he'd sell his soul in an instant—not to mention his growing collection of CD's—for just five minutes alone with Tina Turner. "Never you mind she's old enough to be my mum," he'd say to his colleagues. "My mum look like that, I'd'a never left home."

Barbara turned up the volume and opened the refrigerator. She was hoping that the sight of something inside would stimulate her appetite. Instead the odour of five-day-old plaice made her retreat to the other side of the kitchen, saying, "Jesus bloody hell," with some considerable reverence while she considered how best to be rid of the leaking package of fish without having to touch it. She wondered what other malodorous surprises were waiting for discovery, wrapped in foil, stored in plastic cases, or brought home in cartons for a hasty meal and long since forgotten. From her position of safety, she spied something green climbing the edges of one container. She wanted to believe it was leftover mushy peas. The colour seemed right, but the fibrous consistency suggested mould. Next to it, a new life-form seemed to be evolving from what once had been a plate of spaghetti. In fact, the entire refrigerator looked like an unsavoury experiment-in-progress, conducted by Alexander Fleming with another trip to Stockholm in mind.

With her eyes fastened suspiciously on this mess and the back of one index finger pressed beneath her nose to breathe against shal-lowly, Barbara edged over to the kitchen sink. She rustled through cleansers, scrubbing pads, brushes, and a few stiffened lumps that had once been dish-cloths. She unearthed a carton of rubbish bags. Armed with one of these and a spatula, she advanced to do battle. The plaice went into the sack first, splatting against the floor and sending up a death howl in the form of an odour that made Barbara shudder. The mushy peas-*cum*-antibiotic went next, followed by the spaghetti, a wedge of double Gloucester that appeared to have grown some sort of interesting beard, a plate of petrified bangers and mash, and a carton of pizza which she could not get up the nerve to open. Leftover chow mein joined the mess, as did the spongy remains of half a tomato, three grapefruit halves, and a carton of milk she dis-tinctly remembered having purchased last June.

Once Barbara developed a rhythm to this catharsis of comestibles, she decided to carry it to its logical conclusion. Anything that wasn't sealed in a jar, permanently and professionally pickled, or posing as a condiment unaffected by the passage of time—out with the may-onnaise, in with the ketchup—joined the plaice and its companions-in-decomposition. By the time she was done, the refrigerator shelves were bare of anything that made even the smallest promise of a meal, but she wasn't a mourner for the edible loss. Whatever appetite she may have been trying to stimulate with her sentimental journey through the territory of ptomaine had long since disappeared.

She slammed the door home and tied up the rubbish bag with its length of wire. She opened the back door, shoved the bag outside and waited for a moment to see if it would develop legs and slither off to join the rest of the household rubbish on its own. When it didn't, she made a mental note to handle it later.

She lit a cigarette. The scent of the match and of the burning tobacco did much to mask the residual foul odour of food gone bad. She lit a second match and then a third, while all the time she inhaled the smoke from the cigarette as deeply as she could.

Not a total loss, she thought, nothing for tea or supper, but look at it this way: another job's done. All she had to do was scrub down the shelves and wash out the single drawer and the refrigerator would be ready to sell, a little old, a bit unreliable, but priced accordingly. She couldn't take it with her when she moved to Chalk Farm—the studio was far too tiny to accommodate anything larger than munchkin size—so she was going to have to clean it out eventually, sooner or later... when she was ready to move...

She went to the table and sat, her chair noisily scraping one bare metal foot against the sticky linoleum floor. She twirled the end of her cigarette between thumb and index finger and idly watched the progress of the paper burning, as the tobacco it held continued to smoulder. The occasion of having to deal with this refrigerated putrefaction had, she realised, informed against her. One more job done meant one more item ticked off the list, which put her one step closer to shutting the house, selling it, and taking herself off to an unknown new life.

By alternate days she felt ready for the move and unaccountably terrified of the change it implied. She'd been to Chalk Farm half a dozen times already, she'd paid her deposit on the little studio, she'd talked to the landlord about different curtains and about the installation of the telephone. She'd even got a brief glimpse of one of her fellow tenants, sitting in a pleasant square of sun at the window of his lower ground-level flat. Yet even while that part of her life—marked FUTURE—drew her steadily onwards, the larger part—marked PAST—kept her standing in place. She knew that there was no turning back once this house in Acton was sold. One of the last ties to her mother would be severed.

Barbara had spent the morning with her. They'd walked to the hawthorn-lined common in Greenford and sat on one of the benches that surrounded the play area, watching a young mother twirling a laughing toddler on a round-about.

It had been one of her mother's good days. She recognised Barbara, and although she slipped three times and called her Doris, she didn't argue the point when Barbara gently reminded her that Auntie Doris had been dead and gone for nearly fifty years. She merely said with a wispy smile, "I forget, Barbie. But I'm good today. Shall I come home soon?"

"Don't you like it here?" Barbara asked. "Mrs. Flo likes you. And you get on well with Mrs. Pendlebury and Mrs. Salkild, don't you?"

Her mother scrabbled at the ground beneath her feet, then held her legs out straight, like a child. She said, "Like my new shoes, Barbie."

"I thought you might." They were high-top trainers, lavender with silver stripes on the side. Barbara had found them in a rainbow selection in Camden Lock Market. She'd bought a pair for herself in red and gold—snickering at the thought of Inspector Lynley's horrified face when he saw them on her feet—and although they hadn't had any in her mother's size, she'd bought the lavender ones anyway because they were the most outrageous and consequently the most likely to please. She'd thrown in two pairs of purple-and-black argyle socks to fill up the space between her mother's feet and the shoes, and she'd smiled at the pleasure Mrs. Havers had taken at unwrapping the package and fishing through the tissue for her "surprise."

Barbara had got into the habit of bringing a little something with her on these biweekly visits to Hawthorn Lodge where, for the past two months, her mother had been living with two other elderly women and Mrs. Florence Magentry—Mrs. Flo—who cared for them. Barbara told herself that she did it for the joy of seeing her mother's face brighten at the sight of a gift. But she knew each package served as coin to purchase her freedom from guilt.

She said again, "You like it here with Mrs. Flo, don't you, Mum?"

Mrs. Havers was watching the toddler in the round-about. She was swaying to some interior tune. "Mrs. Salkild messed her pants last night," she said confidentially. "But Mrs. Flo didn't even get crossed, Barbie. She said, 'These things happen, dearie, as we get older so you mustn't worry yourself to bits.' I didn't mess my pants."

"That's good, Mum."

"I helped as well. I got the washing flannel and the plastic basin and I held it just so, so Mrs. Flo could clean her. Mrs. Salkild cried. She said, 'I'm sorry. I couldn't tell. I didn't know.' I felt bad for her. I gave her some of my chocolates after. I didn't mess my pants, Barbie."

"You're a big help to Mrs. Flo, Mum. She probably couldn't get along without you."

"She *does* say that, doesn't she? She'll be sad when I leave. Am I coming home today?"

"Not today, Mum."

"Soon though?"

"But not today."

Barbara sometimes wondered if it would be better to leave her mother in Mrs. Flo's more-than-capable hands, if she should simply pay her expenses, disappear, and hope that her mother would forget in time that she had a daughter not far away. She did continual flip-flops on the efficacy of these visits to Greenford. She went from believing they did nothing more than put momentary plasters on the sores of her own guilt at the expense of disrupting Mrs. Havers' routine to convincing herself that her steady presence in her mother's life would keep her from complete mental disintegration. There was no literature available on either position as far as Barbara knew. And even if she had tried to find it—which she couldn't bring herself to do— what difference would some conveniently removed social scientist's theories make? This was her mother, after all. She couldn't abandon her.

Barbara stabbed her cigarette into the ashtray on the kitchen table and counted the stubs that lay crushed there already. Eighteen cigarettes she'd smoked since this morning. She had to quit. It was unclean, unhealthy, and disgusting. She lit another.

From her chair, she could see down the corridor all the way to the front door. She could see the stairway to the right, the sitting room to the left. It was impossible to avoid noticing how far along the renovation of the house had moved. The interior was painted. New carpet was laid. Fixtures were repaired or replaced in the bathroom and the kitchen. The stove and oven were cleaner than they had been in twenty years. The linoleum floor still needed to be stripped completely and then rewaxed, and wallpaper still waited to be hung. But once those two jobs were taken care of, along with washing or replacing the curtains which hadn't been touched as far as Barbara knew since her family's move to the house in her childhood, she could turn her efforts to the exterior.

The back garden was a nightmare. The front garden was nonexistent. And the house itself needed massive effort: There were gutters to replace, woodwork to paint, windows to wash, a front door to refinish. And while her savings were rapidly dwindling and her own time was limited because of her job, things were still moving slowly forward according to her original plan. If she didn't do something to slow down the wheels of this entire project—initially taken on to guarantee she would have sufficient funds to keep her mother at Hawthorn Lodge indefinitely—the time for being on her own would be fast upon her.

Barbara wanted that independence, or so she kept telling herself. She was thirty-three years old, she'd never established a life of her own unattached to her family and their infinite needs. That she could do so now ought to have been a cause for jubilation at a release from bondage. But somehow it wasn't and it hadn't been since the morning she'd driven her mother to Greenford and settled her into a crisp, new life with Mrs. Flo.

Mrs. Flo had prepared for their arrival in a way that should have set every worry to rest. A welcome sign draped over the narrow stairway's banister, and there were flowers in the entry. Upstairs in her mother's room a porcelain carousel spun round slowly, playing "The Entertainer" in light chiming notes.

"Oh Barbie, Barbie, look!" her mother had breathed, and she rested her chin on the chest of drawers and watched the tiny horses rise and fall.

There were flowers in the bedroom as well, irises in a tall white vase.

"I thought she might need a special moment," Mrs. Flo said, smoothing her hands against the bodice of her pin-striped shirtwaister. "Ease her in gentle so she knows we mean to make her welcome. I've coffee and poppy seed cakes down below. Bit early for elevenses, isn't it, but I thought you might have to be off fairly quick."

Barbara nodded. "I'm working on a case in Cambridge." She looked round the room. It was so clean, crisp, and warm, with the sunlight falling across the daisy carpet. "Thank you," she said. She wasn't referring to the coffee and cakes.

Mrs. Flo patted her hand. "Don't you worry about Mum. We'll do right by her, Barbie. May I call you Barbie?"

Barbara wanted to tell her that no one but her parents had ever used that name, that it made her feel childlike and in need of care. She was about to correct her, saying, "It's Barbara, please," when she realised that to do so would be to break the illusion that somehow this was home and these women—her mother, Mrs. Flo, Mrs. Salkild, and Mrs. Pendlebury, one of whom was blind and the other another victim of dementia—constituted a family into which she herself was being offered membership if she cared to accept it. And she did.

So it wasn't so much the prospect of permanently abandoning her mother that caused Barbara to drag her feet from time to time as it became more apparent that her dream of being on her own was about to become reality. It was the prospect of her own abandonment.

For two months now, she had been coming home to an empty house, something she had longed for during the years of her father's lingering illness, something she had deemed completely indispensable when she found herself left to deal with her mother after his death. For what seemed like ages she had sought a solution to caring for her mother, and now that she had one apparently designed by heaven—God, was there another Mrs. Flo anywhere else on earth?—the focus of her plans had shifted from dealing with an ageing parent to dealing with the house. And when the house offered her nothing more to deal with, she'd be face to face with dealing with herself.

Alone, she would have to start thinking about her isolation. And when the King's Arms emptied of her colleagues in the evening—when MacPherson went home to his wife and five children, when Hale went to do increasingly dubious battle with the solicitor who was handling his divorce, when Lynley dashed off to have dinner with Helen, and Nkata drifted off to take one of his six squabbling girlfriends to bed—she'd meander slowly to St. James's Park Station, kicking at rubbish that blew in her path. She'd ride to Waterloo, change to the Northern Line, and hunch on a seat with a copy of *The Times*, feigning interest in national and world events to disguise her growing panic at being alone.

It's no crime to feel this way, she kept telling herself. You've been under someone's thumb for thirty-three years. What else would you expect to feel when the pressure's gone? What do prisoners feel when they're let out of gaol? How about liberated, she answered herself, how about like dancing in the street, like having their hair worked over by one of those posh hairdressers in Knightsbridge who have their windows all draped in black to show off blow-up snaps of gorgeous women with geometric haircuts that never grow out scraggly or get blown by the wind.

Anyone else in her position, she decided, would probably be brimming with plans, working feverishly to get this house in shape to sell so that she could start a new life which, no doubt, would begin with a wardrobe change, a body make-over courtesy of a personal trainer who looked like Arnold Schwarzenegger with better teeth, a sudden interest in make-up, and a telephone answering machine to keep track of the messages from a score of admirers all waiting to entwine their lives with hers.

But Barbara had always been a bit more practical than that. She knew change came slowly if it came at all. So right now, the move to Chalk Farm represented nothing more than unknown shops to get used to, unknown streets to navigate, unknown neighbours to meet. All of it would be done on her own, with no voice to hear in the morning save her own, no friendly noise of someone puttering about, and especially no sympathetic companion both ready and eager to listen to her assessment of how things had gone on a given day.

Of course, she'd never had a sympathetic companion involved in her life in the past, only her parents who awaited her nightly arrival, not to engage her in avid conversation but to wolf down supper and get back to the telly where they watched a succession of American melodramas.

Still, her parents had been a human presence in her life for thirty-three long and unbroken years. While they hadn't exactly filled her life with joy and a sense that the future was an unwritten slate, they had been there, needing her. And now no one did.

She realised that she wasn't so much afraid of being alone as she was of becoming one of the nation's invisibles, a woman whose presence in anyone's life had no particular importance. This house in Acton—especially if she brought her mother back to it—would eliminate the chance of her discovering that she was an unnecessary fixture in the world, eating, sleeping, bathing, and eliminating like the rest of mankind, but otherwise expendable. Locking the door, handing over the key to the estate agent, and going on her way meant risking the revelation of her own unimportance. She wanted to avoid that as long as she could.

She crushed out her cigarette, got to her feet, and stretched. Eating Greek food sounded better than did stripping and waxing the kitchen floor. Lamb *souvlakia* on rice, *dolmades*, and a half-bottle of Aristide's marginally drinkable wine. But first the rubbish bag.

It was where she had left it, outside the back door. Barbara was grateful to see that its contents hadn't managed to climb the evolutionary scale from mould and algae to anything with legs. She hoisted it up and trudged along the weed-sprung path to the rubbish bins. She lowered the bag inside just as the telephone began to ring.

"What d'you know, my date for next New Year's," she muttered. And then, "All right, I'm coming," as if the caller were telegraphing impatience.

She caught it on the eighth double ring, picking it up to hear a man say, "Ah. Good. You're there. I thought I might have missed you."

"You mean you don't miss me?" Barbara asked. "And here I was worried you'd be incapable of sleeping with the two of us so many miles apart."

Lynley chuckled. "How goes the holiday, Sergeant?"

"In fits and starts."

"You need a change of scenery to take your mind off things."

"Could be. But why do I think this is heading in a direction I might learn to regret?"

"If the direction's Cornwall?"

"That doesn't sound half bad. Who's buying?"

"I am."

"You're on, Inspector. When do I leave?"

CHAPTER TWENTY

I T WAS A QUARTER TO FIVE WHEN LYNLEY and St. James walked up the short drive to the vicarage. No car was parked there, but a light burned in what appeared to be the kitchen. Another shone behind the curtains from a first-floor room, making a tawny glow against which they could see a figure moving in silhouette, distorted Quasimodo-like from the way the material hung behind the glass. Next to the front door, a collection of rubbish waited to be carted away. It seemed to consist mostly of newspapers, empty containers for household cleaning agents, and dirty rags. These last gave off the distinct and eye-watering smell of ammonia, as if testifying to the victory of antisepsis in whatever war of cleanliness had been waged inside the house.

Lynley rang the bell. St. James looked across the street and frowned thoughtfully at the church. He said, "My guess is that she'll probably have to dig through the local newspapers to get some sort of account of the death, Tommy. I can't think the Bishop of Truro will tell Barbara anything more than his secretary told me. And that's counting on her ability to get in to see him in the first place. He could put her off for days, especially if there *is* something to hide and if Glennaven reported our visit."

"Havers'll deal with it in one fashion or another. I certainly wouldn't put strong-arming a bishop past her. That sort of thing is her stock in trade." Lynley rang the bell again.

"But as to Truro's admitting to any nasty proclivities on the part of Sage . . ."

"That's a problem. But nasty proclivities are only one possibility. We've already seen there are dozens of others, some applying to Sage, some to Mrs. Spence. If Havers uncovers anything questionable, no matter what it is, at least we'll have more to work with than we have at the moment." Lynley peered through the kitchen window. The light that was on came from a small bulb above the cooker. The room was empty. "Ben Wragg said there was a housekeeper at work here, didn't he?" He rang the bell a third time.

A voice finally responded from behind the door, hesitant and low. "Who's there, please?"

"Scotland Yard CID," Lynley replied. "I've identification if you'd like to see it."

The door cracked open, then closed quickly once Lynley had passed the warrant card through. Nearly a minute passed. A tractor rumbled by in the street. A school bus disgorged six uniformed pupils at the edge of the car park in front of St. John the Baptist Church before trundling up the incline with its indicator flashing for the Trough of Bowland.

The door opened again. A woman stood in the entry. She was holding the warrant card mostly enclosed in one fist while her other hand grabbed at the crew neck of her pullover and bunched it up as if she were concerned that it might not be covering her sufficiently. Her hair—a long crinkly mass that looked electrically charged—hid more than half of her face. The shadows hid the rest.

"Vicar's dead, you know," she said in not much more than a mumble. "Died last month. Constable found him on the footpath. He ate something bad. It was an accident."

She was stating what she must have known they'd already been told, as if she had no idea at all that New Scotland Yard had been prowling round the village for the last twenty-four hours on the trail of this death. It was difficult to believe that she wouldn't have heard of their presence before this, especially, Lynley realised as he studied her, since she certainly had been sitting in the pub with a male companion on the previous night when St. John Townley-Young had paid his call. Townley-Young had accosted the man with her, in fact.

She didn't move away from the doorway to let them in. But she shivered from the cold, and Lynley looked down to see that her feet were bare. He also saw that she was wearing trousers, fine grey herring bone.

"May we come in?"

"It was an accident," she said. "Everyone knows that."

"We won't stay long. And you ought to get out of the cold."

She gripped her pullover's neck more tightly. She looked from him to St. James and back to him before she stepped away from the door and admitted them into the house.

"You're the housekeeper?" Lynley asked.

"Polly Yarkin," she said.

Lynley introduced St. James and went on to say, "May we talk to you?" He felt the curious need to be gentle with her, and he couldn't determine exactly why. There was something both frightened and defeated in her air, like a horse that's been broken by an ill-tempered hand. She seemed ready to bolt in an instant.

She led them into the sitting room where she turned the switch on a floor lamp to no effect. She said, "Bulb's gone, isn't it," and left them alone.

In the diminishing light of dusk, they could see that whatever personal possessions the vicar had owned, they were gone. What was left was a sofa, an ottoman, and two chairs arranged round a coffee table. Across from them a bookshelf reached from floor to ceiling, empty of books. Something glittered on the floor next to this, and Lynley went to investigate. St. James strolled to the window and pushed the curtains to one side, saying, "Nothing much out there. The shrubs look bad. There're plants on the step," mostly to himself.

Lynley picked up a small globe of silver that lay, unhinged and open, on the carpet. Scattered round it were the desiccated remains of triangular fleshy bits that appeared to be fruit. He picked up one of these as well. It had no scent. Its texture was like a dried sponge. The globe was connected to a matching silver chain. Its clasp was broken.

"That's mine." Polly Yarkin had returned, lightbulb in hand. "I wondered where it got itself off to."

"What is it?"

"Amulet. For health. Mum likes me to wear it. Silly. Like garlic. But you can't tell Mum that. She's ever one to believe in charms."

Lynley handed it to her. She returned his warrant card. Her fingers felt feverish. She went to the floor lamp, changed the bulb, switched it on, and retreated to one of the chairs which she stood behind, her hands curved round its back.

Lynley went to the sofa. St. James joined him. She nodded at them to sit, although it seemed clear that she had no intention of sitting herself. Lynley gestured to the chair, said, "This won't take long," and waited for her to move.

She did so reluctantly, one hand holding on to the back of the chair as if she would pull herself behind it again. Sitting, she was more fully in the light, and it appeared that light and not their company was what she wished to avoid.

He saw for the first time that the trousers she wore belonged to a man's suit. They were far too long. She'd rolled the bottoms into bulky cuffs.

"Vicar's," she said in hesitant explanation. "I don't think anyone will mind, do you? I tripped on the back step just a bit ago. Ripped my skirt up proper. Clumsy as an old cow, I am."

He raised his eyes to her face. An angry red welt curved from under the protective curtain of her hair, marking a path that ended at the corner of her mouth.

"Clumsy," she said again, and she gave a little laugh. "I'm always running into things. Mum should've gave me an amulet to keep me steady on my feet."

She pushed her hair forward a bit more. Lynley wondered what else she was trying to hide on her face. Her skin was shiny across what he could see of her forehead, perspiration either from nerves or from illness. It wasn't warm enough in the house for the sheen of sweat to be realistically from anything else. He said, "Are you quite all right? May we phone a doctor for you?"

She rolled the trouser cuffs down to cover her feet and tucked the extra material round them. "I never seen a doctor these past ten years. I just fell. I'm all right."

"But if you've hit your head—"

"Just banged up my face on that silly door, didn't I?" She backed herself cautiously into the chair and put one hand on each arm. Her movement was slow and it looked deliberate, as if she were digging out of her memory the appropriate way to sit and behave when some-one came to call. But something about her manner—perhaps it was the way her arms moved, like mechanical extensions of her body, or the way her fingers uncurled with an effort and lay flat against the chair's upholstery—suggested that she really wanted nothing so much as to cradle herself, doubled over, until some interior pain went away.

When neither Lynley nor St. James spoke at once, she said, "Church wardens asked me to keep the place up and get it ready for another vicar. I've been cleaning. Sometimes I work too hard and get a bit sore. You know."

"You've been working on the house since the vicar died?" It seemed unlikely. The place wasn't that large.

"It takes time, doesn't it, to get things sorted out proper and to make them tidy when someone passes on."

"You've done a good job."

"It's just that they always look the vicarage over, don't they, the new ones? It helps them make a decision if they get offered the job."

"Is that how it worked with Mr. Sage? Did he come to look the vicarage over before he took the position?"

"He didn't mind what it was like. I s'pose it was because he didn't have a family so it didn't much matter about the house. There was only him in it."

"Did he ever speak of a wife?" St. James asked.

Polly reached for the amulet which lay in her lap. "Wife? Was he thinking of getting married?"

"He'd been married. He was a widower."

"He never said. I thought... Well, he didn't seem much interested in women, did he?"

Lynley and St. James exchanged a glance. Lynley said, "How do you mean?"

Polly picked up the amulet and closed her fingers round it, returning her hand to the arm of the chair. "He never acted any different with the church-cleaning ladies than he did with the blokes that ring the bells. I always thought... I thought, well, maybe the vicar's too holy. Maybe he doesn't think about ladies and such. He read the Bible lots, after all. He prayed. He wanted me to pray with him. He'd always say, Let's start the day with a prayer, dear Polly."

"What sort of prayer?"

" 'God, help us to know Your will and to find the way.' "

"That was the prayer?"

"Mostly. But it was longer'n that. I always wondered what way I was s'posed to find." Her lips curved briefly. "Find the way to cook the meat proper, I guess. Except he never complained about my cooking, the vicar. He said, You cook like Saint Somebody-or-other, dear Polly. I forget who. St. Michael? Did he cook?"

"I think he fought the devil."

"Oh. Well. I'm not religious. I mean the kind of religion with churches and such. Vicar didn't know that, which is just as well."

"If he admired your cooking, he must have told you he'd not be home for dinner the night he died."

"He only said that he wouldn't be wanting any dinner. I didn't know he was going out. I just thought maybe he wasn't feeling right."

"Why?"

"He'd been holed up in his bedroom all day, hadn't he, and he didn't eat his lunch. He came out once round tea time to use the phone in the study, but he went right back to his room when he was done."

"What time was this?"

"Round three, I guess."

"Did you hear his conversation?"

She opened her palm and looked at the amulet. She rolled her fingers against it. "I was a tad worried about him. It wasn't like Mr. Sage not to eat."

"So you heard his conversation."

"Just a tad is all. And only because I was worried. It wasn't like I was listening to *hear*. I mean, he wasn't sleeping well, the vicar. His bed was always thrashed up in the morning like he was wrestling with the sheets. And he—"

Lynley leaned forward, resting his elbows on his knees. He said, "It's all right, Polly. You had good intentions. No one's about to judge you for listening at a door."

She didn't look convinced. Distrust flickered behind the skittish movement of her eyes from Lynley to St. James back to Lynley.

"What did he say?" Lynley asked. "Who was he talking to?"

"You can't judge what happened then. You can't know what's right now. That's in God's hands, not yours."

"We aren't here to judge. That's up to—"

"No," Polly said. "That's what I heard. That's what the vicar said. You can't judge what happened then. You can't know what's right now. That's in God's hands, not yours."

"Was that the only phone call he made that day?"

"Far's I know."

"Was he angry? Was he shouting, raising his voice?"

"He sounded tired, mostly."

"You didn't see him afterwards?"

She shook her head. Afterwards, she said, she took tea to the study, only to find that he'd gone back up to his bedroom. She followed him there and knocked on the door, offering him the food which he refused.

"I said, You haven't had a bite all day, Vicar, and you must eat something, and I'm not leaving this spot until you have a bite of these nice toast fingers I've got here. So he finally opened the door. He was dressed, and the bed was made but I knew what he'd been doing."

"What?"

"Praying. He had this little prayer place in a corner of the room with a Bible on it and a place to kneel. That's where he'd been."

"How do you know?"

She rubbed her fingers against her knee in explanation. "Trousers. The crease was gone from right here. There were wrinkle places as well, where his leg bent to kneel."

"What did he say to you?"

"That I was a good soul but I mustn't worry. I asked him was he ill. He said no."

"Did you believe him?"

"I said, You're wearing yourself out, Vicar, with these trips to London. He'd just got back the day before, see. And every time he went to London, he looked a bit worse than the last time he went. And every time he went, he came home and prayed. Sometimes I wondered... Well, what was he up to in London that he came back so tired and peaky looking? But then, he went on the train, didn't he, so I thought maybe it was just the aggravation of travel and such. Getting to the station, buying all the tickets, switching trains here and there. That sort of thing. Makes you tired, a trip like that."

"Where did he go in London?"

Polly didn't know. Nor could she say what he'd been doing. Whether it was Church business, whether it was personal, the vicar kept the information to himself. The only thing Polly was able to tell them for sure was that he stayed in a hotel not far from Euston Station. It was the same hotel each time. She remembered that. Did they want the name?

Yes, if she had it.

She started to rise, then caught her breath with something like surprise when the movement didn't come easily to her. She disguised a small cry by coughing. It did little enough to hide her pain.

"Sorry," she said. "I'm silly to fall. Got myself real banged up. Clumsy old cow." She inched her way forward in the chair and pushed herself up when she got to the edge.

Lynley watched her, frowning, noting the odd manner in which she held her pullover bunched in front of her with both hands. She didn't stand up straight. When she walked she favoured her right leg.

He said abruptly, "Who's been to see you today, Polly?"

Just as abruptly she stopped. "No one. Least no one that I recall." She made a show of thinking the question over, creasing her brow and concentrating on the carpet as if she would see the answer there. "Nope. No one at all."

"I don't believe you. You didn't fall, did you?"

"I did. Out back."

"Who was it? Has Mr. Townley-Young been to see you? Did he want to talk to you about the pranks at Cotes Hall?"

She seemed genuinely surprised. "The Hall? No."

"About last night in the pub, then? About the man you were with? That was his son-in-law, wasn't it?"

"No. I mean it was. It was Brendan, true. But Mr. Townley-Young hasn't been here."

"Then who—"

"I fell. I got banged up. It'll teach me to be more careful." She left the room.

Lynley pushed himself to his feet and walked to the window. From there he paced to the bookcase. Then back to the window. A wall radiator was hissing beneath it, insistent and irritating. He tried to turn the knob. It seemed permanently stuck. He clenched it, fought with it, burnt his hand, and cursed.

"Tommy."

He swung round to St. James, who hadn't moved from the sofa. *"Who?"* he asked.

"Perhaps more importantly, why?"

"Why? For God's sake—"

St. James' voice was low and perfectly calm. "Consider the situation. Scotland Yard arrives and begins asking questions. Everyone's meant to toe the already established line. Perhaps Polly doesn't want to. Perhaps someone knows that."

"Christ, that's not even the point, St. James. Someone beat her up. Someone out there. Someone—"

"Your hands are full and she doesn't want to talk. She could be afraid. She could be merely protective. We don't know. The larger issue at the moment is whether what happened to her is connected to what happened to Robin Sage."

"You sound like Barbara Havers."

"Someone has to."

Polly returned, a slip of paper in her hand. "Hamilton House," she said. "Here's the phone as well."

Lynley put the slip of paper into his pocket. "How many times did Mr. Sage go to London?"

"Four. Perhaps five. I can look in his diary if you want to know for certain."

"His diary's still here?"

"All his things's here. His will said to give all his belongings to charity, but it didn't say which. The church council said to pack everything up until they decide where to send them. Would you like to look through it?"

"If we may."

"In the study."

She led them back along the corridor, past the stairway. She'd apparently been cleaning spots in the carpet sometime that day because Lynley noticed patches of damp that he hadn't seen when they first entered the house: near the door and in an uneven trail to the stairs where one of the walls had been washed as well. Beneath a bare urn stand opposite the stairway, a strip of multi-coloured material curled. As Polly walked on, oblivious, Lynley picked it up. It was flimsy, he discovered, similar to gauze, with threads of metallic gold running through it. It reminded him of the Indian dresses and skirts he'd often seen for sale in outdoor markets. Thoughtfully, he twisted it round his finger, felt an unusual stiffness to it, and held it up to the ceiling light which Polly had turned on in their progress towards the front of the house. The material was heavily blotched with a rusty stain. It was frayed on the edges, ripped from a larger piece, not cut with scissors. Lynley examined it with little surprise. He put it into his pocket and followed St. James into the vicar's study.

Polly stood next to the desk. She'd lit the lamp on it, but positioned herself so that her hair cast an oblique shadow across her face.

The room was crowded with cartons, all of them labelled, one of them open. This contained clothes, obviously the source of Polly's trousers.

Lynley said, "He had a lot of possessions."

"Not a lot of important stuff. It's just that he was a bit of a hoarder. When I wanted to throw something away, I had to put it in his work tray on the desk and let him decide. Mostly he kept things, especially London things. Tickets to museums, a day pass for the underground. Like they were souvenirs. He just collected odd bits, did the vicar. Some people are like that, aren't they."

Lynley wandered among the cartons, reading the labels. *Just books, loo, parish business, sitting room, vestments, shoes, study, desk, bedroom, sermons, magazines, odd bits* . . . "What's in this?" he asked of the last.

"Things from his pockets, scraps. Theatre programmes. That sort of thing."

"And the diary? Where would we find it?"

She pointed to the cartons marked *study*, *desk*, and *books*. There were at least a dozen. Lynley began moving them for easier access. He said, "Who's been through the vicar's belongings, besides yourself?"

"No one," she said. "The church council told me to pack everything up and seal it and mark it, but they haven't looked things over yet. I expect they'll want to keep the parish business carton, won't they, and they might want to offer his sermons to the new vicar as well. The clothes can go to—"

"And prior to your packing things into cartons?" Lynley asked. "Who went through his things then?"

She hesitated. She was standing near him. He could smell the odour of her perspiration soaking into the wool of her pullover.

"After the vicar died," Lynley clarified, "during the investigation, did anyone look through his belongings?"

"Constable," she said.

"Did he go through the vicar's things alone? Were you with him? Was his father?"

Her tongue darted out to dampen her upper lip. "I brought him tea. Every day. I was in and out."

"So he worked alone?" When she nodded, he said, "I see," and unsealed the first carton as St. James did the same to another. He said, "Maggie Spence was a frequent visitor to the vicarage, as I understand. She was a great favourite of the vicar."

"I suppose."

"Did they meet alone?"

"Alone?" Polly picked at a rough spot on the side of her thumb.

"The vicar and Maggie. Did they meet alone? In here? In the sitting room? Somewhere else? Upstairs?"

Polly surveyed the room as if looking for the memory. "In here mostly, I'd say."

"Alone?"

"Yes."

"Was the door open or shut?"

She began to unseal one of the cartons. "Shut. Mostly." Before Lynley could ask another question, she went on. "They liked to talk. Bible stuff. They loved the Bible. I'd bring them their tea. He'd be sitting in that chair"—she pointed to an overstuffed chair on which three more cartons were piled—"and Maggie'd be on the stool. There. In front of the desk."

A discreet four feet away, Lynley noted. He wondered who placed it there: Sage, Maggie, or Polly herself. He said, "Did the vicar meet with other young people from the parish?"

"No. Just Maggie."

"Did you think that unusual? After all, there was a social club for the teenagers, as I understand. He never met with any of them?"

"When he first got here there was a meeting in the church for the young people. To form the club. I made them scones. I remember that."

"But only Maggie came here? What about her mother?"

"Missus Spence?" Polly shuffled through the material in the carton. She made a show of examining it. It seemed to consist mostly of loose papers filled with typescript. "She never was here, Missus Spence."

"Did she phone?"

Polly considered the question. Across from her, St. James was going through a sheaf of papers and a stack of pamphlets. "Once. Near supper. Maggie was still here. She wanted her at home."

"Was she angry?"

"We didn't speak very long, so I couldn't say. She just asked was Maggie here, sort of snippy, I guess. I said yes and fetched her.

Maggie talked on the phone, mostly Yes, Mummy, No, Mummy, and Please listen, Mummy. Then she went on home."

"Upset?"

"A bit grey in the face and dragging her feet. Like she was caught doing something she wasn't supposed to. She was fond of the vicar, Maggie was. He was fond of her. But her mum didn't want that. So Maggie came to see him on the sly."

"And her mother found out. How?"

"People see things. They talk. There's no secrets in a village like Winslough."

It seemed a wildly facile statement to Lynley. As far as he had been able to ascertain, there were secrets layered upon secrets in Winslough and nearly all of them had to do with the vicar, Maggie, the constable, and Juliet Spence.

St. James said, "Is this what we're looking for?" and Lynley saw that he was holding a small engagement diary with a black plastic cover and a spiral spine. St. James handed it over and went on rooting through the carton that he had opened.

Polly said, "I'll leave you to it, then" and left them. In a moment, they could hear water running in the kitchen.

Lynley put on his spectacles and flipped through the diary from December, backwards, noting first that although the twenty-third was marked with the Townley-Young wedding and the morning of the twenty-second had *Power/Townley-Young* scrawled at half past ten, there was no reference on that same day to having dinner with Juliet Spence. The day before had a notation, however. The name *Yana-papoulis* made a diagonal across the lines for appointments.

"When did Deborah meet him?" Lynley asked.

"When you and I were in Cambridge. November. A Thursday. Was it round the twentieth?"

Lynley flipped the pages forward. They were filled with notations about the vicar's life. Meetings of the altar society, visitations to the sick, the assembling of his fledgling teen club, baptisms, three funerals, two weddings, sessions that looked like marital counseling, presentations before the church council, two clerical gatherings in Bradford.

He found what he was looking for on Thursday the sixteenth, *SS* next to one o'clock. But at that point, the trail went cold. There were names listed next to times further back, all the way to the vicar's

arrival in Winslough. Some were Christian names, some were sur-
names. But it was impossible to tell if they belonged to parishioners
or if they indicated Sage's business in London.

He looked up. "SS," he said to St. James. "Does that suggest
anything to you?"

"Someone's initials."

"Possibly. Except that he's not used initials any place else. It's
always names except this once. What does that suggest?"

"An organisation?" St. James looked reflective. "Nazis come to
mind."

"Robin Sage, neo-Nazi? A closet skinhead?"

"Secret Service, perhaps?"

"Robin Sage, Winslough's budding James Bond?"

"No, it would have been MI5 or 6 then, wouldn't it? Or SIS."
St. James began replacing items in the carton. "Nothing much in
here aside from the diary. Stationery, business cards—his own,
Tommy—part of a sermon on the lilies of the field, ink, pens, pencils,
farming guides, two packets of seeds for tomatoes, a file of corre-
spondence filled with letters of dismissal, letters of application, letters
of acceptance. An application for—" St. James frowned.

"What?"

"Cambridge. Partially filled out. Doctor of theology."

"And?"

"It isn't that. It's the application, any application. Partially filled
out. It reminded me of what Deborah and I have been . . . Never
mind that. It brings to mind SS. What about Social Services?"

Lynley saw the leap his friend had made from his own life. "He
wanted to adopt a child?"

"Or to place a child?"

"Christ. Maggie?"

"Perhaps he saw Juliet Spence as an unfit mother."

"That might push her to violence."

"It's certainly a thought."

"But there hasn't been the slightest whisper of that from any
quarter."

"There usually isn't if the situation's abusive. You know how it
goes. The child's afraid to speak, trusting no one. When she finally
finds someone she can trust . . ." St. James refolded the carton's flaps
and pressed the tape back down to seal them.

"We may have been looking at Robin Sage through the wrong sort of window," Lynley said. "All those meetings with Maggie alone. Instead of seduction, he might have been trying to get to the truth." Lynley sat in the desk chair and set the diary down. "But this is pointless speculation. We don't know enough. We don't even know when he went to London because you can't tell from the diary *where* he was. It has names and times listed, scores of appointments, but aside from Bradford, there's no place mentioned."

"He kept the receipts." Polly Yarkin spoke from the doorway. She was carrying a tray on which she'd assembled a teapot, two cups and saucers, and a half-crushed package of chocolate digestives. She put the tray on the desk and said, "Hotel receipts. He kept them. You can match up the dates."

They found the file of Robin Sage's hotel receipts in the third box they tried. These documented five visits to London, beginning in October and ending just two days before he died, 21 December, when *Yanapapoulis* was written. Lynley matched the receipt dates to the diary, but he came up with only three more pieces of information that looked even marginally promising: the name *Kate* next to noon on Sage's first London visit of 11 October; a telephone number on his second; *SS* again on his third.

Lynley tried the number. It was a London exchange. An exhausted end-of-the-working-day voice said, "Social Services," and Lynley smiled and gave St. James a thumb's-up. His conversation was unprofitable, however. There was no way to ascertain the purpose of any telephone call Robin Sage may have made to Social Services. There was no one there by the name of Yanapapoulis, and it was otherwise impossible to track down the social worker to whom Sage had spoken when, and if, he had made the call. Additionally, if he had paid anyone a visit at Social Services on one of his trips to London, he took that secret with him to his grave. But at least they had something to work with, however little it was.

Lynley said, "Did Mr. Sage mention Social Services to you, Polly? Did Social Services ever phone him here?"

"Social Services? You mean about taking care of old folks or something?"

"For any reason, really." When she shook her head, Lynley asked, "Did he speak about visiting Social Services in London? Did he ever bring anything back with him? Documents, paperwork?"

"There might be something with the odd bits," she said.

"What?"

"If he brought anything back and left it round the study, it'll be in the odd bits carton."

When he opened it, Lynley found that the odd bits carton appeared to be a hotchpotch display of Robin Sage's life. It contained everything from pre-Jubilee-Line maps of the London underground to a yellowing collection of the sort of historical pamphlets one can purchase for ten pence in country churches. A stack of book reviews clipped from *The Times* looked fragile enough to suggest they'd been gathered over a period of years, and going through them revealed that the vicar's taste tended towards biography, philosophy, and whatever had been nominated for the Booker Prize in a given year. Lynley handed a stack of papers to St. James and sank back in the desk chair to peruse another. Polly moved gingerly round them, realigning some cartons, checking the seals on others. Lynley felt her glance repeatedly resting upon him then flitting away.

He looked through his stack. Explanations of museum exhibits; a guide to the Turner Gallery at the Tate; receipts for lunches, dinners, and teas; manuals explaining the use of an electric saw, the assembly of a bicycle's basket, the cleaning of a steam iron; advertisements extolling the benefits of joining an exercise club; and handouts one collects when strolling along a London street. These consisted of offers for hairstyling (*The Hair Apparent, Clapham High Street, Ask for Sheelah*); grainy photographs of automobiles (*Drive The New Metro From Lambeth Ford*); political announcements (*Labour Speaks Tonight 8:00 Camden Town Hall*); along with assorted advertisements and solicitations for charities from the RSPCA to Homeless Relief. A brochure from the Hare Krishnas played the roll of a bookmark inside a copy of the Book of Common Prayer. Lynley flipped it open and read the prayer marked, from Ezekiel: *"When the wicked man turneth away from his wickedness that he hath committed, and doeth that which is lawful and right, he shall save his soul alive."* He read it again, aloud, and looked up at St. James. "What was it Glennaven said that the vicar liked to discuss?"

"The difference between that which is moral—prescribed by law—and that which is right."

"Yet according to this, the Church seems to feel they're one in the same."

"That's the wonderful way of churches, isn't it?" St. James unfolded a piece of paper, read it, set it to one side, picked it up again.

Lynley said, "Was it logic chopping on his part, talking about moral versus right? Was it a form of avoidance in which he engaged his fellow clerics in meaningless discussion?"

"That's certainly what Glennaven's secretary thought."

"Or was he himself on the horns of a dilemma?" Lynley gave the prayer a second look. " '. . . he shall save his soul alive.' "

"Here's something," St. James said. "There's a date on the top. It says only the eleventh, but the paper looks at least relatively fresh, so it might match up to one of the London visits." He handed it over.

Lynley read the scrawled words. "Charing Cross to Sevenoaks, High Street left towards . . . These appear to be a set of directions, St. James."

"Does the date match up with one of the London visits?"

Lynley went back to the diary. "The first. The eleventh of October, where the name *Kate* is listed."

"He could have gone to see her. Perhaps that visit set in motion the rest of the trips. To Social Services. Even to . . . what was that name in December?"

"Yanapapoulis."

St. James cast a quick look at Polly Yarkin and finished obliquely with, "And any of those visits could have served as instigation."

It was all conjecture, based upon air, and Lynley knew it. Each interview, fact, conversation, or step in the investigation was taking their thoughts in a new direction. They had no hard evidence, and from what he could tell, unless someone had removed it, there had never been hard evidence in the first place. No weapon left at the scene of the crime, no incriminating fingerprint, no wisp of hair. There was nothing, in fact, to connect the alleged killer and her victim at all save a telephone call overheard by Maggie and inadvertently corroborated by Polly, and a dinner after which both parties became ill.

Lynley knew that he and St. James were engaged in piecing together a tapestry of guilt from the thinnest of threads. He didn't like it. Nor did he like the indications of interest and curiosity that Polly Yarkin was attempting to hide, shuffling a carton here, moving a second one there, rubbing her sleeve across the base of the lamp to remove spots of dust that didn't exist.

"Did you go to the inquest?" he asked her.

She withdrew her arm from the vicinity of the lamp, as if caught in an act of misbehaviour. "Me? Yes. Everyone went."

"Why? Did you have evidence to give?"

"No."

"Then . . . ?"

"Just . . . I wanted to know what happened. I wanted to hear."

"What?"

She lifted her shoulders slightly, allowed them to drop. "What she had to say. Once I knew the vicar had been with her that night. Everyone went," she repeated.

"Because it was the vicar? And a woman? Or this particular woman, Juliet Spence?"

"Can't say," she said.

"About everyone else? Or about yourself?"

She dropped her eyes. The simple action was enough to tell him why she'd brought them the tea and why, after seeing to its pouring, she'd remained in the study shifting cartons and watching them sift through the vicar's possessions long after it was necessary for her to do so.

CHAPTER TWENTY-ONE

HEN POLLY HAD SHUT THE DOOR BEHIND them, St. James and Lynley got as far as the end of the drive before Lynley stopped and gave his concentration to the silhouette of St. John the Baptist Church. Complete darkness had fallen. Street lamps were lit along the incline that led through the village. They beamed ochreous rays through an evening mist and cast their shadows within the elongated pools of their own light on the damp street below. Here by the church, however, outside the boundary of the village proper, a full moon—rising past the summit of Cotes Fell—and its companion stars provided the sole illumination.

"I could use a cigarette," Lynley said absently. "When do you expect I'll stop feeling the need to light up?"

"Probably never."

"That's certainly a comforting reassurance, St. James."

"It's merely statistical probability combined with scientific and medical likelihood. Tobacco's a drug. One never completely recovers from addiction."

"How did you escape it? There we all were, sneaking a smoke after games, lighting up the very instant we crossed the bridge into Windsor, impressing ourselves—and trying like the devil to impress everyone else—with our individual, nicotinic adulthood. What happened to you?"

"Exposure to an early allergic reaction, I suppose." When Lynley glanced his way, St. James continued. "My mother caught David with a packet of Dunhills when he was twelve. She shut him up in the lavatory and made him smoke them all. She shut the rest of us in there with him."

"To smoke?"

"To watch. Mother's always been a strong believer in the power of an object lesson."

"It worked."

"With me, yes. With Andrew as well. Sid and David, however, always found the thrill of displeasing Mother more than equal to whatever discomfort they themselves might incur as a result. Sid smoked like a chimney until she was twenty-three. David still does."

"But your mother was right. About the tobacco."

"Of course. But I'm not sure her methods of educating her off-spring were particularly sound. She could be a real termagant when pushed to the edge. Sid always claimed it was her name: What else can you expect from someone called Hortense, Sidney'd demand after we'd suffered a whipping for one infraction or another. I, on the other hand, tended to believe she was saddled rather than blessed by moth-erhood. My father kept late hours, after all. She was on her own, despite the presence of whatever nanny David and Sid hadn't man-aged to terrorise into leaving yet."

"Did you feel yourself abused?"

St. James buttoned his topcoat against the chill. There was little breeze here—the church acted as a break against the wind that oth-erwise funnelled through the dale—but the falling mist was frost in the making, and it lay upon his skin in a clammy webbing that seemed to seep through muscle and blood to the bone. He stifled a shiver and thought about the question.

His mother's anger had always been terrifying to behold. She was Medea incarnate when crossed. She was quick to strike, quicker to shout, and generally unapproachable for hours—sometimes days—after a transgression had been committed. She never acted without cause; she never punished without explanation. Yet in some eyes, he knew, and especially in modern eyes, she would have been seen as extremely wanting.

"No," he said and felt it to be the truth. "We tended to be an unruly lot, given half a chance. I think she was doing the best she could."

Lynley nodded and went back to his study of the church. As far as St. James could tell, there wasn't much to see. Moonlight glinted off the crenellated roofline and sketched in silver the contour of a tree in the graveyard. The rest was one variation or another of darkness and shadow: the clock in the belltower, the peaked roof of the lych-gate, the small north porch. It would be growing close to the time for evensong, but no one was readying the church for prayers.

St. James waited, watching his friend. They'd brought away from the study the odd bits carton, which St. James was carrying under his arm. He set it on the ground and blew on his hands to warm them. The action roused Lynley, who looked his way and said, "Sorry. We should be off. Deborah will be wondering what's happened to us." Still he didn't move. "I was thinking."

"About abusive mothers?"

"In part. But more about how it all fits. If it all fits. If there's the slightest possibility that *anything* fits."

"The girl didn't say anything to suggest abuse when she spoke to you today?"

"Maggie? No. But she wouldn't, would she? If the truth is that she revealed something to Sage—something he felt he had to act upon and something that cost him his life at her mother's hands— she wouldn't be likely to reveal it a second time to anyone else. She'd be feeling responsible as hell for what happened."

"You don't sound as if you're keen on that idea, despite the phone call to Social Services."

Lynley nodded. The mist made a penumbra of the moonlight in which his expression was moody, with shadows drawn beneath his eyes. " 'When the wicked man turneth away from his wickedness that he hath committed, and doeth that which is lawful and right, he shall save his soul alive.' Did Sage intend the prayer to refer to Juliet Spence or to himself?"

"Perhaps neither. You may be making too much of nothing. It may have merely been a chance marking in the book. Or it may have referred to someone else entirely. It could be a piece of Scripture that Sage was using to comfort someone who had come to him to confess. For that matter, since we know he was trying to woo people back to the Church, he could have been using the prayer for that. Doeth that which is lawful and right: Worship God on Sundays."

"Confession's something I hadn't thought of," Lynley admitted.

"I keep the worst of my sins to myself, and I can't imagine anyone else doing otherwise. But what if someone did confess to Sage and then regretted having done so?"

St. James mulled the idea over. "The possibilities are so narrow that I think it unlikely, Tommy. According to what you're attempting to set up, the regretful penitent would have to be someone who knew Sage was going to Juliet Spence's that night for dinner. Who knew?" He began to list. "We have Mrs. Spence herself. We have Maggie—"

A door slammed with an echo that bounded across the street. They turned at the sound of hurried footsteps. Colin Shepherd was opening the door to his Land Rover, but he hesitated when he caught sight of them.

"And the constable, of course," Lynley murmured and moved to intercept Shepherd before he left.

At first, St. James remained where he was at the end of the drive, a few yards away. He saw Lynley pause fractionally at the edge of the cone of light cast by the interior of the Rover. He saw him remove his hands from his pockets, and he noted, with some uneasy confusion, that his right hand was balled. St. James knew his friend well enough to realise that it might be wise to join them.

Lynley was saying in a chillingly pleasant tone, "You've apparently had an accident, Constable?"

"No," Shepherd said.

"Your face?"

St. James reached the edge of the light. The constable's face was abraded on both the forehead and the cheeks. Shepherd's fingers touched one of the scratches. "This? Rough-housing with the dog. Up on Cotes Fell. You were there yourself today."

"I? On Cotes Fell?"

"At the Hall. You can see it from the fell. Anyone up there can see anything, in fact. The Hall, the cottage, the garden. Anything. Do you know that, Inspector? Anyone who chooses can see anything below."

"I prefer less indirection in my conversations, Constable. Are you trying to tell me something, aside from what happened to your face, of course?"

"You can see anyone's movements, the comings and goings, whether the cottage is locked, who's working at the Hall."

"And, no doubt," Lynley finished for him, "when the cottage is vacant and where the key to the root cellar is kept. Which is, I take it, the point you're trying to make, however obliquely. Have you an accusation you'd like to share?"

Shepherd was carrying a torch. He threw it into the front seat of the Rover. "Why don't you start asking what the summit is used for? Why don't you ask who goes hiking up the fell?"

"You do yourself, by your own admission. And it's a rather damning one, wouldn't you say?" The constable made a sound of disdain and began to climb into the car. Lynley stopped him by noting, "You seem to have eschewed the accident theory you were espousing yesterday. Might I know why? Has something caused you to decide your initial investigation was incomplete?"

"Those are your words, not mine. You're here at your own desire, no one else's. I'll thank you to remember that." He put his hand on the steering wheel, a prefatory movement to entering the car.

"Did you look into his trip to London?" Lynley asked.

Shepherd hesitated, his expression guarded. "Whose?"

"Mr. Sage went to London in the days before he died. Did you know that?"

"No."

"Polly Yarkin didn't tell you? Did you interview Polly? She was his housekeeper, after all. She'd know more about the vicar than anyone else. She'd be the one who—"

"I spoke to Polly. But I didn't interview her. Not officially."

"Then unofficially? And recently, perhaps? Today?"

The questions hung between them. In the silence, Shepherd removed his spectacles. The mist that was falling had sheened them lightly. He rubbed them against the front of his jacket.

"You've broken your glasses as well," Lynley noted. They were, St. James saw, held together across the bridge by a small piece of tape. "That's quite a bit of rough-housing with the dog. Up on Cotes Fell."

Shepherd replaced them. He dug in his pocket and brought out a set of keys. He faced Lynley squarely. "Maggie Spence has run off," he said. "So if there's nothing else you'd care to remark on, Inspector, Juliet's expecting me. She's a bit upset. Evidently you didn't tell her you'd be going by the school to talk to Maggie. Headmistress thought otherwise, as I understand. And you spoke with the girl alone. Is that how the Yard operates these days?"

Touché, St. James thought. The constable wasn't about to be intimidated. He had weapons of his own and the nerve to use them.

"Did you look for a connection between them, Mr. Shepherd? Did you ever dig for a less salubrious truth than the one you came up with?"

"My investigation stood firm on its own," he said. "Clitheroe saw it that way. Coroner saw it that way. Whatever connection I may have failed to see, I'll put money on its linking someone else to his death, not Juliet Spence. Now if you'll excuse me . . ." He swung himself into the car and jammed the key into the ignition. The engine roared. The headlamps flared. He ground the gears as he shifted to reverse.

Lynley leaned into the car for another few words, which St. James couldn't hear beyond " . . . this with you . . . " as he pressed something into Shepherd's hand. Then the car slid down the driveway to the street, the gears ground another time, and the constable soared off.

Lynley watched him go. St. James watched Lynley. His face was grim. "I'm not enough like my father," Lynley said. "He would have dragged him bodily into the street, stepped on his face, and probably broken six or eight of his fingers. He did that once, you know, outside a pub in St. Just. He was twenty-two. Someone had made fast and loose with Augusta's affections and he took care of the situation. 'No one breaks my sister's heart,' he said."

"That doesn't solve much."

"No." Lynley sighed. "But I've always thought it would feel so damn good."

"Anything atavistic generally does, for the moment. It's what follows that causes complications."

They went back down the drive where Lynley picked up the odd bits carton. Perhaps a quarter of a mile down the road, they could see the tail lights of the Land Rover gleaming. Shepherd had pulled to the verge for some reason. His headlamps illuminated the gnarled form of a hedgerow. They watched for a moment to see if he would drive on. When he didn't, they began their walk back to the inn.

"What next?" St. James asked.

"London," Lynley said. "It's the only direction I can think of at the moment, as strong-arming suspects doesn't appear to be something that's going to have any appreciable effect."

"Will you use Havers?"

"Speaking of strong-arming." Lynley chuckled. "No, I'll have to see to it myself. Since I've sent her to Truro on my credit cards, I don't imagine she'll be hell-bent on getting down there and back in the customary twenty-four police hours. I'd say three days... with first-class accommodations all the way, no doubt. So I'll handle London."

"What can we do to help?"

"Enjoy your holiday. Take Deborah on a drive. Cumbria, perhaps."

"The lakes?"

"That's a thought. But I understand Aspatria's quite nice in January."

St. James smiled. "That's going to be one hell of a day trip. We'll have to be up by five. You'll owe me for this. And if there's nothing to be uncovered about the Spence woman there, you'll owe me in spades."

"As always."

Ahead of them, a black cat slinked out from between two buildings, something grey and limp between its jaws. This the animal deposited on the pavement and began tapping gently in the mindlessly cruel way of all cats, hoping for more tormenting play before a final pounce ended the captive's fruitless hope for survival. As they approached, the animal froze, hunched over its prize, fur bristling, waiting. St. James glanced down to see a small rat blinking hopelessly from between the cat's paws. He thought about frightening the cat away. The game of death it played was unnecessarily heartless. But rats, he knew, were breeders of disease. It was best—if not most merciful—to let the cat continue.

"What would you have done had Polly named Shepherd?" St. James asked.

"Arrested the bastard. Turned him over to Clitheroe CID. Had his job."

"And since she didn't name him?"

"I'll have to come at it from another direction."

"To step on his face?"

"Metaphorically. I'm my father's own son in wish, if not in deed. It's nothing I'm proud of. But there it is."

"So what did you give Shepherd just before he drove off?"

Lynley adjusted the carton beneath his arm. "I gave him something to think about."

.   .   .

Colin remembered with perfect clarity the final time his father had struck him. He was sixteen years old. Foolish, too hot-headed to think of the consequences of defiance, he had risen angrily and bodily to his mother's defence. Shoving his chair back from the dinner table—he could still recall the sound it made as it scraped across the floor and slammed into the wall—he'd shouted, Just leave her alone, Pa! and grabbed his father's arms to keep him from slapping her face another time.

Pa's rage always took root in something inconsequential, and because they never knew when to expect his anger to flare into violence, he was that much more terrifying. Anything could set him off: the condition of a beef joint at dinner, a button missing from his shirt, a request for money to pay the gas bill, a comment about the hour at which he had arrived home the previous night. This particular evening it was a telephone call from Colin's biology master. Another exam failed, lessons incomplete, was there a problem at home, Mr. Tranville wondered.

His mother had revealed that much over the dinner table, tentatively, as if attempting to telegraph her husband a message she was unwilling to say in front of their child. "Colin's teacher asked if there were problems, Ken. Here at home. He said counselling might—"

Which was as far as she'd got. Pa said, "Counselling? Did I hear you right? Counselling?" in a tone that should have told her that she'd have been wiser to eat quietly and keep the telephone call to herself.

But instead, she said, "He can't study, Ken, if things are in chaos. You see that, don't you?" in a voice that pleaded for reason but only succeeded in betraying her fear.

Pa thrived on fear. He loved to feed twigs of intimidation into its fire. He set down his knife first, then his fork. He pushed back his chair from the table. He said, "Tell me about all this chaos, Clare." When she read his intentions and said she supposed it was nothing, really, his father said, "No. Tell me. I want to hear." When she didn't cooperate, he got up. He said, "Answer me, Clare," and when she said, "Nothing. Do eat your meal, Ken," he was on her.

He'd only managed to strike her three times—one hand twisted in her hair and the other smacking harder each time she cried out—when Colin grabbed him. His father's response was the same as it had been from Colin's childhood. Women's faces were meant to be abused with the open hand. On boy children a real man used his fists.

The difference this time was that Colin was bigger. And while he was as afraid of his father as he'd always been, he was also angry. Anger and fear washed his body with adrenaline. When Pa struck him, for the first time in his life, Colin struck back. It had taken more than five minutes for his father to beat him into submission. He did it with his fists, his belt, and his feet. But when it was over, the delicate balance of power had shifted. And when Colin said, "I'll kill you next time, you filthy bastard. Just see if I won't," he saw for an instant, reflected on his father's face, that he too was capable of inspiring fear.

It had been a source of pride to Colin that his father had never struck his mother again, that his mother had filed for divorce a month later, and most of all that they were rid of the bastard because of *him*. He'd sworn he'd never be like his father. He'd never again struck a living soul. Until Polly.

On the side of the road leading out of Winslough, Colin sat in the Land Rover and rolled between his palms the piece of material from Polly's skirt which the inspector had pressed into his hand. All of it had been such a pleasure: feeling the sting of her flesh against his palm, tearing the material so easily from her body, tasting the salty sweat of her terror, hearing her cries, her pleas, and especially her choked sob of pain—no moan of sexual arousal now, Polly, is this what you wanted, is this how you hoped it would happen between us?—and finally accepting the triumph of her numb defeat. He slammed into her, he ploughed her, he mastered her, all the time saying cow bitch sow cunt in his father's voice.

He'd done it all in a storm of blind rage and desperation, frantic to keep the memory and the truth of Annie at bay.

Colin pressed the piece of material to his closed eyes and tried not to think about either of them, Polly or his wife. With Annie's dying, he'd crossed every line, violated every code, wandered in the dark, and lost himself entirely, somewhere between the valley of his worst depression and the desert of his blackest despair. He'd spent the years since her death caught between trying to rewrite the history of her torturous illness and trying to recall, reinvent, and resurrect the image of a marriage that was utterly perfect. The resulting lie had been so much easier to face than the reality that when Polly tried to obliterate it forever in the vicarage, Colin struck out in an effort to preserve it as much as in an attempt to hurt her.

He'd always felt he could continue to cope and move forward in life as long as he had the falsehood. It comprised what he called the sweetness of their relationship, the sure knowledge that with Annie he'd had warmth and tenderness, complete understanding, compassion, and love. It also comprised an account of her illness, one filled with the details of her noble suffering, replete with illustrations of his efforts to save her and his eventual calm acceptance of the fact he could not. The falsehood depicted him at her bedside, holding her hand and trying to memorise the colour of her eyes before she closed them forever. The falsehood declared that as life was taken from her in vicious bits and pieces, her optimism never faltered and her spirit stayed whole.

You'll forget all this, people had said at the funeral. Given time, you'll remember only the beauty of what you had. And you had two wonderful years with her, Colin. So let time work its magic, and watch what happens. You'll heal and look back and still have those two years.

It hadn't happened that way. He hadn't healed. He'd simply rearranged his recollection of what the end had been like and how they'd got there. In his revised version of their history, Annie had accepted her fate with grace and dignity while he had been unfailing in his support of her. Gone from memory were her descents into bitterness. Excised from existence was his implacable rage. In the place of these was a new reality that masked everything he couldn't face: how he hated her in moments as much as he loved her, how he despised his marriage vows, how he embraced her death as his only possible escape from a life that he could not bear, and how in the end all they had to share in a marriage that had once been joyful was the fact of her illness and the day-to-day horror of having to cope with it.

Make it different, he had thought, after she had died, make me better than I was. And he had used the past six years to do so, seeking oblivion instead of forgiveness.

He rubbed the gauzy material against his face, feeling it snag on the scratches that Polly's nails had left. It was stiff in places with Polly's blood and musty with the scent of her body's secrets.

"I'm sorry," he whispered. "Polly."

He'd been steadfast in his unwillingness to face Polly Yarkin because of what she represented. She knew the facts. She also forgave them. But her knowledge alone made her the single contagion he had to avoid if he was to continue to live with himself. She couldn't see this fact. She was incapable of grasping the importance of their leading completely separate lives. She saw only her love for him and her longing to make him whole once again. If she'd only been able to understand that they'd shared too much of Annie ever to be able to share each other, she would have learned to accept the limitations he'd imposed upon their relationship after his wife's death. Accepting these, she would have allowed him to go his own way without her. Ultimately, she would have rejoiced in his love for Juliet. And, thus, Robin Sage would still be alive.

Colin knew what had happened and how she had done it. He understood why. If keeping the knowledge to himself was the only way he could make amends to Polly, he would do that. Scotland Yard would unravel the skein of events in good time once they looked into her access to Cotes Fell. He would not betray her while he himself bore so much responsibility for what she had done.

He drove on. Unlike the previous night, all the lights were on in the cottage when he pulled to a stop in the courtyard of Cotes Hall. Juliet ran out as he opened the car door. She was struggling into her pea jacket. A red-and-green scarf dangled from her arm like a banner.

"Thank God," she said. "I thought I'd go mad with the waiting."

"Sorry." He got out of the Land Rover. "Those blokes from Scotland Yard stopped me as I was leaving."

She hesitated. "You? Why?"

"They'd been to the vicarage."

She buttoned the coat, wrapped the scarf round her neck. She fished gloves from her pocket and began drawing them on. "Yes. Well. I've them to thank for this, don't I?"

"They'll be off soon, I expect. The inspector's got the wind up about the vicar going to London the day before he . . . you know. The day before he died. He'll no doubt be on the trail of that next. And then on the trail of something else afterwards. That's how it goes with these types. So he won't be bothering Maggie again."

"Oh God." Juliet was looking at her hands, taking too much time about adjusting the gloves. She was smoothing the leather against each finger in an uneven motion that betrayed her anxiety. "I've phoned the police in Clitheroe, but they couldn't be bothered to take me seriously. She's thirteen years old, they said, she's only been gone for three hours, madam, she'll turn up by nine. Kids always do. But they don't, Colin. You know it. They don't always turn up. And not in this case. Maggie won't. I don't even know where to begin looking for her. Josie said she ran off from the schoolyard. Nick went after her. I must find her."

He took her arm. "I'll find her for you. You've got to wait here."

She twisted from his grasp. "No! You can't. I need to know . . . I just . . . Listen to me. I must be the one. I've got to find her. I must do it myself."

"You need to stay here. She may phone. If she does, you'll want to be able to fetch her, won't you?"

"I can't just wait here."

"You've no choice."

"And you don't understand. You're trying to be kind. I know that. But listen. She isn't going to phone. The inspector's been with her. He's filled her head with all sorts of things . . . Please. Colin. I've got to find her. Help me."

"I will. I am. I'll phone the instant I have any news. I'll stop in Clitheroe and get some men out in cars. We'll find her. I promise you. Now go back inside."

"No. Please."

"It's the only way, Juliet." He led her towards the house. He could feel her resistance. He opened the door. "Stay by the phone."

"He filled her head with lies," she said. "Colin, where's she gone? She has no money, no food. She's got only her school coat to keep her warm. It's not heavy enough. It's cold and God knows—"

"She can't have got far. And remember, she's with Nick. He'll watch out for her."

"But if they hitchhiked . . . if someone picked them up. My God, they could be in Manchester by now. Or Liverpool."

He ran his fingers against her temples. Her great dark eyes were tear-filled and frightened. "Sssh," he whispered. "Let the panic go, love. I said I'll find her and I will. You can trust me on that. You can trust me on anything. Gentle, now. Rest." He loosened her scarf and unbuttoned her coat. He caressed the line of her jaw with his knuckles. "You make her some dinner and keep it warm on the cooker. She'll be eating it sooner than you can know. I promise." He touched her lips and her cheeks. "Promise."

She swallowed. "Colin."

"Promise. You can trust me."

"I know that. You're so good to us."

"As I mean to be forever." He kissed her gently. "Will you be all right now, love?"

"I . . . Yes. I'll wait. I won't leave." She lifted his hand, pressed it against her lips. Then her forehead creased. She drew him into the light of the entry. "You've hurt yourself," she said. "Colin, what have you done to your face?"

"Nothing that you need to worry about," he said. "Ever," and he kissed her again.

■ ■ ■

When she'd watched him drive off, when the sound of the Rover's engine faded and was replaced by the night wind creaking in the trees, Juliet let the pea jacket fall from her shoulders and left it in a heap by the front cottage door. She dropped her scarf on top of it. She kept on her gloves.

These she examined. They were made of old leather lined with rabbit fur, the skin feather-smooth with the years she had worn them, a thread unravelling along the inner right wrist. She pressed them against her cheeks. The leather was cool but she could feel nothing of her face's temperature through the gloves, so it was much like being touched by someone else, like having her face cupped with tenderness, with love, with amusement, or with anything else that hinted remotely at romantic attachment.

That's what had started all this in the first place: her need for a man. She'd managed to avoid the need for years by keeping herself and her daughter isolated—just Mummy and Maggie taking on the human race in one part of the country or another. She'd diverted both the interior longing and the dull pain of desire by throwing her energies into Maggie, because Maggie was what her life was all about.

Juliet knew she had bought and paid for this night's anguish in coin she had minted from a part of her make-up that had never failed to give her grief. Wanting a man, hungering to touch the hard fierce angles of his body, longing to lie beneath him—to straddle or to kneel—and to feel that moment's delight in their bodies' joining . . . These were the voids that had started her on this current path to disaster. So it was utterly fitting that physical desire, which she had never been able to eradicate completely no matter how many years she refused to acknowledge it, should be what had brought her to losing Maggie tonight.

There were dozens of *if only*'s barking in her head, but she fastened on one of them because, although she wanted to do so, she couldn't lie to herself about its importance. She had to accept her involvement with Colin as the prime mover behind everything that had happened with Maggie.

She'd heard about him from Polly long before she'd ever seen him. And she'd thought herself secure in the belief that since Polly was herself in love with the man, since he was so many years her own junior, since she rarely saw him—indeed, since she rarely saw anyone now that they'd found what she'd come to believe was an ideal location to get on with their lives at last—she stood little chance of involvement or attachment. Even when he came to the cottage that day on his official business and she saw him parked by the lavender on the lane and read the bleak despair on his face and recalled Polly's story about his wife, even when she felt the ice of her detached composure receive its first rift in the face of his sorrow and for the first time in years she recognised a stranger's pain, she'd not considered the danger he presented to the weakness in herself that she believed she had mastered.

It was only when he was inside the cottage and she saw him looking round at the frivolous fittings of the kitchen with such ill-disguised yearning that she felt her heart stir. At first, getting ready to pour them each a glass of her homemade wine, she'd looked round herself to try to understand what was moving him. She knew it couldn't be the superficials—cooker, table, chairs, cupboards—and she wondered at the fact that the rest might be touching him in some way. Could a man be moved by a rack of spices, African violets in the window, jars on the work top, two loaves of bread left to cool, a rack of washed dishes, a tea towel hanging from a drawer to dry? Or was it the finger-painted and oft-moved picture affixed with Blu-Tack to the wall above the cooker: two skirt-wearing stick figures—one with breasts that looked like lumps of coal—surrounded by flowers as tall as themselves and surmounted by the words *I love you, Mummy* in a five-year-old's hand. He'd looked at it, looked at her, looked away, and finally didn't seem to know where to look at all.

Poor man, she had thought. And that had been her downfall. She knew about his wife, she began to speak, and she'd not been able to turn back from that moment. Sometime during their conversation, she'd thought *just this once oh God to have a man that way just this once one more time he's so hurting and if I control it if I'm the one if it's only his pleasure with no thought of my own can it be such a wrong,* and as he asked her about the shotgun and why she had used it and how, she had watched his eyes. She answered, keeping everything brief and to the point. And when he would have left—all information having been gathered, and thank you, madam, for your time—she decided to show him the pistol to keep him from going. She shot it and waited for him to react, to take it from her, to touch her hand as he removed it from her grip, but he wouldn't, he kept the distance between them, and she realised with a sudden dawning of wonder that he was thinking those very same words *just this once oh God just this once.*

It wouldn't be love, she decided, because she was those ugly, gaping ten years older than he, because they didn't even know each other and had not spoken before this day, because the religion she'd long ago forsaken declared that love didn't grow from allowing the needs of the flesh to dominate the needs of the soul.

She held on to those thoughts as that first afternoon together wore on, believing herself safe from loving. This would just be for pleasure, she decided, and then it would be forgotten.

She should have recognised the extent of the danger he represented when she looked at the clock on her bedside table and realised that more than four hours had passed and she'd not even thought about Maggie. She should have ended it there—the moment guilt rushed in to replace the sleepy peace that accompanied her orgasms. She should have closed her heart and cut him out of her life with something abrupt and potentially hurtful like *you're almost a decent fuck for a copper.* But instead she'd said, "Oh my God," and he'd known. He'd said, "I've been selfish. You're worried about your daughter. Let me clear out. I've kept you far too long. I've . . ." When he stopped speaking, she didn't look his way, but she felt his hand graze her arm. "I don't know how to name what I felt," he said, "or what I feel. Except that being with you like that . . . it wasn't enough. It's not even enough now. I don't know what that means."

She should have said drily, "It means you were randy, Constable. We both were. We still are in fact." But she didn't. She listened to him dressing and tried to work up something curt and unmistakably

final with which to dismiss him. When he sat on the edge of the bed
and turned her to him with his face caught somewhere between wonder and fear, she had the opportunity to draw the line. But she didn't.
Instead, she listened to him say,

"Can I love you this quickly, Juliet Spence? Just like that? In an
afternoon? Can my life change like that?"

And because she knew more than anything else that life can
change irrevocably in the instant one is forced to realise its malicious
caprice, she said, "Yes. But don't."

"What?"

"Love me. Or let your life change."

He didn't understand. He couldn't, really. He thought, perhaps,
she was being coy. He said, "No one has control over that," and
when his hand moved slowly down her body and her body rose eagerly
to meet it against her will, she knew he was right. He phoned her
that night long after midnight, saying, "I don't know what this is. I
don't know what to call it. I thought if I heard your voice . . . Because
I've never felt . . . But that's what men say, isn't it? I've never felt
like this before so let me get into your knickers and test the feeling
out another time or two. And it's that, I won't lie, but it goes beyond
and I don't know why."

She had played the fool in the biggest way because she loved
being loved by a man. Even Maggie couldn't stop her: not with her
white-faced knowledge—unspoken when she entered the cottage not
five minutes after Colin's initial departure, with her cat in her arms
and her cheeks fresh-scrubbed from where she'd been brushing tears
away; not with her silent appraisal of Colin when he came to dinner
or took them for hikes with his dog on the moors; not with her shrill
pleas not to be left alone when Juliet went for an hour or two to be
with Colin in his house. Maggie couldn't stop her. And she didn't
really need to do so because Juliet knew there was no hope of per-
manency. She understood from the first that each minute was a memory stored against a future in which he and the love of him had no
place. She merely forgot that while she had lived for the moment for
so many years—on the edge of a tomorrow that always promised to
bring the worst upon them—she'd made sure to create a life for
Maggie that appeared normal. So Maggie's fears of Colin's permanent
intrusion were real. To explain to her that they were also groundless
would be to tell her things that would destroy her world. And while

Juliet couldn't bring herself to do that, she couldn't bring herself to let Colin go either. Another week, she would think, please God just give me another week with him and I'll end it between us, I promise I will.

So she had bought this evening. How well she knew it.

Like mother, like daughter in the end, Juliet thought. Maggie's sex with Nick Ware was more than just an adolescent's way of striking back at her mother; it was more than just a search for a man she could call *daddy* in the darkest part of her mind; it was the blood in her veins declaring itself at last. Yet Juliet knew that she might have been able to forestall the inevitable had she herself not taken up with Colin and given her daughter an example to follow.

Juliet drew off the leather gloves a finger at a time and dropped them onto the pea jacket and scarf that lay heaped on the floor. She went not to the kitchen to prepare a dinner that her daughter wouldn't eat, but to the stairs. She paused at the bottom with one hand on the banister, trying to gather the energy to climb. This stairway was a duplication of so many others over the years: worn carpeting on the flooring, nothing on the walls. She had always thought of pictures on the walls as one more thing to have to remove when they left a cottage, so there never seemed to be a point to hanging any up in the first place. Keep it plain, keep it simple, keep it functional. Following that credo, she had always refused to decorate in a way that might encourage affection for a set of rooms in which they lived. She wanted there to be no sense of loss when they moved on.

Another adventure, she'd called each move, let's see what's what in Northumberland. She'd tried to make a game out of running. It was only when she'd stopped running that she'd lost.

She mounted the stairs. A perfect sphere of dread seemed to be growing beneath her heart. Why did she run, Juliet wondered, what did they tell her, what does she know?

The door to Maggie's room was partially closed, and she swung it open. Moonlight shone through the branches of the lime tree outside the window and fell in a wavy pattern across the bed. On this Maggie's cat was curled, head buried deeply between his paws, feigning sleep so that Juliet would take pity and not displace him. Punkin had been the first compromise Juliet had made with Maggie. *Please, please c'n I have a kitten, Mummy* had been such a simple request to grant. What she had not understood at the time was that seeing the joy of one small wish granted led inexorably to the longing to grant others. They'd been little nothings at first—a doss-round with her girlfriends, a trip to Lancaster with Josie and her mum—but they'd led to a budding sense of belonging that Maggie had never experienced before. In the end, they had led to the request to stay. Which, along with everything else, led to Nick, to the vicar, and to this night . . .

Juliet sat on the edge of the bed and switched on the light. Punkin buried his head deeper in his paws although the tip of his tail twitched once to betray him. Juliet ran her hand over his head and along the mobile curve of his spine. He wasn't as clean as he ought to be. He spent too much time prowling about the wood. Another six months and he'd no doubt be more feral than tame. Instinct, after all, was instinct.

On the floor next to Maggie's bed lay her thick scrapbook, its cover worn and cracked and its pages so dog-eared that their edges were crumbling to flakes in places. Juliet picked it up and rested it on her lap. A gift for her sixth birthday, it had *Maggie's Important Events* printed in large block letters in her own hand on the first page. Juliet could tell by the feel of the book that most of the pages were full. She'd never looked through it before—it had seemed too like an invasion of Maggie's small, private world—but she looked through it now, driven not so much by curiosity as by a need to feel her daughter's presence and to understand.

The first part comprised childhood mementos: a tracing of a large hand with a smaller one traced inside it and the words *Mumy and me* scrawled below; a fanciful composition about "My Doggie Fred" upon which a teacher had written "And what a lovely pet he must be, Margaret" across the top; a programme for a Christmas music recital at which she had been part of a chorus of children who sang—very badly but ambitiously—the Alleluia Chorus from Handel's *Messiah;* a second-place ribbon from a science project on plants; and scores of pictures and postcards of their camping holidays together on the Hebrides, on Holy Island, far from the crowds in the Lake District. Juliet flipped through the pages. She touched her fingertips to the drawing, traced the edge of the ribbon, and studied each picture of her daughter's face. This was a real history of their lives, a collection that spoke of what she and her daughter had managed to build upon a foundation of sand.

The second part of the scrapbook, however, spoke of the cost of having lived that same history. It comprised a collection of newspaper clippings and magazine articles about automobile racing. Interspersed among these were photographs of men. For the first time, Juliet saw that *he died in a car crash, darling* had assumed heroic proportions in Maggie's imagination, and from Juliet's reticence on the subject had sprung a father whom Maggie could love. Her fathers were the winners at Indianapolis, at Monte Carlo, at Le Mans. They spun out in flames on a track in Italy, but they walked away with their heads held high. They lost wheels, they crashed, they broke open champagne and waved trophies in the air. They all shared the single quality of being alive.

Juliet closed the book and rested her hands on its cover. It was all about protection, she said inside her head to a Maggie who wasn't there. When you're a mother, Maggie, the last thing you can bear of all the things that you have to bear anyway is losing your child. You can bear just about anything else and you usually have to at one time or another—losing your possessions, your home, your job, your lover, your husband, even your way of life. But losing a child is what will break you. So you don't take risks that might lead to the loss because you're always aware that the one risk you take might be the one that will cause all the horrors in the world to sweep into your life.

You don't know this yet, darling, because you haven't experienced that moment when the twisting squeezing crush of your muscles and the urge to expel and to scream at once results in this small mass of humanity that squalls and breathes and comes to rest against your stomach, naked to your nakedness, dependent upon you, blind at that moment, hands instinctively trying to clutch. And once you close those fingers round one of your own . . . no, not even then . . . once you look at this life that you've created, you know you'll do anything, suffer anything, to protect it. Mostly for its own sake you protect, of course, because all it is really is living, breathing need. But partly you protect it for your own.

And that is the greatest of my sins, darling Maggie. I reversed the process and I lied in doing it because I couldn't face the immensity of loss. But I'll tell the truth now, here, and to you. What I did I did partly for you, my daughter. But what I did all those years ago, I did mostly for myself.

CHAPTER TWENTY-TWO

I DON'T THINK WE SHOULD STOP YET, NICK," Maggie said as stoutly as she could manage. Her jaw hurt awfully from locking her teeth together to keep them from chattering, and the tips of her fingers were numb despite the fact that she'd kept her hands balled into her pockets for most of the journey. She was tired of walking and muscle-weary from leaping behind hedges, over walls, or into ditches whenever they heard the sound of a car. But it was still relatively early, although it was dark, and she knew that in darkness lay their best hope of escape.

They'd kept off the road whenever possible, heading southwest towards Blackpool. The going was rough on both farmland and moors, but Nick wouldn't hear of setting foot to pavement until they'd put Clitheroe a good five miles behind them. Even then, he wouldn't hear of taking the main road to Longridge where, the plan was, they would get a ride in a lorry to Blackpool. Instead, he said, they would stick to the twisty turny back lanes, skirting by farms, through hamlets, and over fields when necessary. The route he was taking made Longridge miles and miles farther away, but it was safer this way and she'd be glad they'd taken it. In Longridge, he said, no one would look at them twice. But until then, they had to keep off the road.

She didn't have a watch, but she knew it couldn't be much more than eight or half past. It seemed later, but that was because they were tired, it was cold, and the food Nick had managed to bring back to the car park from the town had long since been consumed. There had been little enough of it in the first place—what *could* one reasonably be expected to purchase with less than three pounds?—and while they'd divided it evenly between them and talked about making it last until morning, they'd eaten the crisps first, moved on to the apples to quench their thirst, and devoured the small package of biscuits to answer their craving for a sweet. Nick had been smoking steadily since that time to take the edge off his hunger. Maggie had tried to ignore her own, which had been easy enough to do since it was more than convenient to concentrate on the bitter cold instead. Her ears ached with it.

Nick was clambering over a drystone wall when Maggie said again, "It's too early to stop, Nick. We haven't gone nearly far enough. Where're you going, anyway?"

He pointed to three squares of yellow light some distance across the field in which he stood, on the other side of the wall. "Farm," he said. "They'll have a barn. We can doss there."

"In a *barn?*"

He brushed back his hair. "What'd you think, Mag? We don't have any money. We can't exactly get a room somewhere, can we?"

"But I thought . . . " She hesitated, squinting at the lights. What *had* she thought? Get away, run off, never again see anyone but Nick, stop thinking, stop wondering, find a place to hide.

He was waiting. He dug inside his jacket and brought out his Marlboros. He shook the pack against his hand. The last cigarette popped into his palm. He began to crumple the pack and Maggie said:

"P'rhaps you ought to save the last one. For later. You know."

"Nah." He crushed the pack and dropped it. He lit up as she picked her way up the loose stones and over the wall. She rescued the pack from the weeds and carefully smoothed it, folded it, and put it into her pocket.

"Trail," she said in explanation. "If they're looking for us, we don't want to leave a trail, do we? If they're looking."

He nodded. "Right. Come on, then." He grabbed her hand and headed in the direction of the lights.

"But why're we stopping now?" she asked once again. "It's too early, don't you think?"

He looked at the night sky, at the position of the moon. "Perhaps," he said and smoked thoughtfully for a moment. "Look. We'll rest up here a while and doss somewhere else later. Aren't you feeling clapped out? Don't you want to have a sit?"

She did. Only she was also feeling that if she sat anywhere, she might not be able to get back up. Her school shoes weren't the best for walking, and she thought that once her head sent her feet the false message that their evening's walk was at an end, her feet mightn't cooperate in setting off again in an hour or so.

"I don't know . . . " She shivered.

"And you need to warm up," he said decisively and began to lead her towards the lights.

The field they walked across was pasture, the ground uneven. It was littered with sheep droppings that looked like shadows against the frost. Maggie stepped into a pile of these, felt her shoe slither among them, and nearly went down. Nick righted her with a "Mag, you got to watch for the muck," and then he added with a laugh, "Lucky they don't have cows here." He clasped her arm and offered her a share of his cigarette. She took it politely, sucked in on it, and blew the smoke through her nose.

"You c'n have the rest," she said.

He seemed glad to do so. He picked up their pace to cross the pasture but slowed abruptly as they neared the other side. A large flock of sheep were huddled together against the pasture's far wall, like mounds of dirty snow in the darkness. Nick said in a low voice something that seemed to be, "Hey, ah, ishhhh," as they slowly closed in on the flock's perimeter. He extended his hand before him. As if in response, the animals jostled one another to allow Nick and Maggie passage, but they neither panicked, bleated, nor began to move off.

"You know what to do," Maggie said and felt a tingle behind her eyes. "Nick, why d'you always know just what to do?"

"It's only sheep, Mag."

"But you know. I love that about you, Nick. You know the right thing."

He looked towards the farmhouse. It stood beyond a paddock and another set of walls. "I know with sheep," he said.

"Not only sheep," she said. "Truly."

He crouched next to the wall, easing a ewe to one side. Maggie crouched next to him. He rolled his cigarette between his fingers and after a moment drew a long breath as if to speak. She waited for his words, then said herself, "What?" He shook his head. His hair fell forward across his forehead and cheek and he concentrated solely on finishing his cigarette. Maggie clasped his arm and leaned against him. It was pleasant here, with the wool and the breath of the animals to warm them. She could almost think of staying the night in this very spot. She raised her head.

"Stars," she said. "I always wished I could name them. But all I ever could find was the North Star because it's brightest. It's . . ." She twisted round. "It should be . . ." She frowned. If Longridge was to the west of Clitheroe, with just the smallest jog to the south, the North Star should be . . . Where was its bright shining?

"Nick," she said slowly, "I can't find the North Star. Are we lost?"

"Lost?"

"I think we're going in the wrong direction because the North Star isn't where—"

"We can't go by the stars, Mag. We have to go by the land."

"What d'you mean? How d'you know what direction you're heading in if you go by the land?"

"Because I know. Because I've lived here forever. We can't go climbing up and down fells in the middle of the night which is what we'd be doing if we headed direct west. We have to go round them."

"But—"

He crushed his cigarette against the sole of his shoe. He stood. "Come on." He climbed the wall and reached back over to hold her hand as she did the same. He said, "We've got to be quiet now. There'll be dogs."

They slipped across the paddock in near silence, the only noise coming from their shoe soles crackling against the frost-covered ground. At the last wall, Nick hunched over, raised his head slowly, and examined the area. Maggie watched him from below, hunkered against the wall, gripping her knees.

"Barn's on the far side of the yard," he said. "Looks like solid muck, though. It's going to be messy. Hold on to me tight."

"Any dogs?"

"I can't see. But they'll be about."

"But Nick, if they bark or chase us, what'll—"

"Don't worry. Come on."

He climbed over. She followed, scraping her knee across the very top stone and feeling the corresponding rip in her tights. She gave a little mewl when she felt the quick heat of abrasion against her skin. But to feel a scratch was baby business at this point. She allowed herself neither a wince nor a hobble as she dropped to the ground. It was thick with bracken along the edge of the wall, but rutted and muck-filled as it gave onto the farmyard itself. Once they left the protective cushion of the bracken, each step they took *smick-smacked* loudly with suction. Maggie felt her feet sinking into the muck, felt the muck seeping over the sides of her shoes. She shuddered. She was whispering, "Nick, my feet keep getting stuck," when the dogs appeared.

They announced themselves by yapping first. Then three border collies tore across the farmyard from the out-buildings, barking wildly and baring their teeth. Nick shoved Maggie behind him. The dogs slithered to a stop less than six feet away, snapping, snarling, and ready to spring.

Nick held out his hand.

Maggie whispered, "Nick! No!" and watched the farm-house fearfully, waiting for the door to crash open and the farmer himself to come storming out. He'd be shouting and red in the face and angry. He'd phone the police. They were trespassing after all.

The dogs began to howl.

"Nick!"

Nick squatted. He said, "Hey-o, come on, you funny blokes. You can't scare me," and he whistled to them softly.

It was just like magic. The dogs quieted, stepped forward, sniffed his hand, and within an instant became old friends. Nick petted them in turn, laughing quietly, tugging at their ears. "You won't hurt us, will you, funny old blokes?" In answer, they wagged their tails and one of them licked Nick's face. When Nick stood, they surrounded him happily and acted as escort into the yard.

Maggie looked round at the dogs in wonder as she carefully sloshed through the mud. "How'd you *do* that? Nick!"

He took her hand. "It's only dogs, Mag."

The old stone barn was a section of one elongated building, and it stood across the yard from the house. It directly abutted a narrow cottage on whose first floor a curtained window was lit. This had probably been the original farm building, a granary with a cart-shed beneath it. The granary had been converted sometime in the past to house a worker and his family, and its living quarters were gained by means of a stairway that led up to a cracked red door above which a sole bulb was now glowing. Beneath, lay the cart-shed with its single unglazed window and its gaping arch of a door.

Nick looked from the cart-shed to the barn. The latter was enormous, an ancient cow-house that was falling into disuse. Moonlight illumined its sagging roofline, its uneven row of pitching eyes on the upper storey, and its large wooden doors with their gaps and their warping. As the dogs sniffed round their shoes and as Maggie hugged herself against the cold and waited for him to lead her onward, Nick appeared to evaluate the possibilities and finally slogged through a heavier patch of muck towards the cart-shed.

"Aren't there people up there?" Maggie whispered, pointing to the quarters above it.

"I s'pose. We'll just have to be real quiet. It'll be warmer in here. The barn's too big and it's facing the wind. Come on."

He led her beneath the stairway where the arched door gave entrance into the cart-shed. Inside, the light from above the labourer's front door at the top of the stairs provided a meagre, match-strength illumination through the cart-shed's single window. The dogs followed them, milling about what was apparently their sleeping quarters, for several chewed-up blankets lay in a corner on the stone floor and the dogs went there eventually, where they sniffed, pawed, and sank into the pungent wool.

The cold outside seemed to magnify in the stone walls and floor of the shed. Maggie tried to comfort herself with the thought that it was just like where the baby Jesus was born—except there hadn't been any dogs there as far as she could recall from her limited knowledge of Christmas stories—but odd squeakings and rustlings from the deep pockets of darkness in the corners of the shed made her uneasy.

She could see that the shed was used for storage. There were big burlap sacks piled along one wall, dirty buckets, tools she couldn't have named, a bicycle, a wooden rocking chair with its wicker seat missing, and a toilet lying on its side. Against the far wall stood a dusty chest of drawers, and Nick went to this. He shimmied open the top drawer and said, with some excitement in his voice, "Hey, look at this, Mag. We've had ourselves some luck."

She picked her way through the debris on the floor. Out of the drawer he was taking a blanket. And then another. They were both large and fluffy. They seemed perfectly clean. Nick shoved the drawer partially closed. The wood howled. The dogs lifted their heads. Maggie held her breath and listened for a betraying movement in the labourer's quarters above them. Dimly, she could hear someone talking—a man, then a woman, followed by dramatic music and the sound of gunfire—but no one came in search of them.

"The telly," Nick said. "We're safe."

He cleared a space on the floor, spread the first blanket down, doubling it up to serve as both cushion against the stones and insulation against the cold, and beckoned her to join him. The second he wrapped round them, saying, "This'll work for now. Feel warmer, Mag?" and drew her close.

She *did* feel warmer at once, although she fingered the blanket and smelled the fresh lavender scent of it with a twinge of doubt. She said, "Why do they keep their blankets out here? They'll get messed up, won't they? Won't they get rotten or something?"

"Who cares? It's our luck and their loss, isn't it? Here. Lie down. Nice, that, isn't it? Warmer, Mag?"

The rustlings along the wall seemed louder now that she was at the level of the floor. They also seemed accompanied by an occasional squeak. She burrowed closer to Nick and said, "What's that noise, then?"

"I said. The telly."

"I mean the other . . . that . . . there, did you hear it?"

"Oh, that. Barn rats, I expect."

She flew up. "Rats! Nick, no! I can't . . . please . . . I'm afraid of . . . Nick!"

"Shh. They won't bother you. Come on. Lie down."

"But rats! If they bite you, you die! And I—"

"We're bigger than they are. They're lots more scared. They won't even come out."

"But my hair . . . I read once where they like to collect hair to make up their nests."

"I'll keep them away from you." He urged her down next to him and lay on his side. "Use my arm for a pillow," he said. "They won't climb up my arm to get you. Jeez, Mag, you're shaking. Here. Get close. You'll be okay."

"We won't stay here long?"

"Just for a rest."

"Promise?"

"Yeah. Promise. Come on. It's cold." He unzipped his bomber jacket and held it open. "Here. Double warmth."

With a fearful glance in the direction of the deepest pool of darkness where the barn rats skittered among the burlap sacks, she lowered herself onto the blanket, into the confines of Nick's bomber jacket. She felt stiff with both the cold and her fear, uneasy with their proximity to people. The dogs hadn't roused anyone, that was true, but if the farmer made a final round of the yard prior to going to bed, they'd likely be found.

Nick kissed her head. "Okay?" he said. "It's just for a while. Just for a rest."

"Okay."

She slipped her arms round him and let her body warm from his and from the blanket that covered them. She kept her thoughts away from the rats and instead pretended that they were in their very first flat together, she and Nick. It was their official first night, like a honeymoon. The room was small but the moonlight gleamed against the walls' pretty rosebud paper. There were prints hanging on them, watercolours of frolicking dogs and cats, and Punkin lay at the foot of the bed.

She moved closer to Nick. She was wearing a beautiful full-length gown of pale pink satin with lace on the straps and along the bodice. Her hair flowed round her, and perfume rose from the hollow of her throat and behind her ears and between her breasts. He was wearing dark blue pyjamas of silk, and she could feel his bones, his muscles, and the strength of him along the length of her body. He would want to do it, of course—he would always want to do it—and she would always want to do it as well. Because it was so close and so nice.

"Mag," Nick said, "lie still. Don't."

"I'm not doing anything."

"You are."

"I'm just getting closer. It's cold. You said—"

"We can't. Not here. Okay?"

She pressed against him. She could feel It in his trousers, despite his words. It was already hard. She slithered her hand between their bodies.

"Mag!"

"It's nothing but warmness," she whispered and rubbed It just the way he'd taught her.

"Mag, I said no!" His answering whisper was fierce.

"But you like it, don't you?" She squeezed It, released It.

"Mag! Get off!"

She ran her hand Its length.

"No! Damn! Mag, leave it be!"

She recoiled when he knocked her hand away and felt quick tears come in answer. "I only . . . " She ached when she breathed. "It was nice, wasn't it? I wanted to be nice."

In the dim light, he looked like something was hurting inside him. He said, "It *is* nice. You're nice. But that makes me want to and we can't right now. We *can't*. Okay. Here. Lie down."

"I wanted to be close."

"We are close, Mag. Come on. Let me hold you." He urged her back down. "It feels good just like this, lying here, you and me."

"I only wanted—"

"Shh. It's okay. It's nothing." He opened her coat and slipped his arm round her. "It's nice just like this," he whispered against her hair. He moved his hand to her back and began caressing the length of her spine.

"But I only wanted—"

"Shh. See. It's just as nice like this, isn't it? Just holding? Like this?" His fingers pressed in long, slow circles, stopping at the small of her back where they remained, a tender pressure that relaxed and relaxed and relaxed her completely. She finally slipped, protected and loved, into sleep.

It was the dogs' movement that awakened her. They were up, about, and dashing outside at the sound of a vehicle coming into the farmyard. By the time they were barking, she was sitting up, fully awake, aware that she was alone on the blanket. She clutched it to her and whispered, "Nick!" frantically. He materialised from the darkness by the window. The light from above was no longer shining. She had no idea how long she had slept.

"Someone's here," he said unnecessarily.

"Police?"

"No." He glanced back at the window. "I think it's my dad."

"Your *dad*? But how—"

"I don't know. Come here. Be quiet."

They gathered up the blankets and crept to one side of the window. The dogs were sending up enough noise to announce the Second Coming and lights were snapping on outside.

"Hey there! Enough!" someone shouted roughly. A few more barks and the dogs were silent. "What is it? Who's there?"

Footsteps sloshed across the yard. Conversation ensued. Maggie strained to hear it, but the voices were low. A woman said quietly, "Is it Frank?" at a distance and a child's voice cried, "Mummy, I want to *see*."

Maggie pulled the blanket closer round her. She clutched on to Nick. "Where c'n we go? Nick, can we run?"

"Just be quiet. He ought to ... Damn."

"What?"

But she heard it herself:

"You don't mind if I have a look round, do you?"

"Not at all. Two of them, you said it was?"

"A boy and a girl. They'd be wearing school uniforms. The boy might have had a bomber jacket on."

"Never saw a hair of anything like that. But go on and have a look. Let me get my boots on and I'll join you. Need a torch?"

"Got one, thanks."

Footsteps went in the direction of the barn. Maggie grabbed Nick's jacket. "Let's go, Nick. Now! We can run to the wall. We can hide in the pasture. We can—"

"What about the dogs?"

"What?"

"They'll follow and give us away. Besides, the other bloke said he was going to help in the search." Nick turned from the window and looked around the shed. "Our best hope is to hide out in here."

"Hide out? How? Where?"

"Move the sacks. Get behind them."

"But the rats!"

"No choice. Come on. You've got to help."

The farmer began to tromp across the yard in the direction of Nick's father as they dropped their blankets and started pulling the sacks away from the wall. They heard Nick's father call out, "Nothing in the barn," and the other man say, "Have a go with the shed, here," and the sound of their approach spurred Maggie into a fury of pulling sacks far enough from the wall to create a burrow of safety. She had retreated within it—Nick had as well—when the light from a torch beamed in through the window.

"Doesn't look like nothing," Nick's father said.

A second light joined the first; the shed became brighter. "The dogs sleep in here. Can't say as I'd want to join them even if I was on the run." His torch clicked off. Maggie let out her breath. She heard footsteps in the muck. Then, "Best to have a closer look, though," and the light reappeared, stronger, and shining from the doorway.

A dog's whine accompanied the sound of wet boots slapping on the floor of the shed. Nails ticked against the stones and approached the sacks. Maggie said, "No" in despair without making any sound and felt Nick move a step closer.

"Here's something," the farmer said. "Someone's messed with that chest."

"Those blankets belong there on the floor?"

"Can't say they do." The light darted round the room, corners to ceiling. It glinted off the discarded toilet and shone on the dust on the rocking chair. It came to rest on the top of the sacking and illuminated the wall above Maggie's head. "Ah," the farmer said. "Here we've got it. Step out here in the open, youngsters. Step out now or I'll send the dogs in to help you make up your minds."

"Nick?" his father said. "That you, lad? Have you got the girl with you? Come out of there. Now."

Maggie rose first, trembling, blinking into the torchlight, trying to say, "Please don't be angry with Nick, Mr. Ware. He only wanted to help me," but beginning to weep instead, thinking, Don't send me home, I don't want to go home.

Mr. Ware said, "What in God's name were you thinking of, Nick? Get out here with you. Jesus Christ, I ought to beat you silly. You know how worried your mum's been, lad?"

Nick was turning his head, eyes narrowed against the light that his father was shining into his face. "Sorry," he said.

Mr. Ware *harumphed*. "Sorry won't go far to mend your fences with me. You know you're trespassing here? You know these people could've had the police after you? What're you thinking of? Haven't you no better sense than that? And what were you planning to do with this girl?"

Nick shifted his weight, silent.

"You're filthy." Mr. Ware shone the light up and down. "God almighty, just look at the sight of you. You look like a tramp."

"No, please," Maggie cried, rubbing her wet nose against the sleeve of her coat. "It isn't Nick. It's me. He was only helping me."

Mr. Ware *harumphed* again and clicked off his torch. The farmer did likewise. He'd been standing to one side, holding the light in their direction but otherwise looking out the window. When Mr. Ware said, "Out to the car with both of you, then," the farmer scooped up the two blankets from the floor and followed them out.

The dogs were milling round Mr. Ware's old Nova, snuffling at the tyres and the ground alike. The exterior lights were shining from the house and in their glow Maggie could see the condition of her clothes for the first time. They were crusted with mud and streaked with dirt. In places the lichen from the walls she'd climbed over had deposited patches of grey-green slime. Her shoes were clotted with muck out of which sprouted bracken and straw. The sight was a stimulus for a new onslaught of tears. What had she been thinking? Where were they supposed to go, looking like this? With no money, no clothing, and no plan to guide them, what had she been thinking?

She clutched Nick's arm as they slogged to the car. She sobbed, "I'm sorry, Nick. It's my fault. I'll tell your mummy. You didn't mean harm. I'll explain. I will."

"Get in the car, the both of you," Mr. Ware said gruffly. "We'll do our deciding about who's at fault later." He opened the driver's door and said to the farmer, "It's Frank Ware. I'm at Skelshaw Farm up Winslough direction. I'm in the book if you discover this lot did any damage to your place."

The farmer nodded but said nothing. He shuffled his feet in the muck and looked as if he wished they'd be off. He was saying, "Funny blokes, out of the way," to the dogs when the farmhouse door opened. A child of perhaps six years old stood framed in the light in her nightgown and slippers.

She giggled and waved, calling, "Uncle Frank, 'lo. Won't you let Nickie stay the night with us please?" Her mother dashed into the doorway and pulled her back, casting a frantic and apologetic look towards the car.

Maggie slowed, then stopped. She turned to Nick. She looked from him to his father to the farmer. She saw the resemblance first— how their hair grew the same although the colour was different; how their noses each had a bump on the bridge; how they held their heads. And then she saw the rest—the dogs, the blankets, the direction they'd been walking, Nick's insistence that they rest at this particular farm, his form at the window standing and waiting when she had awakened . . .

Her insides went so calm that at first she thought her heart had stopped beating. Her face was still wet, but her tears disappeared. She stumbled once in the muck, grabbed the Nova's door handle, and felt Nick take her arm. From somewhere that sounded like a thousand miles away, she heard him say her name. She heard him say, "Please, Mag. Listen. I didn't know what else . . ." but then fog filled her head and she didn't hear the rest. She climbed into the rear seat of the car. Directly in her line of vision a pile of old roof slates lay beneath a tree, and she focussed on them. They were large, much bigger than she'd imagined they would be, and they looked like tombstones. She counted them slowly, one two three, and was up to a dozen when she felt the car dip as Mr. Ware got into it and as Nick climbed in and sat next to her on the rear seat. She could tell he was looking at her, but it didn't matter. She continued counting—thirteen fourteen fifteen. Why did Nick's uncle have so many slates? And why did he keep them under the tree? Sixteen seventeen eighteen.

Nick's father was unrolling his window. "Ta, Kev," he said quietly. "Don't give it a thought, all right?"

The other man came to the car and leaned against it. He spoke to Nick. "Sorry, lad," he said. "We couldn't get the lass to go to bed once she heard you were on your way. She's that fond of you, she is."

"S'okay," Nick said.

His uncle slapped his two hands down on the door in farewell, nodded sharply, and stepped back from the car. "Funny blokes," he called to the dogs. "Away with you."

The car lurched round in the farmyard, made a slippery turn, and set off towards the road. Mr. Ware turned on the radio. He said kindly, "What d'you fancy, youngsters?" but Maggie shook her head and looked out the side window. Nick said, "Anything, Dad. It doesn't matter," and Maggie felt the truth of those words pierce through her calm and drip like cold bits of lead into her stomach. Nick's hand touched her tentatively. She flinched.

"I'm sorry," he said softly. "I didn't know what else to do. We didn't have any money. We didn't have any place to go. I couldn't think what to do to take care of you proper."

"You said you would," she said dully. "Last night. You said you would."

"But I didn't *think* it would be . . . " She saw his hand close round his knee. "Mag, listen. I can't take care of you proper if I don't go to school. I want to be a vet. I got to get through school and then we'll be together. But I got to—"

"You lied."

"I didn't!"

"You phoned your dad from Clitheroe when you went to buy the food. You told him where we'd be. Didn't you?"

He said nothing, which was affirmation enough. The nighttime scenery slipped by the window. Stone walls gave way to the bony frames of hedges. Farmland gave way to open country. Across the moors, the fells rose like Lancashire's black guardians against the sky.

Mr. Ware had turned the car's heater on along with the radio, but Maggie had never felt so cold. She felt colder than she had when they were walking in the fields, colder than she had on the floor of the cart-shed. She felt colder than she had on the previous night in Josie's lair, with her clothes half off and Nick inside her and the meaningless promises he'd made creating fire between them.

■   ■   ■

The end was where the beginning had been, with her mother. When Mr. Ware pulled into the courtyard of Cotes Hall, the front door opened and Juliet Spence came out. Maggie heard Nick whisper urgently, "Mag! Wait!" but she pushed the car door open. Her head felt so heavy that she couldn't lift it. Nor could she walk.

She heard Mummy approach, her good boots clicking against the cobbles. She waited. For what, she didn't know. The anger, the lecture, the punishment: it didn't really matter. Whatever it was, it couldn't touch her. Nothing would ever touch her now.

Juliet said in a curiously hushed voice, "Maggie?"

Mr. Ware explained. Maggie heard phrases like "took her to his uncle's . . . bit of a walk . . . hungry, I'd guess . . . tired as the dickens. . . . Kids. Don't know what to make of them sometimes . . ."

Juliet cleared her throat, said, "Thank you. I don't quite know what I would have done if . . . Thank you, Frank."

"I don't think they meant real harm," Mr. Ware said.

"No," Juliet said. "No. I'm sure they didn't."

The car reversed, turned, and headed down the lane. Still, Maggie's head drooped with its own weight. Three more clicks sounded on the cobbles and she could see the tops of her mother's boots.

"Maggie."

She couldn't look up. She was filled with lead. She felt a whispery touch on her hair, and she withdrew from it fearfully, taking a gasping, indrawn breath.

"What is it?" Her mother sounded puzzled. More than puzzled, she sounded afraid.

Maggie couldn't understand how that could be, for the power had shifted once again, and the worst had happened: She was alone with her mother with no escape. Her eyes got blurry, and a sob was building down deep inside her. She fought against letting it out.

Juliet stepped away. "Come inside, Maggie," she said. "It's cold. You're shivering." She began to walk towards the cottage.

Maggie raised her head. She was floating in nowhere. Nick was gone, and Mummy was walking away. There was nothing to grab on to any longer. There was no safe harbour in which she could rest. The sob built and burst. Her mother stopped.

"Talk to me," Juliet said. Her voice was desperate and uneven sounding. "You've got to talk to me. You've got to tell me what happened. You've got to say why you ran. We can't go any further with each other until you do, and if you don't, we're lost."

They stood apart, her mother on the doorstep, Maggie in the courtyard. To Maggie, it seemed that they were separated by miles. She wanted to move closer but she didn't know how. She couldn't see her mother's face clearly enough to know if it was safe. She couldn't tell whether her voice's quiver meant sorrow or rage.

"Maggie, darling. Please." And Juliet's voice broke. "Talk to me. I'm begging you."

Her mother's anguish—it seemed so real—tore a little hole in Maggie's heart. She said on a sob, "Nick promised he would take care of me, Mummy. He said he loved me. He said I was special, he said we were special, but he lied and he had his dad come get us and he didn't tell me and all the time I thought . . . " She wept. She wasn't quite sure what the source of her grief really was any longer. Except that she had nowhere to go and no one to trust. And she needed something, someone, an anchor, a home.

"I'm so sorry, darling."

What a kindness sounded in those four words. It was easier to continue in their echo.

"He pretended to tame the dogs and to find some blankets and..." The rest of the story came tumbling out. The London policeman, the after-school talk, the whispers and rumbles and gossip. And finally, "So I was afraid."

"Of what?"

Maggie couldn't put the rest into words. She stood in the courtyard with the night wind whistling through her filthy clothes, and she couldn't move forward and she couldn't go back. Because there was no back, as she knew quite well. And going forward meant devastation.

But apparently, she would not need to go anywhere, for Juliet said, "Oh my God, Maggie," and seemed to know it all. She said, "How could you ever *think*...You're my life. You're everything I have. You're—" She leaned against the door-jamb with her fists on her eyes and her head raised up to the sky. She began to cry.

It was a horrible sound, like someone was pulling her insides out. It was low and ugly. It caught in her breath. It sounded like dying.

Maggie had never before seen her mother cry. The weeping frightened her. She watched and waited and clutched at her coat because Mummy was the strong one, Mummy stood tall, Mummy was the one who knew what to do. Only now Maggie saw that Mummy was not so very much different from her when it came to hurting. She went to her mother. "Mummy?"

Juliet shook her head. "I can't make it right. I can't change things. Not now. I can't do it. Don't ask me." She swung from the doorway and went into the house. Numbly, Maggie followed her into the kitchen and watched her sit at the table with her face in her hands.

Maggie didn't know what to do, so she put on the kettle and crept round the kitchen assembling tea. By the time she had it ready, Juliet's tears had stopped but under the harsh overhead light, she looked old and ill. Wrinkles reached out in long zigzags from her eyes. Her skin was blotched with red marks where it wasn't pasty. Her hair hung limply round her face. She reached for a paper napkin from its metal holder and blew her nose on it. She took another and blotted her face.

The telephone began to ring. Maggie didn't move. Which way to head was mystery now, and she waited for a sign. Her mother pushed back from the table and picked up the receiver. Her conversation was emotionless and brief. "Yes, she's here... Frank Ware found them... No... No... I don't... I don't think so, Colin... No, not tonight." Slowly, she replaced the receiver and kept her fingers on it, as if she were gentling an animal's fears. After a moment in which she did nothing but look at the telephone, in which Maggie did nothing but look at her, she went back to the table and sat once again.

Maggie brought her the tea. "Chamomile," she said. "Here, Mummy."

Maggie poured. Some sloshed into the saucer and she reached hastily for a napkin to soak it up. Her mother's hand closed over her wrist.

"Sit down," she said.

"Don't you want—"

"Sit down."

Maggie sat. Juliet took the teacup out of its saucer and cradled the cup between her palms. She looked into the tea and swirled it slowly round and round. Her hands looked strong, steady, and sure.

Something big was about to happen. Maggie knew. She could feel it in the air and in the silence between them. The kettle was still hissing gently on the cooker, and the cooker itself snapped and popped as it cooled. She heard this as background to the sight of her mother's head lifting as she made her decision.

"I'm going to tell you about your father," she said.

CHAPTER TWENTY-THREE

POLLY SETTLED INTO THE TUB AND LET THE water rise round her. She tried to concentrate on the warm wash of it between her legs and the gush of it across her thighs as she sank, but instead she caught herself in the midst of a cry, and she squeezed her eyes shut. She saw the negative image of her body fading slowly against her eyelids. Tiny pits of red replaced it. Then black swept in. That's what she wanted, the black. She needed it behind her eyelids, but she wanted it in her mind as well.

She hurt more now than she had this afternoon at the vicarage. She felt as if she'd been stretched on the rack, with her groin ligaments torn from their proper housings. Her pubic and pelvic bones seemed beaten and raw. Her back and her neck were throbbing. But this was a pain that would recede, given time. It was the other pain that she feared would never leave her.

If she saw only the black, she wouldn't have to see his face any longer: the way his lips curled back, the sight of his teeth and his eyes like slits. If she only saw the black, she wouldn't have to see him stagger to his feet afterwards, with his chest heaving and the back of one wrist scouring his mouth of the taste of her. She wouldn't have to watch him lean against the wall while he stuffed himself back into his trousers. She would still have to bear the rest of it, of course. That endless, guttural voice and the knowledge it provided of the filth she was to him. The invasion of his tongue. His teeth biting, his hands tearing, and then the last when he scourged her. She would have to live with that. There was no memory pill she could take to wipe it away, no matter how much she liked to hope there might be.

The worst of it was that she knew she deserved what Colin had done to her. Her life was governed, after all, by the laws of the Craft and she had violated the most important:

> *Eight words the Wiccan Rede fulfil:*
> *An it harm none, do what ye will.*

All those years ago, she had convinced herself that she cast the magic circle for Annie's own good. But all the while in her most secret heart, she had thought—and hoped—that Annie would die and that her passing would bring Colin closer to herself in a grief he would want to share with someone who had known his wife. And this, she had believed, would lead them to loving each other and lead him to an eventual forgetting. Towards this end—which she called noble, un-selfish, and right—she began to cast the circle and perform the Rite of Venus. It was no matter that she had not changed to this Rite until nearly a year after Annie's death. The Goddess was not and had never been a fool. She always read the soul of the petitioner. The Goddess heard the chant:

> *God and Goddess up above*
> *Bring me Colin in full love*

and She remembered how three months before Annie Shepherd's death, her friend Polly Yarkin—with sublime powers that came only from being a child conceived of a witch, conceived within the magic circle itself when the moon was full in Libra and its light cast a radiance on the altar stone at the top of Cotes Fell—had stopped performing the Rite of the Sun and had switched to Saturn. Burning oak, wearing black, breathing hyacinth incense, Polly had prayed for Annie's death. She had told herself that death wasn't to be feared, that the ending of a life could come as a blessing when the suffering endured had been profound. And that is how she had justified the evil, all the time knowing that the Goddess would not let evil go unpunished.

Everything until today had been a prelude to the descent of Her wrath. And She had exacted Her retribution in a form that exactly matched the evil committed, delivering Colin to Polly not in love but in lust and violence, turning the magic three-fold against its maker. How stupid ever *ever* to think that Juliet Spence—not to mention the knowledge of Colin's attentions to her—was the punishment that the Goddess intended. The sight of them together and the realisation of what they were to each other had merely acted to lay the foundation for the real mortification to come.

It was over now. Nothing worse could happen, except her own death. And since she was more than half dead now, even that didn't seem so terrible.

"Polly? Luv-doll? What're you doin'?"

Polly opened her eyes and rose in the water so quickly that it sloshed over the side of the tub. She watched the bathroom door. Behind it, she could hear her mother's wheezing. Rita generally climbed the stairs only once a day—to go to bed—and since she never made that climb until after midnight, Polly had assumed she would be safe when she'd first called out that she'd be wanting no dinner as she entered the lodge, hurried up to the bathroom, and shut herself in. She didn't reply. She reached for a towel. The water sloshed again.

"Polly! You still taking a bath, girl? Didn't I hear the water running long before dinner?"

"I just started, Rita."

"Just started? I heard the water running directly you got home. More'n two hours back. So what's up, luv-doll?" Rita scratched her nails against the door. "Polly?"

"Nothing." Polly wrapped herself in the towel as she stepped from the tub. She grimaced with the effort of lifting each leg.

"Nothing my eye. Cleanliness is next to whatever, I know, but this is taking it to extremes. Wha's the story? You fancying yourself up for some toy boy to climb through your window tonight? You meetin' someone? You want a spray of my Giorgio?"

"I'm just tired. I'm going to bed. You go on back down to the telly, all right?"

"All wrong." She tapped again. "Wha's going on? You feeling queer?"

Polly tucked the towel round her to make a wrap. Water ran in rivulets down her legs to the stained green bath rug on the floor. "Fine, Rita." She tried to say it as normally as possible, sifting through her memories of how she and her mother interacted to come up with an appropriate tone of voice. Would she be irritated with Rita by now? Should her voice reflect impatience? She couldn't remember. She settled for friendly. "You go on back down. Isn't your police programme on about now? Why don't you cut yourself a piece of that cake. Cut me one as well and leave it on the work top." She waited for the answer, the lumber and huff of Rita's departure, but no sound came from the other side of the door. Polly watched it, warily. She felt chilled where her skin was wet and exposed, but she couldn't face unwrapping the towel, uncovering her body for drying, and having to look at it again just yet.

"Cake?" Rita said.

"I might have a piece."

The door knob rattled. Rita's voice was sharp. "Open up, girl. You a'nt had a piece of cake in fifteen years. Somethin's wrong and I mean to know what."

"Rita . . ."

"We a'nt playing here, luv-doll. And unless you intend to climb out the window, you may as well open this door straightaway 'cause I mean to be here whenever you get round to it."

"Please. It's nothing."

The door knob rattled louder. The door itself thumped. "Am I going to need the help of our local constabulary?" her mother asked. "I c'n phone him, you know. Why is it I expect you'd rather I didn't?"

Polly reached for the bathrobe on its hook and slid the lock back. She draped the bathrobe round her and was in the act of tying its belt when her mother swung the door open. Hastily, Polly turned away, unfastening her hair from its elastic binding to let it fall forward.

"He was here today, was Mr. C. Shepherd," Rita said. "He cooked up some story 'bout looking for tools to fix our shed door. What an agreeable bloke, our local policeman. You know anything about that, luv-doll?"

Polly shook her head and fumbled with the knot she'd made in the belt of the robe. She watched her fingers pick at it and waited for her mother to give up the effort at communication and leave. Rita wasn't going anywhere, however.

"You'd best tell me 'bout it, girl."

"What?"

"What happened." She lumbered into the bathroom and seemed

to fill it with her size, her scent, and, above all, her power. Polly tried to summon her own as a defence, but her will was weak.

She heard the *clank-jangle* of bracelets as Rita's arm raised behind her. She didn't cringe—she knew her mother had no intention of striking her—but she waited in dread for Rita to respond to what she didn't feel emanating like a palpable wave from Polly's body.

"You got no aura," Rita said. "And you got no heat. Turn round here."

"Rita, come on. I'm just tired. I've been working all day and I want to go to bed."

"Don't you mess me about. I said turn. I mean turn."

Polly made the belt's knot double. She shook her head to gain further protection from her hair. She pivoted slowly, saying, "I'm only tired. A bit sore. I slipped on the vicarage drive this morning and banged up my face. It hurts. I pulled a muscle or something in my back as well. I thought a hot soak would—"

"Raise your head. Now."

She could feel the power behind the command. It overcame whatever feeble resistance she might have been able to muster. She lifted her chin, although she kept her eyes lowered. She was inches from the goat's head that served as pendant on her mother's necklace. She bent her thoughts to the goat, his head, and how it resembled the naked witch standing in the pentagram position, from which the Rites began and petitions were made.

"Move your hair off your face."

Polly's hand did her mother's bidding.

"Look at me."

Her eyes did the same.

Rita's breath whistled between her teeth as she sucked in air, face to face with her daughter. Her pupils expanded rapidly across the surface of her irises, and then retracted to pinpricks of black. She raised her hand and moved her fingers along the welt that scythe-cut its path of angry skin from Polly's eye to her mouth. She didn't make actual contact, but Polly could feel the touch of her fingers as if she did. They hovered above the eye that was swollen. They tapped their way from her cheek to her mouth. Finally, they slid into her hair, both hands on either side of her head, this time an actual touch that seemed to vibrate through her skull.

"What else is there?" Rita asked.

Polly felt the fingers tighten and catch at her hair, but still she said, "Nothing. I fell. A bit sore," although her voice sounded faint and lacking in conviction.

"Open that robe."

"Rita."

Rita's hands pressed in, not a punishing grip but one that spread warmth outward, like circles in a pond when a pebble hits its surface. "Open the robe."

Polly untied the first knot, but found she couldn't manage the second. Her mother did it, picking at the tie with her long, blue fingernails and with hands that were as unsteady as her breath. She pushed the robe from her daughter's body and took a step back as it fell to the floor.

"Great Mother," she said and reached for the goat's head pendant. Her chest rapidly rose and fell under her kaftan.

Polly dropped her head.

"It was him," Rita said. "Wasn't it him did this to you, Polly. After he was here."

"Let it be," Polly said.

"Let it . . . ?" Rita's voice was incredulous.

"I didn't do right by him. I wasn't pure in my wanting. I lied to the Goddess. She heard and She punished. It wasn't him. He was in Her hands."

Rita took her arm and swung her towards the mirror above the basin. It was still opaque from steam, and Rita vigorously ran her hand up and down it and wiped her palm on the side of her kaftan. "You look here, Polly," she said. "You look at this right and you look at it good. Do it. Now."

Polly saw reflected what she had already seen. The vicious impression of his teeth on her breast, the bruises, the oblong marks of the blows. She closed her eyes but felt tears still trying to seep past her lashes.

"You think this is how She punishes, girl? You think She sends some bastard with rape on his mind?"

"The wish comes back three-fold on the wisher, whatever it is. You know that. I didn't wish pure. I wanted Colin, but he belonged to Annie."

"No one belongs to no one!" Rita said. "And She doesn't use

sex—the very power of creation—to punish Her priestess. Your thinking's gone off. You're looking at yourself like those sodding Christian
saints would have you do: 'The food of worms . . . a vile dung-hill.
She is the gate by which the devil enters . . . she is what the sting of
the scorpion is. . . . ' That's how you're seeing yourself now, isn't it?
Something to be trampled. Something no good."

"I did wrong by Colin. I cast the circle—"

Rita turned her and grabbed her arms firmly. "And you'll cast it
again, right now, with me. To Mars. Like I said you should've been
doing all along."

"I cast to Mars like you said the other night. I gave the ashes to
Annie. I put the ring stone with them. But I wasn't pure."

"Polly!" Rita shook her. "You didn't do wrong."

"I wanted her to die. I can't take back that wanting."

"An' you think she didn't want to die as well? Her insides were
eaten with cancer, luv. It went from her ovaries to her stomach and
her liver. You couldn't have saved her. No one could have saved her."

"The Goddess could. If I'd asked right. But I didn't. So She
punished."

"Don't be simple-minded. This isn't punishment, what happened
to you. This is evil, *his* evil. And we got to see that he pays for doing
it."

Polly loosened her mother's hands from her arms. "You can't use
magic against Colin. I won't let you."

"Believe me, girl, I don't mean to use magic," Rita said. "I mean
to use the police." She lurched round and headed for the door.

"No." Polly shuddered against the pain as she bent and retrieved
the robe from the floor. "You'll be bringing them out on a fool's errand.
I won't talk to them. I won't say a word."

Rita swung back. "You listen to me . . . "

"No. You listen, Mum. It doesn't matter, what he did."

"Doesn't . . . That's like saying you don't matter."

Polly tied the robe firmly until it, and her answer, were both in
place. "Yes. I know that," she said.

*   *   *

"So the Social Services connection made Tommy feel even more
certain that, whatever her reasons might have been for being rid of
the vicar, they're probably connected to Maggie."

"And what do you think?"

St. James opened the door of their room and locked it behind them. "I don't know. Something still niggles."

Deborah kicked off her shoes and sank onto the bed, drawing her legs up Indian fashion and rubbing her feet. She sighed. "My feet feel twenty years older than I do. I think women's shoes are designed by sadists. They ought to be shot."

"The shoes?"

"Those too." She pulled a tortoiseshell comb from her hair and pitched it onto the chest of drawers. She was wearing a green wool dress the same colour as her eyes, and it billowed round her like a mantle.

"Your feet may feel forty-five," St. James noted, "but you look fifteen."

"It's the lighting, Simon. Nicely subdued. Get used to it, won't you? You'll be seeing it more and more at home in the coming years."

He chuckled, shedding his jacket. He removed his watch and placed it on the bedside table beneath a lamp whose tasselled shade was going decidedly frizzy on the ends. He joined her on the bed, shifting his bad leg to accommodate his position of half-sit and half-slouch, resting on his elbows. "I'm glad of it," he said.

"Why? You've developed a fancy for subdued lighting?"

"No. But I've a definite fancy for the coming years. That we'll be having them, I mean."

"You thought we might not?"

"I never know quite what to think with you, frankly."

She raised her knees and rested her chin on them, pulling her dress close round her legs. Her gaze was on the bathroom door. She said, "Please don't ever think that, my love. Don't let who I am—or what I do—make you think we'll drift apart. I'm difficult, I know—"

"You were ever that."

"—but the *together* of us is the most important thing in my life." When he didn't respond at once, she turned her head to him, still resting it against her knees. "Do you believe that?"

"I want to."

"But?"

He coiled a lock of her hair round his finger and examined how it caught the light. It was, in colour, somewhere on the scale between red, chestnut, and blonde. He couldn't have named it. "Sometimes the business of life and its general messiness get in the way of *together*," he settled on saying. "When that happens, it's easy to lose sight of where you began, where you were heading, and why you took up with each other in the first place."

"I've never had a single problem with any of that," she said. "You were always in my life and I always loved you."

"But?"

She smiled and side-stepped with greater skill than he would have thought she possessed. "The night you first kissed me, you ceased being my childhood hero Mr. St. James and became the man I meant to marry. It was simple for me."

"It's never simple, Deborah."

"I think it can be. If two minds are one." She kissed him on the forehead, the bridge of his nose, his mouth. He shifted his hand from her hair to the back of her neck, but she hopped off the bed and unzipped her dress, yawning.

"Did we waste our time going to Bradford, then?" She wandered to the clothes cupboard and fished for a hanger.

He watched her, nonplussed, trying to make the connection. "Bradford?"

"Robin Sage. Did you find nothing in the vicarage about his marriage? The woman taken in adultery? And what about St. Joseph?"

He accepted her change in conversation, for the moment. It kept things easier, after all. "Nothing. But his things were packed away in cartons and there were dozens of those, so there may be something still to be uncovered. Tommy seems to think it unlikely, however. He thinks the truth's in London. And he thinks it has to do with the relationship between Maggie and her mother."

Deborah pulled her dress over her head, saying in a voice muffled from within its folds, "Still, I don't see why you've rejected the past. It seemed so compelling—a mysterious wife's even more mysterious boating accident and all of that. He may have been phoning Social Services for reasons having nothing to do with the girl in the first place."

"True. But phoning Social Services in London? Why wouldn't he have phoned a local branch if it was in reference to a local problem?"

"For that matter, even if his phoning had to do with Maggie, why would he phone London about her?"

"He wouldn't want her mother to know, I expect."

"He could have phoned Manchester or Liverpool, then. Couldn't he? And if he didn't, why didn't he?"

"That's the question. One way or the other, we need to find the answer. Suppose he was telephoning with regard to something that Maggie had confided in him. If he was invading what Juliet Spence saw as her own patch—the upbringing of her daughter—and if he was invading it in a way that threatened her and if he revealed this invasion to her, perhaps to force her hand in some way, don't you suppose she may have reacted to that?"

"Yes," Deborah said. "I tend to think she would have done." She hung up her dress and straightened it on the hanger. She sounded thoughtful.

"But you're not convinced?"

"It's not that." She reached for her dressing gown, donned it, and rejoined him on the bed. She sat on the edge, studying her feet. "It's just that . . . " She frowned. "I mean . . . I think it more likely that, if Juliet Spence murdered him and if Maggie's at the bottom of why she murdered him, she did it not because she herself was threatened, but because Maggie was. This is her child, after all. You can't forget that. You can't forget what it means."

St. James felt trepidation send its current of warning through the shorter hairs on the back of his neck. Her final statement, he knew, could lead to treacherous ground between them. He said nothing and waited for her to continue. She did so, dropping her hand to trace a pattern between them on the counterpane.

"Here's this creature that grew inside her for nine months, listening to her heartbeat, sharing the flow of her blood, kicking and moving in those final months to make her presence known. Maggie came from her body. She sucked milk from her breasts. Within weeks, she knew her face and her voice. I think—" Her fingers paused in their tracing. Her tone tried and ultimately failed to become practical. "A mother would do anything to safeguard her child. I mean . . . Wouldn't she do anything to protect the life she created? And don't you honestly think that's what this killing's all about?"

Somewhere below them in the inn, Dora Wragg's voice called, "Josephine Eugenia! Where've you got yourself to? How many times do I have to tell you—" A slamming door cut off the rest of the words.

St. James said, "Not everyone is like you, my love. Not everyone sees a child that way."

"But if it's her only child . . . "

"Born under what circumstances? Having what kind of impact on her life? Trying her patience in what sort of ways? Who knows what's gone on between them? You can't look at Mrs. Spence and her daughter through the filter of your own desires. You can't stand in her shoes."

Deborah gave a bitter laugh. "I do know that."

He saw how she had grasped his words and turned them round on herself to wound. "Don't," he said. "You can't know what the future has in mind for you."

"When the past is its prologue?" She shook her head. He couldn't see her face, just a sliver of her cheek like a small quarter moon nearly covered by her hair.

"Sometimes the past is prologue to the future. Sometimes it isn't."

"Holding on to that sort of belief is a damned easy way to avoid responsibility, Simon."

"It can be, indeed. But it can also be a way of getting on with things, can't it? You always look backwards for your auguries, my love. But that doesn't seem to give you anything but pain."

"While you don't look for auguries at all."

"That's the worst of it," he admitted. "I don't. Not for us, at least."

"And for others? For Tommy and Helen? For your brothers? For your sister?"

"Not for them either. They'll go their own way in the end, despite my brooding over what led up to their eventual decisions."

"Then who?"

He made no reply. The truth of the matter was that her words had jogged a fragment of conversation loose in his memory, giving rise to thought. But he was wary of a change in topic that she might misinterpret as further indication of his detachment from her.

"Tell me." She was starting to bristle. He could see it in the way her fingers spread out then clutched the counterpane. "Something's on your mind and I don't much like to be cut out when we're talking about—"

He squeezed her hand. "It has nothing to do with us, Deborah. Or with this."

"Then..." She was quick to read him. "Juliet Spence."

"Your instincts are generally good about people and situations. Mine aren't. I always look for bald facts. You're more comfortable with conjectures."

"And?"

"It was what you said about the past being prologue to the future." He loosed his tie and pulled it over his head, throwing it in the direction of the chest of drawers. It fell short and draped against one of the pulls. "Polly Yarkin overheard Sage having a conversation on the telephone the day he died. He was talking about the past."

"To Mrs. Spence?"

"We think so. He said something about judging..." St. James paused in the act of unbuttoning his shirt. He sought the words as Polly Yarkin had recited them. " 'You can't judge what happened then.' "

"The boating accident."

"I think that's what's been niggling at me since we left the vicarage. That declaration doesn't fit in with his interest in Social Services, as far as I can see. But something tells me it needs to fit somewhere. He'd been praying all that day, Polly said. He wouldn't take any food."

"Fasting."

"Yes. But why?"

"Perhaps he wasn't hungry."

St. James considered other options. "Self-denial, penance."

"For a sin? What was it?"

He finished with his unbuttoning and sailed the shirt the way of the tie. It too missed its mark and fell to the floor. "I don't know," he said. "But I'm willing to lay whatever odds you'd like that Mrs. Spence does."

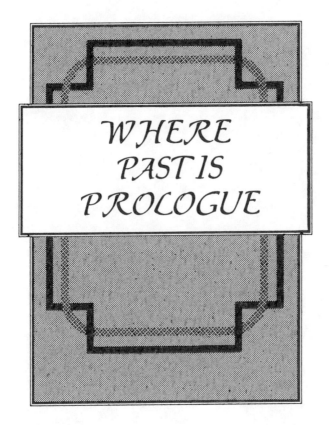

WHERE
PAST IS
PROLOGUE

CHAPTER TWENTY-FOUR

AN EARLY START, INITIATED LONG BEFORE the sun rose above the slopes of Cotes Fell, got Lynley to the outskirts of London by noon. The city's traffic, which daily seemed to become ever more like a Gordian knot on wheels, added another hour to his travel time. It was just after one when he pulled into Onslow Square and claimed a parking space that was being vacated by a Mercedes-Benz with its driver's door crumpled like a defeated accordion and a scowling driver harnessed into a neck brace.

He hadn't phoned her, either from Winslough or from the Bentley. He'd told himself at first that it was far too early—when, after all, had Helen ever risen before nine in the morning if she wasn't compelled to do so?—but as the hour grew later, he changed his reasoning to the fact that he didn't want her to rearrange her schedule just to accommodate him. She wasn't a woman who liked being at any man's beck and call, and he wasn't about to foist that role upon her. Her flat wasn't that far from his own home, after all. If she'd gone out for the afternoon, he could simply toddle onwards to Eaton Terrace and have lunch there. He flattered himself with thinking how liberated all these considerations were. It was far easier than admitting the more obvious truth: He wanted to see her, but he didn't want to be disappointed by Helen's having an engagement that excluded him.

He rang the bell and waited, observing a sky the approximate colour of a ten-pence coin and wondering how long the rain would hold off and if rain in London meant snow in Lancashire. He rang a second time and heard her voice crackle with static from the speaker.

"You're home," he said.

"Tommy," she said and rang him in.

She met him at the door to her flat. Without make-up, with her hair pulled back from her face and held in place with an ingenious combination of elastic and satin ribbon, she looked like a teenager. Her choice of conversation emphasised the similarity.

"I've had the most tremendous row with Daddy this morning," she said as he kissed her. "I was supposed to meet Sidney and Hortense for lunch—Sid's discovered an Armenian restaurant in Chiswick that she swears is absolutely heaven on earth, if the combination of Armenian food, Chiswick, and heaven is even possible—but Daddy came to town yesterday on business, spent the night here, and we sank to new depths in our mutual loathing of each other this morning."

Lynley removed his overcoat. She'd been consoling herself with the rare luxury of a midday fire, he saw. On a coffee table in front of it were spread out the morning's paper, two cups and saucers, and the remains of a breakfast that appeared to consist mostly of overboiled and half-eaten eggs and deeply charcoaled toast.

"I didn't know you and your father loathed each other," he said. "Is this something new? I'd always got the impression you were rather his favourite."

"Oh, we don't and I am, how true," she said. "Which is why it's so utterly disagreeable of him to have such expectations of me. 'Now don't misunderstand me, darling. Your mother and I don't for a moment begrudge you the use of this flat,' he says in that sonorous way he has of talking. You know what I mean."

"Baritone, yes. Does he want you out of the flat?"

" 'Your grandmother intended it for the family, and as you're part of the family, we can't accuse you or ourselves of ignoring her wishes. Nonetheless, when your mother and I reflect upon the manner in which you spend your time,' and all the etceteras at which he so excels. I hate it when he blackmails me about the flat."

"You mean 'Tell me how uselessly you've been spending your days, Helen darling'?" Lynley asked.

"That's just exactly it." She went to the coffee table and began folding the newspaper and stacking the dishes. "And it all came about because Caroline wasn't here to cook his breakfast. She's back in Cornwall—she's definitely decided to return and isn't *that* the decade's best news, the blame for which, frankly, I lay directly on Denton's doorstep, Tommy. And because Cybele is such a model of connubial bliss, and because Iris is as happy as a pig in the muck with Montana, cattle, and her cowboy. But mostly it was because his egg wasn't boiled the way he wanted it and I burnt his toast—well, heavens, how was I supposed to know one had to hang over the toaster like a woman in love?—and that set him off. He's always been as prickly as a hedgehog in the morning anyway."

Lynley weeded through the information for the one point on which he had at least a degree of expertise. He couldn't comment on the marital choices that two of Helen's sisters had made—Cybele to an Italian industrialist and Iris to a rancher in the United States—but he felt conversant with at least one area of her life. For the past several years, Caroline had acted the role of maid, companion, housekeeper, cook, dresser, and general angel of mercy for Helen. But she was Cornwall born and Cornwall bred and he'd known London would wear uneasily upon her in the long run. "You couldn't have hoped to hold on to Caroline forever," he noted. "Her family's at Howenstow, after all."

"I could have done if Denton hadn't seen fit to break her heart every month or so. I don't understand why you can't do something about your own valet. He's simply unconscionable when it comes to women."

Lynley followed her into the kitchen. They set the dishes on the work top, and Helen went to the refrigerator. She brought out a carton of lemon yogurt and prised it open with the end of a spoon.

"I was going to ask you to lunch," he said hastily as she dipped into it and leaned against the work top.

"Were you? Thank you, darling. I couldn't possibly. I'm afraid I'm too occupied with trying to decide how to make something of my life in a fashion both Daddy and I can live with." She knelt and rooted through the refrigerator a second time, bringing forth three more cartons. "Strawberry, banana, another lemon," she said. "Which would you like?"

"None of them, actually. I had visions of smoked salmon followed by veal. Champagne cocktails fore, claret with, brandy aft."

"Banana, then," Helen decided for him and handed him the carton and a spoon. "It's just the very thing. Quite refreshing. You'll see. I'll make some fresh coffee."

Lynley examined the yogurt with a grimace. "Can I actually eat this without feeling like little Miss Muffet?" He wandered to a circular table of birch and glass that fitted neatly into an alcove in the kitchen. At least three days of post lay unopened upon it, along with two fashion magazines with corners turned down to mark pages of interest. He flipped through these as Helen poured coffee beans into a grinder and set it to roar. Her choice of reading material was intriguing. She'd been investigating bridal gowns and weddings. Satin versus silk versus linen versus cotton. Flowers in the hair versus hats versus veils. Receptions and breakfasts. The registry office versus the church.

He glanced up to see that she was watching him. She spun away and dealt with the ground coffee intently. But he had seen the momentary confusion in her eyes—when on earth had Helen ever been nonplussed about anything?—and he wondered how much, if any, of her current interest in weddings had to do with him and how much of it had to do with her father's criticism. She seemed to read his mind.

"He always goes on about Cybele," she said, "which puts him into a state about me. There she is: mother of four, wife of one, the grande dame of Milano, patroness of the arts, on the board of the opera, the head of the museum of modern art, chairwoman of every committee known to mankind. *And* she speaks Italian like a native. What a wretched sort of oldest sister she is. She could at least have had the decency to be miserable. Or to be married to a lout. But no, Carlo adores her, worships her, calls her his fragile little English rose." Helen slammed the glass carafe under the spout of the coffee maker. "Cybele's as fragile as a horse and he knows it."

She opened a cupboard and began pulling out an assortment of tins, jars, and cartons, which she carried to the table. Cheese biscuits took up position on a plate with a wedge of brie. Olives and sweet pickles went into a bowl. To these, she added a splash of cocktail onions. She finished off the array with a hunk of salami and a cutting board.

"Lunch," she said and sat down opposite him as the coffee brewed.

"Eclectic gastronomy," he noted. "What could I have been thinking of, suggesting smoked salmon and veal?"

Lady Helen cut herself some brie and smoothed it onto a biscuit. "He sees no need for me to have a career—honestly, what a Victorian Daddy is—but he thinks I ought to be doing something useful."

"You are." Lynley tucked into his banana yogurt and tried to think of it as something one could chew rather than simply gum and swallow. "What about everything you do for Simon when he gets swamped?"

"That's a particularly sore spot with Daddy. What on earth is one of his daughters doing dusting and photographing latent fingerprints, placing hairs on microscope slides, typing up reports about decomposing flesh? My God, is this the sort of life he expected the fruit of his loins to be living? Is this what he sent me to finishing school for? To spend the rest of my days—intermittently, of course, I don't pretend to be doing anything far removed from frivolity on a regular basis—in a laboratory? If I were a man, at least I could fritter away my time at the club. He'd approve of that. It's what he spent most of his youth doing, after all."

Lynley raised an eyebrow. "I seem to recall your father chairing three or four rather successful investment corporations. I seem to recall that he still chairs one."

"Oh, don't remind me. He spent the morning doing so, when he wasn't listing the charitable organisations to which I ought to be giving my time. Really, Tommy, sometimes I think he and his attitudes stepped right out of a Jane Austen novel."

Lynley fingered the magazine he'd been looking through. "There are, of course, other ways to appease him, aside from giving your time to charity. Not that he needs to be appeased, of course, but supposing you wish to. You might, for instance, give your time to something else he considered worthwhile."

"Naturally. There's fund raising for medical research, home visits to the elderly, working on one hot line or another. I know I ought to do something with myself. And I keep intending to, but things just get in the way."

"I wasn't talking about becoming a volunteer."

She paused in the act of slicing herself a piece of salami. She placed the knife down, wiped her fingers on a peach linen napkin, and didn't respond.

"Think how many birds the single stone of marriage would kill, Helen. This flat could go back to the use of your whole family."

"They can come here any time as it is. They know that."

"You could declare yourself too busy with your husband's ego-centric interests to be able to live a life of social and cultural responsibility as Cybele does."

"I *need* to start being more involved in things, anyway. Daddy's right about that, although I hate to admit it."

"And once you had children, you could use their needs as a shield against whatever judgement your father might cast upon you for inactivity. Not that he'd cast any judgements at that point. He'd be too pleased."

"About what?"

"About having you . . . settled, I suppose."

"*Settled?*" Lady Helen speared a sweet pickle and chewed it thoughtfully, watching him. "My God, don't tell me you're really that provincial."

"I didn't intend—"

"You can't honestly believe that a woman's place is to be *settled*, Tommy. Or," she asked shrewdly, "is it just my place?"

"No. Sorry. It was a poor choice of words."

"Choose again, then."

He placed his yogurt carton on the table. Its contents had tasted fairly good for the first few spoonfuls, but they didn't wear well on the palate after that. "We're dancing round the issue and we may as well stop. Your father knows that I want to marry you, Helen."

"Yes. What of it?"

He crossed his legs, uncrossed them. He lifted his hand to loosen the knot of his tie, only to discover and recall that he wasn't wearing one. He sighed. "Damn it all. Nothing of it. It merely seems to me that marriage between us wouldn't be such a miserable thing."

"And God knows that it would please Daddy well enough."

He felt stung by her sarcasm and answered in kind. "I have no idea about pleasing your father, but there are—"

"You used the word *pleased* less than a minute ago. Or have you conveniently forgotten?"

"But there are moments—and frankly this isn't turning out to be one of them—when I'm actually blind enough to think that it might please me."

She looked stung in turn. She sat back in her chair. They stared at each other. The telephone, mercifully, began to ring.

"Let it go," he said. "We need to thrash this out, and we need to do it now."

"I don't think so." She got up. The phone was on the work top, next to the coffee maker. She poured them each a cup as she spoke to her caller, saying, "What a good guess. He's sitting right here in my kitchen, eating salami and yogurt..." She laughed. "Truro? Well, I hope you're running his credit cards to the limit... No, here he is... Really, Barbara, don't give it a thought. We weren't discussing anything more earth-shaking than the merits of sweet pickles over dill."

She had a way of knowing when he felt most betrayed by her levity, so Lynley wasn't surprised when Helen didn't meet his eyes as she handed him the phone and said, unnecessarily, "It's Sergeant Havers. For you."

He caught her fingers under his when he took the receiver. He didn't release her until she looked at him. And even then, he said nothing, because, damn it all, she was at fault and he wasn't going to apologise for lashing out when she drove him to it.

When he said hello to his sergeant, he realised that Havers must have heard more in his voice than he intended to convey, for she launched into her report without prefatory remarks of any kind, saying, "You'll be chuffed to know that the C of E take police work dead to heart down here in Truro. The bishop's secretary kindly gave me an appointment to see him a week from tomorrow, thank you very much. Busy as a bee in the roses, the bishop, if his secretary's to be believed." She blew out a long, loud breath. She'd be smoking, as usual. "And you should see the digs these two blokes live in. Sodding bloody hell. Remind me to hold on to my money the next time the collection plate is passed round in church. They should be supporting me, not vice versa."

"So it's been a waste." Lynley watched Helen return to the table where she sat and began unfolding the corners of the magazine pages she'd previously folded down. She was pressing each one deliberately flat and smoothing it with her fingers. She wanted him to see the activity. He knew that as well as he knew her. Realising this, he felt the momentary grip of an anger so irrationally powerful that he wanted to kick the table through the wall.

Havers was saying, "So evidently the term 'boating accident' was a euphemism."

Lynley tore his eyes from Helen. "What?"

"Haven't you been listening?" Havers asked. "Never mind. Don't answer. When did you tune in?"

"With the boating accident."

"Right." She began again.

Once she had realised that the bishop of Truro wasn't going to be of help, she'd gone to the newspaper office, where she'd spent the morning reading back issues. There she discovered that the boating accident that had claimed the life of Robin Sage's wife—

"Her name was Susanna, by the way."

—hadn't occurred on a boat in the first place and hadn't been deemed an accident in the second.

"It was the ferry that runs from Plymouth to Roscoff," Havers said. "And it was suicide, according to the newspaper."

Havers sketched in the story with the details she'd gathered from her perusal of the newspaper accounts. The Sages had been making a crossing in bad weather, on their way to begin a two-week holiday in France. After a meal midway through the crossing—

"It's a six-hour ride, you know."

—Susanna had gone off to the Ladies' while her husband returned to the lounge with his book. It was more than an hour before he realised that she ought to have turned up, but as she'd been feeling a bit low, he assumed she wanted some time alone.

"He said he had a tendency to hover when she was in a mood," Havers explained. "And he wanted to give her some space. My words, not his."

According to the information Havers had been able to gather, Robin Sage had left the lounge two or three times during the remainder of the crossing, to stretch his legs, to get a drink, to purchase a chocolate bar, but not to look for his wife about whose continued absence, it seemed, he did not appear to be worried. When they docked in France, he went below to the car, assuming that she would be there waiting. When she failed to show up as the passengers began to leave, he set about looking for her.

"He didn't raise the alarm until he noticed that her handbag was on the front passenger seat of the car," Havers said. "There was a note inside. Here, let me . . ." Lynley heard the noise of pages turning. "It said, 'Robin, I'm sorry. I can't find the light.' There was no name but the writing was hers."

"Not much of a suicide note," Lynley remarked.

"You're not the only one who thought that," Havers said.

The crossing had been made in bad weather after all. It was dark for the latter half of it. It was cold, as well, so no one had been on deck to see a woman throw herself from the railing.

"Or be thrown?" Lynley asked.

Havers agreed obliquely. "The truth is that it could have been suicide, but it could have been something else as well. Which is, apparently, what the rozzers on both sides of the Channel thought. Sage was put through the wringer twice. He came up clean. Or as clean as he could because no one witnessed anything at all, including Sage's trip to the bar or his saunters to stretch his legs."

"And the wife couldn't simply have slipped off the boat when it docked?" Lynley asked.

"An international crossing, Inspector. Her passport was in her handbag, along with her money, her driving licence, credit cards, and the whole bloody bit. She couldn't have got off the boat at either end. And they searched every inch of it in France *and* in England."

"What about the body? Where was she found? Who identified her?"

"I don't know yet, but I'm working that angle. D'you want to place any bets?"

"Sage liked to talk about the woman taken in adultery," Lynley said, more to himself than to her.

"And since there were no stones handy on the boat, he gave her the old heave-ho as her just deserts?"

"Perhaps."

"Well, whatever happened, they're sleeping in the bosom of Jesus right now. In the graveyard in Tresillian. They all are, in fact. I went to check."

"They all are?"

"Susanna, Sage, and the kid. All of them. Lying in a tidy little row."

"The kid?"

"Yeah. The kid. Joseph. Their son."

■　　■　　■

Lynley frowned, listening to his sergeant and watching Helen. The former was supplying the rest of the details. The latter was playing a knife across the wedge of brie in an aimless pattern, her magazines closed and set to one side.

"He was three months old when he died," Havers said. "And then her death . . . let me see . . . here it is. She died six months later. That supports the suicide theory, doesn't it? She'd have been depressed as hell, I'd guess, to have her baby die. And how did she put it? She couldn't find the light."

"What was his cause of death?"

"Don't know."

"Find out."

"Right." She rustled some papers, jotting down instructions in her notebook, probably. She said suddenly, "Hell, Inspector, he was three months old. D'you think this bloke *Sage* might've . . . or even the wife . . ."

"I don't know, Sergeant." On the other end of the line, he heard the brief, distinct snap of a match being struck. She was lighting up again. He longed to do so himself. He said, "Dig a little deeper on Susanna as well. See if you can find anything at all about her relationship to Juliet Spence."

"Spence . . . Got it." More paper crinkled. "I've made copies of the newspaper articles for you. They're not much, but shall I fax them to the Yard?"

"For what they're worth, I suppose so." It seemed little enough.

"Right. Well." He could hear her drawing on the cigarette. "Inspector . . ." The word was not so much spoken as drawled.

"What?"

"Soldier on up there. You know. Helen."

Easy to say, he thought as he replaced the phone. He returned to the table, saw that Helen had cross-hatched the entire top of the brie. She'd given up eating her yogurt, and the salami was still only partially cut. At the moment, she was using a fork to roll a black olive round her plate. Her expression was disconsolate. He felt oddly moved to compassion.

"I expect your father wouldn't approve of your playing with your food, either," he said quietly.

"No. Cybele never plays with her food. And Iris never eats, as far as I know."

He sat and looked without hunger at the brie he'd spread on a biscuit. He picked it up, put it down, reached for the pickle bowl, pushed it away.

He finally said, "Right. I'll be off. I must go out to—" just as she said quickly, "I'm so sorry, Tommy. I don't mean to keep hurting you. I don't know what comes over me or why I do it."

He said, "I push you. We push each other."

She took the ribboned elastic from her hair and played the elastic round her hand. She said, "I think I'm looking for evidence, and when it isn't there, I create it from nothing."

"This is a relationship, Helen, not a court of law. What are you trying to prove?"

"Unworthiness."

"I see. Mine." He tried to sound objective but knew he didn't manage it.

She looked up. Her eyes were dry, but her skin was blotched. "Yours. Yes. Because God knows I already feel my own."

He reached for the ribbon she'd twisted in her hands. She'd bound them loosely together, and he unwove the binding. "If you're waiting for me to end things between us, it's not going to happen. So you'll have to do the ending yourself."

"I can, if you ask me."

"I don't intend to."

"It would be so much easier."

"Yes. It would. But only at first." He stood. "I must go out to Kent for the afternoon. Will you have dinner with me?" He smiled. "Will you have breakfast as well?"

"Love-making isn't what I'm avoiding, Tommy."

"No," he agreed. "Making love is easy enough. It's living with it that's the devil."

■   ■   ■

Lynley pulled into the car park of the train station in Sevenoaks just as the first raindrops hit the windscreen of the Bentley. He fumbled in his overcoat pocket for the directions they'd found among the vicar's belongings in Lancashire.

They were simple enough, taking him to the high street for a brief jaunt before heading out of the town altogether. A few turns past the point where the pre-hurricane, eponymous oaks of the town had once stood, and he was in the country. Down two more lanes and up a slight rise, and he found himself following a short drive labelled Wealdon Oast. This led to a house, with white tile cladding above and brick below, decorated by the distinctive, bent-chimneyed oast roundel attached to the building at its north end. The house had a view of Sevenoaks to the west and a mixture of farmland and woodland to the south. The land and the trees were winter-drab now, but the rest of the year, they would provide an ever-changing palette of colour.

As he parked between a Sierra and a Metro, Lynley wondered if Robin Sage had walked this distance out from the town. He wouldn't have driven all the way from Lancashire, and the set of directions seemed to indicate two facts: He had arrived by train with no intention of taking a taxi from the station, and no one had met him or intended to meet him, either at the station or somewhere in the town.

A wooden sign, neatly lettered in yellow and affixed to the left of the front door, identified the oast house not as a home but as a place of business. *Gitterman Temps*, it read. And beneath that in smaller letters of yellow, *Katherine Gitterman, Prop.*

Kate, Lynley thought. Another answer was emerging to the questions that had arisen from Sage's engagement diary and the odd bits carton.

A young woman looked up from a reception desk as Lynley entered the house. What had once been the sitting room was now an office with ivory walls, green carpeting, and modern oak furniture that smelled faintly of lemon oil. The girl nodded at him, as she said into the thin wire headpiece of a telephone receiver,

"I can let you have Sandy again, Mr. Coatsworth. She got on well with your staff and her skills... Well, yes, she's the one with the braces on her teeth." She rolled her eyes at Lynley. They were, he noted, skilfully shaded with an aquamarine shadow that exactly matched the jumper she wore. "Yes, of course, Mr. Coatsworth. Let me see..." On her desk, which was otherwise free of clutter, lay six manila folders. She opened the first. "It's no trouble, Mr. Coatsworth. Really. Please, don't give it a thought." She riffled through the second. "You've not tried Joy, have you?... No, she doesn't wear braces. And she types... let me see..."

Lynley glanced to his left through the door that opened into the roundel. Into its circular wall a half-dozen neat cubicles had been built. At two of them, girls were pecking at electric typewriters while a timer ticked to one side. In a third, a young man worked upon a word processor, shaking his head at the screen and saying, "Jesus, this *is* screwed for sure. I'll bet a hundred quid it was another power surge." He leaned towards the floor and rattled through a repair case filled with circuit boards and arcane equipment. "Disk crash city," he murmured. "I sure as hell hope she was backing up."

"May I help you, sir?"

Lynley swung back to the reception desk. Aquamarine held a pencil poised as if to take notes. She'd cleared the desk of the folders and replaced them with a yellow legal pad. Behind her, from a vase on a glistening credenza, a single petal fell from a spray of hot-house roses. Lynley expected a harried custodian with dustpan in hand to appear from nowhere and whisk the offending bit of floribunda from sight.

"I'm looking for Katherine Gitterman," he said, and produced his warrant card. "Scotland Yard CID."

"You want Kate?" The young woman's incredulity apparently prevented her from giving his warrant card any attention at all. "*Kate?*"

"Is she available?"

Eyes still on him, she nodded, lifted a finger to keep him in place, and punched in three numbers on the telephone. After a brief and muffled conversation which she conducted with her chair swivelled in the direction of the credenza, she led him past a second desk on which a maroon leather blotter held the day's post, arranged artfully into a fan with a letter opener acting the part of its handle. She opened the door beyond the desk and gestured towards a stairway.

"Up there," she said and added with a smile, "You've put a spanner in her day. She doesn't much like surprises."

Kate Gitterman met him at the top of the stairs, a tall woman dressed in a tailored, plaid flannel dressing gown whose belt was tied in a perfectly symmetrical bow. The predominant colour of the garment was the same green as the carpeting, and she wore beneath it pyjamas of an identical shade.

"Flu," she said. "I'm battling the last of it. I hope you don't mind." She didn't give him the opportunity to respond. "I'll see you in here."

She led him down a narrow corridor that gave way to the sitting room of a modern, well-appointed flat. A kettle was whistling as they entered and with a "Just a moment, please," she left him. The soles of her slim leather slippers clattered against the linoleum as she moved about the kitchen.

Lynley glanced round the sitting room. Like the offices below, it was compulsively neat, with shelves, racks, and holders in which every possession appeared to have its designated place. The pillows on the sofa and on the armchairs were poised at identical angles. A small Persian rug before the fireplace lay centred perfectly. The fireplace itself burned neither wood nor coal but a pyramid of artificial nuggets that were glowing in a semblance of embers.

He was reading the titles of her videotapes—lined up like guardsmen beneath a television—when she returned.

"I like to stay fit," she said, in apparent explanation of the fact that beyond a copy of Olivier's *Wuthering Heights*, the cassettes all contained exercise tapes, featuring one film actress or another.

He could see that fitness was approximately as important to her as neatness, for aside from the fact that she was herself slender, solid, and athletic looking, the room's only photograph was a framed, poster-sized enlargement of her running in a race with the number 194 on her chest. She was wearing a red headband and sweating profusely, but she'd managed a dazzling smile for the camera.

"My first marathon," she said. "Everyone's first is rather special."

"I'd imagine that to be the case."

"Yes. Well." She brushed her thumb and middle finger through her hair. Light brown carefully streaked with blonde, it was cut quite short and blown back from her face in a fashionable style that suggested frequent trips to a hairdresser who wielded scissors and colour with equal skill. From the lining round her eyes and in the room's daylight, despite the rain that was beginning to streak the flat's casement windows, Lynley would have placed her in mid to late forties. But he imagined that dressed for business or pleasure, made up, and seen in the forgiving artificial light of one restaurant or another, she looked at least ten years younger.

She was holding a mug from which steam rose aromatically. "Chicken broth," she said. "I suppose I should offer you something, but I'm not well versed in how one behaves when the police come to call. And you *are* the police?"

He offered her his warrant card. Unlike the receptionist below, she studied it before handing it back.

"I hope this isn't about one of my girls." She walked to the sofa and sat on the edge with her mug of chicken broth balanced on her left knee. She had, he saw, the shoulders of a swimmer and the unbending posture of a Victorian woman cinched into a corset. "I check into their backgrounds thoroughly when they first apply. No one gets into my files without at least three references. If they get a bad report from more than two of their employers, I let them go. So I never have trouble. Never."

Lynley joined her, sitting in one of the armchairs. He said, "I've come about a man called Robin Sage. He had the directions to this oast house among his belongings and a reference to *Kate* in his engagement diary. Do you know him? Did he come to see you?"

"Robin? Yes."

"When?"

She drew her eyebrows together. "I don't recall exactly. It was sometime in the autumn. Perhaps late September?"

"The eleventh of October?"

"It could have been. Shall I check that for you?"

"Did he have an appointment?"

"One could call it that. Why? Has he got into trouble?"

"He's dead."

She adjusted her grip on the mug slightly, but that was the only reaction that Lynley could read. "This an investigation?"

"The circumstances were rather irregular." He waited for her to do the normal thing, to ask what the circumstances were. When she didn't, he said, "Sage lived in Lancashire. May I take it that he didn't come to see you about hiring a temporary employee?"

She sipped her chicken bouillon. "He came to talk about Susanna."

"His wife."

"My sister." She pulled a square of white linen from her pocket, dabbed it against the corners of her mouth, and replaced it neatly. "I hadn't seen or heard a word from him since the day of her funeral. He wasn't exactly welcome here. Not after everything that had happened."

"Between him and his wife."

"And the baby. That dreadful business about Joseph."

"He was an infant when he died, as I understand."

"Just three months. It was a cot death. Susanna went to get him up one morning, thinking that he'd actually slept through the night for the first time. He'd been dead for hours. He was stiff with rigor. She broke three of his ribs between the kiss of life and trying to give him CPR. There was an investigation, of course. And there were questions of abuse when the word got out about his ribs."

"Police questions?" Lynley asked in some surprise. "If the bones were broken after death—"

"They would have known. I'm aware of that. It wasn't the police. Naturally, they questioned her, but once they had the pathologist's report, they were satisfied. Still, there were whispers in the community. And Susanna was in an exposed position."

Kate got up and walked to the window where she pushed back the curtains. The rain was pattering against the glass. She said contemplatively but without much ferocity, "I blamed him. I still do. But Susanna only blamed herself."

"I'd think that's a fairly normal reaction."

"Normal?" Kate laughed softly. "There was nothing normal about her situation."

Lynley waited without reply or question. The rain snaked in rivulets against the window-panes. A telephone rang in the office below.

"Joseph slept in their bedroom the first two months."

"Hardly abnormal."

She seemed not to hear. "Then Robin insisted he be given a room of his own. Susanna wanted him near her, but she cooperated with Robin. That was her way. And he was very convincing."

"About what?"

"He kept insisting that a child could be irrevocably damaged by witnessing at any age, even in infancy, what Robin in his infinite wisdom called 'the primal scene' between his parents." Kate turned from the window and sipped more broth. "Robin refused to have sex as long as the baby was in the room. When Susanna wanted to . . . resume relations, she had to go along with Robin's wishes. But I suppose you can imagine what little Joseph's death did to any future primal scenes between them."

The marriage quickly fell apart, she said. Robin flung himself into his work as a means of distraction. Susanna drifted into depression.

"I was living and working in London at the time," Kate said, "so I had her come to stay with me. I had her go to galleries. I gave her books to identify the birds in the parks. I mapped out city walks and had her take one each day. Someone had to do something, after all. I tried."

"To . . . ?"

"To get her back into life. What do you think? She was wallowing in grief. She was luxuriating in guilt and self-loathing. It wasn't healthy. And Robin wasn't helping matters at all."

"He'd have been feeling his own grief, I dare say."

"She wouldn't put it behind her. Every day I'd come home and there she would be, sitting on the bed, holding the baby's picture against her breast, wanting to talk and relive it all. Day after day. As if talking about it would have done any good." Kate returned to the sofa and placed her mug on a round of mosaic that served as a mat on the side table. "She was torturing herself. She wouldn't let it go. I told her she had to. She was young. She'd have another baby, after all. Joseph was dead. He was gone. He was buried. And if she didn't snap out of it and take care of herself, she'd be buried with him."

"Which she eventually was."

"I blame *him* for that. With his primal scenes and his miserable belief in God's judgement in our lives. That's what he told her, you know. That Joseph's death was the hand of God at work. What a *beastly* man. Susanna didn't need to hear that sort of rubbish. She didn't need to believe she was being punished. And for what? For what?"

Kate pulled out her handkerchief a second time. She pressed it against her forehead although she didn't appear to be perspiring.

"Sorry," she said. "There are some things in life that don't bear remembering."

"Is that why Robin Sage came to see you? To share memories?"

"He was suddenly interested in her," she said. "He hadn't been the least involved in her life in the six months that led up to her death. But suddenly he cared. What did she do while she was with you, he wanted to know. Where did she go? What did she talk about? How did she act? Whom did she meet?" She chuckled bitterly. "After all these years. I wanted to smack his mournful little face. He'd been eager enough to see her buried."

"What do you mean?"

"He kept identifying bodies washed up on the coast. There were two or three of them he said were Susanna. The wrong height, the wrong hair colour when there was hair left on them at all, the wrong weight. It didn't matter. He was in such a nasty rush about it all."

"Why?"

"I don't know. I thought at first he had some woman lined up to marry and he needed to have Susanna declared officially dead in order to get on with it."

"But he didn't marry."

"He didn't. I assume the woman gave him the brush-off, whoever she was."

"Does the name Juliet Spence mean anything to you? Did he mention a woman called Juliet Spence when he was here? Did Susanna ever mention Juliet Spence?"

She shook her head. "Why?"

"She poisoned Robin Sage. Last month in Lancashire."

Kate raised a hand as if to touch it to her perfectly brushed hair. She dropped it, however, before it made contact. Her eyes grew momentarily distant. "How odd. I find I'm glad of the fact."

Lynley wasn't surprised. "Did your sister ever mention any other men when she was staying with you? Did she see other men once things began to go wrong in her marriage? Could her husband have discovered that?"

"She didn't talk about men. She talked only about babies."

"There is, of course, an unavoidable connection between the two."

"I've always found that a rather unfortunate quirk in our species. Everyone pants towards orgasm without pausing to realise that it's merely a biological trap designed for the purpose of reproduction. What utter nonsense."

"People get involved with one another. They pursue intimacy along with love."

"More fools, they," Kate said.

Lynley got to his feet. Kate moved behind him and made an adjustment to the position of the pillow on his chair. She brushed her fingers across the chair's back.

He watched her, wondering what it had been like for her sister. Grief calls for acceptance and understanding. No doubt she'd felt herself cut off from mankind.

He said, "Have you any idea why Robin Sage might have telephoned Social Services in London?"

Kate picked a hair from the lapel of her dressing gown. "He'd have been looking for me, no doubt."

"You supply them with temps?"

"No. I've had this business only eight years. Before that, I worked for Social Services. He'd have phoned there first."

"But your name was in his diary before his calls or visits to Social Services. Why would that be?"

"I couldn't say. Perhaps he wanted to go through Susanna's paperwork in the trip down memory lane he'd been taking. Social Services in Truro would have been involved when the baby died. Perhaps he was tracking her paperwork to London."

"Why?"

"To read it? To set the record straight?"

"To discover if Social Services knew what someone else claimed to know?"

"About Joseph's death?"

"Is it a possibility?"

She folded her arms beneath her breasts. "I can't see how. If there had been something suspicious about his death, it would have been acted upon, Inspector."

"Perhaps it was something borderline, something that could have been interpreted either way."

"But why would he take a sudden interest in that now? From the moment Joseph died, Robin showed no interest in anything other than his ministry. 'We'll get through this by the grace of God,' he told Susanna." Kate's lips pressed into a line of distaste. "Frankly, I wouldn't have blamed her in the least if she'd had the luck to find someone else. Just to forget about Robin for a few hours would have been heaven."

"Could she have done? Did you get a sense of that?"

"Not from her conversation. When she wasn't talking about Joseph, she was trying to get me to talk about my cases. It was just another way to punish herself."

"You were a social worker, then. I'd thought—" He gestured in the general direction of the stairway.

"That I was a secretary. No. I had much larger aspirations. I once believed I could actually help people. Change lives. Make things better. What an amusing laugh. Ten years in Social Services took care of that."

"What sort of work did you do?"

"Mothers and infants," she said. "Home visits. And the more I did it, the more I understood what a myth our culture has created about childbirth, depicting it as woman's highest purpose fulfilled. What contemptible rot, all of it generated by men. Most of the women I saw were utterly miserable when they weren't too uneducated or too impossibly ignorant to be able to recognise the extent of their plight."

"But your sister believed in the myth."

"She did. And it killed her, Inspector."

CHAPTER TWENTY-FIVE

IT'S THE NASTY LITTLE FACT THAT HE KEPT misidentifying bodies," Lynley said. He nodded to the officer on duty at the kiosk, flashed his identification, and descended the ramp into the underground car park of New Scotland Yard. "Why keep saying definitively that each one was his wife? Why not say he wasn't certain? It didn't matter, after all. A postmortem would have been performed on the bodies in any case. And he must have known that."

"It sounds like shades of Max de Winter to me," Helen replied.

Lynley pulled into a space conveniently close to the lift now that the day was long over and the vast clerical staff was gone. He thought about the idea. "We're meant to believe she deserved to die," he mused.

"Susanna Sage?"

He got out of the car and opened her door. "Rebecca," he said. "She was evil, lewd, lubricious, lascivious—"

"Just the sort of person one longs to have at a dinner party to liven things up."

"—and she pushed him into killing her by telling him a lie."

"Did she? I can't remember the whole story."

Lynley took her arm and led her towards the lift. He rang for it. They waited as the machinery creaked and groaned. "She had cancer. She wanted to commit suicide, but she lacked the courage to kill herself. So, because she hated him, she pushed him into doing it for her, destroying him and herself at the same time. And when the deed was done and he'd sunk her boat in the Manderley cove, he had to wait until a female body washed ashore somewhere along the coast so that he could identify it as Rebecca, gone missing in a storm."

"Poor thing."

"Which one?"

Lady Helen tapped her cheek. "That's the problem, isn't it? We're meant to feel compassion for someone, but it does leave one a bit tarnished, doesn't it, to be siding with the murderer?"

"Rebecca was wanton, entirely without conscience. We're meant to think it was justifiable homicide."

"And was it? Is it ever?"

"That's the question," he said.

They took the lift in silence. The rain had begun falling in earnest on his drive back into the city. A snarl of traffic in Blackheath had made him despair of ever getting back across the Thames. But he'd managed to reach Onslow Square by seven, they'd made it to Green's for dinner by a quarter past eight, and now at twenty minutes before eleven, they were heading up to his office for a look at whatever Sergeant Havers had managed to fax from Truro.

They were operating under an undeclared ceasefire. They'd discussed the weather, his sister's decision to sell her land and her sheep in West Yorkshire and return to the south to be near his mother, a curious revival of *Heartbreak House* that Shavians were denouncing and critics were beatifying, and a Winslow Homer exhibition that was coming to London. He could sense her need to hold him at a distance, and he cooperated without much liking it. Helen's timeline for opening her heart to him wasn't what he would like it to be. But he knew that he stood a better chance of winning her confidence through patience rather than confrontation.

The lift doors slid open. Even in CID, the night staff was significantly smaller than the day, so the floor seemed deserted. But two of Lynley's fellow DI's were standing in the doorway to one of their offices, drinking from plastic cups, smoking, and talking about the latest government minister to get caught with his trousers down behind King's Cross Station.

"There he was, poking some tart while the country goes to hell," Phillip Hale was remarking blackly. "What is it with these blokes, I ask you?"

John Stewart flicked cigarette ash onto the floor. "Stuffing some dolly in a leather skirt's more immediately gratifying than solving a fiscal crisis, I'd guess."

"But this wasn't a call girl. This was a ten-quid whore. Good Christ, you *saw* her."

"I've also seen his wife."

The two men laughed. Lynley glanced at Helen. Her face was unreadable. He guided her past his colleagues with a nod.

"Aren't you on holiday?" Hale called after them.

"We're in Greece," Lynley said.

In his office, he waited for her reaction as he took off his coat and hung it on the back of the door. But she said nothing about the brief exchange they'd heard. Instead, she went back to their previous topic, although, when he evaluated it, he realised that she wasn't digressing too far thematically from her central concern.

"Do you think Robin Sage killed her, Tommy?"

"It was night, a rough crossing. There were no witnesses who saw his wife throw herself from the ferry, nor was there anyone who came forward to support his claim of going to the bar for a drink when he left the lounge."

"But a priest? Not only to do it in the first place but then to manage carrying on with his ministry afterwards?"

"He didn't carry on, exactly. He left his position in Truro directly she died. He took up a different sort of ministry as well. And he took it up in places where he wasn't known to the congregation."

"So if he had something to hide from them, they wouldn't necessarily recognise that fact from a changed behaviour since they didn't know him in the first place?"

"Possibly."

"But why kill her? What would have been his motive? Jealousy? Anger? Revenge? An inheritance?"

Lynley reached for the telephone. "There seem to be three possibilities. They'd lost their only child six months before."

"But you said it was a cot death."

"He may have held her responsible. Or he may have been involved with another woman and knew as a priest he couldn't divorce and expect his career to go anywhere."

"Or she may have been involved with another man and he found out about it and acted in rage?"

"Or the final alternative: The truth is what it appears to be, a suicide combined with an honest mistake made by a grieving widower in misidentifying bodies. But no conjecture satisfactorily explains why he went to see Susanna's sister in October. And where in the maze does Juliet Spence fit?" He picked up the phone. "You know where the fax is, don't you, Helen? Would you see if Havers sent the newspaper articles?"

She left to do so, and he phoned Crofters Inn.

"I left a message with Denton," St. James told him when Dora Wragg rang through to their room. "He said he hadn't seen a hair of you all day and hadn't expected to. I imagine about now he's phoning every hospital between London and Manchester, thinking you've had a crash somewhere."

"I'll check in. How was Aspatria?"

St. James gave him the facts they'd managed to gather during their day in Cumbria, where, he informed Lynley, the snow had begun falling at noon and followed them all the way back to Lancashire.

Prior to moving to Winslough, Juliet Spence had been employed as a caretaker at Sewart House, a large estate some four miles outside of Aspatria. Like Cotes Hall, it was in an isolated location and, at the time, inhabited only during August when the son of the owner came up from London with his family for an extended holiday.

"Was she sacked for some reason?" Lynley asked.

Not at all, St. James told him. The house was deeded over to the National Trust when the owner died. The Trust asked Juliet Spence to stay on once they'd opened the grounds and the buildings for public viewing. She moved on to Winslough instead.

"Any problems while she was in Aspatria?"

"None. I spoke to the owner's son, and he had nothing but unqualified praise for her and great affection for Maggie."

"So there's nothing," Lynley mused.

"Not quite. Deborah and I have been working the phones for you most of the day."

Before Aspatria, St. James said, she'd worked in Northumberland, outside the small village of Holystone. There, she'd been a combination of housekeeper and companion to an elderly invalid called Mrs. Soames-West, who lived alone in a small Georgian mansion to the north of the village.

"Mrs. Soames-West had no family in England," St. James said. "And she didn't sound as if she'd had a visitor in years. But she thought a great deal of Juliet Spence, hated to lose her, and wanted to be remembered to her."

"Why did the Spence woman leave?"

"She gave no reason. Just that she'd found another job and she thought it was time."

"How long had she been there?"

"Two years there. Two years in Aspatria."

"And before that?" Lynley glanced up as Helen returned with at least a metre's worth of fax hanging over her arm. She handed it to him. He laid it on the desk.

"Two years on Tiree."

"The Hebrides?"

"Yes. And before that Benbecula. You're seeing the pattern, I take it?"

He was. Each location was more remote than the last. At this rate, he expected her first place of employment to be Iceland.

"That's where the trail went cold," St. James said. "She worked in a small guesthouse on Benbecula, but no one there could tell me where she'd been employed before that."

"Curious."

"Considering how long ago it was, I can't say there's great cause for suspicion in the fact. On the other hand, her life-style itself sounds rather suspect to me, but I suppose I'm more tied to home and hearth than most."

Helen sat down in the chair facing Lynley's desk. He'd turned on the desk lamp rather than the fluorescent lights overhead, so she was partially in shadow with a streak of brightness falling mostly across her hands. She was wearing, he noted, a pearl ring he'd given her for her twentieth birthday. Odd that he'd not noticed before now.

St. James was saying, "So despite their wanderlust, at least they won't be going anywhere for the moment."

"Who?"

"Juliet Spence and Maggie. She wasn't at school today, according to Josie, which made us think at first that they'd heard you'd gone to London and done a bunk as a result."

"You're sure they're still in Winslough?"

"They're here. Josie told us at considerable length over dinner that she'd spoken with Maggie for nearly an hour on the phone round five o'clock. Maggie claims to have flu, which may or may not be the case since she also appears to have had a falling out with her boyfriend and according to Josie, she may have been skipping out on school for that reason. But even if she isn't ill and they're getting ready to run, the snow's been coming down for more than six hours and the roads are hell. They're not going anywhere unless they plan to do it on skis." Deborah said something quietly in the background after which St. James added, "Right. Deborah says you might want to hire a Range Rover rather than drive the Bentley back up here. If the snow keeps up, you won't be able to get in any more than anyone else will be able to get out."

Lynley rang off with a promise to think about it.

"Anything?" Helen asked as he picked up the fax and spread it across the desk.

"It's curiouser and curiouser," he replied. He pulled out his spectacles and began to read. The amalgamation of facts were out of order—the first article was about the funeral—and he realised that, with an inattention to detail unusual in her, his sergeant had fed the copies of the newspaper articles into the facsimile machine haphazardly. Irritated, he took a pair of scissors, cut the articles, and was reassembling them by date, when the telephone rang.

"Denton thinks you're dead," Sergeant Havers said.

"Havers, why in God's name did you fax me this mess out of order?"

"Did I? I must have got distracted by the bloke using the copy machine next to me. He looked just like Ken Branagh. Although what Ken Branagh would be doing making copies of a handout for an antiques fair is well beyond me. He says you drive too fast, by the way."

"Kenneth Branagh?"

"Denton, Inspector. And since you haven't phoned him, he assumes you're squashed bug-like somewhere on the M1 or M6. If you'd move in with Helen or she'd move in with you, you'd be making things a hell of a lot easier on all of us."

"I'm working on it, Sergeant."

"Good. Give the poor bloke a call, will you? I told him you were alive at one o'clock, but he wasn't buying that since I hadn't actually seen your face. What's a voice on the phone, after all? Someone could have been impersonating you."

"I'll check in," Lynley said. "What do you have? I know Joseph's was a cot death—"

"You've been a busy bloke, haven't you? Make that a double and you'll have put your finger on Juliet Spence as well."

"What?"

"Cot death."

"She had a child die of cot death?"

"No. She died of it herself."

"Havers, for God's sake. This is the woman in Winslough."

"That may be the case, but the Juliet Spence connected to the Sages in Cornwall is buried in the same graveyard as they are, Inspector. She died forty-four years ago. Make that forty-four years, three months, and sixteen days."

■   ■   ■

Lynley pulled the stack of clipped and sorted faxes towards him as Helen said, "What is it?" and Havers continued to speak.

"The connection you wanted wasn't between Juliet Spence and Susanna. It was between Susanna and Juliet's mother, Gladys. She's still in Tresillian, as a matter of fact. I had late tea with her this afternoon."

He scanned the information in the first article at the same time as he prolonged the moment when he would have to examine the dark, grainy photograph that accompanied it and make a decision.

"She knew the entire family—Robin grew up in Tresillian, by the by, and she used to keep house for his parents—and she still does the flowers for the church here. She looks about seventy and my guess is she could take us both on in tennis and rout us in a minute. Anyway, she got close to Susanna for a time when Joseph died. Since she'd been through the same thing herself, she wanted to help her, as much as Susanna would let her which, obviously, wasn't a great deal."

He reached in the drawer for a magnifying glass, played it over the faxed photograph, and wished uselessly that he had the original. The woman in the photograph was fuller of face than was Juliet Spence, with darker hair that curled loosely round her head to her shoulders and below. But more than a decade had passed since it had been taken. This woman's youth might have given way to another's middle-age, thinning the face and greying the hair. The shape of the mouth looked right. The eyes seemed similar.

Havers was continuing. "She said she and Susanna spent some time together after they buried him. She said it's something a woman never gets over, losing a child and particularly losing an infant that way. She said she still thinks of her Juliet every day and never forgets her birthday. She always wonders what she might have turned out like. She said she still has dreams about the afternoon when the baby never woke up from her nap."

It was a possibility, as indistinct as the photograph itself, but still undeniably real.

"She had two more children after Juliet, did Gladys. She tried to use that fact to help Susanna see that the worst of her grief would pass when other babies came. But Gladys'd had one other *before* Juliet as well and that one lived, so she could never break through to her completely because Susanna'd always remind her of that."

He set down the magnifying glass and the photograph. There was only one fact he needed to confirm before he moved forward. "Havers," he said, "what about Susanna's body? Who found it? Where?"

"According to Gladys, she was fish bait. No one ever found her. They had a funeral service, but there's sod all in the grave. Not even a coffin."

He replaced the telephone receiver in its cradle and removed his spectacles. Carefully, he polished them on a handkerchief before returning them to his nose. He looked at his notes—Aspatria, Holystone, Tiree, Benbecula—and saw what she had attempted to do. The why of it all, he was certain, remained where it always had been, with Maggie.

"They're the same person, aren't they?" Helen left her chair and came to stand behind his where she could look over his shoulder at the material spread out before him. She put her hand on his shoulder.

He reached for it. "I think they are," he said.

"What does it mean?"

He spoke contemplatively. "She would have needed a birth certificate for a different passport so that she could slip off the ferry when it docked in France. She could have got a copy of the Spence child's certificate at St. Catherine's House—no, it would have been Somerset House then—or she could have pinched the original from Gladys without her knowledge. She'd been visiting her sister in London before her 'suicide.' She would have had time to set everything up."

"But why?" Helen asked. "Why did she do it?"

"Because she may have been the woman taken in adultery after all."

■   ■   ■

A stealthy movement of the bed awakened Helen the next morning, and she cracked open one eye. A grey light was sifting through the curtains and falling upon her favourite armchair across whose back an overcoat was flung. The clock on the bedside table said just before eight. She murmured, "God," and plumped her pillow. She closed her eyes with some deliberation. The bed moved again.

"Tommy," she said, fumbling for the clock and turning it to face the wall, "I don't think it's even dawn yet. Truly, darling. You need to get more sleep. What time did we finally get to bed? Was it two?"

"Damn," he said quietly. "I know it. I *know* it."

"Good. Then lie down."

"The rest of the answer's right here, Helen. Somewhere."

She frowned and rolled over to see that he was sitting against the headboard with his spectacles perched on the end of his nose, letting his eyes travel over piles of paper scraps, handouts, tickets, programmes, and other miscellanea that he'd spread across her bed. She yawned and simultaneously recognised the piles. They'd pawed through Robin Sage's odd bits carton three times before giving it up and going to bed last night. But Tommy wasn't done with it, it seemed. He leaned forward, riffled through one of the piles, and rested against the headboard once more, as if awaiting inspiration to strike.

"The answer's here," he said. "I know it."

Helen stretched out an arm beneath the covers and rested her hand on his thigh. "Sherlock Holmes would have solved it by now," she noted.

"Please don't remind me."

"Hmmm. You're warm."

"Helen, I'm making an attempt at deductive thought."

"Am I getting in the way?"

"What do you think?"

She chuckled, reached for her dressing gown, draped it round her shoulders, and joined him against the headboard. She picked up one of the piles at random and leafed through it. "I thought you had the answer last night. If Susanna knew she was pregnant, and if the baby wasn't his, and if there was no way she could pass it off as his because they'd stopped having sex, which according to her sister appears to have been the case... What more do you want?"

"I want a reason she'd kill him. What we have right now is a reason he'd kill her."

"Perhaps he wanted her back and she didn't want to go."

"He could hardly force her."

"But if he decided to claim the child was his? To force her hand through Maggie?"

"A genetic test would take the wind out of that plan."

"Then perhaps Maggie was his after all. Perhaps he *was* responsible for Joseph's death. Or perhaps Susanna thought he was, so when she discovered she was pregnant again, she wasn't about to let him have a go with another child."

Lynley made a noise of dismissal and reached for Robin Sage's engagement diary. Helen noticed that, while she slept, he'd also rummaged round the flat for the telephone directory, which was lying open at the foot of the bed.

"Then... Let me see." She flipped through her small stack of papers and wondered why on earth anyone would have kept these grimy handouts, the sort that were continually thrust at pedestrians on the street. She would have dropped them into the nearest dustbin. She hated to refuse to take them altogether when the people passing them out always looked so earnest. But to save them...

She yawned. "It's rather like a reverse trail of bread crumbs, isn't it?"

He was flipping to the back of the telephone directory and running his finger down the page. "Six," he said. "Thank God it wasn't Smith." He glanced at his pocket watch, which lay open on the table next to his side of the bed, and threw back the covers. The odd bits went flying like debris in the wind.

"Was it Hansel and Gretel who left a trail of crumbs or Little Red Riding Hood?" Helen asked.

He was rooting through his suitcase, which gaped open on the floor and spilled out clothing in a fashion that Denton would have found teeth-jarring. "What are you talking about, Helen?"

"These papers. They're like a trail of crumbs. Except he didn't drop them. He picked them up."

Tying the belt of his dressing gown, Lynley rejoined her at the bed, sitting on her side of it and reading the handouts once again. She read them along with him: the first for a concert at St. Martin-in-the-Fields; the second for a car dealership in Lambeth; the third for a meeting at Camden Town Hall; the fourth for a hairdresser in Clapham High Street.

"He came by train," Lynley said thoughtfully and began to rearrange the handouts. He said, "Give me that underground map, Helen."

With the map in one hand, he continued to rearrange the handouts until he had the Camden Town Hall meeting first, the concert second, the car dealership third, and the hairdresser fourth. "He would have picked up the first at Euston Station," he noted.

"And if he was going to Lambeth, he'd have got on the Northern Line and changed at Charing Cross," Helen said.

"Which is where he'd have got the second, for the concert. But where does that leave Clapham High Street?"

"Perhaps he went there last, after Lambeth. Does it say in his diary?"

"On his last day in London, it says only Yanapapoulis."

"Yanapapoulis," she said with a sigh. "Greek." She felt a tugging of sadness with the saying of the name. "I spoiled this week for us. We could have been there. On Corfu. Right this moment."

He put his arm round her and kissed the side of her head. "It doesn't matter. We'd be doing the same thing there as we are right now."

"Talking about Clapham High Street? I doubt it."

He smiled and lay his spectacles on the table. He brushed her hair back and kissed her neck. "Not exactly," he murmured. "We'll talk about Clapham High Street in a while . . . "

Which is what they did, a little more than an hour later.

Lynley agreed to Helen's making the coffee, but after her presentation of lunch yesterday, he wasn't willing to endure whatever she might bring forth from cupboards and refrigerator to serve as their breakfast. He scrambled the six eggs he found in the refrigerator and threw in cream cheese, stoned black olives, and mushrooms for good measure. He opened a tin of grapefruit wedges, dished them out, topped them with a maraschino cherry, and set about making toast.

In the meantime, Helen manned the telephone. By the time he had the breakfast ready, she'd gone through five of the six entries for the name Yanapapoulis, made a list of four Greek restaurants she'd not yet tried, received one recipe for a poppy-seed cake soaked in ouzo—"Goodness, that sounds rather terrifyingly inflammable, my dear"—promised to pass along to her "superiors" a complaint about police mishandling of a burglary near Notting Hill Gate, and defended her honour against the accusations of a shrieking woman who assumed she was the mistress of her errant husband.

Lynley was setting their plates on the table and pouring coffee and orange juice when Helen struck gold with her final call. She had asked to speak to Mummy or Daddy. The reply went on at some length. Lynley was spooning orange marmalade onto his plate when Helen said,

"I *am* sorry to hear that, my dear. What about Mummy? Is she there? . . . But you aren't home alone, are you? Shouldn't you be in school? . . . Oh. Well, of course, someone must see to Linus' head-cold. . . . Do you have Meggezones? They work awfully well for a sore throat."

"Helen, what in God's name—"

She held up a hand to stop him. "She's where? . . . I see. Can you give me the name, dear?" Lynley saw her eyes widen, saw the smile begin to curve her lips. "Lovely," she said. "That's wonderful, Philip. You've been such a help. Thank you so much . . . Yes, dear, you give him the chicken soup." She hung up the phone and left the kitchen.

"Helen, I've got breakfast—"

"Just a moment, darling."

He grumbled and forked up a portion of eggs. They weren't half-bad. It wasn't a combination of flavours that Denton would have either served or approved of, but then Denton had always possessed tunnel vision when it came to food.

"Here. Look." With her dressing gown flying round in a whirl of burgundy silk, Helen clattered back into the kitchen—she was the only woman Lynley knew who actually wore high-heeled slippers with snowball tufts dyed to match the rest of her nightly ensembles—

and presented him with one of the handouts they'd been looking at earlier.

"What?"

"The Hair Apparent," she said. "Clapham High Street. Lord, what a ghastly name for a hairdresser. I always hate these puns: Shear Ecstasy, The Mane Attraction. Who comes up with them?"

He spread some marmalade on a wedge of toast as Helen slid into her seat and spooned up three pieces of grapefruit with "Tommy, darling, you can actually cook. I might think about keeping you."

"That warms my heart." He squinted at the paper in his hand. " 'Unisex styling,' " he read. " 'Discount prices. Ask for Sheelah.' "

"Yanapapoulis," Helen said. "What've you put in these eggs? They're wonderful."

"Sheelah Yanapapoulis?"

"The very same. And she must be the Yanapapoulis we're looking for, Tommy. It's too much of a coincidence otherwise that Robin Sage would have gone to see one Yanapapoulis and just happened to have in his possession a handout with the place of employment of an entirely different Yanapapoulis printed upon it. Don't you agree?" She didn't wait, merely went on, saying, "That was her son I was speaking to on the phone, by the way. He said to ring her at work. He said to ask for Sheelah."

Lynley smiled. "You're a marvel."

"And you're a fine cook. If you'd only been here to do Daddy's breakfast yesterday morning . . ."

He set the handout to one side and went back to his eggs. "That can always be remedied," he said casually.

"I suppose." She added milk to her coffee and spooned in sugar. "Do you vacuum carpets and wash windows, as well?"

"If put to the test."

"Heavens, I might actually be getting the better part of the bargain."

"Is it, then?"

"What?"

"A bargain."

"Tommy, you're absolutely ruthless."

CHAPTER TWENTY-SIX

ALTHOUGH THE SON OF SHEELAH YANAPA-poulis had recommended a telephone call to The Hair Apparent, Lynley decided upon a personal visit. He found the hairdresser's on the ground floor of a narrow soot-stained Victorian building that was shoe-horned between an Indian take-away and an appliance repair shop on Clapham High Street. He'd driven across the river on Albert Bridge and skirted Clapham Common upon whose north side Samuel Pepys had come to be lovingly tended in his declining years. The area had been referred to as "Paradisian Clapham" during Pepys' time, but it had been a country village then, with its buildings and cottages spread out in a curve from the northeast corner of the common, and with fields and market gardens in place of the closely packed streets that had accompanied the arrival of the railway. The common remained, essentially inviolate, but many of the pleasant villas that once looked upon it had long since been demolished and replaced by the smaller and less inspired buildings of the nineteenth century.

The rain that had begun on the previous day was continuing to fall as Lynley drove along the high street. It rendered the usual kerbside collection of wrappers, sacks, newspapers, and assorted rubbish into sodden lumps that seemed bled of all colour. It also had the effect of eliminating virtually all pedestrian traffic. Aside from an unshaven man in a threadbare tweed coat who shuffled along, talking to himself and holding a newspaper spread over his head, the only other creature on the pavement at the moment was a mongrel dog sniffing at a shoe that lay on top of an upended wooden crate.

Lynley found a place to park on St. Luke's Avenue, grabbed his coat and umbrella, and walked back to the hairdresser's where he discovered that the rain had evidently put a damper on the hair business as well. He opened the door, was assailed by the eye-smarting odour that accompanies someone inflicting a perm upon another's innocent head of hair, and saw that this malodorous operation of beauty was being performed on the hairdresser's single customer. She was a plump woman perhaps fifty years old who clutched a copy of *Royalty Monthly* in her fists and said, "Cor, lookit this, will you, Stace? That dress she wore to the Royal Ballet must of cost four hundred quid."

"Gloriamus on toast," was Stace's reply, delivered somewhere between polite enthusiasm and heavy ennui. She squirted a chemical onto one of the tiny pink rolls on her client's head and gazed at her own reflection in the mirror. She smoothed her eyebrows, which came to curious points on her forehead and exactly matched the colour of her ramrod, coal hair. Doing this allowed her to catch sight of Lynley, who stood behind the glass counter dividing the tiny waiting area from the rest of the shop.

"We don't do men, luv." She tossed her head in the direction of the next work station, a movement that clicked her long jet earrings like small castanets. "I know it says unisex in all the adverts, but that's Mondays and Wednesdays when our Rog is here. Which he isn't, as you can see. Today, I mean. It's just me and Sheel. Sorry."

"Actually, I'm looking for Sheelah Yanapapoulis," Lynley said.

"Are you? She doesn't do men either. I mean"—with a wink—"she doesn't do them *that* way. As for the other ... well, she's always been lucky, that girl, hasn't she?" She called towards the rear of the shop: "Sheelah! Get out here. This is your lucky day."

"Stace, I tol' you I was heading out, din't I? Linus's got a bad throat and I was up all night. I got no one on the book coming in this afternoon so there's no point to me staying." Movement in a back room accompanied the voice, which sounded plaintive and tired. A handbag clicked closed with a metallic *snick;* a garment snapped as it was shaken out; galoshes slapped against the floor.

"He's good-looking, Sheel," Stace said with another wink. "You wouldn't want to miss him. Trust me, luv."

"Is that my Harold, then, having a bit of fun with you? 'Cause if it is . . ."

She came out of the room, drawing a black scarf across hair that was short, artfully cut, and coloured a white blonde that came only from bleaching or being born an albino. She hesitated when she saw Lynley. Her blue eyes flicked over him, taking in and evaluating the coat, the umbrella, and the cut of his hair. Her face became immediately wary; the birdlike features of her nose and chin seemed to recede. But only for a moment before she lifted her head sharply, saying,

"I'm Sheelah Yanapapoulis. Who is it exactly wants to make my acquaintance?"

Lynley produced his warrant card. "Scotland Yard CID."

She'd been in the process of buttoning a green mackintosh, and although she slowed when Lynley identified himself, she did not stop. She said, "Police, then?"

"Yes."

"I got nothing to say to you lot about anything." She adjusted her handbag on her arm.

"It won't take long," said Lynley. "And I'm afraid it's essential."

The other hairdresser had turned from her client. She said with some alarm, "Sheel, want me to ring Harold for you?"

Sheelah ignored her, saying, "Essential to what? Did one of my boys get up to something this morning? I've kept them home today if that's supposed to be a crime. The whole lot of them got colds. Did they get up to mischief?"

"Not that I know."

"They're always playing with the phone, that lot. Gino dialed 999 and yelled fire last month. Got thrashed for it, he did. But he's nothing so much as pig-headed, like his dad. I wouldn't put it by him to do it again for a giggle."

"I'm not here about your children, Mrs. Yanapoulis, although Philip did tell me where to find you."

She was fastening the galoshes round her ankles. She straightened with a grunt and drove her fists into the small of her back. In that position, Lynley saw what he had not noticed before. She was pregnant.

He said, "May we go somewhere to talk?"

"About what?"

"About a man called Robin Sage."

Her hands flew to her stomach.

"You do know him," he said.

"And what if I do?"

"Sheel, I'm ringing Harold," Stace said. "He won't want you talking to the coppers and you know it."

Lynley said to Sheelah, "If you're going home anyway, let me drive you there. We can talk on the way."

"You listen. I'm a good mother, Mister. No one says different. You just ask anyone around. You c'n ask Stace here."

"She's a bleeding saint," Stace said. "How many times you gone without shoes so those kids of yours could have the trainers they wanted? How many times, Sheel? And when was the last time you had a meal out? And who does the ironing if it isn't you? And how many new frocks d'you buy last year?" Stace drew a breath. Lynley seized the moment.

"This is a murder investigation," he said.

The shop's sole client lowered her magazine. Stace drew her chemical bottle to her breast. Sheelah stared at Lynley and seemed to weigh his words.

"Whose?" she asked.

"His. Robin Sage."

Her features softened and bravado disappeared. She took a long breath. "Right, then. I'm in Lambeth, and my boys are waiting. If you want to talk, we got to do it there."

"I've a car outside," Lynley said, and as they left the shop, Stace shouted after them, "I'm still ringing Harold!"

A new cloudburst erupted as Lynley shut the door behind them. He opened his umbrella, and although it was large enough for them both, Sheelah kept her distance from him by opening a small, collapsible one that she took from the pocket of her mackintosh. She didn't say a word until they were in the car and heading towards Clapham Road and Lambeth.

And then it was only "Some motor, mister. I hope it's got an alarm system on it, else there won't be a bolt left when you leave my flat." She gave the leather seat a caress. "They'd like this, my boys."

"You have three children?"

"Five." She pulled up the collar of her mackintosh and looked out the window.

Lynley gave her a glance. Her attitude was streetwise and her concerns were adult, but she didn't look old enough to have borne five children. She couldn't yet have been thirty.

"Five," he repeated. "They must keep you busy."

She said, "Go left here. You need to take the South Lambeth Road."

They drove in the direction of Albert Embankment and when they hit congestion near Vauxhall Station, she directed him through a maze of back streets that finally took them to the tower block in which she and her family lived. Twenty floors high, it was steel and concrete, unadorned and surrounded by more steel and concrete. Its dominant colours were a rusting gun metal and a yellowing beige.

The lift they rode in smelled of wet nappies. Its rear wall was papered with announcements about community meetings, crime-stopping organisations, and crisis hot lines covering every topic from rape to AIDS. Its side walls were cracked mirrors. Its doors comprised a snake nest of illegible graffiti in the middle of which the words *Hector sucks cock* were painted in brilliant and unavoidable red.

Sheelah spent the ride shaking off her umbrella, collapsing it, putting it into her pocket, removing her scarf, and fluffing up the top of her hair. She did this by pulling it forward from the crown. In defiance of gravity, it formed a drooping cockscomb.

When the lift doors opened, Sheelah said, "It's this way," and led him towards the back of the building, down a narrow corridor. Numbered doors lined each side. Behind them music played, tele-visions chattered, voices rose and fell. A woman shrieked, "Billy, you let me go!" A baby wailed.

From Sheelah's flat came the sound of a child shouting, "No, I won't! You can't make me!" and the rattle of a snare drum being beaten by someone with only moderate talent for the occupation. Sheelah unlocked the door and swung it open, calling, "Which o' my blokes got a kiss for Mummy?"

She was instantly surrounded by three of her children, all of them little boys eager to oblige, each one shouting louder than the other. Their conversation consisted of:

"Philip says we have to mind and we don't, Mum, do we?"

"He made Linus eat chicken soup for breakfast!"

"Hermes has my socks and he won't take them off and Philip says—"

"Where is he, Gino?" Sheelah asked. "Philip! Come give your mummy what for."

A slender maple-skinned boy perhaps twelve years old came to the kitchen door with a wooden spoon in one hand and a pot in the other. "Making mash," he said. "These lousy potatoes keep boiling over. I got to keep watch."

"You got to kiss your mum first."

"Aw, come on."

"*You* come on." Sheelah pointed to her cheek. Philip trudged over and pecked at his duty. She cuffed him lightly and grabbed on to his hair in which the pick he used to comb it stuck up like a plastic headdress. She plucked it out. "Stop acting like your dad. Makes me crazy, that, Philip." She shoved it into the rear pocket of his jeans and slapped his bottom. "These're my boys," she said to Lynley. "These are my extra-special blokes. And this *here* is a policeman, you lot. So watch yourselfs, hear?"

The boys stared at Lynley. He did his best not to stare back at them. They looked more like a miniature United Nations than they did the members of a family, and it was obvious that the words *your dad* had a different meaning for every one of the children.

Sheelah was introducing them, giving a pinch here, a kiss there, a nibble on the neck, a noisy spluttering against a cheek. Philip, Gino, Hermes, Linus.

"My lamb chop, Linus," she said. "Him with the throat that kept me up all night."

"And Peanut," Linus said, patting his mother's stomach.

"Right. And how many does that make, luv?"

Linus held up his hand, the fingers spread, a grin on his face and his nose running freely.

"And how many are those?" his mother asked him.

"Five."

"Lovely." She tickled his stomach. "And how old are you?"

"Five!"

"Tha's right." She took off her mackintosh and handed it to Gino, saying, "Let's move this confab into the kitchen. If Philip's making mash, I got to see to the bangers. Hermes, put that drum away and help Linus with his nose. Christ, don't use your bleeding shirttail to do it!"

The boys trailed her into the kitchen, which was one of four rooms that opened off the sitting room, along with two bedrooms and a bathroom jammed with plastic lorries, balls, two bicycles, and a pile of dirty clothes. The bedrooms, Lynley saw, looked out on the companion tower block next door, and furniture made movement impossible in either: two sets of bunkbeds in one of the rooms, a double bed and a baby cot in the other.

"Harold ring this A.M.?" Sheelah was asking Philip when Lynley entered the kitchen.

"Naw." Philip scrubbed at the kitchen table with a dish cloth that was decidedly grey. "You got to cut that bloke loose, Mum. He's bad news, he is."

She lit a cigarette and, without inhaling, set it in an ashtray and stood over its plume of smoke, breathing deeply. "Can't do that, luv. Peanut needs her dad."

"Yeah. Well, smoking's not good for her, is it?"

"I'm not smoking, am I? D'you see me smoking? D'you see a fag hanging out of this mouth?"

"That's just as bad. You're breathing it, aren't you? Breathing it's bad. We could all die from cancer."

"You think you know everything. Just—"

"Like my dad."

She pulled a frying pan from one of the cupboards and went to the refrigerator. Two lists hung upon it, held in place with yellowing cello tape. *RULES* was printed at the top of one, *JOBS* at the top of the other. Diagonally across both, someone had scrawled *Sod You, Mummy!* Sheelah ripped the lists off and swung round on the boys. Philip was at the cooker seeing to his potatoes. Gino and Hermes were scrambling round the legs of the table. Linus was dipping his hand into a carton of corn flakes that had been left on the floor.

"Which of you lot did this?" Sheelah demanded. "Come on. I want to know. Which of you bloody did this?"

Silence fell. The boys looked at Lynley, as if he'd come to arrest them for the crime.

She crumpled the papers and threw them on the table. "What's rule number one? What's always been rule number one? Gino?"

He stuck his hands behind his back as if afraid they'd be smacked. "Respecting property," he said.

"And whose property was that? Whose property did you decide to write all over?"

"I didn't!"

"You didn't? Don't give me that rubbish. Whoever causes trouble if it isn't you? You take these lists to the bedroom and write them over ten times."

"But Mum—"

"And no bangers and mash till you do. You got it?"

"I didn't—"

She grabbed his arm and thrust him in the direction of the bedrooms. "I don't want to see you till the lists are done."

The other boys shot sly looks at one another when he'd gone. Sheelah went to the work top and breathed in more smoke. "I couldn't go it cold turkey," she said to Lynley in reference to the cigarette. "I could do with other stuff, but not with this."

"I used to smoke myself," he said.

"Yeah? Then you know." She took the bangers from the refrigerator and slid them into the frying pan. She turned on the burner, looped her arm round Philip's neck and kissed him soundly on the temple. "Jesus, you're a handsome little bloke, you know that? Five more years and the girls'll be mad for you. You'll be beating them off you like they was flies."

Philip grinned and shrugged her arm off him. "Mum!"

"Yeah, you'll like that plenty when you get a bit older. Just—"

"Like my dad."

She pinched his bottom. "Little sod." She turned to the table. "Hermes, watch these bangers. Bring your chair here. Linus, set the table. I got to talk to this gentleman."

"I want cornflakes," Linus said.

"Not for lunch."

"I want them!"

"And I said not for lunch." She snatched the box away and threw it into a cupboard. Linus began to cry. She said, "Stow it!" And then to Lynley, "It's his dad. Those damn Greeks. They'll let their sons do anything. They're worse than Italians. Let's talk out here."

She took her cigarette back into the sitting room, pausing by an ironing board to wrap a frayed cord round the bottom of an iron. She used her foot to shove to one side an enormous laundry basket spilling clothes onto the floor.

"Good to sit down." She sighed as she sank into a sofa. Its cushions wore pink slipcovers. Burn holes in them showed the original green beneath. Behind her, the wall was decorated with a large collage of photographs. Most of them were snapshots. They grew out in a starburst pattern from a professional studio portrait in the centre. Although adults were featured in some of them, all of them showed at least one of her children. Even photographs of Sheelah's wedding—she stood at the side of a swarthy man in wire-rimmed spectacles with a noticeable gap between his front teeth—also contained two of her children, a much younger Philip dressed as ring bearer and Gino, who could not have been more than two.

"Is that your work?" Lynley asked, nodding at the collage.

She craned her neck to look at it. "You mean did I make it? Yeah. The boys helped. But mostly it was me. Gino!" She leaned forward on the sofa. "Get back to the kitchen. Eat your lunch."

"But the lists—"

"Do what I tell you. Help your brothers and shut up."

Gino plodded back into the kitchen, casting a chary look at his mother and hanging his head. The cooking noises became subdued.

Sheelah knocked ash from her cigarette and held it under her nose for a moment. When she replaced it in the ashtray, Lynley said,

"You saw Robin Sage in December, didn't you?"

"Just before Christmas. He came to the shop, like you. I thought he wanted a haircut—he could of used a new style—but he wanted to talk. Not there. Here. Like you."

"Did he tell you he was an Anglican priest?"

"He was all done up in a priest uniform or whatever it's called, but I figured that was just a disguise. It'd be like Social Services, wouldn't it, to send someone snooping round dressed up like a priest on the prowl for sinners. I've had my fill of that lot, I can tell you. They're here least twice a month, waiting like vultures to see if I'll knock about one of my boys so they can take 'em away and put 'em in what they think's a proper home." She laughed bitterly. "They can wait till they're grey. Fucking old biddies."

"What made you think he was from Social Services? Did he have some sort of referral from them? Did he show you a card?"

"It was the way he acted once he got here. He said he wanted to talk about religious instructions. Like: Where was I sending my kids to learn about Jesus? And: Did we go to church and where? But all the time he kept looking round the flat like he was measuring it up to see was it fit for Peanut when she comes. And he wanted to talk about being a mother and how if I loved my kids did I show them regular and how did I show them and how did I discipline. The sort of rot social workers always talk about." She leaned over and turned on a lamp. Its shade had been covered somewhat haphazardly with a purple scarf. When the lightbulb glowed, great splodges of glue looked like the Americas beneath the material. "So I thought he was going to be my new social worker and this was his not-so-clever way of getting to know me."

"But he never told you that."

"He just looked at me the way they always do, with his face all wrinkled and his eyebrows squished." She gave a fair imitation of factitious empathy. Lynley tried not to smile, and failed. She nodded. "I've had that lot coming round since I had my first kid, mister. They never help out and they never change a thing. They don't believe you're trying to do your best and if something happens, they blame you first. I hate the lot of them. They're why I lost my Tracey Joan."

"Tracey Jones?"

"Tracey *Joan*. Tracey Joan Cotton." She shifted her position and pointed to the studio photograph at the centre of her collage. In it, a laughing baby in pink held a stuffed grey elephant. Sheelah touched her fingers to the baby's face. "My little girl," she said. "This is my Tracey that was."

Lynley felt hair rise on the back of his hands. She'd said five children. Because she was pregnant, he had misunderstood. He got up from his chair and took a closer look at the picture. The baby didn't look more than four or five months old. "What happened to her?" he asked.

"She got snatched one night. Right outa my car."

"When?"

"I don't know." Sheelah went hastily on when she saw his expression. "I went into the pub to meet her dad. I left her sleeping in the car 'cause she'd been feverish and she'd finally stopped her squalling. When I came out, she was gone."

"I meant how long ago did this happen?" Lynley asked.

"Twelve years last November." Sheelah shifted again, away from the photograph. She brushed at her eyes. "She was six months old, was my Tracey Joan, and when she got snatched, Social bleeding Services did nothing about it but hand me over to the local police."

.   .   .

Lynley sat in the Bentley. He thought about taking up cigarettes again. He remembered the prayer from Ezekiel that had been marked off in Robin Sage's book: "When the wicked man turneth away from his wickedness that he hath committed, and doeth that which is lawful and right, he shall save his soul alive." He understood.

That's what it all came down to in the end: He had wanted to save her soul. But she had wanted to save the child.

Lynley wondered what sort of moral dilemma the priest had faced when he finally traced down Sheelah Yanapapoulis. For surely, his wife would have told him the truth. The truth was her only defence and her best chance of convincing him to turn a blind eye to the crime she had committed so many years in the past.

Listen to me, she would have said to him. I saved her, Robin. Do you want to know what Kate's records said about her parents, her background, and what happened to her? Do you want to know everything, or are you just going to condemn me without the facts?

He would have wanted to know. He was at heart a decent man, concerned with doing what was right, not just what was prescribed by law. So he would have listened to the facts and then he would have verified them himself, in London. First by going to see Kate Gitterman and trying to discover if his wife had indeed had access to her sister's case reports in that long-ago time when she worked for Social Services. Then by going to Social Services itself to track down the girl whose baby had had a fractured skull and a broken leg before she was even two months old and then had been kidnapped off a street in Shoreditch. It wouldn't have been a difficult project to gather the information.

Her mother was fifteen years old, Susanna would have told him. Her father was thirteen. She didn't stand a chance in a life with them. Can't you see that? Can't you? Yes, I took her, Robin. And I'd do it again.

He would have come to London. He would have seen what Lynley saw. He would have met her. Perhaps as he sat talking with her in the crowded flat, Harold would have arrived as well, saying, "How's my baby? How's my sweet mama?" as he spread his dusky hand across her belly, a hand on which the gold wedding band glittered. Perhaps he too would have heard Harold whispering, "Can't make it tonight, babe. Now don't cause a scene, Sheel, I just can't do it," in the corridor as he left.

Do you have any idea how many second chances Social Services give an abusive mother before they take a child? she would have demanded. Do you know how difficult it is to prove abuse in the first place if the child can't talk and there appears to be a reasonable explanation behind the accident?

"I never touched a hair of her head," Sheelah had said to Lynley. "But they didn't believe me. Oh, they let me keep her 'cause they couldn't prove nothing, but they made me go to classes and I had to check with them every week and—" She smashed out her cigarette. "All the time it was Jimmy. Her bleeding stupid dad. She was crying and he didn't know how to get her to stop and I'd left her with him for only an hour and Jimmy hurt my baby. He lost his temper . . . He threw her . . . The wall . . . I never. I wouldn't. But no one believed me and he wouldn't say."

So when the baby vanished and young Sheelah Cotton-not-yet-Yanapapoulis swore she'd been kidnapped, Kate Gitterman phoned the police and gave them her professional assessment of the situation. They'd eyed the mother, measured the level of her hysteria, and searched for a corpse instead of looking for a potential trail left by the baby's abductor. And no one involved in the investigation ever connected the suicide of a young woman off the coast of France with a kidnapping in London nearly three weeks later.

"But they couldn't find a body, could they?" Sheelah had said, wiping at her cheeks. "Because I never hurt her and I never would. She was my baby. I loved her. I *did*." The boys had come to the door of the kitchen as she wept, and Linus crept across the sitting room and crawled onto the sofa beside her. She hugged him to her and rocked him, her cheek pressed against the top of his head. "I'm a good mother, I am. I take care of my boys. No one says I don't. And no one—bloody no one—is goin' to take my kids away."

Sitting in the Bentley with the windows steaming and the traffic hissing by on the Lambeth street, Lynley remembered the end of the story of the woman taken in adultery. It was about casting stones: Only the man without sin—and interesting, he thought, that it was men and not women who would do the stoning—could stand in judgement and administer punishment. Anyone whose soul was not unblemished had to move aside.

You go to London if you don't believe me, she would have said to her husband. You check on the story. You see if she'd be better off living with a woman who fractured her skull.

So he had come. He had met her. And then he had faced the decision. He was not without sin, he would have realised. His inability to help his wife come to terms with her grief when their own child died had been part of what led her to commit this crime. How could he now begin to lift a stone against her when he was responsible, if only in part, for what she had done? How could he begin a process that would destroy her forever at the same time as it ran the risk of also harming the child? Was she, in truth, better for Maggie than this white-haired woman with her rainbow children and their absent fathers? And if she was, could he turn away from a crime by calling its retribution a greater injustice?

He had prayed to know the difference between that which is moral and that which is right. His telephone conversation with his wife on that final day of his life had telegraphed what his decision would be: *You can't judge what happened then. You can't know what's right now. That's in God's hands, not yours.*

Lynley glanced at his pocket watch. It was half past one. He would fly to Manchester and hire a Range Rover. That would get him to Winslough sometime in the evening.

He picked up the car phone and punched in Helen's number. She heard it all when he said her name.

"Shall I come with you?" she asked.

"No. I'm not fit company now. I won't be later."

"That doesn't matter, Tommy."

"It does. To me."

"I want to help in some way."

"Then be here for me when I get back."

"How?"

"I want to come home and have home mean you."

Her hesitation was prolonged. He thought he could hear her breathing but knew it was impossible, considering the connection. He was probably only listening to himself.

"What will we do?" she asked.

"We'll love each other. Marry. Have children. Hope for the best. God, I don't know any longer, Helen."

"You sound horrible." Her own voice was bereft. "What are you going to do?"

"I'm going to love you."

"I don't mean here. I mean Winslough. What are you going to do?"

"I'm going to wish to be Solomon and be Nemesis instead."

"Oh, Tommy."

"Say it. You've got to say it sometime. It might as well be now."

"I'll be here. Always. When it's over. You know that."

Slowly, with great care, he replaced the phone.

THE WORK
OF
NEMESIS

CHAPTER TWENTY-SEVEN

W AS HE LOOKING FOR HER, TOMMY?" DEBORAH asked. "D'you think he never believed she drowned in the first place? Is that why he moved from parish to parish? Is that why he came to Winslough?"

St. James stirred another spoonful of sugar into his cup and regarded his wife thoughtfully. She had poured their coffee but added nothing to her own. She was playing the small cream jug between her hands. She didn't look up as she waited for Lynley's answer. It was the first time she had spoken.

"I think it was pure chance." Lynley forked up a portion of his veal. He'd arrived at Crofters Inn as St. James and Deborah were finishing dinner. Although they hadn't had the dining room to themselves this night, the two other couples who had been enjoying beef Wellington and rack of lamb had moved to the residents' lounge for their coffee. So between Josie Wragg's appearances in the dining room to serve one portion of Lynley's late meal or another, he had told them the story of Sheelah Cotton Yanapapoulis, Katherine Gitterman, and Susanna Sage.

"Consider the facts," he went on. "She didn't go to church; she lived in the North while he remained in the South; she kept on the move; she chose isolated locations. When the locations promised to become less isolated, she merely moved on."

"Except this last time," St. James noted.

Lynley reached for his wine-glass. "Yes. It's odd that she didn't move at the end of her two years here."

"Perhaps Maggie's at the root of that," St. James said. "She's a teenager now. Her boyfriend's here and according to what Josie was disclosing last night with her usual passion for detail, that's a fairly serious relationship. She may have found it difficult—as we all do—to walk away from someone she loves. Perhaps she refused to go."

"That's a reasonable possibility. But isolation was still essential to her mother."

Deborah's head darted up at that. She began to speak, but she appeared to stop herself.

Lynley was continuing. "It seems odd that Juliet—or Susanna, if you will—didn't do something to force the issue. After all, their isolation at Cotes Hall was due to end any time. When the renovation was complete, Brendan Power and his wife—" He paused in the act of spearing up a piece of new potato. "Of course," he said.

"She was the mischief-maker at the Hall," St. James said.

"She must have been. Once it was occupied, she increased her chances of being seen. Not necessarily by people from the village, who would have seen her occasionally already, but by guests coming to call. And with a new baby, Brendan Power and his wife would have had guests: family, friends, out-of-town visitors."

"Not to mention the vicar."

"She wouldn't have wanted to take the risk."

"Still, she must have heard the name of the new vicar long before she saw him," St. James said. "It's odd that she didn't invent some sort of crisis and run for it then."

"Perhaps she tried. But it was autumn when the vicar arrived in Winslough. Maggie was already in school. If indeed her mother had rashly agreed to stay on in the village for Maggie's happiness, she'd be hard-pressed to come up with an excuse to leave."

Deborah released her hold on the cream jug and pushed it away. "Tommy," she said in a voice so carefully controlled that it sounded strung, "I don't see how you can be sure of all this." When Lynley looked at her, she went on quickly. "Perhaps she didn't even need to run. What sort of proof do you actually have that Maggie isn't her real daughter in the first place? She could be hers, couldn't she?"

"That's unlikely, Deborah."

"But you're drawing conclusions without having all the facts."

"What more facts do I need?"

"What if—" Deborah grabbed her spoon and clutched it as if she would use it to strike the table while she made a point. Then she dropped it, saying in a dispirited voice, "I suppose she... I don't know."

"My guess is that an X-ray of Maggie's leg will show it was once broken and that DNA testing will tell the rest of the tale," Lynley told her.

She got to her feet in response, shoving her hair away from her face. "Yes. Well. Look, I'm... Sorry, but I'm a bit tired. I think I'll go up. I'll... No, please stay, Simon. No doubt you and Tommy have lots to discuss. I'll just say good night."

She was out of the room before they could respond. Lynley stared after her, saying to St. James, "Did I say something?"

"It's nothing." Pensively, St. James watched the door, thinking Deborah might reconsider and return. When she didn't after a moment, he turned back to his friend. Their reasons for questioning Lynley were disparate, he knew, but Deborah had a point, if not the one she was intending to make. "Why didn't she brazen it out?" he asked. "Why didn't she claim Maggie was her own child, the product of an affair?"

"I wondered about that myself initially. It seemed the logical way to go. But Sage had met Maggie first, remember. I imagine he knew how old she was, the same age as their son Joseph would have been. So Juliet had no choice. She knew she couldn't pull the wool over his eyes. She could only tell him the truth and hope for the best."

"And did she? Tell him the truth, that is?"

"I expect so. The truth was bad enough, after all: unmarried teenagers with an infant who'd already suffered a fractured skull and a broken leg. I've no doubt she saw herself as Maggie's saviour."

"She might have been."

"I know. That's the hell of it. She might have been. And I imagine Robin Sage knew that as well. He had visited Sheelah Yanapapoulis the adult. He couldn't have known what she would have been like as a fifteen-year-old girl in possession of an infant. He could make surmises based upon her other children: how they were turning out, what she said about them and their upbringing, how she acted round them. But he couldn't know for certain what it would have been like for Maggie had she grown up with Sheelah instead of Juliet Spence for a mother." Lynley poured himself another glass of wine and smiled bleakly. "I'm only glad I'm not in the position Sage was. His decision

was agonising. Mine is only devastating. And even then, it's not going
to be devastating to me."

"You're not responsible," St. James pointed out. "A crime's been
committed."

"And I serve the cause of justice. I know that, Simon. But,
frankly, it gives me no pleasure." He drank deeply of the wine, poured
more, drank again. He placed the glass on the table. The wine shimmered in the light. He said, "I've been trying to keep my mind off
Maggie all day. I've been trying to keep it focussed on the crime. I
keep thinking that if I continue to re-examine what Juliet did—all
those years ago and this past December as well—I might forget about
why she did it. Because the why of it isn't important. It can't be."

"Then let the rest of it go."

"I've been saying it like a litany since half past one. He phoned
her and told her what his decision would be. She protested. She said
she wouldn't give her up. She asked him to come to the cottage that
night to talk about the situation. She went out to where she knew
the water hemlock grew. She dug up a root stock. She fed it to him
for dinner. She sent him on his way. She knew he would die. She
knew how he would die."

St. James added the rest. "She took a purgative to make herself
look ill. Then she phoned the constable and implicated him."

"So why in God's name can I forgive her?" Lynley asked. "She
murdered a man. Why do I want to turn a blind eye to the fact that
she's a killer?"

"Because of Maggie. She was a victim once in her life and she's
about to become a victim of a different sort again. At your hands this
time."

Lynley said nothing. In the pub next door, a man's voice rose
momentarily. A babble of conversation ensued.

St. James said, "What's next?"

Lynley crumpled his linen napkin on the table top. "I have a
WPC driving out from Clitheroe."

"For Maggie."

"She'll need to take the child when we take the mother." He
glanced at his pocket watch. "She wasn't on duty when I stopped by
the station. They were tracking her down. She's to meet me at
Shepherd's."

"He doesn't know yet?"

"I'm heading there now."

"Shall I come with you?" When Lynley glanced back at the door through which Deborah had disappeared, St. James said, "It's all right."

"Then I'll be glad of your company."

The crowd in the pub was a large one this night. It appeared to consist mostly of farmers who had come by foot, by tractor, and by Land Rover to outshout one another on the subject of the weather. Smoke from their cigarettes and pipes hung heavily on the air as they each recounted the effect that the continuing snowfall was having on their sheep, the roads, their wives, and their work. Because of a respite from noon until six o'clock that evening, they hadn't yet been snowed in. But flakes had begun to fall again steadily round half past six, and the farmers seemed to be fortifying themselves against a long siege.

They weren't the only ones. The village teenagers were spread out at the far end of the pub, playing the fruit machine and watching Pam Rice carry on with her boyfriend much as she had done on the night of the St. Jameses' arrival in Winslough. Brendan Power was sitting near the fire, looking up hopefully each time the door opened. It did this with fair regularity as more villagers arrived, stamping snow from their boots and shaking it from their clothes and their hair.

"We're in for it, Ben," a man called over the din.

Pulling the taps behind the bar, Ben Wragg couldn't have looked more delighted. Custom in winter was hard enough to come by. If the weather turned rough enough, half of these blokes would be looking for beds.

St. James left Lynley long enough to go upstairs for his overcoat and gloves. Deborah was sitting on the bed with all the pillows piled up behind her. Her head was back, her eyes were closed, and her hands were balled in her lap. She was still fully dressed.

She said as he closed the door, "I lied. But you knew that, didn't you?"

"I knew you weren't tired, if that's what you mean."

"You aren't angry?"

"Should I be?"

"I'm not a good wife."

"Because you didn't want to hear anything more about Juliet

Spence? I'm not sure that's an accurate measurement of your loyalties." He took his coat from the cupboard and put it on, fishing in the pockets for his gloves.

"You're going with him, then. To finish things."

"I'll rest easier if he doesn't have to do it alone. I brought him into this, after all."

"You're a good friend to him, Simon."

"As he is to me."

"You're a good friend to me as well."

He went to the bed and sat down on the edge. He closed his hand over the fist hers made. The fist turned, the fingers opened. He felt something pressed between his palm and hers. It was a stone, he saw, with two rings painted on it in bright pink enamel.

She said, "I found it sitting on Annie Shepherd's grave. It reminded me of marriage—the rings and how they're painted. I've been carrying it round ever since. I've thought it might help me be better for you than I have been."

"I have no complaints, Deborah." He closed her fingers round the stone and kissed her forehead.

"You've wanted to talk. I haven't. I'm sorry."

"I've wanted to preach," he said, "which is different from talking. You can't be blamed for displaying an unwillingness to listen to my sermons." He stood, pulling on his gloves. He took his scarf from the chest of drawers. "I don't know how long this will take."

"It doesn't matter. I'll wait." She was placing the stone on the bedside table as he left the room.

He found Lynley waiting for him outside the pub, sheltered within the porch and watching the snow continue to come down in silent undulations lit by the street lamps and by the lights from the terrace houses lining the Clitheroe Road.

He said, "She'd only been married once, Simon. Just to Yanapapoulis." They headed towards the car park where he'd left the Range Rover he'd hired in Manchester. "I've been trying to understand the process Robin Sage went through to make his decision, and it comes down to that. She's not a bad person, after all, she loves her children, and she's only been married once, despite her life-style prior to and following that marriage."

"What happened to him?"

"Yanapapoulis? He gave her Linus—the fourth son—and then

evidently took up with a twenty-year-old boy fresh in London from Delphi."

"Bearing a message from the oracle?"

Lynley smiled. "I dare say that's better than gifts."

"Did she tell you about the rest?"

"Obliquely. She said she had a weakness for dark foreign men: Greeks, Italians, Iranians, Pakistanis, Nigerians. She said, 'They just crook their fingers and I come up pregnant. I can't think how.' Only Maggie's father was English, she said, and look what sort of bloke *he* was, Mister Inspector person."

"Do you believe her story? About how Maggie came to have the injuries?"

"What difference does it make what I believe at this point? Robin Sage believed her. That's why he's dead."

They climbed inside the Range Rover, and the engine caught. Lynley reversed it. They inched past a tractor and threaded through the maze of cars to the street.

"He'd decided on that which is moral," St. James noted. "He threw himself behind the lawful position. What would you have done, Tommy?"

"I'd have checked into the story, just as he did."

"And when you found out the truth?"

Lynley sighed and turned south down the Clitheroe Road. "God help me, Simon. I just don't know. I don't have the kind of moral certitude Sage seems to have garnered. There's no black or white for me in what happened. Grey stretches forever, despite the law and my professional obligations to it."

"But if you had to decide."

"Then I suppose it would all come down to crime and punishment."

"Juliet Spence's crime against Sheelah Cotton?"

"No. Sheelah's crime against the baby: leaving her alone with the father so that he had the opportunity to injure her in the first place, leaving her alone in the car at night only four months later so that someone could take her. I suppose I'd ask myself if the punishment of losing her for thirteen years—or forever—fit or exceeded the crimes committed against her."

"And then what?"

Lynley glanced his way. "Then I'd be in Gethsemane, praying

for someone else to drink from the cup. Which is, I imagine, what Sage himself did."

•   ■   •

Colin Shepherd had seen her at noon, but she wouldn't let him into the cottage. Maggie wasn't well, she told him. A persistent fever, chills, a bad stomach. Running off with Nick Ware and dossing down in a farm building—even if only for part of the night—had taken its toll. She'd had a second bad night, but she was sleeping now. Juliet didn't want anything to waken her.

She came outside to tell him, shutting the door behind her and shivering in the cold. The first seemed a deliberate effort to keep him out of the cottage. The second seemed designed to send him on his way. If he loved her, her quaking body declared, he wouldn't want her standing out in the cold having a chat with him.

Her body language was clear enough: arms crossed tightly, fingers digging into the sleeves of her flannel shirt, posture rigid. But he told himself it was merely the cold, and he tried to read beneath her words for an underlying message. He gazed at her face and looked into her eyes. Courtesy and distance were what he read. Her daughter needed her and wasn't he being rather selfish to expect her either to want or accept a distraction from that need?

He said, "Juliet, when will we have a chance to talk?" but she looked up at Maggie's bedroom window and answered with "I need to sit with her. She's been having bad dreams. I'll phone you later, all right?" And she slipped back into the cottage and shut the door soundlessly. He heard the key turning in its lock.

He wanted to shout, "You've forgotten, haven't you? I've my own key. I can still get in. I can make you talk. I can make you listen." But instead he stared long and hard at the door, counting its bolts, waiting for his heart to stop pounding so angrily.

He'd gone back to work, making his rounds, seeing to three cars that had misjudged the icy roads, herding five sheep back over a disintegrating wall near Skelshaw Farm, replacing its stones, rounding up a rogue dog that had finally been cornered in a barn just outside the village. It was routine business, nothing to occupy his mind. And as the hours passed, he found himself more and more needing something to keep his thoughts in order.

Later had come, and she did not phone. He moved about his

house restlessly as he waited. He looked out the window at the snow that lay unblemished in the graveyard of St. John the Baptist Church and, beyond it, upon the pasture land and the slopes of Cotes Fell. He built a fire and let Leo bask in front of it as day drew towards evening. He cleaned three of his shotguns. He made a cup of tea, added whisky to it, forgot about drinking it. He picked the phone up twice to make certain it was still in working order. The snow, after all, could have downed some lines. But he listened to the dialling tone's heartless buzz telling him something was very wrong.

He tried not to believe it. She was concerned about Maggie, he told himself. She was rightfully concerned. It was no more than that.

At four o'clock he could stand the waiting no longer, so he did the phoning. Her line was engaged, and engaged at a quarter past, and engaged at half past, and every quarter hour after that until half past five when he understood that she had taken the phone off the hook so that its ringing would not disturb her daughter.

He willed her to phone from half past five to six. After six, he began to pace. He went over every brief conversation they'd had in the two days since Maggie had returned from her short-lived experience of running away. He heard Juliet's tone as she had sounded on the phone—resigned, somehow, to something he did not want to understand—and he felt a growing desperation.

When the phone rang at eight, he leapt to answer it, hearing a terse voice ask:

"Where the hell have you been all day, boy-o?"

Colin felt his teeth set and made an effort to relax. "I've been working, Pa. That's what I usually do."

"Don't get a mouth with me. He's asked for a wopsie, and she's on her way. Do you know that, boy-o? Are you up on the news?"

The telephone was on a lengthy cord. Colin cradled the receiver against his ear and walked to the kitchen window. He could see the light from the vicarage porch, but everything else was shape and shadow, curtained off by the snow that was falling as if disgorged in an explosion from the clouds.

"Who's asked for a wopsie? What're you talking about?"

"That blighter from the Yard."

Colin turned from the window. He looked at the clock. The cat's eyes moved rhythmically, its tail ticked and tocked. He said, "How do you know?"

"Some of us maintain our ties, boy-o. Some of us have mates that're loyal to the death. Some of us do favours so that when we need one, we can call it in. I've been telling you that from day one, haven't I? But you don't want to learn. You've been so bloody stupid, so flaming sure . . ."

Colin heard a glass clink against the receiver at his father's end. He heard the rattle of ice. "What is it?" he asked. "You having gin or whisky tonight?"

The glass crashed against something: the wall, a piece of furniture, the cooker, the sink. "God damn you ignorant piece of filth. I'm trying to help you."

"I don't need your help."

"Bugger that for a lark. You're in so deep you can't smell the shit. That ponce was locked up with Hawkins, boy-o, for nearly an hour. He called in forensic and the DC who came up there when you first found the body. I don't know what he told them, but the end result was that they phoned for a wopsie and whatever that bloke from the Yard has up his sleeve to do next, it's with Clitheroe's blessing. You got that, boy-o? And Hawkins didn't phone and put you in the picture, did he? *Did* he?"

Colin didn't reply. He saw that he'd left a pot on the AGA at lunchtime. Luckily, it had held only salted water which had long since boiled away. The bottom of the pot, however, was crusted with sediment.

"What d'you think that means?" his father was demanding. "Can you put it together or do I have to spell it out?"

Colin forced himself to sound indifferent. "Bringing in a wopsie's fine with me, Pa. You're in a state over nothing."

"What the hell is that supposed to mean?"

"It means I missed some things. The case needs to be re-opened."

"You damn fool! Don't you know what it means to botch a murder investigation?"

Colin could picture the veins in his father's arms standing out. He said, "I'm not making history. This won't be the first time a case has been re-opened."

"Simpleton. Ass," his father hissed. "You gave evidence for her. You took the oath. You've been playing in her knickers. No one's likely to forget that when it comes time to—"

"I've some new information, and it's nothing to do with Juliet.

I'm ready to hand it over to that bloke from the Yard. It's just as well he's going to have a female PC with him because he'll be wanting her."

"What're you saying?"

"That I've found the killer."

Silence. In it, he could hear the fire crackling in the sitting room. Leo was chewing industriously on a ham bone. He had it locked in his paws against the floor, and the sound resembled someone planing wood.

"You're sure." His father's voice was wary. "You've evidence?"

"Yes."

"Because if you cock this up any further, you're done for, boy-o. And when that happens—"

"It's not going to happen."

"—I don't want you crying to me for help. I'm through covering your arse with Hutton-Preston's CC. You got that?"

"I've got it, Pa. Thanks for having confidence."

"Don't you give me your bloody—"

Colin hung up the phone. It began ringing again within ten seconds. He let it ring. It jangled for a full three minutes while he watched it and pictured his father at the other end. He'd be cursing steadily, he'd be aching to batter someone into pulp. But unless one of his pieces of sweet female flesh was there to oblige him, he was going to have to face his furies alone.

When the phone stopped ringing, Colin poured himself a tumbler of whisky, returned to the kitchen, and punched Juliet's number. The line was still engaged.

He carried his drink to the second bedroom that served as his study and sat down at the desk. From its bottom drawer, he took the slim volume. *Alchemical Magic: Herbs, Spices, and Plants.* He set it next to a yellow legal pad and began to write his report. It flowed easily enough, line after line, piecing fact and conjecture into an overall pattern of guilt. He had no choice, he told himself. If Lynley was asking for a female PC, he meant to start trouble for Juliet. There was only one way to stop him.

He had just completed his writing, revised it, and typed it when he heard the car doors slam. Leo began to bark. He got up from the desk and went to the door before they had a chance to ring the bell. They would find him neither unprepared nor unaware.

"I'm glad you've come," he said to them. He sounded a mixture of sure and expansive, and he felt good about the sound. He swung the door home behind them and led them into the sitting room.

The blond—Lynley—took off his coat, his scarf, and his gloves and brushed the snow from his hair as if he intended to stay for a while. The other—St. James—loosened his scarf and a few buttons of his coat, but the only things he removed were his gloves. These he held and played through his fingers while the snowflakes melted into his hair.

"I've a WPC coming up from Clitheroe," Lynley said.

Colin poured them both a whisky and handed the glasses over, uncaring of whether they chose to drink or not. Not was the case. St. James nodded and set his on the side table next to the sofa. Lynley said thank you and placed his on the floor when he sat, unbidden, in one of the armchairs. He beckoned Colin to do likewise. His face was grave.

"Yes, I know she's on her way," Colin answered easily. "You've got second sight among your other gifts, Inspector. I was twelve hours away from phoning Sergeant Hawkins for one myself." He handed over the slender book first. "You'll be wanting this, I expect."

Lynley took it and turned it over in his hands, putting on his spectacles to read the cover first and then the descriptive copy on the back. He opened the book and ran his glance over the table of contents. Pages were folded down at the corners—the result of Colin's own perusal of the book—and he read these next. On the floor by the fire, Leo returned to gnawing his ham bone. His tail thumped happily.

Lynley finally looked up without comment. Colin said, "The confusion and the false starts in the case are my fault. I wasn't on to Polly at first, but I think this clears things up." He passed the stapled report to Lynley, who handed the book over to St. James and began to read. He went through the pages. Colin watched him, waiting for a flicker of emotion, recognition, or dawning acceptance to move his mouth, raise his eyebrows, light his eyes. He said, "Once Juliet took the blame and said it was an accident, that's what I focussed on. I couldn't see that anyone had a motive to murder Sage and when Juliet insisted that no one could have had access to the root cellar without her knowledge, I believed her. I didn't realise then that he was never the target in the first place. I was worried about her, about the inquest. I wasn't seeing things clearly. I should have realised earlier that this murder had nothing to do with the vicar at all. He was the victim by mistake."

Lynley had two pages left to read, but he closed the report and removed his spectacles. He replaced them in his jacket pocket and handed the report to Colin. When Colin's fingers were on it, he said, "You should have realised earlier... An interesting choice of words. Would this be before or after you assaulted her, Constable? And why was that, by the way. To get a confession? Or merely for pleasure?"

The paper felt weightless beneath his fingers. Colin saw that it had slipped to the floor. He picked it up, saying, "We're here to talk about a murder. If Polly's turning the facts so that I'm under suspicion, that should tell you something about her, shouldn't it?"

"What tells me something is that she hasn't said a word. About being assaulted. About you. About Juliet Spence. She doesn't act much like a woman who's trying to hide her culpability."

"Why should she? The person she was after is still alive. She can tot the other up as a simple mistake."

"With a motive of thwarted love, I take it. You must think a great deal of yourself, Mr. Shepherd."

Colin felt his features hardening. He said, "I suggest you listen to the facts."

"No. You listen. And you hear me well because when I'm done you'll resign from policework and thank God that's all your superiors expect from you."

And then the inspector began to talk. He listed names that had no meaning to Colin: Susanna Sage and Joseph, Sheila Cotton and Tracey, Gladys Spence, Kate Gitterman. He talked about cot death, a long-ago suicide, and an empty grave in a family plot. He sketched the vicar's route through London, and he laid out the story that Robin Sage—and he himself—had pieced together. In the end he unfolded a poor copy of a newspaper article and said, "Look at the picture, Mr. Shepherd," but Colin kept his eyes where he'd placed them the moment the man had started speaking: on the gun cabinet and the shotguns he'd cleaned. They were primed and ready and he wanted to use them.

He heard Lynley say, "St. James," and then his companion began to speak. Colin thought, No. I won't and I can't, and he conjured up her face to hold the truth at bay. Occasional words and phrases pierced through: most poisonous plant in the western hemisphere...root stock . . . would have known . . . oily juice upon cutting an indication of . . . couldn't possibly have ingested . . .

He said in a voice that came from so far within him he couldn't quite hear it himself, "She was sick. She'd eaten it. I was there."

"I'm afraid that's not the case. She'd taken a purgative."

"The fever. She was burning. *Burning.*"

"I expect she'd taken something to elevate her temperature as well. Cayenne, probably. That would have done it."

He felt cleaved in half.

"Look at the picture, Mr. Shepherd," Lynley said.

"Polly wanted to kill her. She wanted to clear the way."

"Polly Yarkin had nothing to do with any of this," Lynley said. "You were a form of alibi. At the inquest, you'd be the one to testify to Juliet's illness the night Robin Sage died. She used you, Constable. She murdered her husband. Look at the picture."

Did it look like her? Was that her face? Were those her eyes? It was more than ten years old, the copy was bad, it was dark, it was blurry.

"This doesn't prove a thing. It's not even clear."

But the other two men were relentless. A simple confrontation between Kate Gitterman and her sister would tell the tale of iden-tification. And if it didn't, the body of Joseph Sage could be exhumed and genetic testing could be done upon it to match him to the woman who called herself Juliet Spence. Because if she was indeed Juliet Spence, why would she refuse to be tested, to have Maggie tested, to produce the documents attendant to Maggie's birth, to do anything possible to clear her name?

He was left with nothing. Nothing to say, no argument to propose, and nothing to reveal. He got to his feet and carried the copied photograph and its accompanying article to the fireplace. He threw them in and watched the flames take them, curling the paper at the edges first, then lapping eagerly, then consuming entirely.

Leo watched him, looking up from his bone, whining low in his throat. God, to have everything simple, like a dog. Food and shelter. Warmth against the cold. Loyalty and love that never wavered.

He said, "I'm ready, then."

Lynley said, "We won't be needing you, Constable."

Colin looked up to protest even as he knew he had no right. The doorbell rang.

The dog barked, quieted. Colin said bitterly, "Would you like to answer that yourself, then?" to Lynley. "It'll be your wopsie."

It was. But it was more. The female PC had come in uniform, bundled against the cold, her spectacles flecked with moisture. She said, "PC Garrity. Clitheroe CID. Sergeant Hawkins's already put me in the picture," while behind her on the porch listened a man in heavy tweeds and boots with a cap pulled low on his head: Frank Ware, Nick's father. Both of them were backlit by the headlamps of one of their two vehicles which blazed a blinding white light into the steady fall of the snow.

Colin looked at Frank Ware. Ware looked uneasily from the PC to Colin. He stomped the snow off his boots and pulled at his nose. He said, "Sorry to disturb. But there's a car gone into a ditch out next the reservoir, Colin. I thought I best stop by and tell you. It looks to me like Juliet's Opel."

CHAPTER TWENTY-EIGHT

THERE WAS NO CHOICE BUT TO TAKE SHEP-
herd with them. He'd grown up in the area. He knew
the lay of the land. Lynley wasn't willing to give him the
freedom of his own vehicle, however. He directed him to the front
seat of the hired Range Rover, and with Constable Garrity and St.
James following in the other, they set out for the reservoir.

The snow flew into the windscreen in constant banners of white,
dazzling in the headlamps and blown by the wind. Other vehicles
had beaten it down into ruts on the road, but ice ridged the bottom
of these and made the going perilous. Even their Range Rover's four-
wheel drive was not sufficient to negotiate the worst of the curves
and acclivities. They slipped and slid, moving at a crawl.

They eased past Winslough's monument to World War I, the
soldier's bowed head and his rifle now glittering white. They passed
the common where the snow blew in a spectral whirlwind that dusted
the trees. They crossed the bridge that arched over a tumbling beck.
Visibility worsened as the windscreen wipers began to leave a curved
trail of ice when they moved on the glass.

"Blast," Lynley muttered. He made an adjustment to the de-
froster. It was ineffectual, since the problem was external.

Next to him, Shepherd said nothing beyond giving two-word
directions whenever they approached what went for an intersection
this deep in the country. Lynley glanced his way when he said, "Left
here," as the headlamps illuminated a sign for Fork Reservoir. He
thought about taking a few minutes' pleasure from mixing obloquy

with castigation—God knew that Shepherd was getting off far too lightly with a request for resignation from his superiors and not a full public hearing—but the blank mask that was the other man's face dried up the well-spring of Lynley's need to censure. Colin Shepherd would be reliving the events of the last few days for the rest of his life. And ultimately, when he closed his eyes, Lynley could only hope that it would be Polly Yarkin's face that haunted him most.

Behind them, Constable Garrity drove her Rover aggressively. Even with the wind blowing and the windows rolled up, they could hear her grinding her way through the gears. The engine of her vehicle roared and complained, but she never dropped more than six yards behind them.

Once they left the outskirts of the village, there were no lights other than those from their vehicles and those that shone from the occasional farmhouse. It was like driving blind, for the falling snow reflected their headlamps, creating a permeable, milky wall that was ever shifting, ever changing, ever blowing their way.

"She knew you'd gone to London," Shepherd finally said. "I told her. Put that into the account if you'd like."

"You just pray we can find her, Constable." Lynley changed down gears as they rounded a curve. The tyres slid, spun helplessly, then caught again. Behind them, Constable Garrity sounded her horn in congratulations. They lumbered on.

Some four miles from the village, the entrance to Fork Reservoir loomed to their left, offset by a stand of pines. Their branches hung heavily with a weight of wet snow caught in the web of the trees' stubby needles. The pines lined the road for perhaps a quarter of a mile. Opposite them, a hedge gave way to the open moor.

"There," Shepherd said as they came to the end of the trees.

Lynley saw it as Shepherd spoke: the shape of a car, its windows along with its roof, bonnet, and boot hidden beneath a crust a snow. The car teetered at a drunken angle just at the point where the road sloped upward. It sat on the verge neither coming nor going, but rather diagonally with its chassis oddly balanced on the ground.

They parked. Shepherd offered his torch. Constable Garrity joined them and beamed hers on the car. Its rear wheels had spun themselves a grave in the snow. They lay deeply imbedded in the side of the ditch.

"My nitwit sister tried this once," Constable Garrity said, flinging her hand in the upward direction the road was taking. "Tried to make it up a slope and slid backwards. Nearly broke her neck, little fool."

Lynley brushed the snow from the driver's door and tried the handle. The car was unlocked. He opened the door, shone the light inside, and said, "Mr. Shepherd?"

Shepherd came to join him. St. James opened the other door. Constable Garrity handed him her torch. Shepherd looked inside at the cases and cartons as St. James went through the glove box, which was gaping open.

"Well?" Lynley said. "Is this her car, Constable?"

It was an Opel like a hundred thousand other Opels, but different in that its rear seat was crammed to the roof with belongings. Shepherd pulled one of the cartons towards him, pulled out a pair of gardening gloves. Lynley saw his hand close over them tightly. It was affirmation enough.

St. James said, "Nothing much in here," and snapped the glove box closed. He picked a piece of dirty towelling off the floor and wrapped round his hand a short length of twine that lay with it. Thoughtfully, he looked out across the moors. Lynley followed his gaze.

The landscape was a study in white and black: It was falling snow and night unredeemed by the moon or stars. There was nothing to break the force of the wind here—neither woodland nor fell disrupted the flow of the land—so the frigid air cut keenly and quickly, bringing tears to the eyes.

"What's ahead?" Lynley asked.

No one responded to the question. Constable Garrity was beating her hands against her arms and stomping her feet, saying, "Must be ten below." St. James was frowning and making moody knots in the twine he'd found. Shepherd was still holding the gardening gloves in his fist, and his fist was at his chest. He was watching St. James. He looked shell-shocked, caught between dazed and mesmerised.

"Constable," Lynley said sharply. "I asked you what's ahead."

Shepherd roused himself. He removed his spectacles and wiped them on his sleeve. It was a useless activity. The moment he replaced them, the lenses were respeckled with snow.

"Moors," he said. "The closest town's High Bentham. To the northwest."

"On this road?"

"No. This cuts over to the A65."

Leading to Kirby Lonsdale, Lynley thought, and beyond it the M6, the Lakes, and Scotland. Or south to Lancaster, Manchester, Liverpool. The possibilities were endless. Had she been able to make it that far, she would have bought herself time and perhaps an escape route to the Irish Republic. As it was, she played the part of fox in a winter landscape where either the police or the unforgiving weather ultimately was going to run her to ground.

"Is High Bentham closer than the A65?"

"On this road, no."

"But off the road? Cutting across country? For Christ's sake, man, they won't be walking along the verge, waiting for us to come by and give them a lift."

Shepherd's eyes darted inside the car and then, with what seemed like an effort, to Constable Garrity, as if he were anxious to make sure they all heard his words and knew, at this point, that he'd made the decision to cooperate fully. He said, "If they're headed due east across the moors from here, the A65's about four and a half miles. High Bentham's double that."

"They'd be able to get a ride on the A65, sir," Constable Garrity pointed out. "It might not be closed yet."

"God knows they'd never be able to make a nine-mile hike northwest in this weather," St. James said. "But they've got the wind directly in their faces going east. There's no bet they could even make the four and a half."

Lynley turned from his examination of the darkness. He shone his torchlight beyond the car. Constable Garrity followed his lead and did the same, heading a few yards in the opposite direction. But snow obscured whatever footprints Juliet Spence and Maggie might have left behind them.

Lynley said to Shepherd, "Does she know the land? Has she been out here before? Is there shelter anywhere?" He saw the flicker cross Shepherd's face. He said, "Where?"

"It's too far."

"Where?"

"Even if she started before dark, before the snowfall got bad—"

"Damn it all, I don't want your analysis, Shepherd. Where?"

Shepherd's arm extended more west than north. He said, "Back End Barn. It's four miles south of High Bentham."

"And from here?"

"Directly across the moors? Perhaps three miles."

"Would she know that? Trapped here, in the car? Would she know?"

Lynley saw Shepherd swallow. He saw the betrayal bleed out of his features and settle them into the mask of a man without hope or future. "We hiked it from the reservoir four or five times. She knows," he said.

"And that's the only shelter?"

"That's it." She'd have to find the track that led from Fork Reservoir to Knottend Well, he told them, a spring that was the midway point between the reservoir and Back End Barn. It was marked well enough when the ground was clear, but a wrong turn in the dark and the snow could take them in circles. Still, if she found the track they could follow it to Raven's Castle, a five-stone marker that joined the tracks to the Cross of Greet and the East Cat Stones.

"Where's the barn from there?" Lynley asked.

It was a mile and a half north from the Cross of Greet. It sat not far off the road that ran north and south between High Bentham and Winslough.

"I can't think why she didn't head there in the car in the first place," Shepherd said in conclusion, "instead of coming out this way."

"Why?"

"Because there's a train station in High Bentham."

St. James got out of the car and slammed the door home. "It could be a blind, Tommy."

"In this weather?" Lynley asked. "I doubt it. She'd have needed an accomplice. Another vehicle."

"Drive this far, fake an accident, drive on with someone else," St. James said. "It's not that far removed from the suicide game, is it?"

"Who'd have helped her?"

All of them looked at Shepherd. He said, "I last saw her at noon. She said Maggie was ill. That was it. As God is my witness, Inspector."

"You've lied before."

"I'm not lying now. She didn't expect this to happen." He flicked his thumb at the car. "She didn't plan an accident. She didn't plan anything but getting away. Look at it straight. She knows where you've been. If Sage discovered the truth in London, you did as well. She's running. She's panicked. She's not being as careful as she ought to be. The car skids on the ice and puts her in a ditch. She tries to get out. She can't. She stands here on the road, just where we are. She knows she could try for the A65 across the moors, but it's snowing and she's afraid she'll get lost because she's never made the hike before and she can't risk it in the cold. She looks the other direction and remembers the barn. She can't make it to High Bentham. But she thinks she and Maggie can make it there. She's been there before. She sets off."

"All of which could be what we're intended to think."

"No! Bloody Christ, it's what happened, Lynley. It's the only reason why—" He stopped. He looked over the moors.

"The reason why . . . ?" Lynley prompted.

Shepherd's answer was nearly taken by the wind. "Why she took the gun with her."

.   .   .

It was the open glove box, he said. It was the towelling and the twine on the floor.

How did he know?

He'd seen the gun. He'd seen her use it. She'd taken it from a drawer in the sitting room one day. She'd unwrapped it. She'd shot at a chimney pot on the Hall. She'd—

"God damn it, Shepherd, you *knew* she had a pistol? What's she doing with a pistol? Is she a collector? Is it licenced?"

It wasn't.

"Jesus Christ!"

He didn't think . . . It didn't seem at the time . . . He knew he should have taken it from her. But he didn't. That was all.

Shepherd's voice was low. He was identifying one more crook to the rules and procedures he'd bent for Juliet Spence from the first, and he knew what the outcome of the revelation would be.

Lynley jammed his hand against the gear shift and cursed again. They shot forward, north. They had virtually no choice in the matter of pursuit. Providing she had found the track from the reservoir, she had the advantage of darkness and snow. If she was still on the moors and they tried to follow her across by torchlight, she could pick them off when they got within range by simply aiming at the torches' beams. Their only hope was to drive on to High Bentham and then head south down the road that led to Back End Barn. If she hadn't reached it, they couldn't risk waiting for her and taking the chance she'd got lost in the storm. They'd have to set across the moors, back towards the reservoir. They'd have to make an attempt to find her and hope for the best.

Lynley tried not to think about Maggie, confused and frightened, travelling in Juliet Spence's furious wake. He had no way of knowing what time they'd left the cottage. He had no idea of the clothes they wore. When St. James said something about having to take hypothermia into consideration, Lynley shoved his way into the Range Rover and slammed his fist against the horn. Not like that, he thought. God damn it to hell. However it ended, it wouldn't be like that.

They got no moment's relief from either the wind or the snow. It was falling so heavily that it seemed as though all of the northwest would be five feet under drifts by the morning. The landscape was changed entirely. The muted greens and russets of winter were moonscape. Heather and gorse were hidden. An endless camouflage of white upon white made grassland, bracken, and heath a uniform sheet upon which the only markers were the boulders whose tops were powdered but still visible, dark specks like blemishes on the skin around them.

They crawled along, prayed their way up inclines, rode the declivities on brakes and ice. The lights from Constable Garrity's Range Rover slithered and wavered behind them, but came steadily on.

"They won't make it," Shepherd said, gazing out at the flurries that gusted against the car. "No one could. Not in this."

Lynley changed down to first gear. The engine howled. "She's desperate," he said. "That might keep her going."

"Add the rest, Inspector." He hunched into his coat. His face looked grey-green in the lights from the dash. "I'm at fault. If they die." He turned to the window. He fiddled with his spectacles.

"It won't be the only thing on your conscience, Mr. Shepherd. But I expect you know that already, don't you?"

They rounded a curve. A sign pointing west was printed with the single word *Keasden*. Shepherd said, "Turn here." They veered to the left into a lane that was reduced to two ruts the width of a car.

It ran through a hamlet that appeared to consist of a telephone box, a small church, and half a dozen signs for public footpaths. They experienced an all-too-brief respite from the storm when they entered a small wood just west of the hamlet. There the trees were bearing most of the snow in their branches and keeping it relatively clear of the ground. But another curve took them into open land again, and the car was instantly buffeted by a gust of wind. Lynley felt it in the steering wheel. He felt the tyres slide. He cursed with some reverence and moved his foot off the gas. He restrained himself from hitting the brakes. The tyres found purchase. The car moved on.

"If they're not in the barn?" Shepherd asked.

"Then we'll look on the moor."

"How? You don't know what it's like. You could die out there, searching. Are you willing to risk it? For a murderess?"

"It's not only a murderess I'm looking for."

They approached the road that connected High Bentham and Winslough. The distance from Keasden to this crossroads was a little over three miles. It had taken them nearly half an hour to drive it.

They turned left—heading south in the direction of Winslough. For the next half mile, they saw the occasional lights from other houses, most of them set some considerable distance off the road. The land was walled here, the wall itself fast becoming just another white eruption from which individual stones, like staggered peaks, still managed to break through the snow. Then they were out on the moor again. No wall or fence served as demarcation between the land and the road. Only the tracks left by a heavy tractor showed them the way. In another half hour, they too would probably be obliterated.

The wind was whipping the snow into small, crystal cyclones. They built from the ground as well as from the air. They whirled in front of the car like ghostly dervishes and spun into the darkness again.

"Snow's letting up," Shepherd remarked. Lynley gave him a quick glance in which the other man obviously read the incredulity because he went on with, "It's just the wind now, blowing it about."

"That's bad enough."

But when he studied the view, Lynley could see that Shepherd was not merely acting the role of optimist. The snowfall was indeed diminishing. Much of what the wipers were sweeping away came from what was blowing off the moors, not falling from the sky. It gave little relief other than to make the promise that things weren't going to get much worse.

They crept along for another ten minutes with the wind whining like a dog outside. When their headlamps struck a gate that acted as a fence across the road, Shepherd spoke again.

"Here. The barn's to the right. Just beyond the wall."

Lynley peered through the windscreen. He saw nothing but eddies of snowflakes and darkness.

"Thirty yards from the road," Shepherd said. He shouldered open his door. "I'll have a look."

"You'll do what I tell you," Lynley said. "Stay where you are."

A muscle worked angrily in Shepherd's jaw. "She's got a gun, Inspector. If she's in there in the first place, she isn't likely to shoot at me. I can talk to her."

"You can do many things, none of which you're going to do right now."

"Have some sense! Let me—"

"You've done enough."

Lynley got out of the car. Constable Garrity and St. James joined him. They directed their torches' beams across the snow and saw the stone wall rising in a perpendicular line from the road. They ran their beams along it and found the spot where its flow was interrupted by the red iron bars of a gate. Beyond the gate stood Back End Barn. It was stone and slate, with a large door to admit vehicles, a smaller door for their drivers. It looked due east, so the wind had blown the snow in large drifts against the barn's face. The drifts were smooth mounds against the larger barn door. Against the smaller, however, a single drift was partially trampled. A V-shaped dent ran through it. Fresh snow dusted its edges.

"By God, she made it," St. James said quietly.

"Someone did," Lynley replied. He looked over his shoulder. Shepherd, he saw, was out of the Range Rover although he was maintaining his position next to its door.

Lynley considered the options. They had the element of surprise but she had the weapon. He had little doubt that she would use it the moment he moved against her. Sending in Shepherd was, in truth, the only reasonable way to proceed. But he wasn't willing to risk anyone's life when there was a chance of getting her out without gunfire. She was, after all, an intelligent woman. She had run in the first place because she knew that the truth was a moment away from discovery. She couldn't hope to escape with Maggie and go unapprehended a second time in her life. The weather, her history, and every one of the odds were dead set against her.

"Inspector." Something was pressed into his hand. "You might want to use this." He looked down, saw that Constable Garrity had given him a loud hailer. "Part of the kit in the car," she said. She looked embarrassed as she tipped her head towards her vehicle and buttoned the neck of her coat against the wind. "Sergeant Hawkins says a DC's always got to know what might be needed at a crime scene or in an emergency. Shows initiative, he says. I've a rope as well. Life vests. The lot." Her eyes blinked solemnly behind the wet-streaked lenses of her spectacles.

"You're a godsend, Constable," Lynley said. "Thank you." He raised the loud hailer. He looked at the barn. Not a sliver of light showed round either of the doors. There were no windows. If she was inside, she was sealed off completely.

What to say to her, he wondered. Which cinematic inanity would serve their purpose and bring her out? You're surrounded, you can't hope to escape, throw out the gun, come out with your hands up, we know you're inside . . .

"Mrs. Spence," he called. "You have a weapon with you. I don't. We're at an impasse. I'd like to get you and Maggie out of here without harm being done to anyone."

He waited. There was no sound from the barn. The wind hissed as it slid along three graduated tiers of stone projections that ran the length of the barn's north side.

"You're still nearly five miles from High Bentham, Mrs. Spence. Even if you managed to survive the night in the barn, neither you nor Maggie would be in any condition to walk farther in the morning. You must know that."

Nothing. But he could feel her thinking. If she shot him, she could get to his vehicle, a better vehicle than her own, after all, and be on her way. It would be hours before anyone would notice he was missing, and if she hurt him badly enough, he wouldn't have the strength to crawl back towards High Bentham and find assistance.

"Don't make it worse than it already is," he said. "I know you don't want to do that to Maggie. She's cold, she's frightened, she's probably hungry. I'd like to get her back to the village now."

Silence. Her eyes would be quite used to the darkness. If he burst in on her and had the luck to shine the torchlight directly in her face on the first go, even if she pulled the trigger, it wouldn't be likely that she'd be able to hit him. It might work. If he could find her the instant he crashed through the door...

"Maggie's never seen anyone shot," he said. "She doesn't know what it's like. She hasn't seen the blood. Don't make that part of her memory of this night. Not if you love her."

He wanted to say more. That he knew her husband and her sister had failed her when she needed them most. That there would have been an end to her mourning the death of her son had she only had someone to help her through it. That he knew she had acted in what she'd believed were Maggie's interests when she'd snatched her from the car that long-ago night. But he also wanted to say that, in the end, she'd not had the right to determine the fate of a baby belonging to a fifteen-year-old girl. That while she may have indeed done better by Maggie as a result of taking her, they couldn't know that for sure. And it was because of that simple *not knowing* that Robin Sage had decided a cruelty-as-justice had to be done.

He found he wanted to blame what was going to happen this night on the man she had poisoned, on his sententious perspective and his bumbling attempt to set things straight. For in the end, she was his victim as much as he was hers.

"Mrs. Spence," he said, "you know we're at the end of it here. Don't make it worse for Maggie. Please. You know I've been to London. I've seen your sister. I've met Maggie's mother. I've—"

A keening rose suddenly above the wind. Eerie, inhuman, it cut to the heart and then took on substance round a single word: *Mummy*.

"Mrs. Spence!"

And then the keening again. It sounded high with terror. It locked round the unmistakable tone of a plea. "Mummy! I'm afraid! Mummy! Mummy!"

Lynley shoved the loud hailer into Constable Garrity's hands. He pushed through the gate. And then he saw it. A shape was moving just to his left, beyond the wall as he himself was now.

"Shepherd!" he shouted.

"Mummy!" Maggie cried.

The constable came rapidly onward through the snow. He charged straight for the barn.

"Shepherd!" Lynley shouted. "God damn it! Stay out!"

"Mummy! Please! I'm afraid! Mummy!"

Shepherd reached the barn door as the gun went off. He was inside when she shot again.

. . .

It was long past midnight when St. James finally climbed the stairs to their room. He thought she'd be asleep, but she was waiting for him as she'd said she would be, sitting in bed with the covers drawn up to her chest and an old copy of *Elle* spread across her lap.

She said, "You found her" when she saw his face and then "Simon, what happened," when he nodded and said nothing except "We did."

He was tired to the point of weakness. His dead leg felt like a hundredweight hanging from his hip. He dropped his coat and scarf to the floor, tossed his gloves upon them, and left them where they lay.

"Simon?"

He told her. He began with Colin Shepherd's attempt to implicate Polly Yarkin. He ended with the gunshots at Back End Barn.

"It was a rat," he said. "She was shooting at a rat."

They'd been huddled into a corner when Lynley found them: Juliet Spence, Maggie, and a mangy orange cat called Punkin that the girl had refused to leave behind in the car. When the torchlight fell on them, the cat hissed, spit, and scurried into the darkness, but neither Juliet nor Maggie moved. The girl cowered into the woman's arms, her face hidden. The woman encircled her as much as possible, perhaps to warm, perhaps to protect.

"We thought they were dead at first," St. James said, "a murder and a suicide, but there wasn't any blood."

Then Juliet spoke as if the others weren't there, saying, It's all right, darling. If I haven't hit him, I've frightened him to death. He won't get you, Maggie. Hush. It's all right.

"They were filthy," he said. "Their clothes were soaked. I can't think they would have lasted the night."

Deborah extended her hand to him. "Please," she said.

He sat on the bed. She smoothed her fingers beneath his eyes and across his forehead. She brushed back his hair.

There was no fight in her, St. James said, and no intention to run any farther or, it seemed, to use the gun again. She'd dropped it onto the stone floor of the barn, and she was holding Maggie's head to her shoulder. She began to rock her.

"She'd taken off her coat and thrown it round the girl," St. James said. "I don't think she actually knew we were there."

Shepherd got to her first. He stripped his own heavy jacket off. He wrapped it round her and then flung his arms round them both because Maggie wouldn't release her hold on her mother's waist. He said her name, but she didn't respond other than to say that she'd shot at it, darling, she always hit her mark didn't she, it was probably dead, there was nothing to fear.

Constable Garrity ran for blankets. She'd brought a Thermos from home and she poured it saying, Poor lambs poor dears, in a fashion that was far more maternal than professional. She tried to get Shepherd to put his jacket back on, but he refused, wrapping himself in a blanket instead and watching everything—his eyes riveted with a kind of dying on Juliet's face.

When they were on their feet, Maggie began to cry for the cat, calling, Punkin! Mummy, where's Punkin? He's run off. It's snowing and he'll freeze. He won't know what to do.

They found the cat behind the door, his fur on end and his ears at the alert. St. James grabbed him. The cat climbed his back in a panic. But he settled well enough when he was returned to the girl.

She said, Punkin kept us warm, didn't he, Mummy? It was good to bring Punkin like I wanted, wasn't it? But he'll be happy to get home.

Juliet put her arm round the girl and pressed her face to the top of her head. She said, You take good care of Punkin, darling.

And then Maggie seemed to realise. She said, No! Mummy, please, I'm afraid. I don't want to go back. I don't want them to hurt me. Mummy! Please!

"Tommy made the decision to separate them at once," St. James said.

Constable Garrity took Maggie—You bring the cat, dear, she said—while Lynley took her mother. He intended to push all the way through to Clitheroe if it took him the rest of the night. He wanted it to be over. He wanted to be clear of it.

"I can't blame him," St. James said. "I won't soon forget the sound of her screaming when she saw he meant to separate them then and there."

"Mrs. Spence?"

"Maggie. Calling for her mother. We could hear her even after the car drove off."

"And Mrs. Spence?"

There was nothing from Juliet Spence at first. Without expression or reaction, she'd watched Constable Garrity drive away. She'd stood with her hands in the pockets of Shepherd's jacket and the wind blowing her hair across her face, and she watched the tail lights of the receding car bob and weave as it lurched across the moor in the direction of Winslough. When they began to follow it, she sat in the rear seat next to Shepherd and never looked away from those lights for a moment.

She said, What else could I do? He said he was going to return her to London.

"And that was the real hell behind the murder," St. James said.

Deborah looked perplexed. "What real hell? What do you mean?"

St. James got to his feet and walked to the clothes cupboard. He began to undress. "Sage never intended to turn his wife over to the authorities for snatching the baby," he said. "That last night of his life, he'd brought her enough money to get out of the country. He was perfectly willing to go to prison rather than tell anyone in London where he'd found the girl once he turned her over to Social Services. Of course, the police would have known eventually, but by that time his wife would have been long gone."

"That can't be right," Deborah said. "She must be lying about what happened."

He turned from the clothes cupboard. He said, "Why? The offer of money only makes the case against her blacker. Why would she lie?"

"Because . . . " Deborah plucked at the bedcovers as if she would find the answer there. She said deliberately, laying out her facts like cards, "He'd found her. He'd discovered who Maggie was. If he meant to return her to her real mother anyway, why wouldn't she have taken the money and saved herself from gaol? Why did she kill him? Why didn't she just run? She knew the game was up."

St. James unbuttoned his shirt with great care. He examined each button as his fingers touched it. He said, "I expect it was because Juliet felt she was Maggie's real mother all along, my love."

He looked up then. She was rolling a bit of the sheet between her thumb and forefinger and watching herself do so. He left her alone.

In the bathroom he took his time about washing his face, brushing his teeth, and running a brush through his hair. He removed his leg brace and let it thump to the floor. He kicked it to lie by the wall. It was metal and plastic, strips of Velcro and polyester. It was simple in design but essential in function. When legs didn't work the way they were supposed to, one strapped on a brace, or took to a wheelchair, or eased along on crutches. But one kept going. That had always been his basic philosophy. He wanted that precept to be Deborah's as well, but he knew she would have to be the one to choose it.

She'd switched off the lamp next to the bed, but when he came out of the bathroom, the light behind him fell across the room. In the shadows he could see that she was still sitting up in bed, but this time with her head on her knees and her arms round her legs. Her face was hidden.

He flicked off the bathroom light and made his way to the bed, tapping carefully in a darkness that was more complete this night because the skylights were covered with snow. He lowered himself into the covers and lay his crutches soundlessly on the floor. He reached out and ran his hand along her back.

"You're going to get cold," he said. "Lie down."

"In a moment."

He waited. He thought about how much of life comprised that very act, and how waiting always involved either another individual or a force outside oneself. He had mastered the art of waiting long ago. It had been a gift imposed upon him with too much alcohol, oncoming headlamps, and the cormorant scream of skidding tyres. Through sheer necessity, wait-and-see along with give-it-time had become his armorial motto. Sometimes the maxims led him into inaction. Sometimes they allowed him peace of mind.

Deborah stirred beneath his touch. She said, "Of course, you were right the other night. I wanted it for myself. But I also wanted it for you. Perhaps even more. I don't know." She turned her head to face him. He couldn't see her features in the darkness, just the shape of her.

"As retribution?" he asked. He felt her shake her head.

"We were estranged in those days, weren't we? I loved you but you wouldn't let yourself love me in return. So I tried to love someone else. And I did, you know. Love him."

"Yes."

"Does it hurt you to think about it?"

"I don't think about it. Do you?"

"Sometimes it creeps up on me. I'm never prepared. All of a sudden, there it is."

"Then?"

"I feel torn inside. I think how much I've hurt you. And I want things to be different."

"The past?"

"No. The past can't be changed, can it? It can just be forgiven. It's the present that concerns me."

He could tell that she was leading him towards something she had thought carefully through, perhaps that night, perhaps in the days that had preceded it. He wanted to help her say whatever it was she felt needed to be said, but he couldn't see the direction clearly. He could only sense that she believed the unspoken would hurt him in some undefinable way. And while he wasn't afraid of discussion—indeed, he'd been determined to provoke it ever since they'd left London—he found at the moment that he wanted discussion only if he was able to control its content. That she intended to do so, to an end he couldn't clearly anticipate, caused him to feel the cold-hot mantle of wariness cloak him. He tried to shed it, couldn't do so completely.

"You're everything to me," she said softly. "That's what I wanted to be to you. Everything."

"You are."

"No."

"This baby thing, Deborah. Adoption, the whole business of children—" He didn't complete the sentence because he didn't know where to go with it any longer.

"Yes," she said. "That's it. This baby thing. The whole business of children. *Being* whole in and of itself. That's what I wanted for you. That would be my gift."

He saw the truth then. It was between them the single dried bone of reality that they picked at and worried like two mongrel dogs.

He'd grabbed it and chewed it for the years they'd been apart. Deborah had been worrying it ever since. Even now, he saw, when there was no need, she was grappling with it.

He said nothing further. She'd gone this far and he was confident she would say the rest. She was too close now to back away from saying it, and backing away was not, in fact, her style. She'd been doing so for months to protect him, he realised, when he needed no protection, either from her or from this.

"I wanted to make it up to you," she said.

Say the rest, he thought, it doesn't hurt me, it won't hurt you, you can say the rest.

"I wanted to give you something special."

It's all right, he thought. It doesn't change anything.

"Because you're crippled."

He pulled her down to him. She resisted at first, but came to him when he said her name. Then the rest of it was spilling out, whispered into his ear. Much of it didn't make sense, an oddly combined jumble of memories and the experience and understanding of the last few days. He merely held her and listened.

She remembered when they brought him home from his convalescence in Switzerland, she told him. He'd been gone four months, she was thirteen years old, and she remembered that rainy afternoon. How she'd observed it all from the top floor of the house, how her father and his mother had followed him slowly up the stairs, watching as he gripped the banister, their hands flying out to keep him from losing his balance but not touching him, never touching him because they knew without seeing the expression on his face—which she herself could see from the top of the house—that he wasn't to be touched, not that way, not any longer. And a week later when the two of them were alone—she in the study and this angry stranger called Mr. St. James a floor above in his bedroom from which he had not emerged in days—she heard the crash, the heavy thud of weight and she knew he'd fallen. She'd run up the stairs and stood by his door in her thirteen-year-old's agony of indecision. Then she'd heard him weeping. She'd heard the sound of him pulling himself along the floor. She'd crept away. She'd left him to face his devils alone because she didn't know what to do to help.

"I promised myself," she whispered in the darkness. "I'd do anything for you. To make it better."

But Juliet Spence had seen no difference between the baby she'd borne and the one she'd stolen, Deborah told him. Each was her child. She was the mother. There was no difference. To her, mothering wasn't the initial act and the nine months that followed it. But Robin Sage hadn't seen that, had he? He offered her money to escape, but he should have known she was Maggie's mother, she wouldn't leave her child, it didn't matter what price she had to pay to stay with her, she would pay it, she loved her, she was her mother.

"That's how it was for her, wasn't it?" Deborah whispered.

St. James kissed her forehead and settled the blankets more closely round her. "Yes," he said. "That's how it was."

CHAPTER TWENTY-NINE

BRENDAN POWER CRUNCHED ALONG THE verge, heading into the village. He would have sunk up to his knees in the snow, but someone had been out earlier than he, and a path was already trodden. It was speckled every thirty yards or so with charred tobacco. Whoever it was out for a walk was smoking a pipe that didn't draw much better than Brendan's.

He himself wasn't smoking this morning. He had his pipe with him in case he found himself in the position of needing to do something with his hands, but so far he hadn't brought it out of its leather pouch, although he could feel the weight of it tapping securely against his hip.

The day after any storm was generally glorious, and Brendan found this one as splendid as the previous night had been frightful. The air was still. The early sun laid down great blazes of crystal incandescence across the land. Frost rimed the tops of the drystone walls. Slate roofs wore a thick coating of snow. As he passed the first terraced house on his way into the village, he saw that someone had remembered the birds. Three sparrows were picking at a handful of toast crumbs outside a doorway, and while they eyed him warily as he passed by, hunger kept them from scattering into the trees.

He wished he'd thought to bring something with him. Toast, a slice of stale bread, an apple. It didn't matter. Anything edible to offer the birds would have served as a marginally credible excuse for being out in the first place. And he'd be needing an excuse when he returned home. In fact, it might be wise to start concocting one now as he walked.

He hadn't thought of that earlier. Standing at the dining-room window, looking out beyond the garden to the vast white pasture that was part of the Townley-Young estate, he'd thought only of getting out, of tramping holes in the snow and driving his feet forward into a forever he could bear to live with.

His father-in-law had come to their bedroom at eight o'clock. Brendan had heard his military footsteps in the passage and had slid out of bed, freeing himself of the anchoring heaviness of his wife's arm. In sleep, she'd thrown it diagonally across him so that her fingers rested in his groin. Under other circumstances he might have found this somnolent implication of intimacy quite erotic. As it was, he lay flaccid and mildly repelled and at the same time grateful that she was asleep. Her fingers wouldn't be drifting coyly another inch to the left in the expectation of encountering what she deemed appropriate male morning arousal. She wouldn't be demanding what he couldn't give, pumping him furiously and waiting—agitated, anxious, then angry— for his body to respond. Tin-voiced accusations wouldn't follow. Neither would the tearless weeping that screwed up her face and resounded through the corridors. As long as she slept, his body was his own and his spirit was free, so he slipped to the door at the sound of his father-in-law's approach, and he cracked it open before Townley-Young could knock and awaken her.

His father-in-law was fully dressed, as usual. Brendan had never seen him otherwise. His tweeds, his shirt, his shoes, and his tie all made a careful statement about good breeding that Brendan knew he was supposed to understand and emulate. Everything he wore was just old enough to indicate the appropriate lack of interest in clothing that was inherent to the landed gentry. More than once Brendan had looked at his father-in-law and wondered idly how he managed the feat of maintaining an entire wardrobe that—from shirt to shoes— always looked at least ten years old, even when new.

Townley-Young gave a glance to Brendan's woollen dressing gown and pursed his lips in silent disapproval at the messy bow Brendan had made when tying the belt. Manly men use square knots to keep their dressing gowns closed, his expression said, and the two tails falling from the waist are always perfectly even, you twit.

Brendan stepped into the corridor and shut the door behind him. "Still asleep," he explained.

Townley-Young peered at the door's panels as if he could see through them and make an evaluation of his daughter's frame of mind. "Another rough night?" he asked.

That was certainly one way to put it, Brendan thought. He'd got home after eleven with the hope she'd be asleep, only to end up tussling with her beneath the covers in what went for marital relations between them. He'd been able to perform, thank God, because the room was dark and, during their biweekly nighttime encounters, she'd taken to whispering certain Anglo-Saxon pleasantries which he found allowed him to fantasize more freely. He wasn't in bed with Becky on those nights. He chose his mate freely. He moaned and writhed beneath her and said, Oh God, oh yes, I love it, I *love* it to the image of Polly Yarkin.

Last night, however, Becky had been more aggressive than usual. Her ministrations possessed an aura of anger. She'd not accused or wept when he came into their bedroom smelling of gin and looking— he knew because he could not hide it—dejected and decidedly love-lorn. Instead, she'd wordlessly demanded retribution in the form she knew he wished least to make.

So it had indeed been a rough night, although not in the manner his father-in-law thought. He said, "A little discomfort," and hoped Townley-Young would apply the description to his daughter.

"Right," Townley-Young had said. "Well, at least we'll be able to set her mind at rest. That should go far to making her more comfortable."

He'd gone on to explain that the work at Cotes Hall would proceed without interruption at last. He gave the reasons why, but Brendan merely nodded and tried to look filled with anticipation while his life drained away like an ebbing tide.

Now as he approached Crofters Inn along the Lancaster Road he wondered why he had depended so much upon the Hall's remaining unavailable to them. He was married to Becky, after all. He'd mucked up his life. Why did it seem a more permanent disaster if they had their own home?

He couldn't have said. It was just that with the announcement of the Hall's pending completion, he'd heard a door slam somewhere on his dreams of the future, as meaningless as those dreams had been.

And with the door's slamming, he felt claustrophobic. He needed out. If he couldn't make an escape from the marriage, at least he could from the house. So out he went, into the frosty morning.

"Where you off to, Bren?" Josie Wragg was perched on top of one of the two stone pillars that gave way to the Crofters Inn car park. She had brushed it clear of snow and she was dangling her legs and looking as forlorn as Brendan felt. She was the word *droop* personified: in her spine, her arms, her legs, and her feet. Even her face looked heavy, with the skin pulled down round her mouth and eyes.

"Just a walk," he said. And then he added because she looked so down-trodden and he knew exactly how that feeling throws one's life into shadow, "Would you like to come along?"

"Can't. These don't work in the snow."

These were the Wellingtons that she bounced upwards in his direction. They were enormous. They looked nearly twice the size of her feet. Over their tops at least three pairs of knee-socks were folded.

"Don't you have some proper boots?"

She shook her head and pulled her knitted cap down to her eyebrows. "Mine've been too small since November, see, and if I tell Mum I need new ones, she'll have a conniption. 'When are you going to stop growing, Josephine Eugenia?' *You* know. These're Mr. Wragg's. He doesn't mind much." She bounced her legs back against the frosty stones.

"Why do you call him Mr. Wragg?"

She was fumbling with a fresh packet of cigarettes, trying to rip off its cellophane wrapper with mittened fingers. Brendan crossed the road, took the packet from her, and did the honours, offering her a light. She smoked without answer, trying and failing to make a ring, blowing out steam as much as smoke.

"It's pretend," she finally said. "Stupid, I know. You don't have to tell me. It makes Mum see red, but Mr. Wragg doesn't care. If he's not my real dad, I can pretend my mum had a big passion, see, and I'm the product of her fatal love. I pretend this bloke came to Winslough passing through on his way to wherever. He met Mum. They were crazy for each other but they couldn't get married, of course, because Mum wouldn't ever leave Lancashire. But he was the big love of her life and he set her on fire the way men are supposed to set women on fire. And I'm how she remembers him now." Josie flicked ash in Brendan's direction. "That's why I call him Mr. Wragg.

It's dumb. I don't know why I told you. I don't know why I ever say anything to anyone. It's always my fault, isn't it, and everyone's going to know it eventually. I natter too much." Her lip trembled. She rubbed her finger beneath her nose and threw her cigarette down. It hissed gently in the snow.

"Nattering's no crime, Josie."

"Maggie Spence was my best mate, see. And now she's gone. Mr. Wragg says she won't probably be back. And she was in love with Nick. Did you know that? True love, it was. Now they won't see each other again. I don't think it's fair."

Brendan nodded. "Life's that way, isn't it?"

"And Pam's been gated for forever because her mum caught her last night in the sitting room with Todd. Doing it. Right there. Her mum put on the lights and started screaming. It was just like a film, Pam said. So there's no one. No one special. It feels sort of hollow. Here." She pointed to her stomach. "Mum says it's just because I need to eat but I'm not hungry, you know?"

He did. He knew all about hollow. He sometimes felt he was hollow incarnate.

"And I can't think about the vicar," she said. "Mostly, I can't think about anything." She squinted at the road. "At least we have the snow. It's something to look at. For now."

"It is." He nodded, tapped her knee, and continued on his way, turning down the Clitheroe Road, concentrating on the walking, putting his energy into that effort rather than into thought.

The going was easier on the Clitheroe Road than it had been on the way into the village. More than one person had forged through the snow, making the walk out to the church, it seemed. He passed two of them—the Londoners—a short distance from the primary school. They walked slowly, heads together in conversation. They looked up only briefly as he passed.

He felt a quick stab of sadness at the sight of them. Men and women together, talking and touching, promised to cause him unending grief in the coming years. The object was not to care any longer. He wasn't quite sure if he'd be able to manage it without seeking relief.

Which is why he was out walking in the first place, pushing steadily forward and telling himself that he was merely going to check on the Hall. The exercise was good, the sun was out, he needed the air. But the snow was deep beyond the church, so when he finally reached the lodge, he hung about for five minutes just catching his breath.

"Bit of a rest," he assured himself, and he scrutinised the windows one after the other, looking for movement behind the curtains.

She hadn't been to the pub for the last two nights. He'd sat and waited until the last possible moment, when Ben Wragg called time and Dora bustled through picking up glasses. He knew that once half past nine arrived, it wasn't very likely that she'd pop in. But still he waited and dreamed his dreams.

He was dreaming them still when the front door opened and Polly walked out. She started when she saw him. He took an eager step her way. She had a basket over her arm and she was wrapped head to toe in wool and scarves.

"Heading to the village?" he asked. "I've just been to the Hall. Shall I walk with you, Polly?"

She came to join him and looked up the lane where the snow lay, pristine and betraying. "Fly there, did you?" she asked.

He fished in his jacket for his leather pouch. "I was going there, actually, not coming back. Out for a walk. Beautiful day."

Some of the tobacco spilled onto the snow. She watched it fall and appeared to be studying it. He saw that she had bruised her face somehow. A crescent of purple on the cream of her skin was going yellow at the edges as it began to heal.

"You've not been at the pub. Busy?"

She nodded, still examining the speckled snow.

"I've missed you. Chatting with you and the like. But of course, you've got things to do. People to see. I understand that. A girl like you. Still, I wondered where you were. Silly, but there it is."

She adjusted the basket on her arm.

"I heard it's resolved. Cotes Hall. What happened to the vicar. Did you know? You're in the clear. And that's good news, isn't it? All things considered."

She made no reply. She wore black gloves with a hole at the wrist. He wished she'd remove them so he could look at her hands. Warm them, even. Warm her as well.

He said in a burst, "I think about you, Polly. All the time. Day and night. You're what keeps me going. You know that, don't you? I'm not good at hiding things. I can't hide this. You see what I'm feeling. You do see it, don't you? You've seen it from the first."

She'd wound a purple scarf round her head, and she pulled it closer to her face as if to hide it. She kept her head bent. She reminded him of someone in prayer.

He said, "We're both lonely, aren't we? We both need someone. I want you, Polly. I know it can't be perfect, not with the way things are in my life, but it can be something. It can be special. I swear I can make it good for you. If you'll let me."

She raised her head and looked at him curiously. He felt his armpits sweating. He said, "I'm saying it wrong, aren't I? That's why it's a muddle. I'm saying it backwards. I'm in love with you, Polly."

"It's not a muddle," she said. "You're not saying it backwards."

His heart opened with joy. "Then—"

"You're just not saying it all."

"What more is there to say? I love you. I want you. I'll make it good if you'll only—"

"Ignore the fact that you have a wife." She shook her head. "Go home with you, Brendan. Take care of Miss Becky. Lie in your own bed. Stop sniffing round mine."

She nodded sharply—dismissal, good morning, whatever he wanted to take it for—and set off towards the village.

"Polly!"

She turned back. Her face was stony. She wouldn't be touched. But he *would* reach her. He would find her heart. He would beg for it, plead for it, he didn't care what it took. "I love you," he said. "Polly, I need you."

"Don't we all need something." She walked away.

■   ■   ■

Colin saw her pass. She was a whimsical vision of colour against a backdrop of white. Purple scarf, navy coat, red trousers, brown boots. She was carrying a basket and ploughing steadily along the far side of the road. She didn't look his way. She would have at one time. She would have ventured a surreptitious glance at his house, and if by chance he was working in the front garden or tinkering with the car, she would have crossed the road with an excuse to talk. Hear about the dog trials in Lancaster, Colin? How's your dad feeling? What'd the vet have to say about Leo's eyes?

Now she made a project out of looking straight ahead. The other side of the road, the houses that lined it, and particularly his simply didn't exist. It was just as well. She was saving them both. Had she turned her head and caught him watching her from the kitchen window, he might have felt something. And so far, he'd managed to keep himself from feeling anything at all.

He'd gone through the motions of the morning: making coffee, shaving, feeding the dog, pouring himself a bowl of cornflakes, slicing a banana, raining sugar on top, and dousing the mixture thoroughly with milk. He'd even sat at the table with the bowl in front of him. He'd even gone so far as to dip the spoon into it. He'd even lifted the spoon to his lips. Twice. But he was unable to eat.

He'd held her hand but it was dead weight in his. He'd said her name. He was unsure what to call her—this JulietSusanna that the London detective claimed she was—but he needed all the same to call her something in an effort to bring her back to him again.

She wasn't really there, he discovered. The shell of her was, the body he had worshipped with his own, but the interior substance of her rode up ahead in the other Range Rover, trying to calm her daughter's fears and looking for the courage to say goodbye.

He strengthened his grip on her. She said in a voice without depth or timbre, "The elephant."

He struggled to understand. The elephant. Why? Why here? Why now? What was she telling him? What was it that he should know about elephants? That they never forget? That she never would? That she still reached out to him for rescue from the quicksand of her despair? The elephant.

And then oddly, as if they communicated in an English that meant something only to them, Inspector Lynley answered her. "Is it in the Opel?"

She said, "I told her Punkin or the elephant. You must decide, darling."

He said, "I'll see that she gets it, Mrs. Spence."

And that was all. Colin willed her to respond to the pressure of his fingers. Her hand never moved, she never grasped his. She simply took herself to a place of dying.

He understood that now. He was there himself. At first, it seemed he'd begun the process when Lynley had laid the facts before him. At first, it seemed he'd continued to decay throughout the interminable passing of the night. He stopped hearing their voices. He drifted out of his body altogether and observed from on high the ending of things. He watched it all curiously, filed it all away, and thought perhaps he might wonder at it later. How Lynley spoke, not as an official of the police, but as if to comfort or to reassure her, how he helped her to the car, how he steadied her with his arm round her shoulders and pressed her head against his chest the final time they heard Maggie cry. It was odd to think he never once seemed triumphant at having his speculations proven true. Instead he looked torn. The crippled man said something about the workings of justice, but Lynley laughed bitterly. I hate all of this, he said, the living, the dying, the whole bloody mess. And although Colin listened from the faraway place to which the self of him had retreated, he found that he hated nothing at all. One cannot hate while one is engaged in the process of dying.

Later, he saw that he'd really begun that process the moment he raised a hand against Polly. Now, standing at the window and watching her pass by, he wondered if he hadn't been dying for years.

Behind him the clock ticked the day onwards, its cat's eyes shifting along with the movement of its pendulum tail. How she'd laughed when she saw it. She'd said, Col, it's precious, I must have it, I must. And he'd bought it for her birthday, wrapped it in newspaper because he'd forgotten the fancy paper and ribbon, left it on the front porch, and rung the bell. How she'd laughed, clapped her hands, said, Hang it up right now, right now, you must.

He took it from the wall above the AGA and carried it to the work top. He turned it face down. The tail still wagged. He could sense that the eyes were still moving as well. He could still hear the passing of its time.

He tried to prise open the compartment that held its workings, but couldn't manage the job with his fingers. He tried three times, gave it up, and opened a drawer beneath the work top. He fumbled for a knife.

The clock ticked and tocked. The cat's tail moved.

He slid the knife between the backing and the body and pulled back sharply. And then a second time. The plastic gave with a snap, part of the backing broke away. It flew up and out and landed on the floor. He flipped the clock over and slammed it hard a single time against the work top. A gear fell out. The tail and eyes stopped. The gentle ticking ceased.

He broke the tail off. He used the wooden handle of the knife to shatter the eyes. He flung the clock in the rubbish where a soup tin shifted with the weight of its fall and began to drip diluted tomato against its face.

What shall we name it, Col? she'd asked, slipping her arm through his. It needs a name. I fancy Tiger myself. Listen what it sounds like: Tiger tells the time. Am I a poet, Col?

"Perhaps you were," he said.

He put on his jacket. Leo dashed from the sitting room, ready for a run. Colin heard his anxious whine and ran his knuckles across the top of the dog's head. But when he left the house, he left it alone.

The steam from his breath said the air was frigid. But he couldn't feel anything, either warmth or cold.

He crossed the road and went through the lychgate. He saw that others had been in the graveyard before him because someone had laid a spray of juniper on one of the graves. The rest were bare, frozen under the snow with their markers rising like smokestacks through clouds.

He walked towards the wall and the chestnut tree where Annie lay, these six years dead. He made a deliberate, fresh trail through the snow, feeling the drifts give way against his shins, the way ocean water breaks when you walk against it.

The sky was as blue as the flax she'd planted one year by the door. Against it, the leafless branches of the chestnut tree wore a diamond cobweb of ice and snow. The branches cast a net of shadows on the ground beneath them. They dipped skinless fingers towards Annie's grave.

He should have brought something with him, he thought. A spray of ivy and holly, a fresh pine wreath. He should have at least come prepared to clean the stone, to make sure lichen had no chance to grow. He needed to keep the words from fading. At the moment, he needed to read her name.

The gravestone was partially buried in the snow and he began to use his hands against it, first brushing off the top and then down the sides and then preparing to use his fingers on the carving.

But then he saw it. The colour caught his eye first, bright pink on pure white. The shapes caught his eye second, two interlocking ovals. It was a small flat stone—worn smooth by a thousand years of river—and it was lying at the head of the grave, tangent to the marker.

He put his hand out, then drew it back. He knelt in the snow.

I burnt cedar for you, Colin. I put the ashes on her grave. I put the ring stone with them. I gave Annie the ring stone.

He reached out with an arm that did its own bidding. His hand picked up the stone. His fingers closed round it.

"Annie," he whispered. "Oh God. Annie."

He felt the cold air sweeping over him from the moor. He felt the frigid unforgiving embrace of the snow. He felt the small stone settle into his palm. He felt it hard and smooth.

ABOUT THE AUTHOR

ELIZABETH GEORGE is a resident of Huntington Beach, California. Her first novel, *A Great Deliverance*, won the Anthony and Agatha awards for Best First Novel, as well as France's Grand Prix de Littérature Policière. She is also the author of *For the Sake of Elena*, *Payment in Blood*, *A Suitable Vengeance*, and *Well-Schooled in Murder*, which was awarded the prestigious MIMI by German authors, critics, and booksellers as the Best Mystery of 1990. She is currently working on her next novel, *Playing for the Ashes*.